A Devil's Dozen

Marian Newell

Bretwalda Books Ltd

For my partner Per,
with thanks for his love and support

First Published 2012
Copyright © Marian Newell 2012

Bretwalda Books
Unit 8, Fir Tree Close, Epsom, Surrey KT17 3LD
www.BretwaldaBooks.com

To receive an e-catalogue of our complete range of books
send an email to info@BretwaldaBooks.com

ISBN 978-1-907791-29-1

Bretwalda Books Ltd

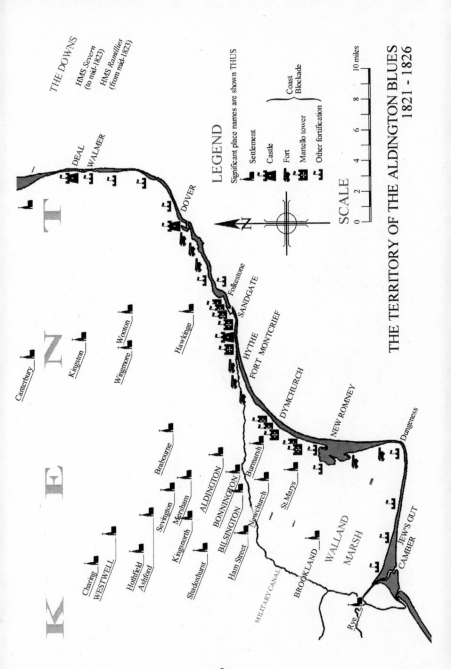

THE TERRITORY OF THE ALDINGTON BLUES
1821 - 1826

THE DOWNS

HMS *Severn* (to mid-1823)

HMS *Ramillies* (from mid-1823)

LEGEND

Significant place names are shown THUS

Settlement

Castle

Fort

Martello tower

Other fortification

Coast Blockade

SCALE

0   2   4   6   8   10 miles

KENT

Canterbury

Kingston

Wootton

Wingmore

DEAL

WALMER

DOVER

Folkestone

SANDGATE

Hawkinge

HYTHE

FORT MONTCRIEF

Brabourne

Sevington

Mersham

ALDINGTON

BONNINGTON

Kingsnorth

BILSINGTON

Charing

WESTWELL

Hothfield

Ashford

Shadoxhurst

Ham Street

Newchurch

Burmarsh

St Marys

DYMCHURCH

NEW ROMNEY

Dungeness

BROOKLAND

WALLAND MARSH

MILITARY CANAL

JEW'S GUT

CAMBER

Rye

3

George

Even the marshes rarely knew such devastation. A storm-soaked February gale howled across the flatlands, tearing at the few scrubby trees which were already bent over by the prevailing winds. Debris whirled upwards, only to come crashing down miles from where it had taken to the air. Dense clouds roiled around the moon, casting terrible shadow-beasts onto the landscape only to blot them out with a blanket of darkness moments later.

Only the keenest of eyes could detect life amidst such desolation, and a pair watched from a low rise. Dark blue and deep set, they belonged to a man named George Ransley. He monitored the action in a series of lightning-lit tableaux. His companions were falling back in stages, engaging the enemy to buy time for each orderly retreat of another few hundred yards. Most had only clubs and knives, pitched against muskets, but they were giving a good account of themselves. The sheeting rain helped, giving rise to poor shots and misfires, as did their familiarity with the marshes that so intimidated their pursuers.

Trailing in the rearguard, two men were doing more fighting than falling back. They would have been too far away to identify, were it not for a limp and a stoop. Smashed by a pistol ball the previous Easter, James Hogben's thigh had mended crooked, while the stoop-shouldered man at his side could only be Cephas Quested. Both would have duck-guns, although time and shot would be too short by then to use them as anything but clubs.

People said that Cephas led the South Kent smugglers, or the Aldington Blues as they were starting to be known, and in many ways that was true. It was he who kept the men in line and he to whom they looked for direction. When sober, he was an inspiring commander who led by actions rather than words. When drunk, as he often was, he was as helpless as a newborn. If there were those in the Blues who thought a leader ought to be more than a towering figurehead with a propensity for passing out all over the parish, they had yet to put their thoughts into words.

George shook his head slowly. Cephas should not have allowed himself to drop behind; he was exposed and individual bravery was in vain if it left the Blues leaderless. Yet courage had its place,

5

drawing loyalty from men who witnessed it. For years, George had managed their intelligence network and devised their strategies but he did so from a position somewhere just outside their number — not for him their bawdy nights out and drunken revelry. He knew that his coolness, a strength in so many ways, could be a weakness in a leader. Men trusted his judgement, it was true, but they would follow Cephas into Hell.

After being driven from their landing site at Camber, most of their men had crossed the marshes and were now working their way towards Brookland. Only the stragglers were anywhere near Cephas and they were too inexperienced to be of much help. George watched a slender figure flitting along the hedges to the east, well clear of the conflict where no one would mark his progress. He trawled his memory for the boy's name. One of his wife's many cousins, he was a Dennard... Tommy — yes, that was it. He couldn't be more than eighteen but his calm under fire boded well for the future.

George scanned the marshes for one last time, the wind whipping sodden hair across his face until his eyes streamed with tears. Unfamiliar shadows dotted the landscape, signifying dropped loads and the huddled bodies of men felled by balls, blades or bats. Both sides had heavy casualties and they had lost most of their cargo into the bargain. There was nothing more he could do to influence the fate of the rearguard but, meanwhile, his task was to save whatever else he could.

He turned away, sighing deeply. It had been a wretched night and he would be spending many an hour pondering how their plans had foundered so badly, whether anyone was to blame and, even if they weren't, whether someone should be held to account. He did not intend the loss of Cephas, if that was the outcome of their night's work, to be the end of the Blues but knew all his skills would be needed to avoid it. With six children, and no reason to think that the second decade of his marriage would be any less productive than the first, he saw no alternative — a father must provide and a ploughman's pay was scarcely enough to put potatoes on the table for such a brood.

Hog

'We've done all we can. It's time we buggered off out of here.'

'I'll not let these bastards off the hook.'

'There'll be other nights.'

No one could accuse James Hogben of being a prudent man but he wasn't in a hurry to hang. He'd escaped the Blockade's clutches once and thought he'd be pushing his luck to bank on it happening a second time. Even so, and no matter how futile he thought the fight, it was hard to leave his leader to face the enemy alone. They were cast in the same hard-drinking mould, and perhaps that was why their friendship had survived three tough decades.

Hog had run with the Blues even before their drabbet working smocks gave birth to the nickname. He was a young man back then, not yet married, tall and strong with a face that, while not handsome, held an appeal for the ladies. He went through plenty before settling early with Ann Kember, as she was then. She was a pretty little thing but, more to the point, her belly was swollen with his child. In those days, things like her good name mattered to him. The intervening years, hard and brutal as they were, had tarnished his character but it was only the last ten months that had plunged him into the depths that he now plumbed.

Little was left of the man who made his marriage vows in the bright and blustery spring of eighteen-hundred-and-eight, within sight of the sea at Folkestone. He knew when he looked into his wife's eyes that she no longer recognised him as her husband. That came as no surprise, given that he barely recognised himself. His loyalty to Cephas was the last vestige of the man he'd once been. He leaned heavily on his left leg, favouring the right where a familiar ache throbbed in the misaligned thigh bone. In pain most of the time, his only relief came from liberal doses of laudanum washed down with alcohol. Months had passed since he last saw the world clearly, his life cloaked in mists that had nothing to do with the damp sea air blown over the marshes.

He weighed up their chances. Perhaps if they had more time, but the preventive men were only minutes behind. They'd shaken off the pursuit once, after bluffing a Blockademan with empty fowling pieces, but the respite would only be temporary. He knew it was hopeless, just the two of them and low on shot at that. Cephas had a loaded musket he'd snatched but that wasn't going to make the difference. No, he had only one choice to make: escape alone or die at a friend's side. Even the younger Hog would have seen little point in throwing away his life in an empty gesture and the older one was long past such idealism.

His deliberations were cut short by footsteps in the darkness ahead. A man was walking as fast as the uneven ground allowed, thinking himself in pursuit of his quarry and clearly not expecting to run into two of them. Hog hefted the fowling piece in his hand, shifting its weight from side to side in anticipation of the approaching target. Anger welled up inside him, fuelled by years of resentment at the grinding poverty of his class and the stupidity of those who signed up to keep things as they were, boiling over into bitter hatred of the unknown man now only yards away.

Like most of the men in the fighting parties, he was swathed in dark clothes from head to toe, with the black mud of the marshes smeared over his already swarthy skin. He stood, poised for action, safe in the knowledge that the wild winter night protected him from detection. His ears told him that the other man was close, then a paler smudge revealed the officer's position. It wouldn't have been the first time that the Preventive Service's fondness for light trousers had saved Hog's skin — in his opinion, any man stupid enough to wear a uniform that marked him out so clearly at night deserved whatever befell him — but this man's trousers were dark. The pale smudge was a Guernsey frock.

Hog hesitated, unsure whether the man was friend or foe and unwilling to find out the hard way. He fixed his eyes on the man, waiting in silence, adjusting his position and timing his move to take full advantage of the element of surprise. He raised the duck-gun, every muscle from shoulder to wrist tensed in readiness, but, before he could land the blow, he heard:

'Shoot the bastards!'

Cephas had judged the man friend and tossed him the musket.

When the man grabbed hold of Cephas, Hog knew the judgement had been wrong. The man was a preventive officer and they were probably surrounded by his comrades. That made his decision for him: there was nothing he could do, a man alone with only an empty duck-gun for protection. Around him, men shouted at each other in confusion but that wouldn't last. He faded silently into the night. It was the first time he'd abandoned a friend and he left another little piece of his soul behind when he did it.

Cob

Further inland, four men ran hunched against the scouring wind, following the line of a ditch. The marshes were at their most treacherous, the night so dark that the gullies criss-crossing the land were barely blacker than the chill air that the men breathed. Even so, knowing the landscape as they did, they were outdistancing their pursuers. Fit and strong, they were capable of running many miles before being overtaken by fatigue.

At the rear, Charles Giles tripped and dropped onto one knee. Looking ahead, he saw his fleeing companions only as faint smudges against the seething sky. A moment later he had staggered to his feet but, just as he lifted his right foot to resume his flight, the clouds cleared from the moon. For an instant, he was thrown into sharp relief. He heard nothing above the howling wind but, before the shroud of darkness enveloped him again, his right shoulder exploded and he lurched forward.

'Damn!' he gasped into the air driven from his lungs.

He struggled for balance and then fell again, this time crumpling onto both knees. The right side of his back burned. He tried to stand, wondering as he did so how bad the damage was. His right leg refused to move. When he moved the left, the right gave way and he toppled sideways onto the rough grass.

'Damn,' he repeated, resignation creeping into his voice.

He expected nothing from his fellows, having known them only a matter of months and being dispensable in their organisation. But, even as he watched the farthest smudge fade from view, he realised it was alone. Before he could understand that, strong hands gripped his arms and hoisted him to his feet. The pain that tore through his shoulder defied description, filling his brain with its heat until conscious thought fled. He head lolled from side to side as he tried to run, his feet flailing uselessly.

'Stay with us, Cob.'

He was surprised to hear concern in the silky voice. As half-

9

thoughts whirled around his head, he tried to recognise the speaker. Who had he been running with? He'd known well enough a minute earlier but now his rescuers were strangers.

'He's all right, saying we gets him out of here.'

'We'll do that.'

Every step jolted his limp body, stabbing through his wound. Confusion closed around him, reality receding into the distance like a circle of light seen from the bottom of a well. He clung to consciousness as he clung to the bat in his hand. He had no idea how much time passed. It seemed as if they'd been blundering through the night for hours when he heard more voices.

'Who've you got there?' An authoritative voice.

'Cob.' The silky voice.

'Bad? The doc'll see to us when he's done with the preventives.'

'Best we gets him clear. He lives, long as we stops the bleeding.'

There was a brief pause.

'All right, but make sure he does. Load him up with the tubs.'

It could have been minutes or hours before he heard a whip crack over the team. He winced as the horses leapt forward but, although his shoulder screamed for mercy, his lips stayed silent. He'd been saved when he could have been left, and they'd hear no complaint from him about that. With his feeble efforts to run no longer needed, he fell back and let the blackness overwhelm him.

He woke to the cool touch of a damp cloth on his forehead. It took three attempts to force his sticky eyelids apart. A blurred figure loomed over him before slowly coalescing into James Quested's distinctive outline; the bulky, stoop-shouldered build was instantly recognisable and the only thing that he shared with his elder cousin. Now a concerned frown dissolved as his flat features settled into a half-smile. Wide grey eyes, reminiscent of a mackerel on the slab, filled with relief.

'About time you comes back. We starts to think you a skiver.'

Cob sipped from the tin cup held to his lips. Water spilled over his chin, only to be dabbed away with surprising delicacy.

'How ... long?'

'Nigh on a week. Fuss you makes, we thinks you're on your way out of this world. All for a scratch, naught worth calling a doctor for.'

Cob settled back onto his pillow, knowing the banter was well meant and sure he had made no fuss, at least while conscious.

'You took care of me ... all this time?'

The silky voice came from the far side of the room. 'Quacks barely left you, Cob. A doctor wouldn't have took half the trouble.'

None of the Blues called Quested or Giles by their given names. 'Quacks' was born partly of respect for his untutored medical skills and partly in mockery at his curious way of speaking, adding an 's' to his verbs as if everything happened in the present, with no thought of past or future. 'Cob' was a straightforward reflection of Giles's occupation as a shoemaker, a trade at which he excelled.

The speaker was leaning against the wall, having turned away from the window out of which he'd been gazing: Paul Pierce. Cob had no trouble recognising his saviours now, two of the best men and firmest friends in the Blues. Pierce's eyes were the same shade of grey as Quested's, and every bit as shrewd, but there the resemblance between the two men ended. Where Quested was tall and lumbering, Pierce was short and stocky. Both had brown hair but, where Quested's was thick and dark, Pierce's was fine and thinning, brushed back severely from a receding hairline.

It was by none of those things that Pierce was identified to strangers; instead descriptions invariably began with the tattoos that writhed down his forearms below permanently turned-back cuffs. The one on the left arm was old and faded, while the other was newer and vividly coloured. Only when he rolled his sleeves up further did he reveal the ugly scars entwined with his adornments. In truth, everything about him was ugly except for a voice that, in stark contrast, had all the fluty beauty of a cock blackbird's song on a spring morning.

Embarrassed by his friend's praise, Quested didn't so much blush as wriggle. 'They says make sure you live, so I makes sure.'

Cob relaxed. Quested and Pierce had risked their lives to save him. It was a good feeling to have friends, to find a place in the Blues with men slightly his senior but more like him in other ways than the youngsters with whom he had failed to bond. He drifted back to the night of the shooting. Remembering the authoritative voice issuing instructions, he realised that even the calculating Ransley had wanted him alive, albeit for his own reasons. But who was it that ran on? Only then did memory fail. Had the man wanted him dead or merely feared for his own life? Perhaps he had not even known a man was down. Only one question mattered. He licked his lips and asked it apprehensively.

'How many did we lose?'

'Four.' Pierce's words were heavy with the burden of bad news. 'Three of the tubmen, old Page amongst 'em, and one of the boys helping on the carts.'

Cob sighed. There'd been all too many losses through the winter and he found himself looking forward to a lull in the trade when the light summer nights arrived. Thinking of the future, he was unprepared for the final blow that Pierce had saved until last.

'They took Cephas.'

His tone said clearly that he saw the man's absence as a permanent state of affairs. No doubt he and Quested had discussed their leader's prospects at some length.

'And they picks up Dick Wraight way out beyond Dowell's Farm,' Quested added. 'Still black with powder.'

That was tough luck indeed, to fall into the preventives' hands when so close to getting clear. Cob nodded, too tired to respond, and drifted back into a troubled sleep where friends were snatched away on every side. Relief at being saved faded into a sense of guilt at surviving when others had not been so lucky.

George

George Ransley stood in the garden of the Bourne Tap, looking across his land towards Bilsington Priory. People said the ruins were haunted but he knew when those rumours started and why.

Cephas Quested was an unimaginative man but he knew the value of having a place off the beaten track where men could meet and store a few tubs. A modest share in their hauls persuaded the elderly landowner, who used the dilapidated abbot's quarters as a farmhouse, to turn a blind eye to their nocturnal comings and goings. New to smuggling then, drawn into the twilight world by his bride's family connections, George casually mentioned to Cephas that most people were afraid of ghosts. He had no doubt that the farmer would be as willing to talk for a tub as he was to keep silent. Before long, a story began to circulate about a monk who wandered the ruins at night, his severed head under his arm.

Impressed by the success of the ruse, Cephas drew George further into his plans. He never acknowledged the contributions in public, later promoting Sam Bailey to second-in-command with Hogben as an unofficial lieutenant, but he relied more and more on his adviser's shrewd counsel in private.

The lack of a formal position did not concern George. With no particular interest in the outward trappings of power, what he wanted was control — and he soon found that his freshly won influence gave him that. Cephas sought his opinions and took his advice, so much so that gradually it became he who decided where and when they would move, which cargo was worth a risk and which wasn't.

Running the Tap as an unlicensed beerhouse, a blind pig as the locals would have it, meant he reaped the best possible rewards from his labours. The spirits they imported were over-proof and he was skilled at letting them down to create a brew that was both palatable and profitable. In the days after a run, the lanes for miles in each direction were littered with men sleeping it off or trying to find their homes when they could barely find their feet. That extra bit of trouble quadrupled the returns, slowly building his fortune until he was wealthier than many of his betters. He might have no grand house filled with precious possessions but, when it came to ready cash, he was comfortably placed indeed.

The partnership worked well for most of a decade. George knew it had two weaknesses, Cephas might shift his loyalty, or he might die. The former might have been harder but even the present situation, sure to end in death, required careful handling. The Blues did not know the extent of his past influence, which might be for the best, but now he had to convince them that he was the man to rally behind. He knew that would not be easy.

During the month since the clash at Brookland, feelings had run high. Not satisfied with four dead and two taken prisoner, Blockademen scoured the countryside for clues to the identities of the hundreds of traders who'd evaded them. George suspected that, for every uniformed officer knocking on doors, there were another two or three spies drifting through the population. It did them no good. Everywhere they heard gossip and boasts, but nowhere did they find names, dates and addresses. When they rode into Aldington in force one night, trying to intimidate the local people into giving up their own, the villagers closed ranks. The authorities found their questions unanswered, their horses unwatered and their searches obstructed. Eventually they rode away, taking only frustration and fatigue with them.

George had been content to let events take their course. He needed the Blues to accept what had happened, and what was likely to follow, and to see for themselves the might of the forces arrayed against them and the need for wise leadership in the future. Only now had he brought some of the best amongst them together for a meeting. His pitch was carefully calculated, inviting them to the Tap to emphasise the advantages that he could offer in an outlet for their wares and easy access from his land to their stores in the ruins. He was relying on Eliza, his wife of twelve years, to ply them with the contents of his extensive cellar, not to mention her delicious baking, giving them a taste of the perks that the Blues would enjoy under his leadership.

He sucked on his pipe pensively. Most of the men awaiting him wanted a new leader as soon as possible. They did not covet the role for themselves, nor did they want their income to plummet while the Blues foundered. George knew he had support from some of the brighter men and thought he could win over the apathetic. That left a few real threats, most of whom would want the eldest of his wife's brothers for leader.

A few years his junior, Sam Bailey was the second of eight children. The Mersham Baileys sprang from the three marriages of Sam's grandfather and the family business was free-trade. Yet George doubted that Sam, despite his lifetime of experience, was the man to lead the Blues. He respected the commander of their bat-wielding scouts, and would gladly retain him in that role, but knew that Sam could not equal Cephas as a leader nor himself as a strategist. They had no one who could fill the captured man's boots as a figurehead, but it was better to have one of the two qualities than neither.

George sighed, having no illusions about the unflattering comparisons to be made. Bailey stood over him by a good four inches and cut an impressive figure, even now that some of his youthful muscle was turning to fat. That was the Bailey legacy: the whole family, man and woman alike, was tall and statuesque, dark and handsome. George was himself dark, with luxuriant near-black curls and deep blue eyes, and, while not of Bailey proportions, he was far from short. Unfortunately, he was equally far from handsome. As

14

coldly rational in his assessment of himself as he was of every other facet of life, he knew that he was downright ugly: a set of prominent and crowded teeth atop a generous paunch, the whole lot perched on long skinny legs. And, if looks weren't enough, he avoided physical confrontation, whereas Bailey's skill and vigour with a swingle — a weapon not unlike a threshing flail — was legendary. The destruction he left in his wake was almost unbelievable for two sticks joined by a few links of chain... until the unbeliever saw the rings of iron studs embedded in the battered ash poles.

George had learned early in life that one as disadvantaged by Mother Nature as he was must be cunning and resourceful to level the playing field, and therein lay his strength. Now he must convince these men that brains were more valuable than brawn. That would be the crux of the matter. He turned to go inside.

Standing in the doorway to the back room, he examined the men knocking back some of his finest Spanish port wine from tankards designed for weaker brews. They were fast drinkers at any time and would waste no time over liquor as smooth as that. As usual, his approach was carefully judged: he wanted them mellow, enjoying his hospitality, but not fighting drunk and, as with so much over recent months, it was a difficult balancing act.

Seeing Sam Bailey's shrewd eyes on him, so dark that they might be black rather than brown, he was still uncertain whether the man wanted the job of leader. There was a chill at the core of his soul that made him hard to fathom. George entered the room and took the only empty seat. The men had gravitated into two camps and now, as he expected, he was between them. He had agonised long and hard over his invitations. Some, like Tommy Dennard, were absent even though he expected them to play a big part in the future of the Blues; they were too young or too insignificant now to merit a vote. Some, like James Hogben, were present even though he would gladly be rid of them; they were too significant to ignore, however much he might have liked to do so. Of the rest, most were solid, dependable men whom he believed he could persuade to his way of thinking, if he could hold their attention long enough to put his case. When quiet fell around the table, he knew he'd scored his first victory. As host, they accorded him control of the meeting. It was down to him to transform that into control of the Blues.

'Well, boys,' he began. 'I think we all know why we're here.'

Some men nodded but others looked less sure. Hogben tipped his chair back on two legs and rested the rail against the wall. He was once amongst the most fearsome of their number, strong and fierce, dark and brooding. George had never much liked him, thinking him stupid and coarse, but he'd felt reluctant admiration for the man's tenacity and single-mindedness. That slight regard had faded in later years, eroded by a degree of brutality unusual even in men of their ilk, but now his distaste was tinged with pity.

When Hogben took the slug at Folkestone, even the authorities considered him incapable of further mischief. Believing he'd been rendered harmless, they released him into a surgeon's care, only to have him abscond at the first opportunity. George could have told them that Hogben would never be harmless while there was breath in his body. Quite the contrary in fact, because the lingering pain had turned him into an opium-eater as well as a drunk. Whatever Hogben saw when he viewed the world through his chemical haze, it probably bore little resemblance to reality.

Still, for all that, Hogben was an unexpectedly honest man. It was he who mustered and paid the tubmen for a run, compensating each one fairly and returning the balance with a full account of how he had disbursed the funds before he went off to drink himself senseless. That was a more important service than it sounded, given that it wasn't easy to find a trustworthy man who commanded the respect of the batmen and could not be intimidated into skimming the weaker men's wages to subsidise the stronger. If Hogben had a redeeming feature apart from his honesty, it was that he could not be intimidated by anyone.

Hogben now growled accusingly. 'Can't wait, can you?'

George gave a slight shrug. 'Would you have us leaderless?'

'We're not damned well leaderless.'

'You think they'll release Cephas?'

Hogben held his eye defiantly. 'Never can tell with a jury.'

'That's true. You're of a mind to persuade them, are you?'

'I won't stand by and let a friend take the morning drop.'

George considered the assertion dispassionately. He was capable of loyalty to a friend but he would not sacrifice the Blues for it. He had no doubt that loyalty figured in Hogben's decision but protecting his own position surely played a part too.

'Cephas knew what to expect if he was taken. We all do.'

Some heads nodded. They all knew the risks and took them without any expectation of daring rescues if their plans went awry. Men sometimes escaped the authorities when angry mobs of kith and kin overpowered the guards who were trying to move them between gaol and courtroom, as had happened in Dover just the year before, but such triumphs were few and far between.

Hogben was not appeased. 'For Christ's sake, Sam, tell the bugger how it is.'

George felt his brother-in-law's stare settle on him, thoughtful but silent. There was still no way to tell whether second-in-command would be enough. Suppressing his doubts, he turned his gaze on Pierce, watching him lean back and evaluate where the men around the table stood on the matter. George was certain there'd been plenty of talk about what was to come next. His own, as yet undeclared, candidacy might have been foreseen but then again it might not. He expected Pierce to be amongst his allies, a man who understood the value of sound information and carefully laid plans, and who was self-motivated enough not to need conventional leadership. If he needed an incentive, he had one in the six children packed into his crumbling cottage in Bonnington.

Pierce cleared his throat before speaking.

'More than fifty men felt ball or blade at Brookland, so they say. God knows but we took our share,' he looked around again, one or two remaining slings and bandages making his point better than words. 'Four of us dead, and one of them. One's all it takes. Someone has to pay or they'll never let it lie. They got old Cephas and I reckon he'll do for 'em. If we let them have him, they'll think we're beaten and we can come back strong. If we don't, well.'

He didn't need to spell out the consequences.

Giles shifted in his chair, nutmeg-brown eyes flitting from face to face and right hand skimming a thatch of hair with the colour and texture of a bristle brush. The young cobbler was well-liked by many of the older men in the Blues but, settled early in both trade and marriage, out of step with his contemporaries. George supposed the young bucks thought him staid or boring but he himself expected their future to rely heavily on the valuable blend of intelligence, restraint and dependability to be found in men like him. For the moment, he noted that Giles's shoulder was much improved but knew it would be weeks before he was hefting tubs as freely as he had before he took a barrel full of shot.

Giles's awkwardness now extended beyond a stiff back. His hand dropped from his hair to his throat, as he kneaded a pair of moles that straddled his Adam's apple.

'I don't know. Cephas is one of us. I mean, well, I wouldn't be here if, well.'

The sharp look that the objection drew from Dick Higgins told George that the man thought his friends fools for hanging back to help Giles. He was no coward and yet he asked nothing of his fellows except that they ask no more of him. Years of poaching had left its mark, physically in a finger joint snapped off by a gin trap and mentally in a knowledge that a poor man's life was worth less than a brace of pheasants. A vivid contrast to Giles, a few years older but far less steady, he was nonetheless a useful man. His skill in negotiating the landscape was equally valuable whether he passed a night in poaching or free-trade. Although well-made, taller than average and flushed with the ruddy colouring of a life lived almost entirely outdoors, it was his character, not his looks, that demanded attention. If other men were candles, Higgins was a lighthouse. For him, there were no half-measures: contentment was joy, anger was rage and love was passion. His company was too good for him to be disliked but no one doubted how fast he would turn on them if he thought he had cause.

George kept a watchful eye on him, knowing that he was unstable but finding that his usefulness outweighed his explosive nature for the present. He returned to the matter in hand. There was a line to be drawn somewhere. Camaraderie was good, uniting men as brothers and making them stronger together than they could ever be alone, but there came a point when a fellow was beyond help and Cephas had reached it the moment that Hogben lost him in the final minutes of the confrontation. Taking a charitable view, Hogben's guilt at escaping, when Cephas had not, was making it harder for him to accept the inevitability of their decision. All the same, George would not risk their lives or their futures to stage a doomed rescue attempt.

'If we could have saved him that night, we'd have done it. But what's done is done. Now's the time to think what comes after.'

Disbelief spread over Hogben's face.

'That's it then?'

He scanned the others contemptuously.

'You're all behind this self-serving sod?'

He appealed to the younger Quested for support.

'Quacks? Damn me but Cephas is your cousin or whatever. Are you going to stand by while he swings?'

George knew then that he'd won the argument. There'd never been much love lost between the Questeds, the elder thinking the younger soft and the younger thinking the elder stupid. The one opposite him was too good a man to find pleasure in his relative's fate but he was unlikely to lose sleep over it. George knew Hogben had lost the hand when he resorted to playing that card.

Quested drew a deep breath. Kinship would not influence his decision but neither would the nature of his feelings for his distant cousin. He was nothing if not fair. Eventually he gave his decision in a deliberate tone that declared he understood its significance.

'I stands with Paul on this.'

Those few quiet words were all George needed.

'Bugger you then,' Hogben said, springing to his feet and banging his chair into the wall. 'Bugger all of you. I'll do it myself.'

He stormed out.

George turned to Bailey, offering him the chance to keep his rank. The keen eyes that met his gaze confirmed that their owner knew what was on the table.

'Will he make trouble?'

'Nothing we can't handle,' his new second-in-command replied. It was a moment or two before he raised a new concern, something that had doubtless occurred to many of them. 'But what if Cephas has his own ideas for getting himself off?'

It was a fair point, given that Cephas wouldn't be the first to turn King's Evidence to save his skin, but George did not believe that would happen. It wasn't so much faith in the man's integrity as certainty of his indifference to death: his legendary binges had taken him close to it often enough but the prospect never seemed to slow him up once he'd tapped a tub. As the locals loved to recount, when one of his drinking mates failed to wake up the morning after they'd fallen down senseless in a wood on a cold night, he had called out cheerily that Clumpy Gardiner had died of what he loved. Cephas loved the trade and George had no doubt he'd die before he betrayed it. There was confidence in his voice when he reassured the assembled men.

'Cephas won't turn approver.'

When no one disputed the declaration, he moved on to consider the men who had not voiced an opinion. Bailey's kin, uncle John and brother Rob, would follow him, regardless of their friendship with Hogben. If blood was thicker than water, then Bailey blood was treacle. While not fond of either man, George did not underestimate their value to the Blues. Tough as nails, they were at the heart of the armed parties. A stranger would surely identify all three as brothers, sharing as they did the same massive build, near-black hair and obsidian eyes, but the likeness did not extend to their characters. If Sam was no better than the other two underneath, he kept a tight rein on his inclinations; he could be a mean drunk but the beaten men he left in his wake were as bad as he was. The younger Baileys were more troublesome, both violent and dishonest. John's sins were usually by omission — he took any and every opportunity to shirk — while Rob's were invariably by commission — little was out of bounds if it entertained him.

That left only James Wilson. Amongst the youngest at the table, the waggoner's mate from Bank Farm was not an easy man to call. On the short side of average, his slender body was lithe and his movements catlike. There was no trace of poetry in George's nature but he'd heard his daughter say that Wilson looked as if he were part of the woodland, with eyes like moss and hair like bark. It was the fancy of a besotted girl, whose attention had already flitted elsewhere, and yet somehow it was not so far off the mark. The man certainly had an uncanny bond with all God's creatures, not least with the horses to which George was also partial.

More prosaically, Wilson's soft speech betrayed a strict upbringing and a weak chest, thee's and thou's delivered in a rasp that declared his life was unlikely to be long and hearty. Yet, for all that, he had a more independent spirit than most of his fellows. He was often overlooked because of his frail body but George did not underestimate the sharpness of his mind. It made sense for Wilson to support his leadership bid, given that Hogben and even Sam Bailey had so little time for the weakling they thought him to be, but George took nothing for granted. He didn't need unanimity but Wilson was respected by some of the men he valued most highly. His support might be useful.

'Bish?'

Bish for Bishop, Wilson's middle name, his mother's maiden name and perhaps a futile expression of her hopes for a future in the church. Even if his class had not barred him from such office, his reflective outlook was better suited to the asceticism of a monk than the political ambitions of a bishop. There was a pause before he spoke and, when he did so, his pensive tone declared he had not yet made a decision. His words were unexpected.

'They'll be seeking to hang Cephas in chains.'

No one replied, every man at the table looking at him in the same bewilderment. He was probably right that Cephas's body would hang in disgrace until the crows picked it clean. When his desiccated remains were finally cut down, they would lie ignominiously in unhallowed ground.

'We can't stand by for that.'

George came to himself with a start, realising that he had been staring, his mouth gaping to reveal the double row of crowded top teeth by which he was often identified. It made no difference to him what happened to a dead man's body and yet, clearly, it mattered to Wilson.

'I doubt he'll be up to worrying about it by then.'

'We can't stand by for it.'

It was an unforeseen obstacle and George wasn't used to being caught off-guard. It had never occurred to him that anyone would care about the fate of Cephas's remains.

'All right. Say I can stop him from hanging in chains.'

'How wouldst thou do that?'

'It don't matter. Say I can? You could check it in the *Chronicle*.'

That was true. Wilson was one of the few who could check in the *Chronicle* if he so wished, given that he read fast and well.

'*If* thou seest to that, thou wilt have my vote.'

George could see that the stipulation had taken all the men as unawares as himself but also that they liked the idea. It meant they hadn't rolled over. They would take their punishment but not humiliation. Fortunately, he had something to bargain with and he wasn't above blackmailing a local magistrate with a troublesome younger brother to advance his cause.

'I'll see to it. So, are we running again?'

Pierce smiled and raised his tankard. 'To the running, lads.'

Toasts echoed around the room and drained tankards soon thumped on the heavy ash table. Eliza brought more jugs, this time filled with beer, and George cautiously congratulated himself. The coup was complete with no blood spilled. The Blues had made a tactical retreat but the war was still on. He rose to his feet, nodded to his men, and left them to their celebrations.

Hog

The Palm Tree public house near Wingmore Court was a regular haunt when the Blues worked in East Kent. Nestled in the Elham valley, it provided a convenient assembly point for runs at Folkestone, Dover and Deal. With a landlord who was both friend and customer to the trade, they could wish for no better base.

Hog had considered all that when he selected the inn for his own meeting but was undeterred. The fact that he regularly mustered men there only made his doing so that night more natural. He'd thought long and hard about the men he'd summoned. Given that he'd recruited half the men in the Blues, he knew them well enough but assessing a man's skills for a run was different from judging his willingness to cross George Ransley. Their new leader had decreed that Cephas would be left to hang and Hog wondered how many of the Blues would go out on a limb to prevent that happening. Knowing that support for Ransley was strongest around Aldington, Hog biased his selection to the east. He expected that to be advantageous in more ways than one.

There had always been a divide in the South Kent smugglers, the men of the marshes on one side and those from the east coast on the other. The marshmen thought themselves above the rest of England, Kent included, while the Deal men saw themselves as the true masters of free-trade. The tension had intensified towards the end of the French wars, when the two halves of the county were combined into one administrative region run from Maidstone far to the west. The marshmen were indifferent to the change, miles to the south as they were, but the east coasters bitterly resented it and brought their resentment into the Blues. Cephas bridged the gap to an extent, with a home in Aldington but roots in Hawkinge. Ransley represented a westwards shift in power, resident in Aldington like his predecessor but born in nearby Ruckinge. By focusing his search on his own home ground, Hog hoped to exploit his men's loyalty to their birthplace as well as their former leader.

He now stood at the bar, drinking lightly for once, waiting for the last of the forty-three men he'd finally settled on. So far, he had said nothing beyond his usual curt greetings and he would do no more until they were outside, safe from eavesdroppers.

They were due to meet at half past eight o'clock but gathering the far-flung mob together was always a time-consuming process. For a start, most were in work of some kind and had little say when their day ended. Few had their own timepieces and each village operated on its own time, taken from its church clock. On top of all that, many men relied on borrowed horses or lifts from friends for part of their journeys. All in all, only a handful of those within walking distance of a rendezvous stood any chance of appearing at the appointed hour. That night was better than some. Hog had been relieving himself a few yards along the lane when the sound of St Mary's clock striking the hour drifted down the valley from Elham. Knowing the hour must be nine, he counted the strokes anyway.

Back in the tap-room, he doubted that more than ten minutes had passed when the last three men came through the door. He would have liked to get straight down to business but they had ridden from Deal and needed a break after their fifteen-mile journey. He watched impatiently while they worked their way through their pies and pints. As soon as the last mouthful disappeared, he made for the door. There was no need to give a signal: all eyes had been on him and the room emptied in his wake. It was a well-rehearsed routine that the locals would barely notice. Even once they were outside, he kept to his familiar pattern. He waited while the mounted men readied their horses then led the way along the valley, north-eastwards as if intending to pick up the Dover road. The fact that he himself was on foot would already have told the smarter men that it was no ordinary night. He thought nothing of walking home from Wingmore but he would have purloined a horse from somewhere if he planned to go via Dover. Nonetheless, they followed without comment. He strode through the night, turning left at Breach and heading up the hillside. Within a quarter an hour of leaving the Palm Tree, his men were sprawled across the resting pasture, the brandy-fuelled fires in their guts staving off any frost that crept through their layers of wool and leather.

He settled himself on a fallen bough from a lone oak. It was a picturesque spot for him to present his case — the full moon high above the ridge behind him and the faces before him bone white in its cold light — but such fancies never crossed his mind. He swallowed apprehensively, far more daunted by what he was about to do than he had ever been by facing a party of preventive men and their muskets. If he got this wrong, he might end up dead or sent to Coventry. Strangely, the second option held more fear for him than the first. Determined to carry on whatever the cost, he cleared his throat.

'There's no run tonight, lads.'

He was sure that much had been clear already but he let them get their mutters out of the way before he continued.

'And there'll be no runs this summer neither.'

That had not been mentioned at the meeting at the Bourne Tap but Hog was sure it was the truth. Ransley had made it clear he intended to let the Preventive Service think it'd won at Brookland, which meant he would not be carrying on with business as usual. Besides, he was a schemer and he had a lot of scheming yet to do.

The men on the hillside began to grumble again. One of the factors Hog had considered when selecting his militia was their need for money. In front of him were some of the most imprudent men in the Blues, most with large families to feed and small incomes on which to do it. Hog knew all about those pressures.

'Our new leader…'

He paused to let the phrase sink in, although he was sure that the news about Ransley had already made the rounds.

'Our new leader wants to let them have Cephas. He thinks, if the bastards think they've done for us, then *maybe* one day…'

He paused again.

'*If* we live that long, we can start trading again.'

The words he quoted had come from Pierce, not Ransley, but he saw no reason to let details undermine his case. The buzz of protest rose. He listened carefully, seeking to pick out the right note of support from the mumbling. He didn't have to wait long for the argument he wanted to make. He pointed at the man in question and repeated his remark.

'"Cephas in't dead yet." That's just what I told the bugger.'

Even Hog did not make a habit of describing Ransley as a bugger, having grudging respect though no affection for the man, but he did so then with a purpose. Each insult that passed unchallenged took them further towards rebellion. He needed to lead his men down a path that would make crossing the inner circle of the Blues seem a sane plan, to take them so far that it became easier to go forward than turn back. To do that, he needed to erode the position that Ransley had built up and avoid any reference to the fact that he had the support of the Baileys. Hog thought the first would be simple enough, given the distance that Ransley put between himself and the rest of the Blues, but was far less certain how to deal with the second problem. That was why these men were hand-picked, many of them resentful of the Mersham Baileys and their influence in the Blues, but he was sharp enough to know that resentment of others did not automatically make them loyal to him, especially since he had been friendly with the younger Baileys until they took the wrong side at the Tap. He chose his opening phrase cautiously, avoiding any suggestion that he thought he knew the gathered men's position, let alone presumed to tell them what it should be.

'I don't know about you lot but I'm not so sure I want a new leader. I mean,' he continued smoothly, without leaving a pause in which he might be interrupted, 'I'm not even sure we need one. I don't reckon Cephas is done for yet. I don't reckon,' he lowered his voice conspiratorially, 'He has to be done for at all.'

He took a moment to study his audience, wondering if they would believe a rescue possible and if they would be willing to risk their necks to attempt one. There were a few whispers but most of them seemed to be letting his words sink in, considering the twin possibilities of standing with or standing against Ransley.

He gave them time.

Eventually a reply came from a group to the right of Hog.

'How's that then? In't like he's in Dover.'

Hog placed the smoke-scuffed rasp instantly and looked for its owner. There he was, a fisherman of middle years, sitting apart from the others with a friend of similar vintage. The pair were notorious for their awe-inspiring tobacco consumption, Smoker never without a skull-bowled Meerschaum and Quids punctuating his sentences with gobs of stained spit. Neighbours and boat-sharers, their decision would be joint as always.

Having been unsure whether to include them, Hog hoped he'd

judged well. They would miss uncustomed tobacco in coming months, of that there was no doubt, and their combined total of thirteen children must make short work of whatever their catches brought in. Set against that was the fact that they were a good deal more cautious than Hog wanted when it came to taking on the authorities. Quick to brand anyone less rash than himself as a coward, he would have dismissed them out of hand, were it not that they risked their lives every time they launched their lugger on a rough night. He'd seen them take a galley across the channel in seas so bad that they could not find men enough for all the oars.

Smoker's next comment hinted at his priorities.

'I'm not out to join him.'

Death on the high seas was one thing, incarceration and execution clearly another. Hog needed to quash such objections if his efforts were to bear fruit. His plan required boats and he wanted Smoker and Quids to sail them, knowing that success depended on having men of their calibre to execute each stage. He was proud of his plan, devised to exploit intelligence that he'd gathered himself. He knew every Blockade watering hole in the Blues' territory and made short work of finding one of Cephas's guards in the Port Arms on the seafront in Deal. A couple of guineas had quickly loosened the man's tongue.

More likely to brood on his faults than deny them, Hog was under no illusion that he could match Ransley's fox-like cunning but he did set store by his contacts and experience. In his opinion, Ransley would do well to spend a little more time in public houses around the coast instead of drifting around in solitary scheming. Now, while Ransley was still trying to find out where the prisoners were being held, after even their families had been refused visiting rights, he knew not just the location but also what was to happen to them next. They were to be moved from His Majesty's Ship *Severn*, at anchor in the Downs off Deal, to Newgate gaol on the first day of April. They would make the journey to Deptford docks aboard the tender, *Industry*. Hog knew the hundred-foot transport well, having seen it bring back scores of raw recruits for the Blockade. When the supply of volunteers for bloody coastal duty far from home dried up in the north and west of England, the Navy cast its net wider and soon began to ship in starving Irishmen as well.

The transfer from the frigate to the city offered precisely the opportunity that Hog needed. Boarding a vessel suited his men's skills far better than attempting a gaol-break. He decided to focus the discussion on that point.

'All we've got to do is board a boat and unload a cargo. What man amongst you hasn't done that fifty times over?'

'And the bastards'll lay down their muskets and help him into a galley, will they?'

The sneer came from Ted Pantry, something of a kindred spirit to Hog in that he liked to take a drink and then savour how badly the world had treated him. They often shared their morose reflections on the state of the country and the abuse of their class. It was characteristic of Ted to exercise his usual sarcasm, without considering its impact on an ally's strategy. Hog took it in his stride, recognising that objections needed to be aired and that it made little difference who aired them.

'I wouldn't trust to it,' he admitted.

'I doubt we'll get near enough to find out.' Another dissenting voice, this time belonging to John Horne. 'They'll be using the *Industry* and she carries four twelve-pounders.'

The Horne brothers, John and Edward — Harry to all — were handsomely built, skilled with a duck-gun and owners of a cart. Always short of money, they rarely turned down the chance to earn a guinea. It was no secret that they had more greed than courage but, so far, the former had proved as reliable as the latter. Best of all, after years of slow progress, they could doubtless be seduced by the chance to distinguish themselves and climb a few rungs. Hog had only to find the right words to tempt them.

He thought the *Industry*'s carronades were the least of their worries. He let his contempt for the ageing vessel fill his voice.

'Aye, if her crew dares fire 'em. She's a year into harbour service and those smashers could be the end of her. Besides, they're only good for three hundred yards and we won't be hanging about when we're that close.'

Smoker tapped out his pipe on a stray chalk boulder. 'And what vessel shall we be?'

Hog had no intention of declaring his plans ahead of time, risking betrayal or plain old careless talk.

'Look, there's a plan and you'll know what it is when the time's right. All I'm asking is whether you're the kind of men who'd stand by while the man who's lined your pockets these past six years gets nubbed? And can you wait months to start earning again?'

A hawking throat-clearing came from the same direction as Smoker's question, the prelude to Quids jettisoning a load of spit before speaking. The spew spattered Smoker's discarded boulder.

'Why now?' Quids asked. His voice was deep, guttural, as if his throat never quite managed to clear itself of saliva.

Hog frowned, misunderstanding the question. When else could you rescue a man but after he'd been taken prisoner? His response was more circumspect than usual.

'When did you have in mind, then?'

'After the trial.' Quids swilled his wad into the other cheek and loosed another string of spit at the boulder. Wiping his lips with his cuff, he added, 'He might yet walk away a free man, without the need for us to do aught.'

That might have been a sound suggestion, but for one thing.

'Good point. I thought the same.' That was a lie: he hadn't considered it an option. 'Trouble is, once he's in Newgate, I don't see how we'd get to him.' He'd made good use of the time since the meeting at the Tap and now intended to use his preparation to impress these men, few of whom knew London any better than he did. 'It's but yards from Newgate to the Old Bailey, and scarce a mile even to the Magistrate in Bow Street. And all the while the streets are busier than Canterbury on May Day. As I see it, we'd mostly likely join him on the scaffold.' He drew a breath before driving home his final argument. 'And, mark my words, that's where he'll end up. They haven't set up their fancy Blockade, with all it's costing 'em, only to throw back their first big catch. If he stood trial down here, it'd be a different thing but with a London jury.' He shrugged, as if the implications of that were clear.

Smoker obliged by raising a possibility that Hog had considered in some detail before rejecting it as hopeless.

'Jurymen can be persuaded.'

'Round here they might,' Hog conceded.

They could arrange for every member of a jury at Maidstone Assizes to receive the required incentive, bribe or threat, within hours of selection. Such an undertaking was beyond them for a Middlesex session.

'There'd be no time for it there. They swear 'em in dozens: we'd never find 'em all and it in't like they'd know us from Adam.'

The noise from the assembled men began to rise again. Hog gave them time to chew over what he'd said. As he saw it, there were three issues: their loyalty to Cephas, their doubts about Ransley, and their need for work that summer. The relative importance of those factors varied from man to man. To his surprise, Smoker was the first to announce a decision.

'You find the men, we'll get 'em aboard.'

Hog felt a tangible ripple of response to the offer. It was the best news he could have hoped for, a guarantee of fast, reliable transport and a challenge to the courage of every man present. Now he needed a response from the armed parties. Just one man might be enough to tip the balance in his favour. As the seconds dragged by, he felt the opportunity begin to slip from his grasp but could think of nothing more to offer in support of his demand for action. Then, from the edge of the gathering, came a voice whose owner Hog had not invited.

'We're in…'

Hog knew the condition before it was uttered.

'…s'long as you're out to free Dick with him.'

Ted Wraight, landlord of the Walnut Tree public house in Aldington: how he came to know of the meeting was almost as much of a mystery as how he came to be overlooked. Hog had appealed to Cephas's cousin but had failed to consider the family of the other captured man. He should have known that the Wraights would not stand by while a cousin hanged, as he surely must with the weight of the circumstantial evidence against him. When Wraight said 'we', he undoubtedly spoke for his three cousins still free and his words were the catalyst that the mob had been waiting for.

'Us an' all.'

Horne's declaration launched a tide of agreement, confirming that Hog had succeeded in the first part of his bid to oppose Ransley. He let out a breath he had not known he was holding. There were plenty of bridges yet to cross but, now that he had men behind him, the optimism of his ebullient side began to gain ground on the cynicism of the world-weary depressive. He began to believe what he had already told Ransley's inner circle.

Cephas would not hang.

George

By a quirk of fate, while Hogben held his meeting near the Palm Tree, George Ransley sat at a table less than an hour's walk away in the Black Robin at Kingston, a welcoming hostelry that he often visited when he wanted to find peace away from the Blues. A dozen miles from Aldington and close to the northern limits of their territory, the only man he occasionally ran into there was James Quested on his way between contacts in Canterbury and land at Hawkinge. George would sip a half of cider, while Quested sank a pint of half-and-half before resuming his journey.

That night, George was alone but awaiting company, in a private room at the back of the inn. The man he was to meet preferred not to be seen with him and the substantial sweeteners with which George regularly plied the landlord guaranteed them the required privacy. The room had one door into the taproom and one to the outside, and it was the latter that George watched.

When the knob began to turn, George tensed. In spite of his carefully laid plans and the absence of any solid evidence to link him with the Blues, he was conscious that feelings still ran high after Brookland and that made him uneasy at telling a magistrate where he would be at a given time. It would take a biased jury indeed to convict him of anything at that point in time but then the Preventive Service might not bother with a trial.

When the door opened, a man stood alone on the threshold. That might have seemed surprising to some but the two men had done business for years and the visitor knew he was in no danger from George. Sir Edward Knatchbull came in, bolted the door behind him and offered his hand. They shook firmly.

George studied Knatchbull thoughtfully. Tall and trim, he bore no resemblance to any caricature of a rural gentleman. Not yet forty, he looked more the eldest son than the squire he'd become just two years earlier, on the death of an estranged father whose main achievement had been to populate the area with almost as many children as unpaid debts. But, if the new squire's delicate mouth held a hint of the dandy, any such notion quickly faded on looking into the sad blue eyes that seemed dark with the burden of baronetship. Only when his mournful gaze had given an entirely false impression of his character did his rich voice, at once mellifluous and droll, restore the balance. Although Knatchbull took both his position and politics seriously, he did not let them deny him the finer things at his family seat of Mersham le Hatch.

'Well now. What's it going to take to put this to bed nice and quiet?' Knatchbull asked, as he filled a tankard from the pitcher on the table. 'Will they pay the piper?'

It irked George to accommodate those who saw themselves as his betters but he was far too shrewd to let petty concerns interfere with good business. Knatchbull wanted him to lead the Blues because he was a lesser evil. Losing access to uncustomed goods would be bad but a vicious gang rampaging across the county would be worse.

Knatchbull met his gaze and waited.

George knew his own position was strong. Like so many others, Knatchbull wanted to preserve his supply. The difficulty was how to balance that desire against the demands of the law that he was duty-bound to uphold.

'There's a price.'

'I suspected there would be. Cephas will hang. It's beyond my power to stop it. An officer died that night.'

'Along with four others.'

'Criminals all.'

George bit his lip. One of the dead was a mere boy, whose sole crime was to lead a team of horses. George recalled the mother's despair when he broke the dismal news in person. Crumpled on the cold stone floor of her kitchen, she seemed not to hear his few words of sparse comfort. He watched her for a minute or two, then reached into his pocket to double the money he'd intended to leave. The boy had been due a shilling for his night's work but it was a sovereign that George set on the table before letting himself out. Suppressing the memory, he returned to the matter in hand.

'They know there has to be a hanging.'

'Then the price…?'

Oddly embarrassed, George passed on the peculiar demand.

'Keep him out of chains.'

The silence was broken only by the loud tick of the long-case clock by the door.

'Do that, and you have my word there'll be no trouble at the trial or the hanging. And I'll wait a while before trading again.'

The additional concession cost him nothing, since he had much to do in the meantime. He saw no need to mention the fact that he had little control over what Hogben might be up to. Waiting while Knatchbull considered his offer, which he believed to be a good one, he reflected that he could apply more pressure if Knatchbull claimed the request was also out of his power.

The other man smiled.

'No need to think about the stick. The carrot looks good to me. I think I can guarantee a Christian burial with his kin. Whose idea was that?' His eyes crinkled in amusement. 'Not yours, I'll wager.'

George bared his teeth, the smile genuine even if his crowded dentition brought it closer to a sneer. 'No, not mine. It came from a better man than me. I'd lose no sleep if the crows ate their fill.'

'Still, it has a certain dignity. Perhaps we owe him that.'

George was surprised by the sentiment but had to admit that he'd done well under Cephas's leadership. He'd intended from the outset to deliver on the promise he'd made to Wilson, to protect the future of both himself and the Blues, but now he became doubly determined, keen to ensure this dignity that seemed so important to Wilson and so fitting to Knatchbull. Taking a sip of cider, he reflected that he might have to call on his second-in-command to ensure that Hogben did not undermine his efforts.

Hog

It took a moment for Hog to recognise the pain in his chest as indigestion, something almost unknown for his robust digestive system. The steak-and-kidney pie he'd eaten at dinner-time was still trying to fight its way past the tension that had tied knots in his intestines over recent days. He tried to clear it with a loud belch, then a still louder fart, but the slight relief was short-lived.

He hadn't fully appreciated the difference between leading and following. In the Blues, and before that in the Navy, he'd recruited and organised countless men. What he had not done was to plan their actions and select the strategy that would save or cost lives. Too brash to undervalue his abilities, he was bitter that his lot in life had never furnished him with the opportunities that turned other men into leaders. He would have to learn by experience — a process that might prove fatal, to himself and to others.

Organising a run might not have stretched him too badly. He knew the Blockade, its methods and its men, as well as any in the Blues. Staging a rescue was a different matter. Too late it occurred to him that he should have asked more questions of the man in the Port Arms. He knew too little of the guards, their routines and their plans for the transfer. He shrugged, a symbolic gesture to cast off his misgivings. It was the first of April and Cephas had been due to leave the *Severn* at dawn. The sun had been up for an hour and, so far, his preparations were unfolding well.

To his surprise, he had all forty-three of the men he'd approached, plus the four Wraights. He doubted he had the unanimous support that the numbers suggested. Some were so desperate for work that no risk could put them off. Others had probably been coerced by companions who felt safer having them implicated than leaving them free to trade information for influence with Ransley.

Even so, his position was better than he'd dared to hope a week earlier. They had two small cutters, *Penelope* and *Dorothea*, each with a fine crew and more than equal to the revenue vessels that patrolled the Channel. True, they had nothing to match the firepower of the *Industry*'s carronades but half a dozen ancient wall-guns were poised to back up an eclectic selection of muskets, pistols and fowling pieces. Despite their age, the weighty long-guns had been deemed fit for service against Napoleon, backing up the cannons atop the Martello towers, and he saw no reason why they should not serve his purpose now. In his grandfather's day, they might have had 20-gun 150-tonners at their disposal, but it was many a long year since the trade flourished like that. In any event, he expected speed and manoeuvrability to count for more than firepower in an ambush. After two hours of lying low in the lee of Foreness Point, they'd eventually spotted the *Industry* sail around the spit and follow the south channel westwards. Smoker and Quids had wasted no time in getting under way.

Indigestion forgotten, Hog's blood began to race. Feeling the brisk easterly tugging at his hair and watching the mist scooting ahead of it, he knew God must surely be on their side. Not only would their pursuit be swift but it would also be cloaked from the look-out's view. Sail canvas snapped overhead while their bow wave bubbled below.

He hadn't stepped aboard a fast ship since his Navy days, and for many years had vowed never to do so again, but Cephas's plight made it necessary and the prospect of his imminent rescue made it pleasurable.

Everything was going to plan. They gained steadily on the tender as they left Margate behind them, drawing near just as the coastline fell into darkness. To the south were the sparsely populated marshes that separated the Isle of Thanet from the mainland proper. The night fisherman would already have landed their catches and few other vessels would be out so early.

Hog's heart pounded, the thrill of the chase overcoming his anxieties about the quality of his information and planning. His thoughts skipped forward, savouring the idea of sailing boldly back to Folkestone with Cephas aboard. He never questioned how the man would evade the authorities once there or how his return would be received by the Blues. All he saw was his own triumph.

His self-congratulation was premature.

'Hard to larboard!' a voice shouted decisively from aloft.

Such initiative would be rewarded with a flogging in the Navy but Smoker responded instantly. The look-out was one of their most reliable seamen and, if he said hard to larboard, that's where they'd go. Men swarmed over the *Penelope*, wrenching her rudder around and sweeping her boom hastily across the deck. There was a sickening moment in which it felt as if she might capsize, her forward momentum threatening to overcome her sudden change in course, but her crew knew what it was doing and saw her through the manoeuvre. As she flanked the unknown obstacle, a vessel coalesced out of the mist about a hundred yards ahead.

Hog had no time to react: he saw a tell-tale flash just an instant before a violent shock wave crashed against his eardrums. Not only was the *Industry* battle-ready but her carronades were already spitting fire. He smothered the panic rising within him. They'd expected opposition; he would not be fazed by its timing.

Relief washed over him as he saw the first ball fall short. Carronades were devastating at short range, but were notoriously inaccurate and often failed to fire their balls over the desired distance. There was no time for complacency though, as another roar announced the next shot. The bastards would find their range in seconds. He peered through the smoke drifting over the water between the vessels. Fifty yards to the north, the *Dorothea* was closer to the *Industry* but safe from the carronades, as she hovered off the bow. A cluster of Blockademen opened fire but their shots posed little risk to the *Dorothea's* crew. The volley of return fire had twice the power and sent two men sprawling on the deck of the *Industry*. The old wall-guns were playing their part, with a longer range and a harder kick than the Navy-issue muskets.

As the *Penelope* cut steadily towards the *Industry's* stern, a ball fell only a few yards short of her hull. Great plumes of spray arched in all directions, soaking the men aboard. Hog was still trying to clear salt-water from his eyes when he heard a ball shatter wood in front of him and then whistle past him, over the deck and into the sea beyond.

'Christ have mercy!' a man wailed, his cry merging into the confusion of wind and water, carronade and long-gun fire.

Hog guessed that a splinter had pierced his flesh and could only hope that it had missed his vital organs. Another ball smashed into the *Penelope*, a square hit near her bow. A covering blast from the *Dorothea* gave the Blockademen something else to think about for a few seconds.

'Fire the wall-guns!' Hog bellowed.

Nothing.

He'd stationed three of his calmest men on the guns, knowing that they would hold their positions and follow his orders. Spirits plummeting as he guessed at the path of the last ball from the carronades, he hauled himself forward to inspect the damage. Before he'd taken three steps, a call halted his advance.

'Guns down. Damage to bowsprit. No lives lost.'

'Damn!' Hog muttered. They'd be lucky to outrun the *Industry* without a sound bowsprit. 'Splice it!' he ordered.

'In hand,' the man shouted back.

'Covering fire from the muskets!'

They were out of range but Hog believed that doing something was always better than doing nothing. They could not just sit and wait to be sunk. The veil of smoke thinned enough for him to see a small party gathered in the bow to make good their damage. Looking past the stern, he saw the *Dorothea* completing a tight turn away from the *Industry*, maintaining her position out of the path of the carronades. She might save herself but offered a poor decoy for them. He needn't have worried. As soon as she completed her manoeuvre, she was headed for them, sailing for a point just astern. He might have known that there was no way that Quids would leave Smoker to face the fire alone.

'Bowsprit braced,' came a yell from the bows.

The reply came from Smoker amidships. 'Hard about.'

'Belay that!' Hog bawled.

'Hard about,' Smoker repeated, relinquishing the wheel to one of his regular crew and coming forward. 'All speed for Folkestone.'

Hog grabbed his shoulder and shook him fiercely.

'We're not done yet. We've not got what we came for.'

Smoker looked at him for a few seconds.

'Nor shall we. Cephas reached Deptford afore ever we set sail.'

Hog frowned. The man could not know that.

'Whatever you paid for your information, the Blockade beat it. Not to mention what their men might make in prize money if they took in even a handful of us after we opened fire on a vessel of the Royal Navy. The only thing now is to send these lovelies on their way back to France and get home before we're missed.'

Smoker had kept his voice low. Hog knew he was being given an opportunity to take advice without admitting he'd done so. The ship was already turning, while men fired blindly into the smoke on their larboard side. But *was* Cephas already lost to them?

'We can't leave him...'

The protest was partly personal, an admission of his pain in leaving one of their own to die, and partly professional, a final attempt to make his plan succeed.

'There's no sense joining him,' Smoker countered. 'It might be All Fool's Day but I'll be damned if I plan on being one of them.'

The words send a shiver down Hog's spine. All Fool's Day? He did not think for a minute that the Blockade had either the time or the inclination for practical jokes, but then again. He thought back to the Port Arms, trying to remember how the guard from the *Severn* had answered his questions. He had no clear memory of hearing the date of April first, whether it had been given fluently or hesitantly, nothing. Perhaps there had been a cruel irony hidden in the lie. Perhaps it was simply the first date that came into the mind of a man suddenly spotting a way to move up a rung on the tortuous path to a decent rank. In the shrunken peace-time Navy, with little prospect of officers being felled by enemy fire, opportunities for advancement were few and far between.

Hearing footsteps behind him, Hog glanced over his shoulder. The Wraights formed themselves into a ragged crescent. Drooping shoulders and downcast eyes declared the failure as painful to them as to him. Yet when Ted spoke, it was to agree with Smoker.

'We knew it was a slim chance, but without surprise on our side?'

So that was it. The Blockade had won. The Blues were finished, falling in behind a schemer just when they needed a fighter. What would Ransley do when faced with a broadside from an array of carronades? How could he negotiate, if they were shot on sight?

Beaten, Hog scowled and then shrugged.

'Please yourselves.'

He strode to the bow, ploughing through the *Dorothea's* wake, and stared into the night. If they could not out-gun the *Industry*, the only path left to them was to out-run her. With nothing left but his despair, he reached into his coat pocket and drew out a flask. Running his hand over its smoothness, he let his pain seep out of the compartment into which he'd forced it. The past few days had taken every scrap of self-discipline he possessed. Not only had he unrelentingly progressed his plans and preparations, but he had done so in a state of total sobriety. Now he longed for the numbing distance offered by the liquor in his palm.

He pulled out the stopper and sniffed the heady concoction, over-proof brandy laced with enough laudanum to calm a cart-horse. A few mouthfuls and none of it would matter any more.

He took a sip.

Too little and too soon for any real benefit, the improvement in his spirits was instant. Decision made, he poured half the flask down his throat. The familiar burning warmed him, as he waited for the indifference that would follow. Afterwards, self-loathing would bring on a melancholy deeper even than his present misery, but that would be tomorrow and he cared only for today.

Quacks

The streets around the Old Bailey, busy at any time, thronged with spectators for the trial of a notorious smuggler. True, many had never heard of Cephas Quested or his gang before the newspapers brought them to their attention but that did nothing to dispel their enthusiasm now the heinous crimes had been exposed, crimes that would have found a far more sympathetic reception amongst the coastal population than they did with a mob of city-dwellers. Most of those gathered knew nothing of the freedom from duties bestowed by Henry VIII on the Cinque Ports of Hastings, Romney, Hythe, Dover and Sandwich, or of the staunch belief of people in Kent and Sussex that it endured to the present, whatever the Preventive Service might think.

The crowds were oblivious to the fact that two of the men waiting outside the court were associates of the accused, one a relative at that. There had been those in the Blues who wanted to attend in force and it had taken all Ransley's authority and Bailey's strength to convince them that a more subtle presence was in order. If they wanted to stay in business, it was better for the judiciary to think them scattered by the loss of their leader. Eventually, after hours of debate, James Quested was chosen to represent the family and James Wilson to ensure that the corpse was treated with the proper respect. Half the Blues now loitered around Aldington, poised to wreak havoc on the local authorities if their counterparts in London failed to deliver the promised concession.

The two men stood at the head of the queue for the public gallery. Quacks had used his considerable bulk and the point of a knife to persuade the men in front to give up their places. People expected the gang to make a showing and most of those waiting had no intention of being caught up in any affray that might result.

Wilson was now reading a newspaper he'd 'borrowed' from one of Quacks' victims.

'What's it say, Bish?' Quacks prompted. He was an astute man, with a dozen business interests outside his involvement with the Blues, but like most of his class he could do little more than sign his own name.

Wilson looked up with a smile. 'If thou wert to believe this,

Cephas has killed more men than Boney. Preventives, farmers, women and children.'

Quacks snorted at the lies. Their former leader was a hard man, there was no denying it, but he knew damned well that his cousin had never killed any women or children. A farmer was slightly more believable, since occasionally those who could not be bribed or intimidated into co-operation became examples to others and there was always a risk that the men delivering a beating would be more zealous than required, or the men receiving it less robust than anticipated. As for preventive men, they knew what to expect when they took on the job. In any case, for each one of them who died, three or four times as many free-traders lost their lives.

'And we would live in pavilions like the King's if we had hauled the half of this.'

Quacks chuckled. The landlord of the Palm Tree had spent a week with family near Brighton and returned with a cheap watercolour of the Pavilion. A bunch of them passed it around, at once awestruck and bemused by the strange spires that had sprouted from the basic structure in recent times, not to mention the onion-shaped domes still under construction. They had to hold Hogben back to stop him pissing on the man's souvenir in a characteristically base protest at the cost of such a pompous creation to a war-torn nation but Wilson was intrigued, continuing to gaze at the painting long after the others had lost interest. If Wilson came into fabulous wealth, Quacks wouldn't be at all surprised if he spent it on a pavilion.

Still, whatever the truth of the Blues' operations under Cephas, the public had been whipped into a frenzy of righteous indignation. Ransley was astute in his judgement that a calculated capitulation would be best all round. They had plenty of support, not to mention customers, across the countryside but hunger for a hanging was something else. No longer a man in the eyes of the excited crowds, Cephas was now merely a distraction from the abject poverty of their everyday lives.

The door to the court opened and the two men used their elbows freely to keep their prime position as the mob surged forwards. Pandemonium quickly ensued, with people jostling for places in all areas of the oak-panelled hall. Oddly, given that many of his ventures were not strictly within the law, Quacks had never been inside a courtroom. He expected solemnity, like a church, but what he witnessed was the noisy, smelly underbelly of humanity, as bad as in any backstreet buttocking shop. He was not fond of crowds, spending most of his life tending his land, sawing timber in his yard and hauling loads across the marshes. A healthy working sweat, or even the reek of a privy, was as nothing next to the stench of scores of strangers crushed into the confined space. Even the busiest market day was better, with the stink able to escape in the open air. When he looked at Wilson, the curl of his lip confirmed that he too was sickened by it. They pushed their way to the front of the gallery and waited for the session to begin.

No sooner had order been established than the room erupted into movement again, as all present rose to their feet for the Judge's entrance. It took fully five minutes for him to restore order and lower the noise to a level where the proceedings could begin, only for it to build again when the defendants were brought in. Scarce an inch apart in height and identical in their leaf-litter hair and eyes, their ruddy faces and stout builds marked them out as countrymen amidst the pale and skinny city-poor of the public gallery. The likeness between them went no further than their features, with the man in the lead almost a decade the elder and reassuringly rotund, while his younger companion was coarse and broad, carrying equal loads of muscle and fat.

The first man was one of the best shots in the Blues. A dab hand at picking off rooks, Dick Wraight often used his talents in defence of a load of uncustomed goods. The fact that he was cousin to the landlord of the Walnut Tree public house in Aldington saw to it that everyone around knew him; his quick wit saw to it that most liked him too. Quacks was sorry to see Wraight hang but, if they could do nothing for Cephas, they could do still less for him. Picked up on the marshes with gunpowder all over his hands and face, his fate was inescapable.

When he saw Cephas behind Wraight, Quacks' first thought was how small his cousin looked. Although he stood upright, refusing to be cowed by the fetters on his wrists and ankles, the restraints eroded his commanding presence into tragic dignity. His brutish strength, so formidable on the marshes on a dark winter's night, was out of place amongst the educated men of the court. His eyes scanned the room slowly as he was pushed roughly towards the dock, his gaze revealing disappointment at finding none of the Blues present. Quacks wondered if he had hoped for rescue. Surely he must realise how futile that would be? They could cause havoc but get him away safely? Unlikely: an attempt would only achieve loss of life — their own and probably others too. In all probability, he would just have company when he danced the Tyburn jig.

The clerk launched the proceedings by reading out the charges against the two men. Up in the public gallery, his rapid delivery blurred into an unintelligible stream of words. From the seemingly endless recitation, Quacks strained to pick out 'assembling', 'smuggled goods' and 'bearing firearms'.

He frowned at that allegation. Most of the firearms they bore were muskets they'd seized from the preventive men themselves. It was not the Blues who had escalated the hostilities but the establishment in eighteen-seventeen of the Coast Blockade for the Prevention of Smuggling by Captain William McCulloch. Before that, only the odd man amongst them carried a duck-gun and then he shot wide, seeking to pin their opponents down long enough for the tubmen and drivers to make their escape. When they began to face more serious opposition, they considered bringing in more firearms of their own but Sam Bailey's old guard preferred bats — wielding the long, studded ash poles did not lay a man open to an automatic death sentence in the same way that carrying a firearm did.

Wraight had taken the stand confidently, turning his most winning smile on the jury before settling a respectful gaze on the judge. He listened attentively while the clerk read the charges, his expression growing ever more shocked and sorrowful. Quacks admired the performance. Few people knew it but Wraight's skill at lying surpassed even his expertise at shooting. For years he'd been an important, if largely invisible, member of the Blues and often it was his guile that ensured the success of their schemes. He was so adept that few of his victims ever knew they'd been defrauded, which was why he remained popular despite making a handsome profit from every fool from Dover to Dungeness.

Meanwhile, Cephas had resumed his examination of the room, studying every face. He had been working along the gallery for a minute or two before his eyes met his cousin's. Quacks had been waiting for the contact and now studied the emotions in Cephas's expression as he held the gaze. He saw that Cephas did not expect a rescue and, after forbidding his wife from coming to court, hoped only that they cared enough to send someone to monitor the proceedings. A flicker in the tired hazel eyes said that his cousin was pleased to find that person was him. Cephas shifted his stare to Wilson but Quacks could not tell how he viewed the presence of one of the least aggressive of their number. He could not know that Wilson was one of only two men who spoke up for him, with the demand that he be spared the ignominy of hanging in chains for public ridicule.

The clerk's voice droned on: 'unlawfully, maliciously and dangerously', 'shooting off and discharging diverse guns'. One accusation followed another until he closed the tenth with, 'in the execution of their respective duties under the statute'.

When asked for his plea, Wraight somehow infused the words 'not guilty' with a rich blend of sincerity and intensity. Studying the jury, Quacks saw them sympathise with the plight of a wrongly accused man and then wonder how Wraight came to be brought in front of them. When Cephas repeated precisely the same plea as his co-defendant, Quacks could detect only defeat in his voice. Glancing back at the jury, he saw that they were as sure of his cousin's guilt as they were of Wraight's innocence. In a fist-fight, few men could better Cephas but, in a court of law, a man who was not just illiterate but also far from articulate stood no chance.

The prosecution launched its case with testimonies from a series of Blockademen from His Majesty's Ship *Severn*. The first was a young master's mate, who bore the impressive name of Charles James Franklin Newton and cut a dashing figure with his immaculate uniform and an old-fashioned greased pigtail tied with black ribbon hanging neatly between his shoulder blades. In a rich bass voice, he conjured a vivid picture of the savage confrontation that had left five of his men wounded and taken the life of a sixth, conveying without bravado his own key role and the extent of the injuries he sustained in the engagement. Although he admitted that he had fired the first three shots of the conflict, he claimed that they were intended merely as warnings and had not been aimed at the men on trial. He went on to describe how he and his men had pursued the smugglers inland towards Brookland, leading to the clash that brought Cephas to trial.

'I saw two men on the left side of the road, apparently with muskets presented at us…' He faltered, in the first trace of uncertainty he had shown during his fifteen minutes of testimony. 'It was rather dark then, it might be nearly five o'clock, but we were close to them and I am sure they had muskets in their hands, apparently presented. We ran after them to catch them but they escaped. In the course of the pursuit, several muskets were fired at us. I observed the man nearest to me run into a field, near the body of men. The men amongst whom he ran were firing from a field on the left side of the road. I saw five or seven men on the right side of the road.'

'I believe you were disguised,' the prosecutor prompted.

'I was dressed in a white Guernsey frock and thick blue Flushing trousers. I stood near our party and one of the men on the right ran down to me and shoved a musket into my hand. He appeared much agitated and said twice, very quick, "Shoot the bastards."'

There was an audible intake of breath around the hall. Up in the gallery, Quacks and Wilson exchanged bleak glances. Being found with a firearm in the midst of such a violent affray was damning enough but Cephas's mistaken exhortation would surely send him to the gallows. His words made him sound like a fool but mistaking an officer for a free-trader was easy to do in the heat of battle on a foul night.

Newton continued his account. 'I seized him by the frock and gave the musket into the charge of John Treader, who was close to me. The man was going to make a noise and, my party being all around me, I gave him to them. It was the prisoner, Cephas Quested. In the confusion, our parties divided.'

His next admission confirmed that Cephas's mistake had not been as stupid as it seemed. 'I endeavoured to join Messrs Digby and McKenzie, who had charge of the prisoner, but I mistook the armed party of smugglers for my own party and was walking towards them.' So Newton had made exactly the same mistake as Cephas had done only minutes before. 'They called out "Who are you?" I fired off my pistol for assistance and then a volley of muskets was fired at me. One ball came into contact with the metal button on the waistband of my trousers. It broke the button, drove through my trousers, cut my skin and I fell. A ball came through my frock and grazed the skin of my left shoulder. I was knocked down by the ball that struck me on the stomach and, as I fell, they called out,

"There the damned bastard drops; there he drops." It was said exultingly. They fancied they had shot me. I got up almost immediately and succeeded in joining Mr Jones and some men who were with him, and we laid down to conceal ourselves till daylight was coming on.'

Newton carried on for a few minutes more in his precise recollection of how the night had ended, and he and his men had eventually returned to the Jew's Gut watch-house with the five tubs they had seized. There they were reunited with Digby.

One of the defence lawyers stood to cross-examine. The witness's account had been persuasive, shocking the jury without resorting to any sensationalism that might have undermined his credibility. Quacks wondered what the defence could do with such a coherent testimony, which was, to the best of his own knowledge and recollection, largely accurate. However, the lawyer had clearly been paying close attention throughout and now he revisited the first part of Newton's testimony.

'The third shot you fired was at them, and before they fired at you?'

Newton considered his answer before replying in the same matter-of-fact tone as before. 'I cannot say. I took no aim. When the two first pistols were fired, it was merely for alarm. I could not see the smugglers. I very likely fired the third in a direction towards them.' Clearly realising that this admission cast the smugglers' return fire in a different light, he added, 'I am certain that Cephas Quested is the man who gave me the musket. I never doubted it.'

The defence lawyer returned to his seat and left his colleague to dispute specific times and places in the witness's testimony. They could not dispute the broad course of events on the fateful night but clearly did not intend to allow the details to go unchallenged. As was often the case, the preventive men had started the firing and their dogged pursuit of the smugglers left the fleeing men with little choice but to fight back, unless they wanted to face the hangman as their friends did now.

The next witness was a young midshipman by the name of Edward Digby. His testimony was as assured as Newton's, and all the more poignant for his direct involvement with the deceased officer, James McKenzie. Like Newton before him, he estimated the numbers of smugglers at two to three hundred but intensified the claim by setting against it their own strength of twenty-five. He then went on to explain how the preventive forces had been separated and what befell McKenzie.

'About half a mile on the east side of Lee's house, I perceived a man on the road, holding a musket downwards in his hand. He saw me. I pursued him and, drawing ahead of my companions, collared him. Men were rising on my right and left, flashing and shouting. Two or three muskets were discharged, the balls of which passed me on my left. A scuffle ensued between this man and me. He extricated himself from me and endeavoured to get the muzzle of his musket to my body but I pushed him off and then discharged a pistol at him as he fled.'

With only the slightest pause for breath, he continued his account. 'I perceived four to six men about eight yards to my right, with muskets in their hands, apparently in confusion. One of them, the prisoner Cephas Quested, came forward and I saw him taken into custody by Mr Newton. At that moment, I heard Mr McKenzie calling for me to come and assist him. I went and observed him in contact with a tall man holding a musket. I wrenched the musket out of the smuggler's hand. We each laid hold of his hands and were hauling him away when musket balls hit both the smuggler and Mr McKenzie. They fell at the same time. I know it was a musket ball that shot Mr McKenzie — he died the midnight following.'

'Did the other man die immediately?' the prosecutor asked.

'Mr McKenzie said to him, "You are shamming" but the smuggler just had life to say "No" and died, I believe, for I left him there.' He went on to describe their return to the watch-house, where they found Richard Wraight held by two other officers.

During his testimony, Digby had alleged that Cephas was intoxicated when taken prisoner. However, under cross-examination by a third defence lawyer, he admitted that his assessment was based only on the smell of the man's breath and that the prisoner had his wits about him as much as his captors. He repeated his claim that he had found swan shot and a fowling piece flint in Cephas's trouser pocket.

That brought the fourth person in the defence team to his feet. Mr Platt was the only member of the legal profession there present that Quacks recognised, a respected figure around Ashford from the local firm of Langham & Platt. Platt studied the witness carefully before putting his question.

'Your wound, I believe, was caused by a ball or a slug.'

'Yes, small shot could not have occasioned it. When I took cover, I heard balls and slugs distinctly pass over me.' Missing the point of the question, he continued, 'Mr McKenzie was killed by a ball. It was impossible from the position of our party that the ball could have come from them.' After a brief pause, as if to make up for the lack of other evidence, he added, 'I should think a quarter of a pound of powder was found on Wraight. It stuck all over his pockets.'

Platt nodded and took his seat again. With his one simple prompt, he had scored the first point for the defence: both prisoners had been found with the accoutrements of fowling pieces, not pistols or muskets. Even if Cephas had passed a musket to Newton, he appeared to have carried no ammunition for it.

Justice Park leaned forward. 'Could the swan shot do harm to an individual?'

'Certainly,' Digby replied, 'If it was fired at him.'

Perhaps Platt missed an opportunity when he failed to emphasise that, while swan shot might do harm to an individual, the individuals in question had not been harmed by such shot.

The next witness for the prosecution was far less convincing than his predecessors. James Hill, a petty-officer, confirmed that he had taken custody of Cephas from McKenzie and delivered him to the watch-house but knew little more. Under cross-examination, he admitted that the night was dark and events confused. He did not know whether the two parties had become mixed together and he had seen nothing in Cephas's hand prior to his arrest.

So far, the jury had heard from one witness claiming that two men presented a musket at his party, from another that the smugglers had been holding muskets but appeared to be in confusion, and from another that he had seen no weapon at all. The picture became muddier still when another petty-officer, John Treader, confirmed that he had seen Cephas pass a fowling piece, not a musket, to Newton and a midshipman, John Jones, testified that he had later received and inspected this weapon, finding it to be loaded with swan shot and powder. None of the fallen preventive men had been wounded by swan shot and so the captured weapon proved nothing.

And so it went on. Witness after witness confirmed the general progress of the battle inland, detailed the injuries they had sustained and the goods that had been seized. They all seemed in agreement that there had been two to three hundred smugglers although, given the darkness and the uncertainty over most other details, it was difficult to see how they reached such a reliable estimate. It fell to a seaman called William Crockford to admit that each volley of shots from the smugglers followed a shot fired by the preventive forces, shots that the witnesses claimed were fired only for the purposes of extending the alarm but shots nonetheless.

Two more seamen, George Mockford and John Nichol, followed Crockford into the witness stand. They gave precise and matching statements of how they had met up near Dowell's Farm, encountered a man alone there, found no direct evidence of his involvement in the affray but taken him, with his agreement, back to the watch-house for questioning. Having only patted the man down for weapons when they captured him, it was not until Digby searched his pockets at the watch-house that powder was found sticking to their linings and smeared over his face. He accounted for this by saying that he had been shooting rooks the previous day and that he supposed that the powder had stuck to his hand when he put it into his pocket and to his face when he wiped it with his hand. Neither of the seamen claimed to have seen Wraight with a weapon at any point during the proceedings.

When the prosecution finally rested, one fact was beyond dispute: Cephas and Wraight had both been taken prisoner in the area on the night in question. However, while the evidence against Wraight was purely circumstantial, there seemed to be no denying that Cephas had handed a firearm to Newton and exhorted him to turn it on the preventive forces. Without a firm link between the weapon and the dead preventive officer, the charge fell short of murder but the penalty for bearing firearms and shooting at the preventive forces was still death.

Perhaps, in spite of the number of witnesses fielded by the prosecution to repeat the details of Wraight's capture as many times as possible, the lack of firm evidence against the man made Justice Park doubt the jury's verdict. Before allowing the defence to proceed, he observed that Wraight's presence at an unseasonable hour upwards of twelve miles from his home, coupled with the discovery of the powder in his pockets, were strong circumstances of suspicion.

Quacks had kept one eye on the jury throughout the long hours of testimony, seeing their doubts laid to rest as the prosecution questioned witness after witness. Not only had their expectation of Cephas's guilt been confirmed but their faith in Wraight's innocence had also been eroded. His capture on Walland Marsh with his hands and face smeared with powder seemed as good as an admission of guilt to them, with the debate over balls or shot apparently passing over their heads. Now the Judge's remarks confirmed that interpretation. Quacks switched his attention to the defence team, wondering what they could possibly offer to undo the damage done by the Blockademen's well rehearsed testimonies.

The jury waited expectantly for Wraight to be sworn in. Instead, the clerk rose to read a statement on the defendant's behalf. Wraight's expression as he waited held something of the devout churchgoer listening to a sermon: solemn in recognition of the seriousness of the matter but filled with quiet faith in the justice of God and man. Even Quacks, who should have known better, could hardly believe that such a man would allow a false statement to be made in his name, but false it was.

The opening words set the tone for the whole account: 'Before I enter upon my defence, I most humbly request that you will discharge from your minds any report that you may have seen in the public prints, tending to prejudice your mind against me, and that you will form your conclusions as to my guilt or innocence upon the evidence that has been, and shall be, adduced to you and upon that only.'

The statement went on to dissect the evidence against him in minute detail, accounting for his movements and justifying them at every stage. Having agreed to call on a man named Thomas Baker near Rye on farm business for his mother, he decided to combine this with visiting a friend in Northland. Attempting to cut across the fields towards Northland, he missed his way and, after trying to recover his bearings for some time, asked for directions from the shepherd living at Dowell Farm. Tired from his travels, he settled down beside a haystack to sleep for a while. The next thing he knew, he was woken by voices. Deciding to proceed to Rye, he resumed his journey but soon met with Mockford and Nichol who took him into custody. As for the powder in his pocket — he had been shooting rooks the day before and some powder must have worked out of the paper into which he had folded it and later been dampened by the breakage of a vial he put into the same pocket. The powder must have stuck to his hand when he put it into his pocket and to his face when he wiped it with his hand.

Nearing the end of the statement, the clerk sipped from a glass of water before reading the closing paragraph.

'I shall now leave my case in the hands of my Counsel to call witnesses on my behalf but, if there should be any whom you think material to the case not called, I trust you will give me credit when I say that, if I had been tried in the county where I was apprehended, I could have had the attendance of ten times the number of witnesses to my character than I can possibly expect in attendance today.'

Quacks saw several jurors waver, then nod sympathetically. They would not like the positions to be reversed, to stand trial on the coastal marshes, far from their friends and family. How could a man prove his value to his community at such a distance from it? Quacks smiled down at his hands: perhaps Wraight might pull off the impossible after all.

Wilson matched Quacks' smile. 'He might yet leave with his life.'

Quacks shook his head slowly. He'd like to believe that but how could a jury acquit a man found, still black with powder, in the midst of an affray in which an officer of the Royal Navy had lost his life?

When Cephas was asked for his defence, he offered just six words spoken in the same flat tone in which he had entered his plea.

'I am innocent of the job.'

'Damn them,' Quacks muttered under his breath. 'Couldn't they do better than that for him?'

Wilson remained silent but the fine frown lines between his eyebrows said it all. The case had been lost as soon as the court heard two, let alone half a dozen, preventive men recount Cephas's words to Newton. It grieved them both to see him go down without a struggle but they knew that this was one battle that he simply did not know how to fight.

The defence concluded its case by calling Wraight's character witnesses. As it turned out, he might have been better off without his mother and her farmer friend. They became bogged down in who took what to whom, and when, making such a poor show of giving their evidence that the prosecution repeatedly asked if they had discussed their testimonies or seen the defendant's written statement that they were so clearly trying to corroborate. The mother's obvious distress at her son's plight went some way to offset the quality of her evidence, casting the prosecutor in a poor light when he tried to put pressure on her. Luckily for Wraight, the last three witnesses — a neighbour, an innkeeper and the shepherd — made a far better job of confirming his movements in the hours before his arrest.

Quacks sighed as they watched the jury file out to consider the evidence they'd heard. If he were on the jury, judging a stranger impartially, he would convict Cephas. He had no doubt that the twelve men serving in that capacity would reach the same decision. He was less certain about Wraight. Disregarding for a moment his own knowledge of the man's involvement with the Blues, his friendship with the neighbour and the contempt in which marshmen like the innkeeper and shepherd held the Preventive Service, he thought perhaps the defence might succeed. The prosecution's witnesses had totally failed to link him to the night's events or to demonstrate that he carried a weapon at any point.

'Will we wait here?' Wilson's soft voice interrupted his reverie.

Quacks shrugged. He had no idea how long a jury might be expected to deliberate. Around them, people were shifting in their seats or standing to stretch their legs but only a handful slipped hastily out, and they in a manner that spoke more of the call of nature than of a prolonged absence from the courtroom. Deciding that they would never regain their commanding view if they gave it up, he nodded.

They did not have long to wait. Whatever the decision, it was clearly unanimous because the jury returned after barely ten minutes. At the court's instruction, the foreman rose to deliver the verdict. He gave it fluently, without any pause for drama.

'We find the defendant, Richard Wraight, not guilty, your honour.' Murmurs swept around the court, only to fade as the spectators sat poised to hear whether the other defendant had been so fortunate. 'We find the defendant, Cephas Quested, guilty.'

The crowd burst into chatter. The prosecutors smiled, seemingly satisfied with partial victory, and shook hands with the defence team. Only the preventive men who'd testified against Wraight glowered, while the judge banged his gavel to restore order. Quacks scowled.

No doubt they were as sure of Wraight's guilt as he was himself, given the number of Blockade spies that had drifted around the marshes both before and after the clash at Brookland. Even so, the Blues had lost four men to their one and now another was to die — how much more blood had to flow? Their anger was the final evidence, if any were needed, that the decision to offer Cephas as a sacrificial lamb was the right one. If he had followed Wraight out of the court a free man, or evaded trial altogether, the war would step up another notch. If he paid with his life and the Blues kept a low profile for a while, they might reach an uneasy truce.

Minutes later, the inevitable pronouncement was made. Cephas was sentenced to hang outside Newgate gaol at a date yet to be set. His body would then be taken to Penenden Heath, where it would hang as a grim warning to smugglers throughout Kent and Sussex of what they could expect if they themselves fell into the hands of the Coast Blockade.

Wraight turned sadly to Cephas, gripped his hand for a moment and then clapped a hand to his shoulder before striding boldly but quickly away from his ordeal. No doubt he would whisk his mother straight back to Kent. There had been no guarantee that he would be spared and it was hardly surprising that he wanted to distance himself from the gallows as fast as possible.

Quacks looked at Wilson, determination in his eye. Unable to influence the public sentence, the plan concocted by Ransley and Knatchbull required duplicity behind the scenes. It was down to them to make that plan work, to fulfil their sense of obligation to a leader who'd put hundreds of guineas into their pockets in the years since the war ended and to ensure that their prosperity continued in the coming era under new leadership. Having expected to remain in the city until the sentence was carried out, they now realised they would have to return when a date had been set, which might be some way off. Delay could only damage the Blues: any possibility of a pardon, however remote, would make it more difficult for Ransley to progress his plans and control dissenting voices like Hogben's. Without wishing his cousin dead, Quacks knew procrastination would benefit no one, not even the condemned man.

Hog

'I hear the South Kents are finished.

The man on Hogben's right didn't move; his eyes remained fixed on the untouched beer on the bar in front of him, leaving Hogben unsure whether he had spoken at all. Hogben took a deep draught from his own tankard. It was the eighth, he thought, or perhaps the ninth. The more he drank, the more he needed to drink, and constantly maintaining a distance from reality became ever more expensive. It was all very well for Ransley to decide to let things cool down but where did that leave men who were less well placed? How was he supposed to feed seven children on thin air?

One of the reasons he stayed out drinking was so that he didn't have to go home and look into their downcast faces. He sometimes wished he were a crueller man — a cruel man would feel no guilt at being a bad husband and a worse father. He motioned the innkeeper to pour another pint, then thought better of it and waved to a bottle of brandy on the shelf. Time for the strong stuff: a few shots of that would numb him to his responsibilities for another night. Taking a blue-glass vial from his inside pocket, he unashamedly poured a generous measure into the caramel-tinted brew. Long past counting the drops, he made no effort to hide his dependency from the indifferent patrons of Rye's Red Lion. Public houses like it littered the coastal towns, providing depraved entertainments to their corrupt clientele, and none was worse than the Lion. Hogben liked it for precisely that reason: he could do what he liked there and no one he knew would see him do it. The Lion was not only far from his home but also from his friends' homes too, and none of them would be seen in such a place anyway. The fact that the inn was in Sussex, albeit only a couple of miles over the county line, increased his sense of security and isolation.

He barely noticed the wretched trade in human flesh being conducted around him that night. The Lion's speciality, if it could be called that, was the final stage of its customers' descent into hell. In the better part of town, a man could spend a month's wages on a few hours with a pretty girl. As he headed towards the seafront, he could save a guinea if he concentrated on poking the fire and didn't look too hard at the mantelpiece; a few more streets and he'd better not look too closely at the fire either. From then on, there were only two paths. A signless house at the far end of the street offered one: where women were too diseased to handle, some men turned to the company of their fellows. Like Hogben, the Lion had no truck with that trade; instead it gave hope to those who were already drawing the wages of their sin. Convinced that lying with a virgin would cure them of their pox, they were the mainstay of its business.

Hogben had tried the treatment himself when he noticed the first of the sores that now encircled his manhood. He tried to be gentle with the flame-haired moppet brought to his room but it was impossible for a man of his size to avoid hurting her. His initial bafflement at the failed cure turned to fury when he returned to repeat it. As he was led to a room, a woman bundled a tearful child down the back stairs. The distinctive auburn locks told Hogben all he needed to know. The misery he endured every time he passed water fuelled his rage as he stormed downstairs and made a good attempt at forcing the proprietor through the wall. Now he enjoyed a standing arrangement for free liquor on his infrequent trips to Rye, provided that he kept his knowledge of the con to himself. A spoonful of pig's blood like the one that deceived him continued to convince others that their troubles would soon be over.

No, there was no need to hide an opium habit from the kind of man who passed an evening in the Red Lion. Hogben took a closer look at the one next to him. The man was unremarkable, an inch or two above average height but otherwise the same brown-haired, grey-eyed, sturdy-built and ruddy-faced type that populated scores of villages throughout the south-eastern corner of England. That was not to say there was no variation — Hogben had to look no further than the Baileys to find marshmen outside the mould — but an observer might expect to see more diversity in a land of ports and harbours. As it was, the thousands of demobilised servicemen had yet to make their mark on the racial mix and few other strangers settled on the marshes.

Hogben suspected he had seen the speaker before but could not place him. Perhaps he was that most contemptible of creatures: a shopkeeper. Hogben shared Napoleon's distaste for the breed. He counted just one amongst his associates, the shoemaker Giles, and deemed him marginally better than the average specimen, given that he crafted his merchandise with his own skilled hands. Even so, it was hardly a proper job for a real man, not like fisherman or farmer, horseman or drover. Hogben's snobbery was ill-founded, given that he had struggled to hold down even the most menial labouring job since his injury and was in danger of becoming the kind of itinerant worker that was only one step up from a tramp.

His alcohol-addled brain was still stumbling from one fragmentary thought to another when the man spoke again.

'Cephas is a hard act to follow.'

This time, there was no doubt. The man had spoken and his words were clearly addressed to Hogben. His voice revealed something else about him: he did not hail from Rye, or at least not originally. Hogben knew instantly, subconsciously, that the man came from even further east than he did himself, not far from Deal unless he missed his guess. He considered his reply, then opted for his usual blend of brash and confrontational.

'What would you know about it?'

The man took a reflective sip from his still-full tankard.

'I know he's set to swing in scarce more than a month. If there was any fight left in the South Kents, they'd've done something before it came to that.'

The man must have good sources to know the news from London already. So certain had Hogben been of the outcome of the trial that he made no effort to find out what had passed in the city. On the contrary, he had deliberately gone where he thought the bad tidings would not reach him. When he eventually replied, his words lacked conviction.

'There's time yet.'

The man smiled at him, a friendly smile. 'You did your best.'

So he knew about the failed rescue attempt. Hogben said nothing: his best had not been good enough. Smoker was right when he guessed that Cephas was already in London. When his wife eventually visited him in Newgate, after the authorities admitted his whereabouts, he was positive that he'd been there since early March. The infamous city gaol was thought to provide better security than a Kentish facility, which it undoubtedly did, and keeping the move secret made rescue doubly unlikely. Not only had Hogben failed in his quest but he had risked forty-three lives with his own when he did so. The knowledge that Ransley's judgement had been sounder than his own festered inside him.

'A fair few men stood with you.'

Hogben didn't even try to keep the bitterness out of his reply. 'Not as many as stood by and did naught.'

'No,' the man said in a low voice, 'Not that many.'

Shifting so that he faced his inquisitor, left elbow on the bar, Hogben let his festering resentment seep into his voice as aggression. 'What's it to you anyway?'

The man shrugged. 'There's a lot of coast between here and Sandwich.'

Hogben frowned, uncertain what Sandwich had to do with anything.

'The North Kents' territory stops there. For now.'

The frown deepened. 'Who the blazes are you?'

'Name's Marsh. Make it Bill.'

He held out a hand, which Hogben ignored.

'Why do you care what's North and what's South?'

Apparently unperturbed by Hogben's rudeness, Marsh withdrew his hand. 'Ever hear of the Burmarsh gang?'

It had been a long time in falling but a penny finally dropped somewhere in Hogben's mind. The crew working out of Burmarsh hardly warranted the title gang, barely managing fifty men on a good night and doing no more than selling on a few tubs to friends and neighbours. If the Blues had buckled in the face of the strengthened Coast Blockade, the Burmarsh lot must be suffering twice as badly. As he thought that, he realised that someone had a vision and the man next to him was only a messenger.

'What if I have?'

'They've heard of you — might have a proposition for you, as a matter of fact.'

'Not interested,' Hogben said bluntly.

'Would it hurt to hear them out?'

Hogben was about to repeat his refusal more forcefully but then hesitated. Taking up with the Burmarsh lot would have been a betrayal of the Blues, except that the Blues were not running. He wondered why Marsh was approaching him, not one of the others, or whether he had already been turned down by the likes of Sam Bailey. Then again, they'd only bring in a man like Bailey if they wanted change at the top. If they already had a leader, they might be looking for men to run their teams. More honest about his failings than most might guess, Hogben was just as objective about his strengths. He was courageous and inspirational when he was working, qualities that could serve another gang just as well as they'd served the Blues.

'Keep talking.'

Marsh gave a slight shake of his head.

'Be in the Shepherd & Crook, tomorrow at dusk.'

Hogben's instant reaction to any instruction was to argue with it. His mouth opened automatically but then he hesitated. It might be a good offer and he had no plans for that night — or any other — beyond maintaining his blood-alcohol level, which he could do in Burmarsh as easily as anywhere else. He nodded his head curtly.

'Good decision,' Marsh said as he pushed himself up from the bar to leave. As he did so, a woman led two girls through the bar-room. They might have been as much as twelve, legally able to consent to the services required of them, but then again they might not. After letting them pass, the man said with no obvious irony in his neutral tone, 'Nice place.'

Hogben watched him leave, wondering how they had known where to find him. Marsh might have followed him but why come all the way down to Rye if he could have said his piece before? Perhaps they valued the anonymity of the Lion as much as he did. Shrugging, he returned to his neglected cocktail of brandy and laudanum.

George

After listening attentively to the account that Quested and Wilson brought back from the London trial, George Ransley headed home in pensive mood. Now he sat astride his mare on a hill to the south of the Bourne Tap. He had been motionless for more than forty minutes but the handsome bay barely stirred beneath him. Accustomed to her master's prolonged introspections, she seemed to match his distant stare and her only movement was to shift her weight from one rear hoof to the other every so often.

The subject of George's deliberations was the poor organisation of the mob now in his charge. Although his schemes had brought them richer pickings and safer runs in recent years, the fiasco at Brookland threw his oversights into sharp relief. The days of the shambling

Preventive Waterguard were gone and the new Coast Blockade clearly had to be taken seriously. He realised he should have seen that from the violent opposition they encountered in the months before Brookland. Even with hundreds of men, each run seemed harder than the last. Now he trawled his memory, trying to understand why he had not foreseen the strength of the preventive forces on Denge Marsh that night. Reconstructing how he'd reached the recommendations he made to Cephas, he realised that he was preoccupied with specifics of earlier affrays instead of their wider significance. The trouble had started at Sandgate in November but, at the time, he'd judged the night a partial success. They lost three men, with a dozen more wounded, but escaped with most of their cargo. Ironically, their own losses were to prove less damaging than those of their enemy, as each death or injury amongst the preventive men brought the service down on them harder.

George always took the men's welfare seriously but he could make only minor adjustments for the run that was already scheduled for the following night at Dymchurch. Luckily, running again so soon gave them the advantage of surprise and they brought in four hundred and fifty tubs, getting clear well before the sentinels could summon reinforcements. That haul went a long way towards filling their orders, sending Cephas off on one of his celebratory binges and giving George time to do some thinking before the next run in December. After careful consideration, he judged that the shingle beach they'd chosen for the November landing was too close to Sandgate, with the old castle and a string of Martello towers hosting the Blockade's men, and to the Divisional Office at Folkestone. If any part of the coast was likely to be patrolled efficiently, it was that one — under the watchful eye of senior officers. If they were to escape the sentinels' notice next time, they had to land on a quieter stretch of coastline.

It hadn't helped that one of their number, a local blacksmith called William Foster who spent his spare time insulting sentinels, gave the Blockade advance notice when he warned the man on duty that his card was marked. Usually, when he wasn't devising and researching plans, George devoted considerable effort on the tricky task of persuading Cephas to adopt new methods. However, in contrast, he found himself adopting one of the oldest methods of all when he sent the Baileys to see Foster. As much as he disliked violence, he blamed the blacksmith for the deaths at Sandgate and intended to send a warning to him and to others like him. When he saw the state of the man a few days later, he was confident that future plans would not be revealed so carelessly.

After hours poring over the sheaves of maps that he had meticulously hand-drawn during his many reconnaissance rides around the area, George knew the next run had to be near Dungeness Point. East or west, he mused through countless rides. There was little to choose between the two, along ten miles of marshy coastline, but slowly he fixed on Romney Sands in the east. The roads there were barely worthy of the name. Even if a sentinel saw them, reinforcements would make slow progress across the waterlogged fields and dunes. It was a hard place to make a landing but local knowledge assured the Blues of an edge over the preventive men who were shipped in from across the kingdom. Thinking to exploit a time when the Blockademen were otherwise occupied, he set the run for early Christmas morning — what trader would object, when a good run would mean fine brandy with his festive dinner?

How cruelly his hopes were dashed. The run was an unmitigated disaster: a man aboard the lugger dead, two preventives wounded and not one tub landed. The blame lay with the master of the lugger, who hovered off Dymchurch for half the evening instead of sliding quietly into Romney Warren just before their rendezvous. George ground his teeth through more than one night afterwards, asking sourly — if rhetorically — whether he had to think of everything. The trouble was that the seaward side of the trade was still living in the past and, with customary disdain for the landward side, paid little heed to the warnings they were given. By the time they woke up to the fact that the Blockade meant business, the trade would be long dead.

Throughout his deliberations, George deployed the best of his men in subtler missions. All around the coast, uncustomed goods slipped through the Blockade's net: packets were crammed into the false bottoms of boats and weighted tubs sunk in the shallows for later retrieval. Trading by stealth was slow, the quantities too small to fill their bulging order book, but it lined the pockets of himself and his stalwarts well enough. By the time he'd let the over-proof spirits down and sold them through the Tap, he turned a handsome profit on his sideline. He sometimes wondered what Cephas would do to him if he discovered the clandestine operations but trusted to luck and the silence of the men he chose. Working on the darkest nights and in the foulest weather, they contrived to pass virtually unnoticed. A load or two was lost when sentinels got too close but not a shot was fired. It would have been better all round if they could have continued that way but customers wanted deliveries and traders wanted paying. Their main business was in spirits, and tubs were far harder to hide than silks, playing cards and packets of tea or tobacco.

Eventually George judged them ready to make another run, forced with armed parties if necessary, and, after further lengthy consultation of his maps, he put forward Denge Marsh to the west of the Point as the location. At the back of the beach was a vast bank of shingle that would hide the working parties from view. Beyond that, the country was criss-crossed with deep dykes that would slow any pursuit on horseback. The trackless wastes were so treacherous that even the Blues needed local farmhands to guide them through the maze; such services were easily arranged, for a small consideration, while the loathed preventive men would find no such assistance at any price.

Almost equidistant from the Kent and Sussex Divisional Offices at Folkestone and Hastings, the stretch of coast between Rye and Dungeness was more sparsely patrolled than most. With sentinels covering as much as a mile of beach apiece, it should be easy to give them the slip. By the time he delivered his full plan for implementation, he was confident they could land their three hundred tubs without disturbing the sentinels in their lonely vigils. He had compiled information from numerous spies over long nights of observation to create a full picture of how the Blockade operated along that stretch of coast. It was worth the time and trouble, given that their cargo would sell for nearly a thousand pounds.

So what had gone wrong? How did they end up with four men dead, two captured and a witch-hunt fuelled by the death of the preventive officer, McKenzie? He scowled at the miscalculation. It had been well past midnight on a dark night when about three hundred of their men swarmed silently down to the beach about five miles west of Dungeness. They could muster half that number again at a pinch and so, by and large, the men he'd called on were solid, reliable types who understood the need for a quiet, profitable run to meet their advance orders and fill their pockets. There was an armed party of twenty-five men on either side of the working party. A few wielded only their trusty ash bats, while some had their own duck-guns, but most carried firearms or cutlasses they'd stolen from preventive men at Sandgate.

Everything went to plan until the sentinel at the Jew's Gut watch-house decided he liked the view from Denge Marsh better. There was no rhyme or reason to it — after weeks of spending half the night perched on a wall there, he or his betters seemed to think that a change would be as good as a rest. Even so, he would not have been close enough to inconvenience them had he not been lucky, or vigilant, enough to be staring out to sea when the lugger acknowledged the all-clear with a single flash. One solitary swing of a lantern condemned six men to death and countless others to injuries of varying degrees of severity. A single warning shot brought preventive men pouring in from east and west. Nothing like the old riding officers, they were not just well trained but highly disciplined: not for nothing was McCulloch known as Flogging Joey — the cries of drunks, thieves and deserters aboard the watch-vessel *Enchantress* beached in Rye Harbour were often heard ashore. Just as it seemed the Blues' luck could get no worse, a revenue cruiser appeared from nowhere and lowered boats filled with reinforcements.

The Blues managed to land their load but even the valiant efforts of fifty armed men could not hold back the hordes of preventive men long enough to send it all safely inland. George would have ordered them to fall back long before Cephas finally admitted defeat. At least two men died because of that delay, with Cephas himself soon to join them in the afterlife. Watching from a vantage point once he reached safety, George saw volley after volley discharged into their men. While some of the preventive forces reloaded, others advanced with cutlasses. The armed parties of the Blues responded with everything at their disposal, keeping their heads and going hard at their adversaries before falling back in formation. Only the training that some had received from the Government to face a quite different foe kept their losses as low as they were. Without the lead of a man like Sam Bailey, they might have lost dozens.

For all his efforts, George's planning had achieved less than Bailey's example. He'd got the Blues into a mess from which only their guts and grit saved them and of one thing he was determined — that would never happen again. His teeth clenched with the

60

intensity of his resolve. Not only would he make sure that his intelligence and strategy were flawless but he would change the way the trade worked. Some of his ideas were new to the Blues but not to the trade itself; he would not be the first gang leader to put his activities on a more businesslike footing, running his own shipping and setting his own schedules. What was new was the way in which he intended to take care of his men.

As well as the boy's mother, he had visited the families of each of the three dead men to offer his muted condolences and compensate them for their loss. He loathed putting a monetary value on men's lives but something had to be done for the women and children they left behind. After Cephas hanged, George would do the same for his wife, Martha — always Pat to her husband for some reason. Eliza had been supporting her through the ordeal, freely offering whatever was needed, but George would not make his own restitution until her husband was dead. To extinguish her hopes before then was too cruel. Satisfied with those arrangements, two things still rankled about the affair.

First was the suspicion that some of the deaths could have been avoided. The exit wound from a musket ball left the back of the boy's head a bloody pulp and a bold sweep of a cutlass disembowelled the eldest of the fallen men, a stalwart scout by the name of Page — nothing could have saved either of them. Not so for the other two. Both were men that George had known for years and both died waiting for the doctor to finish with the preventive men, one bleeding heavily from the gut and the other appearing to fall victim to his dazed senses after a blow to the head. George did not expect the doctor to treat lawbreakers first but now considered his options.

He had seen many men die from their wounds in the same way as happened that night. Of those who survived longer, some were then taken by infection. So, when they managed to get a man to a doctor, what did he do? Thinking about it, George realised that lives were saved in the first minutes after the doctor reached his patients, when he stopped the bleeding, cleaned the wounds and bandaged the casualties for transportation. A man didn't need to be a doctor to do those things. Quested was no doctor but he had saved Giles. George was no doctor either but bitter experience told him that Giles might have died without his friend's care, infection the most likely enemy in his case. Well, what a doctor knew, a doctor could teach.

George made a mental note to ride out to Brookland and pay Dr Hougham a visit. The doctor's home, an imposing double-fronted property called Pear Tree House, was an outward sign of the man's fondness for the good life. George had no doubt that he would be only too willing to provide tuition and equipment for a fee. The next time he came out to an affray on a dark night, he would bring two bags and then the Blues would take care of their own until he was ready for them. In fact, George reflected, it wouldn't hurt to have a word with Dr Beet in Ashford and perhaps others in the coastal towns, just to assure them that a hefty gratuity would find its way to them if they gave their assistance when required, no questions asked.

The second thing that troubled George was the trial itself. What he heard from Quested and Wilson confirmed what he'd already heard from Dick Wraight when he returned triumphant to the Walnut Tree. In a performance of which he was justly proud, he had convinced a jury — albeit a jury of cityfolk — that a man could be found covered in powder in the middle of a battlefield without being guilty of anything. The rook-shooting defence was his own idea and owed no debt to the counsel that he shared with Cephas. George did not fool himself that even the finest barrister could have saved Cephas after his unfortunate exhortation to the young master's mate but he knew that Wraight would almost certainly have joined him on the scaffold were it not for his own inventiveness. Many of the Blues had no such ingenuity and, in his place, they might now have been awaiting death. George did not intend to allow that to happen. He added another note to the list in his well-ordered brain. While local officials might be happy to turn a blind eye and some, like the mayor of Folkestone, had sons in the trade, it was clear that the Blues could not rely on lenience in London. He would retain the best legal counsel that money could buy.

No doubt Knatchbull could advise on the right man for the job, someone who understood the trade and knew where to find the legal precedents needed to defend it to unsympathetic elements in the establishment. They might do worse than Platt: Wilson had remarked quietly on the man's questions regarding the nature of the ammunition that inflicted the fatal wound. Although those questions had not saved Cephas, perhaps it was that careful groundwork that meant the two men had not faced a murder trial. In this case, it had made little difference but such thorough preparation might save a life one day.

George had promised Knatchbull a quiet spell before the Blues resumed their trade. Now he promised himself that they would be unrecognisable on their return. If McCulloch could transform the blundering Waterguard into an effective Blockade, George could transform his ragtag mob into an unstoppable force. All it took was time, money and guile — three things he possessed in abundance.

Hog

The Shepherd & Crook could not have been more different from the Red Lion. At the heart of the hamlet of Burmarsh, it was more like the landlord's home than a public house. That was not to say that it was welcoming, because it wasn't. Hog spent a large proportion of his life in public houses and knew every subtle variation that distinguished them. The Blues had a network of friendly innkeepers, ensuring that they never lacked a safe watering hole on their way to and from a night's work. They drew their men from the whole of southern Kent but most of their core members hailed from the villages to the south of Ashford, centred on Aldington, home of both Cephas Quested and George Ransley. Recently, they'd begun to meet in the Bourne Tap when discussing plans but it was in the Walnut Tree that they blew themselves out. With a convivial host, fine food and varied clientele, it was one of the best public houses Hog knew. Indeed, provided that a man didn't object to a little good-natured debauchery when the hour grew late — and he did not — there were few establishments to compare with it.

Perusing the men in the tap-room around him, Hog detected a very different atmosphere. Gone was the diversity of the Walnut: far out there on the marshes, every man was an agricultural worker of some sort. He saw shepherds and drovers, some carters and ploughmen, but none of the domestic servants and shopkeepers that mingled with them in the Walnut. Hog didn't miss those types of people for their own sake but he did note the insularity of the company. Everyone knew everyone and everyone was keen for it to stay that way. He doubted that the hard-working labourers around him spent their evenings in singing or dancing and, although he did not participate in such pursuits himself, he was not blind to how much they contributed to the atmosphere of an inn. The ranks closed against him made him feel like a trespasser, although he lacked the sensibility to be troubled by his outsider status.

In fact, it rather amused him. It might not be obvious to those who knew him then but, before life had conspired to ruin his character, he'd been an affable and entertaining man. His youthful wit had been well pickled in the years since but it had not deserted him. He saw the irony in the fact that he often avoided hospitable inns, ones where customers took an interest in one another, because people's memories could prove inconvenient if it later suited him to be elsewhere but now he faced the opposite extreme, a roomful of hostile strangers who would certainly remember him. It was an ideal base from which to run a gang, provided the landlord was dependable and Hog had no doubt that he was.

It didn't matter. Having drunk only enough to bring the pain from his leg under control, he was as sober that night as he ever allowed himself to get because he wanted to hear the Burmarsh offer clearly. He had no intention of doing anything that he would later need to deny. He would say nothing, listen to nothing, in the presence of these men that could cause him trouble if it got back to Ransley or one of his cronies — he doubted that the man he had come to meet would expect him to.

He was staring at the second half of his second pint when he felt a tug at his sleeve. His fist immediately clenched in readiness to deliver a blow to whomever might be laying hands on him but he held back when he looked down to find a dirt-streaked waif at his side. The boy was about eight years old, pencil-thin but far too lively to be malnourished. Sea-green eyes flashed with self-importance as he glanced towards the door and then sped outside. Hog drained his tankard lazily. If the boy thought he was running anywhere, he had another think coming. When he left, it was with a measured stride, his manner casual but his eyes monitoring the company in his peripheral vision. A man did not survive as long as he had without learning that the Lord looked out for those who looked out for themselves. His departure appeared to go unpursued.

He maintained his vigilance when he got outside. The sun had not yet set and it was lighter in the yard than it had been in the tap-room. The boy was waiting in the lane, hopping from one foot to the other as if he needed the privy. Hog felt a flash of regret at the loss of his own youth, so distant that it was almost forgotten. He couldn't recall the last time he had felt the excitement that he saw in the young messenger. There was little he had not sampled in his attempts to recapture that verve but he succeeded only in proving that his old self was lost for ever. He shrugged his shoulders, a habitual expression of his determination not to dwell on his disappointments. Someone had heard of him, in a light favourable enough for them to summon him for discussions, and that made him feel better about himself than he had for a long time.

Twenty minutes later, his good humour was becoming strained. He'd traversed a dozen fields, clambered over stiles and struggled through wooded thickets, trying to stay with his nimble guide. He had no idea where he was and an unpleasant awareness of his vulnerability was building inside him. Only the knowledge that there was no need for anyone to drag him halfway to Brookland to kill him kept the anxiety at bay.

Nonetheless, he was on the point of refusing to go any further when he emerged from a behind an untrimmed hornbeam windbreak to see a ramshackle cottage with a lamp in the window. Its small size, and its isolation on the windswept marsh, told Hog that it was more than likely home to a shepherd. Where better to talk to a man whose reliability was as yet unproven? There was no way on God's earth that he would ever find such a place again. He straightened his dishevelled clothes and took a moment to collect his wits. He was not a man who normally worried about the impression he made on others but then perhaps that disregard was part of what had got him where he was now, outside the Blues while Cephas remained securely gaoled. He wanted to be back inside the trade but a return to the Blues, if it was possible at all, required an admission that he had been wrong, which he was not willing to make. He was still sceptical that joining the Burmarsh lot was the answer to his problems but it was the only offer on the table.

While he had been steeling himself for the meeting, the boy had tapped on the door. When it opened, he ran around to the back of the cottage. Hog was pleased to see the lad knew his place, something he thought Ransley's tribe would do well to learn. Not

65

that any of them ever approached him but it still irritated him to see the girl batting her eyes at the younger Blues or the boys pestering to hold their bats.

In the doorway, a man awaited him. Hog would have expected a lackey to search him and escort him inside but something in the bearing of the dark silhouette told him that it was the man he had come to see. He closed the distance between them at a purposeful walk.

'Hogben?'

'And you are?'

For once, Hog's question was devoid of bravado. It was a dispassionate admission of his own identity and reasonably civil request for an introduction.

'Spratford.'

Hog considered the reply. He recognised the name no more than the face. His first reaction was disdain at his contact proving to be a nobody but then he reconsidered. Ransley was well known in Aldington but probably not outside it and yet he seemed to be doing a remarkably effective job of taking over the Blues before Cephas's body was even in its grave. He did not doubt that Spratford was equally well known in the desolate place in which he now found himself. Besides, he was here to listen.

The man stepped back to let him pass. Hog took his time, pleased for the chance to appraise his host. Tall and strongly built, he was somewhere between Ransley and Bailey in both size and looks. There was something of Pierce's compact bulk in his musculature, albeit on a larger scale. He exuded the natural authority that Ransley lacked but his eyes showed no sign of that man's extraordinary blend of cunning and prudence.

Inside the cottage, two men stood against the far wall. Their role was apparent but one look told Hog that they did not have either the power or experience of the Baileys. If they were the best Spratford had, it meant that the Burmarsh lot were as unimpressive as he'd heard but also that it should be easy for him to make significant improvements.

Spratford settled himself into a carver beside the fireplace. He waved to a straight-backed cane-seated chair nearby but Hog declined, intending to retain the psychological advantage afforded by his height and realising too late that Spratford's ease in the face of his caution put him at a disadvantage instead.

'Bill tells me you're not interested in an offer.'

Hog shrugged.

'You're going to stick with Ransley, then?'

Hog hadn't decided how much to say on that score. Even if his future lay elsewhere, he had no intention of betraying his friends in the Blues. He would say nothing that might harm them.

'Marsh said the South Kents are finished,' he replied noncommittally.

'Is that how you see it?'

'They're not running.'

That much was true and public, so he saw no reason not to repeat it.

'So it's not a sham?'

Too late, Spratford tried to extinguish the interest that flickered in his eye. He didn't know the Blues' plans and was gambling on the gossip.

'A sham? What buggering good would that do?'

This time it was Spratford who shrugged. Hog guessed that the man knew the potential benefits of a strategic absence from the fray as well as he did but saw no reason to fill in any blanks that might remain. He changed the subject without subtlety, never his strong suit.

'What're you looking for and why?'

Spratford studied him, making the decision whether to trust him.

'If Ransley can't fill his orders, there's an opening for those as can. How many men have you got waiting for work?'

Hog hesitated, wondering whether to give an answer and, if so, how honest it should be. He wasn't even sure he knew the answer, not having discussed the prospect with the men who'd supported his rescue attempt. Still, he doubted Spratford could step up his operations faster than he could find men in need of a night's pay.

'More than you'd know what to do with.'

Spratford chuckled, clearly unoffended by the gibe or the lack of trust it betrayed, but his expression hardened before he replied.

'But will they follow you?'

'The buggers always have before.'

He watched Spratford weighing his answer. No one could know how events would unfold without Cephas. He had done what few men could, pulling together scores of strangers and using the military training of the few to win victory for the many. Hog sensed his future in the balance and, with his fresh start set to slip from his grasp, knew that he wanted it. It had nothing to do with his loyalty to Cephas and little to do with his resentment of Ransley: overriding everything was his belief that he was as good a man as Cephas had ever been, hampered only by each twist of fate that closed doors in his face even as it opened them for other men. This time, it would be he who passed through the arch of opportunity.

Being as constructive as he knew how to be, he said, 'They're good men. You find cargo and customers, they'll do the rest. I guarantee it.'

After a significant pause, Spratford nodded. 'Marsh'll pass the word.'

Hog nodded. He would still be taking orders but a gang without Baileys offered the prospect of faster progress than he was ever likely to make in the Blues. Accepting his dismissal, he took a step towards the door but then faltered when he realised that he had no idea where he was. At a snap of Spratford's fingers, the boy ran through from the scullery. His mouth was crammed with food, which he was fighting to swallow before facing his employer. If he regularly ate on that scale, Hog thought his stomach must be hosting a heavy burden of worms to keep him so skinny.

'See Mr Hogben back to the Crook.' A faint smile curled his lips as he added, 'The quick way.'

Hog followed the child, glad of the prospect of an easier return journey despite his irritation at the deception. Elated by the prospect of better times ahead, and having no wish to linger in Burmarsh, he decided to ride straight home to Hawkinge. He wasn't sure what kind of reception he'd get from Ann but it was likely to be the warmer for finding him sober for once.

George

George Ransley leaned on the side of the packet boat, bound for France with spirits high. Only two days after Cephas's conviction on a capital charge, his haste might have been unseemly to some. In fact, he had planned the trip weeks before but postponed it until his predecessor's fate was certain. Once all doubt was removed, he saw no value in further delay.

At last, firmly ensconced as the new leader of the Blues, he could begin to do business in the way he believed it should be done. Not for a hundred years had the Kentish coast seen the likes of the trade he intended to slip undetected past the preventive men's noses. Organised and disciplined, his men would thrive on the security that only he could bring them: financial to be sure, with as much as a guinea a week on top of their legitimate earnings, but practical too, through his careful planning and prudent safety measures. Free-trade was about to become a respectable profession although, of course, it was not respectability that George sought. With no regard for the establishment, he had no interest in that kind of approbation. Like most marshmen, he'd dabbled in the trade all his life but there had been two reasons for his decision to commit himself to it as a career a decade earlier.

Foremost were his responsibilities to his family. In eighteen-twelve, even as Napoleon's soldiers fled from the Russians, George faced troubles that were inconsequential to the world at large but seemed insurmountable to him. Married three years, he already had two children when his wife promptly fell pregnant with a third. His meagre carter's wages were stretched to the limit and he had only to look around him to see how things would go from there. Things were bad in Kent and worse still in Sussex, where more poor people depended on the parish for survival than anywhere else in the country. In his judgement, he had no choice but to enter the trade on a full-time basis.

Yet, while the welfare of his family was the most important factor in his decision, it was not the reason that he loved the trade. That was more personal and less logical. It had to do with freedom to make a choice and his refusal to let others control his life, with the special status of the Cinque Ports and his refusal to accept the denial of such hard-won rights, and with the Enclosure Acts and his refusal to tolerate the theft of common land that turned free Englishmen into exploited tenants. It was his protest at his place in the world and he intended to make that protest count. He would do so in a way the rich understood, by making money and buying influence. He had no wish to take lives, turning wives into widows and children into orphans, but he would not live in squalor while his 'betters' squandered the fat of the land.

He chuckled delightedly to himself at the glowing future ahead, theirs for the taking, and then squinted up at the almost painful brightness of the sun high above. Well behaved for once, the Channel reflected the cloudless blue sky and studded it with spangles of sunlight almost like stars. Even his timing was perfect, launching a summer of negotiations and business transactions that would set them up for a winter of highly profitable free-trade. The thrill he felt at the prospect of putting into action his long-planned strategies was as visceral as another man might find in a sporting contest or a sexual conquest. The former had never held much appeal for him and the latter, after more than ten years of servicing an intensely physical wife, could no longer compete with the excitement of his new challenge.

Only the smoke belching from the tall chimney beside the mast marred the glorious day. George had no great fondness for the machines that were beginning to steal work from honest men but he couldn't dispute the fact that packet boats beat oarsmen for speed and sails for reliability. Still, he doubted that steam would ever take the place of the muscle of men and horses. The packet boat's engine devoured coal at a prodigious rate, and that had to be mined by men and hauled by horses. Perhaps they would invent machines to do those tasks. But then they'd need more coal to power the machines that brought the coal… When even his strong head began to spin at the prospect, George abandoned such futile ruminations and returned to the business in hand. Of one thing he was absolutely sure: as long as men breathed, there would be a demand for fine liquor at a good price.

Some years had passed since he last left England but, in his youth, he'd made the trip to France countless times — usually at the oars of a seventy-foot galley heavy with gold guineas worth nine shillings more in post-revolutionary Paris than they were in London. Few people knew of the runs then and even fewer were still around to tell the tale. One or two fell victim to a naval sloop or cutter on patrol, and more were taken by sea and sickness, but most ended their days peacefully in bed. Of those closest to him now, only Sam Bailey and James Hogben remembered the early days. That thought disturbed George's equanimity. Had it been mere nostalgia that made him tolerate a man like Hogben, who could so easily become a threat to them all? He shrugged, as if to cast the doubt off: he'd had his reasons for retaining the Hog. They needed such men if the locals were to be sure that betraying the Blues was unwise, even for a reward that came close to ten years' wages, and he felt for Ann Hogben and the children; without an income from the Blues, they'd be on the parish in no time. He expected Hogben to return to the fold when he found no work beyond it. When that time came, George doubted that he would have the heart to turn the troublemaker away.

The shining chalk cliffs at Dover had not long disappeared to the stern when the flatter contours of northern France blurred the horizon. The land ahead slowly came into focus, revealing a wide harbour crowded with boats and ringed by ships at anchor in the deeper waters. George had not returned to France since the treaty. Then he stepped onto a French beach conscious that it was enemy territory, somewhat surprised by the patriotism stirring in his breast. He'd had no respect whatsoever for the Prince Regent, the politicians or the military — no amount of nationalistic jingoism could make him forget that those men cared nothing for him, his family or his class. Languishing in their great houses, they did nothing while men, women and children died from hunger and disease. It was not only that they failed to deliver salvation but rather that they did not even make the attempt. Nor did he see any sign that the unending death and suffering of the poor disturbed the tranquillity of their lives. There were a few local landowners who showed a sense of duty to their tenants and workers but they were but an island of conscience in an ocean of indifference.

George had been in the Palm Tree on the day that his men studied the watercolour of the Pavilion. He rarely agreed with Hogben about anything but would gladly have joined him in defiling the image of such a monstrous waste of money with waste of another kind. Hundreds of thousands of pounds had been poured into the vain edifice, with thousands more thrown away since on the banquets and balls of a bored fool. George's anger set his teeth grinding, as tension always did. Boredom was a rare experience around Aldington, with most of its inhabitants spending every waking minute in drudgery. True, their occupations were not mentally stimulating but their bodies were so exhausted that their minds barely noticed the deficit. One of the worst things about having too little to eat was the way that thoughts of food played on the mind. The hungry, especially the smaller children, could wile away the whole day in contemplation of one measly potato for supper. They sat by the side of roads, eyes vacant and drool coursing over their chins.

He woke from the unwelcome daydream with a start. Soon there would be work for any man who wanted it. No one — from Aldington to the coast, from Rye in the west to Deal in the east — need starve once the Blues were running again. There was only one cloud on his horizon: Hogben's low profile since his failed rescue attempt and the murmurs of increased activity out on the marshes.

George's gut told him more trouble was to come from the man before they were through. As he saw it, he had three alternatives: send him a warning, order his death or let events run their course. Believing that a warning would only inflame the man's indignation and unwilling to have him killed, he settled for staying out of affairs for the present. Perhaps the preventive men might do him a service for once. Not only would Hogben's death at their hands remove his main problem but it might also convince other doubters that they were safer within than without the Blues.

Hog

On the same day that Ransley embarked for France, two pieces of information reached Hog's ears. The first played on his mind even more than he had expected it to. Marsh had been right: Cephas was to hang in early July. As he had entered no appeal for clemency, there was no question that the sentence would be carried out.

Hog's reaction to the news could not have been more different from Ransley's. Within an hour of receiving confirmation of Marsh's account from a more reliable source, he was too drunk to stand without support. He chose as the site for his excess a public house that he rarely visited, the Valiant Sailor on Folkestone Hill. Perched on the hillside inland of the Warren, it invariably seethed with sailors, valiant or otherwise, and their company was usually an unwelcome reminder of his involuntary stint with the Navy. That night, it seemed more palatable, inducing nostalgia for the camaraderie he'd found amongst his fellow unfortunates aboard a man-o'-war. Having made few such friends since, he lamented the impending loss of one of the best.

'They fired on us,' he moaned to the young man next to him.

The stranger studied him and then, soft hazel eyes tinged with pity, waved for the innkeeper to refill his tankard. Hog frowned, pleased but surprised to be bought a drink. Only when he was halfway through the gift did he realise that the seaman had taken him for a casualty of war, still reliving its horrors six years after its end. He turned the idea over for a minute, wondering whether to hit him for his insolence, but decided that a pint was a pint, whatever the buyer might be thinking. He had sustained no injuries of note during his Navy years and, in his opinion, had survived it intact. There were those who might disagree with that assessment but no one would deny it was a preventive man's pistol that sealed his fate just a year earlier. He drained the tankard.

'I hope you can sleep that off by Saturday night.'

He barely noticed the eastern twang to the familiar voice, at home in Folkestone in a way that it hadn't been in Rye, amongst the softer burrs of Sussex.

'Bugger off.'

Spirits depressed by the poor prospects of a man with whom he'd identified more than any other, his plans for the future suddenly seemed futile. While Cephas led them, he saw evidence that men like them could amount to something but that ray of hope was soon to be snuffed out. He no longer felt any interest in the second piece of information, although he had been eagerly awaiting it before the news from the Old Bailey spread across the county.

'Saturday night,' the voice repeated. Marsh was so close that their upper arms touched. The words were too low for anyone else to hear. 'Ten o'clock in the field behind the Crook. Fifty men or you're out. One chance, no more.'

Hog watched him leave then turned back to his tankard only to find the stranger watching him curiously.

'Bugger off,' he repeated.

The man raised a hand in symbolic surrender, indicating that his interest was only casual. Suddenly lonely, Hog felt a drunken need to unburden himself of his miseries.

'Sorry,' he muttered with uncharacteristic civility. 'Thanks for the beer.'

'You're w-w-welcome.'

The pronounced stammer took Hog by surprise. The man seemed self-assured, tall with passable good looks, plentiful calluses and seaman's garb confirming that he earned his living from the most unpredictable mistress of all, the sea. His voice was entirely at odds with that impression. Had he been closer to sober, Hog would almost certainly have ridiculed him but, in alcoholic solidarity, he felt compassion towards the pitiable man who had taken pity on him.

'Fisherman?' he prompted his new acquaintance.

The man rocked his hand in a gesture of ambivalence. 'Of sorts.'

Hog considered the reply through another mouthful of beer. Seamen were to ports what labourers were to farms: they did whatever was needed, crewing any vessel from ships-of-the-line to humble fishing smacks. He judged his companion too young to have stood against Napoleon but felt confident that he had useful experience, wherever it had been gained: something in his bearing insisted on it.

'Ever do nightwork?' he asked bluntly.

The man frowned. Hog watched him from the corner of his eye, alert to the fact that he might be wary of a trap or planning to lay one. Careless of the risks, never one for prudence where recklessness was an option, Hog waited for the man to make his move.

When it came, the answer was evasive.

'Not in this neck of the w-woods.'

Hog was sure that the accent was Kent — South Kent unless he was much mistaken — but that didn't mean its owner hadn't travelled far and wide since.

'Just got in?' he guessed.

The man studied him again, then finally smiled as if in acceptance of something. 'Aye. M-more w-work up in Harridge but it in't home.'

Harwich — a fine place to run Dutch goods, if ever there was one. Hog considered the point. He needed fifty men in two days hence. Even if all the rebels threw in their lot with him, excepting the Wraights whose interest had been purely personal and ended with Dick's acquittal, that left him seven men short. In reality, he doubted that men like Smoker and Quids would follow him after the failed rescue attempt. He would be down to the men for whom

74

regular work, bringing much-needed income, was the overriding priority. Now one, a seaman who knew the trade, had just fallen into his lap.

'Know the Shepherd & Crook out at Burmarsh?'

'No.' There was a pause before the stranger admitted his interest. 'B-but I could f-find it.'

'Hogben.' Hog held out his hand in support of the perfunctory introduction. For no particular reason, he never gave his Christian name.

'Grey,' the man responded, shaking his hand firmly. 'Datchet Grey.'

If Hog had been in charge, and less distracted by a friend's wait for the gallows, he would have set the run for the night of the trial. With the Blockade's attention diverted and half its best men giving evidence in London, the Burmarsh lot might have made an uncontested run.

As it was, Spratford setting the date four days after the trial gave the preventive men plenty of time to return to Kent and resume their duties. They were probably on alert, guarding against the twin risks of recriminations against their men or witnesses and of the Blues resuming trade as soon as their leader's situation was resolved. They were not to know that the threat came from another quarter. If all went well, they would not be aware of the run at all. If things went less smoothly, Hog would lose no sleep if the Blues took the blame, which they almost certainly would with the landing set for Hythe, the nearest coast to Aldington. That too had not been his choice, at the western end of the most stoutly defended part of the Kentish coast. He would have opted for one of the sparsely patrolled stretches, perhaps south of Deal, but then Ransley had done just that when he planned their ill-fated runs on Denge Marsh.

Desperate for success, both at a personal level to guarantee his future but also in a wider sense to balance the disasters of preceding months, Hog hoped Spratford proved to be Ransley's equal as a strategist. Deep inside, he knew that the man would not. In spite of that knowledge, the thought of abandoning the run never crossed his mind. He waited with his men as he'd waited with his crew before countless naval engagements, concentrating on keeping them calm, quiet and sober, determined that no error of his would bring casualties to their number.

When the signal came, it might have been Ransley's low whistle but, instead, it came from a man whom Hog did not yet know how far to trust. That night, they were to work in two teams, with Marsh leading the Burmarsh men and Hog alongside with his recruits. Each team had forty in its working party, protected by ten men with bats. The order had been to carry no firearms but Hog felt the comforting weight of his pistol beneath his coat, the holster hanging under his armpit from a belt buckled over the opposite shoulder: it was handy but invisible. He glanced at the Horne brothers, standing either side of a cart driven by an elderly man. Their duck-guns, hidden beneath a layer of straw inside the cart, raised his spirits but the age of the driver, an indication of how difficult it had been to find fifty men willing to cross the Blues, quickly depressed him again. If the run went well, and Ransley did not start running again, it would be easier to staff the next run. If it went badly… If the run went badly, Hog doubted he would be invited to make another.

Shoving his worries back into the pit of indigestion that seemed to be a constant companion in his new life, he waved his men forward. If nothing else, at least Mother Nature was on their side. The tides were ideal for their purpose and the weak light of the quarter-moon, while bright enough to light their way, was too weak to draw attention to their presence. Such a perfect night for a run was rare and would normally have brought out the optimist in him but, as it was, the disquieting blend of familiar and unfamiliar things made him uneasy. He was surrounded by tried and tested men, working a stretch of beach that he knew better than the scrap of land behind his own house, but he was depending on strangers for the backup that might save his and his men's lives.

He strained his ears for any hint of danger but all he heard was the surf scouring the foreshore and the distant clunk of oars against hulls. In the dim light, he studied the galleys now less than fifty yards off. They were twelve-oared and clinker-built, judging from the way they sliced through the shallows. Common sense seemed to dictate that a smooth-hulled vessel would be faster but, in fact, the overlapping planks parted the waves with almost no resistance. Spratford must have some useful contacts, if he could arrange for a cargo of eight-score tubs to be delivered so efficiently, but Hog wished the man was more open to advice when it came to their defensive strategy. Divided into two parties, they were spread too thin. Whoever was unlucky enough to catch the brunt of any attack was going to come out of it poorly. On the Sandgate side of the landing, Hog's party was the likely target. He turned his face eastwards, scanning the sands for any sign of movement. If trouble came, he would put serious money on it coming from that direction.

A shot rang out: the alarm.

Hog's eyes flitted over the shadowy dunes from which the sound had come. He could see nothing but clearly the same was not true for the man who fired. The working parties were inevitably exposed, unloading at the waterline with nothing to shield them from view. Hog dropped to one knee, instinctively adopting the most stable position and offering the smallest target area for his enemy. The men around him did the same. Glancing over his shoulder, he saw that the Burmarsh lot remained on their feet.

'Get down!' he hissed. Individually, their lives were of no interest to him but collectively they might make the difference between him being alive or dead when morning came.

Such an early interruption was bad news indeed. If the boats were half-unloaded, they might manage to finish their business before the Blockade forces arrived. As it was, they stood little chance. The safest option was to flash the boats off and abandon the run. Ever confrontational, Hog rarely turned from a fight but he might have considered it that night. However, the decision was not his to make. In response to a hail from the boats, Spratford signalled them to land.

As soon as he heard keel scrape shingle, Hog had his men moving. The working party engulfed the galley, while the armed party fell into formation around them. He was proud of how smoothly his men executed the plan, thanks more to Sam Bailey's training than his own leadership. His relationship with Bailey might be uneasy, seasoned as it was with an unhealthy sprinkling of envy, but he had only admiration for the man's fighting skills and knew that many of the Blues owed their lives to his generosity in passing on his expertise.

At the limits of his vision, he thought he saw movement. That was about right: it wouldn't take long for reinforcements from the station at the nearest tower to reach the sentinel who had fired the alarm. A moment later, he was sure. Blockademen surged forward along the beach. Hog had never decided whether he thought they were brave or stupid but there never seemed to be any shortage of them willing to run right up to a loaded weapon. He reached for his pistol but then left it where it was. They had only a few shots between them: if they resorted to firepower, they'd have to make it count.

Behind him, tubs thudded onto the sands and, seconds later, the first two tubmen headed homewards. Burmarsh was only five miles to the west but that was a long way with a pair of tubs slung across the shoulders. Hog knew that from experience, often having carried such loads twice that distance before his injury. The men's first hurdle would come at the Military Canal, only a few hundred yards behind the beach on this part of the coast and too wide to cross without boat or bridge. Naturally, the bridges were guarded but Hog had been relieved to see Spratford take care of that little obstacle with a sizeable bribe. He'd felt a palpable wave of nostalgia for more secure nights when the transaction brought to mind Ransley's customary words on such occasions.

'You haven't seen anybody, have you?' he would say, while pressing half a crown into the man's palm.

Hog's indigestion took a bitter turn for the worse, as he counted the men flitting along the dunes towards his select band. He saw at least half a dozen, and the true figure was probably twice that. Each would be armed with pistol and musket, cutlass and dirk. The Blockademen were fond of quoting the odds they faced: two hundred smugglers against their twenty-five men, they'd say. They neglected to mention the fact that only a score of the free-traders were usually armed, if that, and most of those with simple ash poles. Now, he had ten men and three guns. He wished the Wraights, or more specifically their fowling pieces, were still at his disposal.

Three more tubmen ran up the beach, two from his party and one from Marsh's. He felt a stab of professional pride at how efficiently his team was working. He glanced along the line of defenders on either side of him. All eyes were on the movements further along the beach.

On the left, without his permission, the Hornes had their duck-guns in hand. Hog couldn't blame them. In little more than a minute, the balls would start to fly past them. Carrying a firearm might not offer much practical protection but it certainly made a man feel better.

On the right, the newcomer was only three places along. As Hog expected, it had been hard to muster fifty men and he found the last handful mainly from amongst the ranks of the retired, some through age and others through infirmity. The new man was altogether more promising. Hog considered the odd name he'd given: Datchet Grey. If that was genuine, Hog was heir to the English crown. He had no idea what the man might be hiding and, an indication of his ineptitude as a leader, it never occurred to him that perhaps he ought to find out.

Another shot split the night: the warning.

'Stand away from the boats,' a voice called.

'Bugger that,' Hog muttered.

Glancing behind him, he found a score of tubmen hastening to secure their loads and flee the beach. About half a dozen tubs remained in the galley, with a few more unclaimed in the surf. An instant's inspection of Marsh's party revealed a much poorer picture, with the bulk of the cargo still in the galley and men loitering aimlessly as if they had all night. Their defenders had no firearms and, in their uneasy positions and loose formation, he could see the conflict between their instincts for fight and flight

'Damn them,' Hog kept up his muttered undercurrent while he assessed the situation. 'Right, those with firearms cover those without. Get in tight as fast as you can and teach these bastards what a bat's for.'

True to form, seconds later, the Blockademen swept forward. If they'd dug in at the edge of their range, they could have picked off his men one by one. With more guns and unlimited ammunition, victory would have been theirs. As it was, they seemed to take a perverse pride in stopping as many balls as possible on their approach to a landing. Far be it for him to disappoint them.

Perhaps the main thing that kept him alive was his unfailing nerve. Balls flew by but he held on to his shot, waiting until he could be sure to make it count. A ball thudded into his left bicep, a brief stab of pain before settling into a steady throb. His ox-hide coat had deflected many an injury in the past and made light work of a musket ball at the limits of its range. There'd be no more than a livid bruise to remind him of yet another near miss.

As he selected his target, he shouted to the men behind him.

'Leave the rest and get clear! Shove that buggering boat off!'

The response was immediate, his own men in obedience born of experience while the oarsmen had been on the verge of leaving before he spoke. They were on long lines from the lugger at anchor in the bay and now their friends aboard sprang into action. With oars lifted, the galleys flew through the water in response to the winding of a capstan back on deck. They made perhaps twice their best rowing speed as the lines sped them out of danger.

Finally seeing a clear target, Hog felled a slight man to one side of the Blockade party. As if his shot had been a prearranged signal, the men around him followed suit, while his fingers flew over the familiar contours of his pistol in reloading. As fast as any man and more careless than most of the explosion that might come from a badly loaded firearm, he disregarded the exposure as he prepared himself to shoot again.

Fortunately, the Blockademen were letting off their usual poorly aimed barrage and he did not expect to sustain a serious wound in the confusion. Trusting to his customary good luck, and heedless of the fact that it had already let him down once, he squinted along the barrel of his pistol and selected another victim. In his peripheral vision, he saw two men fall to the left and then a third to the right. A glance at the new man revealed a pistol in his grip, smoke rising from its firing pan. Checking over his shoulder, he saw both boats well into the distance and the last tubmen at the top of the beach.

'Fall back!' he shouted.

Turning away from the preventive forces, bent double to offer the poorest possible target, he led the retreat as he had led the advance. Like Ransley, he knew the importance of knowing when they were beaten and acting as decisively in defeat as in victory although, unlike Ransley, it had taken countless bloody naval engagements to drum that fact through his stubborn skull. Now his men clustered around him, their confidence apparently unshaken in spite of the night's unpleasant surprises. Putting a brave face on their situation, he kept them moving swiftly towards West Hythe. Once into the roughs beyond the canal, they might shake off their pursuers.

The noise of their own passage drowned out any evidence of pursuit. His frequent backward glances revealed nothing. Still, somehow, he knew the Blockademen were gaining — he *felt* it. Forcing himself to remain calm, he considered the alternatives. The most obvious was to destroy the bridge after they crossed it. Doing so would make them unpopular with the locals but sweeteners in the right quarters would placate them fast enough. However, built from local stone, the bridge was quite literally as solid as a rock.

'Rolfie?' he shouted across the fleeing line. 'Anyone seen Rolfie?'

'Hey, Rolfie!' A man to his right echoed his cry, only for it to ripple away through the ranks.

Richard Rolfe lived in Lympne, not half a mile north of the bridge, but it was not only his local knowledge that Hog sought to mine. With no time to spare, they ran on while the man was found. Just as they turned north, off the road and through the fields on a direct line for the bridge, he stumbled to Hog's side.

'Looking for me?' he gasped.

Fit as they were, even an easy night's trading left them exhausted and it was not an easy night. Most men had done a full day's work before they set out for the rendezvous, some making journeys of as much as twelve miles, only to face hours of waiting, unloading and carrying. The morrow would see them struggling to hold down their regular jobs when they could barely lift their bodies off their mattresses. Rolfe was luckier than some in that regard, working for himself in a trade for which there was a nice, steady demand: monumental stonemasonry.

'The bridge,' Hog gasped back. 'Can we close it?'

'Close it?' Rolfe repeated in surprise. 'What, blast it?'

'Any other way to do it?'

'Well, no, but blast it?'

His voice betrayed his interest in the idea. As well as carving stone, Rolfe had abundant experience of quarrying it. Hog knew he usually carried a quantity of gunpowder because he'd seen it put to good use to create diversions in the past.

'Could you take out a section?'

'Course I bloody well could,' the man retorted, professional pride clearly wounded by the fact that Hog needed to ask.

'Could you do it in time?'

This time, Rolfe's answer was less hasty. He matched Hog's glance to their rear and considered the matter before giving his answer.

'No more chance than a cat in hell without claws,' he finally admitted.

'Bugger.'

'But I could cover a stand.'

It was Hog's turn to mull over an unexpected suggestion. The armed parties making a stand should give the working parties time to get clear. They would probably lose men in the fight but fewer than if they were overtaken in flight. If he was going down, Hog wanted to take some of their foes with him. He knew he was not alone in that sentiment.

'All right, go to it. But keep 'em small,' he added. 'No sense doing half a job if we can't stop the bastards.'

Rolfie waved his acceptance of the point: superficial damage would only inconvenience and impoverish his neighbours. As he lengthened his stride, Hog signalled the other men to slacken their pace. They could not let their pursuers gain too much ground but, while a hint of fatigue might push the Blockademen into a final sprint, it might equally make them become complacent and put less into the chase.

Maintaining a steady jog, he let his mind drift for a few seconds. Was he too old for forced runs, he wondered. Years of heavy drinking had dented his youthful athletic prowess long before his injury accelerated the decline. It was a dim memory now but there had been a time when he thought nothing of making the fifteen-mile journey to Canterbury at an unbroken run. Always short of money, he preferred to spend what little he had in what was then the county town of East Kent rather than on getting there. He might pause on his way to take on liquid, or to pass it, but he had no need of rest. Those days were so distant now that they seemed more like tales he'd been told than a part of his own life. Yes, filled with nostalgia for a life now gone, he was getting old.

Wrenching himself back to the moment, grim as it was, he took another look behind him and then squinted into the darkness ahead. He was relieved at what he saw. The bridge was less than a hundred yards away and the preventive men were still more than twice that distance behind. Like hounds on a scent, their pursuit was relentless but not so swift. Men began to bunch closer around him, recovering the tight formation that had become ragged during their retreat.

'Working parties first over,' he instructed. 'Forget the bloody farm — don't stop moving until you're home. Batmen next: form a defensive line on the far side and beat to snuff any bugger that crosses it. Men with firearms last: we'll hold the bastards back as long as we can. No firing past our own and no falling back till I say so. Clear?'

There was a low chorus of assent from his own men but less conviction from the Burmarsh men mingled with them.

'Make this your last run, if you want to,' Hog snapped, 'But for Christ's sake act like men till it's done. You start a run, you bloody well finish it, so help me. I asked if you're clear?'

There was a little more conviction in the replies this time.

He said, 'Good.' He thought, 'Now let's get out of this mess alive.'

To his relief, every man did as bidden. It was hard to make them out in the darkest part of the night but, at a guess, about half of those who started the night in the working parties took the lead across the bridge. Looking on the bright side, that meant the other half had already left with their loads when the run was abandoned but that still meant half their cargo had either been returned to the lugger or dumped in the surf. Spratford would be lucky to cover his costs with what went inland. Hog discarded that assessment of success, shifting his focus onto saving his men's lives, indifferent now to the profitability of the run. Behind the fleeing tubmen, something upwards of a dozen batmen scurried into their positions on the far side of the canal. The Hornes were on his left and Grey on his right. Beyond Grey was Marsh, a duck-gun slung across his shoulder: so, they were not the only ones to disobey the firearms order. Rolfe knelt at the base of the nearest buttress of the bridge. Hog stopped and squatted at his side.

'They're on our heels. You ready?'

There was a brief silence while the stonemason uncoiled a fuse, rose to his feet and led them over the canal. His reply drifted casually over his shoulder, as if they were discussing the weather.

'Aye, bastards won't know what hit 'em.'

Rolfe headed for a point at the end of the stone wall of the bridge. No doubt all his fuses met there, waiting only for a flame to ignite them.

Hog ducked behind the first reinforcing pier in the stonework and motioned for his companions to do the same. Grey took the one behind him, Marsh behind that, with the Hornes opposite. They would be lucky to get off two shots apiece. The first must wait until the enemy was close enough to see and hit. The second would be hurriedly reloaded, ball loose in the barrel and aim the poorer for it. If they took down two men between them, Hog would count it a triumph.

Up until that point, time had been racing but now it slowed. He knew the preventive men could not be more than a minute or two behind them and the tension of awaiting the first footfall or whisper was almost painful. The blood throbbed in his temple, his brain counting each beat of his heart and then throwing in an unhelpful reminder that any one of them might be the last.

Then it came: the crunch of a boot on loose shingle. From the corner of his eye, Hog saw John Horne's gun-barrel rise in perfect synchronisation with his own. A man materialised from the darkness, stooped in the scant cover of the hedgerow. Hog heard Horne's fowling piece provide a deeper echo to the report of his own pistol. The man dropped into the shadows but whether he was injured or trying to protect himself was not clear. Either way, Hog was reloading before the body hit the ground.

A ball flew past his left ear. He heard another body slump. They seemed to be doing better than he had expected. The last two guns rang out behind him but he saw no sign that their balls found flesh. Three more men scurried forward. Despite his careful aim, his next shot only knocked the musket from his target's hand. Out of time, he returned his pistol to its holster and drew his cutlass. It was a handsome blade, stolen from a lieutenant and a cut above the standard naval issue.

The others' second shots came past in close succession. A string of obscenities announced that one at least had hit something. There was a volley of return fire from the preventive men and then the first lot of gunpowder went up.

'Damnation!'

There was surprise and outrage in the curse. Hog didn't wait around long enough to hear more. Waving the others back with him, they hastily regrouped with the batmen. A second explosion went up, then a third.

'Nice work,' Hog called over to where Rolfe knelt by his fuses.

Grey tapped his shoulder and pointed at the far side of the canal. Hog followed the line of his arm, then saw movement in the fields.

'Bugger,' he growled, before adding an explanation for the others. 'Reinforcements.'

Rolfe looked up, grinned, and then lifted a length of fuse that ran past him. Hog stooped to get a better look. Rolfe raised his taper to illuminate a row of fuses lying one beside the other. The shortest one ended within a yard or so but the others ran beyond the circle of light.

'Thought we should expect more company.'

Hog patted his shoulder, then turned to the rest of their party. 'You know where you're headed. Get moving and keep moving. Rolfie's bought us some time — let's make damned good use of it.'

His words sparked a surge of movement, men streaming away into the night, but he stood firm, cutlass raised to defend the stonemason on whose skill all their lives now hung. He was surprised, but not displeased, to find Grey standing beside him. While Rolfe lit his fuses, Grey reloaded his pistol with a speed that suggested considerable experience of fighting in the dark and under fire. They dropped back a few yards at a time, each pause just long enough to be sure the fuse was burning well. When the eighth was fizzling strongly, they took one last look into the darkness and then turned their faces west and started running. They'd taken no more than half a dozen strides when the first of the delayed explosions went up.

'Fall back!' a voice bawled.

Eight random explosions should buy enough time, Hog thought. It would be a while after the last before the preventive men gained enough confidence to try the bridge again. Putting all their trials behind him, he headed for the rendezvous, the safe haven of Aldergate Farm. The pain from his leg was unbelievable, turning the prospect of a couple more miles into a Herculean task, but he gritted his teeth and set the fastest pace he dared. He would not slow until he was sure they were out of danger.

When they reached the farm more than twenty minutes later, their friends were resting in a field while some of the fittest rounded up stragglers and arranged for provisions from the farmer, a staunch ally. Having done all he could for his men, Hog finally sank onto his good knee and gave in to the nausea engulfing him. Gasping as he strove to regain control, he dribbled sour bile onto the grass. Ten minutes and several mouthfuls of vomit later, he began to feel better. Spitting foul-tasting saliva savagely onto the grass, he forced himself back onto his feet and went in search of the cause of their suffering. As soon as he found it, self-control spent, he unleashed his full fury on Spratford.

'Damn it all! Where in God's name did you get that lot? They've no buggering idea. You might as well line my men up now and shoot them.'

Spratford stared back at him dispassionately, clearly refusing to be drawn into an argument that he could not win. Hog's assessment might be emotional and exaggerated but it contained more than a grain of truth. He kept his response low, only just loud enough to reach Hog's ears.

'I wouldn't have called on you if I had the men I needed.'

Even through his anger, Hog saw the validity of that point but had another of his own that was just as compelling.

'Then there's bugger-all point in running us as two teams, is there? For Christ's sake!' He rolled his eyes dramatically. 'If I knew they needed mollycoddling, I'd have brought a nursemaid with me.'

'I said no firearms,' Spratford said, just as evenly as before.

Hog's reply was far less even.

'If you want men looking to die, find them for yourself.' Stepping closer, he growled right into Spratford's face. 'Before we run again, I want to know who's who and I decide where they work.' Without waiting for a response, he spun to face his men. 'Right, we've got half a cargo and we've already done more than half the work so leave it here for these bastards to haul. We're off.'

With that, he led his team away from the wreckage of their first night with the Burmarsh lot. He doubted that Spratford could do without them but, if the fool thought he could, Hog was prepared to lose the work. Recklessness only went so far and the pathetic disorganisation he'd witnessed that night was well beyond the limit.

Sam

Sam Bailey sat in the kitchen of the Bourne Tap, pensively supping tea while watching Eliza Ransley knead dough. The table squeaked rhythmically as she methodically folded air into the elastic mixture. There were few people on God's earth for whom he had as much respect as he had for his eldest sister. Her husband was ordinarily high on the list but now, believing Ransley's present priorities to be awry, he intended to use her influence to persuade his brother-in-law to change his strategy. He was not fool enough to imagine he could manipulate her and so the first challenge was to convince her. As Ransley was still in France, there was plenty of time to put his case. He'd been hinting at it for a few days but it was the news from Hythe that brought him by that morning.

'You know it's down to George,' Eliza said offhandedly.

Sam cocked his head at her. None of the Baileys took orders in their own homes and he did not believe for an instant that she was the exception. Added to that, he knew Ransley, perhaps better than the man realised, and knew that his marriage was a partnership in a way that was almost unique in their circle. Plenty of their men were good providers who trusted their wives to run their households, and perhaps loved them too for all he knew, but few would discuss their business activities with their women. Eliza played the good wife in company, never revealing what she knew or what she thought, understanding how that would undermine her husband in some of his men's eyes. Sam knew it for an act and admired the wisdom she showed in maintaining the pretence.

'All right,' she conceded, tacitly admitting that she had a say. 'But what makes you think fighting amongst ourselves will help?'

'It wouldn't be amongst ourselves, Lize,' he protested. 'The Burmarsh lot are nothing to do with us.'

'They're traders.'

That was true. It would be a sad day when a Bailey turned against his fellows in the trade. 'But they're taking our business, just the same.'

'George don't think they've got the men for it.'

'What if he's wrong?'

She smiled. 'Don't happen often.'

Sam studied her, thinking carefully before saying something that felt like a betrayal. 'They might be taking care of that.'

'Meaning?'

'The Hog.'

She paused in her kneading.

'Is he with them?'

'That's what I hear.'

She returned to the dough, considering that prospect.

'He's not the man he was.'

'He's still dangerous.'

She smiled again. 'But to who?'

'He had better than two score of men when he went after Cephas. What if they're still with him?'

'Do you think so many will stand against George? It won't get Cephas back.'

'I don't say they're against George but that don't make 'em for him neither. Things have been steady for a ways and now they're

87

changing. George in't the only one to see something for himself in that.'

'But the Hog?'

'Clears the way,' Sam said perceptively. 'The top looks a lot closer without George, and without me.'

'Mmm.'

The murmured agreement told him to back off and let her consider what he'd said. He took a deeper draught from his tankard and moved the conversation onto safer ground in the form of his eldest nephew.

'How's young Georgie?'

Her face lit up with pride. 'More like his father every day. He's learning to do the books, you know. Just ten years old.'

'Smart lad.'

Uneasy with his own reputation for violence, Sam saw nothing wrong with a more intellectual path to prosperity. No such choice had been open to him for, although his father dutifully sent them all along to school whenever they could be spared, books were as much a mystery to him after his education ended as they had been before it began. The deficiency had never troubled him, given that he had no use for reading, but latterly he had begun to realise that knowledge could be as formidable a weapon as a swingle. Georgie was right to look to his father as an example, if he wanted to succeed in a world that became ever more hostile to men like his uncles.

'And Young Sam?' Eliza returned the familial enquiry.

Sam nodded. 'He's a fine boy.'

The words did not do justice to his feelings, to the passion of a man with only one goal left in his life: to raise an heir for the Samuel Bailey name. It had taken his wife three attempts to bear him a son and, though he loved his daughters more than life itself, only the boy gave him a reason for living. Having recently reached his first birthday, the child had few accomplishments to merit his father's esteem but that did not prevent Sam delighting in every tottering step and unrecognisable word. His paternal pride was unaffected by the total lack of any resemblance to himself or his family in the delicate, flaxen-haired boy. He was Samuel Bailey the fourth — nothing else mattered.

Hog

Over the next seven weeks, Hog had plenty of time to rue his hasty words to Spratford. His wife's temper shortened as their meals shrank, while he suffered the twin miseries of near-sobriety and aching hunger. He made the long journey to Rye more often than ever before, aware as he did so that trading too heavily on his promise of discretion might tempt the landlord to find a cheaper way to guarantee his silence — permanently. He was on the brink of despair when Marsh made another appearance.

Now he scanned Eastware Bay, watching as the waves began to recede. High tide had been and gone — where the hell were the rest of his crew? How in God's name men who'd spent their whole lives in East Kent could get lost on their way to Folkestone was a mystery to him… in the middle of the marshes, yes, but a couple of miles from a major port?

'Can't leave it m-much longer.'

In pointing out the obvious, Grey's quiet, hesitant speech inflamed his irritation. Low tide meant a vast expanse of foreshore to traverse before men reached the cover of trees and hedgerows. It might put the carts half a mile from the landing boats. All in all, it spelled the risk of lost cargoes and, worse still, lost lives. Even on a moonless night, the sea reflected enough light to create silhouettes in the empty landscape.

He was about to step forward to flash the lugger in when a disturbance behind him stopped him in his tracks. There was enough noise for a herd of bullocks crunching across the shingle. His heart sank as he realised that his men had finally arrived and they were in no condition to work. He'd known they were not the best of the Blues but he'd underestimated the number of ways in which they might let him down.

Busy with planning the night's work, he'd had no one to do for him what he did for Cephas. It took a strong man to organise the weaker men and make sure that everything was in place for a night's trade. When they had plenty of men, everyone knew there was no point in turning up drunk only to be turned away. His need for men, and his lack of time to supervise them, triggered a vicious circle in which he could neither control them nor do without them. He had not before fully appreciated how many factors contributed to their considerable success under Cephas, with the able assistance of Bailey and Ransley. The high standards of the best did much to improve the behaviour of all.

'For Christ's sake,' he muttered, turning to inspect the late-comers.

They made an uninspiring sight, Ted Pantry in the lead and staggering. Glancing at Grey, Hog felt sudden self-consciousness at the way his command was unravelling for a second time in front of the reserved stranger. The first time, he had felt indignant fury but this time his anger at his men was tempered by the knowledge that it was down to him to pick and discipline them.

Grey did not give him time to wallow in self-recrimination. After a brief assessment of Pantry's antics, he had resumed his seaward vigil. Now he nodded at the lugger. She was setting sail, ready to weigh anchor and get under way. Her master had clearly given up on them, keen to make haste out into the Channel before he attracted unwanted attention. Depending on his arrangement with Spratford or his connection in France, the man might return the cargo or sell it elsewhere. No doubt either way he would recover something for his trouble, not too bad for a sideline on top of his legitimate business.

Without another word, Hog strode over to Pantry and channelled his frustration into a wide punch that made up in power what it lacked in style. Pantry sank to his knees, a string of meaningless gurgles resonating in his throat. Hog was hauling him to his feet, ready to pound the life from his sorry body, when the waif from Burmarsh ran into sight and delivered his message.

'Mr Marsh wants to know what happened.'

'Nothing!' Hog bellowed at him. 'Don't the man have eyes? Nothing buggering well happened.'

The boy cowered away from his flailing arms, not knowing that he had nothing to fear from the wild gesticulations. Hog managed to cool his fury by one or two degrees.

'Tell him…,' he huffed angrily. 'Tell him…'

He tried to think. Spratford had again insisted that they run separate crews and, desperate for work, he'd given in. However, this time the strategy could serve him well. His men had no reason to tell Spratford what had passed — they wanted to get work, not lose it — and Marsh would know only what he reported.

'Tell him some of my men hit trouble on the way here. The preventive bastards took off with their tails between their legs but it was too risky to flash the lugger in, what with the tide and reinforcements more than likely on their way. Tell him to get his men clear, and fast!'

The boy nodded and ran off with barely a sound, as if floating over the shingle.

One thing in Hog's report was true. With the Divisional Office in Folkestone, Blockademen were never far from Eastware Bay. Be that as it may, precisely the same factors that made Folkestone so attractive to legitimate vessels drew free-traders in spite of the frequent patrols. He had not objected to the landing site, one that he had worked time without number before, because it made for swift and easy unloading. If they had worked fast and kept their wits about them, they might have made a profitable run.

Swamped by savage disappointment, Hog turned back to where Pantry was still kneeling on the sand and cradling his chin. He swung his leg back viciously and buried his foot in the man's gut. Pantry rolled onto his side, moaning. He turned away contemptuously, only to find Grey standing at his side and studying Pantry with similar disdain. The night had cost them all in lost earnings and Grey had all but admitted that his need for money was pressing.

'Shh'

A hissed warning brought instant silence. They strained to see or hear some sign of what had sparked it. Hog groaned as he saw shadows huddled just above the high watermark. They moved steadily down the foreshore, ant-like in their resolute column.

'Hold steady,' he muttered to his men. 'No cargo, no case.'

John Horne raised his duck-gun. 'Bearing firearms…'

No more needed to be said on that score. They could hang for that without a tub in sight. For the first time, he saw some sense in old-style runs. Even after years of passing laws to rob poor men of their meagre rights and possessions, the British Government had not yet made it illegal for a man to stand on a beach with friends, a staff in his hand. They might have bluffed their way through a search without their pistols and fowling pieces, not to mention a couple of muskets captured during the run at Hythe.

'Keep back!' he called out. 'We want no trouble.'

There was no answer.

'Keep back!' he repeated.

The advance continued, the column spreading into a fan.

'Hold on to your lives!'

It was a last desperate appeal for sanity. Many lives were lost in vain but few as futile as those thrown away in a fight over non-existent goods.

'F-fools,' Grey snarled. 'Have they naught b-better to do with their time? Is it a crime now to walk on the b-beach at m-midnight?'

Hog considered their position. There was still a chance that the Blockade party did not realise that there was no cargo. Perhaps there was something to be gained from making that clear.

'Fall back fifty paces to the east,' he called to his men. 'Spread out and walk tall. Bats and firearms out of sight.'

The order was met with consternation.

'Do it!' he bellowed, sending a heft kick into Pantry's backside to underline that he meant business.

After a short pause, his followers slowly began to comply. He watched as they did so, soon confident that it was obvious, even in the faint moonlight, that they were unladen and, on the face of it, unarmed. There was no legitimate reason for such a large body of men to assemble on a beach at night but he hoped the Blockade might let it go for once.

While they adopted a defensive formation in their new position, their pursuers were examining the trodden sand of their previous location. There was nothing to be found but the usual detritus dropped and expelled by groups of men waiting for anything. However, the absence of any evidence of a crime was apparently not enough to dissuade them from their course. They surged forward in a full-frontal attack typical of the Blockade.

'Muskets, fire!'

Hog's first order sent a thin volley of shots into the approaching men. Two fell, although one recovered his feet almost immediately.

'Fowling pieces, fire!'

Another volley found its mark. Three men fell, including the one injured before. Still their comrades advanced over them.

'Pistols, fire!'

Hog snarled his final order. Only he and Grey carried pistols so there was no need to shout. Without conscious thought, he aimed low. When the crumpled form juddered twice, he knew that Grey had done the same. They were wasted shots, sent through rage not reason, yet another sign that he was not the leader he wanted to be. Even so, the advance finally faltered. Hog peered past the ragged knot of survivors, expecting to see reinforcements from the next tower in the defensive line at any moment. He was not disappointed: perhaps eight or ten men were making haste along the foreshore.

'To the Warren and scatter,' he told his men. Grabbing Pantry by the shoulder, he shoved him at John Horne. 'Make sure every last bugger gets home. We don't need no approvers to round off our night out.'

He glanced at Grey, wondered if the man would consider another run after two failures, then followed his men into the night.

Quacks

Back in London for only the second time in his life, Quacks had spent the muggy July night wondering whether he wanted to force his way to the front of the crowd to watch his cousin hang at close quarters or wait at a distance, ready to implement the plan that was to satisfy Wilson's stipulation. In the end, it was concern for Cephas that persuaded him to stay back. In his cousin's place, he would not want friend nor family to watch his final reflexive struggles against the noose. He knew the man had asked his wife to stay away from the execution: Martha told him that when she showed him the Bible-shaped snuff box Cephas had carved and given to her as a keepsake at their last meeting. That request, and probably that alone, was true in the letter from the condemned cell, which Wilson had read out the night before. Written in a customarily florid style, designed purely to make a profit for the prison ordinary, it bore no trace of the man alleged to have dictated it. Quacks felt futile anger as he recalled its moralising tone and its warning to the likes of himself.

Dear loving wife,

I am sorry to inform you that the report came down on Saturday night and I was ordered for execution on Wednesday. I sent for Mr Hughes on Sunday and he and the Sheriff came in the afternoon, and, dear wife, they told me it was best for you not to come up. Dear loving wife, I am sorry that I cannot make you amends for this kindness you have done for me, and I hope that God will be a father and a husband to you and your children for ever: and, dear wife, I hope that we shall meet in the next world, and there we shall be happy. And, dear loving wife, I hope you will not fret, or as little as you can help. And father and mother, I send my kind love to you, and to all my brothers and sisters: and, dear brothers, I hope this will be a warning to you, and all others about there. Dear father and mother and brothers and sisters, I hope that you will not frown on my dear loving children. Dear wife, I am happy in mind, thank God for it, and I hope you will keep up your spirits as well as you can.

> *Farewell, my dear friends, I must away,*
> *Death calls me hence, I can no longer stay:*
> *Farewell, my truest comfort here below,*
> *Christ bids me welcome to his heavenly joy.*
> *Farewell, adieu! My grief,*
> *To every trouble death is a kind relief.*
> *Farewell, my fading joys, I go to prove*
> *The endless pleasures of the Saints above,*
> *Farewell, my pains, begone my rousing fears,*
> *In heaven are neither grief nor tears.*
> *All happiness I now resign;*
> *Vain world, farewell! But welcome joys divine.*

So no more from your unfortunate husband,
Cephas Quested

The scene outside Newgate gaol on the day of the execution was too familiar to shock, re-enacted just outside Maidstone on Penenden Heath several times a year. Humiliation was part of the price exacted from those unfortunate, or careless, enough to get caught. It deterred no one, not even the hangmen who had been known to turn to crime themselves despite knowing better than most what awaited them if caught. How ever high the penalty for the few, others kept on in the hope that they would be amongst the many who went unpunished and, of course, they usually were. Most of the Blues accepted the loss of a man as an occupational hazard, just as a fishermen accepted the risk that a friend might be swept overboard in a stormy sea.

Quacks stood at the back of a throng that extended scores deep in every direction. Once again, his companion was Wilson. They had not been close friends before Cephas's capture but the time they'd spent together since had turned mutual respect into friendship, and now he was glad of the quiet company. The crowds sizzled with anticipation at one of the few entertainments open to them. Sellers drifted through the masses, offering food and drink. Later, their wares would be more macabre souvenirs of the day: fragments of the hangman's rope or the hanged man's clothing to go with the letter from the condemned cell. Appetising aromas from the refreshments settled in a thin veneer over the collective stench of humanity. He'd chosen a spot between the crowd and its waste, on raised ground to the north of the execution site with a church at their backs. Moving forward intensified the ripeness of unwashed bodies. Dropping back put them in a moat of effluent where people had relieved themselves.

Beside him, Wilson was eating a toffee-covered apple impaled on a stick. The sickly treats were usually eaten by children but Wilson seemed unperturbed, either by that or by the impending spectacle. Quacks smiled as his friend licked the gooey mixture from his lips. One of the reasons Wilson was so well liked was that he was his own man, reserved and unassuming but unswerving when set on a course. Such mental strength was unexpected in a man who wielded so little physical might, confounding those who might otherwise have bullied or discounted him.

Quacks' thoughts returned to his cousin. He hoped the end would come quickly but did not expect it to. As a child, he'd often watched the rope deliver slow suffocation instead of the intended broken neck. Prisoners writhed in futile attempts to escape its grip, slowly losing control as they passed out. First their bladders emptied, and then their bowels. Of course, fear of what was to come made some let their bladders go before the noose even settled around their necks. Quacks expected that his cousin would face his fate with resignation, taking care of his bodily needs before leaving the prison in the hope of maintaining some dignity in death, ending his life as boldly as he had lived it.

Quacks knew the condemned man had been brought out when movement rippled through the crowd. Before he even heard the customary cry of 'Hats off!', he saw row after row of spectators obey it to give those behind a better view.

Wilson tossed his snack away carelessly. Little flesh remained on the core but a skinny urchin instantly dashed out of the crowd and snatched it greedily. Seconds later, a sucked-clean stick fell to the ground and the child was gone.

From the distance at which they stood, Quacks could see only an anonymous figure mount the steps to the scaffold. It walked erect, looking straight ahead as far as he could tell. The crowd erupted into a cacophony of baying and jeering. Being hanged at Newgate was a hardship all round, hard on Cephas who would have faced a subdued crowd of friends and acquaintances on Penenden Heath and hard on his family, whom he had forbidden to attend. Quacks and Wilson could do nothing to smooth his cousin's path into the next life but they had a plan to ease the family's pain afterwards.

The distant scene played out like a child's game. Unable to see the prisoner's expression or hear the chaplain's words, Quacks was isolated from the reality of what he was witnessing. Used to living in the shadow of his more aggressive relative, it was difficult to imagine that death now stalked the tiny figure on the scaffold. It seemed impossible that the hangman could snuff out the life of a blustering great man like Cephas as easily as a farmer might wring a chicken's neck.

When it came, the end was even more abrupt than a chicken's last reflexive struggles. Too far away for any sound to reach his ears, Quacks saw the body drop and that was all. It swayed slowly from side to side but there was no struggle. Perhaps it was dead — or perhaps the breath was still ebbing from it — he had no way of knowing. Wishing that he had stood closer, he could not even be sure that the corpse belonged to his cousin, although he had no reason to doubt that it did.

A sad, silent presence on the edge of the baying, jeering mass of inhumanity, he turned slowly to Wilson. 'Best we gets on our way then.'

Wilson's light squeeze of comfort on his shoulder was oddly reassuring. A man like Hogben would be bent on revenge, while one like Higgins would fail to see what the fuss was about. Quacks welcomed the presence of someone like himself, who could regret the untimely passing, even of a man he had not personally liked.

They threaded their way through the teeming streets, following a path they'd explored the day before. Corpses to be hanged in chains were taken away for fetters to be fitted and Cephas was no exception.

The difference in his case was that the crowds in London thought he was to hang in chains on Penenden Heath in the wilds of Kent, whereas people around Aldington thought he was to hang in chains outside the notorious Newgate gaol. Perhaps some would be puzzled when he failed to appear in either place but they would probably dismiss it as a misunderstanding. In any event, by the time his body was missed, Cephas would be safely interred in an unmarked grave on consecrated ground. It was Giles who came up with that compromise, balancing the need for anonymity with the Blues' sudden concern for the fate of their erstwhile leader's eternal soul.

It was some time later that Quacks boldly drove his cart up outside a blacksmith's yard and jumped heavily down. In his peripheral vision, he saw Wilson follow suit, delivering a perfect imitation of the swagger in place of his usual catlike grace. They had barely stepped into the yard when a burly man came out of one of the crude wooden buildings along one side, wiping blackened hands on a rag.

'Where're Bill and 'arry?' he asked in a clipped Cockney accent.

Quacks shrugged and steeled himself to attempt something he'd been practising for days. ''ow should I know? Stiff to 'ang on some 'eaf in Kent is all they told me.'

There was no trace of suspicion in the blacksmith's expression when he nodded back at the building he'd come out of. Why should there be? The heyday of the body-snatchers was long past and the fate of the corpse was probably of little concern to him anyway, now that he'd fitted the fetters and earned his pay.

'Smuggler for Pen'den 'eaf,' he confirmed. ''ell of a way, from wot I 'ear.'

Quacks gave a jaded nod, as if to confirm how tiresome the journey would be. In reality, he could barely wait to breathe the fresh Kentish air again after the foul stench of London. He followed the blacksmith into the gloomy interior, where a couple of soot-blackened lamps strove to illuminate his cousin's body. With the slackness of death before rigor mortis set in, Cephas might have been in one of his drunken stupors and Quacks had to suppress an urge to reach out to rouse him. Instead, he forced himself back into his role of driver tasked with taking the body of a convicted felon to its final humiliation. Although Cephas had been wearing a dark jacket and trousers when he mounted the scaffold, they had clearly been appropriated by someone and his body now lay in its underclothes. The garments looked as if they might have been clean on for their owner's last day on earth but they had fallen victim to the usual fate of the hanged man after all. A large yellow stain marred the front, while the smell declared that the rear view would be worse.

'I'll be buggered if I'm pickin' 'im up,' Quacks announced.

The blacksmith grinned. 'That's what the boy's 'ere fer, ain't it?'

Quacks returned the grin, genuinely amused that the task would fall to a man far more refined than himself. Only seven or eight years his junior, Wilson was no boy but the difference in their builds gave an impression of a greater difference. The 'boy' stepped forward and repeated the examination of the corpse.

'You 'eard the man,' Quacks urged him, with a rough shove.

With his cousin as tall and broad as himself, Quacks knew that Wilson would be hard put to lift the body alone. He did not relish administering the beating a junior should expect for failing in so simple a task so he turned back to the blacksmith.

''ow 'bout a nice bit o' the heavy wet 'fore I 'ead off?'

'Now you're talkin',' the burly man agreed.

Quacks led the way towards an inn they'd passed not fifty paces back down the street. It was an unnecessary risk but the day had left him in need of a drink.

When he wound his way back to the yard, two hours and half a dozen tankards later, Wilson was leaning against the cart and drumming his fingers like an impatient wife.

'All right, all right. We gets off home now.'

Quacks' assumed accent had long since slipped, along with his pretence of local origins, but, as luck would have it, the blacksmith seemed as unaware of that fact as he was himself. A long handshake underlined their new friendship, built rapidly on the basis of a shared enthusiasm for porter ale and dominoes. After finally parting company with the reluctance of the inebriated, he hauled himself clumsily onto the cart.

Wilson hopped up behind him and shoved him over sternly. 'The Lord only knows where we'll end the night if thou takest the reins.'

With Quacks still waving to the blacksmith, Wilson urged the champing team smartly out of the yard and set off briskly on a rough south-easterly course through the maze of streets. The day-time masses were now giving way to the people of the night and Quacks watched scenes of drunkenness, prostitution and other vices too numerous to name flicker past his eyes. As the cool air fanned his face, his head began to clear and he started to regret the long, anxious wait he'd given Wilson.

'Sorry,' he slurred.

Wilson glanced sideways, his usual serene expression restored. 'I know what thou wert about. Old Cephas is a fair weight, even after four months in Newgate.'

'He loses no weight in there, not with Martha sending in her baking every week.'

When Wilson did not reply, Quacks fell into silent reverie. Things could have worked out worse for Cephas. With family and friends to bring comforts from the outside and money to buy privileges on the inside, gaol was better for him than for many. There was no knowing how long it had taken life to leave his body but the absence of a struggle and his placid expression in death seemed to suggest it had not been long.

Quacks was still musing on the workings of fate when the city began to give way first to smart villages and then to rural hamlets. Driving two of the best horses from Bank Farm, they hoped to make it back to Aldington before morning. If any man could wring fifty miles out of a team without mishap, it was the young waggoner's mate beside him. Quacks left Wilson to it, sleeping through endless changes of pace and stumbling down at each stop to pass another pint of porter-piss.

Hours later, he snapped to with a start, knowing at once from the erratic swaying of the cart that they had turned off the turnpike road and from the smell of the air that they were nearly home. He peered around for a moment, then guessed, 'Hothfield?'

'Just past Charing.'

That meant only an hour or so before they reached Aldington, even on the poor lanes of home. Realising he had slept soundly from their last stop, although he had intended to take turns in driving, Quacks' guilt flared again. Ahead he saw the sun peeping over the eastern horizon.

'Good work, Bish. They awaits us in the churchyard.'

Wilson nodded.

'The Reverend an' all.' Quacks wasn't sure whom he sought to reassure, himself or his friend. Putting a man into an unmarked grave hardly seemed right but Cephas was to be buried by a proper clergyman in a proper churchyard, in the presence of his family. They could do no more. Still he felt the need to check again with Wilson, a man who spent a deal more time in church than he did himself. 'That counts?'

Wilson smiled. 'Aye, it counts. The Lord hath no need of a marker to find his sheep.'

After pulling over once more to rest themselves and the horses, they set out with renewed determination on the last leg of their long journey. Glad to get home after his second visit to London, Quacks hoped he would never set eyes on the rancid city again. Even so, he was satisfied to have made the trip and achieved their goal.

Two hours later, Cephas was in his final resting place, secure under six feet of earth.

After his fetters were struck off by the blacksmith, his body had been washed and clothed in his Sunday best by his womenfolk. A surprising number of people from Aldington and even villages further afield had got wind of the supposedly secret interment. A steady stream of them filed past the open coffin, some with a genuine wish to pay their respects to a man they'd known all their lives whatever his crimes, others with more interest in the punishment for those crimes. The ghouls were surely disappointed, Quacks reflected, as he saw his kin looking cleaner and more peaceful in death than he usually had in life.

In the rosy light of the dawn, the Reverend John Hollams spoke as respectfully over the coffin of a man who never by choice crossed his threshold as he would for the most devout of his flock. When he filled out the parish register, seeing no need for posterity to record the unseemly haste with which the dead man's family was forced to commit him to the ground, the young curate dated the ceremony for the coming Sabbath. Finally, a group of Blues filled in the grave and laid carefully cut turfs evenly over it. Only a sharp eye would spot the final resting place of their former leader, tucked as it was beneath an ancient yew in a quiet corner of the churchyard.

The Blues had set their price and it had been paid; the score was even. On top of the four men killed at Brookland and a hanged leader, they'd lost Dick Wraight when he decided that one brush with the noose was enough for any man. Nevertheless, bruised but unbeaten, they were poised to make the winter of eighteen-twenty-one their most profitable to date. Quacks had no doubt that Ransley, and not the cousin he had just help to bury, was the man to make that happen.

Hog

Pulling the collar of his coat tighter around his neck against the frosty November air, Hog surveyed the scores of men deployed across the beach at Sandgate. It was the biggest run attempted since Brookland and he'd drafted in casual acquaintances and total strangers alike to meet his quota of two hundred men. Spratford must have called on his entire family and all his neighbours to swell the Burmarsh lot to a hundred. Hog spent days matching men to tasks, mariners in the boats and batmen on the defences. He would have liked more teeth in their bite but, although there was no longer any pretence of avoiding firearms, they still had only a dozen long-guns and about half that number of pistols.

During a series of moderately successful covert runs through the late summer, Hog had slowly persuaded Spratford to agree to some of his terms, so that now he had more information about an impending run and full authority over its defence, but Spratford still retained control over the location and timing.

'Too close to the castle by half,' he muttered.

They were barely out of sight of the ancient fortification, now base to a party of Blockademen. To his surprise, the man at his side nodded grimly in agreement. Perhaps Marsh was becoming as disillusioned as he was about the prospects for expanding the Burmarsh lot. The skills used in a modest covert run were totally different from those needed for a large-scale forced landing. Spratford excelled at collecting orders and scheduling cargoes but he had no idea how to command hundreds of men in an affray. Hog originally dismissed that as typical of a shopkeeper but, having since discovered their leader's naval service was longer than his own, he could only assume that their wars had been very different.

'Too late for the tide too,' Marsh added without inflection.

That harked back to the numbers again. Spratford never allowed enough time for mustering their forces. It took hours to move men, horses and carts across country, to rest and water them, to get them under way again. You didn't just click your fingers and everything started rolling. Hog tried to compensate but there was only so much that he could do, working back from an unrealistic starting point. They should have run a week later, when the tides would suit their purpose far better, but Spratford arranged the cargo before consulting his lieutenants. Hog found his mind drifting back to his nights with the Blues, as it did all too often. Ransley had no military service to his credit and yet his grasp of logistics was uncanny. True, he was of little value in an armed conflict but then he relied on men like Sam Bailey for that: recognising a weakness could sometimes be a strength in itself.

'M-morale could b-be b-better,' Grey added cautiously.

That was at the heart of their troubles. When men lacked confidence in their leadership, there was no guarantee they would stand their ground. Once the line broke, it took a strong commander to recover control and Hog now had no illusions that he was such a man. However, he declined to be drawn on the subject at that moment.

Instead, he asked Grey, 'Can we beat the tide?'

Grey studied the waves for a minute or so. 'Aye, if w-we're lucky.'

'Lucky?' Hog laughed bleakly. 'When were we last lucky?'

'We're still alive.' Marsh's reply carried the same dark humour.

'Let's hope w-we can say the same come the dawn,' was Grey's chilling rejoinder. 'Don't forget, we've the Ninth Lancers to contend with tonight, on top of the p-preventives.'

Their droll evaluation of their prospects was interrupted by the arrival of its architect. Spratford looked far more pleased with himself than his record to date entitled him to.

'Forget them,' he said airily. 'They've ridden west, to the aid of their riding officer friends attending an incident.' If Spratford had a gift, it was his imagination. His diversions had mitigated some disastrous runs and might prove valuable again that night. 'The men are working well,' he added.

That was true. They had started more than an hour behind schedule but had recovered half that through a combination of hard work and favourable weather. Hog waved vague agreement to

Spratford and set off on a tour of inspection. They had three hundred tubs and some packets coming in. They were running their own landing boats out to the lugger, which was one reason they needed so many men, and each of the three vessels must make five or six trips to land the whole cargo. He strode purposefully through his ranks, checking how many tubs had been landed and watching the tubmen shoulder them in pairs. They were to stash the haul in two lots, one to the north-west at Postling and one to the north-east at Alkham, and he was pleased to see that few tubs were spending more than a minute or two on the sands before starting their journey inland. The whole landing site was ringed by batmen, with lookouts posted on the fringes. Everything looked to be in order but he knew how precarious that appearance was. The men needed a few more easy runs to build their confidence but orders had built up through the lean months and they had to land a larger cargo now that winter had arrived.

As tub after tub passed from mariner to tubman, Hog began to feel more confident. Less than a quarter of the cargo to go and there was still no sign of the Blockademen. Picturing them playing cards around a nice warm fire, he hoped they were too comfortable in the castle to concern themselves with what passed outside. The reassuring vision was still before his eyes when a pistol shot shattered his illusions. The status of their operations fresh in his mind, he wasted no time in assessing the options or checking his orders with Spratford. With most of their load safe, he had no intention of risking lives over the few remaining tubs.

'Clear the beach!'

His order was followed immediately, tubmen pausing only long enough to shoulder the last of the loose tubs and then running as fast as their loads allowed, up the foreshore and into the night. Scanning the debris, he doubted their losses amounted to even forty tubs. Rejoining Spratford, he led the batmen in a smooth retreat up the Military Road. That route would take them past the Artillery Barracks but the Blockade rarely got any support from the Army divisions stationed there. Marsh and Grey covered the rear by taking occasional pot-shots at their pursuers but made little impact on the steady hail of fire. The Blockademen should have been able to outdistance exhausted traders, some of whom had been working for eighteen hours or more, but they slowly lost ground. Whether that was because they insisted on shooting at their quarry or because they were out of shape, Hog could not tell.

With no chance of out-gunning their pursuers, he had no alternative but to maintain an aggressive pace all the way to Saltwood Green. Only then did he let his men take a breather.

'As soon as you get your second wind,' he instructed, 'Get clear in twos and threes. Keep to the tracks and fields where you can.'

Most of them didn't need to be told such basics but a reminder never did any harm. They gradually obeyed, friends and neighbours heading off together as soon as they recovered enough to face the next leg of their journeys. Several men injured during the retreat leaned on companions for support. Only when the last group had gone did Hog turn to Marsh and Grey.

'How many did we lose?'

'Two,' came Grey's reply.

Hog glared at Spratford. They had been so close to success but then the choice of landing site had cost two men their lives. His voice was quieter than usual but filled with menace.

'I told you we were too close to the castle.'

'It wasn't–'

Whatever Spratford intended to say was cut off by the sound of hoof beats behind them. They faded into the hedgerow and waited while the noise grew louder. Hog counted nine horses come past at a flat-out gallop. Back from their fool's errand to the west, the Lancers were determined to salvage something from the night.

'We'll be lucky if it stops at two.'

It was as if fate heard his words when two shots rang out. They stood peering down the hillside for a few seconds. Grey swept a hand over his hair, as if the gesture might clear his mind.

'They're headed P-Postling way,' he said slowly. 'How could they know?'

Marsh snorted. 'Looks like one of our men wasn't quite dead.'

'Christ!' Spratford snapped. 'You mean they know where to find it?'

The threat to two-thirds of his cargo seemed to hit a spot that two deaths had failed to reach. The risk of an injured man talking, deliberately or otherwise, was one solid reason why a leader should care about losses amongst his men.

'Aye,' Hog said bitterly. 'You'll turn no profit on this run.'

'We've got to do something.'

'Like what?'

There was a long, uncomfortable silence before he spoke again.

'I'll not be doing anything for you again. I doubt you'll find many as will.'

He set off down the slope to find out who had caught the Lancers' attention, leaving Grey and Marsh to decide for themselves what they wanted to do. A minute or two later, he heard them fall in behind him. Spratford, and his Burmarsh crew, were history. They marched in silence, unanimous about the direction from which the shots had come and eager to cover the ground as quickly as possible.

When they reached the spot, they found one man sitting dejectedly on the verge, miserably cradling a blood-soaked thigh. Hog instantly recognised him as Tom Wheeler. The blacksmith was built for lifting heavy loads, not for running, and must have fallen behind the main exodus. Half-deaf, he probably hadn't heard the Lancers until they were upon him. Indeed, he hadn't heard the three of them approaching but, when he'd caught sight of them, alarm quickly gave way to delighted relief. No doubt, the long walk ahead looked a good deal better with three strong travelling companions to lend their support.

'Lancers,' he volunteered in explanation.

'We saw 'em,' Hog told him brusquely.

'They took Rolfie while we was loading up his cart.'

'Damn 'em,' Hog snarled through clenched teeth, wondering how many more losses and captures were yet to come.

Grey held out a hand to Wheeler.

'Can you w-walk?'

Hog heard the concern in his voice, partly a matter-of-fact worry for the impact of a wounded man, especially one as hefty as Wheeler, on their escape but also a deeper anxiety for a fellow in trouble. Grey rose another notch in his estimation: he too would have tried to save Cephas and suffered after failing in that duty.

Wheeler looked up at Grey sharply, leaning forward to make out his features in the gloom, but said nothing. He nodded and used the hand to haul himself to his feet, his weight almost pulling the smaller man over. Leaning heavily on Grey's arm, he somehow succeeded in matching their pace.

'I'll live,' he muttered but the sharp whistle of breath through his teeth declared how painful their movement was to him.

Hog felt his thigh throb as if in sympathy. He knew that pain and would not wish it on any man, let alone one like Wheeler. They'd first met out on Swingfield Minnis, where the travelling blacksmith was shoeing some horses that the local people grazed on the common land. One look at his massive frame and knotted muscles was enough to make Hog raise the subject of nightwork. He intended Wheeler to join the batmen but, after just one run, saw that his new recruit was no fighter. Disappointment faded fast when he realised the man's value as a tubman: he could unload a galley single-handed, finishing ahead of the other teams, and carry four tubs further than most men could carry two. All in all, he earned twice what he was paid and was well worth saving.

Wheeler's prodigious strength paid dividends now, keeping him going long after a weaker man would have given in to his pain. It was most of an hour before they stopped for rest on Folkestone Hill, not far from the Valiant Sailor but too late for refreshment without prior arrangement. Fatigue notwithstanding, Hog saw Wheeler repeat his inspection of Grey at some length before announcing his conclusion.

'Well, I'll be! I thought it was.'

Grey only smiled enigmatically in return, offering no sign of whether he knew what the man meant or wanted the knowledge shared with their companions.

'Young Tom Gilham from Al'ington Corner, in't it? So what's with this Datchet Grey business?'

Grey — or was it Gilham? — shrugged. It was nothing out of the ordinary for men to trade under an assumed name but that was normally to deceive the authorities, not their fellow traders. Hog was not best pleased to be the exception.

'Well?' he growled, impatient for an explanation.

The young man shrugged again. 'You m-might have b-been anyone that day in Folkestone. B-better safe than sorry.'

'You could've said something since.'

'W-what's in a name? You wanted a m-man f-for a job. I did it b-better than some. F-fair shake, I say.'

There was no arguing with that. Past months had shown men he had known for years to be drunks and cowards when asked to act upon their own initiative. For all his prodigious drinking, he always turned up fit for work and that only made him more critical of those who did not. So what if the new man was Gilham when he claimed to be Grey? He was sober, punctual, efficient and courageous. The night would have gone far better if they'd had another couple of hundred like him.

It was all academic now because Hog meant what he told Spratford. Seven months since his first run with the Burmarsh lot and he'd netted next to nothing. The returns were so poor that even docking the wages of the drunks and shirkers left too little to pay good workers what they were owed. As much as many of them loved the trade, they did not risk their lives for fun: if there was no money, there would be no traders.

No, there was only one way for them to return to the trade and he now resolved to open that door, for his men if not for himself. Rumours abounded that the return of the Blues was imminent. Hog doubted Ransley would take him back — even if he begged and that was something his pride would never let him do — but perhaps he might be lenient towards men whose only mistake was to follow the one who recruited them into the trade in the first place. What blame was there in that?

He glanced over at Marsh. The man had said nothing to Spratford and yet he sat here now with them.

'You sticking with the Burmarsh lot, Bill?'

Marsh did not shift his gaze from the sea, where it had rested since they stopped.

'The trade's finished,' he eventually said in a low voice. 'If not this year then next. There's no future in it.'

'There might be, with the right leadership.'

After another long pause, Marsh finally looked at him quizzically. 'Ransley? You think he'll have you back?'

Hog shrugged.

Marsh resumed his seaward vigil. 'Makes no difference. It's over — one way or another, sooner or later.' He spat at a chalk boulder two or three yards in front of them. 'I hear there's a convict transport short of men up at Woolwich, bound for New South Wales. A year or so, all told, but beggars can't be choosers. There's naught to keep me here, that's for sure.'

Hog picked his ear meditatively, wondering if he could still get work as a mariner, but dismissed the idea. Neither age nor family barred him from the sea but he'd had his fill of orders in the wars and would never again submit to the harsh discipline of that life.

He would sooner starve.

George

Georgeorge Ransley stared coldly at Hogben. One of the dead and five of the wounded were ex-Blues. His anger at the man in front of him was tempered only by the knowledge that the others chose to follow his defection to the Burmarsh lot: no one forced them. Still, he'd agreed to take them back and so only one decision remained.

'And you think I should have you back, why?'

He leaned back in his chair, making the most of the advantage events had given him. Sam Bailey's bulk at his right hand instilled menace into his every word. Hogben was a formidable presence and yet George was confident that his second-in-command could disable him in seconds. Still, never one to leave much to chance, he had two more Baileys beyond the door, in the back room of the Bourne Tap, waiting to step in if he was proved wrong.

Hogben met his gaze, chastened by a bad year in a life replete with them but not in the least bit intimidated. His reply would have seemed even rasher than normal to someone who knew him less well than George.

'I could turn approver.'

No, hating the Preventive Service as he did, Hogben would never turn approver. That was the main thing keeping him alive at that moment. George's sneer conveyed precisely what he thought of the threat but he was unprepared for Hogben's next concession.

'Then because I've made your point for you. What man in his right mind runs with a crew that loses half its loads? There's no money in it.'

George waited, needing a full capitulation, needing Hogben to understand how absolute his failure had been.

The man shrugged. 'And two men lost for naught.'

George saw how much those words, the open admission of his own culpability, hurt when Hogben sullenly added three more.

'Two good men. All right?'

George considered his position.

Hogben was right: he did not need to make an example of the failure. Every man in the Blues had already reached his own conclusion about the botched affray. It wasn't so much the loss of life, common enough in itself, but the obvious poor planning and weak leadership that brought about such total chaos and collapse. When they implemented his plans, they were confident that their landing place, strategy and escape route had all been meticulously researched and shrewdly selected. Yes, they already knew that he was their best chance for safe, profitable running. What he really needed now was a gesture to bring their hearts to the same place that their minds had already reached. Perhaps Hogben's true value was in the opportunity that he presented for such a signal, despite the attendant risk in bringing such an unpredictable character back into their operations.

Finally, George nodded.

Watching Hogben's reaction, the way his muscles relaxed as the tension flowed out of them, and seeing how much the man needed to be accepted back into the only life he knew, George wondered why he insisted on making it so hard for anyone to be a friend to him. Moving matters on, he cleared his throat as he often did before intervening in or changing the course of a discussion.

'I heard young Tom Gilham was with you.'

Hogben's face showed surprise, followed by resignation that few of his recent actions would be unknown to his new leader.

'I heard that too,' he grumbled.

George frowned for an explanation.

'The bugger told me his name was Datchet Grey, damn him.'

A smile crept over George's features. He'd noticed Gilham when he was still a boy, identifying not so much with his stammering illegitimacy as with his resolve to overcome those impediments. He'd heard the youth was seeking his fortune north of the Thames but knew nothing of his return until he surfaced amongst Hogben's rabble. George attached no blame to the affiliation: Gilham had been away and, when he returned, the Burmarsh lot was the only game in town.

'Useful?'

It was a question he'd put to Hogben many times before, knowing that he had a gift for getting to know strangers in public houses and that he was a better judge of character, or at least of skills, than his appearance suggested. Putting the question now confirmed the second chance.

'Aye,' Hogben admitted with only a trace of reluctance at praising a man who'd deceived him. 'Better than he sounds, that's for sure. He's got no love for preventives, so he can't be all bad.'

'I want him with us.'

Hogben nodded. 'He needs the work.'

'He'll get it.' George projected confidence into his instructions. 'The quarter moon next February marks our return. See to it that we can muster three hundred men at short notice.' His eyes narrowed. 'Good men, mind. Fit and sober. Fifty with the courage to stand against a preventive man, bat-in-hand.'

He read Hog's bewilderment. Like so many others, the man believed that the only response to McCulloch's Blockade was more firepower. George did not have to explain himself, and yet...

'It was a firearm that did for Cephas, and don't you forget it. Bats were good enough before and they'll be good enough again. Make the right run in the right place and they won't find us, let alone fire on us.'

George watched as Hogben's eyes flicked from his to Bailey's. His own gaze never shifted. He knew Bailey doubted their ability to avoid clashes with the Blockade but his faith in the loyalty of his second-in-command must appear absolute. The curt nod with which Hogben eventually replied confirmed that they were finally ready to face the future, whatever it might bring. There was only one piece of outstanding business and Hogben raised it now.

'What about Rolfie?'

George had investigated the case against the stonemason.

'The charges'll be dropped to receiving. He'll get the usual fine.'

The terse reply belied the time he'd put into achieving that outcome. In the end, the Blockade case was weak and the local magistrates partial. He was aware of the risk of playing the second card too often.

Satisfied, Hogben made to leave. When he reached the door, he turned back with a trace of dark humour in his eyes. 'Fifty men ready to face a musket with a bat? P'r'aps you might just as well kill me now.' He shook his head. 'You make a go of a return to bats and folk'll be singing songs about you one day.' As the door fell shut behind him, he was still muttering, '...songs about the buggering captain of the buggering bats.'

Paul

Paul Pierce pushed through the bustling crowds, striding eagerly back to where they'd tethered their horses in a side street. Relieved to see them safe, he grinned to the small boy playing marbles a few yards beyond. They'd promised him sixpence to watch the animals and find them if there was trouble, at the same time warning him to stay clear of Tommy Dennard's irritable gelding. It always paid to be careful with a port's many strangers but he was particularly concerned that day, riding his new chestnut filly for the first time. She was a pretty piece of horseflesh, seducing a handsome price from his pigskin purse and leaving him in fear of a theft every time she was out of his sight.

'She's a beauty and no mistake,' Dennard admitted as he tickled her ears. Standing beside the filly, his lively hazel eyes and red-brown mane were an exact match for hers. When she nuzzled him gently, he responded in kind, rubbing his cheek against hers as he spoke. 'Nice nature too.'

Pleased at the assessment of his purchase, Paul tossed the promised reward to the marble-player and made to tighten his girth. He had the utmost respect for his young friend's judgement when it came to horses and would have asked him to look the animal over if he hadn't been so afraid of someone else snapping her up first. Dennard was a man who lived for horses, blessed with an instinct that few men possessed and experienced beyond his years after devoting his childhood to his passion. Some of his knowledge had been hard-won and he still bore the scars of one or two lessons, not that Paul ever saw any sign that he was troubled by his disfigurements. While they were chatting one night, the youngster admitted that the side of a hoof had left the deep vertical indentation on his forehead that he usually credited to the butt of a musket and a stallion's teeth had shaped the weal on his neck that he usually offered as evidence of a preventive man's attempts to garrotte him. Paul smiled at the lies, knowing that a day rarely went by without a pretty girl falling for them.

'No way she's worth what you paid for her though.'

Dennard's love of horseflesh was tempered by a finely honed business acumen. Men said he never paid even half what he later made on a horse, though the lad himself was strangely reticent about his deals. Paul suspected that some were not strictly within the law but knew that others were just a matter of his knowing how to bring on difficult beasts.

Unperturbed by the proviso, Paul shrugged. He knew he'd paid too much for the filly but hadn't been able to resist. His wife had already chided him for the indulgence — saying a mare would be a liability every time she was in season, a fair point to which he had no answer — but business had been brisk and being well horsed was one of his pleasures. What use was money if a man couldn't buy what he wanted with it? A bit of moderation in the Walnut Tree for a while would make up for his momentary weakness.

Beside him, Quested swung onto the big gelding that he'd picked up for a song months earlier. 'You looks a right dandy on her. Turns heads all right.' He grinned. 'Pity they in't ladies' heads.'

Paul grinned back, unperturbed. 'Least I'll get a better class of bugger. No telling whose eye you'll catch on that ugly mule.'

'We're not here to catch anyone's eye,' Dennard reminded.

Paul's smile faded. His friend spoke the truth: Ransley sent them to listen, not to be seen, just three of countless spies scouring the area for the intelligence that kept the Blues ahead of both authorities and competition. With rich pickings and no casualties, not to mention in-fighting aplenty between the many and varied bodies with a stake in the prevention of smuggling, the eighteen months since their return had established him as leader of the largest free-trade empire since the Hawkhurst gang terrorised the Weald a lifetime before. His achievement of a bloodless return to bats had prompted Sam Bailey to recall in the Walnut Tree one night Hogben's remarks on the subject. They'd toasted Captain Bats as the architect of their good fortune, and the name Ransley had barely passed their lips since.

The three of them had spent that day drifting around inns and fish stalls, catching conversations here and there, finding out what was happening, where and to whom. No doubt the clues they'd gathered would give their leader a wealth of new ideas. Paul had enjoyed his day out, comfortable as always in Quested's solid company but content for it to be leavened by Dennard's merry wit. His footloose and fancy-free days were over, with a family to provide for and an employer to answer to, but he felt a vicarious thrill in the youngster's energetic chippie-chasing and horse-trading. His high spirits showed when he led the way out of town at an extended trot, delighting in the filly's springy step, so different from his ageing hunter's steady stride. He'd owned few horses in his life, buying them young and riding them into old age. He looked forward to a long partnership with the eager-to-please soon-to-be-mare.

They'd been riding at a steadier pace for a quarter of an hour when he tilted his head to one side. It was the third time he'd thought he heard something but, whenever he looked back, he saw no one.

'You hears it too?' Quested asked.

Paul nodded. He considered the prospect of pursuit. There was no reason for anyone to follow them and he'd seen no sign that they'd been recognised. Still, it was unlikely they were both hearing things.

'Let's head on down to Abbots Cliff, see if we keep our echo.'

They reached the lane in a few minutes and turned coastward. A fresh salt breeze fanned their faces, its fragrance filling them all with the mixed love and awe of the sea shared by most of their ilk. It brought food and work to the area and sometimes it took a life in payment, an eternal cycle into which they were all locked.

'He's still there,' Dennard said a few hundred yards later. After a pause, he added, 'There's nothing down here but the sea. He's got to be following us.'

'Could be he's on his way home,' Quested offered, in a tone that declared he did not believe his own explanation. 'There's a cottage or two hereabouts.'

Paul nodded his acceptance of the possibility. 'Let's move things on, shall we?'

He urged the filly into an easy canter and took them towards the cliffs. Glancing back at intervals, he saw no sign of pursuit and yet he could not shake off the feeling that they were being followed. He slowed to a trot while he thought, aware of his companions waiting on him, knowing they were as intelligent and resourceful as himself but also that they would defer to his judgement. While never inhibited by his youth, Dennard had a healthy respect for wisdom and experience. As solid as a rock, Quested was willing to stand his ground against any man and yet he was more inclined to throw his ideas into the pot for consideration than to lead his fellows.

Paul reined back and scanned the landward horizon carefully, seeing no movement but expecting the riders to come into view any second. After a moment or two, he launched into a gallop and continued westwards, riding far closer to Dennard's gelding than he'd normally choose to do. Quested matched his position on the far side. He had no need to instruct his friends, sensing that they knew how he planned to handle the situation.

He didn't slow again until they reached some low bushes, and then only enough to toss his reins to Dennard and jump from the filly's back onto the turf. Quested did the same, albeit a lot less lightly, and Dennard urged his skittish mount back into a gallop. The three animals flew on in the same tight formation they'd held for the last few hundred yards, leaving only the faintest traces of what had passed in the dust. It would take a keen eye to notice the evidence and Paul hoped their pursuers would be in too much of a hurry for that. In seconds, he was crouched in the bushes on one side of the track, with Quested hidden in the scrub opposite him.

A minute or two passed before they felt the faint vibrations of approaching hooves. Seconds later and the hoof-beats became audible. There weren't many riders in the party. Paul tensed, knowing that timing was critical. They needed to startle the horses into throwing their riders and then exploit the element of surprise to control the situation. He nearly threw away that advantage when the sight of a lone horseman riding hell-for-leather startled him. He saw the same shock in Quested's face, before they leapt into action as one.

Paul timed his appearance in front of the galloping horse perfectly. It shied away, towards the far side of the lane, then reared back from Quested's threatening waves. The rider stood no chance, his forward momentum at odds with the erratic movements underneath him. He leaned backwards, trying to recover the situation, but he was already short a stirrup and soon lost the other.

Quested reached for the rider as he fell, hurling him to the ground and knocking the breath out of him. While the man gasped like a fish in a net, Quested relieved him of a pistol and dirk.

Studying him carefully, Paul could see that he was little more than a boy, younger even than Dennard. As he thought that, hoof-beats heralded their confederate's return. He reappeared from the dip beyond which he'd disappeared, the horses trotting briskly after he'd brought them carefully back down from the gallop. He rode close, then leapt down to examine their pursuer.

'Just the one?'

Paul shared his surprise. He addressed the youth, who was breathing again but pinned under Quested's knee. 'What did you think you were doing, son?'

The youth writhed, scowled and then lay still.

'Who do you think we are?'

Still there was no answer but frightened eyes flitted to Paul's forearms, showing below sleeves rolled back to the elbows. Paul followed their gaze, recalling the long blade that carved the ugly scar from right elbow to wrist, narrowly missing the veins there, and the shot that peppered the left limb, leaving it bubbled with white scar tissue. An imaginative tattoo-artist in Dover had transformed the long scar into a series of hearts and darts, while the shot-marks disfigured an older mermaid. Someone had clearly described those distinguishing marks to the boy.

Paul rested his boot on their captive's throat, leaned on it menacingly and repeated his question.

'Who do you think we are?'

'B-B-Blues.' The voice was filled with terror but still laced with defiance. Its owner expected to lose his life and yet his hatred burned brighter than ever.

Paul leaned more heavily.

'Who put you onto us?'

'N-n-no one.' He was shaking now.

'Are you with the Blockade?'

That brought the first straight answer. 'Y-yes.' A pause. 'And p-proud of it.'

Paul suppressed a smile. He added an ounce or two to the pressure on the throat under his foot. 'And who told you of my decorations?' He held out the mermaid.

'M-my cousin.' Another pause came before he blurted out the rest. 'B-before he died. After Brookland.'

Paul studied his captive dispassionately. A preventive officer with a grudge was dangerous. Yet who could blame a man for seeking to avenge his kin? He pressed down harder, feeling the power he held over a life, then watched as a dark stain spread across the boy's trousers. He was terrified beyond bodily control and yet still he did not beg or weep.

Paul stole a sideways glance at his companions. Many of the Blues would have delighted in the boy's terror but not them. Dennard stared, fascinated, while there was only pity on Quested's face. What had the boy thought he could do, one against three?

He pulled a large handkerchief from his pocket, used but not disgustingly so, and blindfolded their captive. After roughly binding the wrists, he hauled the boy to his feet. Motioning Quested to throw the bundle across its now-calm steed, he swung into his saddle. The group rode seawards, prisoner bouncing painfully all the way.

Just yards from the precipice, Paul dismounted, took a length of rope from his saddlebag and made for some scrub on the cliff top. He anchored the rope to a stout root and then tossed the free end over the edge. Waving Quested forward, he pointed to the cliff-face below. The big man looked down, smiled, then took a firm hold of their captive's jacket and swung him over the edge. Quested held him in place as if he were a child, while Paul put the rope into his hands and twisted it around his wrists.

'You hold onto this, son, and hold on tight.'

It would be impossible for him to haul himself back up with his hands tied together.

'You yell good and loud. P'r'aps someone'll happen by.'

Paul watched while Quested lowered the boy until his weight was on the rope.

'Then again, p'r'aps they won't.'

Dennard moved forward, the fascination on his face now mingled with disbelief. He looked over the edge, then flashed a broad white smile at Paul. As the three men turned away, they heard a whimper and then a fart. They didn't need to smell it to know that the boy's humiliation was complete.

They had been riding for a while after the wind whipped away the last faint shout when Dennard asked no one in particular, 'Do you think he's still holding on?'

Paul shrugged.

Dennard grinned again. 'You've got a warped sense of humour.'

'He won't be forgetting.'

Quested looked earnest when he said, 'I thinks he hates you all the more now.'

Paul shrugged again. 'He'd better get in line if he wants to do anything about it.'

Dennard laughed. 'Wait till the boys hear about this. A preventive man shitting himself over an eight-foot drop.' At the memory of the ledge in the cliff-face, his laugh deepened. 'Pissing and shitting himself.' He wiped an eye with the back of his hand and repeated the phrase as if he still could not quite believe it. 'Pissing and shitting. Lucky he caught you on a good day.'

Paul smiled. He wasn't a cruel man but the boy deserved a scare for his stupidity: he could have, probably should have, killed him. Some of his fellows certainly would have done so. Even the two friends with him, reasonable and self-disciplined as they were, saw execution as the safest bet. A man who couldn't look death in the eye had no call to be running down men like them.

Tommy

That evening, Tommy Dennard stood outside his cottage, washing in a pail of well water. His skin tightened into goose flesh at its touch, the wooden bucket hauled from far below ground where the warmth of the sun never reached. He scooped a generous slice of soft home-made soap from the jar at his feet and rubbed furiously to build a meagre lather, glancing at the freshly washed shirt hanging from the low-swept eaves as he did so. The welcoming blend of wood smoke, tobacco and beer at the Walnut Tree would be permeated with the smells of men as always, their sweat and breath mingling with subtler traces of bodily products clinging to unwashed clothes. He had grown up with those smells, barely noticing them consciously, and yet he made a deliberate effort to avoid them on himself. Women liked a man who took care of himself and he was content to accommodate them.

As he ran his hands over the hard muscle of his wiry torso, his thoughts flitted to Beau Brummell. Unable to read the newspapers even if he wanted to, all he knew of the society figure came from snatches of ladies' gossip he sometimes overheard at market. Had he known more, he would have found only one shared trait between himself and the fastidious dandy: a talent for spending money faster than he earned it. As it was, he felt a faint pang of envy for a man who could afford to buy the best in clothes and pay someone else to prepare his wardrobe for a night out. His own clothes were well made and well kept but they were of the same coarse cotton and wool that every other man of his acquaintance wore. Only once had he tried something more adventurous, having a shirt made from a length of silk he'd appropriated from one of their hauls. It went down well enough with the girl he was chasing at the time but he soon tired of the constant ridicule it drew from his fellows.

Towelling his body down roughly, his thoughts settled on his current quarry. Her name was Sally and she was proving frustratingly resistant to his charms. He knew that his pursuit of her had become more a matter of pride than lust, which was out of character. Although he enjoyed the thrill of the chase, he was not a man who had to bed every woman he met and preferred to satisfy himself with girls who welcomed his attentions than to coerce them into fulfilling his wishes, whether through actual force or undue pressure. To his credit, Sally had played her own part in the little drama they were acting out, rebuffing his advances until he drew back and then leading him on until he renewed his efforts. As he reflected on that, he realised that she aimed to be the one to catch him for good. He laughed. If he was to be ensnared, it wasn't going to be any time soon. It wasn't for nothing that he dutifully withdrew before his arousal peaked, taking every care to ensure that he was not called upon to pay for his pleasure. Perhaps it was time to move on to pastures new. Besides, he had no intention of devoting that particular evening to one woman: it was his twenty-first birthday and he was hoping to hold a girl for each year, although he doubted he'd get more than a kiss from many of them.

Sometimes he would have welcomed a fellow in his pursuits but he found none in the Blues. Most were keen enough to drop their trousers given half a chance but none shared his love of the subtleties of the chase. He might have hoped for an ally in Gilham, a childhood friend whose return to Kent he'd greeted with enthusiasm, but, while he devoted his youth to exploring the mysteries of what passed between men and women, Gilham's expeditions had been of a more literal and geographical nature. If he had sampled the sins of the flesh on his way, there was no evidence of it. Thinking about that, Tommy recalled that he had noticed one woman eyeing his friend up. Several years older than them, she had three young bastards in need of a father in regular work. He wondered idly if he should warn Gilham: he wouldn't be surprised if his friend was called on to pay for his pleasure the first time he felt the warmth of a woman.

He buttoned the clean shirt and his trousers over it, then ran a brush through the chestnut waves that covered his head and reached down to the nape of his neck behind. The final touch was his jerkin of soft moleskin. It had cost him the proceeds of several nights' illicit labour but was worth every farthing. The knowledge that he looked sharper than just about any man he knew boosted his already healthy self-confidence. Combined with pleasing looks, his cheeky poise made him well nigh irresistible. Feeling desire stirring in his loins, he hoped to find a willing young body to service his needs before the sun rose on the morrow.

When he reached the Walnut Tree, the party had begun without him. On busy nights, with more important men packing both bar-room and taproom, the countless tubmen they called upon to land a haul ended up with barrels in the yard. Now they gathered around him, slapping his back and shouting spit-spattered congratulations in his face. Ordinarily, he would think twice before pushing his way to the front of the crowd, conscious that he occupied a favoured position for his age and wary of risking it by becoming too cocky. That night, however, he knew that the men whose good opinion he sought were waiting inside to celebrate his majority. He paused outside for a moment to collect his wits.

From within came the sound of women singing. He smiled as he recognised the song through the deep rumble of men's voices. It was one of his favourites and they sang it well, a soft contralto weaving harmonies around the soprano's clear melody. He listened, rapt, as they reached the part where the lady tested her lover. A young man's voice sang his words, declaring that he would not give up her token to the masked highwayman.

'The diamond ring is a token won,
I will keep it if my life I lose;'
The women's voices picked up the tale again.
She being tender hearted just like a dove,
She rode away from her true love.

Tommy loved the idea of romance but didn't believe in it. The men he knew were not a persuasive argument. Ransley and Giles probably came closest in their loyalty to their wives but theirs was a pragmatic fondness born of shared experience and mutual dependence. They were not in the habit of making grand gestures or sentimental speeches, at least not when anyone else was around to see. Still, although he would never throw away his life to keep a token from a lady, he was touched by the thought that someone might.

He pushed the door open in time for the last verse, keen to identify the singers and see if their faces were as fair as their voices. The room was heaving, men outnumbering women at least five to one and jostling against one another as they tried to reach the bar or make their way to the door. His hopes of finding twenty-one women to mark his coming of age faded but his spirits remained high, as he recognised some of his regulars in the crowd and several girls broke away from the men they were with to greet him. He returned their kisses but stayed on course for the bar. One of the reasons he was progressing so well in the Blues was that he knew how to build the friendships that counted: there would be time for loving later but first he would pay his respects.

At the centre of the crowd, he saw a rare sight: Ransley leaning against the bar. The man might be an exceptional supplier to half the public houses in southern Kent but he was a poor customer, seldom taking more than half a pint and that usually outside the premises. One of the senior Blues would send out his tankard when they caught word of him sitting on a wall or astride his mare, apparently deep in thought. He might be gone in minutes or linger for hours but, either way, he was never truly *with* them. It was a testament to their respect for his extraordinary mind that they not only accepted such eccentricities in their leader but began to compete for his infrequent company. His presence that night told Tommy he'd succeeded in his quest: he was not merely entering adult life, he was being confirmed into the heart of the Blues — his sole ambition since his first run five years earlier. He trembled as he reached for Ransley's outstretched hand.

'Congratulations, lad.'

Tommy felt a cool, firm grip against his suddenly damp palm. Under the routine birthday greeting, deeper significance stirred. In the twinkle of the deep blue eyes, he saw amusement at his awe. Too overwhelmed to be embarrassed, he nodded his thanks.

Ransley released his hand and reached into his pocket. Coins clinked as he passed a pouch over the bar to Ted Wraight.

'Make it a night to remember.'

With that he disappeared into the crowd, only the tide of thanks marking his passage to the door. Tommy stared after him, staggered by the unexpected public endorsement he had received.

'Well, boy,' a friendly voice spoke close to his ear. 'You got what you wanted. How does it feel?'

He gaped soundlessly.

Pierce laughed. 'Never thought I'd live to see Tommy Dennard lost for words. Well, if naught's coming out, best put something in.'

When Pierce passed his tankard, Tommy stared at it, still stunned, took what he intended to be a sip but then drained it.

'I'll be damned, Paul,' he whispered.

'I don't doubt it,' Pierce said, putting an arm around his shoulders. As the chatter around them returned to its former volume, he added in a low voice, 'You've earned this, Tommy, but don't let it go to your head. It in't the end — it's but the start, if you play on velvet.'

Looking down into the wise eyes of a man who'd seen and done more than he would probably ever know, Tommy nodded slowly. Winning Ransley's approval was vital but he needed friends in his camp as well. The wrong reaction to their leader's favour could alienate men he needed to win over.

Before he could get too anxious about it, he was enveloped by the crowd. His chest puffed out as he scanned the men assembled in his honour: not only those like Pierce and Quested who had coached him in the ways of the trade, but a host of the mariners with Gilham at their head and most of the batmen behind the Baileys. True, such men would not turn down a night's drinking without good reason but their presence at least confirmed that he had not yet given them such cause.

Deciding that being himself had got him thus far, he pushed strategy from his mind and followed his instincts. His best friend in the Blues, or anywhere else for that matter, was the slender man now trying to push his way between the far more substantial bodies around him. Patting Pierce's arm appreciatively, he dived forward and met Wilson halfway. He took the hand that his friend offered but, instead of shaking it, used it to pull him into a hug.

'Well done, Tommy.'

In those few words, joy mingled with a mentor's pride in his protégé.

'I couldn't have done it without you, Bish.'

Tommy was one to acknowledge his debts. It was Wilson who had guided him through his early days in the Blues, passing on suggestions and warnings that paved the way to his acceptance by men who might otherwise have spurned him. Becoming more than an anonymous tubman was hard for a local youngster: Gilham alone had achieved it so young, but then his travels and seafaring skills made him a special case.

Even so, Tommy's friendship with Wilson had nothing to do with his ambitions. Rather, he saw in his friend a reflection of himself, alike and yet different, just as a mirror showed an image that was identical and yet reversed. Wilson was frail while he was vital, pious while he was amorous, and yet they shared the same loyalty and humour, the same passion for horses and love for home. There was nothing he would not do, no risk he would not take, for a man who was more than a brother.

For the moment, he intended to take a drink or two together. Then Wilson would head off home before the smoke in the Walnut became too thick and he would gradually shift his attentions from his plans for the future to his plans for the night. Perhaps too much of his youth had been spent with horses, their company shaping his behaviour more than he knew. Whatever the reason, he was a simple man. His uncomplicated motivations unshackled by any artificial moral code, he needed only to progress within his herd and to mate with his harem.

His birthday party seemed set to fulfil both drives in fine style.

Datchy

It was not much past ten o'clock when Thomas Gilham left the birthday party. He had to be up at dawn the next morning, headed for Folkestone to run a cargo around to the Thames Estuary for a boat-owner by the name of Bolding. His employer knew him not as Gilham but as Carpenter, his father's name and an alias that reflected his sole love in life: woodwork. Around his home-town of Aldington, he was usually known by his real name but, within the Blues, he would forever be Datchet Grey, the pseudonym he'd adopted on the spur of the moment when that chance meeting with Hogben launched him on the course that eventually took him into their midst. For some reason, 'Datchy' stuck.

He was a man who grew identities like other men grew vegetables, dividing his life into compartments and managing his affairs independently within each one. His reasons for doing so had less to do with the felonies he committed than with the taxes he evaded. Adamant that the government had never done anything to help him or his mother, detesting it and all its agents, he refused to pay a penny in tax if he could avoid it.

Consequently, Thomas Gilham owned almost nothing, while Thomas Carpenter, Datchet Grey and half a dozen other occasional personalities accumulated wealth quietly, out of sight of the prying eyes of officialdom. The only levy he calculated honestly was the tithe that he paid anonymously into the parish coffers for the upkeep of the widows, orphans and paupers for whom there was nowhere else to turn.

Now he walked slowly, unable to see the ground by the faint light of the new moon, feeling the effect of the beer now that he was out in the fresh spring evening and thinking about the celebration back in the inn. It seemed as if every man in the village, as well as in the Blues, had turned out to share in the festivities. It was a sign of Dennard's popularity that, while many of the Blues were aware of his less public liaisons, none of them chose to enlighten the husbands of his married conquests. As the evening had worn on, his attention shifted from his friends to the bevy of young beauties who clustered around him, ready to provide whatever entertainment he might require.

Although born in the same year and blessed with the same kaleidoscopic hazel eyes, Datchy was Dennard's opposite in almost every other way. Where Dennard was merry and charming, he was reserved and introspective. He was an enigma, socially disabled by his stammer and yet as accomplished, dependable and courageous as men came. In spite of his more classical features and more muscular build, his diffident nature left him lagging far behind Dennard in experience with women. He didn't usually let it worry him, having no interest in matching Dennard's record and being content with his busy life as mariner, free-trader and talented amateur carpenter. His scant free time was devoted to his widowed mother. Even now, it was not the number of girls that bothered him but rather the identity of a particular girl, daughter to one of the pikeys camped out on Brabourne Down for the summer. He had noticed her in Aldington before, her animated voluptuousness appealing to him in a way that few women did, and now his body began to respond to the memory of her. He normally bore a deep fondness for Dennard, whose uncritical friendship had been a rare consolation in a childhood dogged by bullying and ridicule. However, at that moment, all he felt was envy beginning to fester into resentment.

'Damn him,' he muttered miserably. 'Bastard.'

The sound of his voice, free in private of the stammer that tormented him in public, startled him. He hadn't intended to speak aloud and looked around hurriedly to make sure he hadn't been overheard. Seeing no one, he made an effort to calm down. It was pointless to blame Dennard, especially since he was sure that his friend, as generous as he was lustful, would happily try to convince the girl to lie with him if asked. He couldn't do that, the embarrassment of asking daunting enough without the more profound humiliation of the girl's likely refusal. He was still stewing on his unrequited passion when, at the end of the lane, a woman stepped into his path.

'Good evening, sir.'

She spoke in a breathy murmur, standing so close that he could feel the warmth of her skin, or at least he imagined he could. A tremor ran through his body, shooting down to his feet and then back up to his stomach. It went on from there to do some interesting things in his loins, quickly reigniting his fading arousal.

In his confusion, he had not placed the voice but, when the woman leaned closer still, the moonlight caught her face. Recognising her as an Aldington native some years his senior, the brief flash of ardour abated. She was not like the pretty young moths fluttering so eagerly around Dennard's flame back in the Walnut Tree. Although by no means ugly, her robust rural charm had faded with the passing years, not to mention the burden of bringing up three children.

'Evening, m-ma'am,' was his polite response.

'Miss,' she corrected him huskily.

He nodded his acceptance of the correction, given that, for her, marriage had not come with motherhood. Shifting awkwardly, he wondered how to extricate himself from the unexpected encounter and resume his homeward journey. He felt her arm slip through his.

'Walk me home?'

The slightest upward lilt of her voice barely turned it into a question but he was too gracious a man to refuse, despite his misgivings. Frances Furner lived in a run-down cottage, well outside the village. The half-mile track that led to her door might have been a journey through the darkest jungle, so deep was the apprehension it instilled in him.

'Isn't it a beautiful evening?' she chattered gaily.

'Yes, m-miss,' he agreed.

Hearing the slur in his voice, he regretted the low tolerance for alcohol that meant three tankards took him halfway to drunk. The feminine touch on his forearm felt good, light and gentle, nothing like the firm grip of his mother when he escorted her to church on a Sunday morning. The flutter returned to a region somewhere just south of his stomach.

'You're a handsome man, Mr Gilham.'

He said nothing but debated to himself whether she was just saying that to win him over or really thought so. It shouldn't matter, given that he had no interest in her, but a part of him wanted to know. In truth, he knew he was blessed with passable looks and it wasn't unusual for girls to show an interest in him, until his tongue-tied ineptitude sent them scurrying away in search of a real man. A wave of self-pity swept over him at the memory of too many ill-fated liaisons.

'And a hard worker too, I hear.'

That reputation was well-earned. Hard work held no fear for a man who had no memory of a time when he had not worked hard. He still worked hard, all day every day, even now that his pay from Ransley outweighed his pay from Bolding by a factor of ten.

'All in all, you'd be quite a catch. I'm surprised you haven't already been snapped up.'

With no doubt remaining about her agenda, he still said nothing. Her efforts were pathetic in their transparency, she clearly making the same assumption about him as everyone else did. His irritation at that faded as fast as it flared. About as even-tempered as a man could be, he only ever became truly angry about one thing — the government and anyone stupid enough to serve it in any capacity.

That night he was merely frustrated, both with his inability to pursue the Brabourne girl and with the fact that people could seriously imagine he didn't know what to do just because he didn't do it. His body was the same as any other man's, for Christ's sake, and it had informed him of its needs on a regular basis for long enough.

How stupid did they think he was?

A faint smile touched his lips as he realised that he probably didn't want to know the answer to that question. He knew his stammer, and the ready blush in his cheeks, contributed to his friends' opinions — and that the signs of shyness multiplied when he drew their attention — so he bore their misjudgements in silence. Youthful frustration at his bashfulness had slowly given way to resignation at the role in which it cast him.

He let his companion babble on while they walked, glad that her inconsequential chatter removed the need for a response from him. He felt only pity for her situation, regardless of her own part in its making. Most of the men he knew behaved worse so he wasn't quick to judge, being kind enough to think her more foolish than wicked.

The gloom on the road was nothing compared with the darkness of the track to the cottage. A poplar windbreak blocked the moon's silvery light, leaving the couple to blunder along in inky blackness. Twice she stumbled against him, the trips quite possibly genuine but the exaggerated dependence on his support most certainly not. The third time, she threw her full weight on him just as he stepped forward, leaving him no chance of keeping his balance. He dropped on one knee and braced himself against her pulling him down further.

She persisted for a second, then let go. He heard her sit down heavily and then let out a sharp sigh.

'You might as well get going if you're no use to me.' Her voice was bitter. 'I can see myself home. I've done it often enough before.'

Below the bitterness was hurt. She'd had no doubt she could seduce him and now his unspoken refusal had underlined the inescapable march of time. He shifted from his knee to a more comfortable squat and considered her plight. He thought of a man, firm but fair, who had perhaps faced a similar choice long before.

The seconds passed slowly. She sniffed, not a stage sniff for effect but a muffled whisper of a sniff, refusing to be concealed. Heart aching at the injustice of the world in which they lived, he reached forward and cradled her damp cheek. She tried to turn away but he framed her face with his other hand. She did not resist when he pushed her back against the bank, lifted her skirts and did what she'd asked. His touch was tender, spurred as it was by compassion and not lust. His body obliged readily enough, still charged from its earlier stimulation, but his release was as mechanical as when he brought it on himself.

She gasped obligingly but he did not deceive himself that she felt any more than he did at the brief coupling. A month or two would pass. She would tell him she was with child, whether she was or nay. He would marry her. It happened time without number in villages across the country. It had happened fifteen years earlier and now he would be as firm and fair to her children as his stepfather had been to him. He stood, buttoned his trousers, and offered a hand to pull her to her feet. After seeing her to her door, he touched his cap and left without a word.

Bish

James Bishop Wilson suppressed a familiar urge to cough. The dust seemed to irritate his chest more with every passing year but what use was a waggoner's mate who couldn't work in farmyard or stable? Life was hard enough already, without losing his job. When the burning settled to a tickle, he breathed in cautiously. Gripping his crowbar more tightly again, he prised a worm-eaten board from the base of the waggon he was repairing. Rusty nails squealed in protest as they relinquished their hold on the ageing wood and the board slowly lifted. He relaxed the pressure gradually, long practice enabling him to guess precisely when the nails' grip would fail. When just the tips were still engaged, he set the lever to one side and pulled the plank free with his hands. It was half the weight of a healthy board and he tossed it easily to one side.

He was about to move onto the next board when he caught a movement from the corner of his eye. Looking up, he saw a man emerging from the lane into the yard. An initial inspection revealed the new arrival to be taller and broader than himself. The visitor covered the ground with bold, easy strides and hardly seemed to notice the weight of the large canvas bag he carried over one shoulder. As he drew nearer, Bish could see that his clothes, though dirty, were in good condition. His broad-brimmed felt hat rode low on his brow and his waistcoat was made from a glossy dappled grey hide that Bish guessed was sealskin.

'Aft'noon.' Low and easy on the ear, the voice was as confident as the stride.

'Aft'noon.' Bish echoed the greeting, wishing that his own throat could deliver something more impressive than the parched croak he heard.

'This Bank Farm? John Brissenden's place?'

The visitor spoke with an accent, not far removed from the local dialect and yet totally different to the ear of an Aldington native like Bish. He didn't recognise the inflection but it was not the clipped speech of the Londoners who passed through the area on their way to and from Dover — there was a strange flatness about the vowels but it was still unmistakably the voice of a countryman.

He nodded. 'Art thou looking for work?'

'You got some?'

It wasn't for him to be offering work. He faltered but then found his courage.

'We've need of a groom-come-ploughman. Knowest thou horses?'

The visitor came closer. The tanned leather of his face, taut over high cheekbones, was framed by conker-brown hair that tumbled to his shoulders in careless tangles. His gaze was keen as he studied Bish — warm smoke-grey eyes filled with intelligence and humour, the crow's-feet at their corners making him look older than the life in their depths suggested.

'As well as I know my own father.'

Bish suppressed a smile. The answer was clever, implying a lifelong acquaintance yet at the same time admitting the possibility that the newcomer knew nothing at all about them. Ordinarily, he would have probed deeper with a series of demanding questions that explored the full extent of a man's suitability for any work on offer. Now he did not ask because he wanted no knowledge that he might feel duty bound to pass on. Instead, he held out his hand.

'James Wilson. Most call me Bish.'

'Jem Smeed.'

The newcomer's grip was firm and his vibrant tone made their shared name sound far more exciting than it ever had on Bish's lips.

'I can talk to Mr Brissenden for thee.'

He wished the offer did not sound so feeble. He knew his opinion counted for something on the farm, particularly when it came to horses, but innate truthfulness stopped him from promising more than he could deliver. He steeled himself for derision that never came. Instead, a smile lifted the visitor's lips and creased his eyes.

'I'd appreciate that.'

Bish smiled back. When he realised that he was still smiling inanely several seconds later, he turned abruptly and gestured for Smeed to follow him to the office at the rear of the farmhouse.

The new man's first week at Bank Farm confirmed that Bish was a sound judge of character, even when his professional assessment was influenced by personal motivations. In Smeed's carefully chosen words of introduction, he had detected intelligence and integrity. The days that followed provided ample evidence of the former and nothing to cast doubt on the latter. Perhaps more valuable than either was the ease with which he blended into the farm's team of labourers, working as hard as any without showing up those slower or less capable than himself.

When market day came around, Brissenden instructed Bish to drive him into Ashford. A task that fell to him from time to time, when other business kept the waggoner from making the trip, it was usually more of a treat for him than for Brissenden, who missed his regular drinking companion. That week, it was a disappointment to them both: a long day for small reward and some of the worst horseflesh that Bish had seen in many a long year. Brissenden consoled himself with a liquid supper that made them late home into the bargain.

With his employer snoring peacefully at his side, Bish spent the return journey in the same circular deliberations that had occupied much of his time since Smeed's arrival. The sensation of wanting something that he could not have was far from new but never had it been so intense and persistent. After a lifetime of practice, he thought it had grown easier to ignore that part of his personality but his new temptation made short work of such assumptions. As they turned into the lane that led to the farm, his stomach twisted in cruel knots of impossible yearning, heedless of the knowledge that all the single men would already have left for the Walnut Tree. When the horses instinctively halted outside the farmhouse, he roused his passenger and braced himself while the man stumbled to the ground, making the waggon lurch from side to side.

'G'night, Wilson.'

Brissenden was a civil man, even when drunk and half-asleep, and Bish thought himself lucky to have such an employer.

'Goodnight, sir.'

He clucked to the team, then watched them find some last reserves of energy as they turned eagerly towards the stable. He was no more sentimental about his horses than any man in his business but it was hard not to credit the tired beasts with the same anticipation of a warm bed and a bite of supper that he himself felt. He was about to climb down to open the stable doors when they swung wide. Momentarily startled, he soon recognised the silhouette outlined by the dim lamplight. Settling back onto his seat, he moved the waggon into the low timber shelter. The operation gave him time to compose himself before he spoke.

'Evening. I thought thou wouldst be down the Walnut by now.'

Smeed shrugged. 'Groom, in't I?' He took the lead horse's head and led him inside.

Bish smiled. Smeed just about passed muster as a groom now, after some surreptitious hints when no one was looking, but he certainly hadn't brought much knowledge with him. Thinking back to their introduction, Bish thought it likely that Smeed the elder had been notable by his absence from his son's life.

They worked in amicable silence, he helping to untack the horses and then letting Smeed rub them down briskly while he manoeuvred the waggon into its corner and began to unload its contents. Whenever he worked alongside another man, pride and determination to keep his job made him concentrate all his efforts into controlling his breathing and managing the tasks given to him. Only then, reaching the fifth sack of oats at the end of hard day, did he stagger under its weight. Steadying himself against the waggon, he drew a couple of deep, rasping breaths. He felt the burden lifted from his back and turned to see Smeed shift it easily on top of the other sacks. The man did the same with the others in the waggon, then glanced casually around before speaking.

'I know you're not well, and I know you're worried for your job.' He held Bish's eye. 'You don't need to fret when it's just the two of us. Understand?' He raised his eyebrows questioningly and then added, 'Let me take some of the load for you.'

Bish stared back in disbelief. Why should the man help him out, when he could just as easily curry favour to take his job? Perhaps that was what he had in mind, a scheme to get an incumbent to lower his guard and then turn the situation to his own advantage. Examining him closely, Bish saw no deceit in his expression. All he saw was the same offer of friendship that had been there from the day they met. He silently rebuked himself for his suspicions: the Lord had always blessed him with generous friends and kind neighbours — why should he doubt this man?

'Thanks.' He paused before giving firm acceptance of the offer. 'I will.'

Smeed clasped his shoulder briefly, then returned to his rubbing down. Bish leaned against the waggon, letting his breathing settle into an easier rhythm while watching his new friend's powerful back ripple with the exertion. His interest in those knotted muscles was nothing new, an inclination he had recognised most of a decade earlier but been reluctant to indulge. No one who had shown an interest before had been enticing enough to risk what might come with exposure but now it was as though he were discovering the true meaning of desire for the first time. The powerful urges surging through him paid no heed to his social standing nor even to his life. No, the only thing that kept him rooted to the spot was his fear that he had misread this man and that, instead of reciprocation, he would see disgust written across those handsome features. That he would not be able to bear.

Dick

Crouched in the undergrowth, Dick Higgins held his breath for a few seconds. Even then he could hear little over the blood rushing through his veins. His right temple throbbed. He drew a slow, silent breath and scanned the woods around him.

Damn! He'd probably lost the fellow. The chances were that it was only a local out for a brace of rabbits, and there were more than enough of those on the estate, but a gamekeeper was paid to keep people out regardless of what common sense might say. If he wanted to hold onto his job, Dick couldn't afford to have the locals saying that the estate was easy pickings.

A twig snapped behind him. He swung around, fowling piece rising to his shoulder in one fluid movement and breath held ready to aim a shot.

'That's far enough.'

'All right, Dick. Calm down before you blow my head off.'

He breathed out heavily and lowered the weapon. 'Christ, Tommy! You looking to meet your bloody maker?'

'Just seeing if you're on the square.'

Dick grinned at his young friend, now come forward into the moonlight. 'Decent working man I am now. So, if you're on the lay, go and do it somewhere else.'

'I doubt the master's much interest in the sort of lay I've been a-hunting.'

Dick fell in beside Dennard on his homeward journey. 'Damn me, boy, don't you ever think of anything else?'

'Now 'n' then.' Dennard paused. 'When I've had my fill.'

Dick doubted that situation arose very often.

'You're lucky I didn't have my bloody dog with me. You want to be careful cutting through here.'

'I'm always careful.' Dennard let the double-meaning hang for a second before expanding. 'She's back in the stables with her pups.'

He might have known Dennard had taken the mastiff's whelps into consideration. The lad didn't get away with seducing half the parish's wives without knowing what went on. Curious to know who had provided that night's entertainment, he asked, 'Where've you been?'

'Out Bonnington way.'

The reply was affable but vague. Dick knew Dennard wasn't shy — they'd both dropped their trousers often enough in local hostelries — but his supply of married women depended on his well-known discretion. If a lover wanted an affair kept quiet, nothing would prise the details from his lips. Dick knew him too well to try and wasn't that interested in any case.

There had been a time when he scoured the countryside with something close to Dennard's dedication but that stopped with Rhoda Bailey. That was not to say that he was faithful to her, because he wasn't, but she captivated him in a way that no woman had done before. Their first meeting was enshrined in his memory, her perfect features washed in a golden glow that owed more to his state of mind than to the fine autumn weather. She was visiting her eldest sister, Ransley's wife Eliza. Like everyone else around Aldington, Dick knew the Baileys of Mersham — they were hard to miss, being large, numerous and infamous — but, for some reason, his and Rhoda's paths had never crossed. He stood in the kitchen of the Bourne Tap, staring silently at the raven-haired beauty until Ransley, in the days before he led the Blues, sent him packing with the tubs he'd come to collect. Rhoda's interest was less brazen but her frequent glances in his direction kept his hopes alive.

For days afterwards, he did little but think about her. His thoughts drifted from explicit fantasies of what he wanted to do to that voluptuous figure, his usual response to an attractive woman, to romantic dreams of their future together, a new experience for such a contented bachelor. He debated the risks of tangling with the Baileys and the potential business advantages of being related to them by marriage. He doubted her interest but then remembered those dark eyes flitting over him. Although blessed with ample self-confidence, he did not delude himself that his looks matched hers but he had one indisputable advantage. Like all her kin, Rhoda was tall. If she liked to look up to a man, as many women did, Dick was one of few locals with the height to let her do so. The thought of her full lips upturned for his kiss sent the blood flooding into his groin.

Soon after, he began his surveillance of the Bailey home. He had time in abundance because, although he called himself a labourer, he was a poacher and his vocation left his days free beyond a few hours for sleep. He watched Rhoda as she went about her work at home, and her errands in Mersham and the surrounding villages. He did not consider his pursuit to be spying; in fact, passing through the landscape unseen was such second nature to him that he gave it no thought at all. Nor did he suffer any pang of conscience about the thoughts he harboured while watching her work, whether his eyes were fixed on her shapely backside while she bent to tend to the vegetable garden or on her full breasts while she reached up to pick fruit from the trees.

He considered at great length how he should make his approach. His observation told him two things: firstly, that he was far from alone in appreciating her finer qualities and, secondly, that she was intensely aware of the effect she had on men. However, in a month of careful scrutiny, he never saw her so much as kiss a man. She was nearly a tease, almost but not quite. There was a knowing amusement about her, an acceptance that she could do nothing to change how men thought but that she didn't have to give them what they wanted at every turn.

As his goal seemed to grow more unattainable, so it became more desirable, until Rhoda filled every waking minute of his life. He had his preoccupation with her to thank for his missing finger joint: laying traps was not a job for a man with his head in the clouds. Eventually, he decided that a chance meeting in the fields was as good as any of the more elaborate alternatives he had entertained. Rhoda often cut across country in her wanderings and what could be more natural than to run into a poacher there? His territory didn't extend as far north as Mersham but he had only to wait for Rhoda's next visit to the Tap to stage a plausible encounter on home ground.

He waited until she was crossing the Fright on her return. He had heard strangers conjure up images of a terrifying wilderness when describing Aldington Fright but it was a good place to the local people, some of the last remaining common land free of the Enclosure Acts and a vital source of wild fruit for themselves and grazing for their stock. A bold young woman like Rhoda thought nothing of crossing it alone and, even without her family to avenge her, no local man would take advantage of her isolation while she did so. Dick certainly intended to do no more than introduce himself formally and walk her home, if she would permit him the honour. Such gentlemanly intentions did not survive more than ten minutes in her company.

Dick felt a visceral twitch as he remembered that day. There was a tension between them that had nothing to do with social awkwardness or an inability to find conversation. He had never experienced such primal desire before, rocking his entire world and stripping away what little self-control he possessed, and he saw the same urgency reflected in her darkened eyes, blood-red lips and nipples straining proud against her bodice. Their meeting was a blur to him now, hurtling from greeting through kissing and on to shattering climax, then coming to an abrupt end with his shock at the faint traces of blood he found afterwards. When he staged the encounter, he thought he'd be lucky to get a kiss. When it raced out of his control, he assumed she was far more experienced than he knew. At no stage had it occurred to him that she would give him in minutes what no other man had tasted. For the first time in his life, he felt shame.

Yet she showed no sign of remorse, kissing him tenderly once their passion had passed and asking when they might meet again. Whether it was his shame, or a baser response to the alleviation of his sexual desire, he shrugged off the question. He had the decency to help her to her feet and bid her farewell but that was all. It still amazed him that their relationship had survived that first encounter, not to mention the trials that followed it, but, six years on, they were still embroiled in the same turbulent courtship. Although he was not consciously aware of it, her ready capitulation on that first day was the root of many of their problems since. Unable to accept that he was special to her, he worried that she would not withhold from others what she had so eagerly given to him. Neither her assurances nor the absence of any evidence of her deceit could fully convince him of her loyalty. Yet, through every quarrel and separation, their love seemed only to flare more fiercely.

Thoughts of her brought the same twin stabs of lust and tenderness as it always did. He never tired of how she touched him or how she made him feel. She brought out a romantic streak in him that he hadn't known was there.

It was as if Dennard had read his mind when he asked, 'How's the fair Rhoda?'

'Fair as ever.'

Dick heard the pride in his own voice. Rhoda was a catch, with all her sister's finest qualities and even more striking looks than the rest of the Bailey clan. Of course, he hadn't actually caught her yet and would feel better when their names sat side-by-side on the parish register. They seemed to be out of step on that, as they were on everything else, with her eagerness for commitment waning just as his own finally waxed. Expecting to be forced into marriage when she became pregnant with his child in the early weeks of their entanglement, he escaped that fate because her parents deemed him inadequate as a provider for their daughter. That led to the humiliation of a bastardy hearing, and an order to compensate the parish for raising their child, two shillings and sixpence a week from him and ninepence from Rhoda.

Being rejected then was bad enough but worse was to come when, three years later, Rhoda spent the summer with relatives and did not tell him until afterwards that she had left their second child to be raised as her cousin. Furious at the deception, he took her to task over what she had done without his consent. She had coldly and calmly listed a dozen reasons why she would not be his wife, most of which could be traced back in one way or another to his lack of regular work. Her rational dissection of his life and character provoked many more arguments before, after another bitter separation, he slowly began to see the truth in her allegations.

All of that should now have passed into ancient history. He'd done everything she asked. Not only did he get a job but it brought with it a comfortable, if small, cottage on the estate. Now he had a home but still no wife. Nagging doubts resurfaced as to why Rhoda would not set a date and he glanced uneasily at the good-looking youth striding beside him.

Had he? Worse still, was he?

Living on the eastern side of her employer's Bilsington estate, Rhoda could be said to be 'out Bonnington way'. Dick felt another surge of the jealousy that had only recently put three men in bandages. The priory estate that he patrolled was hardly on the way from Bonnington to Aldington. Perhaps Dennard's route was an ironic joke at his expense.

'Bonnington, you say?'

Friendship had gone from his tone and pride had turned to suspicion.

'Aye.' Dennard studied him and then gave a slow smile. 'No need for that. I haven't been near Bilsington.'

Dick considered the reply. Dennard's cottage on the Fright was a mile or so west of Aldington, making his route more plausible than it at first seemed. Nevertheless, even if he was telling the truth, it meant nothing. If he hadn't been near Rhoda, why not say so? They might have met in Bonnington. His smile only fanned the flames of jealousy. Dick swung the weapon back to cover him.

'I'm warning you. Keep your bloody hands off her. If I find you're dipping it into her, I swear I'll cut the damned thing off.'

The failure of his warning to shift the amusement from Dennard's eyes only enraged him more.

'I mean it.'

Dennard started walking again, ignoring the firearm. 'I know you do. Just be sure you're right this time, eh?'

Rhoda had fiercely denied all three allegations and two of the bandaged men could prove their whereabouts on the nights in question. She'd given him a thorough tongue-lashing the last time, furious that he was making her out a harlot and resolute that she would never be his wife if he didn't learn to control himself. He took a few hesitant steps after Dennard. He didn't want to lose him as a friend but the man was like a ram at rut.

'Tommy,' he called glumly.

Dennard paused for a few seconds, then turned to face him. There was no anger in his expression, only a desire to avoid trouble with a friend.

'Swear it?'

Dennard raised an eyebrow. 'Swear what?'

'That you haven't bloody shagged her, of course.'

There was a long silence, so long that he began to wonder if Dennard had been lying but was not now willing to do so under oath.

'I swear I haven't shagged your intended. Good enough?'

He considered the words: they seemed genuine and unequivocal. Eventually, he nodded.

'Thanks. It's just…well… she means the bloody world to me.'

'So she should,' Dennard assured him. 'She's a good girl.'

'I should've known you wouldn't.'

Dennard gave a low laugh and shook his head.

'No, Dick, you should've known she wouldn't. A little thing like a betrothal wouldn't be stopping me.'

That agitated Dick again.

'How about a little thing like friendship?'

Dennard shrugged. 'What the eye don't see.'

'You're a bastard.'

'No, as it goes, I'm not. I may be a lot of things but not that.' He gave Dick's shoulder a conciliatory slap. 'Fact is, I was cutting a slice out at Lower Hurst Farm. Like they say, a slice off a cut loaf is never missed.'

Dick's anger receded, ebbing like the tide, and he broke into a grin at the good-natured rebuttal. It wasn't easy to stay angry with

Dennard, at least not as long as he kept away from Rhoda and took his slices from other men's loaves.

Bish

'You been to a doctor with your chest?' Smeed asked. Bish looked over at him with a mix of amusement and curiosity. Where would a waggoner's mate get money to see a doctor, even if his life depended on it?

'Thinkest thou me made of money?'

Smeed methodically coiled his fishing line and then cast again, dropping the float neatly in the centre of the stream. 'There's ways to make a guinea. P'r'aps a little nightwork?'

Bish glanced around, even though he knew they were alone.

'No need to be shy about it,' Smeed said in the same low voice. 'A man can't drink at the Walnut without hearing what goes on.'

That was true. Thanks to the drunken boasts of some of the Blues, even a visitor quickly found out most of what passed after nightfall around Aldington. Hogben was one of the worst culprits, his courage and devotion to the trade never in question but his drinking and opium-eating becoming ever more unrestrained. Bish was surprised to realise that he trusted Smeed more than some of his lifelong friends and acquaintances, even with knowledge that could see him hanged. His answer was non-committal but not evasive.

'Hast thou done that thyself?'

'It's been known.'

'I might be able to put some work thy way, if thou wished it.'

'I might be interested, if you did.'

They watched their fishing rods in silence. Bish reflected how friendly silence could be, in the right company. He had no doubt that Smeed could be a dangerous man — he didn't know how he knew it but know it he did — and yet he had never felt as safe as he did now, with this new friend watching over him. Most of an hour had passed when, out of the blue, he answered the question the other man had originally asked.

'No, I've seen no doctor.' He hesitated before expanding. 'My chest has never been right, even when I was a boy. It changeth little but, when it does, it's not for the better.'

Smeed nodded and the eyes he turned on Bish were sad. 'I thought as much.'

'Speakest thou not of it. I have no wish for fuss or worry.'

Smeed nodded again.

'Art thou not in fear of catching aught off me?'

Smeed's eyes crinkled into a smile. 'When Death comes for me, I'm expecting him to be carrying a nice big scythe.'

Bish smiled back. 'Or a musket?'

'P'r'aps.'

Bish knew then that he would be speaking to Ransley about Smeed. With business booming as never before, they needed every good man they could find. For the second time, he would stake his reputation on Smeed for a complex blend of reasons. He had faith in the man's capabilities and he was always willing to put himself out for a friend but, while he had recommended men for farm work before, he had never put someone forward for the Blues. He had always preferred to stay out of the trade's politics, friendly to all and indebted to none, but his reluctance to recruit really had more to do with the fact that lives depended on having the right men in place and he doubted his ability to judge some of the qualities required. Aware that his desires were influencing his thinking, something he had warned Dennard against when he noticed carnal urges overruling the lad's customary common sense, he wondered if he would regret his recent change in policy.

There was nothing irrational in his thinking and nor was he lying to himself, either about his motivations or about his choice in the matter. He knew that only a fool would recommend Smeed in the hope of reciprocated affection and he was no fool. He knew too that he could resist his temptation, that he yielded only because he wanted to do so. Still, in spite of how limited and unsatisfactory mere friendship would be, he wanted Smeed in his life one way or another — yes, he wanted it more than he had ever wanted anything before. Making Aldington a more profitable place to live lessened the likelihood of the man moving on.

It was as simple as that.

Datchy

Within days of announcing his imminent marriage to a woman with whom he had barely spoken, everyone for miles around seemed to know that Frances Furner was expecting Datchy's child. Unable to relate to the idea, feeling no connection between his fleeting release and the new life it had begotten, he felt like an innocent bystander in his own life.

'For Christ's sake! You don't marry a whore like that.' Higgins' exasperation showed in every tense muscle of his body. 'There's not a man in the parish hasn't navigated that stream. What on God's Earth makes you think it's yours? Have you got any bloody idea how many times she's tried that one?'

Datchy said nothing, taking a sip of beer and reflecting how predictable people were. Fran had done what he knew she would do, telling him of his impending fatherhood barely a month after their encounter in the lane. The only thing that surprised him about the news was that he believed it: something in her expression left him in no doubt that she was telling the truth, at least as best she knew it. He had no reason to doubt her fertility and little past evidence on which to judge his own.

He had been uncertain of his mother's reaction but, in hindsight, it came as no surprise. While she studied him in silence, he read the emotions passing across her face in quick succession: disbelief, disappointment and, finally, resignation. The only unexpected aspect was how quietly she took the news. He was relieved when she passed straight over what had brought him to such a sorry pass and began planning the practicalities.

Higgins was certainly running true to form. He was the sort of man who made regular use of loose women but felt no responsibility for any consequences that might follow. In the two years since his return to Aldington, Datchy had seen Higgins take scores of girls in dozens of public houses. Perversely, such public performances made him less likely to be named as a child's father, given that the girls were invariably shared with other men and could have no way to prove which man had given them their trouble.

Datchy finished his pint, letting Higgins curse himself dry before he attempted a reply. When he spoke, it was in a low voice, laced with menace. Even the deep colour in his cheeks could not undermine the earnestness in his tone.

'I'll say this once, b-boys. It's m-my child and she's to b-be m-my wife. You've said your p-piece and I've let you say it. Now let it b-be. If I hear you, any of you, say aught like it again, I sw-wear I'll m-make you answer for it.'

He got to his feet and made for the door. Behind him, he knew that his friends' stunned silence was giving way to amusement, but he bit back the words he'd left unsaid. He would not explain himself. His reasons would make no difference to some. As for the others, he'd sooner have their contempt than their pity. He funnelled his frustration into a call to his workmate for the night.

'Tom-m-my!'

Having missed the exchange, entwined with his latest conquest in the corner of the bar-room, Dennard looked up in surprise. 'Hold your horses. What's the hurry? They in't going nowhere.'

'If you w-want p-paying, you'd b-better start w-work–' Datchy's warning was cut off by the door slamming behind him. Still fuming, he paused outside to listen to the voices within.

The men at the bar were laughing aloud now. 'You heard the man,' Higgins mocked. 'B-b-better b-b-be on your w-w-way.'

'Kiss my tail,' Dennard retorted. With only the door between them, Datchy heard his friend turn his attention back to the girl. 'Well, my beauty, it looks like I shall have to love you and leave you. Shall I find you here tomorrow?'

Although the words were lightly spoken, Datchy heard the tension beneath them — the frustration of a man about to capitalise on an evening's wooing, whose body was still primed for the experience. He felt a flash of satisfaction that he had ruined Dennard's evening, just as Higgins had ruined his, but angrily rejected the cold comfort and set off down the lane. Moments later, noise spilled from the inn as the door opened and brisk footsteps sounded behind him. Dennard drew alongside and thumped his arm.

'Thanks. I was just about to–'

'W-won't hurt you to m-miss a day.'

'C'mon, Datchy. It's not my fault Dick's the way he is.'

'F-for Christ's sake! Get b-back to your lick-spigot. I can find a dozen b-better m-men.'

He regretted the words as soon as he'd said them. It wouldn't be easy to replace Dennard at short notice and he despised himself for lashing out at a friend. He needn't have worried: Dennard just grinned.

'Aye, they'll be lining up at this hour of the night.' He slapped Datchy's back amiably. 'My old mum says all things come to him who waits. Looks like I'll be finding out about that tomorrow night.'

Smiling in spite of himself, Datchy suspected that Mrs Dennard had in mind a delay of more than one night when she urged her son to show more restraint.

A couple of hours later, Datchy strode purposefully towards the beach with Dennard only a few paces behind, leading a horse in each hand, and a score of men bringing up the rear. It was a small mission but still one entrusted to him alone. Ransley had intercepted him on his way into the Walnut Tree a few days earlier. Sitting on the wall at the back of the inn, they'd talked of this and that for a time — or at least Ransley had talked while Datchy nodded and grunted at appropriate points — and then the leader of the Blues came to his point.

'Got a cargo coming in on Wednesday,' he'd said.

Datchy nodded.

'It's only forty tubs. They'll sow them just south of Globsden Gut. It's a good spot there, with only the one sentinel and he keeping to his station.'

Datchy nodded again, in genuine agreement with the proposed location but also because he didn't know what to say and was at a loss to understand why Ransley should be explaining future plans to him.

'I want you to take a crew to creep for them as soon as you can after that, Thursday if the weather's fit. There's not much by way of a moon and there's been a bit of a mist the past few nights.'

So that was what they were about. He and Smoker had brought a boat around to the inlet a few days ahead of time and hidden it carefully in the dunes. Now they were rowing out to retrieve the cargo that had been sunk in the bay and, in no time, it would be headed inland slung across the backs of their most trusted tubmen. He led the group confidently to the vessel and stood back while they hauled it seaward. The men put their backs into the task, waved into place by Dennard in his self-appointed role as foreman.

Without slackening his efforts, Smoker quipped good-naturedly at him. 'Aye aye, sir!' Glancing at Datchy, he added, 'Will there be aught else, Cap'n Grey?'

Datchy grinned at Smoker. 'A sp-pot of supper'd go down a treat afterw-ward.'

The older man took one hand off the boat just long enough to make a crude gesture and then returned to his labours. The hull scraped the shingle as they pushed the vessel into the surf.

With no ship on the horizon to draw a sentinel's attention, Datchy did not expect to be fleeing the scene in haste. Still, rather than be caught with a fast galley, he'd opted for the more mundane smack into which he now hopped with Smoker and Quids. No one could doubt what a score of men were doing on a deserted beach in the middle of the night but certainty wasn't proof. Without an illicit cargo or an illegal boat, no case could be brought. That meant that the window of risk ran from the moment they hauled the first tub into the boat until the moment when the last one disappeared into the night on its way to a paying customer.

He maintained his cautious surveillance of the vicinity while his men rowed towards the appointed spot. Lifting the lantern from where it nestled at his feet, he scanned the surface of the sea for the bundles of feathers used to mark the resting place of the precious cargo. The night was still and dark, the new moon casting only fragments of light onto the black water that lapped at the sides of the boat. A light mist drifted around them, not thick enough to hide their presence but perhaps enough to play tricks on the eyes of a man scanning the sea from the beach. Datchy soon began to enjoy the peaceful search. Every so often, his eyes swept the horizon to ensure they were alone but he knew that Dennard was keeping watch and that his long, low whistle would quickly signal any danger. Catching sight of something to the west, he motioned the two men to row parallel to the shore.

Sure enough, there was a marker. Datchy rose to his feet, grapnel in hand, while the two men set themselves against the sides of the boat for stability. Tossing the iron hook over the side, he began the laborious process of locating the weighted tubs on the seabed below. Barely two minutes passed before he skilfully caught a line for the first of the night's retrievals. Half the haul was to be gin — geneva as it was usually known — and the rest brandy. Datchy would identify the marked tubs and send them on their way to the men who had ordered them. With the time to haul each pair aboard, plus the trips to the shore, he and Dennard wouldn't set out for Aldington with the last batch for hours yet.

Pulling another tub from the depths, Datchy scowled as seawater ran over his gloves, into his sleeves, back down his wrists and into the gloves. As his companions manhandled the cargo aboard, briny cascades poured from the canvas skirts they wore over their woollen stockings. Most of the water spilled harmlessly into the bottom of the boat but, with each tub, a little more found its way into the tops of their thigh-length boots. Creeping was a nasty job in any season and their layers of carefully oiled cloth and leather would slowly become waterlogged. Even with the night as fine as it was, their hands and feet would eventually become numb as their bodies failed to replace the heat that had been leached away.

None of that bothered him. After spending most of his life around boats, cold water held no fear. The hardship of working a cargo only made him appreciate the warm bed that awaited him when he was done. As long as it stayed quiet, he was unconcerned. There were worse jobs to be doing and the guinea that Ransley had promised him for handling the night's business would be going straight into the tin of savings he kept hidden in the wall of his mother's cottage. Becoming a family man would quickly deplete his modest reserves and he planned to take every opportunity to top them up. He deftly grabbed the line on another load and then glanced shoreward with a smile, knowing all too well where his friend's wages would go. Dennard showed no sign of becoming more cautious with women or money, despite regular and public warnings from his mother about where it would all end. Datchy suspected that he might eventually succumb to the right woman but doubted that he would ever learn to hold on to money.

Bish

The clear night air was like a soothing draught in Bish's lungs after the smoky atmosphere of the Walnut Tree. He let it flood the inflamed tissue slowly, giving his chest a chance to acclimatise to its coolness.

'Feel better?' Smeed asked.

He nodded, knowing his friend would catch the gesture in the bright moonlight and that he had already talked far too much during the evening. In the past, the mile walk from the inn to the farm had often stretched ahead like a forced march but now he felt secure in the knowledge that Smeed would get him home and happy in the shared company. The moon hung above them like a freshly washed dinner plate, throwing deep shadows from every rut in the wheel-scarred lane. On the right of the road, they could see over the low hedge and across the shallow valley sloping away towards the Brabournes.

Smeed paused, as if to study the view, but then unbuttoned his trousers and began to piss into the ditch. Bish had been lagging behind and took the opportunity to watch as he closed the gap between them. He couldn't see much, just Smeed's head against the night sky and a dim impression of his hand at his groin, but his body was still quick to respond. Not for the first time, he wondered about Smeed.

Like him, the man was single and, also like him, showed no interest in the local women. Unlike him, Smeed was tall and strong. That seemed to make his aloofness all the more strange. It was too much to hope that Smeed might share his desire and he valued their friendship too much to risk it in trying to find out. He carried on for a few paces, then leaned on a gate and looked out over the countryside. He scanned the low rises, with their patchwork of hedged fields, calmed by their familiarity. The marshes began a mere couple of miles south, bleak and treacherous in their lonely majesty, but Aldington had the cosy feel of home.

The gate creaked as Smeed rested his heavier bulk against it.

'Nice spot.'

Bish nodded thoughtfully. He was an Aldington man, born and bred, and he had never strayed far from his birthplace. In a hoarse whisper, he asked, 'From whence dost thou hail, Jem?'

'North Kent coast, Herne Bay or thereabouts. You know it?'

'No. I've spent my life here in Al'ington.' He sighed. 'I dare say I shall die here too.'

'That'll be a way off yet.'

He gave no answer, not so certain but reluctant to voice his fears. Smeed's hand rested on his forearm. 'You ever think there might

146

be some things you'd like to do before Death comes for you?'

He studied the hand, afraid to move in case he made it move, feeling its weight and warmth through his sleeve.

'See the world? It might be too late for that.'

'P'r'aps what you want is right here. You ever think about that?'

He considered the words, trying to find some other meaning in them than the one that seemed so obvious.

'You're a difficult man to know, Jamie.'

He started at the use of his given name. People rarely used it, and no one had made it Jamie since he was a boy, but it sounded good coming from Smeed.

'What are you afraid of? Me?' A pause. 'Other people?' Another pause. 'Yourself?' A little chuckle. 'Surely not God?'

His skin burned at the gentle mocking. Perhaps Smeed did share his desire and perhaps for him it had not meant years of unfulfilled longing. He felt his hand engulfed in a larger grip. When he did not resist or pull away, he knew he had given his answer to a question as yet unasked. Some of his friends would already have landed their first punch.

'This can't be the first time, can it?' There was no amusement in Smeed's tone now, only curiosity tinged with concern.

His face grew hotter but still he said nothing.

'Well, if it is, you'll be all right with me. I'm good.'

A hint of self-mockery crept into the voice now. Smeed had no doubt that he was good but by saying so he hoped to reassure rather than impress. His free hand came around and cradled Bish's jaw.

'You can say no.'

He couldn't say anything, only tilting his face into the caress, but that was all the permission needed. Smeed's head bent down to plant a tender kiss on his lips, breath a heady mix of tobacco, beer and bacon. For the first time he could remember, no anxiety tainted his desire. He no longer cared that half the men he knew might cheerfully kill him for what he was doing. Lying with Smeed for one night would be worth an even earlier death than he'd been expecting.

From the direction of the village, he heard the lazy clopping of a horse headed their way. Smeed swung astride the gate, offered a hand to help him over it, then led the way towards a copse in the middle of the field. He followed, startled by the ease with which

Smeed had made his move and curious about the casual way in which he was now seeking out privacy for the encounter. If Smeed had read his feelings so easily, how many others had read them too? He stamped on that anxiety as soon as it invaded his consciousness. From the day they first met, what passed between them had been different from what they revealed to others. Even he had not been sure whether he saw unspoken desire deep in Smeed's eyes or merely wanted to see it there. How could anyone else see what they had hidden so well from each other? In any case, he wanted what was coming and he would pay any price for it.

Under the trees, the night was several shades darker. He stumbled twice as he traced Smeed's circuitous path. Somewhere inside him, relief stirred that his companion clearly did not know the copse and was searching for somewhere that suited their purpose. He'd already asked himself if Smeed made a habit of such seductions and felt a pang of envy as he wondered who else might have walked across the same field with him. Knowing some of the regular haunts to which Dennard's conquests followed one another like lambs to the slaughter, he baulked at being drawn into the same trap. It was not so much that he disapproved of such indiscriminate rutting, although there was an element of that in his reaction, but rather that he wanted so much more. The hesitation he saw reassured him: it didn't mean there hadn't been other nocturnal encounters but at least they hadn't been on the same spot.

Finally, finding a patch of moonlit moss that met his requirements, Smeed shrugged off his jacket and spread it on the ground.

'Good enough?' he asked, kicking off his boots.

Bish nodded, his mouth too dry to speak, and followed suit.

'You haven't done it with a man before, have you?'

He shook his head: he hadn't done it with a woman either but there was no need for Smeed to know that.

'Afraid?'

'No.'

While no more than a whisper, his reply was the truth. Hands trembling, heart thudding and groin pulsing, he felt only anticipation and then, at last, Smeed's strong arms around him. If he had a fear, it was just that he would wake before the delicious dream reached its conclusion. He reached hurriedly for his companion's brace buttons, determined before it ended to touch what he had only ever seen:

another man's hard flesh. Smeed leaned back to give him easier access, laughed at his urgent fumblings and then popped the fastenings himself.

With a shy smile, Bish lay back on Smeed's jacket and wriggled out of his trousers. Then, with his arms folded behind his head and his legs parted provocatively, he silently invited his friend to become his lover.

Sam

S am Bailey screwed up his eyes as protection against the wind and peered into the night. The sky was barely less black than the waves and he couldn't see where they met. Somewhere in the blackness, a ship tossed at anchor while landing boats fought across the seething sea. Behind him, men waited with agitated teams for their carts to be filled with tubs and packets. He pushed soaked strands of hair from his eyes, only to have them whipped back again. Retreating as a huge breaker crashed onto the shore, he wondered why he bothered when he was already drenched.

Deafened by the howling wind and roaring sea, he felt more than heard someone behind him. Turning, he saw nothing until a flash of lightning illuminated Ransley's unmistakable figure. Fair-sized, taller than most in fact, he still made an unimpressive sight. Even Sam laughed, something he rarely did, when Dennard once likened Ransley to a cow-hocked plough-horse put out to grass. The comparison was so apt that it had stayed with him ever since, through Ransley's rise to leader of the Blues and entry into local legend, and it still tickled him at the most inopportune moments. Ransley's stomach had grown with the size of their hauls and now he began to resemble a mare in foal.

Ransley's stature might be comical but nothing else about the man inspired ridicule. Sam had never met his equal when it came to planning and executing operations, not in the free-traders, not even amongst the officers under whom he'd fought in the French wars, or perhaps especially not there. He'd never respected any of them the way he respected Ransley, which was the reason he stood by and let him succeed Cephas Quested. He had no regrets: they grew ever richer under Ransley's leadership and he was content to play his part in making that happen.

'By cock and pie but it's a night!' he shouted.

Ransley nodded, his eyes fixed on the point where they expected the ship to be, although there was no way of seeing it in the storm. Sam followed his gaze. As dispassionate as they might be, neither of them wanted to lose men to the sea. Good mariners were too hard to replace.

'How about this Smeed fellow?'

Ransley's hearty bawl barely beat the wind.

Sam flexed the swingle in his hands and watched the landing boat that the newcomer was battling to hold on course for the anchored lugger. Even pitching and tossing as it was, it crept steadily onwards. He leaned closer to Ransley.

'He's no buggering ostler. I doubt he knew which end was the arse till the shit came out.'

Ransley laughed. 'But is he a mariner?'

They watched as the boat was swallowed by the night.

'He'll do,' Sam admitted. 'He's got his head screwed on right.' He considered a moment more before he added, 'Got a way about him, gives the lads confidence. First time out, I had two dozen lined up for Datchy's boat. Couple of trips and they're just as happy either way.'

Gilham might have a diffident nature but he was a first-class seaman and Sam knew they were lucky if, short of a leading mariner to expand the seaward side of their operations, they'd found his equal. The mariner part was easy, but the leading part was harder. Even so, as far as he knew, Wilson had never brought a man into the Blues and he wondered why this one should be the first. He wondered too why a man whose horse-sense was as respected at Bank Farm as it was in the Blues had not objected to an untried ostler when there were dozens of grooms around Aldington. There was no doubting Smeed's value in a boat, and Sam had no problem with what he'd seen of him as a man either, but he distrusted unanswered questions. Knowing that Ransley shared his disquiet in that regard, he suspected their leader knew more about the background to their latest recruit than he chose to reveal. The suspicion did not trouble him: if the explanation was good enough for Ransley, he expected that it would be good enough for him too.

A crash behind them diverted their attention. The moon was still behind cloud but some of its light filtered through, enough to make out the dim shapes of huddled men and beasts behind them. Two slim forms clung to the bridles of the panic-stricken horses hitched to the first two carts. Another sheet of lightning showed a clear circle of white round the eye of the largest animal as it fought against Wilson's grip. It had backed its cart into the side of the larger waggon and now a knot of men fought to disentangle them, keeping clear of the hooves flailing the air around them.

'Christ,' Sam muttered. 'Them devils'll be the death of someone.'

Ransley wouldn't need to hear the words to guess the meaning. Dennard had bought his place in the only way he could, and they admired his spirit and horsemanship, but none of that made them any keener to be near his beasts. Only Wilson was willing to handle them, showing the same serene determination with which he tackled everything. Three more horses owned by one of them meant three less to hire or steal, an advantage too valuable to squander. Now and then, they borrowed horses from Bank Farm without troubling Brissenden for permission but mostly they kept their pilfering farther from home.

Sam watched the two men wrestle and cajole their charges back into something approaching calm. Men feared a preventive officer's pistol but more of their number had been lost to savage seas and panicked horses over the years than were ever felled by the Preventive Service. The Bank Farm men, Smeed and Wilson, were chalk and cheese on the face of it but neither one of them turned a hair at the danger in which their roles placed them. With youngsters like Gilham and Dennard growing in experience with every passing year, the future was looking rosy.

A sudden movement behind the struggling waggoners caught Sam's eye and he peered into the gloom. It was a few seconds before he picked out a figure running towards them, past the slow-moving stream of tubmen trudging up the beach, each carrying a pair of tubs slung front-to-back over his shoulders with one against his chest and the other against his back. The slender outline of a boy confirmed his suspicions. One of their lookouts was coming in with news, a message passed from boy to boy using coded flashes of lanterns. In their case, no news was always good news. Nothing the boy might have to say was likely to be welcome.

Within seconds, Sam recognised the runner as Ransley's eldest

151

son, Georgie. The boy's sole goal in life was to serve in the armed parties and his tireless campaign to achieve his ambition was a regular source of mirth in the Blues. Ransley held out against any involvement at all until he took over after Brookland, only then enlisting his son as a lookout. Sam had wondered about the decision at the time, seeing no reason why Cephas would have objected to the boy joining them earlier. Perhaps Ransley was simply waiting for his son to reach a suitable age but then, at ten, he was already a year or so older than the youngest boys.

To Sam, the delay suggested that Ransley had more faith in his own leadership than in his predecessor's, a view with which he would be the last to argue. It tickled him to see Georgie's delight at belonging to the Blues fighting with his frustration at the insignificance of his role. With his twelfth birthday approaching, the boy was again dropping heavy hints about promotion. Sam's amusement was tempered by the thought of Young Sam making similar demands one day and how he, too, would have to weigh pride in the ambition with anxiety over the consequences.

When Georgie reached them, he was too breathless to speak. Sam waited with barely contained impatience while the boy gasped great lungfuls of air.

'Pre… pre… preventive men,' he finally spluttered. 'Ri…ding… in fast… from… the castle. Along the… lower road.'

Sam frowned at the absence of a vital piece of information but the boy quickly added it.

'Two miles… most.'

That didn't give them long. Sam looked at Ransley, their thoughts running in parallel. Boats at sea, carts and men arrayed on the beach — they needed more time for an orderly withdrawal.

'The chapel?'

Ransley nodded, then shouted to his son. 'How many?'

'A score.' Breathing again, the boy remembered his place. 'Sir.'

Sam's mind sped through the threat and its implications. They had chosen the time and place for the landing carefully, knowing a storm was on its way and that the stretch of beach had not been well patrolled in recent weeks. Everything seemed to go well, with weather worse than the most pessimistic forecast and preventive men apparently content to take refuge in their barracks, but now it was clear that they had plans and information of their own. Sam cursed the number of men headed their way and the inadequacy of the armed parties he'd laid on. Then, wasting no more time, he slipped into his usual role, managing their defences and leaving Ransley to terminate their business as profitably as possible.

'I'll take two dozen.'

He strode up the beach to where the batmen had gathered. They'd seen the boy's arrival and expected to be needed. He moved close, forced by the weather to brief them in a huddle when he'd prefer to do it on the move. A tight circle formed around him to hear the news.

'Twenty preventive men less than two miles off, Sandgate way. Pick up a reserve apiece and let's get over to the chapel.'

Unknown to most of his men, he had a small stock of firearms — mostly muskets captured from the preventive forces over the years — securely hidden from them but he intended to stick with bats that night. Running uncustomed goods usually meant no more than confiscation and a fine, while bearing firearms against the preventives could see them hanged. He wasn't keen on pitching men with clubs against men with firearms but foul weather meant wet powder and poor visibility. Men hurried to join him, swelling his band to nearer thirty than two dozen by the time they left the beach behind.

One of numerous sea defences left to rot after Henry VIII's disputes with the continent nearly three centuries before, Sandgate Castle had recently found a new use as barracks for the Blockade. Without it, the preventive men would spend a cold and miserable winter under canvas, given they'd find no one willing to accommodate them on the marshes.

The Blues were as flexible in their property use as the forces that sought to oppose them. Crypts across the parish bulged with tubs and packets awaiting transportation, curates' consciences kept spotless by a careful combination of strategic absences and selective deafness and blindness. Even the clergy's sense of smell seemed to take a holiday, when torn packets or leaky casks left the air hanging heavy with tea or tobacco, brandy or geneva.

Still, disinclined to push their luck, the Blues did not store weapons in the houses of God. True, the 'chapel' had once served as a nonconformist meeting house but its days of spiritual service were long past. Most of the fishermen who used it for storing nets and other equipment either helped in running goods or bought them, or both, so they had no reservations about partitioning off six feet at the back of the store to make an armoury. With a concealed door skilfully crafted by Gilham, even a diligent search would be unlikely to uncover their plentiful stock of clubs and blades. The watchman would have everything ready for them, warned what to expect by the passing messengers.

It took only minutes to reach the chapel but, even so, Sam knew their foes would be only minutes beyond it. The boy said they were riding fast, as he would expect if they hoped to catch the Blues unprepared, and even a tired horse outpaced a fit man many times over. The watchman met them outside, a lantern in one hand and a battered spyglass in the other.

'I saw the bastards,' he confirmed. 'Be on us in no time.'

The reserves hurried inside to arm themselves and returned quickly, each with the same stout bat and vicious knife that the night's batmen already carried. Several also wore cutlasses. As soon as they were ready, Sam deployed them with curt gestures, knowing every inch of the coastline from Rye to Deal and having a dozen plans perfected for the defence of any given stretch. All were stored in his logical mind, ready to be implemented in the moments between warning and attack.

So it was that men were clustered behind every dune of sand and tussock of grass when the drumming of hoof-beats shook the ground. The horses were moving slower by then, the rhythm of their steady trot on the sand punctuated only by occasional clashes of bits and teeth.

As the preventive forces approached, the batmen closed in, preparing to cut off advance and retreat at once. They would open an escape avenue once there was a prospect of some of the riders calling it a night but, for the present, were intent on stopping them spreading out or making use of the landscape in their defence.

With his brother at his side, Sam leapt across the path of the lead horse, his sudden appearance guaranteed to make it shy. In fact, it was a spirited animal and reared onto its hind legs. Its rider was hard-pressed to keep his seat, giving them the moments they need to capitalise on the confusion. A split second later, screams came from horses at the back of the party. They wouldn't be badly hurt, the batmen intending to use the riderless animals in their pursuit of officers who stayed in the saddle, but a well-judged blow to a sensitive spot worked wonders.

Sam looked up at the belly of the horse above him, then ducked sideways to avoid its hooves. Only the tip of the rider's left boot rested on the stirrup iron. Sam used the side of his fist on the man's shin to send the smooth leather sole sliding off the bar. The man's weight lurched ominously above him. He stepped back, then grasped the man's leg and helped him on his way.

Before the body even hit the ground, Sam set his swingle whirling and flung it downwards with terrifying force. It landed square across the man's back, bringing a crack from his shoulder blade and a whimper from his lips. He swung again, this time breaking the right arm: the man gasped for breath, winded by the first blow and now fighting to spit out the bile brought up by the sickening crunch from the second. Sam jerked his leg back and delivered a savage kick to the arse: the man wouldn't be sitting down for a while, much less riding, not with a cracked tail bone.

Sam moved on to the next man… and then the next. Around him, his kin and Hogben meted out the same treatment, encouraging their fellows to join in the wanton brutality, knowing that fear lost out to blood-lust every time.

Bish

Bish watched as the last tub was manhandled onto the stack in his cart. He had the largest of Dennard's horses in single harness, while the two smaller animals made a decent team for the bigger waggon. There was space enough for another tub or two but he doubted the gelding could pull the extra weight, not to mention the fact that the roads across the marshes were better suited to a light load of hay than to an overloaded cart of liquor.

He glanced along the beach to where he knew the batmen were engaging the preventive men. They would have been out of sight in daylight so there was no question of seeing them through the rain that soaked his cap and ran down his neck, into the first of two scarves wound tightly around it. The one closest to his skin was of the softest lambswool, a gift from his new lover and just about the most precious thing he possessed. He'd never had a beau to buy him gifts of any sort and he was touched by the concern for his health that Smeed's choice implied. A warm feeling that had nothing to do with the snug wool at his throat crept over him when he remembered Smeed saying that the moss-green scarf matched his eyes.

He chuckled.

It was the kind of thing Dennard would tell one of his young consorts, and she would take it no more seriously than it deserved while she decided how much the gift bought for the young buck. The difference was that he had held nothing back from their very first night and so the scarf could only be a genuine gift, given for no other reason than that his lover wanted to give it. In fact, Smeed rarely returned empty-handed from his trips to market, spoiling him with a constant stream of little luxuries.

Bish shifted his gaze seaward for a few seconds, knowing that Smeed would be supervising the loading of his boat from the lugger by now and that the load was likely to be left on the beach when he returned. The man might be sucked into the angry sea before he reached the sands or he might be shot dead when he set foot on them. Bish couldn't stop the icy tendrils of dread creeping through his body but he pushed them to the back of his mind. They were there to do a job, a dangerous job, and they'd do it.

'Ready?' Dennard yelled.

Lit by a glimmer of moonlight from between the clouds racing overhead, Bish didn't bother to pitch his weak voice against the wind and settled instead for a smile and a nod.

He flexed his arms, loosening muscles tied in knots by half an hour of fighting with the gelding, then turned its head landward and set off at an extended trot. They wouldn't hold that pace for long but it was a balance between the strain on his arms, and the horse's mouth, and the risk of pulled muscles and torn ligaments all over its rain-chilled body. The compacted sands cushioned its hooves, making for a soft start, and the wheels rolled easily.

Dennard's team was just as eager and flew past with the larger waggon. Bish let the gelding run with its herd, only starting to ease the reins in when they approached the high-water mark. As he did so, Dennard brought the pair in hand and led the way up to the road. Bish pulled his cap down more firmly over his eyes and settled himself for the drive back to the priory. The tubmen would stash their loads in hiding places dotted all over the countryside, often in holes in the ground that were all but undetectable once the turf was laid over them, sending them on over the coming days as their movements permitted. Some of the drivers would make deliveries to gentlemen and landlords who'd ordered stocks from Ransley. The remainder of the haul would be safe at the priory until Ransley sold it through the Bourne Tap.

He smiled at the thought of a man who rarely touched spirits himself but kept a family of a dozen in fine style on the proceeds of his guile in running them. Ransley would take him to one side later that night, press an earthenware demijohn of the best brandy into his hands, and urge him to take care of himself. Neither of them ever mentioned his health. The free spirits for medicinal purposes were Ransley's way of showing his concern and it was that, more than the over-proof alcohol, that warmed Bish when he poured a glass at bedtime.

Skirting Hythe, Bish followed Dennard west for Bilsington. They took the north road, planning to bear left at Aldington Knowl, while, less than a mile to the south, boats crept along the Military Canal for unloading at Court Lodge. Within an hour of a cargo being landed, it was dispersed so widely that the Coast Blockade was lucky to trace a dozen tubs and fine one or two men for handling uncustomed goods.

Barely a light showed as they clattered through Belle Vue and Court Street. Those who didn't look, didn't see, and that was precisely what the preventive men would hear when they asked. No one would have seen two waggons pass through. No one would know anyone who had been out in the early hours. After all, who would be out on a night like that?

Bish asked himself the same question as he pulled his coat tighter at the neck. Every soaking he endured probably shaved a few more hours off his life. Flicking the whip lightly over the gelding's back, he laughed into the storm; he would never give up the trade, not even for another ten years on his span.

Turning north at Bonnington Cross, he urged the tired horse north towards the Tap. Ransley's land adjoined the priory grounds and a score of fresh and trusted men would be waiting at the house to carry the cargo to its hiding place amongst the ruins, far from passing traffic and prying eyes. The gelding had made the run countless times and sensed the closeness of its journey's end. It trotted eagerly after its fellows as they climbed towards the Fright. It was always the same when they reached the Tap, a firm hand needed to stop the trio carrying on towards their patch of common not far beyond. Bish fought the beast into the rutted yard beside the house, hauled it to a stop alongside Dennard, and then cautiously sat back and let his aching muscles relax.

The weather had settled to a steady, penetrating rain as the waggons worked their way inland. Clouds still scudded across the moon but they were now pale grey with its diffuse light instead of the ominous black that had shrouded the landing. With the lanterns hanging around the yard, there was enough light for Bish to see Dennard's grin as he sprang from his seat. His merriment was infectious, putting men and women equally at ease. Bish had no difficulty in understanding how his friend drew the girls so effortlessly, given that he could easily have been drawn himself if things had been different. As it was, he was happy to count Dennard as one of the truest friends that a man could have.

'Blow me down, what a night!' Dennard was laughing, exhilarated by their adventures, and nearly fell over when Ransley's eldest daughter cannoned into him and threw her arms around him.

The girl was one of a bevy of beauties who were still on the young side for his attentions and he treated them all with the same chivalry, making them feel like ladies but remaining the perfect gentleman. Even the least trustworthy of them, Hogben or the younger Baileys, say, were not fool enough to cross Ransley in that regard. Their leader might not be threatening in himself but he'd know where to buy the worst kind of retribution, just as he knew where to buy any other service he required. Then again, Bish doubted such considerations had anything to do with Dennard's decency. He was a good lad, plain and simple.

'Oh, Tommy,' the girl gushed. 'I'm *so* glad you're safe.'

'Of course, I'm safe, young Miss. You didn't think a bit of a storm would stop me, did you?' He addressed all his smaller admirers as 'young Miss', given that he stood no chance of remembering every name. Doubtless he knew Matilda's but had no intention of playing favourites.

'Father said the preventive men were out.'

Dennard ruffled her hair, achieving his goal when she pulled away petulantly to smooth it. 'Well, your Uncle Sam'll see to them, won't he sweetheart? Now run along inside while we unload.'

With a final flirtatious giggle, the girl disappeared into the house. Having watched the exchange in amusement, Bish climbed down from his perch far more sedately than Dennard had done. He wondered what the children really knew of preventive men or how their uncle would be seeing to them. He was not a violent man himself, his character no better suited to it than his physique, and he usually put the thought of metal-tipped bats buried in bloody skulls firmly out of his mind. Now he considered the picture. He didn't believe a guinea in the pocket was worth a life but then he didn't ask the preventive men to risk their lives the way they did. That night, with Smeed still out in the darkness somewhere, he would have accepted any number of preventive deaths if they were necessary to save his lover's life. Perhaps for the first time, he was truly glad to have men as ruthless as Sam Bailey at their backs while they plied their trade. Knowing his feelings were sinful, he vowed to offer up a prayer for forgiveness later — once Smeed was safe and sound.

He leaned against the cart to catch his breath and coughed into his handkerchief. Dennard stepped closer, rubbed his back and then slapped it roughly, loosening the congestion. Bish coughed twice more, then folded the soiled cloth and slipped it into his pocket. He chose not to spit his sputum on the ground, as most men did, partly from distaste at being surrounded by bodily waste and partly from determination to conceal from his peers for as long as he could the bloody threads with which it was occasionally laced. He wasn't fool enough to think he could hide his general ill-health but he hoped to keep the extent and progress of his disease from all but the most sympathetic of his friends.

'All right?' Dennard asked in a low voice.

He nodded. Seconds later, the yard filled with men ready to unload the cargo. Leaving them to it, he and Dennard unhitched the horses, permitting them a short drink at the trough but careful not to let them bloat themselves while still hot from the exercise, then led them to one side for a rub down before blanketing.

Dennard became calm, reflective even, as he covered the mare's hindquarters with broad sweeping circles of his hand. 'Must have been rough out on the boats.'

Bish nodded, then added a hoarse affirmative.

'They'll get back safe.'

'Aye,'

'Spoiling for a fight though, all that trouble only to leave good liquor on the sands.'

Bish smiled, suspecting that the preventive forces would come out of the night's encounter badly. He'd be happier when all their men, not least Smeed but others like Gilham, were safely away but he felt anxiety rather than fear for their prospects. The gelding shivered under his brushing, and then nuzzled his elbow. He rubbed behind its ears, knowing its momentary gentleness was born of fatigue but rewarding it nonetheless. The next time they met, the animal would again fight him at every opportunity but for now a truce, however brief, was welcome.

Jem

Black walls of water towered over the boat. It rocked from side to side, tipping its occupants first one way and then the other. They held their nerve, fists clenched on oars and mouths set in determination. Jem Smeed crouched at the stern, the steering oar trapped in his vice-like grip, his biceps and triceps screaming from the forces tearing at the wooden paddle. The oarsmen fought to maintain some kind of rhythm against the tempest. He peered past them, straining to see the lanterns burning aboard the lugger, his mind focused on their task without a thought for the frailty of human life or the fact that, in seas as rough as those, a man could drown within a half a mile of the beach as easily as in the midst of an ocean. It was not obstinacy born of stupidity, but rather a cool refusal to give in to the power of the sea. His conviction spread to the men he led, each of them knowing that death might be close and yet drawing strength from his belief that they would evade it.

'Two hundred gallons of geneva,' he muttered. 'And four of brandy. Three hundred pounds of tobacco.'

Many men whispered prayers while they plied their trade but he had little faith in the Almighty. His litany took the form of an inventory of the goods for which they risked their lives. It fixed his mind on the work, perhaps keeping him safe as well as any man's God. None of the goods were of great interest to him, since he preferred beer to spirits and smoked lightly, but the independence and self-respect they brought were valuable commodities.

They were just yards short of smashing into the lugger when he glimpsed a lantern's weak glow through the torrents of water spilling over his sou'wester. He preferred to go bare-headed during a run but rain as hard as it was that night would bring on a headache in minutes, so he accepted the oilskin's protection.

'Hard to larboard,' he bawled.

Only the two men directly in front of him were close enough to hear but they echoed the order forwards, with men following suit until it had rippled to the front of the boat. Not until then did they move as one to turn the craft and bring it alongside the lugger.

The sea close to the hull was a seething cauldron of conflicting forces, waves crashing past the landing boat into the oak planks and rebounding to batter it again on their return. Even his iron-clad stomach rebelled at the shaking, spewing up a reminder of the light cheese supper he'd eaten hours before. He spat bile into the darkness, then looked up at the lugger's deck. There was just enough light in the sky beyond to silhouette the figures looking over the side. His crew flowed as a single organism, some men keeping their places to hold the boat steady while others stood to catch the lines to secure it. A rope ladder hung over the lugger's side and one man moved to its foot to pull it taut. Jem took the lead in swarming up it. He hauled himself over the rail and grinned at the mate of the lugger. It was their third load and he had soon warmed to the man's crude efficiency.

'By Christ, we picked the devil's own night for it.'

Jem nodded. Bad weather was the free-trader's friend. There were no finer mariners to be had and they knew the locale, both sea and land, better than most of the men paid to apprehend them. Even so, there were limits and the growing ferocity of the storm that raged around them came close to exceeding the risk that a sane man was willing to take. As if to punctuate the conversation, one of the lugger's younger crew members picked that moment to launch his supper overboard. Jem and the mate grinned at the prospect of the vomit catching the men below. It mattered little, since the rain coursing over them would wash it away in no time.

'Last load?' he shouted back.

'Nigh on. I wouldn't risk another anyhow, 'f I was you.'

Jem looked up at the sky, just as it was rent by a vivid bolt of lightning. A crack of thunder sent a shudder through his body. Close to the eye of the storm, they were tossed about as if they were toys instead of flesh-and-blood men on a lugger weighing over a hundred tons. He weighed the situation carefully. As much as he disliked leaving a job half done, he was not one for foolhardy risks. It took him only seconds to reach his decision. Better to land nine-tenths of a cargo safely than to sacrifice a good crew for the last few tubs. He gave a curt nod and set about getting barrels and sacks passed down to the boat below, watching every movement and poised to reprimand the first careless move. Despite his high opinion of the men working for him, he saw it as his responsibility, and his alone, to ensure they gave of their best throughout.

He hoped the storm might begin to pass before they cast off from the lugger but the winds only swirled stronger. It was all he could do to stand upright, even with a hand clamped so tight on the rail that his knuckles shone white through the murky night. His men held their places on the ladder with limbs twisted around the rope, the precious cargo passed from one to the next until it disappeared into the darkness below. They were drenched by rain and spray, fresh and salt water blown sideways so hard that the one could not be separated from the other. It seemed an eternity before a cry of 'all full' rippled up the human chain. With one final glance at the cluster of tubs and packets on deck, he resigned himself to leaving them. Half an hour and they'd be safe.

All being well...

He offered his hand to the mate, who shook it and leaned close. 'Regards to Cap'n Bats.'

Jem nodded. 'Good luck.'

The mate gave a grim smile. They'd all be needing a little luck.

Jem swung his legs over the rail and set off down the ladder after his men. He picked his way carefully over the cargo, back to his perch in the stern, then nodded to the men waiting to free the lines. Two men shoved off hard while the rest of the crew carved into the heaving sea with fresh resolve. The sooner they cleared the lugger the better, free then from the risk of being smashed into its hull, left only with the danger of being tipped into the waves and sucked away by the undertow.

The heavily laden boat rode low, each wave adding ounces to its load. They might have to resort to baling but, for now, Jem left all hands on the oars. Men's backs arched and flexed, muscles rippling through their soaked coats, as they heaved and hauled.

On the following day, they would all return to their legitimate employments, maintaining a pretence of work while they nursed strains and bruises from their battle with nature. Only a couple of weeks earlier, Jem had taken three attempts to plough a field with muscles so painful that he could barely hold the plough in contact with the earth, let alone push the blade through it. Long since a friend of Ransley's, Brissenden turned a blind eye in exchange for the odd tub of brandy or pound of tobacco but Jem noted how Wilson avoided pushing his discretion too far and now took the same care himself. Some of their number spent days drunk after a landing, and threatened anyone who dared suggest they should do otherwise, but most were wise enough to realise that co-operation worked both ways. Jem always gave the impression of working, whatever the reality might be. He liked having a job, and a place to call home, even though his pay from Ransley meant he had no need of his paltry groom's wage.

He held the steering oar firmly against the wind but, even so, felt the boat drifting north-eastward instead of holding the northwest line he'd set for the beach. He urged the men on the starboard side to dig deeper, while backing off those to larboard. They battled on, relying on nothing but his sense of direction to get them ashore. The boiling clouds above gave him no guidance but he felt the sands through the night as surely as a horseman felt his steed through the reins.

Ahead, the sound of breakers raking shingle eventually confirmed his internal compass. The oarsmen found a last reserve of energy within themselves and sent the boat flying through the surf but, instead of a score of men clustered around ready to unload, a solitary stocky figure appeared at the bow with a bat tucked under his arm. Jem strode across the cargo and sprang lightly out of the boat to stand beside Pierce in the shallows.

'Preventive men,' Pierce shouted. 'Sam's holding 'em back but they'll break through any time now. Clear the beach.'

Jem frowned. Leaving the remnants of the haul on the lugger had been painful enough, but to lose the load they'd risked life and limb to bring ashore? He offered a compromise.

'At least we can take a pair of tubs apiece.'

'Bats says get clear.'

Jem looked back at his men. He doubted they could hear what was said but they'd have a good idea of what awaited them. He felt Pierce's hand on his forearm.

'They're close. Don't chance it.'

The men in the boat were exhausted. It was the landing crew's job to carry the load. He could not endanger their lives by weighing them down. Finally, he nodded. Leaning into the boat, he projected conviction into a commanding bellow.

'Abandon the boat, boys, and run like hell. I want to see every last one of you in the Walnut come Saturday night.'

There was a moment of stillness while they took in what he was saying, and that the past hour's perilous struggle had been in vain, then they shouldered their oars and did as bidden. He brought up the rear, a knife tucked into one side of his belt and a rope's-end hanging from the other. If the batmen were overcome, the mariners would go down fighting.

Sam

Sam's men had fought on at close quarters for as long as they could, their leader monitoring the skirmish carefully even while slicing the air with his swingle. Sure enough, the rain had penetrated some of the pistols, bringing fortuitous misfires, and it obscured their outlines, bringing misses and flesh wounds in place of mortal injuries. Still, it was only a matter of time before armed riders manage to break through their ranks.

Sam was ready when that moment came, reluctantly swapping his beloved swingle for a bat before commandeering a horse from one of the fallen officers. Joined by his brother and uncle, Hogben and two others, he charged after the rest, most of whom were now headed east towards the landing instead of west back to Sandgate. By his reckoning, sixteen men had kept their seats but six of those had fled westwards, doubled-up with wounded colleagues.

Poised over his saddle with the confidence of a man who'd ridden many a charge, he felt the stolen horse's muscles ebb and flow. For an instant, he wondered if he'd risk his neck to rescue one of his blood-relations but discarded the idea. Speculation had no value.

They were riding flat out beside him with one thought in their minds: how to stop the preventives confiscating their haul.

After blowing a gale for half the night, the storm was starting to fade. The beach was spotted with shifting patches of moonlight. The tide had turned and the surf was erasing the evidence of a hard night's work. A heavily laden boat lay deserted on the sand, the water not yet high enough to rock its considerable bulk. The sand above the waterline had been churned into confusion by the passage of boots and hooves, boats hauled ashore and carts rolling on their way, loads dragged from one spot to another.

For an instant, Sam saw no sign of life. He pushed against his stirrups, wanting more height but not yet ready to slow his mount, when a larger gap in the clouds revealed a dozen men scurrying over the high-water mark. Even at such a distance, he had no trouble in recognising Pierce's compact bulk. The preventive forces swung as one to follow, eager to spill blood in retribution for their losses, not to mention for their failure to do their duty.

The fleeing men stopped abruptly, knowing they'd been seen and seeking cover for a stand. A low growl stirred in Sam's throat. The cornered men were mariners, probably unarmed, and now they prepared to face pistols and swords with only their courage to protect them. Instead of reining back, he urged the horse on at breakneck speed, relying on the sea having swept the sand clear when he had no way of seeing an obstacle that might send his mount sprawling and himself flying to his death.

On his left, his relatives rode as hard as himself, poised over their stirrups with the same ease. Further back, on his right, Hogben struggled to keep pace, his damaged right leg affecting his balance. Two more men followed, staying close to Hogben as usual. He'd lasted in the business longer than most, surviving a score of other injuries over the years as well as the shattered thigh at Folkestone, and Sam knew that inspired confidence in those who valued their lives. Not for nothing was the man known amongst the batmen as the Lucky Pig, although none would be foolish enough to voice the name in his hearing.

He matched Hogben almost year for year in experience but, while Hogben's callous coarseness struck their men as tough, his own cold distance gave the impression that he cared little for his own death and less for theirs. They respected his judgement and followed his plans but they did not come to him for camaraderie. Perhaps, he reflected, they wouldn't have looked to Hogben for it either had they known him better but, on the face of it, his brawling and carousing was more appealing to the kind of man that they recruited to wield a bat for the Blues.

Sam's thoughts were on losses at that moment, in fact, but at a more strategic than personal level. He was counting the cost of losing men like Pierce and Smeed, not to mention the seamen with them. It wasn't easy to find men willing or able to brave seas like those he'd watched earlier. He buried his heels in the horse's flanks, desperate to squeeze out more speed as the preventive officers closed on the men on foot. The officer leading them was a fool to take on even an unarmed group while riders were closing in from behind. He clearly underestimated the men he faced.

The preventive forces split into two groups, one to tackle the trapped men and one to face the riders behind them. Time seemed to crawl as Sam watched — wondering if he had misjudged his charge, if any of the men held loaded firearms and if any of the slugs would find their mark. He felt no fear, just the challenge of pitching his life against theirs.

Then the distance was gone and he was in the midst of them. He dropped into his saddle, sitting tall, his seat deep enough to withstand the fiercest blow. He'd never been knocked from a horse and didn't intend to start now. Spinning the animal broadside into the leading officer's mount, he knocked both horse and rider off balance, then brought his elbow up into the man's jaw with a satisfying crunch. He raised the hand in which he held the bat and slammed the side of his fist into the man's head. The handle of the bat connected squarely with the man's temple, sending him toppling to the ground like a sack of flour.

Seeing his companions engaged all around him, Sam moved on to the next man without hesitation. He found a pistol levelled at him but knocked it flying with the bat before it could be fired. To his right, he saw another weapon trained on him. He let the bat continue in its path, exerting only the slightest pressure to guide it upwards into the raised musket. The first officer drew his cutlass. For an instant, Sam faced the prospect of a blade cleaving the left side of his body open even while a slug was ripping through the right side of his face. Then, as his bat made contact with the pistol, a man rose up behind the first officer and swung something upwards over his shoulders. Every muscle stood out in sharp relief as he brought it whistling downwards, hitting the officer's back with an almighty crack.

Sam doubted he was alone in wondering whether it was wood or bone that made the unearthly noise. Only then did he realise what his fellow Blues were wielding: oars from the landing boat. Realisation hit the preventive officers at the same moment. They turned in disarray, men trying to help their comrades to stay in their saddles while falling over each other to escape.

He was of half a mind to follow, the blood pounding in his ears and gushing hot through his veins. Seeing Pierce and Smeed read the temptation and await a decision, too wise to argue while his blood was up, he sighed and slumped from his fighting stance.

'Looks like they've had enough, boys.'

Pierce nodded his thanks for their intervention, then peered after the withdrawing forces. 'You lose many?'

He looked around, recalling the scene at the tower. 'None dead, far as I saw.' He scanned the beach, doubting that any other officers had showed up at the landing point but knowing there were risks aplenty without them. 'All right here?'

'Aye.' Pierce glanced at Smeed, who now stood with his crew around him. 'Rough enough for you?'

Smeed grinned at his crew. 'How say you, boys? Bit lively?'

The man who'd wielded the oar to such devastating effect wiped his coat. 'Young whippersnapper only went 'n' puked on us.'

'Well, if that's all you've got to complain about, I'd say it was a good night's work,' Smeed said good-naturedly. 'Best start walking. I doubt they left us any ponies.'

There were groans all round as dog-tired men contemplated the long walk home. Most of the mariners lived within a few miles of the coast so it was Pierce and Smeed who faced the longest journeys. Sam noted their stoicism with grudging admiration, then rode alongside Pierce and held out an arm. The man looked surprised for a moment, then swung up behind him, leaving Smeed to accept a similar offer from his brother.

Behind them, the boat rocked in the rising tide. There would be some happy fishermen and beachcombers come morning.

Jem

The air in the taproom of the Walnut Tree was heavy with smoke. Many men around the room held smouldering clay pipes and, although it was still summer, the landlord had lit the first fire of the season for cheer. Fragrant smoke from the previous year's apple prunings curled up the chimney, drifting just enough to scent the atmosphere. Seated beside the fire, his back resting comfortably against the bar and one foot on the fender, was Jem Smeed. He sipped from his regular pewter tankard, savouring the twin pleasures of warm beer and the company of friends. He was sorry that Wilson hadn't felt up to coming with him that night, his chest too sore for conversation or second-hand smoke, but was content to know that the man would be awaiting his return to the farm with the latest news and gossip.

It had been a long time since he'd felt so content with life. His new friends were a rough bunch but most were good men. He surveyed the crowd with quiet amusement. For all his flexibility with storage arrangements in and around his church, Reverend Hollams kept a discreet distance from the inn on such nights. He preferred not to witness the godlessness that pervaded the place when smugglers' pockets were newly filled. That night, temporary wealth had coincided with the passage of a couple of cartloads of fruit-pickers and the Blues aimed to make a night of it. The crueller crew had taken the back room, so Jem shared the smaller space with some of the men he liked best.

The hum of conversation rose as the beer sank and now it was hard to distinguish words from the din. Across the table from Jem, a young girl smiled and shouted into Higgins' ear. She wasn't pretty but there was an appealing sun-flushed freshness to her smooth complexion. Not that Higgins was likely to have noticed, given that his eyes had barely strayed from the firm breasts he was now in the process of revealing.

Jem shared his friend's state of arousal but the object of his desire was on the far side of the room. The boy looked around sixteen, his body on the cusp of manhood with slender turning to lean, developing muscles padding a well-boned frame. Dark gold hair flopped over a dark gold forehead when he leaned forward, only to be tossed back every so often. He was talking to another of his group, a swarthy youth with a year or two on him who sported a spectacularly crushed nose. They were foolish to drink in the inn just then, since there was almost certain to be trouble at some point, but wise enough not to interfere with what went on.

Jem studied the swell of the boy's buttocks in his dirt-streaked trousers, debating if it was worth making a move. The visitors had declared their hand when they chose where to spend their evening. It was no secret what went on around Aldington and ordinary folk were either attracted or repelled. These were clearly attracted. The girls must know what to expect. The boys might be curious, might hope to join the Blues or might, just possibly, have another agenda. Jem had picked up youngsters who found him glamorous before and this boy's furtive glances said he might be receptive. Jem could follow him out when nature called. If he was willing, so much the better. If not, Jem had little doubt he could persuade him to hold his tongue, whether or not he sampled that shapely arse before releasing him.

He returned his gaze to the girl with the good skin. She giggled merrily while Higgins chewed on her nipple. At Jem's side, Giles was leaning on the bar, engrossed in a good-natured argument about the merits of different strains of hops and unperturbed by Pierce's far superior knowledge. The pressure of a thigh against Jem's shoulder only fuelled his desire, a curious cocktail of the feel of a friend's body, the sight of an acquaintance's arousal and the prospect of a stranger's touch.

Higgins leaned forward and swept the table clear with his forearm. Jem was barely fast enough to lift his half-full tankard out of the way before it followed the other items onto the hearth. Higgins pushed the girl onto the table, roughly but not unkindly, and stood for a moment to appraise his prize. Never a particularly heavy drinker and clearly in full control of his faculties at that moment, he unbuttoned his trousers casually with one hand.

Jem took another sip from the tankard in his hand and looked down into the girl's wide eyes, now only inches away, cornflower darkened to violet by her dilated pupils. He supposed she was appealing in her way but she fell far short of Rhoda's sensual beauty, to which he might be impervious but was certainly not blind. Jem knew full well that Higgins was not reacting to the girl's looks but rather to the exhibitionism of their public coupling; he had performed often enough in similar circumstances himself and knew precisely how the atmosphere and audience enhanced the experience. He felt a mixture of amusement and apprehension as he reflected that Higgins would not be so cavalier about where he practised his art if he knew more about the company he was keeping.

Feeling Giles shift beside him, Jem looked up. Giles watched the action for a second or two, then met his gaze. In his eyes was neither lust nor judgement but instead a twinkle of ironic humour, killing Jem's amusement stone-dead, making him wonder just how many of his friends might have suspicions about him. He shivered, understanding what people meant when they said someone had walked over their grave, but held Giles's eye in spite of his unease, trying to see into his mind. He also held his breath.

Giles glanced at the golden boy, then gave a shadow of a shrug.

Jem breathed again, feeling the life flow back into his rigid body. It was fortunate that the men who used their eyes most keenly often used their heads wisely too.

Both men returned to watching Higgins satisfy himself, Jem feeling a rare sense of inclusion as he wondered whether there was so much difference between what he and Giles got from the show. He knew Giles would not follow suit in front of him but then he probably wouldn't have done anyway. The man wasn't faithful to his wife, but he was closer to it than many. He was also selective and Jem doubted the girl's homely looks, even with her alabaster skin and succulent breasts, would meet his exacting standards. In fact, now he came to think of it, Jem had never seen Giles indulge himself in public or where another man had already been. He did not conceal his liaisons but he did not exhibit them either.

It was Pierce who moved closer, ready to take over when their friend was done. Despite his lack of height, his stocky build and tattoos combined to create a fearsome impression but clearly they did not frighten her. Jem had seen his friend buy her a glass of cider earlier in the evening, chatting in his unexpectedly melodious voice, and assumed he must have made a good impression. Pierce proved to be less selfish in his pleasure than Higgins, careful to give as much as he took, and a few minutes passed before he was done.

The girl was in the process of restoring her dignity, knowing that they had no further use for her, when the door flew open and banged against the wall. Hogben swayed in, very much the worse for drink, open trousers and a splash down one thigh declaring he'd made a stop on his way from the bar-room to the taproom. He reached the girl in two long strides and shoved her backwards.

Jem instinctively thrust his hand under her head to cushion it from the split oak of the table.

'Bugger off out of it.' Hogben's words were slurred, testifying to an exceptional intake given how well he held his drink after so much practice.

Jem looked up coolly. He was never keen on the word 'bugger' being used in his vicinity, wary that it might lead people to conclusions he didn't want them to reach. Rising slowly to his feet, he faced up to the lout. He had yet to see Hogben stone-cold sober and despised the kind of man who expected to find solutions to his problems at the bottom of a bottle. Looking beyond, he saw Higgins leaning against the wall, waiting to see how events unfolded. The golden boy stood further along, the fear clear on his face and reflected on the face of his friend beside him. They might have been foolish to come there but they weren't too stupid to see the difference between what had passed and what might follow.

The sad thing, Jem reflected, was that Hogben did not mean to be brutal. As far as he was concerned, his interest was no different from Pierce's. He had not yet grasped the full extent of his decline or the effect that it had on other people, particularly on any woman unlucky enough to take his fancy. Jem glanced down at the girl, saw the horror in her face, and knew that he could not stand by and watch her violated.

He said, 'I think the young lady's had all the company she needs.'

'*I* think it's none of your buggering business.'

Jem stepped forward and shoved Hogben off balance in one fluid movement, motioning behind his back for the girl to get out. She wasted no time, bundling her clothes to her breast and disappearing before Hogben managed to stagger upright again.

'Bastard. You'll pay for that.'

Hogben lunged, missing first with a left jab and then with a right hook. Jem timed his right perfectly, landing a heavy punch on the chin that sent needles of pain through his knuckles and would have felled most men instantly. He followed up with two more but still Hogben clung to consciousness. The two younger Baileys appeared at the door, with a knot of men behind them.

'What the blazes?' Rob demanded.

Jem gave him a grim smile. 'Pig-face told me to bugger off.'

Satisfaction lurked somewhere under Rob's glare. Jem knew that he didn't give a damn about the argument but he'd drunk his fill, had a woman and now wanted a fight to round off his evening. Jem look heavenward as if exasperated, then landed a sudden left before his opponent even realised they'd started. He saw Higgins bury his fist in John's belly, unperturbed by giving away half a foot in height and breadth to the colossus, then there was chaos.

Jem took nearly as many punches as he gave but kept his guard up so few made it to his face. Keeping the upper hand while he worked his way to the door, it was only the sight of Hogben, now laying into the golden boy, that slowed his exit. The brute would have been outclassed by any of their number in his present state but his victim clearly had no idea how to defend himself. The boy held up open palms in protest but made no real effort to block the blows raining down on him. His nose looked set to make a pair for his now-absent friend's and blood streamed from his mouth.

Jem ducked behind Hogben, grabbed his shoulder and spun him around. He waited for a second or two, judged his punch carefully and then put every ounce of his weight behind it. Hogben stayed on his feet for a few seconds and then crumpled. By that time, both bar-room and taproom were in pandemonium so no one noticed that the cause of the brawl was oblivious to it all. Jem nodded towards the door, followed the boy out and shoved him a couple of times until they were well clear of the inn.

'Thanks,' the boy mumbled through swollen lips.

'There's no need to go looking for trouble,' Jem said, passing him a frayed handkerchief. 'It'll find you soon enough.'

The boy nodded and wiped his mouth. 'You want to?'

Jem shook his head curtly.

'I probably don't look so good now.'

The piteous tone made Jem wonder if he'd been right to protect the girl. He might have known the boy would be hopeless in a fight. Cupping the boy's arse in his palm, savouring its firm contours and feeling his loins responding, he hesitated, tempted, but then laughed. 'Some and some but I was only looking. Get back to your friends.'

Jem watched him limp out of the village to the field where the fruit pickers were camped, then turned his face homewards. His decision had little to do with how the boy looked and much to do with the thought of Wilson waiting patiently for him.

When he got back to the farm, he would slip soundlessly into the back of Wilson's tumbledown cottage and creep up the creaky stairs for an hour in his lover's arms. All too soon, he would tear himself away and make a suitably public return to the attic he shared with half a dozen farmhands. He knew they were lucky Wilson had his own cottage, something a single waggoner's mate had no right to expect, but he wished they could make better use of it without his absences being noted.

When Wilson mentioned one day that his mother had worked for Brissenden before she married his father, Jem's mind quickly went where he doubted Wilson's ever had but even his world-weariness had faded during his time at Bank Farm. Brissenden was that rare thing — a good man. If he had a fault, it was his fondness for brandy but then what man had no faults? If his concern for Wilson was more marked than his concern for others, it seemed more likely to spring from compassion for a less fortunate soul than from remorse for any past sins.

Jem lengthened his stride. Never in his life had he turned down such a tempting offer as the boy's but it had already faded from his mind, his thoughts drawn back to the man from whom they rarely strayed for long. He guessed that Wilson would have spent the evening resting, hoping to feel fitter by his return, but asked only that they be together, preferring a chaste embrace with his lover to ecstasy elsewhere.

Dick

Dick Higgins kicked the table leg. Gathered in the back room of the Bourne Tap, ready for one of the meetings that preceded every run under Ransley's regime, the inner circle of the Blues awaited one man. Smeed was late, as he had been several times since the stormy weather and troublesome preventive men at Sandgate put a premature end to their last full night's work. His excuse was heavy ploughing in the fields to the north of Brissenden's holding.

Ransley's hand was firm in some ways but he was pragmatic about the conflicting calls on his men's time. Although Smeed's presence was pivotal to their discussions, Dick knew that nothing would be said to a man who was fast proving to be amongst the most valuable of their number. Ordinarily, that would not have been of the slightest concern to him. He had no interest in either power or responsibility: all he wanted was the money he needed to live well, and he recognised Smeed as the kind of man who could help to make their operations more profitable.

It was a great pity, for Dick and all who knew him, that the same logical reasoning did not inform his personal affairs. Throughout the two weeks since he enjoyed the fruit-picker's attentions in the Walnut, something had been rankling but he must have recalled the scene fifty times before he placed what it was. Smeed had been watching with a suppressed smile, the kind of smile that spoke of secrets and lies, and Dick was at a loss to understand why that should be. As far as he could see, there was nothing amusing about his equipment or his performance. It did not take long for a more sinister interpretation to occur to him.

While the others ate and drank, talked and joked, he glowered at Wilson across the table. If the man was fit, he'd be helping with the farm work but his weak chest got him off the heavier jobs. Not for the first time, Dick thought that he would not have such a sickly creature on his payroll if he were Ransley or Brissenden.

Another half-hour passed before Smeed joined them, slumping into the only empty seat. He took the earthenware jug of beer that Quested passed to him and raised the silver-plate cover to fill the tankard in front of him. Dick studied him carefully. His trousers were dirty but his shirt was clean and he was freshly washed.

'Ploughing late again?'

Dick heard the sneer in his own voice an instant before Smeed's eyes turned on him in surprise.

'Out Grigley's way. We're behind, there's no denying it.'

Dick grunted, knowing he'd be a fool to provoke Smeed but fixated on his suspicions. He was unaccustomed to evaluating the appearance of the men he knew but thought Smeed was probably one of the better looking of the Blues. More to the point, he was smart and growing in status. Dick had never seen him with a woman and now he wondered if he knew why that was. With another glare at Wilson, he satisfied himself with a jeer.

'Maybe if *he* was good for a fair day's work.'

Smeed looked around the gathered men, clearly trying to ascertain whether he'd missed something. Their faces showed the same bemusement as his. There was a long pause before he spoke.

'Nothing to do with Bish. It's ploughman's work. I'm not sure I see what business it is of yours either.'

Dick scowled. He'd passed Bank Farm a dozen times over the past week and seen no sign of any ploughing on the slopes of the East Stour valley. 'I think maybe you lost your bearings.'

Smeed was still staring blankly at him when Dennard laughed. It was a nervous sound, in contrast with his usual merry chuckle. Was it the lad after all? Dennard was handy enough with his fists but Dick had no doubt he could teach him a thing or two. Perhaps now he was worried that Smeed would be helping out.

'Christ, Dick,' Dennard said uneasily. 'Haven't you put that one to bed? Last I heard, you thought it was me giving Rhoda a shot.'

Dick felt a palpable wave of emotion around the table, as men grasped what the argument was about and weighed up the likely outcomes. It had the potential to get very nasty, given that his intended was kin to the Baileys and also, by marriage, to Ransley. Any accusation he made reflected on her as well as the man in question. He glanced hurriedly around the men, lingering on Wilson, wondering if any of them knew what Smeed was up to.

To his left, Hogben and the younger Baileys were grinning, clearly keen to see Smeed taken down a peg or two, although even Dick himself doubted that he was the man to do that. To his right, the men seemed ill at ease. Pierce, Quested, Giles and Dennard were all friendly with Smeed but what they knew or what they thought was not evident. Dick looked again at Wilson, only to find him staring at the table as if to abdicate from the dispute. Finally he fixed Smeed with what he hoped was an intimidating glare.

'Well?'

There was conflict in Smeed's eyes, amusement tinged with annoyance but also with more unexpected anxiety.

'Well what? Maybe you should try asking her before you accuse every man in the parish.'

'Just answer the bloody question.'

'What question?'

'Are you shagging her?'

To his surprise, Smeed answered. His reply was unequivocal.

'No.'

He could accept that. But then again.

'You would say that, wouldn't you? Bastard.'

Smeed glanced at Ransley, as if to ask whether the matter should wait until after the meeting, and got a slight shrug in reply. He rose slowly to his feet.

'Will you think me more truthful if I thrash the living daylights out of you?'

Dick stood to face him.

'You think you're so bloody special.'

Lost for words, Smeed could only shake his head.

Dennard rose to his feet. 'Come on, Dick. Jem's not your man.'

'How would you know? Or was I right the first time?'

His simmering jealousy made him ready to accuse every man at the table, and take them all on at once if necessary.

Hogben took a swig from his tankard and grinned up at him.

'Maybe both of them are at it. You ever think of that?'

It was then that Dick's vision clouded over. He swiped the tankard from Hogben's hand, sending its contents sloshing over the men to his left, then drove Dennard back against the wall and grabbed him by the neck.

'You swore.'

Dennard raised his hands. 'I haven't touched her. Can't you see the Hog's making a fool of you?'

Unrepentant, Hogben continued, 'Could be one at each—'

He couldn't finish the sentence because Sam Bailey gripped his throat and dragged him out of his chair. Glaring right into his face, he snarled, 'Shut your trap before I shut it for you, you worm-eaten shitsack.'

Something in Dick quailed as he saw Bailey toss Hogben back into his chair and Smeed stride towards him. He might have set off more than he bargained for with his suspicions. He felt himself hauled off Dennard and thrown to the ground. Smeed's knee sank into his chest, forcing out the breath and leaving him suffocating.

'I'm not so fond of being made out a liar. What's the matter with you? I've seen you're donkey-rigged but you're acting like a man who can't satisfy his woman.'

When Smeed swivelled a few degrees to get a better grip, his weight shifted from Dick's chest to his gut, forcing beer out of his stomach and back into his mouth. He swallowed desperately, trying not to gag on the bitter fluid.

'Can't you get a stiff and stout without a dozen men looking on? Is that it?'

There was a cruel edge in Smeed's taunts that Dick hadn't heard before. The man was now unmistakably furious about the accusation but there was no trace of guilt in his expression, or even disappointment at the possibility of having his fun curtailed.

'Maybe I should go down Bilsington way for a taste of what you're so worried we're all dipping into. Must be sweet as honey to make you risk your neck warning *me* off.'

His fists closed on Dick's lapels and punctuated each question with a shake.

'Shall I?' Smeed's voice had been rising in pitch with each question but now it dropped to a growl. 'I haven't, I'm not and I won't be.' He leaned closer. 'Don't ever let me hear you speak of me in the same breath as your woman again. Clear?'

Dick could barely move to nod or draw breath to speak.

'Clear,' he mouthed back.

As Smeed rose to his feet, Dick saw the mask drop back into place. No one coming into the room then could have guessed what had passed from looking at the man who took his seat and turned his attention to Ransley, waiting for the meeting to start.

Dick struggled to his feet, torn between beating a retreat and braving it out. His bolder side won and he returned to his chair, careful to avoid catching anyone's eye. He heard little of the discussion, engrossed in his own conjectures. The confrontation was the act of a desperate man but it had revealed something.

Firstly, Smeed was far too angry for a man accused of bedding a woman — anyone would think that he was the wronged party.

Secondly, some of those around the table knew more about it than they were willing to admit.

If the thought of Rhoda's betrayal tore at Dick's soul, the thought of that betrayal being public knowledge transformed it into a point of pride. He would never let a woman make a fool of him in that way.

177

Bish

Bish studied Smeed's back as they returned from the Tap. A casual observer would have seen only a man walking briskly home but he wasn't fooled. Normally they wandered along side-by-side, at whatever pace he could manage comfortably, arms brushing companionably although they were rarely so rash as to hold hands or show affection, even late at night with no one in sight. Now Smeed walked a few paces ahead, maintaining the distance if he tried to catch up but not pulling away if he didn't.

There was no way that he could make out Smeed's tensed muscles in the moonless night but he knew how they looked. The shoulders would be hunched and the brow creased into deep lines. He stopped walking and waited for Smeed to notice. The man took another dozen paces before glancing over his shoulder to see what was keeping his companion. Clearly surprised to see him standing in the middle of the road, rather than stopped by the hedge, he faltered and then turned around.

'All right?'

Bish inclined his head. '*I'm* all right. It's thee I worry for.'

Smeed stared at him for longer than most men would have been easy with but Bish gazed steadily back. Eventually he continued the one-sided conversation.

'Why, Jem? Dick's calling out a different man every week these days. Why art thou troubled by it?'

Smeed halved the distance between them and then examined him, as if wondering whether he was stupid after all. 'Because if they start thinking about what we're *not* doing, it won't be long before they catch on to what we are doing.'

Bish kept the smile off his face. Smeed must be agitated to imagine he hadn't considered that. He might be inexperienced but he wasn't naïve. Long before his lover came on the scene, he'd worried that his lack of interest in women marked him out. Almost all of the men he knew took their pleasures freely and publicly. A few appeared to be faithful to their wives but, in every case, the presence of several children suggested they were well served within their marriages. Even when he met men like himself, he found that most kept a wife to allay any suspicions that might begin to form. That was not an option for him, since he could never make a vow before God that he did not intend to keep.

He said only, 'It had to come, sooner or later.'

Smeed's anger resurfaced.

'Well, I'd sooner it was bloody later. All right?'

He couldn't argue with that but still he was surprised that Smeed was taking the row so seriously. He closed the remaining gap between them and lifted a tentative hand to Smeed's cheek.

'At least Dick hath thought not of it yet.'

'*Yet*,' Smeed repeated bitterly. 'He'll be trouble when he does.'

'I know. I wasn't born yesterday, though some think I was. As like as not, half of the men around that table have guessed already. The other half will be out for blood if they do. I don't stand a chance against them and I fear thou wilt stand up for me instead of saving thyself.' He looked fondly at Smeed. 'But I'll take what I can, while I can, and worry about the morrow when it comes. And I'll say naught if thou wishest an end to it. Thou hast my oath.'

To his surprise, Smeed laughed at the offer. 'Damn me for a horse if I want that. I wasn't thinking of leaving you. I was thinking of leaving with you.'

'Thou wouldst take me?'

Smeed's cursory glance around barely qualified as a precaution but Bish didn't care as he let himself be drawn close. A whisper tickled his ear. 'Course I damn' well would. Would you come?'

'I should be like unto a millstone around thy neck.'

Smeed shrugged. 'Sooner sink with you than swim without.'

Throwing caution to the wind, Bish slipped his arms around Smeed's neck and kissed him before giving his answer. All he wanted was to spend his remaining span with Smeed. When he spoke, there was certainty in his voice. 'To the ends of the earth.'

They resumed their homeward journey, arms linked in shared defiance of the world and its beliefs. For some time, he considered in private what the future might hold for them. His family's fondness for old-fashioned language was the last vestige of a dalliance with the Society of Friends but, dispute with the Church of England long forgotten, recent generations of Wilsons lay alongside their ancestors in the village churchyard. He hoped to share what was left of his life with Smeed but had no wish for Smeed to follow him quickly to the grave. If they were not to lie together in death, he hoped for the company of his kin.

Eventually he broke the friendly silence.

'Jem.'

'Hmm.'

'I told thee once that I've spent my life in Al'ington. I…' He swallowed but then pressed on with his request. 'I always thought to end my days here and rest with my kin in the churchyard.'

'And?'

'If I'm away when it comes, if thou canst… if it's safe… wilt thou bring me back? Please.'

Smeed's arm snaked reassuringly around his shoulders. 'Thou hast my oath.' Although he mimicked Bish's turn of phrase, there was no mockery in the oath. He offered the promise as solemnly as Bish had offered his.

'Only if it's safe,' Bish repeated.

Smeed squeezed his shoulders.

'I mean it,' Bish pressed.

'Only if it's safe,' Smeed finally gave his word.

Paul

Without realising it, Paul Pierce had fallen into step with Giles during the mile-and-a-half walk from his home to the Walnut Tree. They often made the journey together, Bonnington being on the way from Giles's cottage. Rarely a week went by without the Blues finding an excuse for excess at their favourite inn and on this occasion they had to look no further for a justification than Gilham's impending nuptials. For reasons that Paul didn't fully understand, Dennard had insisted on organising a celebration and thrown himself into the task with gusto. Paul had been considering the situation during the walk into Aldington.

'I'm not sure a marriage of necessity is aught to celebrate,' he said as they approached the Knowl.

Giles looked across thoughtfully but said nothing.

'What?'

'Sarah wasn't with child when you wed then?'

'No, she would never hav–'

Paul began boldly but instantly realised two things about what he was going to say. The first was that he might sound naïve and the second was that he might sound critical of his friend's wife. In fact, he'd bedded plenty of women before he married but he was a man of his time, setting one standard for himself and another for his wife. He liked it that Sarah made him wait, even though he had not denied himself pleasures elsewhere while he did so.

More diffidently, he asked, 'Was Mary then?'

Giles smiled, unperturbed by either judgement or question.

'Aye. Not that I'm saying it was a marriage of necessity because we were fixing to wed when she fell. They say patience is a virtue. Can't say I'd know too much about it myself.'

Paul grinned. Giles was devoted to his young wife and his adoration was apt to become apparent when he'd had a glass or two. There was something boyish about the way he threw himself on her mercy and it wasn't hard to imagine her taking pity on him before he'd made an honest woman of her.

'Sorry,' he said. 'I didn't mean, well, you know.'

'Aye, I know. You'd be lying in the road if I thought you did.'

Paul's grin broadened. Righteous indignation could give a man an edge but he doubted even an angry Giles could put him on his back. He was sure, however, that he'd give it a damned good try.

'Besides,' Giles continued, 'You're right about Datchy. I think he'd as soon everyone just let it lie but there's no chance of Tommy giving him a quiet ride to the altar.'

'Still, better that than how Dick's carrying on.'

Giles shrugged. 'She's a hussy. He's only saying it how it is.'

The dispassionate statement took Paul by surprise. He would not have expected Giles to take such a harsh view. As he'd just demonstrated, such an insult would force them to defend their wives and he did not like to see Gilham provoked.

There was a teasing note in Giles's next question, as if he did not expect an answer and might be more interested in whether one was forthcoming than what it was.

'Have you? With her?'

'No.' Relaxed with a trusted friend, Paul let his principles slip and added, 'But I'm one of the few men in the Blues who hasn't.'

'Make that two of the few men.'

Paul laughed but his amusement faded as he regretted the shared slur. 'All that's as may be but praise where praise is due: she's a good mother to those three littl'uns. She could have thrown 'em on the parish like some I could name. I wouldn't be shouting too loud if I was Dick.'

'Or sent them to relatives,' Giles agreed with a wink.

Missing the reference, Paul frowned for an explanation.

'I heard that a young Mersham woman went to stay with a childless aunt and uncle summer before last and, after she returned home, there was a new baby in the house.'

Paul stared, incredulous at finding his friend such a storehouse of gossip. 'How do you come to know so much about it?'

'Comes from having a shop. The local ladies like to keep up with the news.'

'Dick's again?'

'So they say. The popular view is that she's loyal, albeit too free with her favours.'

'It's a pity Dick don't hold to the popular view then.'

Higgins' suspicions, and the damage they were doing to both Rhoda and himself, had become a concern for all who knew the couple. As far as Paul knew, everyone thought the accusations as groundless as he did. It made him appreciate his own rock-solid marriage more than ever. As it happened, he loved his wife dearly but, even if their partnership had been less passionate, he would still prefer stability to the emotional squall that engulfed Higgins.

When the two men reached the Walnut, they could tell from the men already spilling into the yard, and the number of horses tethered nearby, that the party was proving popular. Despite their friends' eternal eagerness to drink themselves senseless, the numbers were probably a fair reflection of the high regard in which the bridegroom was held. Although most thought him too trusting for his own good when it came to his bride, none denied his proficiency as a seaman or his dependability as a friend.

Happy to send Gilham on his way in style, Paul was pleased to see that the evening would be a success. He took the lead in elbowing their way through the crowd inside. At the centre of the throng, Gilham was leaning shyly against the bar while Dennard employed his charms in entertaining men for once. He had just reached the punchline of a joke and the roar of laughter that went up from the listeners was deafening. When he saw the two newcomers, he ushered them to Gilham's side and waved for Wraight the landlord to top up everyone's drinks. Wilson had shuffled along to make room for them and now he and Dennard looked past Paul, as if waiting for something.

'What's up?' Paul shouted.

'Where's Quacks?' Dennard shouted back.

Paul shrugged. 'No idea. I thought he was back home.' Land ten miles to the east, along with numerous part-time jobs and trading enterprises, meant they sometimes saw little of Quested between runs. He wasn't a close friend of Gilham's and Paul had not expected him to make a special journey to attend the party.

Dennard leaned closer. 'Me and Bish ran into him at Ashford market yesterday. He said he'd be in tonight. We thought he was staying with one of you.'

'Not me,' Giles said. 'I haven't seen him in more than a sennight.'

Paul suppressed a smirk. He had a good idea where Quested had been. He could hold his tongue but it would be more fun if he didn't. He trusted the four men with him and the din around them ensured that anything he said would go no further.

Dennard hadn't missed his expression. 'What?'

Paul took his tankard from Wraight's eldest daughter with a friendly smile and then shifted so that he was leaning on his right elbow, facing his friends.

'None of you boys ever wonder why a man goes all the way up to Billham Farm for his cheese when his land buts onto one of the biggest dairy farms east of the Stour?'

'He told me the herbs on the water meadows west of Cheesemans Green give the milk a special flavour.' It was hard to hear Wilson's thin rasp over the far louder voices around him but the innocent belief in his reply came across loud and clear.

'Special flavour, my arse,' Paul scoffed. 'He's had a little milkmaid tucked away up there these past six months… and you know what they say about milkmaids' hands.'

'You're having us on,' said Dennard.

'You think you're the only one who wants a bit of fun?'

'But Quacks? He's always so, well, quiet.'

'They're the ones you have to watch. In and out without you knowing they've been.'

Quested chose that moment to make his entrance, striding across the room effortlessly as the crowds parted before his bulk.

'Evening, lads.'

He did indeed sound a very satisfied man and Paul knew Dennard wouldn't be able to resist goading him. He didn't have long to wait: Quested had only just taken his regular half-and-half from the serving girl when Dennard started on him.

'So, Quacks, is it true what they say about milkmaids' hands?'

Quested choked on the heavy brew and then, wiping his lips on the back of his hand, looked around them. His eye settled on Paul.

'Never has you down for a gossip.'

Paul grinned and shrugged. Giles's talent for gossip put his in the shade but he saw no harm in a joke between friends.

'So that's a yes, is it?'

'Bugger off.'

Quested's ruddy complexion had deepened to beetroot, although Paul knew that had less to do with what they were saying than with the fact they were saying it in front of the young Miss Wraight. The girl waited on them only when her father deemed it safe and would no doubt be whisked away well before anyone started to get out of hand. For a man who'd led such a rough and ready life, Quested invariably showed an almost quaint chivalry to the fairer sex but he needn't have worried, as she'd already moved on to serve men further down the bar and there was no way that she could hear their taunts. Paul watched as his friend tried to ignore them and then had another go.

'So does she squeeze and pull, or does she pull and squeeze?'

Quested stepped forward sharply, grabbed the loose folds of cloth at Paul's crotch and twisted them. 'I'll bloody squeeze you.'

Knowing his oldest friend was well able to take a joke, Paul ran a finger over Quested's lips and spoke in an effete whisper. 'Make it a suck and you're on.'

Quested let go and shoved him away, his brusque manner failing to hide his amusement.

Paul took a sidelong glance at Wilson, curious how he would react, but there was no reading his expression. At Dennard's age he and Quested had been far from the marshes. Before ever they threw in their lot with the Blues, they'd signed up for the war in what Paul then thought was bravery but now recognised as foolishness borne of ignorance. They were on a ship bound for Spain within the week, untrained and ill-equipped, just two of a quarter of a million men in the pay of the British Army.

In those lonely, miserable years, they did things together that they'd never done — or even spoken of — since. Paul felt no shame for the meagre comfort they'd found, knowing they'd go to their graves the same firm friends they'd always been. They returned to chasing the girls as soon as they reclaimed their old lives and, before he knew it, he was courting his wife. Still, although his own choice had been so clear, it was all the same to him if others took a different path. He sometimes debated saying so to certain people but always decided it was none of his business.

Drawing himself back to the reason for the party, he offered his hand to Gilham. In a deliberate attempt to bring some cheer to what he knew could be a daunting night for such a shy man, even without the matters under discussion not half an hour before, he spoke with characteristic generosity.

'Congratulations, Datchy. It'll be the best thing you ever did, if she's half the wife Sarah's been to me.'

He was uneasy likening the bride-to-be to his beloved wife, even obliquely, but was glad he'd made the effort when Gilham seemed to grow an inch at the kind words. Paul felt the firmness of his handshake with some surprise. It was all too easy to make snap judgements about a man who couldn't utter a dozen words without falling over them but the calloused palm and muscular grip that engulfed his hand testified to a life of hard work and skilled craftsmanship.

'Thanks, P-Paul. I aim to m-make a good fist of it.'

The quiet determination in those few words tugged at Paul's heart. A man like Gilham deserved to fall in love as he had, not to pick up a woman after every other man had finished with her, along with the children they'd left in their wake. He made a conscious effort to keep any trace of pity out of his face and voice when he raised his glass to the couple's future.

Bish

Bish stumbled as he tried to keep up with Smeed's long stride out of the bar-room of the Walnut Tree. For once, his pace had nothing to do with his weak chest and everything to do with the amount of beer he'd sunk in celebrating Gilham's coming marriage. Smeed had downed twice as much and yet his progress was only a shade less bold than usual. Bish followed him to the low wall that ran along the yard, climbed up alongside with difficulty and joined him in pissing into the field beyond. The inn's privy was small and filthy, so they rarely made use of it. More often than not, they stopped on their way back to the farm but tonight they couldn't wait.

As soon as one need was satisfied, his mind skipped to another. An evening spent in contemplation of a man settling into domesticity, and all the comforts it was expected to bring, had set him yearning for his own, far less public, pleasures. As usual, he and Smeed had spent the evening with different groups of friends and now he reached clumsily for his lover's arm, prepared for him to shake it off in such a public place under a moon so bright that it might almost have been day but finding himself drawn instead into a passionate embrace. In truth, neither of them was likely to be doing much about it but that didn't stop them feeling the urge. Already unbuttoned, they groped each other eagerly.

The sound of a throat being cleared froze them momentarily, and then threw them apart.

'I never took you two for fools.'

Ransley. The authority of his voice was unmistakable. So was the fact that their behaviour was no revelation to him. Fumbling miserably with his trousers, Bish felt he should have known that Ransley knew. The man knew everything and had probably read the situation in his face the moment he nominated Smeed for nightwork. Now they'd given him the excuse he needed to kick them out of the Blues, if they were lucky, perhaps out of Aldington altogether. He stepped awkwardly down off the wall.

'It'd be best all round if you kept that out of sight.'

Ransley's voice was as calm and even as it always was. Bish saw that Smeed had recovered more quickly than himself and now challenged Ransley with customary confidence.

'You got a problem with it?'

Ransley sucked on his pipe pensively, then let blue-grey smoke trickle upwards from his mouth. 'Not as long as it's him you're doing it to. But you let on to some of them,' he nodded towards the inn, 'You'll be dead before you draw another breath.'

Smeed considered the warning, nodded and touched the brim of his hat. ''Night, Cap'n Bats.'

Bish fell in behind, humiliated by the assumption that Smeed wore the breeches in their relationship and chastened by the thought that perhaps he did, albeit not necessarily in the way that Ransley had implied. He was still stewing on it when Smeed stopped by their gate and looked enquiringly at him.

'You up to it?'

Piqued, he snapped, 'I'm up *to* it but it don't mean I'm up *for* it.'

He felt Smeed study him and then heard his laugh. 'You got the hump 'cause Bats thinks you're my boy?'

Bish glowered.

Smeed's tone softened. 'Don't matter to me what he thinks. You could've said it's the t'other way around, for all I care.' He leaned forward to add in a lust-laced whisper, 'After all, now 'n' then it is.'

Rarely one for anger at any time, Bish felt his annoyance drain away, leaving only insecurity in its wake. He let Smeed pull him close and then buried his face against the man's shoulder.

'This in't about who does what, is it?'

Bish shook his head sadly and then turned to lean on the gate. He always felt more comfortable talking while gazing out over the countryside he loved so well.

'All my life,' he began.

There was a long pause. Smeed took his hand.

'Always sick, they think me half a man at best.'

He couldn't go on, couldn't put his anxieties into words.

'And now, because of me, they think you half a woman too?'

Bish nodded.

'You know that's a lie, don't you?' There was a stern edge in the words. 'Tommy, Paul, Quacks, Cob, and Bats himself, they all rate you with the best.'

Self-pity was no more typical of Bish than anger but now it seeped through him. 'I'm a weakling, however thou turnest it.'

'Takes more courage to fight against the odds than go with the flow when you're built like a Bailey.'

The claim touched a raw nerve in Bish. He'd often envied the bulk and power of the Bailey men. He said nothing.

'You're a stronger man than I am, Jamie.'

Bish let out a bitter snort that declared he did not believe that for an instant.

'I mean it. I've always needed company and I've never been too bothered how I came by it. You don't need anyone.'

His words hurt Bish, making him feel heartless as well as weak. 'Thou art all to me,' he protested.

Smeed cut him off with a curt gesture. 'I know what I mean to you — and the others, too — but you don't *need* us. I never met the man who needed less from his fellows than you. It takes strength for a man to stand alone, let alone play the hand God dealt you.'

'That's blasphemy.'

'It's the truth.'

'He sent thee.'

Now it was Smeed who snorted, although in his case the sound was good-natured. Bish knew he did not believe the Almighty had anything to do with their meeting but not a day passed without a quiet prayer of thanks passing his own lips. There was a flirtatious lilt in his voice when he pointed out the flaw in Smeed's reasoning.

'If the Lord taketh blame for the worst, then surely He deserveth credit for the best?'

'Am I the best?' Smeed flirted back.

'Thou showest promise; that's all I can say for the present.'

Smeed pressed him against the gate, resuming the exploration he'd started outside the inn. Bish offered no resistance, welcoming the intimacy as a confirmation of his value to Smeed and perhaps, by extension, to the world. It was true that he had little need of his fellows, having resolved early in his sickly boyhood that he would not spend his life depending on others, but it was important for him to be needed, to feel he had value in spite of his infirmities.

'I know a nice little copse,' Smeed whispered in his ear.

'Thou hast been taking lessons in courting from Tommy then?'

'You can be the man,' Smeed offered hopefully. 'If you want.'

The offer put Bish's anxieties into perspective. Knowing that there were no rules or limits in their relationship, he wondered why he'd let himself worry about other people's assumptions. For the first time, he was profoundly happy and only a fool would let inconsequential doubts spoil such unexpected fulfilment.

Still, although his heart seemed to have swollen until it pressed against his ribcage, there was no response from lower down. Never having imbibed so freely, he hugged Smeed and admitted, 'I'm not up to it. That was quite a party.'

Instead, secure in Smeed's embrace, he allowed himself to be steered homewards. Denied a more physical outlet, his sensual thoughts drifted slowly towards romance. Half a mile later, he asked, 'Hast thou ever thought of marriage, Jem?'

The sudden tension in Smeed's body told him that he had taken his lover by surprise.

'No.'

One-word answers were nothing new from Smeed, who was far from talkative, but Bish heard the disquiet in this one.

'I meant not with a woman,' he said cautiously.

'That's the only kind there is.'

'I heard...' Bish wasn't sure how to voice the strange things he'd heard in certain Dover bawdy houses.

'You heard what?' Smeed sounded curious now.

Courage failing, Bish tried to back out. 'Naught.'

Becoming playful to tease an answer from him, Smeed wrestled him to the side of the road and pinned him to the bank.

'C'mon. What did you hear? I want to know.'

Bish looked up at him self-consciously, nervous of making a fool of himself over something he'd probably misunderstood and worried that bringing the subject up at all would imply that he demanded more than his lover was prepared to give.

Smeed's manner immediately grew gentler.

'What did you hear, Jamie?'

Bish swallowed. 'That there are places, chapels, where men like us can marry each other.'

As his words sank in, the humour in his lover's eyes turned to sadness. Tender knuckles brushed his cheek, protective arms closed around him and then a voice charged with emotion whispered into his ear. 'They're not what you think, Jamie. Not chapels, just molly houses, that's all.'

'But they call them chapels. I've heard them.'

189

'Aye, that they do.' There was a strange tightness in Smeed's voice. 'You'd call them blasphemy. Would your God want to be witness to half a dozen men lying together, with a score more watching at the door? Or pretending to a birth, with a doll?' His cheek pressed close to Bish's. 'That's all there is for men like us. That or a rope.'

Bish fought familiar disappointment. From the start, his few forays into the hidden world of his own kind had always brought the same disillusionment. With no desire to lean against a wall in a dark alley while a stranger thrust his way to satisfaction, much less simper around in a dress, he'd been no more than a traveller in a foreign land. He felt a stronger affinity to the best of the Blues than to any of the men he saw on seedy backstreets in the bustling harbours of Kent. Now, although never an overtly emotional man, he'd drunk enough to overcome his inhibitions and, with little practice at holding his drink, feared he might weep in sheer frustration. Such a display would embarrass him, even with only his lover to witness it, but, when he felt moisture on his cheek, he knew it had not spilled from his own eye. He held Smeed tighter, comforted by company in his disenchantment with their lot.

Several minutes passed before Smeed spoke again. When he did so, his voice had almost returned to normal, with his rough-edged accent sending a shiver down Bish's spine just as surely as it had on the day that they first met.

'I can't give you a wedding, Jamie, but I can give you my word — forsaking all others and till death us do part. May your God cast me into hell if I break it.' His tone was totally earnest, leaving Bish in no doubt that the promise was sincere, but it lifted when he added, 'And, while we're talking about it, maybe He can see to it that death don't part us any time soon.'

'Don't, Jem,' Bish chided affectionately before kissing his cheek. 'Thou hast my word too, forsaking all others and till death us do part.'

Afterwards, Bish had no idea how long they'd lain together on the grassy bank, exchanging kisses and murmured assurances of love. A wedding night with neither wedding nor consummation and yet still the most magnificent night of his life.

Datchy

D atchy's night was as sleepless as his friends', but his thoughts were far less peaceful. Even an owl's hoot outside sounded like a taunt. Just as the bird would swoop silently on a mouse in the field, so Fran had swooped on him. All his life, he'd striven to be like the owl but, once again, his role was that of the mouse.

How could he feel trapped when he had been neither deceived by Fran's seduction nor blind to the consequences of giving in to her? If he was ensnared, it was only by a kind heart and sense of duty. His life had been transformed by his stepfather and, now he had the means to do the same, what right had he to turn his back on her children? Still, he had thought that doing the right thing would bring more satisfaction than it did. Thinking about what lay ahead just made him sick with nerves.

A sudden cramp down his right leg put an end to his musings. The spasm in his thigh muscles drew the leg up sharply and forced a grunt of pain from his lips. He shifted his weight slowly, trying not to wake the man beside him. Dennard muttered something and then threw an arm over his chest. The misdirected embrace brought a smile to his face, as he recalled a memorable coach journey a few years before. Packed in like sardines, they were all seamen bound for ships at anchor in Harwich. As was the custom, they doubled up in whatever beds they could buy cheapest. He shared a large double with two other old hands, all three of them dropping instantly into sound sleep and prepared to turn discreet blind eyes to whatever state their companions might awake in. Their peaceful slumber was interrupted by a scene on the landing outside their room. He stumbled out, bleary-eyed, only to find a youngster in tears and a man desperately trying to silence him. Allegations of the kind the lad was making could easily see the old salt in the pillory and Datchy had no qualms in taking the man's part. In all likelihood, it was a genuine mistake but, if not, the greenhorn might as well get used to it before he was a hundred miles from England. On most ships, he would find a civil refusal served him far better than a public protest. Only on land did people insist on acting as if a man did not have the same drives as any other male of its species; at sea, pragmatism reigned supreme.

It was more unusual, but by no means unknown, for friends to share a bed so close to home. Although surprised by Dennard's offer, he was not in the least wary of accepting it. He knew that his friend's impulses were firmly focused on the fairer sex and fulfilled too frequently for a substitute to be required. The offer was merely a part of the preparations for his bachelorhood to end on a high note. With his mother's views on the demon drink voiced loudly and often, no good friend would send him home after an eve-of-wedding party at which he was supposed to down every drink given him, a duty that he performed admirably until the last few began to come straight back up again.

His spirits rose a little as he remembered the party, or at least parts of it. Before the event, he'd tried to talk Dennard out of organising it: he was embarrassed by the circumstances, and by his bride-to-be, but even more by the idea of being the centre of attention and having everyone make lewd jokes about what he had done or would be doing. Afterwards, he was glad that his friend had blithely ignored him. Never had he been so drunk on land but, inhibitions — and stammer — cast to the wind, he loved every minute of it. Now, wondering if he would sober up in time for the wedding ceremony, he raised a hand experimentally to see if his muscle control had improved since his friend helped him into bed. It seemed promising until he tried to move the arm lying across his chest and dropped it as he did so.

Dennard stirred and grunted. A few seconds passed before he spoke, voice heavy with sleep and slurred from a night's drinking.

'You all right there?'

Still buoyed up by his party and glad to have company, Datchy did not intend to presume further on the friendship. He kept his reply brief.

'Aye.'

If he thought Dennard would be put off so easily, he was wrong. He heard his friend shift to get more comfortable for talk.

'What's amiss?'

'Naught.'

'Worried for tomorrow?'

Today, Datchy thought. The night was half gone and it was already his wedding day.

'Aye,' he conceded.

'There's no need to listen to Dick, you know.'

Higgins had seized his last chance to try to sway Datchy from his course. It was Dennard who insisted he hold his tongue, saying that the party was no place to be criticising the bride-to-be.

'I know.'

'It's no secret that this is no love match. But it seems to me a man like you has his reasons for what he does.'

'The others think me a fool.' He was surprised at how fluently the words flowed from his mouth, wondering if speaking was always so easy for other people.

'Some do. I was with them at the start, thought you'd got caught out right quick. There's more to it though, in't there?'

Datchy said nothing.

'How old were you when your old lady got wed?'

So, some at least had guessed his motives. It was also no secret that he'd been born on the wrong side of the blanket. He might be frustrated by his diffidence as a man but it was nothing compared with the painful shyness he'd suffered as an illegitimate child. His stammer then had not been a brief hesitation on a few sounds but rather a series of delays so pronounced that listeners tired of waiting even before he despaired of making himself understood. And then there had been the bed-wetting, way past an age when it was expected. There was a long pause before he replied.

'Seven.'

'And the old boy was good to you, wasn't he?'

Datchy felt a rush of nostalgia as he remembered how William Hill's kind and patient supervision slowly built his self-confidence. It was work, not talk, that brought them close. Datchy learned his carpentry skills from his step-father and he loved the silent hours they spent side-by-side in the tiny workshop behind their cottage. Although they spoke little, talking to other people slowly became easier and finally even the bed-wetting stopped.

'Aye.'

'There's no shame in wanting to do the same for those littl'uns.'

Datchy was silent.

'Any man can fall for a pretty face and tell the world he's in love. What you're doing takes far more character.'

'Could be it's easy to do but hard to live with.'

'Ah.' Dennard's tone revealed he'd grasped what was ailing his friend. 'Fran's all woman. She'll feed you, clothe you and keep you warm of a night. Matches that started out a lot more promising have left a man colder than you'll be. Take my word for it.'

Datchy's cheeks burned at the intimate knowledge that made his friend so sure. Dennard was more discerning now but he'd worked his way through the likes of Fran Furner when he was barely a man. In truth, few in the Blues who wanted the pleasure hadn't had it. It wasn't beyond the bounds of possibility that some of them had fathered the children whom Datchy worried for.

Dennard's soft laugh came through the darkness. 'And don't you be stewing on that. I've had Dick's intended…' There was a pause, as if he were remembering something, and then he added, '*Before* she was his intended, and half the others' women too. But you be keeping that between us.'

Datchy was faintly surprised about Rhoda, sure she was as obsessed with Higgins as he was with her, but suspected the lapse had taken place during one of their numerous estrangements. Plenty of men fell victim to Dennard's charm in one way or another, so it was small wonder if a sad and lonely woman succumbed. Although he would never repeat what he'd just heard, it was a comfort to know that many men's wives had secrets. He turned onto his side and pulled the covers closer around himself.

'Thanks for the party.'

'No need for thanks — I had a fine time.'

'Me too.'

'You liked the girl? I wasn't so sure about that.'

Datchy smiled. Yes, he had liked the girl and her appearance was well-timed. Earlier and he might have baulked at performing in front of a hundred men; later and he might have found the spirit willing but the flesh weak.

'Aye. I liked the girl. I always liked that one.'

It was the pikey's daughter from Brabourne Down.

'I know. I saw how you looked at her.'

Datchy was swamped by a wave of camaraderie almost as strong as his earlier sexual ecstasy. It felt good to have a friend devote so much time and effort to his happiness. If ever Dennard settled down, his wife would be a lucky woman.

'No wedding plans for you then?'

Dennard's answer was so slow in coming that Datchy had given up on it when it did.

'No man knows the future. I haven't met my bride yet. That's all I'll say.'

The thirteenth of September dawned brightly. The sun was already well up in a cloudless sky when Datchy felt Dennard shaking his shoulder. He rolled over irritably, feeling that he had only fallen asleep moments earlier. In reality, he'd dozed off soon after the conversation with Dennard and had slept soundly for nearly seven hours. Skimming shallow waves of sleep, he dreamed of mermaids on a hazy vision of a tropical island, based only on what he'd heard from sailors on the docks. It was hot, hotter even than the hottest summer day Datchy could remember, and a particularly beautiful mermaid held up a shell and began to pour cool water over him, except that when the water reached his skin, it was freezing cold.

He jolted awake in confusion, finding the blanket he clutched soaked and Dennard standing over him with a pan of water. He shoved his friend backwards roughly and shook his dripping hair. The movement set his brain spinning inside his skull. He lunged to the right and shot a cascade of watery vomit over the stone floor.

'B-b-b-bloody b-b-b-bastard!' His heart sank to find his stammer back, made worse than ever by his teeth chattering.

Dennard laughed and set the pan down. 'Can't have the bride waiting for the groom. Anyhow, we best allow plenty of time for you to m-m-make y-y-your v-v-vows.'

'Go f-f-fu…' Datchy bit his lip and tried again. 'F-fu… Hell, go and have a roll!'

Still laughing, Dennard squatted and rested a hand on his shoulder. 'You all right this morning?'

Hearing the concern, Datchy relaxed. 'Aye. Thanks.'

Dennard squeezed his shoulder and then went off to rummage for something they could eat. Datchy watched him while he pulled on his trousers. The ancient hovel was a mess, and breakfast was likely to be plain and stale, but he could think of nowhere better to spend the night before his wedding. Friends like Dennard were rarer than hens' teeth. Pushing aside the suspicion that he had dreamed of mermaids because they lured men overboard from the safety of their ships into treacherous seas, he steeled himself to face the business of the day.

By the time they set out southwards, bound for Bilsington, the nausea had receded while his stomach battled the heavy bread and fatty bacon Dennard had dished up. By the time they passed the priory, his brain no longer pulsed against bone and he began to notice the birdsong echoing through the woods on either side of the road. A magpie cackled at its mate, sending a green woodpecker swooping off through the trunks with a screech of alarm. He no longer felt alarmed by his own prospects, his nocturnal anxieties fading in the light of day. Never having harboured romantic dreams, he forsook nothing to take Fran as his wife. He'd seen her with her children often enough, a kind and loving mother, and he had no reason to think she'd be any less tolerant and caring towards her husband. With no expectation of her nagging or neglecting him, things might be much worse.

He saw his mother peering anxiously out of the front door as soon as they came within sight of home. Face filled with relief, she ran to the gate and began scolding him almost before he was close enough to hear her. No one envied him his mother, just as no one envied him his wife. He and Dennard grinned at each other: his friend's mother was a good deal quieter than his own but they were as bad as each other when it came to lecturing their sons. Now he submitted to her fussing, folding himself into the tin bath and then dressing in his freshly pressed Sunday best. Dennard lounged about throughout, passing soap, brushes or facetious remarks as the mood took him.

Datchy was glad to have a friend at his side during a day that meant far more to his womenfolk than it did to him. Since his hasty betrothal, his mother and his future wife had busied themselves with the countless preparations all women seemed to think essential for a wedding. They spoke to him only to demand money or instruct him to acquire items they had been unable to procure. Unconcerned by his minor role in the proceedings, he was pleased to see them getting along so well. He'd wondered how his mother would take his news, no stranger to the disgrace of illegitimate motherhood but now defensive of her hard-won respectability, but she seemed happy to offer the same chance to her prospective daughter-in-law that she had found in her late husband, something that relieved but did not surprise him. Under a hard shell developed against a tough life, she was a kind woman: were that not so, he would not be as devoted to her as he was.

She was still fussing over him, dabbing at his hair with damp fingers and tightening the cravat that he had just loosened, when Dennard announced that they should be making tracks for the church. Only then did Datchy's nerves return with a vengeance. Struck with an urgent need to urinate, he made a dash for the privy but the liquid he passed would barely have filled a thimble. He stood in the garden for a few moments, trying to collect himself. People got married all the time, he reasoned, many in circumstances like his own. Life would go on: the only difference was that he would return to a different house each evening after work and give a chunk of his earnings to a different woman. He could still work away from home and he could still do nightwork. He could still bed other women, if he chose, although he saw no reason to think that would happen any more often after marriage than it had before.

Dennard leaned out of the kitchen window.

'C'mon, Datchy. He who hesitates…'

'Only f-fools rush in…' Datchy mumbled the retort to himself, realising that he'd decided his future in a few seconds on a dark night when he was half-drunk. He wondered how that could have happened, so far from impulsive as he was, but then discarded the doubts. Striding boldly indoors, he kissed his mother and followed Dennard into the lane.

A few minutes later, he walked through the lych-gate and into the church, ready for the minister to bind him to a woman he barely knew for the rest of his days. He stopped, stunned, at the back of the church. Neither he nor Fran had much by way of family and so he'd expected a modest gathering to listen, subdued, while he went through the motions of paying for his sin. Instead, almost every pew was full on both sides of the aisle. Scanning the faces, he saw his whole life arrayed before him. It seemed as if half the local population had turned out, not to mention a fair proportion of the Blues. All of the mariners were there, many with wives and children he'd never even met. In the last of the groom's pews, he recognised Ransley's unique figure. Beside him stood his wife, arms cradling her ninth baby, flanked by their other children in order of age.

'Good turnout,' Dennard said in a low voice.

'Aye,' he agreed. 'You have to pay 'em m-much?'

'A man can be too modest, you know.'

'W-what w-would you know about it?'

Dennard jabbed him lightly in the ribs, then shoved him down the aisle before he could retaliate. He didn't feel modest at that moment. What he felt was some pride and a lot of happiness in having built the life he had from such inauspicious beginnings. It was then that the satisfaction of sharing that began to sink in. For the first time, he looked forward to married life with anticipation outweighing trepidation.

Looking back later, it was as if time sped up at that instant. He waded to the front of the church through a sea of Christian good wishes and dirty jokes that had no place in the House of God. There was no agonised wait for the bride, with the organist starting to play almost as soon as the minister took his place. Even the ceremony flew past, the minister tactfully prompting him for agreement rather than requiring him to repeat the declarations.

In a whirl of a day, only one thing stood out clearly in memory: the sight of his bride coming down the aisle.

One of the things he had been ordered to acquire was a bolt of silk cloth. That in itself would not have been too difficult but his mother was insistent that it should be sea-green, for his trade. Oddly enough, he rather liked the fanciful notion, and so he did not object, but the demand presented difficulties even to a man with his contacts and cost him three times what he might have paid Ransley for a bolt in another shade.

All such prosaic considerations faded away when he saw what the two women had done with it. Fran was barely recognisable, swathed in a dress that hugged her plump breasts in the skilfully gathered silk and then encased her shapely body in a smooth sheath. Her russet hair, as shiny as the best turned-out horse at the county fair, was piled high and edged with dainty ringlets. Behind her, wearing a flounced dress and a huge smile, Delia clasped a spray of white roses to match the bouquet in her mother's hand. She was escorted by her two small brothers, Jimmy and Willy, who looked far too solemn for their matching silk shirts.

In the groom's eyes, the bride looked like a fine society lady. If the fashions she'd copied were not the latest, and the presence of her three little bastards might appal their betters, he neither knew nor cared. If he'd been ashamed of her at his eve-of-wedding party, he was ashamed of himself for it on their big day. She had done him proud, and he valued that. When the minister gave him permission, he drew her into his arms and did something that he had not yet done: he kissed her.

The kiss might lack love or passion but it was filled with appreciation and respect. As he held his bride, Datchy began to understand Dennard's reassurances. He might never know romance but he would have a dutiful wife at his side. Life would not be perfect and yet it could still be good. He kissed her again, then put his arm around her waist and swept her off to their wedding breakfast.

From that day forward, she was his wife and her children were his children: he would brook no comment on her past or their parentage. Something told him that his friends would not expect him to.

Quacks

A cheery blaze crackled halfway up the chimney in the Giles family's sitting room. As a matter of fact, it was really their only downstairs room unless you counted the tiny lean-to kitchen out back. Upstairs, two bedrooms were crammed under the low roof, one for the parents and one for their two little daughters. It wasn't that Cob was a poor provider but rather that he and his lovely young wife were dedicated to making a success of his cobbler's shop up in the village. He invested whatever money they didn't need for food in the best tools and hides, while she steadfastly insisted that their humble home was just perfect for her and the girls. Modestly successful in his own enterprises, Quacks would be the last man to argue with their priorities.

He drained his glass and then belched appreciatively. There was little to beat an evening in the company of good friends in a home kept as beautifully as Mary Giles kept hers. She waited on him and Pierce attentively while they demolished a supper of cold pork and apple pie, then acted the good wife and disappeared into the kitchen while they moved on to a half-anker of brandy they'd bought at the Tap. He was glad they'd decided to make a night of it after Gilham's wedding, especially as the alternative was a chaotic evening in Bonnington with their combined hordes of children. With no need of husbands getting underfoot, their wives at least had the benefit of Pierce's comfortable bed while they themselves would have to make do with Giles's floor.

Quacks watched Giles walk over to the fire and sink to his knees in front of it with the exaggerated caution of the inebriated. Ransley had cut the brandy generously for them, leaving it well over-proof. For a slight man, Giles could put away a prodigious amount of beer but he was susceptible to spirits, usually becoming both garrulous and amorous as his blood turned to alcohol.

Pierce grinned from the far side of the hearth.

'Been sniffing the corks again.'

Giles was oblivious to their amusement, concentrating intently on the large log he was trying to push into the already full grate. A shower of half-burned fragments fell from the fire just as the door from the kitchen opened. His wife surveyed the scene in dismay, then rushed in and pushed him aside.

'Charlie Giles!' she upbraided him while sweeping the glowing embers from the rug with her foot. 'You'll burn this cottage down before you're done.'

Giles crawled back to her, struggled to his feet and put an arm around her waist. 'Don't be like that, missis. I was just getting the place nice and warm for my friends.'

'It's already as hot as Hades,' she snapped. 'Are they devils?'

Quacks watched placidly. Mary was a fine woman, only given to a sharp tongue when her husband deserved it, as he did then. The risk of a fire was not to be taken lightly, although in fact he and Pierce were sober enough to make sure it didn't come to that.

Giles's mind had wandered from her scolding to her other attributes. She slapped his right hand away from her buttock only to find his left on her breast. Her cheeks flushed prettily as she struggled to free herself from his advances. Quacks looked away, embarrassed for her when Giles's enthusiasm began to manifest itself more obviously, but Pierce's grin only broadened. It was odd, Quacks had to admit. He thought nothing of watching a man, married or not, take a woman over a table in the Walnut Tree but it didn't seem decent when the man was pawing his own wife in his own home.

Mary was winning the battle and finally threw her tipsy husband off. She ran for the door before he could grab her again, calling back in a half-hearted attempt at anger, 'Behave yourself or you'll pass the winter sleeping in the pigsty.'

'Just a kiss,' Giles pleaded as the door slammed in his face. He weaved forlornly back to his chair, rearranging his groin as he did so. He sounded puzzled when he added, 'We haven't got a pigsty.'

'You're a dirty bugger, Cob,' Pierce said with a wink to Quacks. 'What man feels his own wife in front of his friends? It's disgusting, if you ask me.'

Giles said nothing, dejectedly caressing his glass.

Pierce's mouth had just opened to comment when there was an indistinct thud at the front door. Quacks saw his friend tense even as his own body froze. It was past midnight and few people were about. The sound might have been made by an animal but most wild ones would be too timid and most dogs would be put off by the scent of the big old mongrel chained up out the back. Unfortunately, it was stone deaf and would sleep peacefully through the arrival of a troop of preventive officers.

Giles's ears had heard the noise but it was a few seconds before his brain caught up. 'More visitors?' he slurred cheerfully, hauling himself back onto unsteady legs.

Already standing, Quacks shoved Giles back into his chair and moved to one side while Pierce prepared to throw the door open.

When he did so, there was no one in sight.

They waited in silence, listening for any sound that might betray a trap. Quacks held his breath, then motioned Pierce to do the same. The fire crackled twice and Giles wheezed behind them. He frowned, then caught the sound again: laboured breathing outside. He stepped forward, mindful of the risk but unafraid, and looked around cautiously. It was not until his third sweep that he saw something huddled on the road. Glancing down, he saw a short branch just beyond the threshold. Unable to reach the door, the fallen man must have thrown it in a last attempt to get help.

Quacks was at his side in eight long strides, kneeling beside him and turning him carefully. The night was too dark to see the face but Quacks' fingers felt the stickiness of blood coating the hair and skin. He gathered the wounded man into his arms and managed to regain his feet with support from Pierce. He went quickly inside and set the casualty down on the rug, a cushion under his head. Even with firelight and candles, it wasn't easy to identify him. Quacks thought he knew but it wasn't until he wiped the mud from the right hand that he was sure. He raised it a few inches, drawing Pierce's attention to the missing top portion of the second finger.

'Christ Almighty,' Pierce muttered.

Whether it was the bloody wreck on the floor or the draught of cold night air Quacks didn't know but Giles had sobered up fast. His face was ashen as he stared down at the mangled flesh.

'Preventive men?' he asked no one in particular.

His wife came back in at that moment, presumably having heard the door. She swayed at the sight that met her eyes, leaning instinctively on her husband. The arm he slipped around her waist then was filled with strength and reassurance in place of the lust she had so recently escaped.

He kissed her cheek and said, 'Set Quacks up, will you, missis?'

She nodded, drew a deep breath and set about obeying him.

Quacks stripped off Higgins' coat and boots, then ran his hands over every inch of his body. 'Broke, I'd say,' he murmured as he explored one arm. 'Broke… cracked…'

And so the catalogue went on. When Mary returned with rags and warm water, he began the long task of cleaning up their friend. The clock on the mantelpiece marked the seconds with solemn ticks. It struck the hour twice before Quacks was done.

Pierce and Giles, who had sat in shocked silence throughout, helped him lift Higgins onto a makeshift bed that Mary had made up in the corner of the room.

'Will he live?' Giles asked sadly.

Quacks tucked the covers around the wounded man and felt his forehead. Not surprisingly, he was cold from shock but it was too early to know if a septic fever would set in.

'God knows. Who in the name of the Devil would do this?'

The savage beating bore none of the hallmarks of the Coast Blockade and, in any case, they hadn't encountered any preventive men since the run at Sandgate. Ransley's strategy seemed to be delivering just what they wanted: profitable, peaceful business. Local people could afford a few luxuries and tradesmen of all kinds prospered, as the Blues threw their illicit earnings around. Even the Blockademen were in work, when four-fifths of their shipmates were discharged with no prospects. As far as Quacks could see, everyone did well out of the trade.

A faint whisper came from the grotesquely swollen lips. Quacks leaned closer, until Higgins' shallow breathing tickled his ear. He sat back and looked at his friends. 'He wants Miss Bailey.'

The estate on which Rhoda Bailey worked was little more than a mile away, at the far end of the village. With servants' quarters short in the main house, she had a room in one of the lodges but calling on her in the middle of the night would still put her job, and what was left of her reputation, at risk. Nevertheless, although Higgins was unlikely to know if she was beside him or not, it might be her last opportunity to see him alive.

'I'll take Mary along to call for her,' Giles said and went through to the kitchen, closing the door behind him.

Quacks and Pierce had to wait nearly an hour before the front door opened again, the tense silence between them a world away from the friendly quietness they'd shared during the evening. Quacks spent the time reflecting on why anyone would want to beat a man like Higgins to the edge of death. Although given to contemplation, he'd never had reason to dwell on Higgins' character but now he found no answers in his memories. Higgins was volatile and lusty but his faults were balanced by courage and wit. He might easily pick up some bruises in a brawl, or from a jealous husband in his younger days, but Quacks had never seen him do anything to earn the brutal assault needed to inflict his present injuries. They knew men capable of delivering such a lesson, although Higgins was a skilled fighter and it would probably take two or three to overpower him so completely.

Giles came through the door first, his wife behind him and with an arm around Rhoda. When the women stepped into the candlelight, things began to fall into place. A bruise coloured Rhoda's left eye, the lids of which were swollen shut. Tears had reddened the other.

'The fool never struck her?' Pierce asked in disbelief.

Giles gave a slight nod.

Quacks sighed. It wasn't the crime that shocked — they knew many men who beat their women far beyond the single blow that had left its mark on Rhoda — it was the damned fool choice of victim. The moment his fist connected, Higgins must have known he'd pay a high price for his jealousy.

Rhoda stood by Higgins' inert body, leaning on Mary and shaking with silent sobs.

Giles leaned on the wall by the fireplace. 'Couldn't get much sense out of her. Seems they argued out past the church, then she ran into

Rob and John on their way back from the White Horse.' He shrugged.

The rest was easy to guess. They resumed their vigil, prepared to wait for as long as it took for the girl to recover.

Mary bustled around, taking Rhoda's coat, finding her a chair and then plying her with tea into which she splashed a generous measure of brandy from the tub on the table. Eventually Rhoda calmed down and sat beside her betrothed, her fingers resting tenderly on the back of his hand, clear of the splints on the broken fingers. When she spoke, it was of her own accord.

'I never meant this to happen. I wouldn't have told them but, well.'

Pierce picked up his chair by the back rail and set it down a few feet from her. He sat backwards on it, elbows resting on the rail, and spoke reassuringly.

'It's not your fault, girl. Dick's been carrying on something alarming for months. Any man amongst us would know as soon as he saw your face.'

She sniffed. 'But I was angry with him. I was so tired of him going on. I wished someone would teach him a lesson.'

'Wishing don't beat a man nigh on to death.'

Quacks was touched by his friend's concern for the girl. It wasn't her fault that Higgins saw disloyalty behind every innocent remark or changed plan, any more than it was her fault that her kin were about as brutal as men came. Nonetheless, he wished she'd managed one or both sides better. He studied her profile, evaluating her in a way he had not done before. The right side of her face was unmarked and it was beautiful: eyelashes long and coal-black, nose straight and delicate, lips full and red. Perhaps if she were not so tempting, Higgins would not be so convinced that men were tasting her charms every time his back was turned.

Quacks had no intimate knowledge of Rhoda's private affairs but the only gossip he'd heard related to her relationship with Higgins, the bastard child she'd borne openly by him and the childless aunt suddenly blessed with a baby. He shook his head silently, never having known that two people so much in love could bring such misery to each other. With his own marriage as placid as his nature, he could not imagine living at the centre of such a maelstrom.

'The past few months, it's been one row after another.' She dabbed her eyes with a small handkerchief edged in home-knitted lace. 'First those two boys from up at the Cross and then the one from Lodge Court. I hardly knew them.' She looked at Pierce in bewilderment. 'Then Tommy — I hadn't even spoken to him since May Day.'

'I know,' Pierce soothed.

'Today was worse than ever. I think Mr Gilham's wedding must have set him off because it started after we passed the church when he was walking me home. It was about Jem Smeed this time.' Her eyes widened with disbelief. 'Can you imagine that? He's not even int're–'

Quacks smiled grimly as she stopped short of something that was never discussed, although he doubted he was the only one who had suspicions about the rising star within their number. He supposed a woman with Rhoda's charms soon spotted when a man was not susceptible to them. He hoped she had also stopped short of telling Higgins why Smeed was ruled out.

'What did you tell him?' Pierce prompted.

'I said Mr Smeed's a gentleman, not like him. I said, well,' she paused.

'Yes?'

'I said it was ridiculous, that he might as well say I was spooning with the Hog.'

Pierce's face remained earnest but Quacks couldn't keep the smirk from his own. When he glanced across at Giles, he saw that his friend was failing just as badly. Rhoda could not have picked a worse thing to say if she'd tried. Thinking of Hogben touching her was enough to tip Higgins over the edge in his recent frame of mind and, however tragic the consequences, the image of his rage was irresistibly comic.

'Then he hit me,' she said in a small voice. 'He *hit* me.' Her outrage flared briefly, until she looked again at how the blow had been avenged. 'Will he live, Mr Quested?'

Quacks shifted forward in his seat. 'I can't say, Miss. A Bailey boy knows how to give a beating, that's certain sure, but Dick's young and fit.'

Giles cleared his throat. 'Does he have something to live for?'

One of the things that bound the three friends together was their shared pride in their work and love for their families. Even so, although Quacks cared for his own wife Jane as deeply as Giles cared for Mary, he would never ask such a personal and romantic question.

He stared at the floor as they waited for Rhoda's answer.

'Oh, yes.' She shuffled her chair closer to the bed. 'Seeing him like this, I know how awful it would be to lose him. He said we must set a date for the wedding, then he'd stop being jealous. I said he must stop carrying on first, then I'd set a date.' She sobbed again and leaned over the unconscious man. 'A year from tonight, Dick, that's the date. You have to be there, you can't leave me now.'

Mary stroked the girl's hair comfortingly. 'What man wouldn't come back for you, my girl? We'll do all we can for him and let the good Lord do the rest.'

'A year from tonight, Dick,' Rhoda whispered again, as though repeating her wish could make it come true.

Datchy

Datchy swiped his left hand across his streaming forehead, then lifted his right from the steering oar for just as long as it took to wipe the palm on his thigh. Glancing anxiously up at the sky, he cursed their bad luck with the weather. The stifling summer days had ended in storms every other day for weeks but that night the humidity soared without bringing a drop of rain.

He'd spent a rare day off helping Higgins extend his pheasant pens, taking as payment a bundle of beech poles from the previous winter's coppicing to make legs for some chairs he was working on. He'd done the lion's share of the work when he saw how Higgins' rheumatism was playing up with all the rain. Although he had little time for men who hit their women, even he doubted that Higgins deserved the beating he'd received: the Baileys stopped short of crippling him, but left him with bones that would remind him of his transgression throughout every cold and wet spell for the rest of his life.

They'd watched the thunderheads build while they laboured, confident that their nightwork would be shrouded by a curtain of heavy rain. Fate seemed to toy with his nerves when the storm, which looked set to break at dusk, was still brewing a full four hours later. A trickle of sweat rolled down his spine and into the cleft between his buttocks. He shifted position, then scratched at the sore skin where his coarse trousers chafed. He and Smeed had waited as long as they dared but, in the end, it was the tide that dictated their schedule. The only blessing was that the thick clouds obscured the moon but some of its diffuse rays crept through to cast shadows — faint but enough to give a preventive man a target.

A thud came from the bows. One of the oarsmen, no doubt as uncomfortable in the heat as he was himself, had let his oar bang against the hull when he shifted on his bench.

'Keep it down,' Datchy muttered.

'Hoist a bloody sail, then.'

The retort was muttered, too, but he heard it clearly enough. Their galley was spritsail rigged, with two masts of equal length, but the sails were stowed and he had no intention of hoisting them. A taunt in Quids' deep rumble made a reply unnecessary.

'Would you have him hoist a bloody flag while he's at it?'

'Bugger you.'

'You should be so lucky.'

A soft plop followed Quids' words as, without his usual hawking, he jettisoned a load of spit over the side.

Behind them, the lugger they'd unloaded was under way but making slow progress in the calm before the storm. She was carrying almost full sail but there was little wind for the canvas to catch. Datchy watched her drift with the current, expecting she'd need her oars to reach open waters where the conditions might be better. Before the night was out, she would surely have more wind than she wanted.

Turning his attention forward, he saw Smeed's boat beached and half-empty. As pleased as he was to see his friends so close to safety, he was sorry to see them at all. His boat was a quarter of a mile from their Dungeness landing site and, by rights, the beach should have been cloaked by the squall that had failed them so dismally. Many was the time mariners had prayed for a storm to hold off until they reached a safe harbour and he saw the irony in his hopes for foul weather on a run.

The oarsmen pulled steadily, sending the boat slipping swiftly and almost silently towards the surf. Datchy looked uneasily along the foreshore, first to the north, where the long expanse of Romney Sand and Dymchurch Wall separated them from the Kent Blockade's base in Folkestone, and then to the west, where the marshes made an effective barrier against the Sussex Blockade's base only ten miles away in Rye. Ransley's sources had brought no news of major operations planned for that night, and so he did not expect a threat from either direction. No, the risk came from the station on Dungeness Point. Their landing site at North Land was carefully chosen to fall between the two sentinels at the lighthouse and the Great Stone. There should have been no way they could be spotted but the unexpectedly clear conditions left them badly exposed. The minutes crept slowly by, marked only by the sweep of the oars.

Smeed's crew shoved their empty boat back out into the surf and struck northwards for secure moorings beyond the Warren. A dozen men who lived along the coast from Romney to Dymchurch kept a watchful eye over the small fleet of smacks, galleys, luggers and cutters, ensuring they were watertight and moving them between moorings when rumours came of preventive men checking the area for illegal vessels or suspicious loads.

Ashore, the last of the first team of tubmen shouldered their loads and scurried away over the mudflats. The advantage that Denge Beach offered in remoteness was partially offset by the vast expanse of foreshore to be traversed before men reached solid ground navigable with a rig but, as they were landing only eighty tubs, Ransley opted instead for using tubmen without carts. The fighting party maintained its position, encircling the trodden sand that marked the first half of the night's work. The second score of tubmen were hidden amongst the low dunes, delaying their appearance until there was a load for them to shift.

Another trickle of sweat dribbled from Datchy's hairline, traced its way over his left temple and down his cheek, then fell from his jaw onto the back of the hand he rested on his thigh. He did not envy the oarsmen, let alone the tubmen facing a ten-mile walk with a load swung fore-and-aft across their shoulders.

His reflections were cut short when the beach finally drew close. He jumped into the water while it was yet thigh-high, stifling the gasp that the sudden coldness brought to his lips, and began to push while his men were still rowing. As soon as the keel hit the sand, others joined him in the water and sped the load into the shallows. Barely clearing the surf before they were surrounded by eager tubmen, his men drew slightly to one side to take a breather before they made for the Warren in their friends' wake. Quids spewed a treacly mess of well-chewed tobacco onto the wet sand at his feet and began to prepare another wad, and a lad from the crew of his fishing smack turned his back to send a stream of piss nonchalantly into the waves, while their companions took pinches of snuff from a box that a man of middle years offered round.

Datchy was pleased to see their ease in the midst of an operation, minds fixed on their objective while they worked but swift to exploit the chance for a moment's rest. He gave a mock salute in response to a wave from Pierce, who was supervising the loading in one of Ransley's rare absences. Too far off to see clearly in the gloom, he could just about make out Sam Bailey's towering figure with the batmen. He knew he wasn't alone in being exhilarated by a big landing, when hundreds of men came together with almost military precision, but sometimes a modest run with a few friends was even better. There was enough risk to set the butterflies fluttering in his stomach but not enough to make him doubt he'd live to see the sun rise on another day.

The tubmen were on form, collecting the tied pairs of tubs at a rate of knots. Datchy carried no timepiece but reckoned twenty men were loaded and clear in less than a minute apiece. Pierce helped to launch the boat, then watched as they made their way into open water before he rejoined the fighting party, which was still in position when Datchy turned his boat northwards.

Afterwards, he could not say how long they had been rowing when he heard the first shot. Job done, or so he thought, he'd had no reason to track the time. Possibly it was minutes, or perhaps mere seconds, but when he twisted to look back at the landing site, he saw the fighting party holding off a pair of sentinels. Jumbled emotions ran through him: disappointment at an easy night spoiled, frustration at the stagnant weather that had denied them the protection they expected, anger at the preventive men interfering once again but, through all that, faith that Bailey would send the men packing, alive but with their tails between their legs. He turned back to his men and opened his mouth to urge them on. Before he could speak, another shot rang out.

'C'mon–' he began, then stopped.

Quids was staring wide-eyed at him, gripping the oar with white knuckles. As he stared back, tobacco-stained saliva flooded over the man's chin. A moment later, Quids slumped forward. All hands sat frozen, as if time itself had stopped, until, knowing that their salvation rested with him, Datchy snapped to with a start.

'Pull!' he shouted far too loud. 'Put some distance between us and the murdering bastards!'

Harsh words, and probably the wrong words as he didn't even know if Quids was dead. All he knew was, with no means to fight, they must fly. Alone, his anger might have sent him running towards a preventive man with a knife in his hand but, with a crew depending on him, he could not afford the luxury of rage.

Only when he was sure that they were out of sight of the beach did he clamber over to Quids and check his breathing. Life had not yet departed but, unless he missed his guess, it soon would. He looked up at his crew and saw his despair mirrored in their eyes.

'Strike out for Folkestone,' he said, his voice cracking with sorrow. 'He may yet see home.'

That was every sailor's hope in adversity, to survive long enough to see home one last time. Throughout the journey, he cradled Quids against his chest, pressing a rolled-up handkerchief against the wound to staunch the flow of blood as he'd seen Quested do. The young lad who had pissed so casually into the sea not an hour earlier glumly took the steering oar, while the others hauled as hard as they had on the outward leg. The boat, now empty, skimmed over the water. As if things weren't bad enough, heavy drops from the leaden sky heralded the arrival of the overdue storm — too late to do them any good.

At last, when the night was at its darkest, Datchy delivered Quids into his wife's arms and watched helplessly with her while death claimed him. The worst night of his life finally came to an end when he broke the news to Smoker, just returned by land from Romney after restoring the first boat to its hiding place. The news was not the only thing that he broke with his words; the hearty fisherman seemed to shrink as he took it in and Datchy knew that his character would be forever altered by the loss of his old friend.

Jem

The back room at the Bourne Tap was filled with smoke and noise from the dozen men crammed around the ash table that half-filled the space by itself. Jem Smeed leaned back to let Eliza Ransley refill his tankard from the large pewter jug she carried. She was an imposing woman — tall and handsome like her kin, shrewd and crafty like her husband — but few in the Blues seemed to realise the extent of her influence over their activities. He nodded his thanks as she expertly took his beer within a hair's breadth of the brim. She served as well as any woman he'd seen and drank faster than any he'd known. While Ransley took no more than half a pint of the weakest brew on offer, his wife downed geneva like water and yet Jem had never seen her the worse for it: she was often vulgar and raucous but never out of control. Her fondness for the company of men was evident, as was their response to her mature but sultry looks, but she soon set straight any admirer who dared to imagine himself doing more than dance with her.

When she had teasingly whirled him around the Walnut one night, he saw her register the friendship that was all he had to offer. Used to attractive women noting his lack of interest, he was not especially concerned. For reasons he did not fully understand, they rarely felt the need to make trouble for him and she proved no exception. He doubted she had raised the subject with her husband but, if she had, he knew she must have been confident of the casual reaction that he later witnessed.

The firearms argument had been raging for hours, since they met at dusk to discuss the future of the Blues in the face of a changing Preventive Service. Plenty of solid points were made on both sides of the debate but, right at the heart of the matter, Quids' death divided them into two camps: those who believed that more weapons would bring more deaths and those who saw equal firepower as their best chance at survival. So far, he'd said nothing, listening instead to what his companions had to say. He examined them one by one, considering what he'd learned of each man during his time in Aldington.

The Baileys were out in force. The biggest, John, was a lazy so-and-so, keen to reap the rewards of their runs but too idle to contribute much to their plans. Jem had little time for him, suspecting his enthusiasm for firearms sprang only from the belief that they would make his life easier. The younger of his nephews, Rob, was a hothead and not the first man Jem would want to see with a musket in his hand; he was the sort who might easily end up killing someone by accident. The elder, Sam, was another matter; his brooding intensity spoke of harsh experience, something that Jem knew all about.

Then came Pierce, Giles and Quested: dependable men, handy in a corner but just as adept at devising and executing strategies. Not obvious members of a gang with a reputation like the Blues, they were vital to its smooth running and paid their way every day with the information and ideas they delivered. All three were fearless, too, earning Jem's friendship as well as his respect. They had not yet declared their views on firearms.

Facing Jem was Dennard, a man whom he trusted to a degree that he rarely accorded anyone. The same intuitive grasp of the consequences of thought and deed that sealed Dennard's lips on personal matters was making him wary of a change that could as easily be their downfall as their salvation.

To Dennard's right was Gilham, Jem's closest friend if men so reserved could be considered close. Gilham's status had grown with his own, his usefulness in a boat never in doubt but his other skills now held in equally high regard. Jem wasn't sure if his friend blamed himself or the Blockade more for the death of a shipmate, but his fury was evident in his fierce advocacy of a return to arms.

Then there was Higgins, whom Jem thought a lucky man — lucky to survive a Bailey beating to start with and then lucky twice more, in working for a man who'd have him back after his bones knitted and in wooing a woman who'd have him back after a blow from a closed fist. To everyone's relief, marriage had mellowed him, steadying his nerves but leaving his vitality intact. Jem liked him, the coarse company and crude humour taking him back to his Navy days, but liking was not trusting: the sharp tongue could too easily turn to his affairs. Still, all in all, he was less unsure about giving Higgins a musket than he would have been a year before.

Next to the threat of exposure was the secret. Jem knew Wilson's views intimately, of course: he disliked firearms but worried for his friends as the men of the Coast Blockade became more confrontational. Jem, in turn, worried for him: his poor health put him at risk from any assailant but a musket in his hand was no guarantee of safety. It was all moot, since Wilson would refuse to carry a firearm and, if forced to do so, would not fire it.

To Dennard's left was Hogben, a man Jem despised and judged as dangerous to the local people as to the Preventive Service. Needless to say, Hogben favoured firearms but he was just about the last man Jem wanted to see holding one. He was puzzled that Ransley kept Hogben in the Blues at all, let alone in their inner circle, but there had to be a reason. Perhaps the man simply knew too much to be cast out and had too many friends to be killed quietly. Although Wilson's knowledge of what passed after the attempt to save Cephas Quested from the hangman was patchy, his account of it made Hogben's return to the Blues seem all the more surprising. The only explanation he'd been able to offer was that Hogben and Ransley went back a long way. Loyalty — even if misplaced — was something Jem well understood.

And, finally, Ransley himself. Jem had profound respect for the man now known by all as Captain Bats. He might not know the reasoning behind some of their leader's decisions but never for a moment did he doubt that there was an astute and logical basis for every one. He trusted Ransley, not in the sense of believing him to be of good character but rather in the sense of knowing him to have just about the soundest judgement of any man he'd known. Ransley had said nothing during the present debate, instead listening to his men argue and watching who stood where and why. Now he cleared his throat, a customary prelude to his intervention in a discussion. The Blues fell silent.

'And you, Jem, what do you think?'

Jem had been as silent as his questioner and it was characteristic of Ransley to notice his abstention. He considered his answer thoroughly before giving it, although he'd long known where he stood. One reason that he'd so swiftly progressed to the heart of the Blues was that he never gave a hasty opinion and never appeared to be seeking control or influence. It was a position he'd judged carefully, and well.

'I think things are changing,' he said in a measured tone. 'There are more preventives than in the old days, better organised and better armed, and they become ever more careless of men's lives. The time is coming when traders must make a choice: bear firearms or throw in the towel.'

There were growls of approval from men around the table who wanted to bear arms and thoughtful looks from those who doubted the wisdom of such a move. It was Giles who spoke, his tone neutral and his words a question rather than a challenge.

'And what do you know of the old days, Jem? You've been with us scarce two years.'

'That's true,' Jem admitted. 'But I'd been around before.'

He caught Ransley's eye on him. The admission was not news to their leader. Ransley might not know where he had been but clearly knew that he had not been green when he joined them.

'I know the North Kents were slow to take up arms, and I know they're no more.'

'You ran with them?'

There was a trace of awe in Gilham's question. The collapse of the infamous North Kents, following a bloody clash at Margate some months after Brookland, was watched closely throughout Kent and

215

Sussex. The *Chronicle* reported that a crowd of more than forty thousand people gathered on Penenden Heath to see four of the leaders hang on a bright April morning in eighteen-twenty-two. Another fourteen men escaped with transportation, if that could be called an escape. The gang's demise did not affect the Blues directly but there were changes afterwards. With the locals out of action, Ransley extended his operations north towards Deal and even Sandwich on occasion. For another, with no North Kents, they were no longer known as the South Kents. They'd always had many epithets, to which the Blockade added the Brookland Gang after the battle fought there, but it was the name the locals used that eventually stuck: the Aldington Blues, the Blues for short.

'For a while.' Jem glanced at Sam Bailey. 'Done a lot of things in my time.' He saw a flicker of understanding in the guarded eyes. 'Even when you were armed at Brookland, it was a close thing. It could have finished you.'

'But it didn't,' Giles prompted in the same reasonable tone.

'No, but think again of what passed last month. Shall our scouts stand by while the bastards shoot our tubmen and mariners like rooks? How many more like Quids before we can't find men to load a cargo, let alone serve as scouts? The time's coming when a man might as well hang himself as stand fast with just a bat in his hand. Every man in the armed parties needs the same musket and pistol as the preventive man he faces.'

Most of his listeners nodded in agreement. The lieutenant who shot Quids had been running along the beach to join his fellows in the fight against the armed parties. Three men saw his approach and watched him stop, look out to sea and then deliberately fire on the boat. They'd been powerless to stop the cold-blooded murder, a hundred paces from the killer with only bats in their hands. Had those bats been muskets, Quids might have lived. So furious were the witnesses at the wanton act that they willingly took the risk of testifying at the inquest, naturally being somewhat selective about their own role in the proceedings but solemnly — and truthfully — emphasising that the boat was empty and the lieutenant opened fire without cause or warning. Their testimony swayed the jury, which recorded a verdict of Wilful Murder, but not the Coroner, who accepted the lieutenant's plea that he shot in self-defence and allowed the Navy to spirit him away.

Giles remained unconvinced.

'The North Kents bore arms and yet they still fell.'

'Like I say, they left it too late. Too little, too late. The King's mustering an army against us. Either we fight or we roll over.'

'I don't stand against the King,' Pierce chimed in.

'Good f'nothin' piss-maker,' Hogben scoffed.

No one commented on the matter of pots and kettles.

Pierce repeated low and firm, 'I don't stand against the King.'

Ransley drew a hiss of breath. 'Nor does any man amongst us.'

That was the truth, though not necessarily through any sense of loyalty or patriotism. It was one thing to unload tubs cheek-by-jowl with the enemy during the French wars, under cover of night and weather, but quite another to talk treason bold as brass in front of witnesses.

Ransley's deep blue eyes twinkled when he added, 'But a preventive man's a different animal all together, in't he lads?' He didn't wait for their reply, turning shrewd eyes on Jem. 'Can you kit us out, if we take that path?'

Jem once again considered his reply before he gave it. He had the knowledge and he could make the contacts. After a minute, he gave the slight nod that he knew might seal their fate.

George

George Ransley's bay mare cantered effortlessly along a drover's road south of Broad Oak, her rider flowing with her movement as if they were one beast. Occupied with a growing, if illicit, business empire, his other activities had dwindled into nothing but, though his horse-trading days might be long gone, the passage of time did nothing to diminish his love for the animals. His eye for horseflesh rivalled Dennard's and went deeper than mere conformation and temperament. When he bought the mare as a filly, he had noted her elegant gait and graceful changes of pace and stride. Careful schooling had refined them further during their six-year association and now he regarded her as the most perfect mount he'd ever owned. The substantial offers he received for her from time to time confirmed that he was not alone in that opinion.

The man he rode to visit had been one of the worst horsemen he knew, something that made some in their circle question his sudden appointment as a groom two years before. Paradoxically, that answered rather than raised questions for George, who saw behind it a motivation that lay outside his area of interest. He did not doubt that Wilson's brain had been working in harness with his groin when he decided to put Smeed forward for the Blues. While there was no great harm in taking on a poor groom with a handsome face, Wilson would not be careless with his friends' lives. George knew he would first have measured the man against a demanding yardstick. Inevitably, there were some in the Blues who disliked Smeed, though so far from envy of his rapid rise rather than for more divisive reasons, but George doubted there were any who seriously questioned his value to them.

It was that value he now sought to exploit. A week had passed since their meeting at the Tap, a span that implied his decision had been reached more easily than it had. In truth, he hadn't slept soundly since the meeting, or for some nights beforehand. He saw the reintroduction of firearms as a personal failure but knew of no other way to safeguard his men's lives, the goal that had been so dear to him in the aftermath of Brookland. Eventually, the balance in his mind tilted, slowly but decisively.

He sat straighter and felt the reins with his fingertips, all it took to bid the mare slow to a trot. As she did so, he rose rhythmically for a few strides and then sat to take her down to a walk. While she snorted heavy breaths of the warm morning air, he squinted through the hedge at his side. The hawthorn leaves were old and dark, cobwebs masking their early summer glory, while the occasional crisp leaf already fell from the beech canopy. A squirrel scrambled through the branches overhead, frantic in its larder-building though winter was yet distant, sending more leaves tumbling in its wake.

The mare had been walking briskly through the green tunnel for a quarter of an hour before George saw what he was looking for. A team of dusty bay Shires threw themselves into their yoke, urged on by a lean figure in a low-brimmed hat fighting the plough behind them. He watched for a minute, seeing his estimation of Smeed confirmed in the beasts' hard labour. No doubt they had been dutifully cared for by the man who supervised them and they rewarded his conscientiousness with their best efforts on the sticky clay soil. Noting how small even a tall man appeared alongside the heavy horses, George understood how daunting they might seem to a man who had not grown up around livestock as most of the locals had. In reality, the team was an excellent example of the Shire breed, as sound in temperament as it was in the conformation that had won several prizes at fairs around the county. Nevertheless, too wise to take a risk when none was needed, he dismounted and tethered the mare to a hornbeam bough. She was only recently out of season and the Shires were breeding stock: taking her close to the stallion was unlikely to make Smeed's task any easier. After easing his bulging saddlebags over his shoulder, George strode over the fresh furrows, stepping between the ridges so as not to crush the loose soil. He was within twenty yards before Smeed spotted him.

'Whoa!' the ploughman called to his team. 'Whoa.'

When they were steady, he took off his hat and swiped a sleeve across his streaming brow.

'Getting warm,' George remarked in lieu of a greeting.

'Aye.'

George pulled a flask from his pocket and held it out. In response to a frown from Smeed, clearly doubting the merit of spirits for a working thirst, he said, 'Just a drop of cider.'

Smeed gave a curt nod of appreciation and took a long pull from the flask before handing it back. George capped it and returned it to his pocket.

'On foot?'

George suppressed a smile. No talker himself, he was still no match for Smeed when it came to brevity. There had to be curiosity behind the two words, given that he rarely walked anywhere except when his plans for a run dictated he must, but there was no hint of it. He nodded to where the stallion was sniffing the air and stamping a rear hoof, the movement shaking the half-yard of flesh that had unfurled below its belly.

'My mare's not long past her season. I didn't think you needed any excitement to spice up your day so I left her down the bottom.'

Smeed nodded his appreciation a second time. His calmness confirmed George's original opinion: if anyone could turn a novice into an expert stock man, Wilson was the man to do it. No longer chary of his charges, Smeed handled them almost as confidently as he did a boat. He would know, as George did, that the stallion's mood was akin to a man watching an attractive woman in his local public house: interested but not about to run off just yet. Pulling out a handful of the sliced carrots he was rarely without, George fed the animal and then its mate.

'How do you find the work?' he asked through their crunching.

It was as close as he would get to a personal question but he was interested in the answer, having ploughed many a field in his younger days. Smeed thought for a while before giving his reply.

'I like being outdoors in my own company.'

That might have sounded like a rebuff but George did not take it that way. He, too, liked being outdoors in his own company.

'I never saw myself as a gentleman's valet or aught like that.'

There was a thread of wry humour in the clarification and George wondered if Smeed meant that he did not see himself stooping so low as to dress a man who should be able to dress himself or if he thought his interest in undressing men might make him ill-suited to such a role. They had not alluded to that side of his character since the chance meeting behind the Walnut Tree, partly because they rarely spoke in private but more because it was not something George felt needed to be discussed. Discarding the possible opening, he settled for a simple answer.

'Nor I.'

Smeed's open gaze, settled directly on him, seemed to confirm that they were in agreement on more than their choice of occupation. He was now waiting to hear the real reason for the visit, confident that it had as little to do with his personal life as it did with the caller's social calendar. George petted the Shire mare's nose, knowing how to tickle it just right so that she leaned into his caress, putting off what he had to say because it pained him to set the change in motion. Eventually, glancing back at Smeed, he saw that the man had guessed what was to come and also why it was so slow in coming.

'I don't see another way,' he finally admitted. 'Not any more.'

'Nor I.'

'I've a mind to bring 'em in, quiet like. Best be ready but…'

Smeed's nod conveyed his understanding, both of the path they were taking and of his caution in striding down it too hastily.

'You know who you can rely on…?'

Smeed nodded again but said, 'There's plenty to be done before we have need to worry about that. How many do we seek?'

'Two hundred each, pistols and muskets.'

Smeed raised his eyebrows but said nothing.

'If we store them in fifties, on hand for our best spots, there'll be less risk of getting caught with them. And there'll be losses and breakages.'

'True enough. But two hundred, twice over? That'll take some gold.'

George acknowledged the cost with a slight nod; while there was no shortage of redundant firearms after more than two decades of war finally came to an end, the risks involved in running them put the price up at every turn. He lifted the saddlebags from his shoulder, feeling the value in the weight but barely hesitating before handing them over. Their contents could whisk Smeed and Wilson to a new life in the colonies if they chose to cross him but he deemed neither man capable of such duplicity.

'Use as much as you need.'

There was no need to add caution or restraint. Smeed would take no more than was his due in expenses and he would pay no more than he must for the firearms, or the information that led him to them. If he felt a need to explain himself to his companion, George had no problem with Wilson knowing their plans. Otherwise, only those needed to implement them would hear a murmur from Smeed… and his accomplices would be as carefully chosen as if George had made the selections himself. Decision made, he would squander no more sleep on the matter, putting it out of his mind until Smeed told him where their new weapons were stashed. Only then would he ask Bailey's opinion on the best locations for their new, highly secret, armouries.

Jem

Jem Smeed reclined against the grassy bank, a stem of cock's foot between his teeth, and surveyed the sky overhead. Not a thread of cloud marred the vast azure expanse and yet storm clouds were gathering, metaphorical if not literal. He frowned, wondering at the wisdom of throwing in his lot with the Blues. He didn't need to, had no dependants and could live on the pittance he was paid. For him, it was a matter of pride, of not bowing to a system that decreed he should live in poverty while fools of better birth squandered England's wealth on wars with France. Now the wars were over and the men who hadn't died in their country's service had been discarded, often homeless and jobless. The frown turned to a scowl before he moved on from such fruitless deliberations.

He thought, instead, of the man he was waiting to intercept. Sam Bailey, eldest of the Bailey boys, father of three, brother-in-law to Ransley and second-in-command of the Blues. Where their leader was hard-nosed, his deputy was plain hard. Things had gone downhill since the halcyon days when Jem first ran with the Blues but, so far, he'd witnessed none of the action, not even on the night they lost Quids. Nevertheless, although he had yet to see the fierce fighter that lurked beneath the disciplined exterior, he'd seen the absolute obedience Sam inspired in the batmen. The rest — the versatility with a swingle in particular — he'd heard from Wilson. He'd have known most of it anyway from the murky depths of Bailey's eyes, in which he saw keen intelligence, cool disdain and, just occasionally, a jaded sense of humour. Below those, almost hidden, were traces of pain and disillusionment. Those were qualities that Jem recognised all too well and, if he'd owned a mirror, might have seen in his own gaze.

Obtaining firearms for the Blues was well within Jem's abilities but that was only half the problem. He had no intention of passing them around freely, only for men to take drunken pot-shots at anything that moved. He intended that, like it or not, they would submit to training and to rules as to when and how the weapons would be carried and used. He couldn't enforce that alone and saw Bailey as his best chance for success. Ransley's authority went a long way in the Blues but he did not inspire the same fear as the Baileys: one of them in his corner would let Jem sleep easier. Of course, his sleeping arrangements could get him killed as it was; now he might be giving the worst of his acquaintances another reason to come after him.

He had settled himself on a straight stretch of lane, just off the Fright. When Bailey started to drink in earnest, he never stopped while he was still standing and the previous evening had been no exception. After a heavy night at the Walnut Tree, he invariably passed that way on his return home late the next morning. He farmed a small piece of land near Bilsington, which gave him more freedom than most in his travels and nocturnal pursuits. In fact, his role in the Blues had expanded to fill most of his time and less than half of his holding was still cultivated.

Jem recognised Bailey's hat long before he'd have recognised the figure riding around the distant bend. The hat was a curious contraption woven from straw, which might have once held a more conventional shape than the strange twist it affected now. Better suited to harness than saddle, Bailey's cob rolled from side to side as it wandered towards Jem. Its leisurely pace suggested that Bailey's head was none the better for his excesses.

When Bailey eventually drew alongside, he raised a hand to the straw abomination. A contemporary of Ransley's, his old-world manners often struck Jem as not just quaint but out of place amongst men of their ilk.

'Morning.'

Jem nodded. 'Sam.'

'Waiting on something?'

'Wanted a word.'

Bailey considered that for a few seconds, then dismounted in a symphony of creaking leather. He loosened the girth on his saddle, then sat on the opposite bank. The ten-foot channel of dried mud ruts between them underlined that he hadn't yet decided the wisdom or length of any conversation they might have.

'What can I do for you?'

Jem considered what he wanted Bailey to do for him. 'You're for the Blues arming up,' he began. Erring on the side of caution, he saw no need to relate Ransley's specific instructions at that moment. 'Seems like Bats is going that way in his thinking too.'

Bailey fixed a hard stare on him but Jem didn't flinch under the evaluation.

'So what?' Bailey asked at last.

'Are we talking about a militia or a mob?'

There was a long silence, so long that Jem began to doubt he'd get an answer, but eventually it came: curt and wary.

'Meaning the Hog? Or my brother?'

'Meaning anyone who'll have no sense with a musket in hand.'

Bailey's eyes glinted with the sharp humour Jem had noted before. He barked a short laugh before saying, 'Meaning half the Blues.'

223

He settled more comfortably, hands clasped and elbows on his knees. 'You see it getting out of hand?'

Jem shrugged, then replied in a lighter tone. 'Often seems to get out of hand.'

'You never get out of hand,' Bailey said quietly. 'Got other arrangements, have you?'

Jem faced his stare in silence.

'None of my business?'

Jem shrugged again. As it happened, Bailey's arrangements were no more public than his own. It was common knowledge that there was little domestic bliss in his household and yet Jem had never seen the man indulge himself anywhere else. His evenings at the Walnut Tree were usually spent in solitary drinking that led to one of two outcomes, melancholy or violence. The melancholy was pitiful to behold, as he seemed to watch ghosts more real than the flesh and blood around him. The violence was cold and mean, yet only ever directed at troublemakers well able to take care of themselves. A Bailey was unlikely to find many opponents of his own size to assault but women, children and old folk were all equally safe from Sam's rages.

Bailey seemed as engrossed in his thoughts as Jem. At last, he sighed. 'The Lord knows I'm no saint, and I'll lose no sleep over the life of a preventive man, but I'm not looking to see Al'ington torn apart like Goudhurst was.'

The pitched battle fought in that village eighty years before lived on in local memory. The Hawkhurst Gang thought it could please itself, and for a long time it did, but, eventually, enough was enough. The local people, long supportive of a man's right to challenge his crippling burden of taxes, drew the line at brutal murders on their doorstep.

'What have you got in mind?' he asked.

Jem hadn't formed a plan as such, only the realisation that something needed to be done. 'I'm not decided,' he admitted. 'It'd be a start to make sure they can shoot straight. We may not be able to stop cold-blooded murder but we can cut the chance of an accident.'

Bailey's ready nod confirmed that he'd have no problem helping on that score.

'You served?' Jem asked casually.

There was a short pause before Bailey nodded again. So, they did share experience. 'You?'

Jem gave an affirmative grunt. In a risky strategy, he decided to gamble on some camaraderie.

'I wasn't discharged as such, officially so to speak.'

Amusement flickered briefly through Bailey's eyes, before the shutters came down again. He said only, 'A lot of men weren't.'

Jem exhaled. He'd been right about shared history and felt easier knowing Bailey was at least partly on his side. With luck, he'd have a respected voice arguing with him for sanity when they made the transition from bats to guns.

Sam

The frown that Sam Bailey wore during the rest of his homeward journey owed more to Smeed's words than to a hangover. He couldn't deny that things were changing, however much he might want to. He was bone-tired: tired of farming, tired of the trade, tired even of beer and women. His concern now was not for his fellows, nor even for himself.

No, the only thing that made the effort of living worthwhile was his children. The frown faded a fraction when he pictured his little angels. He aimed to give them everything that children of their class were denied and that was the sole reason he still braved the sea, the weather and the preventive forces. Running with the Blues could bring in more money in a night than the farm did in a month. That was all well and good while it lasted but what if he was wounded or killed on a moonless beach one night? Who would provide for them then?

That was why he wanted a firearm in his hand when he faced the preventive men. He'd beaten consciousness from dozens of men with his swingle, hand to hand, pitting his skill and strength against theirs, but now they pointed a musket at him and pulled the trigger from afar. They started it and now, by God, the Blues would finish it. He smiled grimly. The struggle would never end, not while the Government tried to tell men what they could and couldn't have, and what price they would pay for it. The goods changed, and the gangs came and went, but there would always be someone willing to ensure that supply met demand.

Unconcerned by the Blockade's casualties, he was troubled by the spectre that Smeed raised. He had no wish to see the people of the parish thrown into the middle of an armed conflict, needless to say not his own and his friends' families but also those of his foes. Even as embittered as he was, he would not wish on any man a loss that he could not contemplate for himself. He might beat preventive men into the boggy soil without compunction but he would never harm a hair on their children's heads. He knew the same could be said of almost all the Blues, doubting only a few.

His brother, Rob, was too reckless by far. Sam didn't see him as a bad man but knew he could be dangerous. It made no difference if a slug lodged in a child's tender body landed there by accident or design: the child would be just as dead. Hanging around with their young uncle John didn't help, as they often goaded one another into doing things they'd never have done alone.

That left Hogben. He was the only core member of the Blues about whom Sam had real doubts. Few knew how far he'd already gone and no one knew his limits. Sam had once asked Ransley why he let Hogben back into the Blues. As brother-in-law, second-in-command and lifelong friend, he thought he had a right to know. If the decision had been his, Hogben would have paid with his life for inciting mutiny after Brookland. Ransley had pondered the question for a long time, as if it had never occurred to him before, although Sam knew the decision must have been as considered as everything else he did. Eventually he said just four words.

Fear keeps us safe.

The practical benefits of that were obvious. Cowed locals did as they were told and did not inform. Ransley was operating like a military commander and so far it had paid dividends. Sam understood the strategy but also its risks. People could only be pushed so far. He'd seen military men pushed too far and the results weren't pretty. None of them could control Hogben and, one day, he might push someone too far. The price might be high.

Privately, Sam hoped Hogben would pick a victim unwisely. There were men amongst them who could deal with him, and no one would shed a tear if they were given a reason to do so. Indeed, if his little angels were at risk, he would kill the man himself. However, it was not his domestic life that he expected to provoke the confrontation that began to seem inevitable.

His thoughts shifted to Smeed's closed stare in response to being questioned about his arrangements. It was the defiant stare of a man declaring that his personal affairs were not a topic for discussion, which was just about the only line he could take, but Sam doubted it fooled many of their closest associates. Unbidden, his brain had chewed on the unanswered questions that disturbed him so in the months after Smeed joined them, until suddenly it had tossed him an answer on a quiet night in the Walnut Tree.

Smeed had been at the bar with Pierce and Giles. They had been too distant for Sam to hear their conversation clearly but their stances revealed that Smeed and Pierce had been arguing one view, while Giles had been fervently but affably putting another. Nothing unusual in that: Smeed often spent his evenings with the two men, and Quested too when he was around, although his habitual reserve kept him on the outside of their tight-knit friendship.

Wilson had been seated at a table in the far corner of the tap-room, playing dominoes with Dennard. His sudden laughter, no doubt in response to one of Dennard's jokes or tales, had drawn brief glances of mild curiosity from several men but Sam's gaze had remained fixed on Smeed. He had not consciously been thinking about his doubts and yet his subconscious had quickly sought to back up suspicions that had been drifting unacknowledged in its depths. When Smeed's shrewd grey eyes had moved to rest on Wilson, Sam realised that he already knew the answer to his questions.

In that unguarded moment, Sam had read emotions any man would recognise in a fellow looking on a woman. Shock had rooted him to his chair for a moment, still staring, then he had recovered enough to tear his eyes away. He had studied the floor at his feet intently while trying to bring his reaction under control, then he had mumbled a formless excuse to his companions and stumbled to the back door. Outside, the yard had been dark under the dying moon. He had stood at the rear boundary, as if to relieve himself, but his trousers remained fastened. Eyes raised to the stars, he had considered what it meant to him to rely on a man of the kind he now knew Smeed to be. It had taken less than half a dozen runs for he and Ransley to realise what an asset they had in him and, since then, Smeed had become steadily more valuable. Confident Ransley had beaten him to this latest revelation, he could only assume that it made no difference in their leader's estimation. With no more concern for propriety or custom than Ransley, he had been surprised at his own reaction. Why should another man's desires disturb him so deeply?

Closing his eyes in the dark, he had let the memory fill his mind. He saw Smeed's pleasure in Wilson's happiness — but then a close friend might feel the same. He saw the minute signs of attraction — but then wide eyes and flushed skin might just as easily stem from the dim warmth of the inn and a glass of ale. Only a fullness of crotch that he barely registered when shifting his gaze, along with an instant change in pose to disguise it, seemed indisputable.

Yet he had still not confronted the source of his horror. No man who'd served at sea could be shocked by something so commonplace as a man seeking pleasure in another man's body. Deprived of their wives for years on end, with the few women aboard taken by one man or by many, plenty preferred the company of friends.

But that was the heart of the matter, he thought uneasily.

There was no shortage of women around Aldington. True, many new men remained in the southern counties after the wars but he doubted they were any more numerous than the local men who failed to return from military service. No, if he chose, a man with Smeed's looks could easily threaten Dennard's supremacy with the ladies of the parish.

Sam had slowly faced up to what he had seen in a gaze that he was fast wishing he'd never witnessed. He gave it no name but, if he had, it would have been love.

Smeed felt for Wilson as a man felt for a wife.

Recalling that night, Sam permitted himself a rare smile. He hadn't known that a man who'd seen the worst that men could do to one another in battle could be shocked by a tender glance between friends, whatever it signified. He had not adjusted easily to his new understanding, keeping an even greater distance from the two men than was his custom and planning runs to minimise any contact with them. Only much later did he see that his anxieties had been entirely misplaced. While he tortured himself with worries about being caught alone with one of them, worse still if it happened while he was at piss, he never stopped to consider whether their concern for each other might endanger others if a run went badly. By the time that objection struggled past his more visceral reactions, he already knew the answer to it.

Time and again, Smeed proved himself amongst their most reliable and resourceful men. Not only would Sam now stake his own life on him but, if needs must, he would even trust him with the lives of his little angels. A year had passed since the revelation in the Walnut and he no longer dwelled on what went on between the two Bank Farm men. On the odd occasion that seeing them together brought such images to mind, they troubled him no more than those far-off shipboard liaisons borne of necessity.

He was not sure why he hinted at the subject when he and Smeed met on the road. Was he trying to build a firmer alliance on some sort of truth? If so, perhaps shared history was a better foundation for that. Certainly, if they were to bring firearms into the Blues on a large scale, Smeed made as good an accomplice in the task as he could hope to find.

Jem

Jem Smeed handed his reins to the ostler, confirmed he'd be collecting his horse the following day and then strode off towards the docks. He'd brought the oldest of Brissenden's mongrel farm-horses, its mane and tail untrimmed and its tack decrepit. Dover was no more than a den of thieves and he'd been careful to bring nothing that any sane man was likely to covet.

As for himself, he wore a fish-scented smock full of holes, which he'd borrowed from Gilham, over work-soiled trousers. He'd spent the ride across from Aldington slipping into his new persona and now little of his customary self-assurance was to be seen. No one would notice, far less remember, one more tired and scruffy fisherman around the bustling port.

He knew his precautions were excessive but the thought of a noose around his neck was apt to make a man edgy. Dover was nowhere near as daunting as Portsmouth or Chatham would have been to a man seeking to evade the authority of the Admiralty but the naval presence was still strong enough to make him wary, though not to stop him acting on Ransley's instructions. In fact, he was pleased to be asked, both for the control that his role gave him over the quality and use of the firearms they brought in, and for the need to revisit an area that he had avoided for all too long. Most of his memories of Dover were happy ones.

Fifty yards from the quay, he ducked into a narrow alley. A motley assortment of ancient buildings lined the street, their first floors projecting above his head so that only a thin strip of sky showed beyond. A gully ran down the centre of the cobbles, carrying a mixture of human effluent and fish guts down to the sea. The particular stench, as it stewed in the scorching late-summer sun, might have choked an unfamiliar visitor but brought waves of nostalgia to a man who'd grown up with it.

After dodging around a child squatted over the gully, Jem made a series of dogleg turns until he came to the Anchor public house. He looked up at the weathered boards, taking in the vague outline of an anchor on a sign that probably hadn't seen a lick of paint in his lifetime, then pushed open the unoiled door and went inside. Even as he crossed the threshold, he grew in height and confidence. With any familiar faces he might find in the gloomy interior almost certain to be friendly ones, he had no need of anonymity. The beard he'd grown in preparation for the trip might hide his face from the new acquaintances he hoped to make but he doubted it would deceive many old ones, who'd seen him use the same trick before.

'Bienvenue, étranger!'

The bellow from behind the bar instantly confirmed that the inn held nothing but friends that day. Jem strode over, drawn to a spot he'd occupied during many a long evening of tall tales, and leaned on the battered oak counter. Almost as if by magic, a tankard of beer appeared in his hand. He studied its familiar dents for a moment, wondering at how readily it sprang into use, before replying to the speaker.

'Long time, Phillippe.'

He kept his voice steady, betraying no trace of the surprise he felt at his delight in the renewed acquaintance. Seeing the Frenchman's large brown eyes shining with the same pleasure, he tried to reckon up the time since his last visit. He wasn't one for counting but it seemed an age, part of a life that felt as distant as the childhood brought back by the crowded fish-strewn streets. He'd had his reasons for leaving that life behind but those reasons did not stop him feeling regret at the friends he'd left with it.

'Do they still look?' he asked

'Sometimes a rumour brings trouble for a time.' Phillippe gave a slight shrug. 'But His Majesty has no need of men now, so they do not look very hard.'

That was as Jem expected. The Navy had more men than it wanted since the wars came to an end. The press gangs were gone, and the topsman was never short of necks for his noose, so why look for men who had long since fled its clutches? He relaxed, content to bask in the familiar surroundings and the company of a friend more loyal than most he had known since.

'What news?' he asked, settling in for the long chat that he knew his question would launch.

He had time and he wanted information. Phillippe excelled at frittering both. In a few hours, he would know as much about events in Dover as the most vigilant resident. Meanwhile, he intended to enjoy the uncomplicated company of a man who shared his predilections. In fact, he reflected, it was the extent of their shared tastes that had precluded more intimacy between them. They'd often wooed and bedded beautiful youths side-by-side but neither of them felt that kind of interest in the other.

Reflection brought revelation, a sudden understanding of why his liaison with Wilson had sometimes seemed strange. Not since he was a boy, at the beck and call of his elders, had Smeed lain with a man. As soon as he was old enough to pass for a man, he took boys on the brink of manhood into his bed just as others had taken him into theirs — it never occurred to him to do otherwise. Only his pursuit of Wilson broke the pattern but, enchanted by his quarry, he never paused to question the chase. Looking back, he wondered if he had been hunter or quarry. Wilson's boyish body, slender and fine-boned, might have baited the trap but it was something quite different that sprung it. No boy Jem had known, and there'd been plenty, had Wilson's wisdom and insight. He'd felt many things for those boys, lust and affection amongst them, but nothing approaching the esteem in which he held Wilson.

For the first time in his life, he was neither the boy nor the man in a relationship and, while he wasn't sure what that made him, he was sure he liked it. Without doubt, he wanted to please his lover but he wondered if there was more to it. He liked the confidence the role gave Wilson, and that seemed a natural enough feeling, but more unexpected was the peace that he discovered in the rare surrender of control. It wasn't literal surrender — he could have thrown Wilson off in an instant at any time — but more like a token of his trust.

Nevertheless, as exquisite as their lovemaking was, it was only a small part of what they shared as lovers in a more profound sense. Belonging to Wilson made Jem feel as if he belonged everywhere — in the Blues, on the farm, in Aldington and on earth — and took his life in a new and deeply satisfying direction. If he had sometimes guided Wilson's early attempts at lovemaking, he had just as often been guided by his lover's murmured words of passion and devotion, sentiments that he'd never voiced before but cautiously began to echo. His faith in a lasting bond between men like them had developed in much the same way as his skills as a groom: slowly, steadily and with the final success largely due to Wilson's influence.

'And you?' Phillippe asked, when he had exhausted his store of gossip. He lowered his voice. 'How are things with you, *mon ami*?'

Jem thought about that, then smiled broadly. 'Good, Phillippe, good.'

Phillippe chuckled. 'Ah, the union of hearts and hands.'

Jem laughed at the quote, recalling how much it had amused Phillippe in a context quite unforeseen by its originator, an old preacher, and nodded.

'I rejoice for you.'

'And you?'

Phillippe shrugged. 'I have a pretty little bed-warmer, but he is young and I am not.'

Jem didn't reply. Remembering his dalliances with boys like that in the past, how he helped so many come to terms with what they were and then watched them move on to pastures new when their confidence grew, he thought again of how different things were for him now. Wilson seemed to accept his desires with the same serenity that he accepted his poor health, waiting until Jem came along only because he had wanted — or been wanted by — no one else enough before. Jem might be more experienced when it came to ways of expressing their feelings but he had nothing to teach Wilson about the feelings themselves. Nonetheless, their time together might be as brief as Phillippe's fragile liaison. Jem pushed that from his mind, knowing that it was better to savour the present than to grow old worrying for the future.

232

'The last time I had tidings, you ran with the North Kents. But they are no more.'

'I heard that too,' Jem teased. He didn't go on immediately, enjoying holding out on his friend, but then became more serious. 'I'm over in Aldington now.' He saw the instant recognition in Phillippe's eyes and added, 'Groom-come-ploughman.'

The chuckle again. 'How does a man who fears *les chevaux* find work as a groom?' He studied Jem, puzzled, and then smiled with the realisation that the position had not been gained on merit. 'Ah, I see. Two birds in one hand.'

'With one stone,' Jem corrected automatically. The excellence of Phillippe's English was due in part to his patient tuition during the man's first months in Dover.

'Quite so. And you are here on business?'

Jem nodded. The afternoon had sped by in Phillippe's entertaining company but he was in Dover for a purpose and could put it off no longer. 'The days when a man could protect himself with a bat are passing. The time is coming when slugs must be met with slugs.'

Phillippe frowned. 'But what when slugs are met by rope?'

'They have to catch a man to hang him.'

'I do not have so many friends that I can afford to lose one of the best.'

Jem ignored the protest and moved the conversation on.

'Is the Dutchman still trading more than fish?'

Shaking his head sadly, Phillippe said, 'He danced for *le bourreau* two years ago.' He remained obstinately silent.

'Come on, Phillippe. If you don't point me in the right direction, I'll have to ask around. Could be risky.' Seeing annoyance at the emotional blackmail flicker across his friend's face, he added, 'I'll be just as dead if I'm shot one dark night.'

Phillippe's irritation slowly gave way to resignation. 'If you don't die of the pox first,' he said before falling into another, more pensive, silence.

Even sipping slowly as he was, Jem emptied his tankard before his friend spoke again.

'There are two possibilities,' Phillippe eventually admitted. 'An *Irlandais*, Finney, out by Castle Jetty and a *Portugais*, Oliveira, on the west side of the harbour. Oliveira is the better man but Finney is

233

more likely to meet your needs.'

Jem nodded his thanks, touched by how uneasy Phillippe was at helping him get into trouble. Though twenty years his senior, the Frenchman had always been an equal, not the mentor he was to some. Now, as ever, Jem spoke as a friend.

'Only the old fear death, Phillippe. We are not so old, are we?'

Phillippe stared at a stain on the table. 'Not you, but I, maybe.'

Jem leaned close. 'I'll wager you don't feel so old when you lie with your pretty little bed-warmer on a cold night.'

Phillippe's rakish grin took years off him, reminding Jem of the men they were when they met in Marseilles. '*Non*, then I am young once more.' He glanced up and then back to the table. 'But there is no fool like an old fool. I love him.'

That came as no surprise to Jem, seeing easily into his friend's heart and hoping the boy was wise enough to value what the man offered. He said nothing and stood to offer his hand. Another wave of nostalgia engulfed him when he felt the callused palm that pressed against his own.

Phillippe gave a parting warning. 'Take care, *mon ami*. Hard times are coming for men such as us. What was a comfort on a distant battlefield becomes an abomination when a man returns to his beloved England. And the people tire of the King's *dépravation*, wishing he were one-tenth the man his father was.'

Jem knew his friend spoke the truth. He'd lost count of the young men he'd comforted, and been comforted by, in the dark years even after the wars and yet now he dare not reveal his true self even to those he respected most as friends. All around him, he saw that the wealthy were dissolute and the poor were strained to breaking point. When those rebellious feelings found an outlet, there would be casualties and anyone who did not fit into the new society might be caught in the backlash.

'And you, *mon frère*.'

He held the handshake for a few more seconds, conscious that every parting might be the last, then made to leave. Phillippe raised his glass in farewell.

'*Á l'amor che muove il sole e l'autre stelle.*'

A man of Phillippe's sophistication was wasted in the backstreets of Dover. If a passing seaman spoke Italian, it was only enough to cajole or bribe a woman into bed and not to recognise quotations from the *Divina Commedia*. But Jem understood and his heart swelled with the realisation that, for the first time, he had found a love that moved not just sun and stars but the whole of creation. He'd forgotten how good it was to be with someone who could believe such a love possible for them.

After he left the Anchor, Jem headed east for Castle Jetty. He knew that Phillippe would prefer him to try Oliveira before Finney but guessed that four hundred firearms would be well beyond the limited capabilities that the Frenchman had implied. While the Portuguese might be the better man, approaching two sellers instead of one brought twice the risk. There was no reason why the transaction should turn sour, lucrative as it would be for the seller, but logic provided no guarantee. A man unable to fill an order might demand a deposit from the buyer and then top it up with a reward from the authorities as an approver.

Jem walked purposefully along the harbour-front, just one of hundreds of seamen going about their business. Some were busy aboard boats moored to the quays, mending nets, painting salt-scoured woodwork or gutting fish. Others matched his deliberate pace, those headed east staying with him while those headed west flashed briskly past. Still more leaned on walls and posts, drinking or smoking, talking or simply watching. Now and then, poorly concealed in alleys between sheds and shacks, he glimpsed more personal activities being conducted in what passed for privacy in a sailor's life: men at piss or shite, men with women kneeling before them or crushed beneath their thrusting bodies, even one with a boy who might have turned Smeed's head, had it been for turning.

What he saw brought back his life as it had been for almost as long as he could remember. Everything was familiar, with a hundred jobs that he could do with his eyes shut, making his choice to become a landsman, with every day a battle against his ignorance and inexperience, seem almost bizarre. It came as small surprise to him to feel no regret over the decision but he was startled to realise that his contentment had almost as much to do with Brissenden and Ransley as with his Jamie. There was a similarity of sorts between his life at Bank Farm or within the Blues and life aboard a ship. Men's fates were bound together, relying on each other to maintain the prosperity that benefited them all. Myriad trades came together to work a farm or run a cargo, just as they did to sail a ship. He was part of a team, his contribution interwoven with those of his friends, and that was how he liked to live. He needed the sense of community, dependent on no one but in partnership with all.

Now his peace was disturbed by apprehension about his mission. At the top of his mind was his own immediate safety. An ill-chosen word in the wrong ear could land him in all kinds of trouble, either with the sort of men who ran guns or the authorities paid to stop them. Below that stirred subtler concerns.

Mindful of his prospects, he sought to impress Ransley with the cost and efficiency of his dealings. He hoped to retain a fair slice of the gold in the bulging saddlebags that were buried beneath the moonlit moss of his personal heaven, the site of his most precious memories become the site of his heaviest responsibility too. He told Wilson of Ransley's plans as soon as he returned from the fields and they went together to hide the gold that night. He buried it two spades deep and Wilson artfully restored the moss so that even a man looking for the spot would have difficulty in detecting the joins. Surveying their handiwork, he felt a thrill of excitement at the hidden treasure and then surprise at the emotion, alien to a man as far from mercenary as he was. He gripped Wilson's arm and, firmly though not brutally, forced him onto the moss. Wide green eyes gazed up at him curiously throughout his hard and needy assault, as he took without asking and brooked no refusal. When he eventually reached to share his pleasure, only moments before it peaked, the man beneath him caught his wrist and held it off. Never, through all his anonymous and empty contacts, had physical satisfaction been sullied by such desolate loneliness. Pulling away afterwards, he was sure that exerting his dominance over his lover had destroyed what they shared — and the certainty had already begun to tear him apart.

Then Wilson's hand, still clasping his wrist, pulled him closer.

'Let not the love of money taint thy heart, for it is the root of all evil.'

In an instant, he had glimpsed what it would be to lose his Jamie. Loss would come all too soon and needed no help from him. Beside it, wealth paled into insignificance. He held his lover close, trembled at the horror of parting, and then, when his wits finally began to return to him, made love with his heart instead of his greed.

236

In their shared sighs, he felt their union as intensely as he had foreseen their separation.

The canvas belt fastened firmly around his waist as he strode through Dover contained only a hundred sovereigns — more than enough, he hoped, to loosen tongues and grease palms on his way. He'd already saved a few of the heavy coins by talking to Phillippe, who would have been cut to the quick by any offer of payment.

Ahead, Castle Jetty jutted out into the sea, with Dover Castle high above on its promontory of solid rock. At first, it seemed to Jem a strange spot for an illicit operation, right under the noses of the Army and Navy forces stationed in the fortress. On the other hand, men rarely hanged merely for talking and doubtless that was all Finney did in the shadows of the ancient stronghold.

When Jem reached the jetty, he found three men rolling a pair of dice on its weathered oak. He studied them, seeing a fair menagerie represented in their number. One put him in mind of a doe-eyed milch cow, deep of voice and slow of thinking. The second was more like a fast carriage-horse, fidgety and highly strung. The third could only have been a ferret in a former life, black eyes shifty and pointed canine teeth longer than the incisors between them. Jem imagined Wilson's likely warning about the deceptiveness of appearances but suspected nonetheless that he was looking at some of Finney's cohorts. He stood behind the ferret, too close to be ignored, and waited for a reaction.

Rather than challenge him directly, the ferret snaked forward, picking up the dice on his way, and rose while twisting to face him in one fluid move. The dark eyes flitted over his person, noting every detail. When the bovine companion made to get up, bony fingers bade him stay where he was. Jem saw that the ferret was as sharp as his looks implied: he knew that Jem was no fisherman and that he was no threat.

'I seek an Irishman.'

'Then you're a lucky man. There's no shortage of 'em in Dover.'

The accent put the ferret's birthplace nearer London than Ireland.

'The Irishman I seek goes by the name of Finney.'

'A common enough name for an Irishman.'

Jem was not in the mood for games.

'I have business on the west side of the harbour. Tell the Irishman he can find me there. But by then, of course, my business may be done.'

The shifty eyes hopped to Jem's waist, lingering on the thickened belt just visible through the ragged smock while their owner speculated on what might be carried in such an accessory.

'No need for haste, friend. You'll find no finer supper in Dover than in the Prince Alfred and you must pass by it on your way.'

Jem nodded. He'd noted every building he'd passed, including the public house that the ferret named. It was a typical harbour-front establishment: rough and dirty but sure to offer good value for money. The beer would be better than the food but both would go down well enough. He retraced his steps, certain that his first contact would be fruitful. It was confidence not so much in his ability to judge a man on first sight but rather in Finney's hold over his territory. If he was the kind of man that Phillippe had implied, no cutpurse would dare to cross him for a few coins when the deal on offer might be worth so much more, as indeed it was.

The inside of the Prince Alfred was no better than the outside. It was all spit and sawdust, with nothing in sight that could not be washed down or swept off. Even so, the reek of fish was overwhelming, seasoned with a trace of vomit. Jem knew that his transition to landsman was complete when he noticed the stench: had he come ashore from the cramped quarters of a man-of-war, the inn would have seemed sweet enough. The welcoming nods he received from the men he passed quickly reminded him that his old life was more than hard labour in mean conditions. Mariners were friendly folk, with seamanship respected across the gulf between military and civilian life. Jem had seen able seamen slot into naval service in days, while soldiers with many years of service were mocked mercilessly if they made poor sailors.

He leaned on the bar and waited until he caught the innkeeper's one good eye. The other was glass, no secret given that it was a poor match its more mobile counterpart.

'Pie and pint.'

'Meat or fish?'

Even that choice exceeded Jem's expectations.

'Whichever's the fresher.'

The innkeeper grinned, a toothless but genial leer, and disappeared through a door. He was back in seconds, a pewter plate

238

in his cloth-wrapped hand. Jem studied the food while the man drew his pint. Flakes of assorted fish-flesh steamed in a watery sauce, below a thick layer of lumpy mashed potato. It was hot, ample and free from any obvious contaminants: a fine supper, as the ferret had promised.

The innkeeper set a brimming tankard beside the plate.

'Thruppence.'

Considering his meal a bargain at twice the price, Jem tossed the coins to the man and began to work his way through the mound. A crust had formed over it while it sat on the stove but, inside that, the food was tasty and tender. He ate steadily, momentary squeamishness forgotten as his appetite reasserted itself. Not until he had mopped up the last of the sauce with a chunk of yesterday's bread did the innkeeper return.

'You seek the Irishman?'

Jem nodded.

'Upstairs.'

The innkeeper's eye rolled in its socket, suggesting that the stairs were through the door from which the meal had appeared. Jem followed the direction. Beyond the door was a passageway. On the right was a room in which every surface was buried under the debris of cooking and eating, clean and dirty dishes piled on top of each other, wherever a space could be found. To the left, steep stairs threaded upwards into the low roof. He stepped onto them cautiously, wary less of a trap than of the jaw-level lintel. With the walls barely half a yard apart, he had to twist as well as stoop to move on. By this time, he was puzzled. He had no fear of confined spaces: going to sea so young left some boys haunted by such terrors but for most it drove them clean away. Even so, he'd never met the man who preferred to stoop when he might stand straight. If he were selecting a base for his operations, it would certainly not be in the eaves of an inn that was poky even for a dockside watering hole.

At the top of the stairs was an open door. Just inside, the ferret was perched on a small, scuffed chest of blackened oak. He looked up nonchalantly, eyeing the knife in Jem's belt and then stroking the pistol that lay across his lap. The message was clear enough: visitors need not disarm but one sudden move would see the ferret shoot first and ask questions later. Jem inclined his head to pass through the doorway, steadying himself on the frame, then stopped in his tracks.

He took his first clear look at the attic room. It was as small as he expected and yet it seemed quite spacious. Not until he took another step did he begin to see the reason for the illusion. The top of the table under the window was at least three inches lower than usual, yet the straight-backed chair beside it was in perfect proportion. Beside an empty grate was a similarly diminutive leather-covered armchair, its occupant shielded by its winged back. Near to it was a three-legged stool, the only standard-sized piece of furniture in the room.

'Will you be standing there all day?'

The voice left Jem in no doubt that he had found the Irishman. He moved forward more boldly, though still hampered by the rafters. His questions tumbled away when he saw the man in the chair. The torso might have belonged to a normal man but the arms coming from its shoulders, while as thick as Pierce's were scarce long enough to rest on the arms of the chair. The legs would not have reached the ground, had the seat of the chair not been some six inches lower than usual.

Jem immediately understood that the room was designed as much for visitors' discomfort as for its occupant's comfort. Anywhere else, the dwarf would look out of place but here it was the visitor who felt uneasy and clumsy, unable to stand straight or move freely. The dwarf motioned him to the three-legged stool. Judging it to be the lesser of two evils, Jem accepted the offer, placing himself below his host's eye level, playing the game as the dwarf wanted it played. He came to no hasty conclusions about the man based on his stature, but he read the elaborate charade well enough. Most of Finney's kind played to men's sense of humour, hoping for some charity in exchange for lifting their spirits. He clearly did not settle for that, instead using his cunning to combat his congenital disadvantage and paying other men for the force he could not wield himself. The strategy, and to some extent the reason for it, was not so different from Ransley's. Jem had deliberately kept his expression blank, guessing when he was only halfway up the stairs that something was out of kilter and maintaining a tight hold on his reactions from that point. He was pleased to note that Finney could read nothing in the gaze that he had allowed to run over his host in exactly the same way as he would with a man of less uncommon appearance.

If there was a customary prelude to his interviews, Finney cut through it when he spoke.

'My friend tells me that you asked for me by name. Now where would you have heard that, I wonder?'

'From a friend.'

'A friend here in Dover?'

Jem shrugged. He saw his source as none of Finney's business and would say nothing that might bring trouble on Phillippe.

'No matter,' Finney chirped. 'But it is not Finney you seek?'

'A means to an end,' Jem admitted.

'And the end would be?'

Jem hesitated. He'd seen such deals done before but he'd never conducted one himself. Sitting in a room with a total stranger, he was nervous of declaring his order but saw little to be gained from beating around the bush.

'Firearms.'

Finney inclined his head to one side. 'A revolutionary?'

Jem hoped that he kept his face free of emotion, as he felt first amusement and then anger at the suggestion. He had served his country faithfully, until circumstances stripped that privilege from him, and he would no sooner stand against it than take his own life; no, his fight was not with England nor even directly with its King, though his opinion of the man was little more charitable than Hogben's. He knew that he had let his composure slip when Finney continued.

'No, no, to be sure — a businessman like myself.'

This time Jem nodded. Any likeness between him and Finney went no deeper than a desire for a mutually satisfying transaction but he was content to smooth the path to that end.

'How many?'

Jem looked straight into Finney's eyes as he spoke, hoping to read truth there when he declared his order.

'Muskets and pistols. Two hundred.' He paused. 'Of each.'

Finney was good: his face barely moved. Only a slight widening of his pale, heavy-lidded eyes revealed his surprise. He held Jem's gaze for a second or two, before answering with a question.

'You'll be coming from out Al'ington way then?'

Jem neither confirmed nor denied the suggestion.

'Not too many Men of Kent can afford to eat these days, let alone to be throwing their money around like that. Four hundred, you say?'

Jem gave a slight nod.

'Won't be cheap.'

'Good weapons at a fair price. If you can't supply 'em, say so.'

Finney laughed soundlessly, revealing teeth like tombstones.

'What if our notions of a fair price differ?'

Jem had a firm idea of what he would pay but had already decided to thrash out the details before settling on a price.

'English muskets on the India pattern but we'll take French pistols if we must, short not long. All for inspection before we take them. And, if they need running, we'll run 'em ourselves.'

Finney studied him. 'I see you're a man who knows what he wants.' After a pause, he laughed again. This time the humour reached his eyes. 'I like that. But I've listened to your terms, so now you listen to mine. Two guineas apiece, quarter now.'

His tone declared that the price was not subject to negotiation.

Jem had set himself a limit of two pounds apiece. He skipped through the arithmetic: four hundred at two-pounds-two-shillings apiece... eight hundred extra shillings, that was... four... no, forty... pounds. He weighed it up: the price of a galley and they lost those often enough, abandoned when the Blockade got too close.

'A hundred pounds now.'

More in total, less in advance, he reasoned. Besides, he'd brought only a hundred sovereigns so they must serve. He was uneasy handing over even them but it was a fair way to do business. Most of their run goods were paid half in advance so less than an eighth was more than fair, but Ransley's customers had known him for years while this deal stood on shakier foundations.

He endured Finney's continued appraisal for most of a minute.

'French pistols?' Finney checked.

He nodded.

'Then we have a deal. A hundred down, seven hundred and forty on delivery.'

Jem rose, unfastened the belt and laid it on the table, and then offered his hand. Finney hesitated, as if surprised, but then extended one of his stubby limbs to shake on the deal. Jem guessed that few men touched his stunted flesh by choice but did not share that reluctance. He had doubts aplenty about Finney but they owed nothing to his form.

'Where shall I be sending news?'

Serious talk over, the exaggerated brogue returned. Jem had already considered the question. Even now that agent had guessed the identity of customer, caution seemed prudent.

'There's a boat-owner in Folkestone by the name of Bolding.'

Finney nodded. 'I've heard the name.'

'A Tom Carpenter crews there. Leave word with him.'

With nothing more to be said, he headed down the narrow staircase. Not until he got outside did he let himself relax, exhaling heavily. Only then, after the deal was done, did he admit to himself how apprehensive he'd been about it.

In need of a drink, he had no intention of hanging around the Prince Alfred to get one. Instead, he set out for the Anchor. Business concluded and burden gone from his waist, he could settle to some serious reminiscing before heading inland in the morning. Rarely did he have the chance to let go as fully as he planned to do that night but he doubted any man drinking at Phillippe's would be disturbed by anything he might say or do.

Bish

Bish Wilson watched his lover's float bobbing as a fish robbed his hook. Smeed was normally a dab hand with a rod, teasing his prey into taking a nice big bite and flicking the hook deftly into its flesh. That afternoon, he barely seemed to notice the shoal around the ground-bait that he was absent-mindedly tossing into the water.

They often went fishing. An enthusiast since childhood, Bish now found it gave a convenient cover for spending time together without attracting suspicion. Sometimes, engrossed in each other, they didn't even unpack their bags; other times, they fished without interruption and took home a fine supper. Never could he recall a day when Smeed had sat so preoccupied. The mood dated from the trip into Dover, and he wondered what could have happened there to cause it.

Eventually he decided he'd wondered long enough.

'Dover hath many memories for thee, Jem?'

Smeed started, then looked across as if to gauge the reason for the question. Bish returned the gaze openly. He was mildly curious, as surely anyone might be about a lover's past, but not jealous. Smeed made him happier than he'd ever been. If Smeed had made others happy before, that was no business of his. With no interest in finding happiness in other arms himself, he hoped Smeed felt the same but he did not demand it. Although bound by his own promise of fidelity, he knew many men broke similar vows made in the sanctity of God's house. Smeed might have underestimated the difficulty of turning away from temptation. He'd be disappointed but his feelings would be unchanged. No, only the news that Smeed preferred another's arms would cause concern for himself and he doubted Smeed would have waited for days to tell him so. That left only concern for Smeed, and he was more than happy for it to show in his eyes.

'There's no one else, Jamie. I gave you my word.'

'I never thought there was.'

Smeed rolled a stem of grass between his palms. Finally he said, 'I went to see an old friend.'

'A man like us?'

The slow smile that crept over Smeed's face brought back a shadow of his usual self. 'I don't know any other men like you.'

At once embarrassed and delighted, Bish stared at his feet.

'Yes, a man like us. I met him long ago, in Marseilles. Later, we had rooms in a boarding house in Dover.'

'Another mariner?'

'No, he kept an inn in Marseilles and does the same in Dover.'

'A Frog?' Bish failed to keep the surprise out of his voice. Having grown up with bedtime stories of the wickedness of Frenchmen, he'd met few since to make him think again.

'Aye, Jamie, a Frog. The wars were madness then and they're over now.'

That gave an opening for Bish to ask about something he'd wondered before. 'Wert thou not too young for the wars?'

He watched Smeed toss another handful of bait into the river, waiting to see if he'd get an answer. Several minutes dragged by.

'Let it lie. Forget I asked it of thee.'

Smeed set down the tin of bait and pulled his legs up to his chest. Arms around his shins and chin on his knees, he sighed.

'Aye, I was too young — just a boy, third class, in the last days. Too young to see what I saw and that's the truth.'

Ten years had passed since the peace treaty. Bish studied Smeed, wondering how old he'd been then. Twenty-seven himself, he'd assumed Smeed was the same or older. But seventeen was hardly likely to make him a boy in the Navy's eyes, although Bish was no expert on the finer points of rank.

'How old wert thou then?'

Smeed did not look up. 'When I went to sea? Eleven.' A shadow of a smile crossed his face. 'I couldn't wait — said I was thirteen so they'd take me on. I've always been taken for older than my age.'

Bish tried to imagine that. Like most children of his class, he'd been working at eleven himself but he was luckier than many, going to school during the quieter times of year. 'What was it like?'

Smeed opened his mouth to reply but then reconsidered. There was another long pause while he thought. Bish guessed it was a question for which he had a ready answer but that he was opting for the truth this time.

'Hard,' he admitted finally.

'Cruel?'

Smeed thought again. 'Sometimes, but mostly just hard. No worse for me than for others.'

Bish said nothing, letting the silence draw more.

'The worst at the start was the food. Biscuit so hard it took hours to soften. At least soaking it drowned some of the weevils.'

Bish's lip curled involuntarily. 'And later?'

'Huh?'

'Thou said *at the start*. What came later?'

Smeed shrugged.

'Floggings?'

Smeed gave an ambivalent wave. 'Not as such. It was a decent crew and I was a fair volunteer. Felt a rope's-end now 'n' then, but a starting when it's needed can be the making of a man.'

Bish frowned. There was something Smeed wasn't telling him. 'What does a boy, third class, do?'

'*Whatever* an officer tells him to do.' Smeed spoke the words with no inflection, reinforcing the impression he was concealing something by the absence of any variation in tone or rhythm.

'Like a steward?'

Smeed gave a half-nod.

'Serving meals and suchlike?'

245

Smeed repeated quietly. 'Whatever an officer tells him.'

As realisation dawned, Bish felt a surge of anger at what had been done to a boy too young to give his consent even if he wanted to, far from home and with no one to call on for help. Of course, the men were not to know that Smeed was so young if he'd lied about his age. Anger was slowly supplanted by a nasty doubt.

'Is that why you…?' Bish didn't know how to ask his question.

'Why I turned out a molly? No.'

'How canst thou know?'

'Because I've known plenty who went through the same and didn't turn out that way. I've seen boys cry themselves to sleep night after night, hating every minute of it. I never hated it. Even when it hurt, I never hated it.'

Bish stared at his hands, horrified and yet fascinated. Years had passed before he discovered that some other men shared his inclination, most in addition to more conventional appetites. The idea of ships filled with such men intrigued him.

'They do it a lot, do they? At sea?'

The question made Smeed laugh. 'Christ, yes. They do it a lot anywhere where there are men without women. A fresh young volunteer hardly has time to sleep.'

'Oh, Jem.' The two words overflowed with compassion.

Now it was Smeed who frowned, clearly puzzled by his pity. 'There's no cause to be worrying over it now, Jamie. It's long past and it wasn't all bad either. I saw half the world and met some good sorts. There was one lieutenant treated me like a prince, used to bring me parcels of food from the Captain's table and presents from his shore leaves. There were good times aplenty.'

His expression had lifted and brightened still more when he added, 'I served in the Marines later.' The momentary pride fell away sharply when he pre-empted any reaction from Bish. 'Routine stuff, mostly patrols off British North America. I was born too late for the glory days, the Nile, Trafalgar. I only got in because they were short-handed after a storm.'

The regret in his voice was palpable. What Navy man wouldn't give his eye teeth to have served under Nelson, the greatest admiral that Britain, perhaps the world, had ever seen? But, of course, Smeed was just a baby when those victories were won.

'So thou wert not discharged after the treaty, with all the rest?'

The coastal counties had been flooded with surplus seaman when the Navy shrank during the first years of peace. Wages plummeted and crime rocketed, as hundreds of thousands of men tried, and all too often failed, to rebuild their shattered lives.

'No.' A long pause. 'I wasn't discharged at all. I deserted off Marseilles, not half a year after I made the Marines.'

Bish considered the reply, surprised but not shocked, with no military background to inject emotion into the idea of desertion.

'You hear me?' Smeed demanded.

'I hear thee. I'm thinking thou hadst your reasons.'

'Oh, I had a reason. A damned fool captain trying to sink his ship and a crew driven to mutiny before my eyes. We were ordered to open fire but we wouldn't do it. There's no place in the Marines for men who can't obey orders.' A snarl twisted his lips. 'But don't you be thinking me a hero. I did it because I wouldn't die for naught — not to help the crew nor to save the ship.'

Bish knew the bitterness wasn't directed at him or, if it was, only in the absence of the men Smeed held to blame. 'I think thee no hero. I think thee a man, a fine man but a man just the same.'

'Don't you understand? If they'd caught me then, if they caught me now, I'd be hanged for mutiny or shot for cowardice.'

Bish watched as the anger guttered, leaving behind it only shame. He replied in the same reassuring tone as before. 'If refusing a death in vain is the measure, most men are cowards.'

'You're not afraid to die. I saw that as soon as I saw how things were with you.'

Bish coiled up his fishing line and set his rod to one side. 'It's a different thing. I've long known that my time here would be shorter than most. It's true that I don't fear it, any more than thou fearest death coming for thee in the night forty years hence. There's no sense in fighting what can't be changed.'

When Smeed made to reply, Bish raised a hand to stop him.

'But when we haul a load across the marshes, preventive men on our tails, I feel the same as any man — the hope we'll get clear and the fear we won't. I'm not ready to give up my life now, while it's worth living. When it becomes a burden, then I'll let it go.'

He paused.

'Truth be told, Jem, those feelings are more than half the reason owling hooked me. I don't need the money, what with my job and

247

no kin to support, but I like the feeling of snatching my life back. It makes me feel like I've some say in when I go.' He looked fondly across at Smeed. 'So now thou knowest me for a fool, eh?'

Smeed shuffled closer. 'If you're a fool, I'm a coward.'

Bish took his hand before returning to where the conversation had started. It startled him to realise that the lover in whose confidence and experience he felt so secure was some six years his junior, close in age to Dennard. But then it was small wonder if he seemed older than his years, alone at sea from childhood and then adrift on the run in a foreign land.

'So Dover brought it back for thee?'

'Aye. It was Phillippe put me up in Marseilles, helped me pass myself off as a local fisherman. That's how I learned most of my seamanship. When I made for England, he came with me. He thought he might do better here than in what was left of France, picked up the licence for an inn on the docks. You know as well as I do that trade never stopped, whatever the Government said — there's plenty of Frogs down there and always will be.'

'He put thee on to the Irishman?'

Smeed nodded. 'He always knows what's what.' When Smeed's grip tightened, Bish felt his mood shift from regrets for the past to thoughts of the present. 'It don't trouble you how things might lie between Phillippe and me then?'

'Trouble?' Bish pondered. 'No… I have faith in thy word but…' He faltered before giving an undertaking that would be painful to keep. 'If the Lord has forgiven my sins, then surely I must forgive thine. If thou needest aught I can't give…' He spread his hands in frustration at trying to put such complex sentiments into words. Finally, he concluded by saying, 'I don't own thee.'

The grin that crept across Smeed's face then was only too familiar. They'd done no fishing worth speaking of up to that point and they'd be doing no more after it.

'Oh, aye, I think you do.'

Datchy

Datchy Gilham chewed on the heel of a loaf his wife had risen early that morning to bake. He was thankful that Dennard had proved wiser than Higgins when it came to the ways of women. Fran had been running a home since soon after Delia's birth and she was well practised in it. Once he'd moved his ready-made family into a better cottage closer to the village, she kept it with a pride that surprised him. She asked only one thing of him and, provided he did that tolerably well once or twice a week, everything went like clockwork. Her attentiveness meant that, while he was not in love with her, he had grown fond of her in a more familial way.

For his part, he devoted his spare time to carpentry, filling their home with every comfort that could be made from wood. He saw the admiration with which his wife watched their furniture take shape and her delight in the toys he made for the children. If he occasionally wondered what she did for warmth when his work took him away, as it often did, he said nothing. He lacked the passion for jealousy and saw little practical difference whether the children he expected to appear at regular intervals were his or not. So far, he had no cause for suspicion. Only a sennight short of nine months after the night he took pity on her, their first child arrived. If the timing of Louisa's birth were not proof enough, her pretty hazel eyes seemed to confirm her parentage beyond doubt. She was adorable and he adored her.

He no longer cared who thought him a fool. Many of the men now rowing the two galleys to France under the leadership of himself and Jem Smeed would not have started their day as well as he had. He woke to find his wife caressing him and barely had to move while she straddled his hips to take him to satisfaction. He dozed contentedly for an hour while she clattered in the kitchen, then emerged to face an enormous breakfast and travelling provisions fit to sink a smaller craft.

Datchy looked at Smeed's back, hunched over the steering oar of the lead galley. He knew that Smeed had made the same assumptions about him when they met as most men did but their shared expertise meant they'd spent many hours together since and friendship had blossomed. Smeed was one of the best seamen Datchy had known, possibly one of the best men as well. In him, competence and confidence did not combine to bring arrogance as they so often did. A self-contained man, he did not reach out to other people and yet there was a dependability about him, an impression that he would put himself out when it counted. Although he was not overtly kind or charitable, he was trustworthy in a way that some of the Blues were not.

Datchy was far from the innocent that most of his friends took him for. With no doubt that Smeed had also left home with his itches thoroughly scratched, he had a good idea who'd done the scratching. He could see the appeal of such an arrangement, free from expanding hordes of children to provide for, but it wasn't an option for him.

Smiling to himself, he realised that he would miss the home comforts that he was so fast taking for granted. He doubted too many men could keep house as well as his wife did. In contrast to his huge parcel of bread and cheese, cold meat and pasties, fruit pie and cake, Smeed carried a Spartan bundle of dry provisions that only the Navy would call food.

He extracted a crumbly chunk of ginger cake. He loved ginger cake and finding his new wife excelled at making it was one of the happiest moments of his adult life. It was easy to acquire spices in his line of work, so marriage to a woman who knew how to use them made a fortuitous partnership. At the starboard oar in front of him, Smoker faltered in his stroke, his eyes fixed on the cake.

'Stone me, Datchy. How much more have you got down there? Is this your idea of torture, wafting your wife's baking under our noses while we work?'

The words might have come from the Smoker of old but the tone was different, its humour subdued by the pall of sorrow that had hung over him since the death of his fishing partner a month before. Datchy had seen such partnerships severed by the sea, though never by a musket ball, and doubted the shadow would ever pass fully. He studied the aromatic sponge regretfully, then broke it in two and stuffed half into his mouth and half back into the parcel. He would gladly have shared it with Smoker but a dozen others would make short work of his supplies.

Reluctantly abandoning thoughts of his stomach, he returned to the job in hand. They opted to collect the shipment from France themselves for two reasons. The first was financial: why pay others to do what they had the skills and vessels to do themselves? The second was discretion: the more people who knew about the shipment — what it contained, who collected it and where it went — the more exposed they became. Now only Finney and a contact in France knew of the transaction. The former was an unavoidable risk but the latter was unlikely ever to come to the attention of the authorities in England. Ransley had undoubtedly told his wife and probably Sam Bailey too but, otherwise, only the men making the run and the men meeting them with carts on their return knew of their mission.

The weather seemed settled. If it held, the voyage would take two or three days. As a child, Datchy had heard stories of guinea boats that could make the narrowest Channel crossings in five hours or less but they were making a far longer crossing and their vessels were not guinea boats. Even so, only a swift cutter in a favourable wind would be a match for their unlicensed twelve-oared galleys. Newly acquired by Ransley, the *Venus* and *Cupid*, along with their sister vessel *Mercury*, were amongst the largest galleys Datchy had ever seen. The boat-builders had used every trick of the trade to wring speed and manoeuvrability from the oarsmen's labour. Clinker-built hulls in smooth fir parted the sea as easily as Moses' staff, making them an instant seizure target for both customs and excise services.

Datchy liked jobs like this one, where their crews were made up of the best of their men. He and Smeed had no need to watch every move, on the lookout for shirking or stupidity. They all knew what had to be done and shared the responsibility for doing it. Nights when they needed to muster a hundred men in boats were a different matter, with the mates having to keep a sharp eye out for theft, violence and plain idiocy.

It was hardly surprising that Smeed had approached him about the run, indeed they had no one else with a comparable blend of skills in seamanship, free-trade and armed combat, but he'd noted his friend's concern about his state of mind following Quids' death. He suspected Smeed thought the change of scene would do him good and, gazing across the tranquil sea around them, realised that he did feel better than he had since that wretched night.

He glanced at Smoker, wondering if anything would help him and wishing for a moment that his friend had gone with Smeed. The fisherman had automatically stepped forward for the *Venus* under his command and he had just as automatically accepted him. It wasn't easy to watch his pain, especially with a seasoning of guilt at having failed to prevent the murder, but Datchy was too good a friend to ease his own misery at another's expense. Smoker had only his routine and his friends to see him through his grief and Datchy wanted to be there for him, generous with whatever meagre comfort his presence might give.

Using a skill learned early in life, he shut out the unpleasant thoughts and focused on the beautiful day they had for the first leg of their journey. The weather was clear and calm, with a brisk north-easterly at their backs to send them on their way. He and Smeed had researched the trip thoroughly and knew that a squall brewing in the North Sea was almost certain to overtake them during the following day. Their plan was to make fast progress while unladen, keeping careful watch and dodging any vessels that might come into view. They honed their strategy while passing fishing smacks, and had a chance to test it when they crept past a revenue cutter headed for Dover. After a busy morning, they'd seen nothing more than a distant sail for hours. He could see the coast on both horizons, and judged their position level with Brighton to the north and Dieppe to the south.

Their destination was Cherbourg, once a key port in Napoleon's invasion plans but now fallen into the same postwar malaise that infected France as well as England. With the only trade left to most of the inhabitants being the illegal transport of goods across the Channel, it was no surprise to anyone when Finney named it as the delivery point.

The peninsula on which the port grew up was one of many strategic vantage points disputed by England and France over the centuries and so, when Smeed said he knew it well, Datchy guessed that his familiarity had military connotations. He, too, knew Cherbourg well but his business there had been commercial. His memories of the town were fond, involving a skinful of cheap brandy and a highly versatile whore who had shown him things far beyond his youthful imagination. The backstreets offered just about anything a man might desire and it amused him to think that Smeed might have been about his pleasures in a neighbouring establishment at the same time for all they knew.

His spirits lifted at the thought of the other boat's commander. He enjoyed the camaraderie he had with Smeed, their shared outlook and similar approach to their duties. They'd discussed the run, quickly finding themselves agreed on a swift outward voyage, direct entrance to Cherbourg where their galleys were perfectly legal, a more cautious return voyage under cover of the bad weather and finally a covert landing near Romney.

He knew his improved mood was fragile when the pleasure of partnership was marred by sadness at the severance of the far longer association between Smoker and Quids. He knew he must shake off the sorrow and regret — one grieving man in a crew was more than enough — but he was at a loss how to do it.

Jem

Jem Smeed sprang from the boat onto the jetty, looped the rope in his hands and dropped it over a post. He waited while the oarsmen climbed out more steadily, knowing that the stiffness he felt from sitting was nothing next to their fatigue after a couple of days at their oars. Gilham joined him, watching as their men stretched limbs and tried to straighten crumpled clothing.

They were well ahead of schedule, with nearly ten hours before they were due to pick up the shipment. Jem was sure that they were no keener than he was to be caught with a consignment of firearms so any break must come before the collection.

'Listen up, lads,' he said, voice low. They drew closer, mindful that there was no need to tell everyone on the dock of their plans. 'I'll take first watch. Go rest your heads and fill your bellies while there's time, take a turn in cock lane if you want, but have a care with the booze. Unsteady on your feet — half-pay. Unfit to take an oar — no pay. Clear?'

They nodded, some with reproachful expressions at the suggestion that they might return the worse for drink. For his part, while he trusted them with his life in most situations, he had no illusions about the difficulty of keeping seamen sober on even a short voyage. While his own leaves were generally devoted to his search for pretty young boys, and occasionally fine food, many of his shipmates wasted half of theirs in drunken stupors. However, knowing that a good half-dozen of the men were as steady and conscientious as Smoker, he had faith in them to keep things under control and judged they were better left to savour their pleasures without the feeling that they were being watched over.

Nodding at a church clock beyond the harbour, he said firmly, 'Back here by eleven.' Then, indicating two pairs of men to take the later watches, he added, 'Five till nine, nine till we cast off.'

They could not leave the galleys unattended but, with no reason to expect a violent assault, two guards seemed ample. The pairs combined the oldest and youngest men in each crew, balancing wisdom with vigour, and he intended to take the rest of the men with him when they collected the cargo, needing their backs to carry the load and perhaps their fists in its defence. He had not discussed the specifics with Gilham, expecting that they would be broadly in agreement as usual but not presuming to give him orders as to how he should spend his time ashore.

The men drifted away, breaking into loose groups as they wandered towards the town. Watching them go, he reflected that Cherbourg harbour could just as easily have been an English port. Further inland, he'd seen more differences between French and English villages but harbours had more in common with each other than with their land neighbours.

'I'll wait with you,' Gilham offered, settling himself on a low stone wall and reaching into a pocket for his pipe.

'No need.'

'I know.'

Welcoming the company, Jem took a seat a yard or so along the wall. He felt for his own pipe. Neither of them were heavy smokers but a shared bowl would help to pass the time. Gilham offered his tobacco pouch but one sniff told Jem that it held Ransley's coarsest flake, hardly surprising given Gilham's thriftiness. He shook his head and passed his own pouch, containing a fine blend of Virginia leaves twisted in true sailor's fashion, a gift from Wilson that he would not be quick to pass around a crowd. He never smoked in his lover's presence, out of concern for his health, so the gift had initially startled him. Only later did he realise that Wilson liked the scent of tobacco on him, perhaps precisely because it was a pleasure that he was denied. Gilham sniffed the open pouch, then smiled and filled his briar.

They sat, puffing companionably, for a while.

'You'll take a b-break when they relieve us?'

Jem nodded, exempting neither of them from the need for food and rest.

'Hungry?'

Jem shrugged. His meagre rations were adequate, no more.

Gilham wandered over to the *Venus* and rummaged through his bags in the stern, returning with a large slice of apple pie in each hand, his pipe clamped between his teeth. Jem made short work of his piece, all the while knowing that he would only feel hungrier when his digestive juices began to flow after eating it.

'Your wife bakes a tasty pie.'

'Aye, she does that.'

Jem studied him for a few seconds before putting a question.

'Do you find wedlock to your liking?'

There was a far longer pause before Gilham answered.

'Aye, it in't so b-bad when all's said and done.'

That was typical of Gilham's dispassionate nature. Jem rarely felt free to discuss his affairs but the description of Wilson that he gave Phillippe when he returned to the Anchor after meeting Finney had brimmed with love and lust. Noticing Gilham's eye on him, he hastily pushed such thoughts out of his mind, wary that something might show in his expression. His friend laughed.

'What?' Jem demanded, feeling the heat rise in his cheeks.

'I've no complaints. Keeping a wife suits me b-better than a turn in cock lane. I don't see you b-bound there neither.'

The remark caught Jem off-guard. 'I—'

'Aye, you,' Gilham teased, then sobered. 'Truth to tell, I never saw one of your k-kind stick with just the one before.'

Jem bridled instinctively, only ever having heard the phrase *one of your kind* as part of an insult or threat before, but then realised that his companion knew no polite word for what he was. He looked at the ground, then out to sea, then back at the ground again. Just when he thought he knew Gilham, along came a demonstration of just how frank a shy man could be.

'Some do,' he began defensively but then admitted, 'Not many.'

'Strikes m-me folk don't m-make it easy. The longer you stick with it, the m-more chance of trouble. An alley in Dover's safer.'

Jem seized the opportunity to see how close trouble might be.
'How many know?'

Gilham shrugged, gesturing expansively with his right hand.

'Too many?'

'M-most wish you no harm.'

'Only takes one.'

'You'll have warning. There's p-plenty like me, who'll p-pass the word if they hear it.'

The unexpected assurance touched Jem deeply, bringing a sense of security he had lacked since his desertion deprived him of the only community he'd ever known. He nodded his thanks but Gilham waved them away. Returning to silent puffing, they waited for the second watch to relieve them and tried not to think about their midnight appointment.

Finney's instructions for collecting the cargo were precise. Jem had a clear picture from the information that Gilham relayed to him, word-for-word as far as he could judge. Seeing how confidently the man now walked beside him, he was sure that their route was as clear to Gilham as it was to himself. He'd spent hours before the run, and most of his time in Cherbourg, considering how careful he needed to be. In the end, he could see no reason for Finney to deceive them. Firearms were not so hard to come by and they were paying a fair price for a large order. As far as he could tell, Finney was no more likely to betray them over it than they were to sell one of their customers short. Profit today was good, of course, but not at the expense of a living tomorrow.

That was why they now set out in one party, leaving only the four guards with the galleys, two on watch and two taking a rest. The instructions took them into whatever the people of Cherbourg would call a warren, where rows of dilapidated workshops underlined how the port's fortunes had suffered.

'A crapping castle for Crappos,' one of the men laughed, pleased with his pun.

Having found more friends in France than England after the sudden end of his naval service, Jem disliked hearing Frenchmen called either Frogs or Crappos but passed no comment. It was true enough that their surroundings bore some resemblance to a privy, containing little but decaying waste of one kind or another, human and otherwise. In his opinion, that was more a cause for sadness than mirth, revealing as it did that the poor of France had fared no better — perhaps even worse — than their counterparts in England, despite a revolution that was meant to improve their wretched lot.

'I like it,' another countered. 'Got a woman for a copper — better looking than the wife and willing too.'

'*Any* woman's better looking than your old lady,' the first man pointed out, getting a gale of laughter from the others.

'Bugger off,' the second man said nonchalantly, seeming to think more that a response was expected than to care what his companions thought of his wife.

'Button your lips, boys.'

Jem kept his voice good-natured, as if objecting only to the noise, and tried not to think about the circumstances that might make a woman work the backstreets for coppers. He'd never had the least compunction about paying for his sexual adventures but he'd always given a fair price for a clean boy in a well-run molly house. He had his own, largely selfish, reasons for that, from a preference for taking his time in pleasant surroundings to a desire for safety, both from the pox and from those who found his kind an affront to the laws of God and man, but the welfare of the boys who entertained him certainly figured in his thinking. Perhaps that was selfish too as, in his experience, boys who enjoyed their work delivered a far better service than their less fortunate brothers. No matter how deeply he might love Wilson, he still remembered some of those nights fondly, best of all when two or three youngsters competed for his favour — and for the sixpences with which he rewarded their trouble.

They walked another two streets in silence, until a right turn revealed the end of their search. The warehouse in front of them looked at first glance to be as run down as its neighbours. The sign over its doors was so peeled that only the first two letters were legible: it had once read SCIERIE — sawmill. There was nothing to suggest that the building had fulfilled that function in many a long year and yet, as they drew nearer, Jem's sharp eyes spotted evidence of recent use in some capacity, from footprints and wheel-tracks in the mud to a new padlock on the double-doors. Looking sideways at Gilham, he saw the same recognition.

They strode forward, motioning their men to wait. Smoker stood squarely as the unofficial foremen of the group, succeeding in looking formidable even without any weapons. That was another thing which Jem had considered long and hard: whether to arm at all and, if so, with what. Eventually he decided there was little point in facing arms-traders with arms of any kind. They could not match even the most modest private army and he judged it best not to try. He carried the ubiquitous seaman's knife in his belt, as did Gilham and most of their men, but that was only because he felt naked without it.

The directions took them to a side door. Finding it unlocked, he entered cautiously, wondering what strange specimen of mankind he might be about to meet. Gilham followed equally warily, some way behind to gain time to react to whatever might happen.

'Good evening, gentlemen.'

Jem had no preconceptions of what their contact would sound like, but a well-educated English accent took him by surprise. The figure perched on a bench in a circle of greasy lamplight was no less unexpected: tall, slim and immaculately dressed. More to the point, it was familiar, although his companions would have no reason to recognise the fine features so admired in some circles. Jem stepped forward confidently, responding in kind.

'Evening.'

He did not intend to reveal that he knew the man's identity but must have let something slip. The man nodded acknowledgement, not of Jem's identity — which he could not know and was doubtless indifferent to — but of the pretence.

'I believe we are holding a consignment of goods for your employer, on behalf of an agent.'

The opening gambit was cautious, admitting no knowledge of the nature of the consignment and no responsibility for any transaction agreed between two absent parties.

Jem nodded, content to follow the man's lead.

'I am advised that there is a balance of seven hundred and forty pounds owing on the consignment.'

Jem nodded again, glad he'd had Wilson confirm Finney's figure. Numbers were not his strong point and he struggled to convert pounds and guineas. At a loss to see why a sovereign must be worth a pound when it was worth a guinea before, he shared Gilham's belief that it was a Government trick to take money from the poor, although he had no idea how such a trick might work.

The young man stood and held out a hand, signalling that he awaited payment. While his posture just about passed muster for a dandy, he'd have needed to exercise more caution had he grown up in Jem's circles.

'We'll check 'em first, if it's all the same to you.'

The hand waved disdainfully and then flicked at the shadows.

'As you wish.'

Men as yet unseen began to carry crates forward into the circle of light. While Gilham stepped back to summon their own men inside, Jem opened the first of the longer crates. Inside were packed the India-pattern muskets he'd ordered, interleaved barrel to stock. He counted twenty quickly enough, then counted the boxes and made it ten. That seemed right. Taking a musket from the box, he began to inspect it, only then glancing up at Gilham. Having seen his friend at his woodwork, he knew how easily figures came to him. Gilham gave the slightest nod. If the ten crates of each size contained the same twenty weapons, their order was complete.

'Open 'em up,' Jem told his men. 'Make sure there's twenty good'uns in each.'

While they did so, he and Gilham selected a few at random for closer checks. He would have been happier to fire them but that could only draw unwanted attention. Instead, he settled for sighting down the barrels and checking the moving parts. Gilham matched his scrutiny, asking for a second opinion on one with a sticky hammer. The muskets looked nearly new, hardly surprising since the East India Company ordered them in thousands and shipped them all over the world as a precautionary measure. The pistols were poorer, cheap French naval models of which many had been well-used. Jem examined some of them carefully but knew that the two-guinea price had been reached only by his concession on the pistols. Short-barrelled as ordered, and with many good shots in them yet, he saw no reason to reject them.

The dandy picked one up and sighted at a mark on the wall.

'A crude weapon but effective, I believe.'

Jem could easily imagine the pair of fine pistols kept immaculate by a valet in readiness for a duel that would probably never come. By comparison, their weapons were crude indeed.

Eventually, he rose from his inspections, swung the knapsack from his back and passed a package to the man.

'You will forgive me if I make my own checks?'

Without waiting for an answer, the man began to unwrap the thick brown paper. Trusting Wilson's calculations and counts, Jem carried on with the business in hand.

'Close 'em down tight, lads. We don't need to be tipping 'em out on the dock for all to see.'

Eager to be on their way, it took all his self-control to stand still while the payment was counted and the crates sealed. He hoped he looked more seasoned on the outside than he felt on the inside, as he concluded his first arms deal and prepared to start a war in Kent.

Minutes later, they were back in the deserted street. He and Gilham walked just behind their men, carefully watching the buildings around them for any sign of trouble. Only when the disused saw-mill disappeared uneventfully from view did he let himself relax. Gilham slapped him lightly on the back and leaned closer to whisper.

'Didn't show.'

Jem looked at him, about to deny his apprehension, then realised he was wasting his time with a man who knew the signs of nervousness better than most.

Gilham leaned closer again, this time to ask a question.

'You knew him?'

Surprised by his friend's keen eye, Jem wondered if he was slipping but did not try to deny the acquaintance. 'Know of him.'

'Aught I should know?'

It was a fair question, given that Gilham took seriously his part in the run, but Jem felt an obligation to the gentleman as well as to his friend. After careful consideration, he decided he could say why he recognised their contact without saying who he was. He let the distance between them and their men grow a yard or two.

'You know of the *Code Napoléon*?' he asked.

Gilham gave something that started out as a nod and then turned to a shrug. 'It's what passes for law in France, in't it?'

Jem smiled at the casual prejudice that the reply revealed. In one significant respect, the *Code Napoléon* struck him as a good deal more just than what passed for law in England.

'Aye. There are things that'll see a man hang in England that don't turn a hair here in France.' He gave a meaningful glance. 'Our betters don't like hanging their kin so exile's the next best thing.'

Gilham digested that for a few seconds, then grinned. 'So will he deal fairer with one of his own?'

Jem returned the grin, pleased to find Gilham easy enough to joke about it. 'Doubt he sees me as one of his own. But he's one of the better ones, always paid his bills and treated people fair from what I heard, and I've no reason to think aught's changed there.'

'Well, we checked 'em over careful enough. All that's left is to get 'em home.'

Although they lengthened their stride to catch up with their cargo, Jem did not expect trouble while they remained within French jurisdiction. He thought their problems would begin only when they came within the grasp of His Majesty's forces.

Datchy

If Datchy had worried about his mental fitness for the run on the outward voyage, he had no time for such introspection on the return leg. The squalls that had started before they reached Cherbourg continued to blow in every few hours. Each was short and sharp, not much of a worry to crews as experienced as theirs but still to be taken seriously. More to the point, his soaked clothes — and the cold flesh inside them — played on his mind far more than the loss of men, past or future. He looked again at the load beneath his feet. The crates were tightly packed into the bottom of the hull, holding the galley deep and steady in the water, and wrapped in three layers of oilcloth that should keep them a lot drier than the men transporting them.

He put their position around halfway home and the time close to dawn. While they enjoyed the twin benefits of darkness and a brief respite in the weather, most of the crew had gone through the palaver of emptying their bowels over the side. A man could twist at his oar to pass water but more substantial waste products took more time and effort. When the last man was done, they resumed their east-north-easterly course. Fifty yards to larboard, Smeed's crew were slower to get back to their oars but followed in their wake before they fell out of sight.

The north-easterly wind was stronger and steadier now, making them work harder for every mile they travelled and throwing each band of rain straight in their faces. While the *Venus* led, the *Cupid* tucked in behind them. When his crew began to tire, Datchy dropped back to let Smeed's crew take the brunt of the weather for a while. The wordless teamwork warmed his heart, though his hands and feet remained as cold as ever.

'Datchy!'

The urgent whisper instantly caught his attention.

'Ahead!'

He twisted instinctively to look over his shoulder at Smeed, who was staring past him into the darkness, then whipped around to search for the danger. The dim outline of sails was coalescing in the gloom, the ship-rigging suggesting a frigate on patrol. Though carrying little sail, it was scudding along at a fair speed.

'We'll head north.'

Smeed had no sooner spoken than the *Cupid* began to peel off to the northern side of the oncoming vessel. Datchy took the *Venus* south, in another of their agreed strategies. One vessel was less visible than two and, if captured, left half their cargo bound for England. Unspoken was the hope that a free crew might come to the aid of its captured friends. Such an attempt would need to be carefully judged but a slim chance was better than none.

With every man dressed in dark clothes from head to foot, skin blackened, and no sail above them, Datchy knew they were all but invisible. Provided they kept quiet, they stood every chance of being passed unseen. Once they were well clear of the frigate's course, he bade his men lay down their oars and wait in silence.

He peered northwards, satisfying himself that he could make out no trace of the *Cupid* in the darkness. Glancing periodically to the east, he monitored the frigate's progress. He tensed when the colours fluttering from her mast, combining the Union Jack with the crown of the Preventive Service, confirmed that she was a revenue vessel on patrol. Some of the tension abated when he saw her decks ablaze with lanterns: the more light aboard, the less chance of a sharp-eyed lookout spotting them in the gloom beyond. He'd just noted that there were more crewmen in evidence than he expected when he saw an unwelcome sight.

A single man stood in the bows, seemingly firing into the sky. Datchy knew the significance of that before a puff of smoke declared it. A second later, an explosion overhead illuminated the sea for half a mile or more in all directions. There were only two reasons to send up a sky rocket: to summon other vessels or to search the surface of the sea for something. Neither explanation was good news for two galleys trying to hide in the shadows.

Datchy looked sideways at the preventive men scurrying around the deck. He was relieved to find their attention focused to the west, suggesting they expected to find another vessel there. There was nothing he or Smeed could do but wait, keep their men and boats silent, and hope no one looked their way. He could not have asked for better men: all stared at their feet, as if the slightest motion or even the white of an eye might betray them. He doubted that possible over the distance but followed their example.

The sky rocket fell slowly, fading as it did so.

His stomach rumbled but, when he passed the wind building inside him, he did so silently. He only realised how nervy he was when the ludicrous notion of being given away by a belch over such a distance nearly made him laugh aloud — even Hogben's notorious bodily functions did not carry that far. Recovering his self-control with difficulty, he held his breath while the frigate passed between his position and the spot for which Smeed had made. Then, just as he felt his crew begin to relax, a shout drifted across the waves separating them from the frigate. A crewman pointed towards them.

'Blast,' he muttered.

Through no fault of theirs, an eye had fallen on them just before the protective darkness enveloped them once more.

'Galley to larboard,' came the distant call.

Datchy wasted not a moment. The frigate had already almost passed them and could not start its pursuit without realigning its sails. Even when it had, the north-easterly wind would do it little good.

'Heave to, boys. Let's see how fast this b-beauty can fly.'

He filled his words with encouragement, turning the order into a challenge to his men's skill and strength. Moving as one, his crew began to row as if they had just set out after a week's rest. Had he not seen it with his own eyes, he would never have believed that they'd been battling the weather for hours. He was confident that Smeed's men were doing just as well somewhere off to the north. He divided his attention between holding their course steady against wind and tide, and monitoring the situation astern.

The frigate wallowed while its crew worked the rigging, starting to drift in a jagged circle. His spirits lifted, as he saw men struggling with the manoeuvre having been taken by surprise, and he felt certain of out-running them. Then his confidence was ripped away by the sight of a cutter joining the fray from the west. The pieces instantly fell into place: here was the vessel that the frigate had been signalling — the damnedest luck had taken them right through the rendezvous.

The commander of the cutter must have been quick off the mark because he sailed straight past the frigate and used all his momentum to pursue the fleeing galley. Datchy hoped that the *Venus* remained the only quarry — that the *Cupid* was already safely on its way. Nothing he could say would be as strong an incentive as the fore-and-aft rigged vessel now in hot pursuit.

'Cutter astern. And she's a f-fast one.'

He began to count aloud, just ahead of their strokes, setting a rhythm that he judged would put them ahead of a vessel that, while swift, was fighting a headwind. The men drew deep strokes through the fractious waters, their layers of clothing pulled taut over the bulging muscles of their shoulders and upper arms. He scanned their faces, looking for signs of fear or fatigue that might cost them precious knots in speed. All he saw was determination as they dug deeper to meet the pace he'd set. Glancing back at every fifth count, it was another twenty strokes before he was sure they were pulling away. He gave no hint of that in his urgent count, knowing that they could not afford to give away a yard.

To the north, he still saw no sign of the *Cupid*. With no time to search for friends, he resigned himself to making the rest of the voyage alone. Looking forward, he drew a sharp intake of breath at the sky ahead. A squall far worse than they'd yet faced snuffed out the stars and stirred the sea into a seething pitch-like stew.

'Storm ahead,' he called, adding wryly, 'Twix the devil and the b-blue sea, 'cept it in't b-blue.'

The oarsmen did not slow one whit, almost flying into the tempest. Rain and wind were no pleasure cruise in a galley but they were more than an inconvenience to a cutter under full sail. Datchy gave a grim smile when the first gust of spray stung his face. Another backward glance showed the cutter's commander reconsidering the pursuit. Had he known that they carried two hundred firearms, he might have reached a different decision but Datchy was not surprised to see that the man deemed a few tubs poor reward for the loss of his fine vessel. The last two things he saw before they were swallowed by the storm was the cutter taking in its sails to ride it out and the *Cupid* closing in from the north to face it with them. The risk of being smashed together was offset by the promise of survival if they lost one of the galleys: they could all reach home safely in one vessel, though perhaps without the load that had cost Ransley so dear.

In truth, Datchy barely considered the prospect of losing either crew or cargo. He'd ridden out storms that made this one look like a summer shower and joined his men in lashing himself to his position in readiness. Nerves long gone, he felt only exhilaration as Mother Nature took hold of them.

Sam

Sam Bailey stared in disbelief at two boards hanging from a post-and-rail fence fifty paces ahead. Little remained of the clumsy circle chalked onto the right-hand one, the wood splintered by a cluster of hits. The board to its left was untouched.

He kicked the man lying at his feet, who was a relative of his wife's but none the better for that.

'It's not my fault,' Ted Pantry whined. 'It's this bloody—'

Sam gave him no time to make the excuse, snatching the weapon and reloading at a furious pace. Raising it to his shoulder, he effortlessly placed a ball straight through the pristine bullseye. The India-pattern muskets were well-made and lightly used, as accurate as any of their kind. Despite his initial resentment at not being consulted before the deal, Sam had no problem with Smeed's choice of weapons. The 39-inch barrels on the muskets sacrificed some manoeuvrability for accuracy but the pistols compensated for the loss. Sam had no love for French firearms, or indeed for anything from a country that had taken so many British lives, but he approved of the short-barrelled service pistols that sat neatly under men's jackets, protected against rain and spray. In recognition of that benefit, the Blockade was in the middle of switching its men from long to short pistols but the Blues would soon take the lead.

'There's nothing wrong with the damned tool. It's the bloody workman that's at fault.' Catching Smeed's smirk from the corner of his eye only fuelled his impatience. 'All right, *you* make a marksman of the bastard. It's all very well when you're teaching the likes of *him*.'

Him was Giles. The shoemaker had never picked up a firearm before they began the training designed to prepare for a darker future. He listened intently as Smeed explained the principles, watched closely as he demonstrated how to clean, load and fire a musket, and then emulated the procedures perfectly on first or second attempt. Pupil already shot almost as well as teacher and, with practice, seemed set to become the best amongst them.

Sam matched Smeed for knowledge and clarity but he trailed badly when it came to patience. In contrast to Giles, Pantry was a poor student, inattentive and inept, exhausting his teacher's goodwill long before they got as far as firing at targets. Having eventually bullied him into following instructions, Sam was at a loss to understand how every ball missed the board when the man was braced securely against the ground and holding the weapon steady as a rock while firing.

Smeed reached for the musket that Giles had just reloaded and passed it to Pantry. Sam knew that Smeed loathed the lazy shepherd, despising like himself all those in their number who saw the trade more as a way to get something for nothing than a chance to better themselves, and yet there was nothing but encouragement in his instruction.

'Take it slow, Ted. Let's see what we've got.'

Clearly determined to show that the fault lay with the weapon, or with his teacher, Pantry did indeed take his time. Sam followed Smeed's inspection of his posture and movements, seeing nothing amiss in them, and yet the shot was as clear a miss as its predecessors. It was lucky they had no shortage of ammunition, thanks to a contact in the Blockade who, for a substantial consideration, redirected part of every consignment.

Smeed shrugged, apparently as puzzled as Sam.

'It's too far away.'

Pantry's whined excuses were starting to wear Sam down.

'For Christ's sake, if you let a preventive man get any closer, it'll be you taking the slug,' he snarled.

Giles had been watching thoughtfully and now he scrambled to his feet and strode towards the fence. Their targets hung only a yard or so from a post and he inspected the hazel pole for a few seconds before waving for them to join him. Sam huffed at Smeed's instant compliance but then grudgingly set off after him. Pantry did not move, doubtless too idle to bother.

When they reached the fence, Giles pointed at the post. Four shots formed an erratic line down the middle third of the pole. They weren't closely grouped, and two of the six shots fired were missing, but they'd have been good enough, if they'd been a couple of cubits to the right.

'What the blazes?' Sam demanded. 'Is he too bloody thick to know a target when he sees one?'

'I think that's the trouble.' Giles was diffident in the face of his temper. 'I don't think he does see it, leastwise not as you or I do.'

Sam glared at the offending holes, wondering how a man could systematically shoot wide of his target like that. 'How –?' he began.

'Don't matter how,' Smeed cut in briskly. 'Damned if we want a man firing a yard to the left of what he aims to hit. Just as likely to fell one of our own that way.'

'He won't take it kindly,' Giles pointed out.

'He'll do as he's damned well told,' Sam snapped.

He glared at the restraining hand that Smeed put on his sleeve when he turned to head back, but failed to make him move it.

'Don't make it personal.'

Smeed's warning was reasonable, wise even, but Sam bridled at being guided by a man who was years his junior, especially in front of a tradesman.

'Don't tell me my business.'

Smeed moved his hand but his frown was no better.

'What? No point beating about the bush: the man's no use.'

'Make five hits in six shots a condition of joining the fighting parties.'

Sam opened his mouth to argue, then faltered. It wasn't a bad idea. They already had a dozen who could meet that standard with a little practice and others, like Pierce and Quested, whom he had not yet called for testing only because he knew what he'd find. He ran through the men in his mind, considering whether such a standard would eliminate any that he wanted to keep. His kin shot as well, if not better, than he did and Hogben, whose exclusion could only cause trouble with his cronies, would not be far behind, so long as they made sure he was reasonably sober when they tested him. A snag insinuated its way into his mind.

'If Ted sees what the problem is, he might shoot a yard to the right to pass the test.'

'Can you see him working that out all by himself?' Some of Smeed's carefully concealed contempt surfaced in the question.

'No,' Sam admitted. 'No, I can't say that I can.'

He knew Giles would say nothing, no friend of Pantry's and — more to the point — as sensitive as they were to the dangers their men would be facing, without being shot by their own side. He led the way back to where Pantry lay, clearly wondering what had passed but lacking the drive or initiative to find out. Sam surprised himself with the casual support that he managed to inject into his final words to Pantry.

'Not too bad after all, Ted.' Picking selectively at the truth he added, 'The grouping's not so bad and we can work on the accuracy another time. Let's call it a day for now.'

Pantry looked startled but quickly accepted the early release. Brushing bits of grass from his thighs, he made his way back to the rest of their men who were loitering by a stream, Giles trailing behind him. It was Smeed who had suggested working with the men two at a time, making them easier to handle and quicker to learn, and Sam realised he was starting to rely on the man's intuition in managing difficult situations.

Seeing the next two men heading out to take their turn, he did not expect the coming session to be difficult at all. When they arrived, he settled back to watch Smeed's demonstration again, grown fluent with repetition. Making no assumptions about what men might or might not know, Smeed presented their agreed way of doing things quietly and firmly. The implication was that men who proved unable to follow orders would soon find themselves back shifting tubs at a few shillings a run, although the pair with them now already had valuable skills and were being tested more as backup than with the expectation of a change in role.

Gilham made no objection to the routine, watching with an apparently open mind and then repeating the procedures as shown. Sam had no doubt that Smeed could see as well as he could that their latest student had handled a musket before. He matched Smeed's speed in biting the end from the cartridge, trickling some powder into the firing pan and then sending the rest down the barrel with the ball behind it. Finally, he dropped the paper wrapper in for wadding and rammed it home solidly.

Equally diligent, if far slower, Dennard was much daintier when it came to ramming the wadding down the muzzle. Sam noted the lack of force with wry humour, wondering whether the boy's handling of horses or women was to blame for his gentle touch. Smeed closed a strong hand over his fist and thrust the rod downwards with twice the force that the lad had wielded.

'Pack it down hard. You don't want the ball rolling out while you're taking aim, let alone have the thing blow up in your face.'

Dennard accepted the advice with a nod, repeating the operation with the required vigour. It was rare for him to need to be told anything twice and Sam expected him to prove a useful addition to the fighting parties, if they had to call on him.

Gilham opted for the more upright of the firing positions they had offered, resting on one knee with the butt of the musket tucked tight into his shoulder. Dennard copied his every move. They shot in unison, Gilham putting a hole only inches from the centre of Pantry's board while Dennard splintered the left edge of Giles's well-worn target.

Gilham was already reloading. Sam grinned at him.

'Could we be teaching grandmother to suck eggs?'

There was no trace of resentment in Gilham's response. 'I can use the p-practice. It's been a while.'

Sam found it easier to acknowledge Gilham's proficiency now that his stammer had faded to little more than a brief pause before certain sounds. He would be pleased to have the man working for him, if that was the way events unfolded. Having found his mark, Gilham's second shot was dead-centre and Sam expected the remaining four to match it.

Dennard's second shot was also better but he groaned in frustration at the over-compensation that took it past the chalk circle, close to the right edge of the board. Smeed patted his shoulder in consolation.

'Next one'll see you there, mark my words.'

The words were prophetic. Dennard's third shot nibbled at the edge of the circle and his last three all passed just within its circumference. Sam heard the deep affection in which Smeed held his student in his gruff words when he took back the musket after the last shot.

'You fire a good stick, Tommy, but mind that's only half the story. If you serve in the fighting parties, take the same care of your firearms as you do of those damned ponies of yours. A misfire could cost your life.'

Dennard's grin at the concern for his welfare hid neither his pleasure at being valued nor his acceptance of the warning. Sam envied his inability to worry, not for a moment mistaking it for rashness or stupidity. He realised that even he was susceptible to the lad's charisma, when he found himself hoping that they would not be putting a musket in his hands: not only would that increase the risk of a mortal wound but it might also turn a charmer into a killer. Knowing the toll that killing had taken on his own character, he had no wish to take another down that road.

Watching the two young friends walk away, waiting for another pair to take their place, Sam's gut churned in hatred of the Blockade that forced them to take ever more drastic measures to make a living. As resigned as he was to the need for firearms, he was still almost as disappointed as Ransley by it. They'd agreed their approach, admitting to only a small number of weapons while they trained men in their use and making no mention of any plans to arm the Blues on a large scale. He wondered if the strategy fooled anyone, but then thought again of Pantry's stupid face staring up at him and suspected that it probably did.

He glanced at Smeed, saw the same turmoil in his expression, and then shrugged it off. They would do what they could and then trust to, what? Luck, he supposed, since he thought Smeed had no more faith in the Almighty than he did. On the other hand, Smeed was surely protected by more fervent prayers than the rest of them put together. Perhaps they would all be safe behind that heavenly shield.

Datchy

Datchy's stomach churned with apprehension. The sensation was a world away from the fluttering he felt whenever he had to speak in front of more than one or two men. He was man enough to recognise it as fear, not mere anxiety, even though it was an emotion that had rarely troubled him since he reached manhood. Gazing past the men at the oars, reluctant to look them in the eyes, he wondered if he was losing his nerve. In an effort to pull himself together, he repeated the words with which he'd been reassuring himself all night. Any man would be nervous, on his first run after a break of two months following the loss of a man. That was probably true and yet his sudden fear still surprised him, when he had rowed to France for the firearms without a second thought.

The circumstances were too similar, he concluded. There were three galleys, rather than the two of the night that Quids was shot before his eyes, and they were sowing a crop not landing a cargo, but it might otherwise have been a repeat of that fateful run. The unusually fine October weather was no better for concealing a run, although at least there was barely a moon.

He'd been through the last run in his head hundreds of times in the weeks since it happened. He was in command of the galley, so a death in its crew had to be his fault. He'd relaxed his guard too soon, thinking they were away when the threat was yet to materialise, but, even under his harshest analysis, he doubted that he could have done better. Even if he'd guessed that an officer would open fire on an unladen boat without so much as a warning, he'd still have judged them too far from the shore to make a target. Even if he'd ordered his men to pull harder, they'd only have been a few yards further out, not enough to make a difference.

Yet still he felt guilty at failing to do something, even if he could not identify what that something might have been. Shoving the thoughts angrily into the darkest recesses of his mind, he forced himself to concentrate on their present task. He'd be damned if he'd lose a second man while lamenting the first.

Once again, he commanded the *Venus*. The loving connotations of the name went some way towards soothing his jagged nerves. They'd unloaded a lugger anchored outside British jurisdiction and were

271

now sowing the crop off Globsden Gut. The mission took him back to happier times, when he'd crept for just such a crop with Smoker and Quids, while Dennard waited with horses to whisk it inland. Now his vigil over the men who were dropping weighted tubs overboard was tense, when before it had been casual. He stared northwards, thinking again that he saw movement but unsure if it was anything more than the waves.

The *Venus* had the riskiest spot, close to the Tower 27 station at Dymchurch, while her sister vessels faced only the more modest Little Stone station on the Warren. Smeed had offered to take the northern flank but Datchy had refused, guessing the concerns that lay behind the offer and determined to prove that they were unfounded. Whether the proof was for Smeed or himself he had yet to decide.

'Blast,' he muttered.

This time there was no doubt. He'd seen faint starlight glinting on something metallic. The straight edge and steadiness of the reflection left him certain that it had not come from the sea. He glanced southwards, trying to gauge how close the other galleys were to completing the run but they were too distant and the night too dark to be sure.

'How close?' Smoker did not pause in his work.

Datchy looked again. 'Two hundred yards.'

Another pair of tubs found their way almost silently over the side, with just the gentle gurgle of the water as it enveloped them. They had few choices: finish sowing or take the remaining tubs with them, row along the shore or away from it. They could hardly strike north, headed straight for a boat full of armed Blockademen and rowing south would lead their pursuers towards the *Cupid*. That left the open Channel as the only option. Datchy watched the galley draw closer, visible now and then when the swell lifted it higher in the water. On its current heading, it would pass close to their present position and could not fail to spot them. Experience told him that it was on patrol and headed down to Denge Beach, where it would probably haul ashore for a break before heading back to Dymchurch. If they fled before being detected, it must encounter the next galley, which had reached its position after the *Venus* began sowing and would be working for some time yet.

Datchy knew that the same considerations had passed through

Smoker's agile mind, and that others in the crew were probably not far behind. When he glanced at the man, he found Smoker's eyes already on him, shrewd, sad and bitter. If they'd carried firearms, they'd have engaged the enemy but without them?

'Make no sound,' he said softly, 'But m-make haste.'

The crew silently followed his instructions, increasing the speed of their work without a murmur. Perhaps a minute dragged by before the last pair of tubs sank into the depths. The men crept back to their oars and turned the galley east in response to his hushed commands.

'Take us out quietly.'

He hoped to gain some distance before showing themselves to divert the pursuit from the others. The strategy was sound, seeing them a hundred yards east before the Blockade galley faltered in its course. Seconds later, it was flying towards them.

'Pull with all your m-might, boys!'

His crew needed no second bidding, putting their backs into long, even strokes that sent the *Venus* slicing through the waves. Datchy monitored the gap between the vessels, dismayed when it began to close. The *Venus*, as fine as she was, had been built to haul a heavy load. The Blockade galley was lighter, with fewer oars but wielded by men at the start of a shift not the end of a long night's work.

'Faster!' he urged.

He saw in their pained faces and strained muscles how hard his men tried to deliver the power he needed but it was to no avail. Progress was steady, and might even have taken them to France if required, but speed was beyond them. The Blockade galley nibbled away at the distance, closing from a hundred to fifty yards and then halving it again.

Datchy fingered the pistol slung beneath his smock, which he'd taken to wearing again in spite of Ransley's standing order not to bear firearms now they had men trained in their use. The urge to open fire on the bastards was hard to resist. Through the fog of anger, he knew such feelings would only see more of his own men dead in the long run. That alone prevented him from taking a life there and then. Once it was clear to them all that they would soon be overtaken, he announced his plan, such as it was.

'When they come upon us, let them take us.' He cut off the tide of dissent with a sharp gesture. 'That'll leave the other b-boats free and clear. Say naught,' he paused for emphasis, '*Naught*, I tell you. They have thirteen men in an empty galley and no more.'

While his words sank in, he drew his pistol and dropped it calmly over the side. They carried no cargo and no arms. Yes, the galley was illegal: it would be seized and someone would be fined. Ransley could handle that with his eyes closed. What they needed now was to stay calm. It took all his self-control to remember that during the boarding and he watched Smoker apprehensively, wary that the Blockademen's crude insults and rough handling might easily send the grieving man over the edge. He needn't have worried. Whether through obedience or determination not to take his friends to the grave with an empty gesture, Smoker meekly allowed himself to be searched, bound and shoved back at his oar.

The lieutenant in charge of the Blockade galley was unremarkable, of middle years and average appearance. In the early days, promotion was so rare that lieutenants invariably boasted long experience or huge potential. Only after a legal loophole left locals refusing to permit illegal searches under the command of petty officers had every station been headed by a lieutenant. Datchy suspected the man holding a pistol on them owed his rank to circumstance not merit. His next order confirmed it.

'Houlihan, take the helm. Keep watch while we retrieve the goods.'

Of course, the officer's options were limited. Without a cargo, the case against his prisoners was weak. Even so, leaving a single man to guard thirteen, even a man as experienced and heavily armed as the one picking his way across to the steering oar appeared to be, was a colossal risk and Datchy intended to make the officer pay for it. From where he'd been forced to his knees in the bow, he watched the other galley set off to where they'd sown their tubs, pondering whether his friends would yet be clear but not once looking in their direction.

The two boats had not long parted company when a shot rang out from the beach. Again the Blockade galley faltered in its course before striking out in a new direction. The lieutenant had clearly decided that the sunken tubs could wait while he assisted the shore party. Datchy glanced at Smoker, saw their thoughts were once more running in parallel, and waited in silence for the galley to disappear from view. The guard's eyes were fixed on him, in the expectation that any threat would come from his quarter, so he left

Smoker to monitor the waters to the south for any sign of whether their friends intended to join the fray.

Time crawled slowly by but they remained alone. Occasional shots came from ashore, widely spaced as only the Blockademen had firearms, but grew more distant. He guessed the fighting party was leading the Blockade forces into the marshes, goading them with bats and stones to give the seamen time to escape.

He considered their position. His crew sat at their oars, hands bound but feet free. He was tied more securely, cramped in the bows and too far from their captor to attempt any kind of attack. He studied the man that the lieutenant had addressed as Houlihan. He was hale and hearty, steady and unlikely to panic, and carried the standard issue of two pistols, a musket and a cutlass. Three shots and he'd be down to a blade. How to make him expend them without killing someone? Any action on Datchy's part might make him fire on a crewman to regain control. Seeing one of his fellows walk away from Quids' murder unpunished was hardly likely to make him more careful of traders' lives. Datchy wondered whether to gamble on his original strategy but knew it was risky: they could be linked to the sown tubs or to the fighting parties on shore. Even without firearms, they might face transportation.

Finally, preferring to die for his actions than for the lack of them, he gathered his bound legs beneath him and slipped nimbly over the side. He could imagine the consternation behind him. The sea was calm enough but plenty of seamen could not swim at all and few would attempt it while bound hand and foot. Neither Houlihan nor the crew would have expected such a move. He wriggled through the water, totally at ease in its chilly embrace, making slow progress but in no fear of sinking while buoyed up by the air in his lungs. His plan was simple and depended as much on the responses of his ally and his victim as on himself.

Reaching the stern, he wriggled more vigorously, heading towards the surface with all the power he could muster. He broke through with a satisfying splash, half-expecting his head to be split open by a musket ball as he did so, but there was no sound and no pain. He fell back in the water, shaking the hair from his eyes, hoping the manoeuvre had given the momentary distraction that Smoker needed. When his vision cleared, he found Houlihan was staring directly at him. His eyes narrowed involuntarily against a shot that never came. Looking more closely, he saw that the man was grinning. Closer still and he saw the grin was a gape. Smoker's right forearm was tight around Houlihan's throat, blocking the passage of air. The man's eyes grew wider. Datchy watched life ebb away, feeling nothing — no personal satisfaction but no urge to put an end to his friend's vengeance either. He held Smoker's gaze as the fisherman put his left hand, still bound to the right, to Houlihan's head and forced it sharply to the side. A brittle crack pronounced death.

Smoker drew Houlihan's cutlass, tossed his body over the side and, without a word of justification then or later, hauled Datchy aboard and set about freeing them all.

With no one in sight to pursue them, they rowed south for their moorings near the Warren, Datchy at the steering oar, half-stunned by what had passed but already rehearsing how to break the news to Ransley. After they'd hidden the galley, before they headed home, he briefed his crew on the half-truth he planned to tell. Smoker had acted to save them all, struggling against the Blockademan while bound with no intention of taking life. It was not his fault that Houlihan's frenzied resistance had forced him to kill or be killed. The crew nodded soberly. They were men Datchy had known for years, reliable and wise to the ways of the trade. Acutely aware of the divisions and disagreements within the Blues, they would stand behind him when he defended Smoker's actions.

Feeling no pity for the dead man, Datchy intended to make Ransley see how close they'd come to capture, how easily the charges might have become capital, and how futile it was to face a pair of pistols, musket and cutlass with a bat. And yet, in spite of all that, he regretted the shift they must make. Ransley's hold over the trade was slipping, with the Blockade forcing him into a head-on conflict just like the one that had cost Spratford his Burmarsh operation. Datchy knew Ransley outclassed Spratford by a wide margin: what he did not know was whether that margin was wide enough.

John

John Bailey paused to lean on a tree. It was mid-afternoon but he'd barely stopped drinking for three days. He didn't much like being as drunk as he was at that moment but then he didn't much like admitting he couldn't keep up with his nephew either. Now he watched as Rob passed him, gait steady in spite of matching him drink for drink. The sound of retching interrupted his train of thought. He turned to see Hogben, bottle in hand, deposit a pool of vomit in the middle of the lane. They'd all watered the verges liberally during their slow journey to nowhere in particular but, until then, they'd kept it all moving downwards. Hogben grimaced, rinsed his mouth with another swig of brandy and then spewed it onto the vomit.

Locked in drunken fascination, John didn't avert his eyes when Hogben dropped his trousers and added a lake of diarrhoea to the filthy mess. The faeces were unrecognisable as such, almost completely liquid and a strange shade of green. Not long before, when Hogben had passed out half-naked after one of their binges, John had inspected the impressive collection of sores surrounding his genitals. He had no idea what diseases the man was carrying and preferred to keep it that way.

There were better men in the Blues. In fact, almost all the Blues were better men than Hogben had become. There'd been a time when John wanted their friendship but nothing he did ever seemed to be good enough. He was in the Blues because he was a Bailey but, as the years passed, he found himself more and more outside their number. He could trace that back to Brookland. Since Ransley succeeded Cephas, brains and cunning were valued more highly than strength and bravado.

John scowled. A stripling like Dennard had more say than he did. Ransley sent Dennard scouting for information and put faith in the intelligence he brought back; never was he himself accorded such respect. He thought Ransley would have got rid of him and Rob long before if not for Sam being his deputy but he wasn't sure, given that Hogben was kept on too. He gathered a generous globule of spittle and sent it earthwards, as if that could purge the bitter jealousies and resentments seething in his befuddled mind.

A glance told him that Rob's state of mind was far removed from his own. Bailey characters were often intensified by alcohol. Eliza became more high-spirited, Rhoda more sensual, Sam more melancholy and John more bitter. Rob became even more carefree, or careless, than usual. Now he was fingering the pistol in his belt and looking into the distance.

John followed his gaze. Cattle.

He felt his spirits lift, not averse to a little target practice. After all, what was the point in making off with weapons before Sam could stash them away if they didn't shoot something with them? He never considered whether they might be doing just what their leaders feared they would do once armed, or how their sprees might damage the Blues. So what if maliciously wounding cattle was a capital offence? Most of their business transactions, and half of their other pursuits, would see them swing if caught — another cow here or there made little difference.

'Hey, Hog!' He looked over his shoulder to find Hogben trying to clean himself up with a handful of dock leaves. 'A guinea says you can't hit a cow from a hundred paces.'

'Damn you!' Hogben struggled back into his trousers. 'I can outshoot the pair of you any day of the week.'

'That so?' Rob goaded. 'Better make it two then.'

Drunk or sober, they were both better shots than Hogben and he already owed them more than twenty guineas apiece. Winning was easier than collecting, of course, but they were content to add to the unpaid tab. John took the lead, determination in his stride and no thought of the cattle's owner in his mind.

Fifty yards on and he studied the target more closely. Thirty or more shorthorns clustered in the middle of the field, chewing the cud and staring placidly, oblivious to the fate that awaited them. He eyed the distance, gauging it as near a hundred paces as made no odds. Leaning on the gate, he felt it sag as the others joined him. A less substantial barrier might have buckled under their combined weight but the fresh young timbers barely creaked.

Rob pulled out his pistol and sighted casually before checking the bet. 'A guinea then?'

'Aye,' Hogben growled. 'A buggering guinea.'

'Apiece?' John prompted.

'Aye.'

'You first then.'

They stood back to give Hogben space. Elbows planted on the top rail of the gate, he shifted his weight from one leg to the other, his ample backside wobbling.

He was about to fire when Rob spoke again. 'Head or what?'

Hogben made a big show of being interrupted. 'Bugger me!'

'Well? There's a guinea on it, when all's said and done.'

Hogben resumed his posturing, speaking through clenched teeth as he took aim. 'Middle of the flank.'

He squeezed his trigger on the word 'flank', clearly hoping for a precise hit to underline his point. Instead, a dark spot appeared on the cow's haunch. Its pained bellow reached their ears a moment after they saw it stagger.

Rob patted Hogben's shoulder, as he took position. 'Not bad.'

The first cow was still moaning when Rob trained his pistol on the flank of another in the herd. Only domestic animals were stupid enough to stand and wait while someone shot them one at a time. The explosion from Rob's weapon was followed in an instant by another bawl. This time, the victim fell to its knees and its distress was almost matched by Hogben's.

'Bugger me!' he wailed at the dark hole dead-centre.

John stepped forward and raised his pistol. For no particular reason, he aimed for the same spot. His shot was barely an inch from Rob's, sending the animal sideways into the mud.

'You owe the sod a guinea too,' Hogben crowed.

John nodded absently. The terms of the wager were ambiguous but he had no interest in betting against Rob. The contest was mainly to pass the time and, as much as they'd like to take Hogben's money, neither of them truly expected to collect.

'Best of three?' Rob offered, reloading. 'Double or quits?'

Hogben nodded and tried again. He cursed as his first shot totally missed its mark, then nodded grim satisfaction when the second hit home in a red-and-white heifer. Satisfaction faded when he saw the wound, while centred nicely in a white patch on the animal's flank, was off-centre overall.

Rob felled two more animals with shots as precise as the first.

John matched Rob with his first slug but wandered by a couple of inches with the second. He surveyed the scene. Six beasts badly wounded and one dead. He shrugged, resumed their journey and called back over his shoulder, 'Three guineas apiece, Hog.'

'Bugger off is it,' Hogben protested, as he hurried to catch up. 'Three shots, three guineas.'

John sighed. For a man who rarely paid his debts, Hogben was a surprisingly bad loser. 'Apiece, we said.'

'My shots were as good as yours.'

'And the one that missed?'

'Damn all! All right, one buggering guinea.'

'Three apiece, Hog,' Rob repeated John's demand. His voice was quiet but there was a cold edge to it that said fun was past and dividends were not open for discussion.

Hogben ignored the tone. 'Three and one. Like it or lump it.'

Rob did not react but John knew he wouldn't let the matter lie. They'd walk on for a while, distance themselves from the damage, then beat Hogben senseless. Rob's blood could stay up for hours, but John doubted he'd be showing such restraint that day.

It was not much more than half an hour before it happened. Hogben was a few yards ahead, when Rob abruptly strode forward and yanked him around by the shoulder. John cracked his knuckles, debating for a moment whether he wanted to join in the fray and then deciding that it was just what he needed to vent his spleen. He closed in as Rob landed his first punch, sending Hogben spinning round to take a jab. Their double-act was well-rehearsed. Some of the past beatings had been in earnest, the worst dished up to Higgins as a lesson not to strike Rhoda, but this was mostly recreational, just a hint that Hogben should honour his debts.

When they moved on, they left Hogben crumpled in the road.

'The Oak?' Rob asked, flexing his fingers to ease the pain.

John's loins stirred, with an enthusiasm they showed only after a fight. Violence did for him what wine did for many. The Royal Oak, close to home for Rob in Mersham, would be full of labourers with small chance of having a woman. He shook his head.

'I'll be getting back.'

He didn't voice the reason. They knew each other inside out, with little need for words at all and none for explanations.

John's return to consciousness brought with it a fearsome headache. It was dark outside but then the March days were short and the window was tucked below the eaves of the roof. A great believer in the restorative power of the hair of the dog, he reached for a bottle of brandy he'd put on the table before forcing his wife, Katherine, into bed. Her side was empty now, perhaps because of the hour or perhaps because of the state of him. Traces of sweat, booze, piss and vomit accosted even his saturated and drowsy nostrils, so he had no doubt they had choked her when he claimed what was his right as her husband hours before. She'd probably taken the children to her sister's, her usual refuge when he was in his cups. Although he never beat her, he was a disgusting drunk — taking whatever he wanted, whenever and wherever he wanted it. His sheer size made him impossible to repel and his clumsy rutting left her with bruises enough without the need for blows.

When he stumbled downstairs, shivering, the bitter cold in the house told him he'd slept for hours. He was peering through the kitchen window, contemplating an icy visit to the privy, when the church clock began to strike the hour. Spotting a bucket by the back door, he decided to pass on getting frozen and instead sent a stream pounding onto its staves while he counted the strokes. Eight. It clearly wasn't eight o'clock in the morning, and he was too sober for it to be the evening after the shooting contest, so he guessed he'd lost a day, not for the first time. The night's run was upon him, with barely enough time to make a poor meal from stale leftovers before setting out for the Royal Oak at Pedlinge Green. He left the bucket for his long-suffering wife to empty.

He and Rob usually went to runs together but Rob had already said he wasn't going. John had thought twice about it but a guinea was a guinea, and it wasn't as if he had anything better to do.

As it was, a couple of hours later but only seconds after going into the Oak, he was wishing he'd stayed in Bonnington. Sam was in his face before he could even call for beer.

'Where've you been?'

John shoved him aside but Sam grabbed his arm.

'I asked where you've been.'

'I heard you.' John jerked free and snapped his fingers at the serving girl. She edged a tankard of beer towards him.

'Were you out Mersham way yesterday?'

'Mind your own damned business.'

'It is my business when…' Sam lowered his voice. 'When you and my fool brother bring trouble down on all of us.'

'It's you telling all and sundry,' John pointed out.

'Then it *was* the pair of you! For God's sake!' Sam snapped. 'What's the matter with you? We're free-traders, not common criminals. Jesus Christ!' He shook with rage as words failed him.

Dennard crossed the narrow room in three furious strides. News had obviously got around. He might be a horseman but the wanton killing of any beast clearly stuck in his craw. 'Three dead, another likely on its way and a calf lost. Don't you have a care for the time and money a man puts into a herd like that? Not just old Bower but his father before him. Damn you! Damn the lot of you!'

John swallowed, only then realising how repugnant such acts were to some in the Blues. With many of them working the land, although few with much by way of cattle, they respected the skills and labours of an honest man. They didn't see him for the fool he was, scrabbling in the dirt for a living too poor to feed his family. Scowling as the anger surged through him, John didn't know whether it was for them or himself.

Ransley had said nothing but studied him, his calm authority silencing the others. When he spoke, his voice was cold.

'Mark this — we need the people of this parish a good deal more than they need us. All the preventives are wanting is a witness and we'll be choked by a hempen quinsy before you can say parsnips.'

John tried to hold Ransley's stare. All trace of the customary shrewd humour was gone from the dark eyes, their warm violet crystallised into steely blue. Eventually, John's gaze dropped to the floor. He had no answer, knowing that their behaviour had been stupid, pointless and, worst of all, dangerous.

'It was the Hog started it.'

His attempt to shift the blame was as stupid and pointless as the shootings. Even if Hogben had been the ringleader, they should have stopped him.

Ransley's voice became chillier. 'And where is he?'

John shrugged uneasily. 'We parted up by Sevington Court.'

'Indeed.'

John could read nothing in the single word with which Ransley terminated the conversation. He had expected an ultimatum, a warning that he would be out of the Blues if it happened again, and was surprised to be dismissed so lightly. He left them despondently, his spirits even lower than they had been before the drunken diversion, and made for a solitary table in the corner.

He was still staring at an untouched tankard of beer half an hour later, when he began to see the predicament in which their leader was placed. Forcibly ejected, men like himself would only become more resentful than they already were, and a witness could come from within their number as easily as from without. The rush of relief he felt on realising the power in his hands was quickly tempered by two thoughts. The first was that he did not like being cast in the role of traitor. But then, on the other hand, if that was how they saw him anyway, why disappoint them? The second was that there was only one way to ensure a man stopped making trouble, whether by taking pot-shots at cattle or by informing on his friends. Any power he wielded could be taken away — suddenly and permanently. He couldn't see Sam letting it come to that but the man was clearly furious at the position they'd put him in. He picked up the beer and sipped it, dejection slowly coalescing into determination. He would make the night's run and show that he was worth having in the Blues. Perhaps he could regain some kind of respect. Failing that, at least it might postpone any action they might be planning against him.

Midnight found him sighting down the barrel of a duck-gun, as cool and calm as the men on either side of him. Having said little to anyone since the earlier exchange, he kept a distance from his usual cronies and took position beside his brother-in-law. Despite the time it had taken for Higgins to recover from the lesson that John had helped to deliver, he seemed to bear no grudge. Perhaps it had been best for everyone in the long run. Eighteen months earlier, exactly a year after the beating, he and Rhoda finally married. Along with the rest of his clan, John thought her mad to marry a man as volatile as Higgins. He was amazed to see how, for reasons that remained a mystery to him, vows made in the sight of God achieved something that promises made in private never had. For Higgins, marriage brought trust and, if there was discord in his household, none of his in-laws saw any sign of it. Judging by the bloom in Rhoda's cheeks and the baby she suckled with such adoration, she was a very happy wife.

It was a good job that someone was happy, John reflected bitterly, since everything else was rapidly going sour. They were short of men, what with Rob at home nursing a thick head and Hogben off

God-only-knew-where. Of course, the beating they'd administered might have made it hard for Hogben to join them, even if he'd wanted to. There was no malice in the thrashing but they might have been too brutal in their intoxication. Quested was absent, too, engaged elsewhere as he often seemed to be. Men were leaving faster than they could be replaced. There was a newcomer that night, a Deal man who said Hogben had told him to meet them in the Oak. Their acceptance of him, albeit only as a tubman, underlined how far they'd fallen since the time when it was a privilege to be taken into the Blues.

John's mood was sombre, free of the blood-lust that normally permeated his nights in the trade. For the first time, he had some understanding of the courage needed to face a foe rationally, taking time to consider the risk of death amongst friends and the consequences of death amongst enemies. Calling on his skill with unfamiliar self-discipline, he waited for each opportunity and then took careful aim. Cautious for once, the preventive men were barely within range so it was through no fault of his that most of his slugs missed their mark. By the faint light of the new moon, he saw that his fellows did no better. His resolve strengthened in a desperate need to prove that he could do more than pepper the broadside of a cow with lead. He peered into the night, the weapon warm against his cheek after being cradled for so long.

A preventive officer shifted position to get a clearer shot, dark coat parting to reveal a white-clad thigh. John focused on the light smudge, feeling as if the rest of the world had spun away, leaving only himself and his target. Without so much as twitching another muscle in his body, he closed his forefinger on the trigger. The weapon thudded against his shoulder but he kept his eye on the white smudge, watching as a dark hole opened at its centre. Then the spell was broken. The target became a man, hands flying to the wound, musket falling to the ground and body following it down.

'Good shot,' Higgins called.

John let out his breath in a deep sigh and started reloading. It would take more than one good shot to prove anything to these men but at least he'd made that one shot, accurately placed to prevent the man from giving chase just as Smeed instructed.

Thinking of the man whose systematic training had taken those who'd listen close to military efficiency, John glanced along the line to where Smeed stood not far beyond the waggon being loaded, in a group of men who were sighting carefully and loosing precise shots against the distant preventive officers. The gunfire had agitated the team hitched to the waggon and now they fought against the slight figure holding them.

Wilson had missed more runs than he'd made through the winter and his hollow-eyed frailty was an unwelcome reminder of how closely they all looked at death on a run. He'd always been sickly but this was the first year his winter pallor had persisted into spring. His corpse-like appearance revolted John, making him steer as clear as he could, but Smeed's loyalty never seemed to waver, he standing ever more firmly at his fading friend's side.

Those thoughts flew through John's mind as fast as his fingers flew over the weapon he was reloading. Just as he finished, the thunder of falling tubs snapped his attention back to the waggon. The horses had made a break for it and, though Wilson clung on and forced them back to a halt, he was too late to stop the half-loaded cargo raining onto the men behind the waggon. Order was restored in seconds and loading resumed but one man stayed down, another kneeling beside him. John couldn't recognise either of them but, looking along the line again, he saw that Smeed was no longer in position and Wilson now stood a yard or two in front of the horses with a duck-gun raised to his shoulder. John watched as the man shot blindly into the darkness and then threw the empty weapon at one of the scouts on the far side of the working party. He frowned at the sudden display of anger, never having seen Wilson behave like that — or fire a gun — before. Shrugging off his puzzlement, he resumed his vigil, waiting for another chance to make a slug count. It was years since he'd used so few during a run. It was also years since he'd made a shot like that one. Flushed with pride, he closed one eye and sighted again. An instant later, he was face-down on the sand with an intense fire where his shoulder had been. He had not even seen his adversary take aim.

He knew it was only a slug that hit him but it felt more like a cannonball. Never having been shot, he had not experienced the pain that he was so adept at handing out. Time seemed to slow, while he looked down on events as if somehow outside them. He wondered idly whether shooting to maim was so humane after all, and then passed out.

Quacks

James Quested had spent the night of the Hythe run in a hayloft above a cowshed, but couldn't have been happier. His affair with the milkmaid, a nineteen-year-old by the name of Esther, was still going strong. He was as surprised as anyone, honest from the start that he'd never leave the wife he loved, but Esther seemed content with his monthly visits. When he eventually suggested she should be seeking a husband of her own, she laughed gaily and told him she most certainly was. Only then did he realise the arrangement was as convenient for her as for him.

In Ashford for a few days, acting for one of his employers, he had a choice between trying to conclude his business early and hurrying down to the marshes for a run with the Blues, or enjoying the entertainments in town and spending a leisurely night in Esther's arms. He smiled wryly, realising that adventure and profit now held less allure than warmth and comfort, and wondered if it meant he was getting old. Whatever it meant, he did not regret his decision. Rising early as always, Esther laid her magical hands on him before putting them to more mundane use. He generally dozed for another hour before going on his way but that morning his lie-in stretched nearer to two. It was past seven o'clock when he rode across the fields to the south, ready to join the Stone Cross road beyond Cheesemans Green. Although their liaisons were something of an open secret, with several of Esther's friends and fellow workers turning a blind eye, he kept a low profile, wanting neither to give Esther a bad name nor to disrupt his own comfortable life.

He whistled tunelessly while his gelding meandered slowly across the rough grassland, the soft ground giving under its weight. He was in no hurry, his belly full and his loins quiet, and it was nearly an hour before the road came into view. He made for an opening in the hedge beside a solitary beech tree; it had been a tight squeeze when he first started calling on Esther but now the gap was wide enough for two horses to pass through side by side. He didn't know if the widening was a result of his visits alone, or whether someone else shared his route.

Following a familiar routine, he reined back in the lee of the hedge and dismounted. Throwing his reins over a broken branch, he took a few strides along the field boundary, unbuttoned his trousers and squatted. It was the symbolic end of the visit, leaving his feelings for Esther behind with the products of her hospitality and resuming his journey with thoughts of wife and children.

Occasionally, usually while listening to the sermon on a Sunday morning, he felt a stab of guilt about Esther but it soon faded in the certainty that few men took their wedding vows literally. He knew that neither of his closest friends did and, while he followed no man blindly, the knowledge salved his conscience. On top of that, he did not consider what passed at Billham Farm adultery: as strong as the temptation was, he stopped short of that with Esther just as he had with mistresses before her. There were sound practical reasons for his self-control, with moral absolution merely an unexpected if welcome side-effect.

When he needed it, he found further justification in how the affair began. He met Esther at a country fair when Jane was expecting their third child, Theo. All Jane's confinements were difficult, progressing through every possible sickness and swelling, and culminating in long, painful deliveries. Rather than trouble her, he did what any decent man would do: he extended his gander moon to include the time before, as well as after, her delivery. There was no shame in a man meeting his needs outside his marriage through consideration for his wife, and that was precisely what he planned when he bought supper for Esther and escorted her home. On the way, he tasted her body for the first time. Undeniably sweet as it was, he was at a loss to explain why he was still seeing her three years on. Earlier gander moons had not brought such sinful consequences but then none of those girls had combined beauty and zest for life in quite such an irresistible package. He might even have fallen in love if Esther took him seriously, making still worse trouble for himself, but she never treated him as anything but a diversion, albeit a pleasant one, and that kept him in his place as a passing entertainment. He was glad of it too — he had no wish to hurt his wife or destroy his marriage.

He continued southwards, over the crossroads at Bliby, headed for Bilsington. He almost always dropped in on Pierce and Giles on his way home, which was how Pierce came to know about Esther in the first place. Combined with his business activities, calling on friends gave him news to pass on to Jane, helping to justify his absences even though she never asked for explanations if he did not offer them. His visits to Bilsington were not mere excuses, of course; he enjoyed seeing his friends as much as his mistress. He would not be seeing Giles, who was in Canterbury on business of his own that day, but he was eager to see Pierce and check that all had gone well the night before. The gardener would be in one of his half-dozen retreats around the estate, spots where he could snatch the odd nap with little fear of discovery. Early spring meant he was probably in one of the glasshouses, hidden behind stacks of seed trays with sacks of potting compost blocking the aisles to ensure that he heard anyone who might approach.

Quacks had gone no more than quarter of a mile beyond the crossroads when he saw a bundle by the roadside fifty yards ahead. Urging the gelding into a steady trot he stared intently at the dark outline, closing the distance by half before he was sure that his first impression was correct. Having nursed more fallen men than he could count, he easily recognised a body for what it was. No fool, he looked around carefully as he approached, not willing to pass by a sick or injured man but not blind to the potential for a trap. In fact, the area was rarely troubled by footpads and highwaymen because of the Blues. He knew there were those who now thought their presence too high a price for such immunity but he was unlikely to be threatened, whether any accomplice in the bushes was inside or outside the Blues.

Even after he dismounted and stood over the body, he still had not placed the man at his feet, hunched as if he had dropped to his knees in agony and passed out before he could even stretch out on the ground. Every inch of clothing was covered with foul-smelling mud, which also caked hair that was probably dark. Bracing himself carefully, he slipped one hand under the shoulder and the other under the hip, and rolled the body onto its side. It retained its foetal coil, muscles rigid and jaw clenched in an ugly sneer that made the face difficult to identify — difficult but not impossible.

Quacks let out a low whistle. He'd seen Hogben in a bad way before but this was beyond anything he'd encountered in the past. He placed two fingers on the filthy neck and took the pulse, letting his eyes roam over the patient in silent evaluation while he did so. Finding the heartbeat erratic, he shook his head mournfully. There was nothing he could do about that so he carried on making his checks, finding no broken bones but a truly staggering array of cuts and bruises. Only a body of such prodigious strength and iron constitution could withstand the abuse that its occupant threw at it so regularly. A lesser man would probably be looking at an early grave but he expected Hogben to outlive them all.

Ignoring the stink, Quacks settled Hogben on his back and used his own jacket as a makeshift pillow. He eased the stiff limbs into rest and then went back to his gelding and rummaged through his saddlebags. He sighed, finding nothing of use in luggage that contained little more than a change of stockings. Returning to Hogben's side, he checked the man's vital signs again and then muttered words that he doubted the patient could hear.

'Best if we heads on down to Paul like I plans. Maybe he finds you a corner on the estate.'

It took him some time to get Hogben's prone form onto the horse, which became more skittish with each failed attempt.

'Law! You carries some weight, Hog,' he grumbled, as he finally got the burden in place across the pommel of his saddle.

Mounting carefully behind the patient, he gathered his reins and urged the animal forward at a much smarter pace than they'd managed thus far that morning. He could not have left any man to die by the roadside, friend or foe, but there was also cold logic behind his decision. Unaided, Hogben might fall into the hands of the authorities and then, bereft of his senses, he might give away information that could prove costly to the Blues. Quacks did not expect Pierce to risk his job for Hogben out of the goodness of his heart but he did expect practical considerations to force him to help in spite of his personal disdain for the unconscious man.

As he rode, Quacks considered Hogben's plight. Unknown to most, their acquaintance dated back to childhood. Born less than five miles apart, they'd spent some time at school in Hawkinge, although not enough to teach them much more than how to write their names and read a few scriptures. Six years his senior, Hogben was strong and athletic in those days. Quacks had felt the flush of admiration so typical of a small boy for an elder, but he doubted that Hogben had noticed him then or connected him with those times since. He recalled their shared history only because it gave him an insight into Hogben's despair that few possessed.

In eighteen-hundred-and-ten, two years after he married Ann

290

Kember, Hogben fell foul of a press gang on his way back from Folkestone docks. It was weeks before his wife, mother to one small child and already suffering the sickness that warned her of another on its way, received the customary brief notice of her husband's enforced service in the Royal Navy. Hogben did not return home until after the treaty and, in a sense, he never returned at all. Quacks saw little sign of the energetic youth in the bitter man who returned to Acrise in the spring of eighteen-sixteen; he suspected that Ann barely recognised the husband that the Navy gave back to her. Even so, there was presumably still something between the couple because five more children appeared in the six years following Hogben's return. It was only after the affray in which his thigh was shattered that the new arrivals ended with little Annie.

Before the injury, Quacks had occasionally wondered how much say Ann had in her unending cycle of childbirth. Naturally, and with some justification, he viewed the fifth baby that his own wife was carrying as a totally different matter. For one thing, his family could live comfortably on his legitimate earnings — almost handsomely when his illicit income was added to the pot. He was proud of the roof he put over their heads, a rambling cottage with a pretty parlour for his wife to entertain her guests and three large bedrooms for them, their sons and their daughters. Not even Ransley kept his family in better style. For another, Jane was an affectionate woman and any blame for the regular interruptions to their marital routine must rest as squarely with her as with him. He went along with every tip that she brought back from her visits to Sarah Pierce but, although the tricks seemed to slow the flow of little Pierces, they proved useless in his household — worse than useless in his view because, if they were to have a child every year anyway, they might as well make love whenever they wanted.

Returning to thoughts of the foul load slung across his horse's withers, Quacks recalled how, after her husband's injury, Ann Hogben had shown she wielded more control than anyone knew, finally deciding that enough was enough. Quacks guessed the reason for her change of heart, having spotted Hogben's opium-eating almost as soon as it began and knowing from his time in the army how the habit could affect a man's character. In Hogben, whose temperament had always been explosive, it added a new facet to the cycle of embittered sobriety and shameless drunkenness; his bouts of self-loathing and fear of persecution were an unwelcome burden for a woman already struggling with the task of bringing up too many children on too little money.

Although Quacks had brought back horrors of his own from the bloody conflict that the country had won at such cost, his service differed from Hogben's in several key respects. Firstly, and most importantly, he signed up of his own free will — he had no one to blame but himself for the decision he'd made. Secondly, and almost uniquely in his experience, he and his closest friend had fought side by side throughout their service and lived long enough to come home together. Thirdly, he left no wife and children behind; imperfect as he might be, Jane got what she expected when he became her husband five years after his return, following a long and steady courtship quite unlike the whirlwind romance on which Pierce embarked almost as soon as they reached Kent.

In fact, although Quacks had not considered the point and would not have been an objective judge if he did, the Peninsula War had left its mark lightly on Pierce and himself. They were more serious when they left the army than when they joined it, but then six years was supposed to make a man not just older but wiser too. By letting their deep friendship take the place of family ties during their service, they retained the humanity and warmth that many others left on the battlefield. With no act or emotion unshared, and even after years of marriage, it was hard to say whether they were closer to their wives or each other. Now he had absolute faith his friend would help in this latest unpleasant task.

Sam

Prostrate on top of a sand dune, Sam Bailey peered at a pair of preventive men wandering along the beach towards Fort Twiss, with a third following a few steps after them. Out of sight behind him were a dozen of his best men, each with a musket in his hand and a pistol in his belt. A mile to the east, at Shorncliffe, eighty men were working a cargo under the vigilant eyes of a score of batmen. Beyond that, another armed party led by his uncle, John, kept watch over the Sandgate road. Sam hoped that his new strategy would enable them to hold back Blockade reinforcements without inflicting mortal wounds, while the batmen dealt with the small party based at the closest Martello tower. With luck, they would silence the sentinel before he could get off a warning shot and have an easy night.

Eastware Bay was deserted, with no ships at anchor and no one in sight except the Blockademen. The moon had waned to a fine crescent and its light barely touched the beach. Based on his surveillance over the past few nights, Sam was confident that a fourth man stood close to the water's edge as he usually did for the first part of his watch but he could see no trace of the sentinel in the darkness. Only the other men's movements enabled him to pick them out, their swinging cutlasses catching the faint starlight from time to time. They seemed to be headed towards their comrade but were still some distance from his customary position.

At that moment, a flash illuminated them. The two men in the lead were turned towards Sam, backs to the breeze, leaning together to shelter a flame from which they were lighting their pipes. Sam doubted the flame was visible to the sentinel beyond them, obstructed by their bodies as it was. It was barely enough to reveal them to him. He was sure they were in uniform but the only detail he could discern was a lieutenant's epaulette.

No sooner had he identified the rank than a shot rang out from the east. Experience told him it had been fired at the landing site, not by John's party beyond. As the men protecting the working party were armed only with bats, he guessed it was a sentinel's alarm to broadcast his discovery of a landing in progress.

Sam grinned to himself. The fellow would be disappointed if he thought his comrades would come running from all directions. He raised himself onto his left elbow and began to lift his right arm to signal his party to take up their positions at his side. As he did so, another shot rang out, this time far closer and directly in front of him. He peered into the darkness, sure he could not be seen and puzzled what they could be firing at; even Giles couldn't hit a target in the next town. Thoughts jostled through his mind: it might be a response to the alarm, but that wasn't standard practice, and there was no point giving an acknowledgement, only to arrive at the scene with an empty weapon.

His musing was cut short by an angry shout.

'You damned fool! What do you fire for?'

There were several seconds of silence before the reply drifted towards Sam. The sentinel's muted voice betrayed his realisation of his blunder.

'I didn't know who was coming. I hailed but there was no answer.'

If there had been a hail, it must have been a quiet one. The first voice spoke again, less loud but no less angry.

'Were it so, if they were smugglers, why did you fire without an act of violence?'

Sam would have been interested to hear the answer to that one. The Blockade claimed that its men observed a general order that stated, 'No one shall fire without violence being first offered'. He'd seen that order flouted more times than he'd seen it obeyed and now these officers had seen it for themselves. Any explanation the sentinel might have been formulating remained unuttered, as the man who'd been following the officers cut in.

'Good God! Mr Dyer is shot!'

Sam waited while the fallen man's comrades gathered around and inspected the body. In less than a minute, he knew the lieutenant was dead. Worming his way back to his men, he led them in falling silently back to Shorncliffe. There they found the working party in flight, tubs strapped firmly to their backs, with the armed party behind, ready to tackle the Blockademen who were driving them inland. Although they were under steady fire, the fleeing men used every possible cover offered by the landscape to minimise their exposure. Few slugs found flesh and, although one or two men were lightly peppered with shot, the long range left little force in the missiles.

Throughout the retreat and later regrouping, Sam cursed his misguided strategy. He'd tried to be clever, concentrating more on avoiding conflict than triumphing over it, but the risk to the batmen was too great. Never again would he ask them to face muskets with ash poles. If the Blockade wanted war, they could bloody well have it. His anger was still flaring brightly when he reached his bed hours later.

On a rough hewn kitchen table, a woman was spread-eagled with one man holding her wrists and another her ankles. A third man stood between her legs. Her screams echoed between the whitewashed stone walls.

A small, dirty child stood pressed against one of the walls, tears washing clean streaks over its grubby cheeks. Its eyes were wide, unblinking as if pinned. Its hands were over its ears. Its mouth was open but no sound came out.

The features began to melt. Black hair turned fair, brown eyes became blue and tanned skin faded to freckles. A stranger became a daughter... then the room fell silent. The child's eyes opened wider, if that were possible, and the horror in them deepened. Then a vast crimson crater opened where the face had been.

Sam sprang upright in bed, eyes staring wildly into the darkness and body drenched in the sour sweat of fear. The crescent moon in the window had barely moved since he'd dropped into bed, dog-tired after the night's events. Beside him, his wife turned over, disturbed but not awakened by his movements just as she had been when he came home. Their lives ran in parallel, the activities of the one scarcely impinging on those of the other. He slipped out of bed and let himself out of their room. On the landing, he silently lifted the latch on the door to his children's room and went inside. The youngsters were tucked up in one big bed, Sarah and Katie at one end and Young Sam at the other. Each of the girls clutched a well-worn rag doll close to her breast, while their brother clasped a pig-like creation that they had crafted for him and insisted was a dog.

Sam studied their faces and saw that their dreams were as peaceful as his were savage. They had never seen anything to give them terrors like his and, while he breathed, they never would. He left them to their slumbers, making his way downstairs, collecting a bottle from the kitchen and going out into the night. He sat on the low wall in front of their cottage and took a swig of brandy. The child's face was still vivid in his memory, quickly supplanting the reassuring sight of his angels safe in their bed.

'What in God's name are you doing? You're in the Royal Navy, for Christ's sake!'

His outraged demand still rang in his ears but it had not prevented the fishing village from being razed or the child's face from being demolished. It wasn't just one child. After so long, Sam wasn't even sure if there had been a particular child against a particular wall or a particular woman. But men he'd fought beside for years, men he considered friends, became animals after the enemy's retreat.

Regularly assigned to the boarding parties because of his size, he'd hacked through Frenchmen, young and old, but those were men fighting for their country just as he fought for his. He could not join in what followed.

He sighed and took another long pull from the bottle. In the months afterwards, he tried to wash away the memories with alcohol but it only intensified them. For a time, his life was an unbroken cycle of depression when sober, hallucinations when drunk and the dream when asleep.

The passing years dulled the memories but sleep could still reignite them as vividly as ever. He had no doubt what had triggered the return of the dream: the sight of a preventive man panicking and killing his own officer. A part of him found it pathetic, confirming the fallibility of their adversaries, but another part of him knew how easy it was for a man to make a mistake like that when he feared for his life. If the sentinels of the Blockade, many of them seasoned naval men, were getting that jittery, he'd be a fool to imagine that his forces were in any better shape.

If the Blues had an advantage, it was in the continuity of their leadership. Having survived Quids' death, their faith in Ransley seemed unlikely to waver but, if times had been tough for them, they'd been worse still for the Blockademen. Within two weeks of Houlihan's demise, the newspapers carried an obituary for the Blockade's commander, Captain McCulloch. Rumours about his health had circulated for years, with the high pressure and long hours of his position exacerbating the asthma that finally claimed his life at forty-five, an age that seemed uncomfortably young to a man nearing his fortieth birthday as Sam was. McCulloch's replacement, a Captain Pigot, arrived within days but had since made little mark on the local population. Those who'd complained about the sound of regular floggings aboard His Majesty's ships might have expected a more enthusiastic welcome from the Blockademen for their new leader but Sam knew from experience that a harsh captain was often held in higher regard than a weak one. McCulloch might have been a hard taskmaster but he was dedicated, efficient and unswervingly loyal to the men under his command. In contrast, Pigot's priority was his career and harbour gossip soon ensured that everyone, not least his men, knew it.

Sam sighed. How many men would meet their deaths in the dark days ahead? He did not expect to die at the Blockade's hands — he was too canny and experienced for that — but even he did not have eyes in the back of his head. If he was looking forwards to repel the enemy, he couldn't be looking backwards at the same time, watching for an error of judgement from one of his own. If death came from that quarter, he wondered if he'd even know his life was ending. One minute, he'd be there, musket in hand, and the next — oblivion.

All too aware of the difficulties of controlling men who were conditioned to wound and kill, his thoughts returned to the dead cattle. How long would it be before the worst of his men tired of killing cows and ended a human life? He wouldn't mourn the death of a preventive man but he didn't underestimate its consequences either. How much more damage would be done if an innocent resident of the parish died? Or, worst of all, a child? Whether their demise came from within or without, he began to believe that the days of the Blues were numbered.

A noise from behind startled him. His wife, Sarah, closed the front door softly behind her and joined him on the wall.

'The dreams again? I thought they'd stopped.'

Her warm palm covered the cooler flesh on the back of his hand. He made no move to accept her comfort and said nothing in response to her concern. After a while, she drew the hand back.

Of the bottle, she said sensibly, 'You know that won't help.'

Anger welled up inside him. Yes, he knew it wouldn't help. Nothing damned well helped. Still he said nothing. He always said nothing. He'd never told her about the dream, what had happened in France, or indeed anything of his torments. He hated what his distance had done to her but saw no escape from his isolation.

The soft sigh before she spoke again was barely audible.

'Don't stay out too long.'

With that, she went back indoors.

Christ, why did she always have to say the same thing? Why did she come out at all, knowing she could do nothing for him? They could do nothing for each other. If it weren't for his angels, he would rue the day she'd taken pity on his drunken despair and he'd taken pity on the plain face that was unlikely to win her a husband from the depleted ranks of his generation. They never discussed it so he didn't know if she felt the same way. Perhaps a man who put food on the table, rarely laid hands on her and worshipped their children was enough for a woman like her. There was no point in asking since, if she had other needs of a husband, he was not the man to meet them.

He knew that his demeanour had given birth to some lurid rumours about his military past. The bitter irony of that wasn't lost on him. Until his desertion, he'd done nothing wrong — every shot he fired was aimed at the enemy in defence of his country — but then came those villages. Afterwards, he lost faith, though faith in what he could not be sure, never having been devout, but certainly in his fellow man and perhaps in life itself. He hadn't planned to desert but, when a bright summer's day found His Majesty's Ship *Bulwark* at anchor in the Medway off Chatham, home suddenly called with a force he could not resist. Sent ashore for provisions, he turned his face to the south-east and simply started walking.

He sometimes wondered what the Blues would make of his past, if they knew it. Was he a coward for deserting or was he a fool for taking orders in the first place, from men who cared nothing for people of his class? Then again, with no answers himself, it hardly mattered what anyone else thought.

Cob

Mid-May and a touch of summer was already in the midnight air. Charles Giles leaned against the side of the Herring Hang house at Dymchurch, watching the sea's fickle fingers stroke the sand. Its gentle swoosh barely reached his ears.

The free-trade season was drawing to a close, most nights too clear to risk a landing. Cob was never sure how he felt about that. His wife, Mary, was a thrifty woman so they always had money put by for quieter times. Yet he missed the nights spent hauling tubs up beaches, often under cover of the foulest weather, waves crashing around them and wind plastering spray-soaked hair to their faces. They'd expected rougher weather for their present operation but strong winds had blown it over too quickly, leaving them uncomfortably exposed as they awaited the incoming boat.

Never before had he felt the camaraderie he'd found in the Blues, a sense of belonging giving him a place in the world that nothing else had. Being the best shoemaker in the district gave him a measure of pride and material comfort, but none of the glamour that came with being a Blue. He delighted in his double-life, relishing the wealth and respect it brought, not to mention its pleasurable fringe benefits. He enjoyed a smooth French brandy as much as Ransley. If it was accompanied by a particularly fine cigar, so much the better. And, occasionally, he rounded his evening off with an hour in the arms of a pretty young maid. He loved his wife far too much to make a habit of that but he was no monk and knew she did not expect him to be.

Life had been perfect. Ransley had done well to keep the Blues in check for as long as he had, bringing in haul after haul safely and efficiently. Of course, the men enjoyed the proceeds of their labours — their drunken revelry was known across the county — but the women they took, and the men they brawled with, were no better than themselves.

Only over the past twelve-month had things begun to pall. The shift started subtly, a few murmurs of complaint from locals at too much being taken for granted, but slowly built until now Cob questioned his own involvement. He'd never felt the slightest compunction at breaking laws he believed were unjust in the first place but now he saw some of his fellows stealing from people who could barely afford to put food on the table as it was. There were rumours of rapes from girls too afraid to complain. With a beloved wife and three daughters of his own, he had no time for men who took what women were not willing to give.

In the shadows between the houses clustered behind the sea-wall, six or seven score of their men waited for Ransley to signal the arrival of the boat from France. They were expecting several hundred pounds of tobacco, on top of the hundred casks of spirits originally planned. With Cob were Dennard and Gilham, both carrying muskets issued by Sam Bailey. There'd been a time when they were rarely amongst the armed parties but they were being called upon more and more often to defend the men working the cargoes. The reason was simple: they were good shots with cool heads. Cob had noted how reluctant Bailey and Smeed were to rely on the likes of Hogben; Sam did not seem even to trust his own kin. It proved easier to find horsemen and mariners to replace Dennard and Gilham in their former duties than to match their blend of dependability and determination in a tight corner. Cob might already have left the Blues had it not been for men like them. They'd never discussed where things were headed, but increasingly found themselves arguing the same corner each time events conspired to cause more dissent in the Blues.

Now he was glad to have reliable friends at his side as he prepared to fend off another assault. It was becoming ever harder to land goods safely, as the preventive forces became more organised and the coastline bristled with their numbers. Nearly half the trade now went through other channels, using myriad tricks that their smartest men spent hours devising and vessels cunningly modified to provide a hundred hiding places. The problem with such strategies was one of quantity: it took many concealed loads to match a big haul on a dark night.

With customers across the county, the Blues worked ever harder to meet the demand they'd created. They all knew that, if they didn't deliver, others would start to muscle in. That would lose money in the present and become dangerous in the future. So, they used ever less reliable men in ever greater numbers and Cob saw the strain of controlling them begin to etch itself deeply not only on Ransley's face but on those of his lieutenants, Sam Bailey and Jem Smeed. It became harder to recover weapons after a night's work, with Bailey adamant that his arsenal would be kept secure but powerless to prevent men like Hogben fading into the night with a pistol jammed into their belts.

Cob's thoughts were interrupted by a movement ahead. At first he saw nothing, but Ransley's top-heavy form became visible as soon as he left the shadows between the houses and stepped onto the beach. Cob shifted his gaze out to sea but saw nothing. Minutes dragged by, all of the men poised to react to their leader's signal, before a call drifted in on the faint breeze.

Cob stepped forward, finding himself in a tide of like-minded men as they began a routine polished by countless repetitions over the years. He and the other scouts flowed into a horseshoe formation under Sam Bailey's directions, their eyes fixed on the empty beach around them and their backs to the tubmen lined up ready to unload the boat that was now visible to all.

A movement amongst the beached boats not fifty yards away caught his eye. Before he could raise the alarm, a shot rang out. Without so much as flinching, Cob raised his musket to his shoulder and waited for a target to shoot at. A man stood to fire over one of the up-turned boats. Cob eyed him along the barrel of his weapon. The head was clear against the moonlit sky. He held that in his aim for an instant, then lowered the weapon a fraction. He normally favoured an initial shot in a man's gun arm but the distance meant he could not guarantee his aim. Now he aligned the barrel with the man's abdomen, relying on a painful gut-shot to put him out of action without killing him. He squeezed his trigger finger smoothly.

The officer's musket thudded hollowly onto the boat's hull, as his hands flew to his side. It was a good shot, for the weapon and the distance, doing no permanent harm but giving the wounded man something other than their cargo to think about.

Beside him, Dennard and Gilham shot into the night with similar precision. He was already reloading when they crouched to do the same. After the noise of the first volley, it seemed as if silence had fallen but slowly his ears began once more to register waves breaking on sand and barrels knocking on planks as the tubmen worked on. Amongst those everyday sounds, metal rasped against metal as ramrods pounded musket balls home.

Cob looked up to see their opponents advancing. Cursing the hours of practice that gave them an edge, he kept at his task as calmly as if he were putting a new heel on a worn boot. Staying down on one knee, he again took careful aim. This time, he focused on the shoulder of a man whose musket pointed straight back at him. Even as he adjusted the trajectory of his barrel, he saw the other man adjust his. For an instant, it was as if they were alone on the beach, locked together in single-combat, aims matched shoulder for shoulder. The moon hung high in the sky behind him and Cob knew that darkness shrouded his dirt-blackened face, while his opponent's shone bone-white. Hands steady on the stock, Cob began to squeeze, hoping that his slug would find its mark before its counterpart buried itself in his own flesh. As he did so, two things happened almost at once.

The face of his adversary split open down the left side. A dark river sprang into life and immediately burst its banks, flooding over his jaw and soaking invisibly into the cloth of his coat. The force of the shot threw the man backwards, closing his finger on the trigger of his musket as he fell. Time seemed to slow to a crawl as Cob saw the barrel of the weapon lift and then the flash as it fired. He tried to throw himself to the ground but his body was too slow to respond.

He could not even cry out when his throat opened to the cool night air. He gasped for breath as he fell, gagging on the blood that filled his mouth and then choking as it ran into his windpipe. For the first time, his firm grip failed in an affray and his weapon fell to the ground. He slumped over it in the long shadow cast by the landing boat. He doubted anyone noticed as he toppled silently from his kneeling position.

Quacks

James Quested knelt anxiously beside Giles. In the chaos after the preventive men opened fire, no one had seen him fall. It was pure luck that Pierce had stumbled over his body as they cleared the beach. His whistle brought Quacks running and they'd hauled their friend to safety, not knowing if he was alive or dead, not willing to leave him to the enemy either way.

'How is he?' Pierce whispered.

Quacks ran rough hands over the torn flesh at their friend's throat. The light was too poor to depend on sight for a diagnosis. The copious amounts of blood spilling over his fingertips made him fear the worst. He shook his head in despair.

'Looks bad. Throat's tore open.' He raised his eyes to meet his friend's gaze, although Pierce was just a dim outline in the shadows. 'Don't know as we dares move him.'

Pierce looked cautiously over the hedge that shielded them from view. The preventive men had propped their own casualty against the wall and were scouting around to see if there were any fallen men to be captured. They would soon be joined by others.

'No choice. There'll be no defending Cob, with a slug in his neck and its mate in that fellow's face.'

There was no need for him to point out that being caught meant being hanged.

Quacks considered that while exploring the wound. Always prepared for trouble on a run, he pulled a wad of clean rag from his pocket. With an assured touch, unfazed by the darkness, he deftly bound the bloody neck. When a final examination of Giles' body revealed no more injuries, he tried to sound optimistic.

'Least there's naught else amiss, far as I can tell.'

It was small comfort but better than nothing. Quacks knelt on one knee and lifted Giles onto his shoulder. Although the casualty was a fraction of an inch taller than him, he was lighter by easily two stones — their only good fortune so far. Quacks rose slowly to his feet. He and Pierce shared the same powerful build but how far could they carry even a light man on a dark night across rough country? He headed inland at a steady pace, spirit yearning for flight but sense saying that more haste would bring less speed.

Pierce's urgent whisper came from close behind. 'We've got to get well clear of here, somewhere no one'll connect the wound with what's passed. The preventive men won't let this go easy.'

'It's a musket ball. Most'll see it for what it is.'

They strode on in silence. A year or two earlier and they'd have been confident no one would talk around Aldington. Now Quacks was not so sure. Giles was popular enough, as indeed were he and Pierce, but there were still those who would see the incident as an opportunity to rid the area of the Blues.

'If it's not one thing, it's another,' Pierce muttered.

They weren't having much luck, it was true. The Devil had looked after his own for years but now he seemed to be taking a break from his duties. Quacks' medical skills had been in demand more often than either his aim or his cart in recent months.

Another half-hour passed before he paused to look around.

'Don't looks like they're following us,' he offered hopefully.

'They'd have been with us by now,' Pierce conceded. 'They'll search on horseback, come the dawn.'

That would almost certainly be futile. The rough grass and saturated bogs of the marshes would swallow any evidence of their passage. The dykes between fields were too broad for a horse to jump, meaning that pursuers made no better — and often worse — progress than their quarry. The impassable landscape and lack of good roads was precisely the reason why Aldington lay at the centre of Kent's most profitable smuggling ground. Even so, an injured man meant the Blockademen would scour every village from Hythe to Warehorn, pressuring the weak and bribing the greedy, hoping that someone saw a wounded man carried home.

Quacks dropped to his knee again and laid Giles on the ground. There was no need to feel for a pulse, as the breath rasped past the wound in his neck.

'He's still breathing,' Pierce said unnecessarily, an unfamiliar thickness in his voice.

Quacks kept his eyes on his patient, thinking how much the quiet shoemaker had come to mean to them in the few years they'd known him — perhaps even more to Pierce. He himself had been friends with Pierce since they squandered their youth running wild in Canterbury, he happily following his younger companion's lead into countless scrapes, but the distance between his home in Hawkinge and Pierce's old-fashioned cottage in Bonnington meant they saw less of each other. Giles's shop was a short walk from the estate where Pierce worked as a gardener, so the two men often shared a pot of tea or a pitcher of beer. Now Quacks realised that his patient's death would be a double blow; he'd be losing one friend and letting another down.

'Even if he beats the night, chances are he dies later.'

'Do you want to leave him?'

'Not an earthly. Just wants you to know what I knows.'

Pierce nodded, then knelt to pick up their casualty. He almost matched Quacks' ease in hefting their precious cargo into place. There was nothing odd in his silence but something in his bearing as they walked on told Quacks that the man was deep in thought. He waited for the outcome. Eventually, Pierce cleared his throat.

'Cob's got an aunt in West'ell, on his mother's side. Don't remember her name, if he ever said it, but I don't see how anyone would connect him with her.' There was a short pause before he added, 'Even if they know who they're looking for.'

On the far side of Ashford, Westwell was most of fifteen miles from their present position. Quacks thought about the distance. They'd do better on horseback but their horses were hitched to a cart that he hoped was well on its way back to Aldington. With luck, the beasts had escaped the affray unharmed but Pierce had brought his old hunter and Quacks had no great fondness for the lumbering cross-breed he rode. In any event, they could be of no help in their masters' current plight.

'We could borrow one of Tommy's.'

Even as he said it, Pierce's voice made it clear that he didn't honestly see it as an option. Quacks didn't bother to respond. They might all end up dead, trying to wrestle one of them into submission in Dennard's absence, even if the horses were back on the common after the run. Instead he voiced his own opinion.

'I says we stays clear of Al'ington, goes by 'amstreet and Shadoxhurst. They never picks us up out that way. The less they know, the safer Cob'll be in West'ell.'

He had barely finished speaking when they reached the first of the countless dykes they'd have to traverse in the hours ahead. Without the planks with which they usually spanned the broad ditches, each would add precious minutes to their journey. They slid down its steep sides, Pierce struggling manfully under the burden of Giles's limp form. Taking a bold stride into the black water, Quacks drew a sharp breath that whistled past his teeth. As his boots sank into the mud, the level rose to the top of his thighs.

'B-b-bugger me. That's d-d-damned cold for May.'

'You should worry,' Pierce grumbled from behind.

Looking back, Quacks saw the water was waist-high on his shorter and heavily laden friend. He shrugged. 'No doubt we gets wetter before we sees the sun again.'

He waded on, shuddering as the water sapped the warmth from his body. On the far side, the slope down from the field was gentler, ending in a narrow strip of bank. When they had clambered out, Quacks perched on the edge and began to wash off the dark earth he'd used earlier to black his face. After rubbing for a while, he looked up at Pierce. 'Better?'

Pierce's teeth flashed in the gloom. 'Makes all the difference.'

Hearing the sarcasm, Quacks looked down at himself. It was too dark to see much but he took Pierce's point. Soaking wet and covered in mud, carrying a wounded man across the marshes, what else could they be but free-traders? Still. 'Don't hurt to try. I sees old Dick Wraight talk himself out of the Old Bailey, an' the powder's still on his hands that night.'

Pierce said nothing but set Giles down. His acceptance of Quacks' point was confirmed when he washed first his own face and then Giles's. There wasn't enough light for them to judge the result but it was worth a try. Wearing a disguise, without any other crime being proved, could lay them open to a death sentence under the tangle of conflicting laws that was British justice.

Once they'd climbed the slope and resumed their journey, Pierce cleared his throat. He must have used the time they'd spent negotiating the dyke to consider Quacks' suggested detour through the villages west of Aldington because he continued the conversation as if it had never been interrupted.

'It's a devil of a way. And if we try for horses, we could draw them right down onto us.'

'We makes it.'

'There must be a dozen dykes before we clear the marshes.'

'Nearer a score, and we've to cross the canal, but we makes it.'

Pierce's smile showed again, grimmer now. 'If you say so, Quacks, if you say so.'

They plodded on. It would be a long night, but they'd both carried heavy burdens through long nights before. It was Giles they feared for.

Paul

Years had passed since Paul Pierce's last visit but little had changed. Larger than Aldington, Westwell was mostly clustered between two cross-roads. The fine weather had held and the early summer sun was high in a cloudless noon sky. Paul rolled his shoulders as he walked, trying to ease the aches that hours carrying a full-grown man had left in his knotted muscles. Clothes damp and muddy after crossing the marshes, he adopted the easy air of a farm labourer to whom such discomforts were nothing new.

Sweeping the village with casual glances, Paul gave a fair impression of a man without a care in the world. Only the hand that occasionally rubbed his face betrayed any unease — although he and Quested had checked each other at daybreak for tell-tale signs of the blackening they'd washed off in the dyke, he still worried someone might notice a smudge. Concentrating on the job in hand, he realised he knew nothing of Giles's aunt beyond a hazily recalled conversation about her love of gardening and her problems with slugs. He'd passed on tips for repelling the greedy gastropods but that was of little help now. The only potentially useful snippet he could bring to mind was a passion for *Dianthus*, the old cottage garden favourites often known as pinks. He now had the fool's errand of looking for a garden with a generous crop of pinks, even though it was too early in the year for them to be in flower.

Their only good fortune was that Quested was the best man to stay with the injured Giles and Paul was the best man to be trying to identify an unknown woman by the contents of her garden. Just about everything else that could go wrong had gone wrong.

He touched his cap politely to a pair of elderly ladies, scanning their faces as he passed in the hope of spotting some resemblance to his wounded friend but finding none. Their voices were thick with the local dialect, making them seem unlikely relatives. Giles was well-spoken for those parts, although there was no guarantee that his aunt shared that trait.

Paul had inspected the road from the south on his way into the village and now he completed his circuit of the road that ran east-west through it. He'd seen odd clumps of pinks in many gardens but nothing to suggest the ardent love affair with the species that Giles had implied. The clumps could easily be gifts to friends and relatives from an eager propagator in their midst. As he turned north, he faced the grim prospect that the aunt could have died or moved house, or perhaps simply lost interest in pinks. The road he followed was a narrow dirt ribbon with only a few cottages dotted along its length. They were tiny but not in bad repair.

A satisfied smile crept over his face as he squinted at one fifty yards ahead. He'd been examining each garden carefully for the evidence he sought but knew now that he need not have bothered. His doubts evaporated. Only one garden could possibly belong to Giles's aunt. Still too distant to see what was in the beds, he already recognised the silver spears protruding from pots and troughs balanced on the low wall and steps beyond. He lengthened his stride, covering a yard with each step.

Kneeling by a large pot on the top step was an ample figure, a shapeless woolly jumper stretched to bursting point by a vast bosom and a homespun skirt pulled almost as tight by equally immense hips. Paul had expected a frail crone, far removed from the huge woman before him. He ran quickly through half-remembered conversations to check whether that was fact or assumption. Finding nothing to support his prejudice, he cleared his throat.

She looked over her shoulder at him and began the laborious task of struggling to her feet.

'Morning, missus.'

307

'That it is,' she confirmed, familiar nutmeg-brown eyes sparkling with wit from deep craters in a moon face.

Paul had been wondering how to introduce himself. His eyes came to rest on a clay dish set into the soil of one of the borders. Two slugs floated in the scummy brown liquid. He nodded towards it. 'A beer trap?'

She followed his gaze, then nodded. 'My nephew knows a gardener down Bilsington way gave me that tip. Works a treat on the little so-and-so's.'

Paul had the opening he needed. 'Would your nephew go by the name of Charles Giles?'

She frowned. 'And who might you be?'

'The gardener down Bilsington way.' The frown lines on the woman's face deepened, her wariness clear. He had no proof to offer but perhaps Giles had given his name. 'Pierce. Paul Pierce.'

'Why didn't you say so, young man?' She bustled down to the gate with surprising speed and threw it open. 'Come on in. I'll have a pot brewing in no time. I've a thousand questions for you.'

If only his mission had been so innocent. There was nothing he'd have liked more just then than to sip tea and talk about plants but there was no time. He shook his head, stepped up to the gateway and lowered his voice. 'Cob needs a place to stay.'

Her sharp eyes darted anxiously to his. 'Where is he?'

'Half a mile down the Hothfield road. With a friend.'

'He's h-hurt?'

Paul nodded. They expected Giles to die and he felt the burden of bringing him to this woman's home for his passing.

'Bad?'

He nodded again. There was no point dressing it up.

Two or three seconds passed while the woman fought her emotions, then he saw steely resolve spread over her features. She looked further along the lane in the direction he'd been headed, out of Westwell.

'See that oak? There's a path from it down to the Kennington road. Fifty yards west along the road and you'll pick up another path headed Dignash way. Bear right at the first fork and it'll bring you out south of Westwell with no one to see you but sheep.'

'We'll have him here in no time.'

Paul couldn't improve Giles's prospects but intended to get him to his kin before he passed on. He strode away, trying to look unhurried but covering the ground deceptively fast. The woman's directions proved accurate. The path meandered along field edges but it would take far more than that to deceive Paul's sense of direction. He did not join the road south out of Westwell, instead jogging through the fields in the shadow of the hedgerows. On the far side of the third field stood the stately elm under which he'd left Quested ministering to Giles. By the time he was halfway across the field, he could see a man hunched over a body. Relief washed over him. His friend would be unlikely to be tending a corpse so carefully, although there was no knowing how close death might be. The thought filled him with urgency and he covered the last hundred yards at a flat-out run.

'How is he?' he gasped, as soon as he drew near.

'No worse than he was.'

The terse reply was misleading. Paul could see Quested felt more optimistic than before. Giles was holding his own. If he was going to die from loss of blood, he'd probably have deteriorated. He might still die if the wound turned septic but the signs seemed better than they had in the darkest hours of the night.

'You finds her?'

Paul had forgotten his own good news. 'Aye.' He turned to look back the way he'd come. 'There's a path cross-country from here, comes out near her place. Saw a shepherd but three fields off.'

They exchanged weary smiles. Perhaps their luck was turning. Quested knelt and hauled Giles onto his shoulder before rising. He was clearly dog-tired but Paul had already done the extra distance there and back, so he would carry their friend the last mile. Only when they reached the north road did Quested carefully set Giles on his feet. They each took an arm around their shoulders and walked him along the lane. With luck, anybody watching from one of the widely spaced cottages would think they were seeing a drunk friend home. No decent working man would be in that state at noon but it was nothing unusual for some of their associates.

They surveyed the lane in both directions before turning into the aunt's garden and hurrying towards the door she opened for them. She bustled off into the kitchen while they got Giles inside. A blanket covered the largest chair and two more sat folded beside it. Quested settled Giles as comfortably as he could, prised off his boots and then covered him to the chest with the blankets.

Paul watched his friend feel the hands, check the pulse and then remove the caked bandage from the neck. His stomach churned at the bloody mess beneath. He wasn't in the least squeamish, having plunged a blade into many a man's flesh, but it was a different thing to see a wound that might end a friend's life.

The aunt brought through a large bowl of water, rags stiff from repeated boilings draped over her arm. She set the bowl on the table beside Quested, watched his careful examination of the wound for a few seconds, then stepped back to let him to work. Something in his calm bearing and experienced touch clearly reassured her that her nephew was safe in his hands. A minute or so passed before she fetched a bottle from a cabinet. An easily recognisable sketch on the label tied around its neck declared its contents as potato wine. Spirits were more conventional but Paul hoped that wine had the same purifying properties.

Time crawled by, as Paul watched Quested tease the musket ball from deep inside their friend's throat and then gently cleanse the wound. Eventually, his patience gave out. 'Well?'

Quested was never one to be hurried and now he finished his examination in silence. He sorted through the clean rags and selected some that met his requirements. After folding one into a pad, he dressed the wound and bandaged the neck again.

Finally he stood back and studied Giles.

'The ball sticks in the muscle.' His surprise was plain. 'Hardly nicks aught that matters. I thinks maybe he makes it after all.'

Paul said nothing, having no words for his relief and not trusting his voice anyway.

The aunt supported herself on the back of a wooden chair, suddenly ashen, as if the whole thing had only just sunk in.

'Thanks be,' she said in a dry whisper.

Cob

When Cob opened his eyes, sunlight flooded through the window, bathing his aunt's living room with its warmth. He raised a hesitant hand to his bandaged throat, thinking of what Quested had said when he first came around and, in the hoarse whisper left to him, demanded to know what had happened.

'Close call, Cob. You draws the slugs like a cat on heat draws the toms — that makes six by my reckoning.'

There was none of the mocking humour that Cob had woken to after Brookland but, instead, the relief of a friend whose worst fears had thankfully not been realised. In the silence that followed the words, he'd heard Quested's thoughts: too close.

It had been far too close, taking him within a hair's breadth of death. He picked up the musket ball that was lying in a shallow dish on the low table at his side. Rolling it between his fingertips, he pictured the rough lead sphere lodged in his throat and thought how easily it could have ended his life. With no stupidity or bravado in him, he'd always known the risks he ran and his decision to continue had been a logical one, based on carefully weighed costs and benefits. Now, with the sun on his face and a yearning for his wife at his side, he made a new calculation. He did not want to die, simple as that. He was not afraid but he no longer believed that comfort or glamour was worth the loss of his life.

His aunt bustled through the door from the kitchen.

'Ah, Charlie, back with us proper at last?'

He nodded. He'd slept a lot over the week or two she'd been tending him but, once Quested was satisfied that he'd live and went back to his own affairs, she was beside him every time he woke. When he took a turn for the worse one day, she had a doctor before he could protest, without a thought for the fee she might face. Luckily the doctor subscribed to Ransley's no-questions-asked policy, so the bill went to the Blues and Cob's convalescence went unreported. Now she set a breakfast tray on the table beside him and began pouring tea.

Cob swallowed, building up to a whisper. 'Thanks, Dace.' Her name was Daisy but she was Dace to all who knew her. 'I'm sorry to bring my troubles here.'

She brushed his apology away. 'Pshaw! What are family for if not to look out for each other?' She helped him sip milky tea from the cup she held to his lips. 'Mary's been asking after you again, sends her love. She's been wanting to come since Mr Pierce got word to her but Mrs Pierce is making sure she keeps up appearances. You're away in Canterbury looking at a new tannery there and taking in the fashions.'

Cob sipped more tea resignedly. If the Preventive Service had lost men, he had to stay out of sight until he could act normally. The Blues had no way of knowing whom the preventive officers were watching. If Mary visited, she might put them onto him. Without evidence, suspicions were only that.

Daisy was looking at him intently. 'Is it worth it, son? You do well enough with your shoemaking, don't you?'

His throat lubricated by the warm liquid, his reply came more easily. 'I've been asking myself the same question, Dace. I'm not ready to be parted from Mary and the girls, I'll say that.'

'Will they let you go so easy?'

He thought for a moment she meant the Preventive Service but soon saw it was the Blues she feared. It was then he realised how terrible their reputation had become.

'Aye, there's still enough good ones to be sure of it.'

'Mr Pierce and Mr Quested seem fine gentlemen,' she admitted.

'The best,' he agreed. 'Don't believe all you hear, Dace. Even now, there's still more of their kind than the other.'

Dickon

'**B**astards.'

Dickon Wyor delivered his verdict in a resentful growl, directing fierce kicks at tussocks of grass as he wandered along the verge beside the road into Aldington. He scowled up at his brother, Billy, who was running nimbly along the top rail of the fence beyond the verge. A cubit broader than his brother, Dickon was not built for balancing on fence rails. At that particular moment, he was not in the mood for it either.

'Get down from there, damn you.'

Billy paused atop a post, stared at Dickon for a few seconds with pretty grey-green eyes that his brother thought would suit a woman better, then leapt down in a graceful arc. Rising to his feet in a continuation of the same deft manoeuvre, he frowned.

'What the devil's got into you?'

'Nothing.'

'You've got a flea in your ear over something.'

'D'you *want* to carry tubs for the rest of your life?'

Under the anger in the demand, there was the petulance of a child denied a toy. Billy's broad grin only inflamed the emotions.

'Well? *Do* you?' Dickon pressed.

'I've got more life left than you.'

There was barely two years between them.

'You won't have if you keep that up.'

Dickon set off at a smarter pace.

Billy trotted at his side, grinning again.

'How many down so far this year?'

'What?'

'How many men down?'

'In the Blues?'

'Where else?'

Dickon considered the question. 'I dunno. A few.'

Billy nodded sagely. '*Quite* a few. Bailey and Giles go without saying but they're not the only ones. Smeed with the tubs, and that weakling with him neither use nor ornament. By my reckoning, two of the old 'uns took slugs out by New Romney and another half dozen felt a cutlass. It was worse still at Dymchurch.'

Times were hard, of that there was no doubt. It only intensified Dickon's irritation at being rejected for the armed parties.

'So?'

'So it won't be long before they have to take who they can get.' Billy hopped back onto the fence. 'You.'

Dickon wasn't keen on being portrayed as the bottom of the barrel but did not object because his single-track mind had latched onto something else in what his brother had said.

'Us.'

Billy said nothing.

'Us?' Dickon repeated, as a question.

Billy laughed. 'I don't know about that.'

'Coward.'

The laugh came again. Dickon knew he was wasting his time trying to bait his brother. Billy could goad him into doing things he later suffered for, but it never worked the other way around.

'Why not?'

'Oh, I'm not ready to take a piss where I can't whistle yet. Taking pot-shots at preventives'll see you swing in no time.'

'You think they'll let you off if you say you wasn't carrying arms?'

Billy shrugged. 'Maybe.'

'You think it'll come to that?'

Billy's smile slipped for an instant, revealing a glimpse of the sharper, darker side he rarely showed. 'Bad times, big brother. And they'll get worse before they get better.' The grin slotted back in place. 'But unless you're thinking of working for a living…'

No, whatever else, Dickon was not thinking of that. His father worked for a living through every daylight hour of his life, except those he spent sitting bolt upright in a pew in his threadbare Sunday best, and Dickon had worked too. They'd been lifting potatoes, while eleven-year-old Billy followed behind putting them into a sack. The sky above was dark with thunderheads.

'Best crack on, son. When that breaks, there'll be hailstones the size of your fist.'

Dickon had been looking down at the soil when his father spoke. As he raised his eyes and opened his mouth to answer, there was a flash. He had no time to close his eyes and so he saw each moment of his father's death. Then, it felt as if time had slowed down; later, it was as if it had taken no time at all. One moment, his father's kind and patient voice filled his ears; the next, the smell of burning flesh filled his nostrils. Dickon had no memory of the minutes he and Billy spent trying to wake the lifeless body, or of their tortuous progress back to the house, dragging the charred corpse behind them. He had a vague image of his mother's face, contorted with horror and grief, but only one thing lodged firmly in his mind: her appeals to the Almighty.

As the days passed, Dickon and Billy passed through shock, denial and grief but they never quite made it through anger. Seeing the deadly bolt of lightning as an unjust punishment of a righteous man, Dickon turned his wrath squarely on the Lord. Billy went a step further, dismissing God as a fairytale for a cruel world. Their protests began with a refusal to attend the funeral service and ended with a total rift from a church that soon wanted no more to do with them than they wanted to do with it.

Knowing nothing they did mattered, that their fate would be as arbitrary as their father's, they were impervious to the doubts and fears that might inhibit their peers. By the time they joined the Blues, they were as hated as they were feared.

'Speaking of a living,' Billy said. 'What are we to do for dinner?'

Dickon pushed his gnarled hands deep into his pockets. Having toiled through six winters before his early retirement, he had the swollen knuckles of a much older man. The two farthings he retrieved would not be buying them much of anything. He glanced up at Billy, who tossed him a ha'penny for his collection. Their pay from the run was gone; what they hadn't drunk in the hours immediately afterwards, they'd lost at cards later.

'Old woman Wraight makes a fine pie.'

Billy's words evoked a tempting picture of those delectable pastries, an image that set Dickon's stomach rumbling.

'A penny won't buy us much at the Walnut.'

'Who said aught about buying?'

For the first time, Dickon's face mirrored his brother's grin. They were Blues: they could take what they wanted. Who dared stop them? Looking ahead to Aldington, he lengthened his stride.

Like any public house worth its salt, the Walnut Tree was a barometer of life in the village. As Aldington prospered from the money the Blues brought in, the inn prospered with it. At dinner-time, there was never an empty seat as tradesmen and ploughmen working in less distant fields called in for a jug of beer and plate of bread-and-cheese. Meat pies and fancy cakes were beyond many men's pockets but the landlord, Ted Wraight, was a good host and made sure there was something for the humblest of them, even if only a plain baked potato from the bottom of the oven. Evenings were lively but mostly good-natured, with a seemingly endless round of celebrations at the slightest excuse.

Lately though, things had changed and the Wyors were a part of the change. It wasn't many years since landlords throughout the parish had boxed their ears but anyone who might have taken them in hand then was too fearful of the consequences to do so now. Such fears were not entirely justified. Plenty in the Blues had no time for the likes of the Wyors, but they were usually occupied elsewhere. Having built up the sprawling empire that was the Blues, they were too busy to control what went on between runs while men idled their time away in drinking and fighting.

Dickon scanned the taproom contemptuously, noting how men looked away as soon as they identified his brother and himself. After a lifetime in Aldington, even a short one, he knew all present. Most

315

had been in the trade at one time or another but many had dropped out during the years of open war with the Blockade, which made them cowards in his eyes. He strode up to the bar.

'Pie and pint for two.'

The words were a common greeting in a public house, usually made as a friendly request. Dickon's demeanour turned them into a threat. When Wraight stared uneasily at him, he glared back.

'You deaf, man?'

It was not the first time he'd gone into the Walnut Tree for a meal without the means to pay for it. To start with, caution made him claim he thought he had more money with him or he'd left it behind by mistake. Wraight hadn't believed the excuse the first time and, by the third, wanted to see their money before he served them. The unexpected, if subtle, defiance confounded Dickon on one occasion but simply elicited a threat the second time.

Far from perceptive as he was, even Dickon understood the conflict in Wraight's expression as he faced him that day. An innkeeper could not afford to feed the neighbourhood for free but to object could lead only to injury, disability or death. On top of that, the inn would be wrecked and its trade decimated. After a sullen pause, Wraight poured the beers and went through to the kitchen. A few seconds later, he returned and shoved two plates at them, each filled with a generous wedge of cold pork pie.

Dickon took a large bite and chewed noisily with his mouth open. Without finishing the mouthful, he slurped from the tankard and swallowed food and drink together, then belched.

'Not bad,' he admitted, 'But this place is a hole.'

He kicked a chair into a table, sending a rummer of sack wine hurtling to the floor where it broke into three pieces, spilling its contents over the floor. He took another bite from the pie, repeating the same disgusting process to ingest it, and reached for a crudely modelled plaster horse on the mantel. He perused it scornfully, then turned and tossed it into the fireplace.

'A bloody disgrace, in fact.'

Wraight stared at him, his face frozen into a mask, but made no move to stop him. Dickon looked around the room again, his gaze alighting on a couple seated by the window, their dinner still on the table. He sauntered over and made a show of studying the woman, who was young and fair but of no particular interest to him for her looks. He reached out and ran his hand over her cheek.

She shuddered, staring up at him with wide grey eyes that flicked nervously to her husband and then to the table. Dickon knew she was torn between her hopes of defence and her fears for her husband. She was right to fear for the man, given that he was physically and mentally outmatched by an opponent with no scruples of any kind. Dickon caressed her breast roughly. She said nothing, biting her lip until a drop of blood seeped from it.

Several men shifted in their seats. Dickon monitored their movements in his peripheral vision, relishing the scene he was creating. He loved the power that their inaction gave him, knowing they could overpower him if they acted together and yet knowing they would not act because of the individual risk required for a collective triumph. Men like Sam Bailey or Jem Smeed would stride over and thrash a lesson into him, and he would not be able to stand up to them while they did it, but these men lacked the skill and strength for fighting and, far more importantly, they lacked the guts for it. That was what divided the retired traders from the Blues. It was pathetic.

'Why don't you go on home, boys? You've had your fun.'

Dickon spun to face the speaker, whose voice was unfamiliar but whose face he instantly recognised. It was one of the retired traders he despised, perhaps the worst of them, a man who'd shown the white flag to the Preventive Service back in eighteen-twenty-one and handed southern Kent to Ransley in the process.

'Bugger off, Spratford.'

Turning back to the couple, he took a bite of the fruit pie that still sat untouched on their table. When a sharp tang of rhubarb stung an ulcer inside his cheek, he spewed the pie back onto the plate and spat savagely on it.

'Come on now, son.'

Spratford's words might have been friendly but his tone was filled with loathing. Dickon turned towards him, slowly, letting a humourless smile spread over his face.

'I'm not anyone's son, old man, least of all yours.'

Spratford did not back down. It was almost as if he became bolder when he saw that reason would not save the day.

'Some of us are trying to make a go of things around here. We're not going to stand by while you and your kind ruin us all.'

Dickon spat on the floor between their feet.

'We?' he asked contemptuously.

Spratford did not look around for support, perhaps knowing he was unlikely to find it. Instead, he held on to his dignity.

'All right, I'm trying to make a go of it. My shop's doing well and I plan to keep it that way.'

'You call a few measly cuts of horse meat doing well?'

Spratford did not react.

Dickon stared at him and then, with exaggerated deliberation, swept the contents of the couple's table onto the floor. No one moved, as earthenware split apart and pewter rattled into stillness. Spratford stood as still as the pewter, the dilemma plain on his face: call the bluff or back down and lose face for ever.

Dickon saw something to admire in the decision when it came but, admiration notwithstanding, had no intention of being turned out of a public house by a butcher. He let Spratford take his arm and walk him to the door. Then he twisted sharply, threw him off and landed a heavy punch on his jaw. Snatching him by the lapels, he used his forehead to smash Spratford's nose while his knee pulverised his groin. Letting the limp form fall to the floor, he took one more look at the patrons of the Walnut Tree.

'No one pushes me around. It'll go easier if you remember that.'

Content with the havoc he'd wrought, he went into the kitchen with Billy behind him as he had been all along. While Wraight watched from the doorway, they helped themselves to a whole meat pie and fruit pie apiece and almost kicked the back door off its hinges on their way out. Wandering down the lane, they devoured the meat pies hungrily.

'Fine pie,' Billy said. 'I knew the old hag made a fine pie.'

Dickon released a loud and painful belch.

'Bugger's given me indigestion.'

Billy's only reply was a grin, while he savoured his own dinner.

They drifted on. There were days yet before the next run and, until then, they must make their own entertainment. As they were headed south, there was a good chance that the White Horse at Bilsington would host their next showdown, unless Pierce or one of the Baileys happened to be on hand to intervene. Dickon wanted preventive men to quail at his name but, for the time being, local innkeepers would have to suffice.

Bish

In the taproom of the Palm Tree, Bish's knuckles shone white as he gripped the handle of an earthenware tankard. His forehead burned hot while his body shivered as if it were December not June. He knew he should have stayed behind at the farm but he'd missed several runs during the winter and was determined to do better now that summer had come.

Smeed had not yet arrived with Sam Bailey and the weapons. Instead Dennard sat at his side. Bish was conscious that the two men, lover and friend, left him alone as little as they could. One of them was usually on hand to offer discreet support when his strength failed, as it so often did of late. Striving to maintain his independence, all the time knowing it was being eroded, he felt a pang of self-pity. The weaker he grew, the harder it was to refrain from bemoaning his lot or blaming the Almighty. He countered the blasphemy by reminding himself that God had sent him not only tribulations but also comfort in his torment, not just in the men who watched over him with such care but in all the friends who stood by him even now he was of precious little use to anyone.

He looked around the inn. Arriving with Dennard before the crowd, he'd bagged a table by one of the front windows so that they could monitor the Blues arriving. They'd since been joined by Gilham and Higgins. The night's haul was not ambitious, only about a hundred tubs, and yet they struggled to muster three score men to work it. With each run, fewer good men turned out and more tough strangers appeared. Hogben found most of them, rough men looking for work around the harbours in Folkestone, Dover and Deal. Most were itinerant, with no ties to the area or concern for the locals. Many had been hardened by naval service, embittered by being discarded when Britain's hour of need had passed. With none of Jem Smeed's self-control or Sam Bailey's honour, they were dangerous men and he gave them a wide berth.

Even with their falling numbers, the Blues took the Palm Tree from bustling to uncomfortably crowded but they would soon be on their way. With no payment from Ransley for men who showed up too drunk to work, they were sober enough not to alarm the inn's regulars. Once Blues were running wild with money in their pockets, decent people often preferred to stay at home. In the fading twilight, Bish saw two men striding along the lane with an empty cart rolling briskly behind. The ugly but willing gelding in the traces confirmed what he already knew. Two outlines, one tall and one short, both brawny — Quested and Pierce.

Bish watched as Quested listlessly tossed the lead rein over a scrubby hawthorn near the window. Although he knew the man capable of deep and varied emotions, few found expression — men had to look carefully into those fishlike eyes before deciding if one of his quiet asides was a friendly quip or a grim warning. Now a cloud of gloom hung over him and Pierce, and they brought it in with them. After collecting beers from the bar, they headed over.

There'd been speculation earlier about whether Giles would make the run. Now the answer was clear: he'd have been with them if he was coming. A month to the day since he took a slug in his throat, he was back with his family in Bilsington and almost fully recovered. He told those who asked that a boil on his neck had become infected during his trip to Canterbury, laying him low for a fortnight and preventing him travelling home. Bish doubted there were many around Aldington who believed the story but few would say so and at least it offered an explanation for the raw wound on his throat. The thought that one of the most courageous in their number had lost his nerve was scarcely less incredible. He said nothing, leaving Dennard to confirm their suspicions.

'No Cob?'

The answer was a barely perceptible shake of Pierce's head.

'Still not fit?'

'He's fit enough,' Quested replied. Softly. Sadly.

The men around the table, and those standing behind, were silent. Losing Giles was a blow. Not even Higgins, who'd been picking off rabbits in the dark since childhood, could match him as a shot and few surpassed him for ingenuity. Every man amongst them was a little less safe without him at their backs and they all knew it. Or at least most of them knew it.

From where he stood with his nephew in a group by the door, John Bailey had listened to the exchange. Bish saw the conflicting emotions cross his face, knowing he'd tried to do better since the cattle business and seeing how difficult his choice of friends made any improvement. Loyal to his cronies, and bitter at the perceived unfairness, he was defensive when they were blamed for every bad turn the Blues' fortunes took. He chose a poor time to vent his mounting resentment.

'Damned coward! A scratch and the rat abandons the sinking ship.'

The metaphor seemed apt to Bish, seeing his own decline mirrored in the Blues. They were sinking and nothing that anyone could do would stop them — not George Ransley, not Sam Bailey, not even his beloved Jem Smeed. While glum resignation seeped through him, he realised that Bailey's outburst had kindled a totally different reaction in most of his companions.

Before he could marshal his confused thoughts, Pierce was on his feet. He'd landed a swift left and right before anyone, least of all Bailey, could react. Seconds later he was at the man's throat. His hands gripped the thick neck like a vice, blocking even the slightest flow of air. Bailey seemed not to notice, as he gripped Pierce's wrists and pitched his might against the smaller man's strength. With nine inches difference in their heights, the outcome of a contest between the tallest and shortest men in the Blues might seem to be a foregone conclusion but no one who knew Pierce would underestimate his skill and determination in a fight.

Rob Bailey uncoiled lazily from his casual pose against the wall. Bish tensed, unsure if he would intervene but not giving much for Pierce's chances if he did. He needn't have worried. Quested mirrored Rob's movement, warning that he would join the fray if necessary but would not escalate the argument himself. No one in his right mind would want to see the dispute spread — if the men of the armed parties fought, the injuries were unlikely to stop within their number. Bish doubted his friends could hold their own against the Bailey contingent, their strength being more in coolness and accuracy under fire than in pure physical power.

Long seconds limped by. Rob Bailey looked on but held back, as the two men strained. Bish watched as Pierce fixed a fierce glare on Bailey and fought to maintain his stranglehold. So focused was he that he did not anticipate Bailey's change in tactics. The first he knew of Bailey's raised knee was when it engaged with his groin. He released his grip in an instant, folding at the stomach and covering his crotch instinctively, if belatedly.

Bish doubted there could be a man in the room who did not

flinch. None of them was a gentleman by any definition but few would expect one of their fellows to deliver such a blow. Pierce wasted no time on his pain, unfolding as fluidly as he'd folded and landing a forceful right hook on Bailey's jaw as he did so. It caught his victim unawares, dropping him to his knees.

Pierce eyed Rob Bailey defiantly, daring him to have a go. Rob held the gaze briefly, then shrugged and smiled. Not given to taking things as seriously as his uncle, he'd let it go for now. There'd be other fights.

Pierce returned to their table and lowered himself cautiously into his chair. 'Fool.'

'Aye.' Only the faintest glint in Quested's cold grey eyes underlined the humour when he added, 'But not the only one.'

Pierce looked up sharply.

'Lucky you already has plenty o' littl'uns.'

Pierce relaxed, grinning in admission that attacking a Bailey was not the smartest thing he'd ever done and that the damage to his private parts might easily have been permanent.

Bish smiled at the rapport between the pair, the ease with which Quested soothed Pierce's rage. On the floor, Bailey shook his head in an effort to clear it. Bish watched out of the corner of his eye, seeing resentment and frustration simmering just below the boil. Frictions within the Blues multiplied with each passing day. When the end came, he had the uneasy feeling that there would be no shortage of willing helpers for His Majesty's men.

Bailey's friends did nothing as he gathered his wits. Rob held out a hand to help him to his feet but he ignored the offer, clearly furious that his nephew had not taken his part in the dispute, and leaned on a chair for support. Still dazed, he stumbled over and loomed above Pierce, his height and bulk accentuated by the fact that Pierce was seated while he stood.

'Your time's past, old man. Things are changing. If you ever lay a finger on me again, you'll pay with your life.'

Pierce did not dignify the threat with an answer. Bristling with suppressed fury, John stalked out of the door. Rob followed without hesitation, throwing away a night's wages as he did so.

Bish wondered how they could afford to show up so rarely and then walk out with the job not done. He had his own ideas on the matter but had failed to turn up any evidence to support them. The tougher men in the Blues regularly used threats of violence to obtain the horses, waggons and boats they needed for their work. Such tactics were a mainstay of the trade and hurt no one, provided that the locals had the sense to turn a blind eye and enjoy the tobacco or spirits they were left for their trouble. Bish suspected the younger Baileys had expanded these activities and now demanded payments for a new range of services, mostly in the form of promises about what they would *not* do. He despised such crimes, and knew he'd find plenty of support for that view within the Blues, but as yet he'd been unable to turn up anything he could take to Ransley as proof something needed to be done. Few people in the area would speak out against such dangerous men, at least while the demands left them enough to live on.

Returning to the confrontation he'd witnessed, he considered John Bailey's parting shot. Only in his mid-thirties, albeit with a hairline that added ten years, Pierce was hardly an old man by anyone's reckoning. Given that he and Bailey were only months apart in age, it was not his years that provoked the insult but rather his place in the old guard, the men who were content to do things Ransley's way. Bish was in that number, as were all the men at the table, although two — Gilham and Dennard — were not yet twenty-five. Their outlook had more to do with their time in the Blues than their years on earth. Fierce fighters from the start, the Baileys preferred to face muskets with muskets but, nostalgic for the days when half a dozen batmen had been enough to protect a cargo, few others welcomed the escalating violence that was fast turning eighteen-twenty-six into the worst year of their lives. Bish sighed, longing for a past that he knew was gone and doubting his own place in whatever future was replacing it.

Gilham had been sipping his beer contemplatively. 'M-m-maybe Cob's got the right idea.' He glanced up at Higgins and then hastily scanned Pierce and Quested. Addressing the family men, he continued, 'W-we've got res-p-p-ponsibi–' He grimaced and then added deliberately, '-bilities.'

The recent deterioration in Gilham's speech confirmed that he was feeling the pressure of making one forced run after another. Even at his best, it was unusual for him to attempt a word that gave him such trouble but no one was in a joking mood. They stared at the table. Bish glanced up at the same time as Dennard and, when their eyes met, saw his own uncertainty reflected in his friend. They had no responsibilities but that didn't mean they wanted to get killed, or indeed to kill anyone else. Dennard was less troubled about the prospect of ending a preventive officer's life than Bish would have been, had he been in the fighting parties, but didn't seek to deal that final blow if he could avoid it.

It was Pierce who put a check on their despondency, ever the professional whatever his feelings or doubts.

'Maybe so,' he conceded. 'But now's not the time to be thinking on it. We're here to do a job tonight and we're going to do it.' He gave Gilham a hard look. 'You want to get back to that baby of yours, you keep your mind on the here and now.'

Bish smiled. Gilham's exhilaration at his second child being a son, proudly baptised Thomas after himself, was almost as intense now as it had been in the first days after the birth. He regularly quizzed Pierce and Giles on his latest anxiety about the admittedly small but otherwise healthy infant, clearly regarding the Bilsington friends as the epitome of fatherly virtues. Bish wouldn't argue with that assessment. Only Ransley had more children than Pierce. Gilham wouldn't presume to ask their leader for advice and Ransley, excellent provider as he was, preferred to leave the rearing of his countless offspring in his wife's capable hands. It was an approach favoured by most men in the Blues, with Pierce and Giles amongst a handful who took a more equal share in the yoke of parenthood. Each had a youngster only a year or so older, if far more solidly built, than little Tommy and so they brought fresh experience to Gilham's questions. Being denied the satisfaction of fatherhood was Bish's only regret about his personal affairs but his poor health meant that he did not dwell on what might have been. Even if he were made differently, he would have preferred not to sire children only to leave them fatherless after a few short years or, worse still, to pass on to them the infirmities that had dogged his own brief life.

'Here we goes,' Quested said.

The other five men followed his gaze. Ransley stood with Sam Bailey but there was no sign of Smeed. Usually Ransley came inside to organise his men while his two lieutenants took a cart to fetch weapons from one of their numerous secret armouries around the coast. Now that they had more firearms than men to fire them, they dispersed their weapons as widely as possible, both to minimise the distance for which they had to be carried and to avoid them all be seized at once if information about their whereabouts fell into the wrong hands. Always cautious, their leaders became more and more secretive about their plans and hiding places. Now that the Blues were more of a rabble than a gang, information was guarded as carefully as gold.

'Jem not running tonight?' Pierce asked.

Bish frowned, then shrugged. Smeed had left Bank Farm at the same time as he set out to meet Dennard. With his fever still showing no sign of abating, it was the last night that he wanted to be out alone in their ever more dangerous world.

Sam Bailey hauled himself onto Quested's cart and began to turn it around in the narrow lane in front of the inn. Ransley strode towards the door. He was out of sight for a moment and then appeared in the doorway behind the gaggle of fighting men still gathered there. He looked around appraisingly, giving abrupt little nods of acknowledgement in response to the many eyes on him, then jostled past the Baileys' cronies and headed towards Bish and his companions.

'Quacks,' he said tersely. 'Go with Sam.'

Quested drained the last inch of his half-and-half, then left without a word.

Bish looked up at Ransley, longing to ask after Smeed but wary as ever. Ransley deliberately evaded his gaze and glanced around the room, raising his eyebrows a shade as if to ask why everyone was waiting on him.

'What's up, boys? There's some drinking time yet before we make tracks.'

He nodded to the landlord, a signal for more ale. It was something he did from time to time, apparently without reason, but a trick Bish had seen him use before to occupy those he did not want to involve. Most of his men were too keen on a free drink to question his motives. Others subscribed to the view that what they didn't know wouldn't hurt them. Only a few were more suspicious, or curious, and more troublesome for it.

In the uproar that followed the renewed hospitality, Ransley sat in the chair that Quested had vacated and addressed Pierce. 'You might tell Quacks that he don't have to save every drunk he finds by the wayside.'

It took a moment for the comment to register. Hogben had missed the last two runs, since the momentous drinking binge and subsequent beating that brought him so close to death. It was the first time his escapades had interfered with his lifelong love, the trade, and it was sad confirmation that he'd lost the fight to control his pain and the addictions it had brought in its wake.

'The Hog back tonight?' Pierce asked.

Ransley nodded.

'Trouble?'

Ransley gave an ironic tilt of his head. Where Hogben went, trouble was never too far behind. 'The Horne girl.'

Bish shifted uneasily in his chair. The Hornes had been around the Blues for years, longer than he had himself, but they remained outside the inner circle. The reason for that was simple: Ransley didn't trust them. Bish supposed the Hornes knew that — certainly others did. Even in easier times, they'd never been privy to plans and hiding places. Their skill with their duck-guns meant they were sometimes used in the armed parties but they were paid and dismissed long before they neared home. They were dangerous because they were cowards. The tubmen could not rely on them to stand their ground if the Blockade was gaining the upper hand and no one could rely on them keeping secrets if taken prisoner.

None of that explained the night's excitement. Mary Horne could not have been less like her brothers, a pious young woman who saw physical death only as a gateway to everlasting spiritual life in paradise. Bish shared her faith, even if he savoured earthly ecstasies alongside the promise of heavenly bliss.

'Unlucky bitch,' Higgins muttered.

Bish started, only then seeing what should have been obvious. The girl was as beautiful as she was devout. It was an ethereal beauty that he associated more with angels than with any acts that might interest Hogben. With his own desires lying elsewhere, and his ability to appreciate beauty for its purity as well as its sensuality, such a possibility hadn't entered his head. He couldn't imagine any man violating a body that its occupant so clearly kept sacred unto God but now saw that the other men around the table did not share his naïvety.

'Nothing,' Ransley searched for a word to convey his meaning without having to speak of matters on which he preferred to remain silent, 'lasting.'

Bish assumed he meant the girl's innocence remained intact.

'John called in on his way to meet Harry,' Ransley added by way of explanation.

So, Hogben's fun had been interrupted. Ransley's audience looked on expectantly. John Horne was no match for Hogben on the morning after, let alone the night before. It was a mystery how he'd escaped with his life, let alone his sister with her innocence.

'God's own luck but Jem happened by right about then on his way to Sam's, heard the ruction and stepped in.' Only then did Ransley glance casually at Bish, as he would at the friend and workmate of any man on whom he was reporting. 'They look worse than they are but Horne's another matter.'

So that was why Ransley sent Quested with Sam Bailey, his medical skills once again in demand. The night was going from bad to worse. By the time Bailey got back with the firearms, they'd be a couple of hours behind schedule and the new moon would be high in the sky. Not only that but, without the younger Baileys, they'd be short of experienced men in the armed parties and have to rely on hotheads and sixth-raters, as Smeed would call them. Dickon Wyor, who'd been itching to get his hands on a musket for weeks, might get his wish on a night like this one was becoming.

'What was the Hog doing over there?' Pierce asked. 'Some route that puts Bilsington between Folkestone and Walmer.'

Ransley shrugged. Hogben ranged far and wide, with few men inclined to try to stop him. All preferred him to be far from their own patch. Many would rather he was well away from Bilsington and the neighbouring villages, home to half their families.

'Keep this quiet. The girl's safely away with Cob's wife. As far as you know, the Hog was here with us. As he will be.'

Bish tapped the rim of his tankard edgily, none too keen on covering for such a brutish act. His unease did not pass unnoticed.

'What would you have me do? Put him before the magistrate?'

The question was fair. Hogben knew too much to be cast out. Bish knew Ransley would gladly be rid of the man, sorry Quested had saved him before and sorry Smeed had not killed him now. Bish shivered at the thought — murder could be hard to hide and he'd rather Hogben live than his lover hang. Perhaps, if there was no lasting damage to Miss Horne, it was a time when least said was soonest mended.

Suddenly he felt tired, desperately, wretchedly tired of it all. He'd told Smeed that he'd give up his life when it became a burden. He hadn't reached that point yet, but perhaps the time had come to give up this part of it. He wondered if he could persuade Smeed to pack it in too. They might go to Marseilles, where he'd said it was warm all year round. It might buy them a few more months, even years, together.

For now he resigned himself to getting through what promised to be a long and dismal night. He ran through a few calculations. Bailey would do well to make the trip to Bilsington and back via his armoury in less than an hour. Then another hour or so unloading the cargo. Maybe the same again to take a laden waggon back to the priory and then at least half an hour for the walk home. He couldn't see himself getting to bed inside four hours and it might be far longer. Making a deliberate effort to stop his hand from shaking, he took a sip from his mulled ale, grateful that the landlord was an old friend who took special pains for him. The heady mix of herbs and spices soothed his throat and chest, bringing faint numbness to dull the soreness.

Hours later, with knees wobbling and stomach spinning sickeningly, Bish noted that his estimate for their night's work was proving to be close to the mark.

The long-case clock in the inn had not long finished striking midnight when Quested's cart rattled up for the second time. Perched atop it were Bailey and Hogben. Knowing something of Bailey's loathing of Hogben's unbridled lust, Bish guessed the two men had shared a long, silent ride. It would have surprised no one if Hogben disappeared on the way; indeed, Bailey's restraint was more remarkable than any assault would have been.

By his reckoning, it was about half past one when they finally began to load their cargo. On top of his fever, the extra hours spent sipping his intoxicating herbal remedy had left him halfway to drunk. He hadn't realised the extent of his inebriation until there was some confusion about a pair of rummers at the turnpike house and Ransley angrily told him he was a fool to put them at risk over something that was of no use anyway. He remembered admiring the engraved glass goblets, thinking how fine they'd look on his mantelpiece, but had no memory of taking them. Still, he could hardly deny that he had done so when they were standing proudly on the seat of his cart. Ransley paid off the turnpike man but, as they left, Bish put the rummers by the gate in shame. He would always have felt he'd stolen them from a neighbour, whether or not money changed hands after the fact.

Waiting while the goods were loaded, only his fingers twisted tightly in the mane of the horse beside him stopped him from falling to the ground. Almost midsummer and yet he felt worse than he had in the clutches of the seemingly endless winter. From his earliest memory, winter was a time of coughs and fevers but then summer brought him close to the hale heartiness that most countrymen took for granted. Now, for the first time, the season brought no respite. Now, also for the first time, anxiety stirred in his breast for what that might mean.

Somehow, through it all, he'd managed to keep his job. He knew there were many reasons for that, some to his credit and others down to pure luck. A skilled and conscientious man, long years of hard and diligent work meant that no one watched over him or checked what he did. Having long since realised that such a reliable mate could take care of the carts and other equipment without supervision, the waggoner was usually busy on Brissenden's work elsewhere. In his absence, Smeed unobtrusively took on the tougher jobs but he was not the only one to help. Other men around the farm sometimes offered Bish a hand and no one expected him to do any heavy labour.

As far as luck was concerned, Brissenden liked his brandy and so a tub every once in a while worked wonders. For years it had bought his silence about the affairs of the Blues and now it bought tolerance for Bish. The farm's prosperity made it easy for its owner to be magnanimous. There was plenty of work of all kinds, even within Bish's shrinking capabilities, and there was no financial pressure to let workers go. All in all, things could have been far worse and he knew it.

The time would come when he could not hold down a job of any sort — and perhaps a time would come when he'd no longer care — but for now he needed to feel useful and clung both to his legitimate job and to his less respectable activities. He'd always refused to think about how things would end for him, determined to live life to the full for as long as he could. Now doubts gathered deep inside him. The end was closer than it had been and he was not ready to face it. A shudder ran through his body, not exactly fear but a bitter cocktail of dread and dismay.

He glanced past the men loading his cart, to the ring of musket-bearers watching the darkness for the all-too-familiar sight of preventive officers. In the moonless night, he could not distinguish one man from another. He knew he should be glad that his lover was safely back in Bilsington, supervising the cover-up of Hogben's excesses, but instead he felt lost without the comfort of that square-shouldered silhouette.

He no longer even had Dennard's cheery company in his driving, although they usually caught and hitched the horses together as they had that night. The beasts were still unruly but wise handling had mellowed them to the point where a competent driver could manage them without incident. As Dennard became more valuable in defending their cargoes than in hauling them, drivers came and went for his ponies. All good men in their way, none was the match of the man they replaced.

Bish reflected on the changes, feeling sorrow both for the escalating conflicts that made large fighting parties necessary and the skill with a musket that put Dennard in their midst. Almost every run of the past half-year had met with stiff opposition from the Blockade. Bish knew for certain that two officers had been injured in March and another in May, on the fateful night that Giles fell. It was only a matter of time before a preventive officer died and his fellows swarmed over the marshes as they had after Brookland. Then the investigation had met with a wall of silence but much had changed in the five years since.

His heart sank when a shot rang out along the beach. He was in no shape for yet another forced run. With his mind fixed solely on his team and his load, he let the ensuing chaos pass over his head.

He heard Ransley's urgent shout as if in a dream.

'Don't fire, but, if you do, fire low!'

He heard more shots, and then a volley of curses from several different men. Amongst the profanities, he picked out Dickon Wyor's name. Presumably he had fired, and not low at that. Bish tried to shut that out of his delirious mind, concentrating on the fact that Smeed, probably awaiting them back at the Bourne Tap, was not there to die and that a slug could only hasten the fate that was already beckoning to him.

No one noticed when Bish did not follow the returning men into the Tap. Outside in the yard, clinging to the hot horseflesh at his side, it was all he could do to stay on his feet. He and the spirited gelding had long since come to an understanding and now the beast stood docile under his weight, as if it sensed his need for support. He was determined to rub it down and return it to the common as usual but the strength of his mind could do nothing in the face of the weakness of his body. Inside the house, the angry voices raised in argument began to fade as nausea rolled through him. In his fever, he had no sense of time but the shivers running through the horse told him he'd been standing there for a while.

A door slammed and footfalls echoed in the yard, empty but for Bish half-hidden beyond the trough. The steps were at once deliberate and aimless: an angry man planting his feet firmly but with no idea where he was going — anywhere but in the midst of the warring factions. Suddenly the footfalls turned in Bish's direction. He tried to rouse himself, not wanting his fellows to see the state of him, but needn't have worried.

'Christ, Bish! You all right?'

Dennard was beside him in an instant. Bish fell against his friend, fighting to stay conscious.

'A-a-all r-right,' he echoed weakly.

'You look it,' Dennard muttered, hauling him over to the wall. 'C'mon, lean here, just for a minute.'

Bish didn't move a muscle, not daring to shift his weight, knowing that he could not recover his balance once lost. Dennard bustled around the horse, stripping its harness and rubbing the dried sweat roughly from its cold skin. The activity confused Bish, whose dedication to his stock matched Dennard's but who would surely put a friend before a horse. He needn't have worried. Dennard returned in no time, helping him to the horse's flank and then boosting him effortlessly onto its back.

'God knows but you're just a bag of bones these days.'

The words were intended to be light-hearted but they were too close to the truth. Bish felt an unfamiliar burning in his eyes and blinked back tears. He would not feel sorry for himself. In fact, it was not willpower but friendship that drove out his self-pity. Dennard hopped up lightly behind him, shifting close so that his body provided support and warmth like a cradle. The gelding seemed to shrug off its tiredness, setting out in a smooth jog quite unlike its usual fighting trot.

His drowsiness irresistible, he settled back and drifted. He wasn't truly asleep, feeling the security of Dennard's grip and the fluid movement of the horse beneath him, but he managed to relax for the first time since he set out early that evening. Unable to track the passage of distance or time, only the familiar turn into Bank Farm aroused something in his subconscious. He stirred.

'Aye,' Dennard confirmed in his ear. 'Nearly home now.'

Bish tried to speak but his rasping breath carried no sound.

'Shh. I know where you live.'

Still agitated, Bish gasped again. 'Not cott-age.' Feeling a momentary relaxation in Dennard's tense concern, Bish guessed that his friend was smiling.

'I know. The new Mrs Weaver told me how generous you'd been, giving up your beautiful cottage for her and her husband, sharing that nasty little room with Mr Smeed.' A chuckle tickled Bish's ear. '*Very* generous.'

Bish felt his face burn with embarrassment. He'd witnessed a thousand far lewder exchanges but no one made such comments to him, not from knowledge of what he did but rather from pity for what they thought he, as an invalid, could not do.

There was no time for him to worry about it. Dennard reined back behind the stable block and sprang to the ground. Bish let himself slither down, relying on his friend to keep him upright. For the second time, Dennard propped him against a wall while he tended to the horse. A couple of miles at a steady pace meant the gelding was just pleasantly warm so a blanket from the stable was enough to stave off a chill.

Seconds later, Dennard helped him into the little room. Was it nasty? He'd never been happier than during the time that he and Smeed had shared it. It saddened him to think that others saw their home as a hovel. When Dennard had lit a lamp, Bish looked around with fresh eyes. The door was set into the short side of a rectangular room, perhaps ten feet wide and twice that in length. At the far end, a narrow bed ran along each side. In the gap between the beds stood a tall oak chest of drawers and a rag rug made by his sister. There was a window by the door, although of course no light came through its thick diamond panes now. A small stove stood in a chimney-breast to the right and two wooden armchairs faced it. There was a table and two cane-seated chairs against the wall opposite the stove, with an array of shelves above them weighed down by the paraphernalia of everyday life.

A plain little room — what farm worker had much better, although obviously a couple with half a dozen children needed a bit more space — but nasty?

Dennard helped him towards the end of the room, looked at the beds and grinned. Bish felt the heat hit his cheeks, knowing his friend was asking *Which one? Does it matter?* He waved weakly at the right, then submitted as Dennard stripped his top-clothes, helped him under the covers and propped him with pillows. He lay gasping, willing his breathing to settle, while Dennard raked the glowing embers in the stove, stoked it up and put on a kettle to boil. In happier days, Bish's partiality to a nice cup of tea had been a standing joke and he'd always taken the gibes in good part, stacking up his packets of choice teas and leaving the tobacco for his friends. He was starting to feel better by the time Dennard came over and dropped heavily onto Smeed's bed.

'It's not nasty.' A soft laugh. 'Mind, you've seen my place.'

It was unnerving how often Dennard seemed to read his mind. If he'd ever had ideas about keeping secrets, he'd been a fool. The lad had probably known his feelings from the first time they met, and yet their staunch friendship had blossomed in spite of them.

Dennard surveyed the blue-striped curtains and tablecloth, then the patchwork quilts that Bish himself had hemmed, after carefully halving the double that his mother had made for the big bed back in the cottage. The mantelpiece above the stove bristled with a multitude of small plaster dogs left by a maiden aunt. A generous bunch of cornflowers filled a jug on the table. When the kettle began to whistle, Dennard brewed tea without passing any further comment on the domestic arrangements. He put the heavy earthenware mugs on the chest and made to settle himself on the empty bed, then thought again and kicked off his boots first.

'You heard what passed?' he checked.

Bish nodded.

'Won't just go away. More preventive men every run. If they don't get us, there's them amongst us'll do the job for 'em.'

Bish nodded again. Most of the old hands were coming to the

same conclusion. They might be shot or hanged by the King's men. They might be shot or stabbed by their own men. Only recently had Bish begun to consider a third possibility. With the reward that had long stood for information on smugglers, they might be turned in by one of their own. Doubt and mutual suspicion were becoming a way of life. He thought again of the men that Hogben was bringing in to replace their losses. Any one of them might have a secret agenda. Free-trade paid well in comparison with almost anything else a working man might tackle but it'd take a lot of nightwork to match what the Blockade could offer a traitor.

Bish sucked in air cautiously and then gave a shallow cough to clear his throat of mucus.

'My last.'

Dennard glanced across at him, made as if to speak, but then nodded. There was a profound sadness in the hazel eyes that usually danced so merrily, too great to hide or deny.

'Jem?'

Bish gave a slight shrug. They had not discussed it. Perhaps the time had come when that needed to change.

'I don't blame you,' Dennard admitted, 'But it's a sorry pass. First Cob, now you. There'll be others — you heard Datchy. Maybe I should think on it too.'

Bish repeated his shrug. His hand was forced, finally admitting he might be a danger to his friends as well as to himself, but perhaps he'd have made the same choice as Giles anyway. He didn't know.

They sipped their tea in silence.

Some time passed before they heard a man's stride outside, faltering as he reached the tethered horse. The door opened noiselessly and Smeed's fight-swollen face appeared in the gap, taking in the teapot and lamplight, then seeing Bish in one bed and Dennard slouched across the other. If a momentary doubt passed over the startled features, Bish could not have sworn to it but he knew Smeed quickly deduced what had passed. Dennard surely knew it too but he spoke up anyway.

'Bish came over bad back at the Tap. I brought him home, thought I'd better hang around till you got in.'

Smeed nodded. 'Thanks.'

He closed the door and came to sit on the bed. Even Bish, usually so sensitive to those around him, didn't know when but, at some point, they'd reached a tacit understanding. Dennard knew about them. They knew he knew. He knew they knew he knew.

When Smeed spoke again, his tone confirmed the knowledge. At the head of an armed party, he was almost as powerful a presence as the commanding Sam Bailey — both men projected the force of their personalities through their voices to keep their men in line. Off-duty with friends like Pierce and Giles, he spoke in his natural voice — firm but muted, with stronger traces of his birthplace. Only with Bish did a hint of softness creep in, revealing a complex blend of tenderness for a lover and concern for an ailing spouse. Bish had never expected anyone else to hear that hushed tone but Dennard heard it now.

'I said you weren't fit, mule.'

Bish smiled weakly. He knew he had a name for stubbornness when his mind was set but the nickname was Smeed's alone.

Dennard yawned. 'Well, I'd better be getting along.'

There was no unease in the announcement, just an exhausted man eager to reach his bed.

Smeed nodded. 'Thanks again. Sorry I wasn't there to look out for him.'

Dennard gave something that tried to be a grin but turned into a grimace. 'You had your hands full. God only knows who put a musket in Wyor's hands this time.'

Bish remembered then that Dennard had found him only because he'd come out to let his temper cool down. Not prone to angry outbursts, their current straits were pushing even him to the limit. Yes, it was time for that conversation with Smeed.

Dennard stood, stretched, then leaned over and squeezed Bish's shoulder. 'Take care of yourself, eh?'

Bish nodded and managed a hoarse whisper of thanks.

Dennard waved his gratitude away and headed for the door. Smeed let him out and bolted it securely behind him.

'Tommy's a good man,' he said unnecessarily.

Bish read the reassurance in the comment. Smeed knew the depth of the friendship between him and Dennard, perhaps Smeed even knew he'd once wished for more than friendship, but he surely also knew that any such desires were far in the past. He wanted no one but Smeed and the man was too clever and too confident to manufacture problems where there were none, especially when they had problems enough.

His earlier tearfulness returned with the sudden realisation that he was long past giving anyone cause for jealousy. No one, man or woman, would ever again be attracted to his wasted body. Even Smeed's steadfast love could not overcome the revulsion that the living felt for the dying: eyes that had always gazed lovingly into his when their bodies joined now stayed resolutely closed during their rare intimacies. That would have hurt more had he not been so sure that the image in Smeed's mind was not of another lover but of himself in good health.

'Need anything?'

Bish shook his head.

Smeed stripped quickly and slipped into the bed beside him.

'You should see a doctor.'

'T'would change naught,' Bish mouthed almost soundlessly.

'It's consumption, in't it?'

Amazingly, neither of them had uttered the word before, as if not saying it somehow stopped it from being true. Bish nodded. It was consumption and he had reached the beginning of the end. And he wasn't as easy with that idea as he'd thought he'd be.

'How bad were you taken?'

There was just a hint of a tremor in Smeed's voice. He was also too clever to lie to himself, about the health of his lover any more than the state of the Blues.

'Bad. I'll not run again.'

Smeed hugged him. 'Good. You know I fear for you.'

Bish ran a finger over the cuts and bruises peppering Smeed's face. 'I fear for thee too.'

'Want me out as well?' There was surprise in Smeed's voice, but perhaps more at the question being asked than its nature.

Bish hesitated. He'd never asked Smeed to change because of their relationship and baulked at doing so now. Finally he settled for a compromise and mustered his meagre energy to put his case.

'Another marsh winter will be the death of me.' He steadied his breathing. 'But, God willing, I might see it through in Marseilles.'

Even as he spoke, it startled him that he was not talking about a place to pass the winter — he was talking about a place to die. He didn't know what response he expected but Smeed's warm smile came as a relief. He gave no reply but his tender kiss promised that

336

autumn would find them headed south to a land where the climate might be kinder and, even if it was not, the law allowed a man to nurse his lover without shame or subterfuge.

Relaxed with strong arms around him, Bish pondered Smeed's initial surprise, almost reluctance, and then ready agreement. It wasn't long before he worked it out. Smeed would not, could not, run from a bad situation but he had no problem in making a conscious decision to take his sick lover abroad for the winter three months hence. Bish smiled, knowing that Smeed would not be the man he loved without that resolve and determination.

Sam

Who the devil gave Wyor a musket ?'

Only inches away, Smeed spat the demand in Sam's face. Few men would stand so close or shout so loud. Sam felt his grip on his temper begin to slip. Each run was worse than the last and, if there was one thing he didn't need, it was Smeed telling him how it was his fault. He glared down at his accuser, glad that even the tallest of the others fell several inches short of Bailey proportions, and snarled his reply.

'For Christ's sake! Three years ago, we could muster five hundred men at a day's notice. Now we've to look hard for eighty. That's scarce enough to run a cargo, without fighting for it an' all. The bugger's a fair shot — what d'you expect me to do?'

'He'll kill someone before he's through. Then we'll all swing.'

'Then we'll bloody well swing, damn you!'

Smeed's fists grabbed his lapels and yanked him still closer.

'I'll be damned if I'll hang for the likes of that blasted shitsack.'

Sam gripped Smeed's wrists and forced him backwards. Men all around the stable-yard at the Bourne Tap watched them strain against each other. Knowing they were evenly matched in skill and experience, Sam had no doubt that he could overpower a man whom he outweighed by several stones but, when he did so, the achievement gave him little satisfaction. The rage burning inside him was only fuelled by the knowledge that Smeed was right — another forced run and another preventive man carried off, in a bad way by the look of it, and that could only bring the Blockade down on them harder than ever. Desperate for an outlet for his pent-up turmoil, he shoved Smeed mercilessly into the wall and crushed the air from his chest. The onlookers tensely drew closer around them but no one intervened.

'What if it's one of us that falls next time?' Smeed gasped.

Sam was sure that thought had occurred to others too, as Wyor shot past them to reach his targets. Even a perfect shot like Giles would be a fool to take risks like that. No man's aim was infallible, let alone at night, and, even if it was, their weapons were not accurate enough to take chances. But then again, without enough guns in the armed parties, men would be shot or hanged by the Blockade. Did it matter how they died?

'Then he falls. If you can't live with it, go bugger yourself.' His words were cold and mean, low but loud enough to be heard by those watching, but then he leaned forward and dropped his voice to a barely audible growl. 'I doubt that cripple can do it for you.'

Sam saw the fury in Smeed's eyes and then felt it flow through the man's tensed muscles an instant before he was thrown backwards. He might have regained his balance if Smeed had not cannoned into him. Even as they fell to the ground in a tangle of flailing limbs, part of him was protesting that the fight was pointless. He wasn't angry with Smeed and mocking the man's sorrow gave him no pleasure.

'What in blue blazes goes on here?'

Sam heard the words through a red mist that somehow filtered out both the meaning and the identity of the speaker. He buried his right fist in Smeed's gut.

'And what're you lot waiting for?' the voice demanded. 'Haven't we troubles enough that we need make more for ourselves?'

The next thing Sam knew, a hand grasped his collar and hauled him off Smeed. He spun around, ready to take on the newcomer as well, but found himself looking down the barrel of a pistol. Focusing with difficulty, he saw Dennard's face behind the hammer. He paused, panting, and debated whether to call the bluff. Before he could decide, Smeed moved behind him. Turning to face a renewed attack that never came, he found Gilham holding the point of a knife to Smeed's throat.

Ransley stepped between them. 'Now what's this all about?'

Sam opened his mouth angrily. Then he closed it again. He had no idea what it was all about.

'Well?' Ransley stared at first at him and then at Smeed.

Smeed glanced at him, then answered sullenly. 'Nothing.'

'Nothing?' Ransley raised his eyebrows.

Sam sighed, then gave his curt agreement. 'Misund'standing.'

Ransley studied them for a few seconds, then looked around the assembled men. Unlike his predecessor, he rarely exerted his dominance over the Blues but he did so now. Drawing himself up to his full height, he held the silence just long enough for his men to feel uncomfortable, then spoke briskly.

'Indeed? Now listen to me and listen well. Our enemy is the Preventive Service. If there's fighting to be done, it's with them. Let that be an end to it.'

There was a finality to his tone that brooked no argument.

Smeed gave a surly nod and strode out of the yard without a word. If he resented the rebuke, he clearly didn't intend to make an issue of it.

Even in the wrong, Sam didn't expect to be taken down a peg in front of his men. He knew he could do worse than follow Smeed's example but instead, scowling and cursing, he stalked round to the unlicensed public house at the back of the Tap. He was in no mood for pleasantries when he banged his fist on the table for service.

'Brandy, damn it!'

'You know what you can do with your curses, Sam Bailey. We run a civil house here.'

Sam treated Eliza Ransley to an even more gruesome scowl.

'And your ugly looks too. Whose dog's dead this time, then?'

'Yours if you don't mind your business, woman.'

She held aloft the glass she'd filled, indicating that he'd leave her premises dry if he didn't answer her question and in language she found acceptable. He glared up at it, then pulled a stool to the table resignedly. He'd never won an argument with his sister in his life and he didn't expect to start now. She set glass and bottle down in front of him and pulled up another stool. Her voice was low and calming when she spoke again.

'Another bad night?'

Sam nodded, drained the glass and let her refill it. His hand shook as he picked it up and his breath came out in a shuddering sigh. Their family had run uncustomed goods for as long as anyone could remember, certainly way before his grandfather's time. It had been the way of things in Kent for hundreds of years and he couldn't see why it must change. Why was it so important to snatch away a man's only chance of a decent life for himself and his family? And why the hell did it have to happen in his lifetime?

'Christ, Lize. They were everywhere. Each time, there's more of them and less of us.' He stared into the brandy. 'Cob and Bish gone, Paul 'n' Dick say nothing but all of a sudden they're too busy, and God alone knows where John and Rob were tonight. And as for the new ones coming in.' He shook his head in despair.

'And there you are at Jem's throat,' she scolded.

'Don't you start. I've already had a dressing-down from your husband.'

She smiled sadly, her dark eyes reflecting his own doubts and fears. 'Is the end coming, do you think?'

Rubbing his face wearily, he gave a shrug that said more yes than no, then downed the brandy in one. For him, the most unsettling event of the evening took place during their return along the turnpike road. A man leaned from the window of his bedchamber and began to wish them good night and good luck but, when he saw the armed party behind the working party, his good wishes turned to threats. The threats themselves were foolish, setting one duck-gun against a dozen muskets and pistols, but the vehemence with which he denounced them sent a chill through Sam. It was a bitter reminder that they could no longer count on support from their neighbours, who wanted nothing more than an end to the savage conflict between Blockade and trade that threatened their safety and damaged their property.

Now he said only, 'P'r'aps it'd be best all round if it was.'

'That don't sound like my brother talking.'

'I'm tired, Lize. Dog-tired of it all.'

'Would Sarah and the littl'uns be all right, with just the farm?'

'Got a bit put by. It'd be hard but they won't starve. You?'

'Oh, you know George. We're ready for a few rainy days. He don't do it for us, not any more.'

Sam nodded. Even knowing little of his brother-in-law's arrangements, he guessed they'd show the customary prudence. Ransley certainly didn't piss his money against the wall like some of their fellows.

340

'But how will the younger ones manage?' she asked.

Sam shrugged. 'Same way as t'other folk.'

'With nothing but a sack of potatoes to feed a family for a week?'

'They don't care, Lize, the toffs.' He raised his hand to forestall her response, knowing what it would be from the many times they'd had the same conversation over the years. 'All right, so there's the odd one like Knatchbull — and Cosway looks like he'll make a fair landlord for the priory estate too — but they're a drop in the ocean. Most of 'em don't care if we live or die, so long as there's another to take our place. Once they get more of their damned machines, they'd won't even need to worry about that.'

When she refilled his glass, Eliza poured one for herself.

'Now their blasted wars are over, they don't even need us to go and die for 'em.'

Eliza's hand closed over his and they stared at the stained tabletop in silence. The world was changing and there no longer seemed to be room for the likes of them.

Billy

Billy Wyor followed a few yards behind his brother, as he often did. People tended to overlook him in the wake of Dickon's broad and manly frame. He'd even heard himself described as a head shorter, when in fact he gave away less than an inch in height. Their features were as different as their builds, with Dickon's eyes a warm oak-bark hazel while his were cool pebble-grey, Dickon's hair owl-tawny while his was flax-gold. The contrast was only strengthened by their characters. Dickon was ebullient but volatile; new acquaintances usually took to him, until he beat the men senseless in a fit of rage or took the women in a bout of lust. Billy, on the other hand, rarely made new acquaintances because people barely noticed him lurking in his brother's shadow, which was fine by him, since it meant they never connected him with their stolen possessions or violated womenfolk. But, for all their differences, they were as twins in their arrogance and cruelty.

Billy glanced over at their new playmate. Well into his middle years, Hogben's battered body testified to numerous past abuses. Far worse than the limp was the thread-veined skin and haunted eyes that told of years as a drunk and opium-eater. Both Wyors had recognised the signs as soon as they met the man who was surely the most repulsive example of humanity they'd ever find and yet, at the same time, highly entertaining to be around. They'd never seen a man who could drink like him and, once he was awash with booze, there was nothing he would not do. They occupied their spare time in running bets on what they could taunt him into trying next. At that moment, they were all out of their senses after two days of unbroken drinking.

Billy's pockets were full from his latest victory. Even Dickon had not believed what Hogben would do to a cow for a wager and now Billy had his brother's pay from the last run as well as his own. He rubbed the right side of his ribs ruefully, conceding to himself that an honest day's work might be easier than the battle they'd had holding the cow down while Hogben proved his point.

The image brought a surprising reaction from his groin. He had no desire to try the experience for himself but the memory of Hogben's deplorable satisfaction reminded him that it was a day or so since he'd forced himself into a reluctant serving girl behind an inn on the far side of the Brabournes and he was now ready for more. Unfortunately, his libido was far less reliable that Hogben's, which rarely faltered even when pickled in alcohol and opium. Billy risked failure with even the prettiest young girl unless the contact was cloaked in the fear and pain that stoked his ardour. He was musing on how to contrive a union in which he might find such fulfilment, when a forward glance revealed a blurred figure ahead. A few strides later and his well-oiled vision distinguished skirts. He felt another pulse of interest from his groin.

Hogben came to his right side as Dickon drew level on his left.

'How's about it?'

The Wyors grinned at each other. Their shared enthusiasm for taking what was not given freely was one of the things that bound them together. Hogben raped women because no sane woman would let his diseased body near her. Billy had heard talk that the man hadn't always been that way and, just occasionally, thought he glimpsed some faint regret at how things had turned out.

His brother, Dickon, was a different matter. It was as if he saw it all as a game, with nothing to choose between fighting a man and raping a woman. If the woman accepted her lot, he left her unharmed. Billy was aware, of course, that his own need for violence went beyond that but did not dwell on it. He'd always needed an appetiser to move things along and cared little for what it meant for his chosen target. His body throbbed in anticipation of the treat that might await it now.

When he looked ahead again, the figure didn't seem to be much nearer. There was a good chance that she would turn back when she saw the state of them. He led the other two men in a clumsy advance. The figure did indeed turn back but, even as drunk as they were, they gained on her. Billy wasn't so far gone that he couldn't see how odd that was. He squinted, bringing her into focus for an instant, and realised she was not so much walking as shuffling.

Damnation, he thought, a cursed cripple.

The thought did not interrupt his pursuit. Deformity was of less concern to him than the woman's state of mind when he forced her to comply with his demands. Dickon reached the woman first, seizing her arm and jerking her around to face them. With the movement came a sharp crack, punctuated by a screech. Billy's surprise at the easily broken bone was quickly supplanted by shock as he saw the woman's face. He was still taking in the wrinkles lying over wrinkles when Hogben gripped her neck in his huge paw.

'Crone!'

The single word was filled with wrath, as if it was the woman's fault that she did not meet their requirements. He threw her backwards, the force lifting her feet clear of the ground and then sending her flat-backed into the dirt. More bones cracked.

'For Christ's sake, Hog. She could be your grandmother.'

Dickon's words might have been a plea but the laughter underpinning them gave the lie to that. Billy hesitated, revulsion at the wasted flesh fighting with arousal at the terror in the wide eyes. He studied the woman's motionless body, debating whether sampling it was out of the question. She was still conscious, her gaze fixed on him as if her fate was in his hands. It wasn't — the others would do as they pleased anyway. Even without that abdication of responsibility, he would still have slept peacefully at night, lacking as he did a conscience to be troubled by the growing brutality of his sins. He stepped over her, bent down and ripped her worn blouse open. Taking in the shrivelled breasts and papery skin stretched across prominent bones, he scowled. Finding her body as bad as her face, his revulsion defeated his arousal.

'Piss!' He looked at her again, then up at Hogben. 'She'd be no good to a blind man.'

He found himself shoved aside as Hogben took his place over the woman. Repeating his action, Hogben yanked up her coarsely woven skirt and tore her drawers off with a brutal flourish.

'No chance.'

His brother's firm declaration echoed the revulsion Billy felt. He was about to move on, hoping for greener pastures elsewhere, when Hogben spoke.

'How old are you?' he asked the woman.

She tried to answer but only dry breath puffed over her lips.

Hogben drew his pistol and pointed it at her face. 'How old?'

She managed a whisper. 'E-e-eighty-one.'

Hogben considered that for a moment, then made to push the pistol back into his belt. Without even thinking about it, Billy grabbed it by the barrel, swept the butt in an arc and cracked it into the woman's skull.

Her eyes closed without a murmur.

Billy watched her thick blood soak slowly through her thin hair, feeling a visceral sense of satisfaction not unlike the sexual relief he'd been seeking.

'Why d'you kill her?' Dickon asked, mild curiosity in his voice.

'She'd lived long enough.'

Hardly seeming to take in the crime, Hogben spat on the woman's lax face and then lumbered on with Dickon following behind. Billy stared at the body for a few seconds, unsure of the real reason that he'd ended her life, then shrugged and joined his companions. She had nothing to complain about. Most people didn't get eighty years. He didn't expect to.

George

George Ransley crouched in the bows of the *Venus*, watching the oarsmen take her swiftly towards the shore. It was unusual for him to come ashore in a boat landing a cargo but there'd been some confusion with his contact in France so he'd gone aboard the lugger to smooth the deal. They were headed for a point close to the bathing machines at Dover, risky in that it was at the heart of a major port but appealing because of a weakness of the Blockade force stationed in the casements, a shelter partway up the cliffs. It was a notoriously difficult base, reached by badly worn steps that made fast progress impossible. Thanks to the slow response of reinforcements to an alarm, traders had evaded capture several times before and George hoped to exploit the flaw again. He also hoped, after several months working the coast between Deal and Walmer, that a sudden appearance at Dover would be unexpected.

There was an even stronger reason for his strategy that night. The first Deal and Downs Regatta was only eleven days away and he knew that Captain Pigot had committed half his officers aboard the *Ramillies* to organising the event. A fair proportion of the gentry and judiciary of East Kent were to be entertained on board the old man-of-war, the preparations for which provided an excellent diversion from the officers' everyday duties. All in all, he felt more optimistic about the run than he had in a long time. Even the stillness of the starlit night could not dampen his hopes for a trouble-free night of profitable trade.

Sensing his mood, and knowing the thinking behind the choice of landing site, the men were working better than ever. Everyone was grateful for the promise of an easy night after a series of forced runs. As they ploughed through the surf, he scanned the bathing machines for the all-clear. It was half a minute before he spotted the lantern perched atop them and gave a low call.

'Hallo there, you ashore!'

There was no response.

'You ashore!' he repeated.

Again nothing.

He examined the beach and saw Smeed at the steering oar in the stern do the same. There was no sign of trouble.

'Hallo, ashore!' he called a little louder.

At last, he saw movement by the bathing machines. A moment later, shadows swarmed down the foreshore towards their vessel. Fifty tubmen closed in, while a small fighting party fanned out in a protective formation at the perimeter of the site. Sam Bailey headed the cluster to the west while Gilham led those to the east. George frowned when he saw how the men were divided, with the best under Gilham and the worst under Bailey. Looking harder, he saw the reason for that: Dickon Wyor was in Bailey's party and few men wanted to stand anywhere near him when he held a musket. Still, Bailey would do his best to keep the youngster in line, and he had his brother and Hogben on hand to help him do it.

'Here we goes,' Quested's deep voice came from just beyond the bow. 'Tom, you takes the first pair. Ted, you next.'

The tubmen followed his guidance, shouldering their loads and setting off up the beach at a brisk walk. Quested soon had them moving apace. George was standing beside him in the shallow water, watching his men work, when the peace was shattered by a shout from the east.

'Stop, you bastards! If you stir a peg, I'll blow your brains out.'

There was a flash but no report. The Blockademan's pistol had snapped, though whether through damp powder or a lost ball George could not know. A second shout came from the west.

'Pickett? What vessel is it? Can you see?'

The first man had no time to respond. His questioner, presumably seeing something of them in the faint starlight, fired a shot almost before he'd finished speaking, provoking a volley from Bailey's quarter. George cursed under his breath, seeing his hopes of a quiet night dashed once more. While Bailey's men reloaded, Gilham's flowed forward in a smooth advance, intent on taking the sentinel before he could fire again.

From his position beside the *Venus*, George saw Gilham lead his party in thrusting at the sentinel with their muskets while he, cursing fluently, slashed at them with his cutlass. Dennard reached to try to catch the cutlass after it swept past him. Missing his grip on the guard, he must have caught the blade because he clasped his hands together and screamed at the sentinel.

'Damn you, bastard! That was my bloody hands!'

With the sentinel slicing the air at random, the other scouts dodged his blows and tried to get past his panic-stricken defence. George had no doubt that Gilham would just have soon put a slug through the man's head but, instead, he resolutely battled on, abiding by Smeed's instructions to use minimum possible force.

On any other night, it would have been Smeed at the head of the second fighting party and Gilham in the *Venus*. George was not sure why they'd switched that night but suspected it had something to do with the argument he'd witnessed between Smeed and Bailey. He considered ordering them to take their usual places but decided against it, judging them equally skilled in both roles and accepting that Smeed and Bailey might be best apart if personal feelings were running so high.

Gilham was shouting at the sentinel. 'For Christ's sake, there's no use in striking every b-bastard who comes within reach.'

Another shot came from the west. George looked at Bailey's men, who had reloaded and were poised ready to fire on the new assailant. If the Blockademan was carrying the standard pair of pistols, without a musket, he now held two empty weapons. The unmistakable outlines of the two Baileys had just moved forward to tackle the foe when another in their party fired. There was no time for anyone to react, as an answering shot came from the east.

George peered into the night, trying to see where it had come from. The sentinel was still holding off the scouts and so there was only one explanation: reinforcements. With more than half of their cargo already on its way inland, and only a small fighting party in place, there was no point in facing a major assault, if one was on its way. Wasting no time, he ordered the retreat.

'Shove off the boat! Get clear!'

Quested shouldered a pair of tubs and ushered the last of the tubmen from the beach, while Smeed and three of the mariners shoved the *Venus* out to sea. George patted Smeed's shoulder in encouragement, then fell in behind Quested to supervise the delivery of the cargo for counting near the Palm Tree. As they cleared the foreshore, another shot came from the east. Glancing back, he saw the fighting parties in retreat with no sign of pursuit. By the time they regrouped, he expected to be well clear.

Only minutes later, he was on his cart with Georgie driving the team swiftly along the Canterbury Road and Quested not far behind. Some of their men rode horses alongside, while others ran and the injured rode in the carts. All in all, he reflected, it might have been worse. They'd lost no men and landed the better part of their cargo. The mariners would sow the rest somewhere for later collection. Even so, his deep sighs during their journey expressed regret at the trouble along with his relief at their escape.

Jem

Jem Smeed raised his hand to the door of the Walnut Tree, then paused with his fingertips resting on the split oak. The inn was the site of some of his happiest memories of his time in Aldington, perhaps of his time on earth. Only his private moments with Wilson surpassed the friendly gossip and rowdy parties he'd shared with friends in what had been the best public house for miles around. On the walk from the farm, he could almost have convinced himself that nothing had changed — the warm summer evening like countless others and the fields as bountiful as ever — but then reality intruded.

Before he left, he'd helped Wilson into bed and brewed a pot of his favourite tea. It had been another bad day for Wilson, forehead burning and limbs trembling. Maintaining any pretence of work became ever more difficult but Brissenden made no complaint. Quite the opposite in fact, when he decided all the tack needed cleaning and told the waggoner to set Wilson up with everything he needed on a stool in a snug corner of the stable. Seeing his lover labour for days over something he could have done in his sleep before, Jem began to feel as if his heart were being scooped out of his chest piece by piece with a teaspoon.

Sometimes he wondered how much more he could take, but the wondering only added guilt to the burden under which he was already buckling. He despised his selfishness when Wilson bore his trials with such fortitude but still there were times when he nearly packed his bag and walked out of Aldington just as he had walked in so casually three years earlier. Nothing in his hard and dangerous life compared with the pain of watching Wilson's flesh waste away before his eyes. Pain had turned to anguish earlier that evening, when he guided Wilson from chair to bed and found his grip encircling a bicep with room to spare. The sorrow that engulfed him then, as he tried to detect in those skeletal remains the boyish figure that had so appealed to him when they met, flooded through him again and it was a moment before he dared to push on the door to the public house.

Even the wood seemed to share his suffering. Ted Wraight still ran the inn but he was a changed man. Gone was his pride in the establishment and his concern for the customers. Gone were most of the customers, scared off by the new face of the Blues, and gone was his friendship for those who remained. The door was dented from drunken demands to open out of hours and covered with the mud that Wraight's wife had washed away each morning in better times. A dirty-stable smell hung in the air, where men barely troubled to step outside to relieve themselves any more. The Wraights themselves were showing the strain, their health failing under the weight of their anxieties, and Jem wondered how much longer they'd hold on to the place.

Only Wilson kept him in Aldington, when all his instincts told him to put as much distance between himself and the authorities as possible. Part of him still hoped they might spend the winter in Marseilles as they'd planned but he was slowly accepting the fact that, although Wilson was better some days than others, he was unlikely ever again to be well enough to make such a journey. There was an unremitting ache of regret deep in his gut that he'd waited too long. If they'd left when it was first suggested, Wilson might be a few months further from death and he himself would not have been present at the murder of a preventive officer.

Within hours of the Dover run, they knew that a Quartermaster had died in the affray. No one was sure how it happened or who fired the fatal shot. The sentinel with whom Gilham's party had battled was still alive and cursing when they fell back, so it had to be one of the unseen men further off, probably a victim of a chance hit in the darkness.

Perhaps it was traces of his military training that made him think of this death as a murder, while others before it were casualties of the war against the Preventive Service. From his position by the *Venus*, Jem could not be sure what happened but he had little doubt that there had been no need for the preventive man to die. They might have overpowered him with bats and certainly could have shot to wound. Jem had no love for the Preventive Service but he had no desire to kill its men either. More importantly, he knew that the death would only make matters worse for the Blues. That was confirmed when Wilson had read the next day's *Chronicle* to him in a hoarse whisper.

Like all the local papers, the *Kentish Chronicle* barely deigned to report on injuries and losses amongst the King's men in years gone by. The tone of its latest article marked a shift in editorial, and probably public, opinion. Jem's heart sank as he heard it.

ANOTHER DREADFUL AFFRAY

Early on Sunday morning (July 30th) a smuggling boat, heavily laden with tubs of spirits, arrived off Dover and in a short time the crew, with the assistance of several other men, endeavoured to run the cargo. A man, however, belonging to the Blockade Service peremptorily ordered them to surrender, declaring if they did not he would fire: the threat was only laughed at by the smugglers and the man immediately discharged his pistol in the air, while the smugglers unceremoniously set to work and removed the whole cargo, consisting of 200 tubs, which were secured by several persons on the beach, and the boat immediately put off. We regret to say that, the moment the preventive man fired his pistol for the purpose of obtaining assistance, one of the men on the beach fired his also and shot the poor fellow through the head. No trace can be obtained of the boat.

It wasn't an accurate report. Things had been far more confused than that, with two preventive men present from the start and the first shot not clearly fired as an alarm. From what Jem heard afterwards, the fallen man had taken a while to die and his wounds were in his chest rather than his head. Nonetheless, while the reporter's use of the word 'peremptorily', once Jem had asked his lover what it meant, perhaps suggested that the preventive man should have offered some justification or authority for his order, the choice of 'unceremoniously' and 'poor fellow' served to illustrate the shift in public opinion about the Blues. Gone was the unconditional support of the mobs who freed imprisoned free-traders in years past. Gone were the times when no magistrate in Kent or Sussex would convict a free-trader, even with an eyewitness, and the days when killing a preventive man was self-defence. Jem doubted that any man amongst them would evade the noose if placed at the scene.

He was not surprised. Along with so many others, he'd seen the way things were going and now his sole cause for surprise was that he was still around to be caught up in it. If only the dead man had approached from the other side of the working party, Gilham's group might have silenced him without a shot fired. If only they'd had more good men like Giles that night.

Jem sighed: 'if only' would get him nowhere. He pushed on the door. Inside, the tap-room was unswept and the fireplace still contained the debris from a fire lit months earlier. Tables were coated in dried beer and ash littered every surface. It was busy enough, with a couple of dozen men present, but the atmosphere was hardly the convivial buzz that a man looked for in a public house. Jem scanned the group, confirming what he suspected — all were Blues. He craned his neck to see into the bar-room and found it empty. So a wretched bunch of them had come together to see what was to be done after the disastrous run. Taking a tankard from a sullen-faced Wraight, he headed over to where Dennard and Gilham sat in a corner.

'Ev'ning.'

The two men nodded grimly. There was a short silence, unusual for them and accentuated by the fact that no one else was speaking around them either.

'How's Bish doing?' Dennard asked, his hands swathed in dirty bandages after his brush with the sentinel's cutlass. Thankfully, the damage was superficial and Quested assured him there'd be no permanent loss of movement.

'Not so good.'

Silence fell again but it was not absolute. In the space left by the absence of normal activity, small noises seemed louder. There were the sounds of men swallowing beer and then of belches as they released the gas from it, not loud ones intended for others to hear but suppressed ones that normally would pass unnoticed. There were scuffles as they shifted position, and sometimes thuds as their boots caught the furniture. It was as if everyone was waiting for something, although nothing had been arranged.

Jem had been staring at his untouched beer for some time when the door opened again. The Baileys came in and repeated his scrutiny of the room while they waited to be served. He studied them. Of course, they were as tall and broad as ever but somehow

351

even they seemed less hale and hearty. If he wasn't mistaken, they'd all shed some weight and now he noted that, while their hair and eyes were as dark as ever, their complexions looked faded — they were just as careworn as everyone else.

It was unusual for Sam to walk into Aldington with his kin, even though John's cottage in Bonnington was only a mile or two from his own in Bilsington. They were probably closing ranks now trouble loomed. Perhaps reconciliation was in Sam's mind when he came over with his drink. He nodded to all but spoke to Smeed.

'Jem.'

'Sam.'

Those were the first words they'd addressed directly to one another since the fight at the Tap. Their mutual antipathy hadn't helped at Dover, one more thing to deepen Jem's guilt-ridden depression.

'You were right.' Sam spoke flatly, the admission seemingly painful enough without adding a note of apology.

Jem shrugged. Being right gave him no satisfaction in this case, added to which he wasn't sure he had been right.

'Could've been anyone.'

Their words were deliberately obscure, useless as testimony even if Wraight dared to repeat them. No one seriously thought he would. He was locked into the same miserable cycle as they all were, making half his living from the trade and tied to it through family, even if such links were largely in the past. There was no crime lower for a man of the marshes than turning King's Evidence on a free-trader.

'No,' Sam countered. 'You were right.'

Rob took a step forward. 'I heard Big Flash was talking in the White Horse dinner-time, bragging about hitting what the rest of us missed. Won't matter if he did or he didn't, if he's set on telling everyone he did.'

Everyone present knew who he meant by 'Big Flash'. True they had plenty of loud-mouthed bullies to choose from but the pun could only be intended for one of the lightning-bereaved Wyors; 'Big' meant Dickon, which went almost without saying as Billy was a lot of things but not usually stupid.

The Baileys' demeanour underlined the gulf between them and the Wyors. They were hard, savage even, but they were not reckless, at least not when they were sober. They would not be looking to put

352

their necks in a noose, and neither would they be blind to how many men they might take with them if they did so.

Jem stared at Sam, hearing again the words that had really got his blood up: *that cripple*. Part of him couldn't understand why it should trouble him so much. Through no fault of his own, Wilson was a cripple and using a different word wouldn't make it any less true. His anger sprang from somewhere deeper, his resentment of the contempt shown to Wilson by men like the Baileys year after year, just because they'd been blessed with strong and healthy bodies while his was frail and sickly. But as puny as his body might be, Wilson's mind was many times more agile than theirs. He would not ignore a warning from someone as reliable as Jem, lover or not, and nor did he underestimate the damage that fools like the Wyors were doing, both in cruelty towards the local people and aggression towards the preventive men.

Nonetheless, it was too late for recriminations. Short of praying for a corpse to be raised from the dead, Jem saw no way to change what had passed. But, if they lay low and kept quiet, what could be proved? The night was so dark that Jem could not say with certainty what passed — how could a witness do better? There'd been a reward for information on the trade for years — why should anyone claim it now?

Jem came to himself with a start and realised that he was still staring at Sam, who held his eye, steadily but not defiantly.

'Then you'd better shut him up and make a good job of it.'

Sam gave a slight nod, as if that opinion had confirmed his own, and then inclined his head towards the door. Rob and John drained their tankards in single draughts and headed out without a word. No one doubted for an instant that the arguments they presented to the Wyors would be compelling.

Sam pulled up a chair to join them. 'What about next Sunday?'

'Tell Bats to call it off.'

'He'll say he's got orders.'

'Damn his orders.'

'They won't be expecting us to run again so soon.'

Jem stared again, this time in disbelief. 'Of course they won't. That's because only a lunatic would push their luck like that. Are we lunatics now?'

'We can lie low after, wait for things to die down a bit.'

Jem wasn't sure later whether he meant to give voice to his thoughts but somehow the words just came out. 'It's never going to die down. Christ, you know that as well as I do. They're out to put an end to the trade and they won't stop till they've done it. Pigot don't care how many of his men die in stopping it so why in God's name would he care how many of us go down with 'em.'

Sam's eyes narrowed. 'Are you saying you're out?'

Jem hesitated. Was he saying that? He'd never run from a risk in his life but he'd never set out to be hanged either. Finally he nodded. 'I suppose I am.'

Looking around the table, he saw that his companions — while not surprised — were still somehow shocked. As resourceful as many of them were, they'd come to rely on him during his few years in the Blues and now they wondered how they'd manage without his leadership. He hoped they'd find they couldn't, not for his ego but for their safety. Perhaps he was letting them down but then again, if they followed his lead and dropped out as well, perhaps he was saving their lives. He shrugged.

'Let Bats make the call. I'm off home.'

Datchy

Datchy sat on a long-abandoned tub, musket butt-end to the ground, cleaning its long barrel with a rag wrapped around the ramrod. Over fifty of the Blues were dotted around the field, some talking, others occupying themselves with routine chores like his. A couple of hundred yards south-east of their position, Ransley awaited a galley bearing a hundred tubs of French gin. As Datchy swept the rod up and down, he glanced at the sky above. There was no moon and only the faint light of the stars illuminated the world below. He hated the wait before a run: it gave a man too much time to think about the prospect of the night being his last.

Before his marriage, he never questioned his involvement with the Blues but the balance had been so different in those days. His work was more often as mariner than scout and, even when called on to defend a cargo, the blows he inflicted with his stout ash pole took no lives. They rarely faced more than an ill-prepared sentinel and, on a good night, threats or bribes saved the need for violence.

After he gained a wife and three stepchildren, all looking to him to deliver more than the poverty-stricken illegitimacy that had dogged their short lives. As if that were not enough, he soon had two youngsters of his own: his daughter Louise had no sooner been weaned than her mother's belly began to swell again. He'd accepted that with the same pragmatism that he greeted every turn of fate, working harder in anticipation of another mouth to feed without giving much thought to the new arrival, but that all changed the instant he set eyes on his son. Nothing had prepared him for the pride and delight the tiny baby inspired in him, powerful feelings that he could not begin to describe and expressed instead through his hands. From babyhood, Tommy was surrounded by an expanding horde of wooden toys, most far too old for him, as his father arrayed before him the wonders of the world beyond their modest home. It was because of Tommy that Datchy agonised over the risks he took during his nights with the Blues but it was also because of Tommy that he delayed pulling out: he wanted his son to have everything but, as skilled and hard-working as he was, he would be able to do little more than feed his family on his honest wages.

Having cleaned the barrel until no trace of powder could possibly remain, he began to load the musket. With no use for a gun between runs, he passed his to Sam Bailey at the end of a night's work to be stored safely out of troublemakers' reach. The small anchor he'd carved into the stock of a musket in each store identified it as his and it was always returned to him when they prepared for a run. Each time, he checked the weapon over carefully and cleaned it meticulously. Many of the youngsters were careless about such things but Datchy took his lead from the older men with military service behind them, knowing they had their reasons for the rituals that he noted with his usual keen eye.

He sighed deeply.

'No heart for it, Datchy?'

The voice was Dennard's and came from a few yards to his right. The night was so dark that Datchy could see no trace of his friend in the shadows but had heard him flop down some quarter of an hour before, with a muttered oath about the dampness of the grass. He himself was probably visible as a lighter smudge in the blackness, given that he'd come straight from work and, with no opportunity to change into his customary dark blue, still wore his waterproof canvas smock. The smock had once been white but a thick layer of grime now toned down its brightness.

Datchy considered his answer. He'd never had the heart for murder and that's what the papers were calling Quartermaster Morgan's death. Finding it easier to deflect than answer the question, he threw it back.

'Have you?'

There was a pause before the reply. 'No, can't say I have.'

'Sam could be right, that they won't expect us to run again so soon.' He didn't believe that.

'Or they might have every station on alert.'

'Aye, they m-might at that.'

They sat in wretched silence, doubting the wisdom of the night's run but trapped by their loyalty to Ransley.

'Why don't he call it off?'

Datchy had wondered about that. The Blues' main asset during his and Dennard's time was in Ransley's logic and adaptability. Where Cephas Quested had relished a fight, his successor did all he could to avoid confrontation, seeing the trade as a business and basing his decisions on a rational assessment of the rewards of success and the price of failure. Now he was acting out of character, letting the Blockade push them down a path that could lead only to destruction. Datchy thought he understood something of how the transformation had come about.

'Rem-member a year since, when that b-bastard shot Quids?'

'Aye,' Dennard's voice trailed off while he recalled the details. 'Millett. That was the bugger's name. But they paid for that one.'

'True, but I'd say that's when B-Bats gave up on keeping it peaceful. They take one of ours, we take one of theirs, b-but tit for tat'll see us under the daisies in no time.'

It wasn't exactly tit for tat, given they all accepted the risks that went with their occupation and inflicted no premeditated revenge, but he knew the Blockademan, Houlihan, lost his life because of Quids' death. Without it, Smoker would not have strangled the man with his bare hands and Datchy would not have stood by while he did it. The man might still have died, thrown overboard to take his chances, but he would not have been murdered. When a jury evened the score with a second Wilful Murder verdict, Datchy realised that support had not so much shifted away from the Blues but rather that the locals were sick of living amidst such violence and wanted only for it to stop.

A low whistle, echoed at intervals across the field, put an end to their conversation — their cargo had arrived. Datchy gave one more vicious stab with the ramrod and then slid it back into its housing. With fifteen men in the armed parties that night, they might outnumber any opposition, if they were lucky, but that advantage would be offset by the Blockade's superior firepower. Each preventive man carried two pistols in place of their one, with a cutlass to slice the flesh of any man who got in close enough. On top of that, in spite of Bailey and Smeed's best efforts, the Blues were not professional soldiers, with nothing to do with their time but drill. Pushing his doubts and fears back into the pit of his stomach, Datchy rose to his feet and headed for the beach. Around him he felt, more than saw or heard, his friends surge forward. Their progress was marked only by soft thuds from boots on turf, faint rustles of grass stems against trousers and the odd grunt, or muttered curse, as men stumbled on the uneven ground.

In less than a minute, the rough pasture under his feet gave way to a band of shingle above the high-water mark that crunched with each step. It made walking hard and noisy, so that each man hurried to cross it with a few long strides. Feeling a flash of relief when the soles of his boots found the wave-washed sand of the foreshore beyond, Datchy followed Dennard to the westward side of the formation. The beach was fractionally lighter than the field had been, with no trees to deepen the shadows and the pale shingle to reflect the sparse starlight. Anonymous black shapes coalesced into a horseshoe, with the working party inside and the open end towards the sea. Ploughing through the surf was a large galley, sitting deep in the water. Datchy took his place at the end of the line, one of the worst positions as he must stop the enemy working around their defences and had no one to protect his left flank. He was glad to find Dennard on his right.

If he hated the wait before a run, the wait during it was a close second. The armed party stood in silence, eyes probing the darkness, ears straining for the slightest warning of attack. All he heard were the sounds of the working party behind him: the swoosh of hull on sand, muttered greetings, the thump of the crew's boots against the hull and the swish of the working party's legs through the shallows, the sound of wood on wood as tubs were swung over the side and the laboured breathing of the men shifting them. Holding his musket across his body, the stock in his right hand and the barrel resting on his left palm, his only movement was to transfer his weight from one leg to the other. Listening intently, he kept his body as relaxed as he could, needing his muscles to move freely if opposition appeared.

One after another, tubmen set off up the beach, toiling over the shingle bank as the weight of the tubs slung across their chests and shoulder-blades drove them deep into its shifting surface. Some twenty men had made the trip when they were followed by two carts. Datchy recognised one as Quested's, which Sam Bailey had used earlier to fetch the weapons, and guessed the other was Ransley's, although it was far too dark to read the former owner's name emblazoned across its side: 'Thomas Chaucer of Tenterden'. Ransley's eldest son, Georgie, had occasionally driven a cart for a while but it was Wilson's departure that turned him into a regular in the working party. He was a smart lad, already doing most of his father's paperwork at just fifteen years of age, and Datchy hoped that his own son would make him as proud one day.

As the carts wallowed on the bank, Datchy reckoned up the haul so far. Say, a score in each cart and forty with the tubmen… that made eighty. That left another score or so to land. Some of the tension drained from his body as he savoured the thought of their first unforced run since February, when the sentinel on duty had sounded the alarm loud enough but the slow response of the lieutenant in the Grand Redoubt Station at Dungeness saved their bacon. Datchy later heard talk on the docks that the officer had a rupture at the time and could barely walk. Whatever the truth of it, he was suspended soon afterwards.

No sooner had he thought of success than a shot rang out from the far side of the horseshoe. Sam Bailey's fury-filled growl followed it in an instant.

'Damn it, Flash!'

'It wasn't me,' Dickon snapped back.

Another shot. Bailey's voice again.

'Hog?'

'There's something out there,' Hogben replied.

'Then for Christ's sake wait till you can see what it is,' Bailey snarled. 'We're not here to take pot-shots at bloody seagulls.'

'It wasn't no buggering seagull.' Metal rasped on metal as Hogben began to reload.

'And what are you going to do about it with two empty guns in your hands, you—'

'Shh!' Ransley's hiss cut the argument short.

Behind them, a lantern winked twice in the darkness. The shots had alarmed the crew of the waiting ship and it was now recalling its galley in readiness to sail. With the benefits of stealth now squandered, the sounds of hurried unloading intensified. Tubs were tossed carelessly in the surf, to be picked up if they didn't split on impact.

Casting aside the disappointment that briefly incapacitated him, Datchy resumed his vigil. Like Bailey, he'd assumed the stray shot came from Dickon Wyor but it sounded as if the beating he'd had a few days earlier might have slowed him up a bit. A moment later, all conscious thought fled from his mind as the instinctive part of his brain took over. His heart sank as he placed a familiar sound ahead but his lips dutifully hissed a warning to the line.

'M-men ahead. At least two. Twenty yards west, just above the foreshore.'

The loading stopped and everyone listened.

There was no need to for them to strain; the sound of two men running came clearly across the beach. Datchy frowned. The Blockade's training methods were a mystery to him. Lone officers often ran up and ordered them to stop work, seemingly oblivious to the fact that they had two shots at best in the face of a dozen armed men. How many times had the fools disregarded Ransley's warnings to hold their fire and keep their lives? It was almost as if they wanted to die. Had he been old enough for the wars, he might have lain down his life in defence of his country but there was no way that he would ever throw it away on serving the Revenue or understand the kind of man that did.

Spurred into life by the imminent arrival of the authorities, the tubmen resumed work. Eyes forward, he waited for the threat to materialise and an opportunity to arise. Then, before he could absorb the cry that came from behind him, something cannoned into the back of his legs. Staggering, he kept his feet but clenched his fists reflexively. His ears filled first with the blast of his own musket and then with answering shots from ahead.

Already on the verge of falling backwards, he was toppled into the surf by something thudding into his midriff. Deafened as he fell by the blast of Dennard's musket, he lay defenceless as the breakers rippled over his face and then, after filling his nose and mouth, rolled back still clawing at his hair. He knew he could easily drown in the few inches of water but couldn't move.

Before he'd fully registered the danger he was in, strong fists grabbed his smock and hauled him to his feet. He was surprised at the ease with which Dennard righted him, with even a lean man like himself a heavy burden when soaked to the skin. As he reached vertical, he retched and sprayed seawater over his friend.

'Damn you!'

The deep voice that cursed him was not Dennard's. Datchy forced his stinging eyes open and strode forward without waiting for his vision to clear. The man was a stranger and there was only one kind of stranger on a beach at night. He drove his full weight into his opponent through his outstretched arms. Taken by surprise, the man took a step back and gave him the advantage. As his senses returned, Datchy found that he was still clutching his musket. Spent and soaked, he doubted it would be firing again that night but it had its uses. He spun it around, gripped the barrel with both hands, and began to sweep the stock from side to side. On only the third arc he felt it connect with a satisfying crunch. Through blurred tears he saw the figure before him crumple and, swinging his improvised club upwards, he prepared to finish it off.

In the split second when his arms reached the top of their travel, he stood vulnerable. His gut and groin were exposed, ready for a slug or blow to stop him in his tracks, but it was an officer's head that did the job, first as a battering ram into his belly and then flying up to crack his jaw more powerfully than a fist ever could. Datchy tasted blood as his teeth closed on his tongue. He groaned, partly in pain and partly in despair as his newly cleared vision fogged over again. His assailant was still close — too close for him to land a decent punch, even if he could have thrown one, but just right for him to raise a knee sharply into the man's groin.

Without waiting to judge the success of his manoeuvre, Datchy pressed his advantage, more clumsily this time. He and the officer stumbled across the foreshore, flailing against one another with more rage than accuracy. Pursuing the man onto the shingle bank, he lost his footing. Dragging his opponent down with him, he grabbed at the throat, seeking a grip that would enable him to choke the life out of the fellow.

The firing grew more sporadic, as men had few opportunities to reload their spent weapons. As Datchy grappled with his man, a brief silence ended in an ear-splitting roar. Glancing round, his eyes drawn involuntarily by the powerful explosion, he saw the lieutenant who'd failed to apprehend him standing with a blunderbuss in hand. The polished brass of the flared barrel, glinting in the faint light, was designed to spread shot so wide that it was well nigh impossible to miss with it, even in the dark.

'Bugger me! Oh, Christ!'

The pained wail came from within the working party. It took Datchy a few seconds to place the voice as one of their tub-carriers, a good sort by the name of Bushell. He pitied the man if he'd been in the way when the blunderbuss spewed out its load of coarse shot. Before he had time to act on his concern for Bushell or vent his anger on the man in his grip, any order left in the scene ebbed away. Blockademen with loaded guns resumed fire and the others renewed their hand-to-hand combat. The armed party fell apart under the onslaught, stalwarts left with empty guns while lesser men ran from the beach.

Datchy returned his attention to his own fight just in time to catch a punch on the left side of his jaw. Fury swept over him and he threw the man down the shingle bank and then staggered after him. Swinging the musket again, he landed it heavily on the man's temple. His victim crumpled without so much as a whimper.

'Bloody bastards,' Datchy muttered as he turned back to help the pinned-down working party, stammer banished by fury.

The galley was now fifty yards from the beach, pulling away fast. Leaving the rest of the cargo strewn in the surf, the tubmen were trying to fall back landwards but the Blockademen were not about to settle for a seizure of goods. Datchy pulled a cartridge from his pocket and tossed the waxed paper wrapper to one side — with luck, it had kept the contents dry enough to fire. He bit off the end and then, careless of the risk of a misfire, trickled powder into the damp priming pan before pouring the rest into the barrel with the ball. With no time to ram the charge, he rapped the butt sharply on the ground. As he prepared to fire, another party of Blockademen arrived from the east. The armed party on that side was in disarray and he'd already seen Harry Horne and several others flee past him. Knowing he must make his shot count, he kept the barrel inclined upwards so as not to lose the ball and studied the scene carefully. Most of the men were getting clear but a few were clustered close to the water's edge. He could not be sure whether they were friend or foe. A few yards nearer to him, Ransley's unmistakable form turned to address those fleeing. He projected every ounce of his authority into his words.

'Come back, you bastards, and shoot them! They've got one of our men!'

Datchy had never doubted how much Ransley hated to lose a man but he knew that some had never forgotten how he left his predecessor to hang. Something in the present urgency spoke of compensation for past failure but Datchy had no doubt that there were shrewd practicalities not far below any emotion. A prisoner, especially a badly wounded prisoner, might be a threat to them all.

He immediately ran down the beach in response, saw Dennard do the same, and then dropped on one knee to a stable firing position beside his friend. They raised their muskets and fired into the cluster of men around Bushell's prone figure. Ransley scurried forward with two other men, straight into a volley of fire from the officers joining the fray from the east. Datchy watched their leader falter, unwilling to let a man fall into the Blockade's hands but unable to prevent it.

'It's no good,' Dennard shouted. 'Get back.'

Ransley and his companions did not retreat. Driven by instinct rather than logic, Datchy ran forward to intercept the officers closing on their leader. Almost blinded by his desperation, he beat them furiously with his musket. Throughout his assault, he vented his loathing for all things governmental in a torrent of muttered curses. He was still raining blows onto his opponents when he realised Dennard was trying to haul him away from the carnage.

'They're clear. Make tracks before we take a blinder.'

Side by side, lurching unsteadily against each other, they ran across the sand and onwards into the fields. Behind them, he heard the sounds of a chase but had no doubt that they could lose their pursuers. Through the years, one thing never changed: they were

362

local, lightly dressed, fit from endless hard work and desperate to keep their lives and provide for their families. The Blockade could never quite overcome those advantages.

They blundered on, through field after field, running lightly over the poles bridging the dykes and then tossing them away so that the Blockademen must wade or turn back. Only at Boulter's Bridge did they drop to their knees, gasping for air. Datchy rubbed at his belly, surprised to find his clothes appeared intact but wincing at the pain. The bruise was underneath his belt and he guessed that he would find the cheap buckle badly scarred when he had light to examine it. He was lucky it had not been the blunderbuss discharged at him: no buckle could halt its broadly scattered pellets. A few minutes passed before the blood pounding through his temples began to slow. He staggered to his feet and out of the shadows to examine his musket. The silvery starlight was little help and he explored the weapon more with his fingers than his eyes. Experimenting with the hammer, he found he could no longer cock it.

'B-bugger it!' he snarled, sending the gun spinning away.

Perhaps it had been repairable, perhaps not. There was no way to know now, with it lying where it had fallen in a pitch-black field beyond the hedge. The pointless gesture did nothing to calm the tumultuous emotions roiling inside him.

Bushell had carried tubs for the Blues for most of ten years. He did nothing another man could not do just as easily and his loss would have no effect on their operations, but for one thing. Solid and trustworthy, a man who used his eyes and ears more than his mouth, there'd been no reason to conceal anything from him so, while he was not specifically included in their planning, neither was he excluded. Thanks to his long service, he could probably give the Blockade more than half their names and hiding places.

When Datchy fought so fiercely in his defence, he'd been thinking less of the wounded man than the cost of his capture. Bushell could put the noose around their necks and, while Datchy would bet his life on the man's loyalty, a prisoner with a smashed kneecap was not the safest of receptacles for such knowledge.

'Datch—' Dennard began.

Barely hearing him, Datchy snapped. 'Blast! They've got us now. I sw-wear they've got us now.'

Whether it was his dread of their plight, the exertion of their flight, the impact of the slug or the draught of sea-water, he was suddenly engulfed by a wave of nausea. He doubled over and threw up the supper without which his wife never let him leave the house for a run. Then, after wiping his mouth on his sleeve, he spat into the darkness and strode off without another word.

Tommy

Tommy Dennard trudged along the lane to Bank Farm. Not so long ago, he'd never had cause to call on Wilson at home. They met at the Walnut Tree, or on the Fright to catch the horses, or in church — wherever their lives took them. His visits had become more frequent as his friend had become more frail. Now he made the short journey two or three times a week, his heart always heavy at what he might find when he reached the room behind the stables.

That morning was worse than usual. A sulky September sky and chilly easterly wind did nothing to lift his spirits, shouting as they did that summer was past and winter only just around the corner. He was drained, having spent the hours since he got back from the night's run tossing and turning without finding rest. Scarcely a month after Bushell, they'd lost another man and now rumours circulated about strangers asking questions in public houses across the marshes and even around Aldington. No one expected the locals to talk under normal circumstances, some too loyal to the trade and others too afraid of the traders, but a five-hundred pound reward might make them think again.

He stopped at his friends' door, finding it as neat as always. He knew Smeed washed the paint and scrubbed the step, careful to make sure their home did not reflect, and thereby underline, Wilson's decline. It might have seemed a wifely role but for the rough efficiency with which it was undertaken, which spoke more of the naval life. Tommy rapped his knuckles lightly on the wood, nodding absently to two men who were crossing the stable-yard.

Smeed opened the door. Although worry had aged him, the past half-year having brought little but heartache, Tommy thought he looked less tired than at their last meeting. It was still early, not long after dawn, but he looked to have slept well and was already dressed for a day in the fields, where there was still harvesting to be done. He gave a welcoming smile and stepped back.

Everything inside was as it had been, homely and cosy. The rich smell of coffee almost hid a faint sickroom smell from a bed too long slept in. Wilson was also dressed, sitting at the table with scrambled egg and a slice of bread in front of him. He gazed over, eyes bright with delight but skin too taut for much of a smile.

'Tommy!'

The usual surprise, thinking himself fortunate to have a caller when everyone else thought him about as unlucky as men came.

'Bish,' Tommy answered, taking care to keep his voice steady and encouraging. 'Looking good this morning.'

It was a half-truth. Wilson was wasted, his clothes hanging from his shoulders like a scarecrow's and his neatly tied cravat only emphasising how thin his neck had become. On the other hand, he was out of bed, trying to eat and looking happy. Tommy wished he had not brought his cares along to spoil a good day. The Blues' problems were no longer of any concern to his friends.

'Coffee?' Smeed offered.

'Aye, if it's on. All right for time?'

Smeed nodded. 'Got an easy day for a change. We've been putting in the hours to stay ahead of the weather.'

The rain was not far away — Tommy could sense it in the air — but it was later than expected in coming. He took the seat opposite Wilson and looked more closely at his friend.

'How are you feeling?'

'I'm fine. Don't trouble thyself on my account.'

He left the other half of his plea unspoken. Tommy knew he spent much of his time worrying about Smeed, hating to be a burden but knowing the man would not leave, even if he found the courage to ask him to. Smeed set down the coffee and a bowl of sugar, then pulled an easy chair nearer and rested his weight against the arm. Tommy had shovelled in three large spoonfuls of the sugar before it occurred to him that things might be tight now Smeed was no longer doing nightwork. He faltered before stirring but Smeed only grinned, confirming their good cheer.

'That's the least of our worries. Take another, if you've a mind to.'

Tommy shook his head, then thought better of it and ladled in a fourth spoonful. Stirring vigorously to dissolve it, he glanced up at

Smeed. The man was watching him astutely, already aware that it was more than a social call, but it was Wilson who spoke.

'More trouble?'

Tommy nodded. 'But no sense bringing it here. I see that now.'

Wilson leaned forward earnestly.

'Thou hast shared our burden. Let us share thine now.'

Tommy rubbed at his eyes almost as if to forestall tears of despair. They were sometimes closer than he wanted to admit.

'They've got Harry Horne. Tom Piety brought the news back to the Tap after last night's run — he only escaped by the skin of his teeth himself. The damned fools managed to get lost in the fields, not two miles from the bloody Castle at Walmer, and then Harry asks a bastard Blockademen the way home, if you can believe it.'

Smeed's gaze dropped to the floor.

'He'll talk, won't he?'

Smeed shrugged.

Tommy cursed, then nodded apology to Wilson whose views on blasphemy grew stronger as his day of reckoning approached.

'He's tougher than he looks,' Smeed said.

'He let them take him with a duck-gun. He's looking at a rope and that's been enough for better men than Harry.'

Smeed met his eye thoughtfully.

'Then p'r'aps it comes down to what he'll say.'

Tommy chewed on that. A prisoner might well get himself off with just a few names. Whose would they be? Hogben's for sure, both for the beating he'd given Harry's brother and the fate he'd intended to inflict on his sister, but who else?

'I doubt that helps me much. I've served in the fighting parties a score of times this year and Datchy too. Only Cap'n Bats and Sam have done as much.'

'Oh, Tommy. I wish thou hadst stopped back in the summer when thou thought of it.'

Tommy managed a laugh. 'Always easier looking back.'

That was not really the point. Along with Gilham, he'd seen where things were headed, and they were both shaken by Smeed's departure, yet they'd still turned out in August and then again in September.

'Why didst thou stay with it?'

He'd thought about the question before, unsure of his reasons.

Only one thing was clear in his mind.

'Captain Bats took me in, made me into something. I couldn't let him down. I thought, well. he's never been far wrong before. I thought it'd all come out right in the end. Somehow.'

Smeed's jaw clenched. 'He should have had more sense.'

'He couldn't back down. I never saw him let someone force his hand like this but he just can't let them win.'

'They'll win, Sooner or later, one way or another.'

Wilson's eyes, now seeming far too large in his pinched face, had been fixed on Smeed while he spoke but turned abruptly on Tommy. They held a complex blend of urgency and reluctance.

'Give it up. Please. I can't, don't make me see thy...'

There was desperation in the plea, a horror he'd never shown as his own death drew nearer. Realising that his capture, or death, would add to the pain of a man who'd suffered so much clarified Tommy's thinking. He had no wish to die, of course, but nor did he want to inflict such grief on his friends and family. He nodded.

'I think I knew it was over. I just needed someone to say it.'

Of course, dropping out was no guarantee of safety. With two men in Blockade cells, it was unlikely to make much difference. Nonetheless, his heart felt lighter for having made a decision.

'I'll be all right. There's plenty Harry likes less than me.' As an afterthought: 'I've never touched his old lady. Who would?'

His popularity might yet save him, provided that no jealous husbands were amongst those who came forward. Thinking of women brought another reassuring thought to mind.

'He won't name you either, Jem. Not after what you did for John and Mary.'

Smeed held his eye, then glanced quickly at Wilson. It was clear he intended the suggestion to go unseen but Wilson was having one of his best days in weeks, as alert and sharp as he'd ever been. He said nothing but gave a soft sigh. If he did not want to witness a friend's death, how much worse to be the cause of his lover's?

Tommy tried to put a brave face on it. 'There's been talk now and then, I'll grant you, but the tough'uns don't believe it of you and the righteous sort don't believe it of Bish.'

After considering his words for a while, Smeed seemed to find some comfort in them. No doubt he already knew that few men expected to find a molly leading them into battle. That, and the fact that there was no man more pious than Wilson in the Blues, meant they did not make a likely couple in most eyes. A faint smile touched Smeed's lips and Tommy could guess the kind of memories that amused him. Knowing Wilson's loving nature, and having bedded plenty of girls who shared it, he could imagine how satisfying their romantic life had been until sickness shattered it.

He glanced uneasily at Wilson, hoping that his reassurance would not fade on contemplating the moral judgement hidden beneath its surface. He'd never seen the slightest sign of guilt about Smeed in Wilson before but wondered if fears for the afterlife might change that. He was happy to see nothing but relief in the smile that Wilson gave Smeed, whose eyes crinkled momentarily in response but then narrowed in a frown.

'Talk to Datchy. Make him see sense.' He cleared his throat, before adding gruffly, 'Those young'uns need their old man.'

Tommy knew Smeed was worried far more for his friend than for the children. Admitting to anxiety did not come as easily to him as to Wilson but his concern was no less sincere.

'No need. He got there quicker than me — losing Bushell nearly did it for him and last night was the clincher. And I doubt he'll be the only one. Maybe Bats'll call a halt to it after all — who knows?'

Smeed nodded, his satisfaction at Gilham's decision clear.

The sun chose that instant to peep between the clouds, sending a shaft of light through the window to bathe them in its autumnal glow. Irrepressible as always, Tommy's spirits lifted.

'You know what that means. I'll have to look for a proper job.'

Wilson laughed and exchanged a glance with Smeed. Tommy could see there was some private joke in the suggestion he was about to voice. When he spoke, there was a teasing lilt in his tone.

'Why dost thou not seek a position as a coachman?'

'A man who knows horses and cuts a dash can make a pretty penny at that, in the right household,' Smeed added.

Tommy looked from one to the other twice before he was sure he'd understood their meaning right. His cheeks grew hotter at the thought, making Wilson laugh aloud. The rare sound brought back Tommy's grin, overshadowing any embarrassment.

'Maybe so,' he said slowly, as if giving the idea serious thought, 'But if anyone's to be watching my arse in a pair of breeches, it'll be the mistress of the house — make no mistake about that.'

Smeed smiled and rested a casual hand on Wilson's shoulder.

'Then she'll be a lucky woman, for it's a fair view.' He stood up and stretched before Tommy could object to his lewdness. 'I'd better show my face before dinner-time. Stay if you've naught else on. Jamie'll be glad of the company.'

Tommy nodded readily. He often sat with Wilson when Smeed was busy. Sometimes it was a hard duty, watching a decline he could not halt, but that day was different, with Wilson well enough for friendship in place of nursing. They might do some light work with the horses or go fishing: it mattered little — each good day was a blessing to be treasured.

George

Probably one of the most cunning and ingenious men in the parish, if not the county, George Ransley was not a match for some of his men in one respect. Never having lived the life of a military man or common thief, he did not spend his nights in a cautious sleep with the proverbial one eye open. He kept a fine brace of bulldogs to do that for him, a duty they fulfilled with admirable diligence. Under their watchful gaze, the Bourne Tap echoed with the rhythmic snoring of its master and mistress. Harmonies came from the attic room shared by the two eldest boys, Georgie and John.

A thud on the door roused George from a slumber that was, as always, untroubled by any dreams he'd remember. With his business being what it was, disturbances in the middle of the night weren't as strange to him as they might have been to some. Still, somewhere deep in his befuddled mind, he knew all was not well.

He was not yet fully awake when a sustained pounding resounded through the house. It dawned on him then what was amiss. Anyone approaching at night was greeted by a volley of barking. Even regular visitors would shout from the lane sooner than try to reach the front door when the dogs were loose.

He whispered to his wife, wide awake now.

'Stay out of sight.'

In the darkness, he felt a familiar tension, one that told him precisely what he could do with his orders. He rolled onto his side and stroked her cheek fondly.

'I mean it, love. If they're come, no amount of money, talk or threats will make 'em go. Shield the children and let me face 'em.'

He took a moment to savour her rough hand clasped around his, to memorise the touch that he'd felt almost every day of their long marriage but might now never feel again. They'd made a formidable team, her handsome vigour paired with his shrewd intelligence, united by the knowledge that they were stronger together than apart. He knew they were about to be parted but could not foresee how long the separation might last or, indeed, if it would ever end.

He kissed the hand and then got out of bed, hissing as the chill October night found his legs beneath his nightshirt. His feet had barely touched the floorboards when a final blow, far louder than before, fractured the door. The oak split with a shriek and a bolt clattered onto the stone floor. Moments later, boots tramped through the house. The bedroom door flew open to reveal a tall shadow in the hallway. The faint moonlight did not reach him but it glinted menacingly off the pistol in his outstretched hand.

George had a similar pistol hidden in a drawer. Had he woken faster, he might have reached it but now the chance was gone. He let that thought go as soon as it struck. He could not take on a band of armed preventive men and, if he wanted to try, he would not choose his home to do it in. Instead, he watched calmly as the intruder came in, checking either side of the doorway as if he expected the leader of the Blues to sleep with an armed escort.

More men came in and checked every last inch of the room. Only when they stood holding George's pistols and musket, and cautiously nodded to say they were done, did the officer pull a sheet of paper from inside his coat. George had no doubt that it was an arrest warrant, although it was far too dark for the officer to read from it and so instead he kept his announcement simple.

'George Ransley, alias Captain Bats, I am Lieutenant Samuel Hellard of the Royal Naval Coast Blockade for the Prevention of Smuggling. I arrest you on suspicion of the murder of First Class Quartermaster Richard Morgan at Dover on the night of the thirtieth of July. You will be taken to His Majesty's Ship *Ramillies*, and from there you will be handed over to the proper authorities.'

At his signal, two of his men stepped forward. One was short and held a pair of handcuffs. The other was a head taller and stout with it, a human anchor to which George found himself being linked.

Even if he had a chance to dispatch the man, he would not make much progress with such a burden. Perhaps he could hack the man's arm off at the wrist but he'd need a decent knife to do it.

In reality, he did not envisage having an opportunity to escape. After the Blockade had waited so long to find something to charge him with, only a fool would let him go. This Samuel Hellard looked no fool. If anything, he looked most like his namesake, Sam Bailey: hardened and resolute. No doubt it was his spies who'd been asking their questions and offering their gold throughout the area since Morgan's death, putting a stop to the trade a month before. If he was to be brought down by someone, there seemed no shame in falling to a man such as the one before him.

Hellard selected half a dozen men, clearly not at random but on what basis George could not tell.

'Take him back to the *Industry*. The rest of you with me. There's plenty left to do before this blasted night is over.'

George looked at him sharply but said nothing.

Hellard laughed. 'Aye, Bats. You'll have company, damn you. Once the bastards start, it's hard to stop their tongues a-flapping.'

'How many?' George kept his tone even, refusing to give the man more satisfaction than he'd already found in his triumph.

Hellard hesitated, then shrugged. 'You'll know soon enough, when you're sharing a cell with the murderous dogs.'

Ignoring the men surrounding him with pistols raised, George started to put on the clothes he'd laid out for the morrow as he did every night. With no intention of parading in front of the entire Coast Blockade in his nightshirt, he dressed quickly but without haste, waiting pointedly when he needed the handcuffs removed to complete his attire. Only when he'd settled his shooting jacket in place did he obey their order to go onto the landing.

He was sorry that his children's last sight of him might be as a captive but, determined to retain whatever dignity he could, he was relieved that Hellard had let him finish dressing. Georgie and John stared sullenly at the preventive men but their younger brothers and sisters looked more fearful than resentful.

No doubt there'd be plenty of time for beatings, floggings or even torture later but perhaps Hellard shared his view that there was no need for small children to see that.

Bish

'Christ!'

Bish watched Smeed worm his way backwards down the slope.

'What couldst thou see?'

'The whole place is crawling with 'em. We'd better lie low by the river till this blows over. Least we'll have water and fish there.'

Bish doubted that the search would blow over until the last of them was taken in. Feelings had been running too high for too long. He let out a rare curse for Hogben and the Wyors. If anyone was to blame for their plight, it was men like them. Even after the fatal shot, fewer drunken brawls and local girls abused and they might not be in this mess.

He and Smeed did not yet know whether their names were on the preventive men's list — all they had were garbled reports of a raid on the Bourne Tap and a warning that the preventive men weren't through yet. Smeed had thrown a few meagre supplies into his canvas bag, put on three layers of clothing and hurried them out of their room. Bish tried not to hold him up but was painfully aware that, barely able to dress himself, he was nothing but a liability to the man who meant more to him than any other.

'Go on without me, Jem,' he'd croaked. 'Thou couldst get clear by thyself.'

Smeed hadn't dignified that with an answer, instead tucking an arm around him and hauling him onto his feet. 'It's only a mile or two, no worse than walking home from the Walnut of a night.'

The reassurance brought scant comfort. It was months since he'd made that trip with less than a dozen stops for breath.

Ever since the June night when he finally conceded that he was of no further use on a run, his health had declined steadily. He would have been out of the Blues long before, were it not for Smeed and Dennard standing so firmly at his side. Now he would have given anything to trade places with Dennard: in flight with a fit friend like that, Smeed would've had a good chance of escaping. He tried to banish the growing fear from his mind, fear not for himself but for those he cared about. After expecting a slow and painful death for so long, he knew a hangman's noose could only hasten what was already coming to him but seeing it end the lives of his friends was a completely different matter.

Gasping for breath, he tried begging. 'Please. Get thyself away.'

Smeed checked their surroundings again, then dropped to a crouch. 'I couldn't live with myself if I left you. Don't ask it.'

Bish felt the tears prick his eyeballs but he didn't weep. He took Smeed's hand and held it against his cheek.

'Thou hast been all I ever wanted. Naught will change it.'

They stumbled on, he leaning ever more heavily on Smeed's unfailing support. The eastern horizon was starting to glow when they reached the river. He sank gratefully onto a mossy bank, trying not to draw the deep breaths he craved, knowing they'd only inflame his lungs. He still wished that Smeed would save himself but knew he could not have left if their positions were reversed. Perhaps, against the odds, they'd slip through the net.

He wished, too, that they knew more about the threat. Most of their information came from local papers that he painstakingly read out to Smeed, pausing every few sentences for a sip of the watered-down brandy that did not so much slow his deterioration as blur his awareness of it, and the reports ranged from scant facts to wild speculation, rarely agreeing on the details. They waited anxiously for the Friday papers after the first Blues were seized and then Smeed sat impassive as he listened to the reports that had finally sent them into hiding. He'd bought both local papers but the news was just as bad in each.

The *Chronicle* had opted for what seemed to be a factual account of the raid. Certainly Ransley and 'several others' — seven as far as they could tell — were missing.

CANTERBURY, OCTOBER 20TH:

A considerable party of armed seamen was landed from two vessels in Dymchurch Bay, in the night of Monday last, accompanied by their officers and (we are informed) a smuggler who had been previously taken by the Coastal Blockade, and who has given important information relative to the 'Fighting Party' who have on several occasions protected the running of contraband goods, on different parts of the coast of this County and Sussex.

On proceeding to Aldington, Bilsington and Ruckinge, they captured in his bed, the 'Captain Bats' and several others, whose residences and persons

After reading the report, they thought the informant must be Bushell or Horne. Bushell seemed unlikely, given that a month in custody with a smashed and later amputated limb seemed to have drawn nothing from him, but there was every chance that Horne had turned King's Evidence to save his own skin. Of course, once he did so, Bushell might see no harm in adding a few details for a share in the blood money.

Horne's betrayal filled Bish with a festering anger that he could barely contain, a corrosive emotion he'd never felt before and was ashamed of now. His only defence was that it sprang from concern for others, mainly Smeed but other friends too, and not himself.

As ever, the *Express* took a more sensational tone than the *Chronicle*, speculating about the future path of the investigation and careful to get the word 'murder' in twice. As he read it, Bish saw Smeed's scowl. Until then, as far as Smeed was concerned, the Preventive Service had declared war on their business activities and a death in war was not a murder. Only now did Bish see his doubts about this particular death.

MURDER OF MORGAN

This morning (18th October) intelligence was brought to Dover that one of the party concerned in the murder of Morgan, of the Coast Blockade, had made disclosures implicating, some reports say twenty, others thirty, in the barbarous action; but it is certain that eight persons are now in custody on this information. A Reward of £500 was offered for their apprehension at the time, and a reward is said to have tempted the informer, an inhabitant of Deal, to come forward voluntarily and give information.

That had set them speculating on the identity of the Deal man but they could think of no likely candidate. Neither of the captured men came from there and neither had come forward voluntarily. At the heart of the trade in Kent for generations, Deal was the last place that any trader expected to give birth to an approver. Not only that but, more than twenty miles to the east of Aldington, it had witnessed few of the Blues' clashes with either the preventive men or the public. If they were to find sympathy anywhere, Deal should have been that place.

Now Bish could only hope that things were not as bleak for Smeed as he feared. Assuming the worst, he'd dreaded that the searchers knew everything about the Blues. Now he wondered if their information extended only to the leaders but, even if it did, that was small comfort. While he was insignificant, Smeed had become both important and well known as he armed and helped train the men. An informant was unlikely to overlook him.

Bish knew Smeed had the rumours about them on his mind when he decided they should run before he was even sure that they were being chased. It was one thing to maintain a front of mere friendship when they worked and traded side by side but devotion was harder to hide when a sorrowful man tended his dying lover. Dennard had done what he could, acting as if such care for a friend was the most natural thing in the world, but their only real defences were their recent low profile and people's reluctance to speak of something so unspeakable.

That reluctance could crumble at any time. Once a man had decided to take the risk of betraying the Blues, it took seconds to add a name to the list for personal reasons. Without that anxiety, Smeed might have left him at the farm, thinking the risk to his health from flight greater than the chance of a popular and retired member of the Blues being amongst the arrests. With it, especially having been unable to ascertain the identity of the new informant, he judged there was a strong chance Bish's name was on an arrest warrant somewhere not far from his own.

George

George Ransley sighed. Two weeks in Newgate gaol was long enough to know that incarceration didn't suit him. It might be months before they were tried and he wondered if, by then, he might be looking forward to a nice quick hanging. He'd never been one to lament the past, believing it dead and gone, yet now even his self-control faltered. Looking forward, he saw nothing but misery and death. Looking back, he saw missed opportunities and the seeds of bitter regret.

Perhaps, if he'd understood his own men better or foreseen how first McCulloch and then Pigot would use theirs, things might be different. Waiting in the dock, he swore softly at himself for the wasted emotion. Even if he'd swayed individual events, bringing them to the gallows earlier or later, their downfall was sealed at the moment that Richard Morgan breathed his last.

Whether it was the death of a particularly fine officer or just a death too many, it set in motion events that he'd been dreading. In an instant, the forces they'd evaded for so long came together in one mission: to bring down the Aldington Blues. Hellard, a man as single-minded as he was foul-mouthed, was dogged in his pursuit of the men who, more by accident than design, had brought one of his best young officers to such a savage and untimely end.

Beside George stood the others captured so far: Dennard, Gilham, Giles, two Baileys — Sam and Rob — and both Wyors. Preventive officers still scoured the countryside for men not yet apprehended. George hoped they were long gone. He supposed that he, and some of the men beside him, deserved what was coming. Although he'd never killed a man himself, it was the defence of his business activities that had ended a life. His hardest men had sent plenty of preventive men from the service as invalids but, until Quids' death changed the rules, there'd been no killings since Brookland. Even so, while there might be justice in a life for a life, all their lives for Morgan's?

He glanced to his left. Originally more in demand for their skills with horses or boats, Dennard and Gilham had joined the armed parties only in recent months and then only through necessity. They were no danger to the people of the parish.

And Giles? He'd contributed as much as George to many of their schemes, and was a fine shot into the bargain, but he'd already abandoned that life so what merit was there in hanging him? Was it justice or vengeance that took a reformed man's life? Pleading for clemency was unlikely to help him. The only men willing to testify to his decision to quit the trade, and to his absence on the night in question, would be his fellow accused. None of the free Blues would come forward, and probably no one would believe them if they did.

376

Even without the change of heart, he had not long recovered from the shot to the throat he'd taken in May by the night of Morgan's death. As it was, his friends knew that his decision to bow out ran deeper than a taste of his own mortality; he was almost as concerned about the suffering heaped on the parish by some of their number as by his own prospects. Still, whatever they might know, they would never be able to convince anyone else of it.

George surveyed the court. At the defence desk, he and his fellows were represented by Mr Platt of Langham & Platt, senior partner now that old Langham had gone on to a better place, and the assistant at his side. Platt was a heavily built man with steel grey hair that flowed in waves from the crown of his head and then merged seamlessly with an impressive set of whiskers around his jaw. In a hurried consultation before the hearing, he'd barely had time to tell them that Sir Richard Birnie would be presiding. He considered the Chief Magistrate a humane, if ambitious, man but warned that he was impervious to bribery and dedicated in his campaign to repress crime. They could expect an impartial, but not charitable, committal hearing in his courtroom.

George shifted his gaze to the man at the bench. With a large nose as his only distinctive feature, he looked unimpressive but George knew better than most how foolish it was to make snap judgements based on the body that a man was given by God.

Then, across the aisle from Platt was Mr Jones, solicitor to the Admiralty. He was an imposing man, barely into his middle years, whose cool and businesslike manner gave George no fresh hope for a way out. Jones stood and cleared his throat. Far from being a nervous gesture, it was one designed to draw the court's attention.

'It is now my duty to enter on the charges affecting the prisoners who were charged with the Wilful Murder of Richard Morgan, a Quartermaster in the Preventive Service on the thirtieth of July last near Hythe, on the coast of Kent. The prisoners are also charged with unlawfully assembling in arms, with the intention of running smuggled goods, on the Kentish coast.'

He shuffled the papers on his desk.

'On the occasion of the murder of Morgan, an inquest was held in Dover, and the jury who sat on the body returned a verdict of Wilful Murder against some person or persons unknown. With a view to establishing the charge of murder against the prisoners, I now call a material witness, Michael Pickett.'

The clerk to the Court moved forward, Bible in hand, waiting until the witness had taken the stand to administer his oath. When he was done, Jones began his examination.

'Please state your occupation for the court, Mr Pickett.'

'I am a seaman in His Majesty's Ship *Ramillies*, and was employed in the Preventive Service on the coast of Kent.'

'Now, sir, I ask you to relate as precisely as you can the events you witnessed on the night in question.'

George noted Pickett's eye on him, then saw the man stand taller and collect himself before proceeding in a measured tone.

'On Saturday night, the twenty-ninth of July last, I was stationed on the coast of Dover, opposite to the bathing machines. I saw Quartermaster Morgan that night — he was the visiting officer of the party to which I belonged. After being at the station for three-quarters of an hour, I saw Morgan coming from the westward and walked towards him on my beat. I heard some people who were coming on a French galley hailing some persons on shore. I knew the vessel as a French galley from her length, and noted her because it was unusual to see such a vessel on the coast.' He paused, as if in doubt. 'To the best of my belief, the people in the galley cried out "John ashore" or some such exclamation. They hailed in this manner three times and on the third occasion they were answered from behind the bathing machines. I ran towards the galley when I saw her approaching the beach. I took a pistol in my right hand on full cock, and stood by the bows of the boat until such time as I saw the working people surround the galley on both sides.'

Jones raised a hand to interrupt the testimony. 'What, may I ask, do you mean by "working people"?'

'Those persons on shore who answered to the hail of the boat, sir.'

'I see. Please continue.'

'There were about fifty of the working party besides the armed party. The latter drew up in a line on the beach at high watermark, and the working party ran down in a line to the galley. There were six or seven men belonging to the armed party.'

'You could see all this clearly? Even at that hour?'

'It was the latter end of the moon, sir, but the stars were sufficiently bright to distinguish persons at the distance of fifty yards.'

'I see.' Jones waved a hand to bid the witness continue.

'I saw some of the men in the galley hand out two tubs and put them on a man's shoulder. I cried out to the party, "You —"'

Pickett faltered in his testimony and George felt amusement ripple through the men standing with him. They remembered well enough what the man had called them.

'Well,' Pickett mumbled, 'I named them for the dogs they are and then I said, "If you stir a peg I will blow your brains out."'

'And what was their response?'

'I attempted to fire a warning shot but my pistol flashed in the pan, before I received an answer. You see, sir, there was nothing in the pistol but powder.'

'And this was when Quartermaster Morgan intervened?'

'Aye, sir. Morgan hailed me and asked what boat it was but, before I could give an answer, he fired his pistol for an alarm.'

'Where was the deceased at this time?'

'He was about fourteen yards beyond me, in the act of running towards me.'

'What followed?'

'The armed party of smugglers then opened fire at Morgan, and he fell. They fired a volley and I heard two or three shots after that. I was in the act of priming my pistol when one of the armed party came up to me with a musket and asked, "What are you up to? I'll do you." I thought he was about to shoot me too but, instead, he turned the butt end and struck me. I held up both my hands and the man knocked the pistol from my grasp. I told him that I was not in dread of him. When he raised the musket again, I drew my cutlass and gave him a cut across the shoulder. At that, he returned to the armed party and they continued working the tubs.'

The magistrate leaned forward. So far, he'd said nothing, leaving the clerk to move the proceedings along and using the odd curt gesture to convey his wishes. When he spoke, his deep voice still carried traces of formative years spent in Scotland half a century earlier. 'So the smugglers still meant to carry away tubs from the galley?'

'So it seemed,' Pickett agreed. 'I turned round and struck another of their party. I thought that I must have cut him across the neck because he had only a cravat on. Yet I was but one man. As soon as one of their number got a tub on his shoulder, he ran with it to the town and other men came down to fetch more. There were thirty-eight tubs seized that night and lodged in the Customhouse. Some of the tubs contained brandy, others gin–'

'Yes, yes,' Jones cut him off. 'But what happened next on that fateful night?'

'After I struck the second man, I struck at a third who snatched a hold of my cutlass in order to get it away. I drew it through his hands, causing him to run screaming towards the beach. I then struck two or three more, until a man who I believed to be one of the heads of the party cried out, "There is no use in striking all the bast –"' Pickett shrugged apologetically to the bench. 'He questioned the parentage of his own men and then shouted, "Shove off the boat". Thus it was my poor efforts that kept the men from taking more of the tubs away.'

'What was the condition of the deceased at this point?'

'He lay about fourteen yards off. I ran to him and asked if he were killed. He answered, "Oh, God". He lay upon his back, with a pistol at each side of him. I took up the pistols and loaded them, saying I would have satisfaction for him.'

'Had the pistols been discharged.'

'Aye, sir. Both of them. I ran as far as the bathing machines, after the party, but I did not come up with them. Then I saw a man run across the beach from the eastward. I thought him a smuggler but found him to be Quartermaster Prendergast. I told him that Morgan was shot. On our return, we found him dead. Then we went up the beach. I said I had got some tubs but he said, "Damn the tubs! Let us follow the party". We pursued the smugglers but did not come up with them. Then we met Lieutenant Hall and he sent me back to my station.'

'I believe you attended the coroner's inquest at Dover, where a verdict of Wilful Murder was returned against some person or persons unknown. Is that correct?'

'Aye, that it is.'

'Did you observe the dress of the smugglers on the night in question?'

'I did, sir.'

'What were your observations?'

'The man who first came out of the boat wore such a jacket as the prisoner George Ransley wears now, a sort of shooting jacket made of fustian. The man who struck me with the musket wore a similar coat. The rest of the armed party appeared to be in dark dresses, blue or black coats and dark trousers. The man I last struck had a red cap on. Some of them had light green jackets such as the prisoner, Samuel Bailey, has on. I could not swear to the man who struck me with the musket but he was like that prisoner.'

Pickett raised his hand to point.

Jones translated the gesture into words. 'Let the record show that the witness has identified Charles Giles.'

The identification was scarcely conclusive. More than half of the Blues might be described as like Giles: brown hair, medium height, medium build. Of those brought before the magistrate, the Baileys were clearly out of the question. Dickon Wyor was too broad and his brother probably too fair, although that might not count for much on a dark night. George gazed down at his paunch and reflected that it was not only age and colouring that put him out of the running. Even so, that left both Dennard and Gilham. Neither had the falsely accused man's brushlike thatch but then most of them wore hats on a run. Dennard shared the sallow complexion and Gilham bore a similar collection of moles on his neck. George hoped that a jury would see it for the poor identification that it was, no proof of Giles's presence at Morgan's death. It was strange that Pickett recalled their clothes with such confidence but their faces with so little certainty, failing even to identify George's distinctive features.

Jones turned to the stand. 'You may step down, Mr Pickett. I now call Peter Prendergast.'

Jones shuffled his notes while the witness was sworn in and then made his customary opening. 'Please state your occupation for the court, Mr Prendergast.'

'I was one of the Quartermasters of His Majesty's Ship, *Ramillies*.'

'Please relate the events you witnessed on the night in question.'

'I was stationed at the boat houses. From there, I heard firing at the bathing machines and so I proceeded in that direction, discharging my pistol by way of alarm as I did so. On my way, I met Michael Pickett, who told me that Morgan was shot. On reaching the spot where Morgan lay, I found that he was quite dead.'

'Thank you, Mr Prendergast. You are excused.' Jones turned to the magistrate. 'That concludes the prosecution's evidence in proof of the murder having been committed on the night in question, by a gang of smugglers. It is now our intention to show that some of the prisoners at the bar were present when that murder took place. For this purpose, I call on Edward Horne, an accomplice who has since come forward as an approver.'

The courtroom erupted into chatter at the identity of the informer. While the men at his side cursed Harry under their breath, George remained stony faced as the traitor was sworn in. Although he'd known the man for years, he'd never trusted him. He wished now that he'd followed his instincts and excluded him altogether. Sighing, he reflected that a five hundred pound reward would loosen most tongues. There were only two sane reasons for a man to turn down such wealth, either because he would not dance for his masters at any price or because he did not believe the sum would be paid. George himself subscribed to both views.

Horne stood uneasily before the court, rigid facial muscles distorting his features. He clearly did not take what he was doing lightly, as indeed only a fool would. Support for the Blues might have guttered but it was not yet extinguished — turning King's Evidence might save him from a noose but a man could die in many ways.

'Please state your occupation for the court, Mr Horne.'

'I'm a labourer at Ruckinge.'

'That would be near Ashford, I believe?'

'That's right.'

'And are you acquainted with the prisoners?'

'Aye, I know 'em. I was with 'em at Dover that night, all excepting Cob – I mean Giles, there.'

'How did you come to be in that location?'

'I got a message from Cap'n Bats–'

'The prisoner George Ransley?'

'That's right. He wanted me to meet him at Lydden, at an inn not five miles from Dover.'

The magistrate leaned forward again. 'You said in your statement that you had known Ransley for nearly ten years and met him by appointment before.'

For the first time, Platt rose to his feet. 'If it please your Honour, I submit that, unless Mr Jones means to bring forward other charges than that of murder, it is not necessary for the witness to state the business on which those appointments took place.'

Jones responded quickly. 'I do not mean, certainly, to confine myself to that charge. I have at least thirty distinct charges against the prisoner Ransley, and I mean to bring several.'

'It is not exactly fair, I must say, and not customary with the Crown, to excite prejudice against a prisoner in this manner.'

The magistrate sat back and cast a shrewd eye on Platt. 'I regret that any question of mine should be the cause of exciting such observations.' Regrets notwithstanding, he waved for the examination to proceed.

'Well, like I say,' Horne continued. 'I met Ransley between nine and ten o'clock at night at Lydden.'

'Witness,' Jones began, 'In answering the question I shall now ask, you are not to name any persons but those present. My object is that the names of persons not yet apprehended shall not be made public.'

Horne nodded his understanding but then said, 'None of the prisoners but Ransley was at Lydden that night. We met others there and then went with them to the Palm Tree, about eight miles from Dover.'

'That is a public house, is it not?'

'Aye, a good one too.'

'Indeed,' Jones said wearily. 'What happened at this highly regarded establishment?'

'We met with all the prisoners, except Giles. There must have been between fifty and sixty men assembled there besides.'

'Were the men bearing firearms?'

'Perhaps a dozen to sixteen had them, yes. Sam Bailey had a musket and so had Tommy Dennard, Datch – I mean, Thomas Gilham, Rob Bailey and Dickon Wyor.'

George considered the answer, contrasted with Pickett's account of six or seven in the fighting party. He thought Pickett was nearer the mark, given that it was a modest run with only fifty in the working party, but could not remember with certainty. Sam might know, if their fate rested on disputing the details later.

'And you went from there to the coast?'

'We did.'

'What followed when you reached the coast.'

'Well, we proceeded towards the bathing machines between twelve and one o'clock that night. A boat was on shore. I was stationed at the back of the bathing machines near the road, with others who were armed. I heard no hailing but Ransley shouted "Hallo, come on!" As he was the commander of the party, we began to carry away the uncustomed goods, consisting of brandy and other spirits, from the galley. Then we were interrupted by pistol fire. We returned fire and I heard afterwards that a man of the name of Morgan had been shot.'

From his account, Horne seemed not to realise that George had been aboard the galley. There was no particular reason that he should, given that he was not involved in the arrangements for collecting the cargo from the lugger.

'You were yourself armed, Mr Horne?'

'Aye, I was. I carried a fowling piece.'

'How many shots were fired?'

'There might have been five or six.'

'Might have been?'

'It all happened fast, like. It's not so easy remembering. I saw the man who was shot fall though.'

'Did you complete your operations afterwards?'

'No. We carried off about seventy tubs but we couldn't work the whole cargo, on account of the Blockade. We weren't engaged more than five minutes when we were obliged to leave the shore. We took the tubs to the Palm Tree and counted them. The armed party was in the road to prevent surprise. Ransley was with the other party, counting the tubs. There was thirty to forty rods distance between the two.'

'The firearm you carried was your own?' Jones asked.

'No. I borrowed it off Sam Bailey. He usually makes up the ammunition.'

'What happened after the tubs had been counted?'

'They were put into carts and carried away, same as always. I went nearly all the way home with Ransley, to within nearly two miles of his house, but he would not show me where they were to be concealed so I left them into his charge.'

George smiled. His doubts about Horne now justified, he had no regrets about shutting him out of the heart of the Blues. The man had not only allowed himself to be captured but had gone into custody with a duck-gun in hand. Without the firearm, the evidence against him would have been weak and Platt could have negotiated a fine, as he'd done so many times before. Still, so far, he'd testified against only a few men when he could have named fifty. It was as if he was doing as little as he must to save his neck.

'When did you next see Ransley?'

'About a week later, when he paid me twenty-three shillings for the night's work.'

'Do you know what the rest of the party received?'

'No. They were not paid in my presence.'

Jones turned once more to the bench. 'That concludes my questions, your honour.'

Platt rose for his cross-examination. 'Pray Horne, where do you come from now?'

Jones immediately lodged an objection. 'I am really very sorry to interrupt the learned counsel, but I am afraid I must oppose the line of cross-examination I presume he is about to follow.'

Platt countered just as quickly. 'If you, Sir Richard Birnie, as the Magistrate sitting here, say that nothing shall be said against the character of this witness, I am of course bound to submit. If the prosecutors are afraid of his character being exposed, they are right to prevent that exposure. Perhaps I could show that this witness is the very man who fired his gun at Morgan. How can anyone say he is not the man? I mean to say that none of the prisoners were present on that occasion.'

George clenched his teeth to prevent a grim smile spreading across his face. Platt knew his job but it would take a miracle to persuade a court that all of them stood falsely accused. The only way anyone but Giles could prove he was elsewhere that night was through a bribe and the Preventive Service could outbid a humble free-trader; even poor Giles was sunk because only his wife could confirm he was at home and who would be convinced by the testimony of a man's wife?

Still, the point was worth making. Horne's arrest early in September meant that he currently resided in Maidstone prison. His motive for turning King's Evidence was clear enough, if Platt could persuade the Judge to admit the witness's circumstances into court. That now looked unlikely.

'I have made out a case against the prisoners sufficient, I think, to call for their committal,' Jones protested.

'The magistrates cannot see that there is sufficient evidence to send these men to prison. I consider it a great hardship that the prisoners who have already been in custody so long, since the seventeenth of this month, should now be committed on such evidence. Here is Giles, one of the prisoners against whom there is not a shadow of evidence.'

Birnie acknowledged the point with a nod. 'You had better, Mr Jones, produce any evidence you have against the prisoner Giles at once.'

'I must send for a witness to the Tower.'

'And I must urge the Court to grant the prisoner Giles the discharge to which he is entitled. The warrant was for the death of Morgan and there is nothing to implicate Giles in that transaction.'

Jones referred quickly to his now-crumpled notes. 'I charge Giles with being armed and near Dymchurch, on the coast of Kent, on the eleventh of May last, when William Wynn was shot.'

The Magistrate's eyes twinkled as he challenged the assertion. 'Are you prepared to prove that case?'

'I will prove it within an hour.'

George drew a deep breath and glanced across at Giles. That case quite likely could be proved. He wondered how many other witnesses Jones had tucked away. Most of his men could be tied to something if men like Horne started to turn King's Evidence. He followed the others as they were led back to a holding cell while a messenger was despatched to the Tower for the witness. He spent the wait deep in thought, while the others argued over what had already been said and what the new witness might yet say. Knowing that it was only a hearing, its purpose solely to decide what would follow and not to hear their defence, he saw no value in speculating on how they might counter the evidence offered against them. Once they knew the extent of the Crown's case, then they could discuss the options with Platt but he feared those options might prove to be limited indeed.

Just within the hour, the prisoners were marched back into court, now with a view to proving that Giles was implicated in smuggling. This time, the witness sworn in against them was not one of their own. William Wynn was a preventive man through and through.

Jones once again introduced his witness. 'Please state your occupation for the court, Mr Wynn.'

'I was a seaman on board the *Ramillies*, stationed at the Herring Hang, in the parish of Dymchurch on the eleventh of May last, and employed with others to prevent smuggling.'

Jones nodded his approval at the precise statement. 'What happened on that night?'

'I was sent out about ten o'clock and stationed on the beach. About twelve o'clock, a party of smugglers came to the Herring Hang house. A boat came in. I was about a hundred yards from her but I could see her quite plain and also the men in her.

'To the best of my judgement, a hundred and fifty men came down to the coast. They were armed and fired on me. I fired at them in return. A volley came at me while they rushed to the beach. There was a second volley, while they were working the tubs, and I took a slug in the face. Two of my men, Whelan and Regan, came to my aid. Some of the tubs were seized. Whelan had a shot lodged in his coat pocket. Regan was not wounded. The smugglers escaped. They left a fowling piece behind.'

George frowned at the account. It had all happened so fast and he'd been on the far side of the boat being unloaded, unable to see much beyond the armed party engaged with the preventive men. He could not be sure who had fired first and now wondered if the young officer could be any more certain.

'Thank you, Mr Wynn. You are excused. I now recall Mr Edward Horne to the stand.' He waited while Horne took Wynn's place and was reminded that he was still under oath. 'Mr Horne, do you recollect a transaction that took place at Dymchurch on Saturday eleventh May?'

'Aye, I recollect it well enough. I went to Ransley's house at Al'inton Fright for the purpose of being on look-out. All the prisoners, except Rob Bailey and the younger Wyor were there. I left the house about seven or eight o'clock and went to Herring Hang, a distance of seven or eight miles. I got to the seashore some time between twelve and two in the morning.'

'Were the men present at the seashore armed?'

'Sam Bailey, Dennard, Gilham and Giles were armed. Ransley was not.'

'And what passed that night?'

'Ransley went forward to look out for the boat. He hallooed to us and we all ran over to the boat. Those who were armed were stationed at each side of the boat, to protect the men as they landed the cargo.'

'Were you one of the loaders or one of the guards?'

Horne hesitated, before admitting, 'Guard.'

'So you were armed?'

'Aye.'

'Where did you obtain the firearm you carried?'

'I don't recollect.'

'I see. Can you recollect the nature of the run goods?'

'Eighty to a hundred casks of spirits, as I recall.'

'But your activities were interrupted, were they not?'

'Aye, they were that. There was firing on the beach between the Blockade and our party while the casks were landing. Giles was wounded and lost his firearm. Ransley had told me to carry away any of the party that might be shot so I carried Giles forty or fifty yards, then walked him on a bit further. When we arrived at the high road, we met with Ransley. He put Giles in his cart, and drove him away.'

George scowled. Bad enough that Horne had turned approver but his testimony was a pack of lies. He'd never put himself out for a wounded man in his life — it was Pierce and Quested who carried Giles fifteen miles to Westwell, without a horse let alone a cart.

As for the catalogue of who was where and when, George doubted he could recall that accurately for every transaction himself and put no faith in Horne's version of events. They generally worked at least one night a month through the summer, far more through the winter, often with over a hundred men in action. Who was to say precisely who was where at a given time, unless there was something remarkable like the Westwell rescue?

It was then he saw the fix they were in. Some of their number had squandered the friendships that protected them and now the posted reward gave a good reason for men to speak out. Having committed themselves, the last thing witnesses wanted was for accused men to be released to serve retribution on approvers. They would say whatever was needed to secure a conviction.

He saw no way out of a guilty verdict, followed by a round of hangings the like of which the county had not seen for years. He studied Platt thoughtfully, knowing his reputation as a fine lawyer was well deserved but wondering what he could possibly do in the face of such overwhelming odds.

Meanwhile, Jones continued questioning Horne.

388

'What was the nature of the wound?'

'He took a slug in the throat.'

'What were you paid for your services?'

'Twenty shillings. The tubmen got seven shillings apiece.' Horne paused, then added, 'We generally spend the money we get at Ransley's house.'

The magistrate once more leaned forward. 'Why, what house does Ransley keep?'

Jones supplied the answer. 'He keeps a sort of public house but I am informed by the magistrates that he is not licensed.'

Platt was on his feet in an instant. 'Really! I must say this is raising an unfair prejudice against the prisoner, Ransley. I perceive that those gentlemen are taking notes. I am fully aware of the utility of reporting, but I fear that those loose assertions may injure my client if they go forth without comment to the public.'

Jones waved his acceptance of the objection. The point had been made and no ruling could erase it. 'I call the arresting officer, Smith, to the stand.' A minute or two later, he resumed his case. 'I believe you took the prisoner, Giles, into custody at or near to Bilsington, in Kent, on the morning of the seventeenth of the present month. Is that correct?'

'It is. He gave his name as Wood, but afterwards acknowledged it to be Charles Giles.'

'And did you examine the prisoner at that time?'

'I did. I looked at his neck and found the mark of a wound, which he accounted for, by saying it was the effect of a blister.'

'Thank you.' Jones called his next witness, William Spillane, to take Smith's place. He waited patiently while a sad young man limped into the stand and accepted a chair offered by the clerk. He leaned heavily on a stout cane, his jaw set in a firm line as he winced with each step. His right leg dragged, his injuries clearly leaving him unable to lift the foot clear of the ground.

'Now, Mr Spillane, you also served on the *Ramillies*, stationed near Dymchurch. Please tell the court what took place in August last, when you were yourself wounded.'

'I was on duty on the sixth and went out at dark.' He paused, drawing breath slowly and gripping the rail in front of him with a shaking hand. 'At one in the morning, I saw two shots fired at Half-East Road. I ran towards the spot and saw two flashes.' He wiped his shining brow with a handkerchief. 'The first man I met was Wynn, then I saw a party of men on the beach about thirty or forty yards off–'

'How many men would you say were in the party?'

'There must have been eighty to a hundred of them.'

'And you approached?'

'Aye. I saw a boat in the neighbourhood, then I heard two shots come from the shore.' He frowned at the recollection. 'I judged them to come from the boat. I ran up and the party fired on me very smart.' He swallowed. 'Wynn and me both fired back, then they fired again in return. I was wounded in the arms and side.'

'I understand that shot was extracted from your back as well, Mr Spillane.'

'That's right.' His eyelids drooped from the effects of laudanum, his pupils so dilated that the irises appeared black, and yet his pain was clear to all. 'Still gives me gyp, truth be told.'

'I'm sure that all here today can see that for themselves. Please, go take your rest. I call Lieutenant Johnstone to the stand.' This time, the exchange took longer, as Spillane struggled to get to his feet. A deep frown creased Jones' brow as he watched the young man's suffering. When the formalities were finally over, he prompted his new witness. 'Please state your occupation.'

'Officer on the *Ramillies*.'

'Are you able to confirm the severity of the injuries sustained by Mr Spillane?'

'I am. He was confined five weeks to his bed and there's doubt he'll ever return to active duty.'

'Were you involved in the affray that night?'

'I was. I heard the firing and rushed amongst the men who were working the cargo, discharging a blunderbuss. I saw two of the fellows fall. One, Bushell, has since had his leg amputated from the shot he received on that occasion. His companions tried for a rescue but we secured him.'

'Can you identify any of your assailants?'

'No, the night was so dark that it was impossible to distinguish faces. I saw a man in a white frock wound one of my officers, Joseph Shord.'

'And you pursued these men?'

'Yes, into the marshes and picked up three muskets. One was loaded with forty slugs but the others were broken. All the men

390

escaped but they left fourteen barrels of foreign gin in my possession.'

'Thank you, Lieutenant. I recall Edward Horne.' Once again, witnesses changed places and the clerk reminded Horne that he was still under oath. 'So, Mr Horne, do you recollect this incident?'

'I do, sir. We were running goods between Dymchurch and Hythe. We met at Ransley's that night and then set out in company with all the prisoners, except Giles and Rob Bailey. There were fifty or sixty men on that occasion.'

'These are sizeable numbers of men,' Jones commented.

'Aye. When eighty or a hundred tubs are to be run, fifteen or sixteen armed men are needed to protect the men who carry off the casks. That night, Dennard, Gilham and the elder Wyor had muskets.'

'How were these armed parties organised?'

Horne frowned, confused.

'Well, who issued the weapons? Or did men carry them at other times?'

'No, most were only armed for runs. Sam Bailey kept the weapons in between.'

'And what time did you reach the shore?'

'Between twelve and two.'

'Was Ransley armed?'

'No. He never carried arms, leastwise not as I ever saw.'

'What followed?'

'Ransley called out to me and the others to come up. We landed part of the cargo but the Blockade stopped us landing more. I saw the Blockade signals along the coast. We'd worked about eighty tubs by then. We took them up in carts and guarded them for four or five miles.'

'And how much were you paid this time?'

'One guinea.'

'Thank you. That completes the evidence presented by the prosecution.'

Birnie looked at Platt. 'Well, you've heard the case against your clients.'

'I have, your Honour. I suppose the prisoners must be committed for trial. My advice to them, therefore, would be to say nothing at present.'

'And wise advice it is too,' Birnie said with barely concealed amusement.

George breathed out deeply. It could have gone better. They might beat the murder case but the charge of bearing arms would probably stick. If it did, they'd hang just as surely as if they were convicted of the murder. Any hopes they might have entertained of a more dramatic escape were dashed when Jones spoke again.

'If it please your honour, the prosecution deems it necessary for the prisoners to be confined in a place of more security than any afforded on the sea-coast of the county of Kent. It is a notorious fact that smugglers have broken open or pulled down every prison in that part of the country.'

Birnie nodded his agreement. 'Indeed. If I recall correctly, a mob broke open the gaol at Dover not five years since, rescuing close to a score of their associates in the presence of several magistrates and in broad daylight. I commit the prisoners into the custody of Newgate prison to take their trial for the murder of Quartermaster Richard Morgan, and on other charges of carrying arms on the coast of Kent with a view to running smuggled goods.'

Lieutenant Johnstone had remained in the courtroom after his testimony and now rose respectfully to his feet. Birnie nodded permission for the man to speak, now that the official business of the court was over.

'It's the Cinque Ports again, sir. Even the magistrates down there think they've a right to uncustomed goods. Many's the time I've had difficulty finding a single one of them to back a warrant. They're all in it themselves, you see, smuggling that is.'

Birnie nodded again and turned to one of his officers. 'Ruthven, on your arrival in Kent, it will be your duty to find magistrates to back the warrants. Be sure not to apply to one of the magistrates of the Cinque Ports, lest he give information to the persons accused. Only recently, Bond went before one of the mayors to get a warrant signed and was detained for some time; in the interim, the mayor gave information to the wife of the smuggler, who immediately absconded. Incredible it may sound but I have the affidavits to prove it. Go before some of the magistrates of the county who I believe are most of them honourable men.'

Yes, George reflected, times had changed. Local people were less ready to cover for them and the authorities were less ready to trust them when they did. The world he'd grown up in was gone and there was no place for him in the tightly regulated one that was taking its place.

Paul

Sarah Pierce gave a little sigh as she pulled a thread tight and clipped it off with her teeth. Her husband watched her fold the darned stockings neatly, stretch her stiffened shoulders and then glance up at the mantelpiece above her chair.

'We might as well go to bed as waste candles.'

Her words prompted a reflexive stirring in his groin. Perhaps some men might grow bored of a wife who carried seven children in little more than a decade of marriage and still invited their attentions with the same phrase. Not so Paul Pierce. He liked it that she let him know what she wanted, and that she still wanted it after so long. He knew many men who got little at all at home and many more for whose wives it was a weekend chore as tiresome as blacking the stove. He was a man of routine himself, usually seeking out his wife once a week and a change once a month. Sarah was less predictable, with this invitation on a Tuesday night not at all out of the ordinary.

'Waste not, want not,' he agreed and made for the door.

A full moon hung high in the sky outside, casting deep black shadows beyond the privy each time the clouds cleared for a few seconds. He left the door open for light and directed his flow into the smelly pit below the smooth beech seat he'd worked himself. He dutifully wiped any splashes off with the rag hanging on the wall, recently washed as always. Sarah kept a comfortable home for him and he had long since learned that a man's life could be a lot more rewarding if he went along with the little things that were so important to a wife.

He stood in the middle of the garden for a while, barely noticing the thunderheads building overhead as he pondered the events of the past month. He was already mourning the loss of so many friends, seemingly sure to end their days at the end of a rope. Young fools like the Wyors had got them where they were and Paul felt only resentment for them. Experienced men like himself, George Ransley and Sam Bailey had taken a calculated risk and lost; he expected them to be as pragmatic as he would be in their place. More grievous were good men like Dennard and Gilham, robbed of what should have been long lives to come. Worst of all were his dearest friends, first Giles and then later Quested. Still, although he knew that his life would never be the same again, he would somehow face up to the losses just as he had when friends fell all around him on the battlefields of Spain.

He rolled his tense shoulders thoughtfully. He still had a job he loved, a family he adored and a wife who could get him excited with ten little words. Thankful not to have lost everything, and pushing recent troubles from his mind, he went inside and climbed the steep stairs and narrow ladder to their room in the roof. From the two main bedrooms, he heard the deep breathing of the small children and a giggle from one of the older ones. The walls of the old fashioned cottage were two feet thick but the boards between the floors had gaps a half-inch wide, not a bad thing when the heat rising from stove and fire took the edge off the chill upstairs. His offspring knew full well what an early night meant but Paul was unperturbed. There was nothing more natural and, if he felt anything, it was pride in his marriage.

When he reached the bedroom, Sarah was already in their bed. He studied her by the flickering light of the candle, her glossy brown hair freshly brushed and her white lawn nightdress crisply ironed. She'd never been a beauty but the young Paul had been drawn by the life and wit that still danced in those wide amber eyes, offering his marriage proposal within days of their first meeting and then campaigning relentlessly for months to secure her acceptance. As his wife, she worked hard from dawn till dusk, and often beyond, yet somehow she managed to leave all that behind when she became his lover after nightfall. Her delicate bone structure and porcelain complexion was a tantalising contrast to his own sturdy build and weather-beaten skin.

He pulled his shirt over his head and peeled off his trousers. After looking at Sarah for so long that she frowned as if to ask if he was all right, he lifted the sheets and slid in beside her, his night-chilled flesh eager for her warmth. He knew that recent weeks had been as hard for her as for him. Jane Quested and Mary Giles were amongst her dearest friends and, even while she tried to comfort them in their separation from their husbands, she dreaded the possibility of losing her own. Sharing her fear for the future, both theirs and their friends', he needed to hold her close.

A square of moonlight shining through the small window in its thatched gable gave light enough for loving and, thinking of thrift not modesty, he leaned across her body to blow out the candle. He put his lips to hers, feeling their softness yield to his exploration. Her hot mouth tasted of their broth-and-bread supper. His would be the same, with a layer of brandy and tobacco on top. He stroked her gently, desire mingled with a need to reassure her that everything would, somehow, be all right. For the few precious minutes that their bodies were entwined, he could almost believe it himself.

'You're a good husband,' she told him earnestly as he fell beside her satisfied.

Was he? Could a man who had regularly broken his marriage vows be a good husband? Of one thing he was sure.

'Not as good a husband as you are a wife.'

When she snuggled close to him, he wondered if perhaps he was a good husband after all. He loved his family and provided well for them. He'd never raised a hand to his wife and only thrashed his children when they deserved it. It was his father who ingrained into him the belief that only a weak man hit a woman and he was thankful for that now. He had a wife who was not afraid to tell him when he could do better, as husband or lover, father or gardener, and his life was the richer for it. His strong embrace slackened only when sleep overtook him.

Waking with a start, he knew from the pale smudge in the corner of the window overhead that he hadn't slept for more than a couple of hours. The moon was now cloaked in roiling black clouds and rain could not be far away. He couldn't tell what had woken him but a prickling at the back of his neck said it was not one of the routine sounds of family life, a child's dreams or a baby's hunger. He'd risen for those so many times over the years that he barely reached consciousness when he did so. If he'd needed confirmation, his wife's steady breathing provided it. She was always the first to wake at a cry from one of her brood but now she slept on. He strained his ears in the silence, hoping he was mistaken and all the while certain he was not.

The first indication was a rustle in the garden. Even through the rough winds that were bringing the storm their way, Paul knew the sound was too heavy to be a bird and too clumsy to be a cat. It might be a fox or a badger. He often shovelled fox scats onto the compost heap when he tidied their plot and, while the badgers were more careful in their personal habits, he sometimes saw their tracks along the back hedge. He liked badgers and left their sett, just inside the wood, alone. The only disturbance the badgers ever saw from the Pierce family was a party of observers tucked in silent wonder behind a bank to watch cubs play at dusk. A badger could easily make the rustle he'd heard but, if it had, it would never have woken him. He listened on.

Then he heard it. A low murmur, no words, just the rumble of a man's voice. Paul froze, alternatives running through his mind. A thief? Well, clearly not *a* thief, unless the man was prone to talking to himself. Paul could not begin to imagine who might rob him. He'd lived in the ramshackle old cottage for all his married life and most of his neighbours were friends. In any case, only a fool would try to rob one of the Blues and anyone who didn't know of his involvement in the notorious gang would have no reason to rob him anyway — a gardener with seven children to provide for was hardly likely to have the Crown Jewels in a cupboard.

He was surprised at the speed and calmness with which those thoughts flashed through his mind. He slipped his hand over Sarah's mouth. Her eyes flew open in panic, then filled with faith and fear in equal measure when she identified him. He put his lips close to her ear and formed his breath into words so soft that a man a yard away would not have heard them.

'Men outside. I'll get onto the roof, see what's what.'

She nodded her understanding, her trust never wavering. If the men were a threat to his family, they'd have to come through him first and she knew it. If they were a threat of another kind, he would fade into the night and she would spin them a yarn. Any such escape was likely to be temporary but it never hurt to have time to find out the charges and concoct a story. An unprepared man was far more likely to incriminate himself.

Paul slipped soundlessly out of the bed and lifted a chair cautiously under the window. Thankful now for the low ceiling on which, even with his modest height, he'd often cracked his head after a night's drinking, he released the latch and swung the window open.

He'd thought about the need to escape the house before, although fire was more on his mind at the time than the forces of the law, fitting a new frame and keeping both latch and hinges well oiled ever since.

Still wearing only his underclothes, he gripped the solid beechwood and raised himself slowly through the opening. His work as a gardener easily offset the effects of his indulgences as a Blue, keeping his body better muscled than some boys half his age. Below him, Sarah held up his shirt and trousers. He took them, letting his fingers brush hers, and then shut the window without a sound. Her fingers secured the latch while he hurriedly dressed.

Less than five minutes had passed since he woke but he did not doubt how short time was. In fact, he was surprised the men below were taking as long as they were. He inched his way down the thatch, uncertain whether it was a curse or a blessing. The steep angle of the smooth rushes made it a potential death-trap even for a man as agile as himself but it also meant that few would expect him to attempt an escape by that route. As a gust of wind threatened his balance, he wondered at the wisdom of it himself.

Bracing his foot against a gable, he leaned as far as he dared and surveyed his garden. Leaves still clung to half the trees, providing plenty of cover for intruders. At first he saw nothing but then a figure flitted along the front hedge and across the vegetable garden. Another matched its progress on the other side. Both disappeared into the blackness behind the house.

His gaze leapt back to the front of the house, drawn by the movement of two men walking boldly up the path. Their boots made no noise on the herringbone brickwork he'd pieced together years before from the ruin of an even more ancient cottage along the lane. The moon lit them brightly, while a chimney stack threw his position into deep shadow. Dark coats over white trousers, and reflected light from brass buttons and raised muskets, left no room for doubt in his mind. Seeing their plan and waiting for it to unfold, he found himself counting. He'd reached thirteen when boots thundered into his front and back doors at once.

Smiling grimly, he scurried across the roof under cover of the noise. The men might be surprised how long it would take them to kick down his doors, fashioned as they were from thick oak planks he'd acquired from a fog-bound lugger that missed the lighthouse at

Dungeness. They were probably the most solid part of his house and, bolted securely at top and bottom, played their part in ensuring that he was never woken by a blade at his throat as he'd known happen to others.

The respite bought by the solid barriers would be short-lived though. The garden was swarming with preventive men. Paul couldn't believe the numbers they'd sent to take one man from his bed. There was no way that he could break through the cordon, even with the darkness and the advantage of knowing every inch of the area. When they began bringing more lanterns and scouting around the outside of the house, he knew that his exposed position on the thatch offered no security either. He worked his way cautiously back to the window and tapped.

When the window opened immediately, he knew Sarah had guessed from the noise that escape might be impossible and was waiting on his decision. He lowered himself through the opening.

'Over a dozen,' he whispered.

They looked at each other, in growing desperation. Trapped in a cramped cottage with no cellar or attic and hardly a square inch of space not filled with a bed, chair or table.

'The oven,' she whispered back. 'It's the only place.'

Built into the side of the vast inglenook was a traditional baker's oven. Sarah used the small oven in the stove for meals but fired up the big one when doing a day's baking. Unfortunately, as she'd spent that very day stocking the pantry with an array of cakes and pastries, the brick-shrouded ironwork would still be holding the heat of her labours. Paul considered the suggestion. It was barely a chance but she was right: there was nowhere else.

They hurried down the ladder, past the children who were gathered silently in the bedroom doorways with eyes wide at the noise and what it meant for their father. Paul could do no more than give a reassuring smile as he made for the hiding place.

Seconds later, crammed into the sooty oven, he cursed himself silently but fluently while she moved the log basket back into its place in front of the oven door. There was nowhere near enough heat left to burn him but the air was stifling. Sweat began to trickle down his spine in no time, making him wonder how long he could endure the confinement.

They'd talked about what might happen if the preventive men

were not satisfied with their first catch but reached no agreement on what to do. They wondered whether to move somewhere safer but it was hard to leave so much behind. After twelve years hard work on the estate, he would become no more than an itinerant labourer without references. So they carried on, hoping for the best, a strategy he could now see for the folly it was. Wretched at failing to protect his family, he waited to see if his wife could turn the men away.

Sarah was already at the front door. He heard her unsteady voice raised to challenge the men, demanding to know by what right they came banging on her door in the middle of the night.

'Lieutenant Samuel Hellard of the Coast Blockade, ma'am.' The shout was brusque but civil enough. 'Open up.'

'W-what do you want?'

'Open up, ma'am,' the voice insisted.

'But it's the middle of the night.'

'I know the hour, ma'am. Just open the damn–' There was a brief pause before the request came again, a little more evenly this time. 'Just open the door, ma'am.'

Paul heard her draw the bolts and open the stout door.

'What do you want?' Her voice was more controlled now.

'Mrs Pierce?'

'Yes.'

'Where's your husband?'

'He's away.'

'Is that so?'

'Yes. He's in Canterbury, on estate business. He's the head gardener, you know.'

Paul smiled at the promotion his wife gave him. The lie about Canterbury was presumably the first thing that came into her head, the same story they'd used for Giles six months before.

'I see. Well, you won't mind us taking a look around then, will you.'

'You don't have any ri–'

'Here's my right,' the voice cut her off. Presumably the man was thrusting some piece of paper into her face, an authorisation that she could not read even if she wanted to.

Paul listened while she admitted the men. In no time at all, he heard chairs skidding across floors and drawers banging as they tore his home apart. What they expected to find in the drawers was beyond him but he shut all that from his mind and focused on keeping absolutely still and drawing as few breaths as possible.

The search was thorough. The men crashed around the ramshackle cottage, as if their quarry might be tucked invisibly into a corner somewhere. The air in the oven was sickeningly stale by the time they began to file out of the front door.

Sarah did not tempt fate by gloating. In fact, he heard no voices at all until most of the footsteps had faded into the garden. He was picturing Sarah closing the door behind the last of them when a gruff voice spoke. The accent declared the speaker was no local, probably thanks to the Blockade's policy of posting men far from friends and family who might corrupt them from their duty.

''old on, sir. These ol' cottages 'ave them big fireplaces. I've 'eard of men 'idin' up the chimneys.'

Paul's heart sank as boots tramped back through the house. Less than a yard away, a man rummaged around the inglenook, grabbing the poker from its hook and then thrusting it up the chimney. Paul was glad his backside wasn't in the way when he heard the vicious stabs dislodge soot and loose brickwork alike.

'Naw,' the man called out. 'Nuffink 'ere.'

His final thrust brought a small avalanche of debris from the chimney, making him cough and stumble backwards into the log basket. Paul's heart skipped a beat, his fate in the balance, then it dropped like a lead weight when he heard the rasp of the iron lever on the oven. Hopes dashed, he knew the search was over.

He put up no resistance, having no intention of starting a fight with his wife and children in the firing line. They stood in a dejected huddle while he was bound. He looked at each of them in turn, beginning and ending with Sarah, trying to convey strength and reassurance through his own calm determination. Then he was shoved through the door, his shoulder catching the frame for the first of the many bruises he was expecting to acquire.

His legs hobbled, he stumbled down the path and into the lane. When the impatient man behind him gave him a hefty shove, he cannoned into another prisoner waiting in the shadows.

'Sorry,' he muttered to the anonymous figure.

'S'all right.'

It took Paul a moment to place the voice as Ted Pantry's.

'Bad luck, Ted.'

'Aye, can't say as I've ever had any other kind.'

Paul did not reply. Pantry liked to complain and, for once, had something to complain about. As they waited in the darkness, listening to the wind tear at the trees until their boughs creaked, large drops of rain began to fall. So began a hellish night: hours toiling through mud, broken only by raids to pick up more luckless Blues. By dawn, they'd been joined by John Bailey and Dick Higgins. Paul wouldn't normally choose either man's company but then again, on that night, he'd rather have had no company at all.

If he'd hoped for a respite at their journey's end, he was to be disappointed. When they reached the docks, a tender awaited them. A flash of lightning revealed it as the *Industry*. He stumbled up the gangplank blind, unable to see anything past Bailey's bulk. Once on deck, he stepped alongside and found two petty-officers waiting to relieve their exhausted comrades. The first was much of an age with Paul and wore an expression that blended boredom with resentment at getting soaked on their account. The instant Paul's gaze shifted to the second man's face, he knew they'd met before. While they often encountered preventive men, the circumstances were not generally conducive to remembering a face. He knew he was in trouble as soon as he placed the youthful features. They'd been younger still when he last saw them, the freshness of boyhood still upon them, blindfolded and wailing as Quested lowered the man over the edge of Abbots Cliff.

The steely edge that crept into the already sharp eyes told Paul he'd been spotted. He suspected that the man had surveyed every batch of prisoners in the hope of finding his humiliator amongst them. He barely saw the officer move before the tip of a bat found his solar plexus. All reason fled from his mind as it filled with pain. It had been a long night and it was not over yet.

Jem

Jem Smeed sat huddled in a half-soaked blanket, his arms around Wilson's shaking body. The makeshift tent he'd fashioned from sailcloth and branches billowed in a wind that was climbing to gale force. Winter had started early, strings of bitingly cold nights broken only occasionally by raging storms that lasted just long enough to soak man and beast to the bone before the weather turned again and froze them to the marrow. Tonight's storm was fast building into the worst he'd seen in England. If only the arrests had come in summer, when the nights were warm. If only they'd come a year earlier, when Wilson was strong. If he were alone, he'd be a hundred miles from Aldington but Wilson was past running. Jem knew his only chance was to leave his lover and yet he could not do it. He pulled the man closer. If he left, he'd never see him again. It was that simple. The only way for Wilson to evade capture was through death.

As it was, Jem expected them to hang together. He pressed his chest against Wilson's back and his lips to the cold, clammy cheek. His own body warmth seeped into Wilson's chilled body without seeming to raise its temperature at all. There was no doubt they must find shelter. Wilson would not survive without it.

His lips close to Wilson's ear, he spoke softly. 'We've got to find somewhere warm and dry to hide. It's no good out here for you.'

Wilson's head moved a fraction of an inch to the side. His voice was just a rush of air with no resonance. 'They'll take thee. Let me go now, and then get thyself clear.'

Jem blinked against the tears that threatened to overcome him. Wilson was ready for death; it was he who was not. He, a man who had faced death ten times over and meted it out to others more often than that, could not let this man surrender to it or face it alone. His reply was a bald statement of fact. 'I can't. Besides, it's my fault we're here. If I'd taken you to Marseilles like you ...'

'No!' Wilson protested as firmly as his condition allowed. 'We said in the autumn. It was no fault of thine that I was past travel long before that.'

'We should've gone when you said it.'

Bony fingers clawed at his hand. 'I wish it, Jem, but for thee not me. I wish thou wert free but there's naught to help me now. I'll not be sorry to end my days here where they began.'

Jem clasped him wretchedly, seeing the truth in his words but still awash with regrets for the choices he'd made. He struggled onto his knees, wrapped the blanket around Wilson and then, sweeping the wind-whipped shelter to one side, rose to his feet with his lover across his arms. There was no weight to him, always slight but now wasted.

'Let's go home.'

He set off for Bank Farm. Even loaded, he could make the distance — only a couple of miles — in an hour. They'd find a snug corner in an outbuilding, where Wilson would be warm at least.

As he strode across the dark landscape, his burden barely conscious, Jem thought back over his time in Aldington. He remembered the first day, when he'd nursed a tankard of beer in the Walnut Tree, wondering what to do now he'd reached the lair of the last great gang of free-traders. Wraight brought out a plate of food, nothing fancy, just bread, cheese and pickles. He stood looking out of the window while Jem ate, giving every appearance of a contented man. The inn was packed with farmers, labourers and tradesmen. Life in Aldington looked good.

'Wanting work?'

Those simple words took Jem into Wilson's life. Wraight said Brissenden needed another man and directed him to Bank Farm.

Jem remembered their meeting in vivid detail, how Wilson had looked up from his repairs, moss-green eyes set like jewels in flawless fair skin. Their attraction was instant, across fifty yards, and yet weeks passed before he was sure Wilson wouldn't run if he made a move. It'd meant so much to him that he took more time and put more effort into his pursuit than ever before.

Three years on and he hadn't touched another man, even when Wilson's appetites faded with his health, doing no more than look at even the most tempting stranger who subtly signalled interest. He'd never felt such devotion, lust long since abating at the sight of Wilson's fleshless body but love growing deeper with each day. Now he was ready for their lives to end together. Three wonderful years, loving his Jamie and running with the Blues. Who could ask for more? Nothing lasted for ever and he didn't expect it to.

When he reached the farm, he headed for the old stables. They weren't used much since he and Wilson had helped build a new

403

block eighteen months before. When visitors' horses filled the main stables, the plough-horses were moved into the old buildings but otherwise they were mostly used for storage.

He slipped inside, confident he had not been seen, and headed for the bins beyond the stalls. He set Wilson down tenderly on a workbench that ran along one wall, lit a lamp, then began lifting lids. In the corner, a bin was empty but for a couple of wood mice feeding on a sprinkling of oats. He caught them deftly and tossed them onto a stack of straw bales, then lined the bin with some dusty horse blankets that had been tossed over one of the stalls.

Not daring to risk attracting attention by hauling a bucket of water from the well with the creaking winch, he took some from the horse trough. In summer, it might have been scummy and foetid but it now brimmed with fresh rainwater. He drank his fill, then helped Wilson to sip from the ladle before stepping outside again to return it to the well and relieve himself. Holding a bucket for Wilson to do the same, he felt none of the emotions he might have expected at ministering to the helpless man — only a desire to bring whatever comfort he could. Quickly and methodically, he stripped off their oilskins and the wet outer layers beneath, stowed them out of sight, and then dried their hair and skin as best he could with grubby rags.

Finally, exhausted, he checked to make sure that nothing was out of place, blew out the lamp and lifted Wilson into the bin. He dropped in the remaining blankets and climbed in himself. Once he settled the lid into place, the darkness was absolute. It took a few minutes to get settled on his back, head cushioned by the blankets underneath him, arm around Wilson at his side and three blankets on top of them. Wilson's breathing still rasped but began to settle now one lung was draining of fluid. Jem shifted until they were as close as they could get and began to stroke Wilson's hair. He wasn't sure if Wilson was unconscious or asleep but he was alive and out of pain, and that was enough. Slowly he felt the heat of his body begin to warm first the space and, eventually, Wilson.

They'd be caught, of that he had no doubt. Preventive officers still searched relentlessly and they'd returned to known haunts like the farm more than once. They'd be back and he'd hang. He hoped Wilson would have passed on peacefully in his arms by then. That was all he asked and he offered it up in a bitter prayer. He wanted nothing for himself but demanded that for Wilson.

Jem jerked awake. He hadn't slept properly in two weeks and had only dozed throughout the night; not until the hour before dawn had he found a deeper rest. He knew immediately that the end had come. Thuds and crashes echoed around the stable outside the snug bin in which he lay with his arms around Wilson. He shook the sick man gently.

'Jamie. Jamie, wake up. They're come.'

Wilson stirred and murmured hoarsely, 'Run, please run.'

'Too late for that,' Jem whispered, brushing the top of the man's head with his lips. After one final embrace, he rearranged them so that they looked more like men sharing body heat on a cold night and less like lovers.

He was only just in time. The lid to the bin flew open. He screwed up his eyes against the light and found himself looking into the startled face of a young preventive officer. A second or two passed, then the man threw the lid against the wall and raised his pistol.

'Got the bastards!'

His shout brought men running from all directions.

Jem made to stand but stopped when he saw the man's finger trembling on the trigger. Inexperience and youth came together in excitement at being the one to capture the fugitives and fear of failing in his duty. Jem knew he could easily get himself killed and he had no intention of letting that happen while Wilson still needed him. He raised his hands slowly.

'Get out of there!' The officer shouted the order, even though he was barely a yard away. 'Slowly!'

Jem did not move. He glanced down at Wilson, then spoke in a soft, persuasive tone. 'My friend's sick. Let me lift him out.' He moved his hand tentatively, as if to indicate Wilson.

'Don't move!'

A second officer joined the first. He was older and examined Jem with a steady eye. He looked into the bin and repeated the examination on Wilson.

'The bastard looks dead to me.' He raised his pistol. 'Easier to finish it now.'

Jem studied him calmly. Perhaps that would be best for both of them. If only he could be sure they'd shoot Wilson after they shot him; he could not let him fall into their hands alone. He knew the older officer had seen his indecision, and his lack of fear, when he relaxed his grip on the pistol and let the barrel drop.

'All right, damn you. Get him out–'

The youngster at his side tensed and made to interrupt.

'Keep it slow. If I think I see steel, you die.'

It was a statement more than a threat.

Jem nodded and dropped to a squat, hampered by the close confines of the bin. Wrapping a blanket around Wilson, he stood up with the living skeleton in his arms. He stepped over the edge of the bin, feeling the tension abate as the preventive men saw his hands occupied and his concern for the man in them. He wouldn't be tossing Wilson to one side to attack them and the more experienced officer knew it.

The men and women of Bank Farm were gathered outside in the stable-yard, news of the capture having spread fast. Jem set Wilson down on his feet, supporting him while he struggled for balance, and then glanced around the sullen faces in the group. He was pleased to see they got no entertainment from watching the detested preventive men bind their workmates. Some of the women wept. Jem knew their tears were for not him, a relative newcomer and inclined to keep his own counsel, but for Wilson, a man they'd known all their lives and loved like a brother. Weeks on the run had eroded what was left of his broken constitution and now he looked close to death. It was small wonder that the onlookers were aggrieved. The young officer only fuelled their resentment when he signalled their departure by shoving Wilson forward and pitching him into the dust.

Men around the yard inched forward, loath to provoke trouble but loyal to their friend and Jem, even bound as he was, tensed to lunge for the officer. At that instant, Brissenden strode out of the farm office and elbowed his way through the men in his path.

'Fred!' he bellowed. 'Get ol' Mags tacked up.' He stopped just inches from the young officer and glared at him. 'You'll put Mr Wilson on a horse and treat him right on your way to wherever it is you're going. He's a better man than you'll ever be, m'lad.'

The youngster opened his mouth to protest but his superior cut him off with a curt wave of his hand and spoke sharply to Brissenden. 'Suit yourself but, take my word on it, the bugger's not so good that he won't hang.'

Brissenden turned away disdainfully and spoke to the farmhand leading an old plough-horse out of the new stables. 'Go with 'em, Fred. Make sure they treat him fair, then bring Mags back after.'

So it was that Jem had company on the long walk to Hythe. The farmhand took Mags's head, while Jem walked by her flank, raising his bound hands to steady Wilson whenever he seemed in danger of falling. Around them swarmed a mass of preventive men determined to prevent their escape.

Hours passed before Fort Moncrieff came into sight. It was nearly noon by the time they stopped outside the sprawling complex of ugly buildings shared by the Blockade and Army. Only after two of the preventive men had helped Wilson down with decent good grace did the farmhand clap a hand on Jem's shoulder in farewell and turn the elderly mare back towards Aldington.

Watching her ample hindquarters recede into the distance, Jem knew utter defeat for the first time. There would be no escape and, as a key member of the Blues, he would hang for Morgan's death, as surely as he'd seen Rolfe, Wilsden, Fagg and Meredith of the North Kents hang four years earlier. Then, he'd been just another follower but, now, he would pay the price for being a leader. Then, he'd been just another anonymous figure in a sea of spectators standing in subdued silence as the procession passed. He'd been surprised by the silence, having heard as a boy from his shipmates about the jeering mobs outside Newgate on a hanging day. Penenden Heath was different, the crowds drawn from country not city and mostly sympathetic to the condemned men. He'd be the last to deny that times had changed, and with good cause, and he wondered what he might face on his journey to the scaffold.

The elder officer barked orders at the men of the fort. Jem could see from their responses that the man was held in high regard. Somewhat short and stocky, he was in his middle years, much of an age with Ransley, with an all-too-familiar bearing — the man had doubtless devoted his life to the Navy. The single epaulette on his right shoulder identified him as a lieutenant, although the regulation tricorne hat was missing to reveal a closely cropped salt-and-pepper thatch. In Jem's day, many men still wore pigtails as he had himself, and he'd noted the ban on them a couple of years earlier with amusement. The Navy liked to control every aspect of its men's lives, down to when they shaved and how they wore their hair.

The lieutenant held his eye for a few seconds before speaking.

There was a grudging admiration in his voice. 'You're the last.' He glanced at Wilson, crumpled at the base of a wall, before continuing. 'Christ knows how you stayed out of sight with him in tow. Why bother? He's dead as it is, damn him.'

Jem shrugged. 'What sort of man leaves a friend in a tight spot?'

There was a pause before the lieutenant nodded. When he spoke again, his voice was brisk and businesslike. 'I take it you're not interested in the reward then?'

Jem gave the slightest shake of his head.

'Ever seen a flogging?'

'Aye. One or two.'

'Make you talk?'

'Doubt it.'

'Hellard.' The lieutenant's introduction was perfunctory. 'I can see he's Wilson, so that must make you Smeed.'

'Aye.'

'Right, well, you're headed for the Smoke. The *Industry*'ll take you as far as the *Ramillies*, off Deal.' There was a distinct note of satisfaction in his voice when he added, 'You won't be short of company there, mark my words.'

Jem raised an eyebrow, knowing better than to speak other than in response to a direct question.

'Hogben and Wheeler. Amongst others.'

Jem considered the news, unconcerned by Hogben's capture but disappointed that the blacksmith had suffered the same fate. He knew Wheeler well because he'd become a firm friend of Wilson's in the years he'd shod the farm's horses. As well as their old-fashioned ways and unexpected good manners, they shared a fondness for China tea — a taste Jem himself had never acquired. Sometime driver or tubman, Wheeler's special task was to fix whatever needed fixing on a run. Jem had seen him prop a cart against one huge shoulder while he changed a broken wheel, as if it were the easiest thing in the world.

Shifting his thoughts back to the present, Jem wondered who else awaited them on the *Ramillies*, and tried to guess the final tally. Eight in the first raid and then, by his reckoning, three more on the tempestuous November night that his own flight began. During his stealthy forays for food, he heard enough to know that Pierce and Pantry had been taken, along with John Bailey.

Hellard had been watching him in silence but now seemed to relent. 'Sixteen, all in. Not counting the bloody turncoats.'

With that, he turned away and waved forward the midshipman who was waiting to supervise the transport. Jem went to help Wilson, wasting no energy on wondering who had turned King's Evidence or what kind of case the Blockademen had against him. His sole purpose in coming days would be to shield his companion from the worst of their troubles. He could do no more and he would do no less.

Quacks

'Ugh!'

Quacks jolted into wakefulness, casting around in the gloom for the reason that his restless sleep had been interrupted. With a harbour crew of more than three hundred men, His Majesty's Ship *Ramillies* was crowded enough without her abundant population of rats. Until he came aboard the 74-gun veteran of Ushant, Quacks had never given rats a second thought, simply shooting or poisoning them if they threatened his wartime rations or peacetime profits. Now, however, chained below decks while they ran freely over his body, he was rapidly developing a hatred of the disease-ridden rodents.

'Someone outside.'

Pierce's words were matter-of-fact but carried comfort and reassurance to his friend. A slight whistle now accompanied his soft voice, courtesy of a tooth lost during the beating that had marked his arrival on board. Quacks had been appalled to see the state in which it had left him, then saddened to discover that his warning on that distant day had been justified. He saw his own regret and relief mirrored in his friend's eyes when they were reunited, each sorry to see the other captured but pleased to be together once more. They faced their incarceration with the same stoicism that had seen them through the Spanish years.

When the door was thrown open, smoky lamplight silhouetted two more prisoners in the corridor beyond. There was no need to see their faces to recognise them, a slight figure leaning heavily against a taller man who managed to support him with a forearm in spite of his shackled wrists. Quacks shuffled closer to Pierce, making room at his side for the newcomers to join him. It was not for him to say how they would be arranged but the guards mostly took the line of least resistance. They did so now, letting themselves be steered into chaining the ailing man next to Quacks and his companion beyond. No one spoke until the door was barred and the guard's footsteps faded into the distance.

'Bish?' Quacks prompted gently.

There was no reply. After a few seconds more, Smeed spoke in a voice thick with emotion.

'He's scarce with us.'

That much had been obvious but Quacks heard more in those few words. Smeed had done his best, trying to keep Wilson free but finally facing the fact that they were going nowhere and winter was no time for a sick man to sleep rough on the marshes.

In something closer to his normal voice, Smeed asked, 'Who else've we got here?'

Pierce answered for the other men. 'Paul, Dick, Hog and Tom the Blacksmith. John was with us but they moved him out.'

'Not a squeal?' Smeed's tone declared that he found that hard to believe.

Pierce laughed. 'Not a chance. He was giving 'em hell. They probably decided Newgate was welcome to him. But Ted Pantry sang soon enough.'

'No surprise there then. They got anyone else against us?'

'The word is Harry Horne told 'em where to find us but didn't give 'em any names they didn't already know. And Jim Bushell said naught till after they took the first lot.'

Quacks caught the admiration in the words. When they learned the extent of Bushell's injuries back in August, they wondered how long it would be before he talked. Losing a leg was an ordeal any time and a prison in the belly of a naval vessel was the last place he'd want to face it. Having since seen Lieutenant Hellard at work, Quacks doubted he'd twist a knife in an open wound to get information but Bushell had still done well to remain silent.

'You all right, Paul?' Smeed had clearly detected something other than admiration in Pierce's voice.

Pierce laughed it off. 'Aye, been catching up with an old friend.'

'Sounds like a friend you can do without.' Smeed answered in kind

410

but soon returned to business. 'So where'd they get the rest?'

'Don't know. Rumour has it they've got a secret informant.'

'The Deal man?'

'Maybe. Then again, maybe that was just a blind. More likely from Aldington or thereabouts, if you ask me.'

Sharing Pierce's opinion that their nemesis came from within their midst, Quacks nodded, the gesture lost in the darkness. He shifted to examine the man at his side. They wore the worst kind of fetters, heavy and linked by bars that made movement difficult and painful. Chains linked the bars to the deck, making it hard to change position and impossible to stand. Even the simple act of relieving themselves had become an obstacle to overcome and they all bore the stench of the overspill. During their first days aboard, they'd tried to maintain a semblance of decency but, as everything grew filthier, they slowly became less particular.

His examination found Wilson's skin and clothes drenched in sweat, his temperature raging while his body shook with chills. The man needed to be washed, dried, dressed in clean clothes and wrapped in warm blankets. More than any of that, he needed fluids to prevent further dehydration.

'When does he last have aught to drink?' Quacks asked Smeed.

'Around noon. They watered us before the tender left Hythe but I couldn't get much into him and half of that came up later. I told them he needed blankets but...' His voice shook with anger.

Without the basic necessities, Wilson would die. Of that there could be little doubt. Quacks cast around for a temporary solution. He would gladly have given up his jacket but, with his hands manacled and no means of slitting the seams, could not remove it. He was still thinking when the clank of chains told him that a man was struggling against his restraints in the darkness and, seconds later, Higgins spoke.

'Here, give him this.'

Quacks felt Higgins' feet moving against his own. Guessing that his friend was trying to kick something closer, he worked his own feet against them. It must have been a couple of minutes before his fingertips finally brushed against the heavy cloth of Higgins' cloak. They all still wore what they'd been wearing when captured and, as Higgins had been taken while patrolling the estate, he had several layers of warm and waterproof clothing. Quacks did not argue, immediately tackling the tricky task of wrapping a fettered man in a cloak while fettered himself.

It was Smeed who acknowledged the gesture. 'Thanks, Dick.'

'I was too hot anyway.'

Higgins sounded distinctly on edge. Not a generous or thoughtful man by nature, perhaps being seen to do a good turn made him uneasy. On the other hand, their current plight was enough to make any man anxious. Quacks smiled, both in amusement at Higgins' response and in relief at being able to offer some care to Wilson. Swathing his body in the insulating material would improve his prospects considerably, although there was still the problem of getting fluids into him. They had only one source of liquid, one that he knew crews sometimes resorted to at sea but felt unable to propose.

'How bad does he need a drink?' Smeed asked.

'Bad,' Quacks said flatly.

'When will the guards be back?'

'In the morning, if they feels like it.'

'No chance of calling them?'

'Down here?'

Quacks held no hope of mercy, or even fairness, from their gaolers. While Hellard seemed decent, albeit crude, he was a busy man and the guards were content to do as little as they could get away with during his frequent absences. With the *Ramillies* as overcrowded as it was, their dungeon was sandwiched between the provisions on the orlop deck where no one would even hear their muffled shouts. Of no further use after being questioned, prisoners were simply cargo awaiting transport to Newgate.

Had William McCulloch still headed the Blockade, Quacks had no doubt he would have taken a profound and personal interest in them. As it was, only Hellard matched his zeal in the crusade against smugglers in general and Blues in particular, a passion kept warm by the scores of injuries inflicted on his men in the years since Brookland. If McCulloch was watching from the afterlife, his frustration at missing their capture by a mere twelve months would know no bounds. Having sacrificed his health and risked his family's safety in his uncompromising pursuit, he would now see victory go to an ambitious post-captain who saw the Coast Blockade only as a stepping stone to future promotion and not as a personal quest for justice. Captain Pigot had not so much as inspected his prisoners, leaving Hellard to organise their capture, interrogation and transport virtually single-handed.

'They needs to get him to a doctor,' Quacks said bitterly.

Smeed's reply was equally bitter. 'They think he's past help.'

They settled into a sad silence. Once or twice, Quacks heard Smeed shifting beyond Wilson but thought he was comforting his ailing friend. He had guessed long before that the bond between the two men ran deeper than friendship but he thought about that no more than he thought about the others' relationships with their wives. Like many things in his life, it simply *was* and he had no views on it, one way or another. A few minutes passed before Smeed's fingers brushed his hand.

'Try him with this. It's not water but it might serve.'

Careful not to drop the slim flask offered, Quacks rightly assumed it'd held spirits that Smeed managed to slip past the searches. He debated the wisdom of administering them for, while their medicinal qualities were proven, they were no substitute for water and might make matters worse. As soon as he felt the warmth in the metal, he knew that the spirits were long gone. Smeed had delivered what he'd been too reticent to suggest.

It took almost as long to get the liquid into Wilson without spillage as it had for Smeed to provide it so discreetly. Quacks' knowledge of survival medicine was patchy and, acquired in the army, included less experience of water shortages than most seamen had. In the years since, he'd nursed patients through many dangers but the one hardship that the people of the marshes never faced was thirst or drought. He knew that prolonged dependence on second-hand water could endanger life but thought the benefits would outweigh the risks for the present. He knew that Smeed would not have offered the solution if he did not think it better than doing nothing.

With his active business life, Quacks was more aware of the date than some of his fellows. He knew precisely when he'd been captured and was fairly confident that he had not lost track of the days since. By his reckoning, it was early on the twenty-third day of November, a Thursday, when Lieutenant Hellard returned to the *Ramillies*. Whatever the date, they'd endured three more hellish days of constant confinement and irregular rations since Smeed and

Wilson joined them.

Hellard was not pleased with what he found. The extensive vocabulary he employed in expressing his displeasure was a revelation to his prisoners, though not it seemed to his men; if breaking the third commandment consigned a man to hell, they were sure to have company there. It was the closest thing to entertainment they'd seen since their arrests, indeed for some time before, and watching their captors being taken down several pegs lifted their spirits from despondency to mere misery.

Quacks would have enjoyed the spectacle more had he not been worrying over his patient. Amazed at the tenacity with which Wilson clung to life, when plenty of stronger men would long since have surrendered, he did what little he could to help. Part of him knew it was pointless, aware that they were looking at when — not if — he died, but neither the friend nor the medic in him could give up hope until death claimed its prize.

When Hellard eventually exhausted his repertoire of abuse, he returned to the cell and stood in the doorway, glowering at the state of his prisoners. Quacks had encountered Hellard's like in the army. As much as he hated the Blues, and the violence that he believed they had wantonly inflicted on some of his best men, he was a career naval officer and the ideal of honourable engagement was etched deeply into his character. He hoped with every shred of his being that they would hang but he would treat them as men until that happened. Plenty in the Blues understood that code and, in their own way, lived by its tenets. Quested felt a sense of kinship for the man, as he watched integrity slowly triumph over the need for vengeance.

Voice low but threatening, Hellard addressed the two guards waiting behind him. 'Clean them up before you put them on the bloody *Antelope*.' He studied Wilson's prone form. 'Is he dead?'

Quacks took it upon himself to answer the question. 'No.'

Hellard raised the lamp in his right hand and repeated his inspection more carefully. The light revealed a cloak wrapped around the pale figure, scarves rolled into a pillow for his head and a damp handkerchief crumpled in Quacks' fist.

'You're watching over the bastard?'

Wondering where the questions were leading, Quacks glanced uneasily past his patient. If anyone was to answer for Wilson, it

414

should be Smeed. The slightest nod told him that Smeed wanted him to continue his care, if that was to be permitted, whatever that meant for him. He looked back to Hellard and nodded.

'Is he fit for travel?' As if realising the question was ludicrous, given that Wilson was fit for nothing, Hellard clarified. 'Will he die before he reaches London, damn you?'

Quacks considered the point. It was easy to think nothing could be worse than conditions aboard the *Ramillies* but, if the *Antelope* was as small as the *Industry* that brought them aboard, that might be a costly error. And, with the season well towards winter, even the short passage from the Downs to Deptford might be rough.

'Aye, I thinks he might.'

'Will a few days' rest and rations make any bloody difference?'

They could do no harm, of that he was sure. 'Aye. They might.'

'Then you'll stay here with him, scrub this shithole out and get the bugger fit to stand trial. You understand me?'

There was no missing the malice underlying the concession, offered for one reason only. Hellard wanted to deliver his full complement of prisoners into the justice system, to be held to account for their crimes against his men, not to watch them die anonymously in the bowels of a depot ship.

Decision made, Hellard prepared to leave. 'The rest of you worthless shitsacks, get up on deck.' As he turned away, he growled, 'Light irons on the ones for transit. Leave these two free.'

'But…' one of the guards began, his protest immediately dissolving in the face of Hellard's furious glare.

'Damn you, man! I'll be hanged if I'll have my blasted orders questioned.'

'Yes, sir!'

The hasty capitulation saved Hellard the need to formulate any further threats. He stalked off down the corridor, leaving the guards to follow his instructions — which they did, resentfully.

Quacks parted from his friends grimly, apprehensive at staying behind when Wilson's death might leave him alone within days but determined to nurse the man until the time came. His regret at being separated from Pierce was as nothing to the sorrow he saw in Smeed's eyes. Still unconscious, Wilson could not have felt the strong grip on his damp hand and the lips that brushed lightly over it before Smeed followed the others above decks.

George

George Ransley shivered as he stood with the other accused men. The three months in gaol awaiting trial, first Newgate and later Maidstone, had not been as unremittingly wretched as he had expected. As miserable and intimidating as Newgate was, worse even than it had been when Cephas was imprisoned there, a part of him felt a perverse sense of pride at being deemed significant enough to merit its security. The precaution was born of bitter experience, given that the authorities had managed to lose two sets of prisoners in close succession when crowds rioted over smuggling cases in Dover. Nonetheless, pride notwithstanding, the crumbling hell-hole was an education in subjects he could do without — vermin, disease and insanity — and the prospect of hanging had soon looked less bleak. By the time they were moved to the new gaol at Maidstone in early November, he was of the view that any change could only be for the better. For once, he was not disappointed. With larger, cleaner and better segregated quarters, and their families bringing in food to supplement the meagre rations, they were comfortable, if bored and apprehensive.

Since his arrest, their number had swelled to sixteen. When Eliza made the long journey to visit him in Newgate every Thursday, she brought accounts of each fresh capture along with her other news. George was dismayed but not surprised, having known that few of his men would flee the marshes, no more able to face being cast adrift from their families than he was. Only Smeed was bound by no familial ties and, with his contacts and experience, well suited to making a bid for freedom. Even hampered by Wilson, he was still the last to be caught. Six months earlier, the two men might have been in France instead of gaol but Wilson's failing health had kept them in Kent and now left them both facing the hangman.

George looked sadly at Wilson. The man stood shaking, Smeed at his side trying to shield him from the draft that blew down the dank corridor. It was a miracle that he was still with them, if a life so painful and fragile could be called a blessing. When it became clear that he would not live long enough to take his punishment, Platt argued for him to be released but it was to no avail. Although

Quested refused any credit for the improvement in Wilson during their two weeks aboard the *Ramillies* after the others left, George was confident that his care had as much to do with the remission as the improved rations and warm blankets that they finally received. With his only comfort that Eliza and the children were safe back at the Tap, George pitied Smeed's frustration in the face of his lover's inexorable deterioration. Already settled in Maidstone, he had not been privy to the reunion between Smeed and Wilson but assumed it was as restrained as their conduct had always been. Only in that one unguarded embrace behind the Walnut Tree had he ever witnessed a trace of their intimacy and, even having seen it, he still found it hard to cast Smeed in that role. In any event, although their arrangements could scarcely be a secret from most of those with them now, such matters seemed trivial when men awaited death.

Looking back, George had no idea what the authorities were up to with their movements. He and the seven men captured on that first night in mid-October had been interrogated aboard the *Ramillies* for a week or so and then, when it became clear that they had no intention of making a deal with their captors, were sent on to London. They arrived in Newgate before the month was out and, within days, faced their committal hearing. Afterwards, they were joined by the newly captured John Bailey, who brought news of the other November arrests, but their other friends were still with the Blockade in the Downs when they were moved to Maidstone. He knew now from Pierce's account that his party had not arrived in London until the end of November and he was baffled why they had not been taken straight to Maidstone. He could only suppose that their committals had to be conducted in Bow Street Magistrates Court, given that Quested and Wilson were also shipped all the way around to London, only to be brought back to Maidstone two weeks later. Whether by accident or design, it meant that they were not together in one place at one time until a few days earlier. It would have been virtually impossible to free them all with one rescue attempt, even if such an enterprise had been planned. Perhaps that was precisely what the Blockade had intended its schedule to achieve.

After careful consideration, George had entrusted his fate to Platt's judgement and advised his men to do the same. The barrister's plan was audacious, designed to achieve the best outcome for the largest number, but it required them to act together, offering a chance for those on the most serious charges but requiring a brave gamble from the men facing only lesser counts. Unsurprisingly, Pierce, Quested and Giles stood as firmly beside the others awaiting trial as they had in every affray, while Wilson would willingly have sacrificed what was left of his life for any of them; the others, John Bailey and Dick Higgins, threw in their lot with their kin out of familial loyalty. All were apprehensive, even the smartest questioning the wisdom of their strategy, and now they waited to see if Platt could deliver what he hoped. George was by no means sure that the plan would succeed but he knew their advisor was right about one thing: they did not want the Preventive Service to parade wounded officers before a jury. Their defence could do without the names of fallen men being turned into young faces and crippled bodies.

With some seventy-odd witnesses poised to testify, few on the defendants' behalf, there could be little doubt that some of the charges would stick. Even though most of the witnesses were reluctant, there only because they'd been subpoenaed — or speened, as they called it — the cumulative weight of their testimonies must surely be irresistible. Once convinced that there had been smuggling and bearing arms, what juryman would doubt murder? And what difference would it make, when bearing arms against the King's men carried the same penalty? In George's opinion, with the authorities determined to send out a clear message to anyone thinking of stepping into the Blues' shoes, the noose was inevitable but then so was their attempt to evade it. Although those not directly involved in killings had sometimes seen death commuted to transportation in the past, such clemency now was beyond their hopes.

When Platt came to check on the group, he adopted his customary confident and professional bearing. Although they were now recovering in the better conditions of Maidstone, George had no doubt that his long-standing business associate had noted every scab gained and pound lost in Newgate but, if he did, he gave no sign of it.

'For what it's worth,' Platt said amiably, 'You're set to go down in history as the last of the great free-traders. You should see the crowds outside, waiting on your fate.'

His bravado brought some cheer to the younger men. They'd rather keep their lives but, if they were to lose them anyway,

419

notoriety had some appeal. George was too old to care about such frivolities but he liked seeing even a trace of hope in them.

Platt continued with his briefing. 'Sir James Park is presiding. That's your first real piece of luck in this business. He's a fair man and he's spoken out before on the trade, telling all who'll listen that the fault lies with those who buy and not those who sell. You couldn't hope for a better ear to hear your case.' George noted that Quested and Wilson, like himself, decided against pointing out that Park was in fact the man who had sentenced Cephas to death six years before. But then Platt knew that, of course, having been in court himself that day. George hoped that the similarities would not extend to their sentences. Platt nodded to the far side of the defence desk. 'You know Mr Clarkson, who is assisting me. And the Counsel for the Crown is the Solicitor-General, Mr Twiss, with the assistance of Mr Knox.'

The Blues looked over at the man preparing to send them to the gallows. He cut an unremarkable figure, about forty and with heavy brows over dark eyes set deep in a round face. George noted Platt's hesitation, the pause while he let his clients take in the two men about to prosecute them, and then saw the indecision behind it. A moment later, mind made up, Platt gave a conspiratorial grin and leaned closer.

'Don't let Twiss worry you. He can talk the hind leg off a donkey but he can't conjure a case from thin air. Believe me, I've seen the depositions and he knows more about where you take a drink than about events on the nights in question. Your friends gave him little that he had not already discovered through the unidentified informant who facilitated your capture and who I understand to be a local man outside your number. Horne, in particular, always claims to have been in the eastward party when the westward party was firing and vice versa. I cannot say whom he seeks to protect but his testimony is less than convincing.'

The words did little to lift the spirits of the dejected group. Few free-traders walked away from the charges they faced. Unperturbed, Platt lowered his voice still further.

'I once heard a little rhyme about our friend, Mr Twiss. Darned if I remember it all but it went something like this — 'twould puzzle the sages of Greece to unriddle, which flows out the fastest his verse or his piddle, and 'twould pose them as much to know whether or not, his piss or his poems go quickest to pot.'

Pleased to see the ditty bring weary grins from some of his men, George returned Platt's smile. The solicitor was doing his best to ready them for their ordeal. He concluded with a warning.

'As I say, don't let Twiss worry you. And *don't...*' he paused for emphasis. 'Let him rattle you. I want civil answers when you're called on to speak. No more, no less.'

George permitted himself a moment's grim satisfaction. He had done his research carefully when he selected Langham & Platt to represent the affairs of the Blues and he was glad of it now. He knew from past experience how quick-witted Platt was and now he saw that he was well-informed too. He knew whom he faced and, doubtless, what they intended to throw at him as well. There was no guarantee that he could save his clients but, if he could not, George doubted that anyone else could do better.

Justice Park took his seat on the Bench at nine o'clock and the room was instantly filled in every part. It took a quarter of an hour for the court to come to order, what with the noise from outside and the hordes to seat inside. Eventually, the clerk rose to read the charges. He was a faded wisp of a man in comparison to the outdoorsmen he accused, sandy hair thinning and pale skin barely touched by the sun. Picking up a sheaf of papers from his desk, he cleared his throat and began to speak in a lilting tenor that was as unexpected as it was clear.

'The prisoners on trial this morning are the sixteen persons indicted on charges connected with the murder of Quartermaster Richard Morgan, at Dover, on the thirtieth of July last.'

The clerk perused the papers in his hand unhurriedly.

'The first charge is brought against the following men: Ransley, George, 44 years of age.'

He paused for the bailiff to motion the accused man forward and then, while George led the way to the bar, continued to name the men charged with him. His words were almost drowned out by the clanking of their irons, the chains between their legs dragging on the bare boards of the courtroom.

'Bailey, Samuel, 42; Bailey, Robert, 30; Gilham, Thomas, 24; Dennard, Thomas, 24; Hogben, James, 43; Smeed, James, 23.'

Only then did George discover Smeed's youth. He saw the shock ripple through his companions. The man who had armed them and helped lead them, standing as firmly at his left hand as Sam Bailey did at his right, was younger even than Dennard. Smeed only grinned when he saw their surprise.

'Wheeler, Thomas, 32; Wyor, Richard, 19; and Wyor, William, 18.'

The clerk waited until the ten men stood shoulder-to-shoulder in the dock and silence fell once more.

'The prisoners are charged with assembling with other persons unknown, to the number of eighty, armed with firearms, at the parish of St James the Apostle, of the Port of Dover, in the county of Kent, on the thirtieth of July. The prisoner, Richard Wyor, did then and there unlawfully, maliciously and feloniously, shoot Richard Morgan, a person lawfully employed in the prevention of smuggling, and did give to the said Richard Morgan, three mortal wounds under the left pap of his breast, of which wounds he languished, and languishingly did live for the space of one hour, and then did die.'

He paused for breath before going on.

'The other prisoners are charged with being present, aiding, assisting and comporting the said Richard Wyor, in the commission of the said murder.'

'How do the prisoners plead?' the Judge asked.

George glanced at Platt, knowing the procedure well enough but awaiting his Counsel's signal nonetheless. Only when the solicitor gave a slight nod did he take the lead in entering his plea. He spoke slowly and deliberately, keeping his voice firm but low.

'Not Guilty.'

Each of his companions echoed the plea, even Gilham answering without hesitation. Only when all of the accused had spoken did Platt lean over to speak to Twiss. His words were murmured, far too quiet for George to hear from the dock. Judging from the way in which the court officers were frowning and leaning closer, even those nearest to the prosecution and defence could not follow the exchange.

The minutes ticked past as the consultation went on. Twiss had initially seemed startled and then began to shake his head slowly. Platt's bearing became more earnest, his expression making it clear that he was endeavouring to convince Twiss that his proposition was the only reasonable course of action. Soon it was Justice Park who began to frown, clearly becoming impatient to know what deal was being done in his courtroom. He drummed his fingers lightly on the Bench, warning Counsel that some explanation had better be forthcoming.

George watched intently, knowing what Platt was attempting but less than half convinced he would succeed. Even if his proposition were to be accepted, it was only a battle won and not the end of the war; their fate would lie with a higher authority. He studied Twiss, feeling the anticipation rise inside him as he willed this man to accept their offer. It was a gamble, with their lives as the stake, but even a slim chance was better than none at all.

When Platt stopped speaking for the last time, Twiss held his gaze for most of a minute. George saw in those deep-set eyes a complex blend of emotions: reluctance to play into their hands, resignation at the weakness of his own hand, a desire to achieve a conviction of some sort and, most of all, a longing to put an end to the Blues. George knew that the prosecutor was assessing whether it was worth pressing a flimsy case for murder when a lesser charge could achieve his main objective. Finally he gave a decisive nod.

Only Platt's triumphant glance at George revealed his satisfaction at the assent. Businesslike as ever, he passed a note to the clerk for the Bench. George turned his scrutiny on Justice Park, as the Judge read the note and considered its contents. His expression showed that, as yet, he did not understand the strategy but that he had grave misgivings about it. George had no idea whether Park had the authority to intervene or whether he must agree to the motion accepted by the prosecution. Park gave little outward indication of his uncertainty, using an authoritative tone to order the remaining prisoners brought from Newgate prison.

When they arrived, George remained at the bar with Sam Bailey, Smeed, Dennard and Gilham. They were joined by John Bailey, Higgins, Pierce and Wilson.

The clerk cleared his throat before embarking on another long indictment. 'The prisoners are charged with assembling, with numerous other persons unknown, on the sixteenth of March, at New Romney, armed with firearms.'

He barely paused before adding a second count.

'The prisoners did then aid and assist in the landing and running of uncustomed goods. They did feloniously, wilfully and maliciously shoot at Patrick Doyle and Cluryn Macarthy, persons employed by his Majesty's Customs for the prevention of smuggling.'

George watched Justice Park while the charges were read out. His eyes were still fixed on the man in whose hands their fate rested when the Judge repeated his earlier question.

'How do the prisoners plead?'

The first to be arraigned, John Bailey stood at the head of the queue to answer. There was an expectant pause before he spoke. The plea they had agreed to enter was a hard one for a man to give, knowing that his life would hang by a thread once he had spoken. Bailey did not flinch but, for the first time in George's experience, his voice was devoid of bluster or bravado. He faced the might of the legal profession with a quiet courage far more impressive than the savagery he had shown to the men of the Preventive Service in the past.

'Guilty'.

A murmur ran around the room. George's gaze returned to Justice Park in time to see him frown and raise a hand to stop the proceedings.

'I am aware that the prisoners are in the hands of able and learned gentlemen of the bar or I should explain to them the consequences of pleading Guilty; but, as they are so assisted, I have no doubt that they act under the advice of their Counsel and I shall interpose no opinion of my own.'

George noted Platt's slight nod at the recognition of his professional expertise. He saw that Twiss was following events with the same curiosity as he felt himself, noting the minute signs that revealed each participant's opinion on the proceedings.

One by one, each man echoed the plea. Wilson spoke last, teeth clenched to stop them from chattering but just as resolute as the others. The Judge's frown deepened.

There was a short pause before the clerk read out more charges of a similar nature. All related to running uncustomed goods, bearing firearms and, in some cases, shooting at preventive officers. None referred to the murder of Richard Morgan. The clerk passed through the shootings of Wynn and Spillane, along with two other men, Brady and Millings.

George remained at the bar with his second-in-command throughout, while his men shuffled to and fro as directed by the bailiff. Only two others were charged with every offence: Gilham and Dennard. George shifted his weight from right foot to left. The prosecution had certainly been busy since the committal, presumably following up information elicited from approvers by the promise of a reward. If he'd doubted Platt's word about the quality of Horne's testimony, the length of the list confirmed there was no point in dwelling on the man's duplicity. As sure as he could be that Horne would not have informed on Quested or Smeed, in gratitude for their assistance on the night of Hogben's attack on his sister, George thought it likely that it was Mary Giles' kindness to the young woman afterwards that made Horne so adamant that Giles was not present at Morgan's death — which was of course true.

Some of the information might have come from James Bushell. Judging by the delay before their arrests, he'd not been much help to the preventive men but he could hardly be blamed for letting something slip during the interrogation that must surely have followed the amputation of his leg. The combination of pain and fever was guaranteed to loosen even the most loyal tongue.

One thing that puzzled George was the inclusion of Wilson in the charges. The man's plea, given under oath before God and surely hard for him to utter, was not a lie to benefit himself but it did exaggerate his role in their runs. Not only had he never carried a firearm, or even a bat, but he was a hard man to dislike. George suspected the evidence came from someone with petty concerns of a private nature, something he despised because Wilson was more virtuous than any of them in every other way. Still, the verdict of the court was of less consequence to Wilson than to most, his death a far greater worry to his friends and family than it was to him. Even as he thought that, George saw that the same logic could have condemned Wilson: he was already dead — why not give his name rather than that of a man with brighter prospects? Backed into a corner, he might have done the same himself, however unfair it might be.

All in all, given the long list of charges and the number of his men facing them, George thought there must be at least one more approver. He'd heard so many rumours on that score that he paid little heed to them any more. Some had the Blues undermined by a spy who had been reporting their movements for half a year; the mystery man variously hailed from Deal, Walmer or Dover. Others had an Aldington man who, despite the risk to himself and his family,

425

spoke out in defence of a community being torn apart by violence. Others had a conspiracy, with the Sussex gangs collaborating with the authorities to put their rivals out of action. George knew that for nonsense, partly through his contacts in those gangs and partly from an objective assessment of the risks and rewards of such a strategy. With free-trade in Sussex under as much pressure from the Blockade as it was in Kent, freeing the authorities to concentrate on activities there would be no help. Added to that, like the Blues, they were short of men and had no capacity to capitalise on any opportunities that might arise in Kent.

George had considered exacting payment from the approvers for their betrayal. If he could have dispatched them before the trial, giving himself and his men a hope of acquittal, he might have done so but Horne and Bushell at least were kept carefully guarded in gaol. Hellard had no intention of letting all his hard work in apprehending the fugitives go to waste and took personal charge of protecting the evidence. It would be easy to wreak revenge on any of the witnesses after the trial but George found himself with no appetite for more fruitless bloodshed.

Abandoning such thoughts, he dragged himself back to the proceedings. To every charge, he and his men entered the same plea, irrespective of whether or not they had been present on the night in question. In fact, as far as he could recall, the charges were substantially correct. Some men in the armed parties had evaded the law, and some of the accused were rarely armed but, by and large, they had indeed assembled, borne arms and, when necessary, shot at preventive officers.

Only when all the charges had been read, did the position become clear. Fourteen of them were guilty by their own admission of smuggling and bearing firearms. Ten would stand trial for the murder of Richard Morgan; of these, only Robert Bailey and Thomas Wheeler were not charged with other offences.

George felt the tension across his chest as he realised that the decisive moment had come. His future, and the futures of the men around him, all hinged on the coming minutes. He stood firm at the bar, waiting while the other nine defendants were mustered around him. Sam and Rob Bailey stood on his left, along with Hogben and the Wyor brothers. To his right were Smeed, Wheeler, Gilham and Dennard.

While the jury was being empanelled, George thought about his co-defendants. It was strange how they'd taken their places, their positions reflecting their roles in what had passed. The men at his left hand had protected the lives of the Blues time after time and yet it was largely their fault that they all now faced death as close as they ever had. They were dangerous men and George could not blame the people of the parish for wanting to be free of their worst excesses. The group on his right was a different matter, not one of them a risk to the local community and Wheeler perhaps the most grievously out of place. True, he was there on the night of the murder but he was not even in the armed parties. Inoffensive as he was, his presence was more of a mystery than Wilson's.

George had no wish to die but it was as much for his fellows as himself that he now gripped the bar grimly in both hands and waited for the drama to unfold.

When the jury was in place and the court was ready to hear the case, the Solicitor-General stood. The room had fallen quiet, with both participants and spectators confused when each set of charges was met with pleas of Guilty, but now the quiet deepened into silence. All present awaited Twiss's opening statement in anticipation.

All, that is, except for the defendants. Only they and the counsels for prosecution and defence knew what to expect and now they waited for the first phase to be delivered. Platt had been adamant that he could bargain on their behalf and now George held his breath, the suspense almost unbearable.

Twiss addressed the Judge as if no one else were present. 'If it please the Court, since the prisoners have entered pleas of Guilty to other charges, by which they have forfeited their lives to the laws of their country, it is not my intention to offer any evidence against them on the charge of murder.'

Murmurs rippled around the courtroom, as people tried to grasp the significance of the statement. If the men were to hang for admitted smuggling offences, the prosecutor was saying that there was no sense in trying them for murder. Justice Park banged his gavel; it took several attempts to restore order.

George returned to his study of Park's expression. He saw that the judge had guessed what was coming. Knowing that there was more at stake than the precise nature of the crime for which the accused men would shortly be hanged, Park said nothing, raised a hand to still the crowd, and then fixed his attention on Twiss.

The prosecutor continued evenly. 'I cannot say that their lives will be saved but, as far as my recommendation would go, they should have the benefit of it. At all events, they will most probably be sent out of the country for the remainder of their lives.'

The murmurs broke out again, louder this time, as the spectators realised that two of the accused men, Robert Bailey and Thomas Wheeler, were about to be wholly acquitted because they had been indicted solely for the murder. Park had to pound the Bench to regain control. Silence restored, he motioned the clerk to put to the bar the fourteen prisoners who had pleaded Guilty to smuggling offences.

George watched as Bailey and Wheeler were singled out. Neither man could hide his relief or joy, nor did he expect them to. Tom Wheeler's steady gaze settled on Wilson in brief and final farewell before he left the room without a backward glance. Rob Bailey lingered longer, his eyes darting restlessly between his brother and uncle, then muttered a promise to visit soon. George had no doubt that the commitment would be honoured: the Baileys had many faults but their loyalty to each other knew no bounds. His own feelings were in turmoil, part of him rejoicing for the freed men but another part bitterly jealous of their good fortune. He wished that it were he who would take the afternoon coach back to Ashford, yearning for his wife's kisses and his children's hugs to soothe away the sorrows and deprivations of the past three months. Valiantly trying to suppress his misery, he let the clerk push him into line. On one side of him were John and Sam Bailey, Dennard, Giles, Gilham, Higgins, Hogben, Pierce and Quested. On the other, Smeed and Wilson stood with the Wyor brothers. After all his years of meticulous planning, their fates had been decided by pure chance. Along with a dozen others never arrested, the acquitted men were guilty of the smuggling charges not extended to them and yet now they walked free. George knew that he and the men beside him might never taste freedom again.

Justice Park perused his notes in silence for some time before beginning his address. Finally, he cleared his throat and the court fell silent to hear what he had to say. He fixed his gaze on the prisoners.

'You have pleaded Guilty to an offence of a most heinous nature, the commission of which struck terror into every well-disposed mind. You assembled in numerous bodies to aid in the running of uncustomed goods, and in so doing, fired upon persons who were only doing their duty. Perhaps, in the darkness of the night, it might be difficult to fix the crime of murder on ten of your number but still you have confessed your guilt of a very serious offence. Perhaps no human eye saw the hand that actually committed the murder, and I doubt not that the Solicitor-General has exercised a sound discretion in the decision, but it is manifest that he has dealt with you most humanely for, if any of you had been convicted of the murder, you certainly would have been executed.

'I am in no way a party to the course that has been adopted. I should not myself feel warranted in recommending you to the mercy of the Sovereign, though the Solicitor-General has promised to do so and doubtless will keep his word.

'You have admitted that you assembled in gangs of as many as eighty — a gang numerous enough to overawe the peaceable part of the community. These things cannot be suffered to go on with impunity. I trust that the present proceedings will have a proper effect and convince offenders that the arm of the law is long enough, and sufficiently powerful, to reach and punish even the most distant and desperate.

'It must be made known throughout the country that, if an offence of this nature were again committed, no mercy would be shown to the offenders. I now repeat what I said to the Grand Jury: if persons in the higher stations of life were not to purchase smuggled goods, there would be an end to smuggling but many persons labour under the delusion that defrauding the Revenue is no crime. It is a serious offence against the laws of man, and a breach of the laws of man is also an offence against the laws of God — and smuggling can lead to the commission of the greatest crimes, even the crime of murder.

'If the mercy of our gracious Sovereign is extended to you, I trust you will receive it with due gratitude, and be still more grateful to God, whom you have so grievously offended. For my part, I sentence you to death. You are to be severally hanged by the neck until you be dead, on Monday the fifth day of February next.'

A clock struck the half-hour just as the clerk recorded the termination of the Assizes, the trial of the Blues having taken only an hour and a half. As George followed his men past the Bench on

429

their way back to gaol, he heard Park mutter wryly.

'Well, when I came into court this morning, I expected to be detained until Tuesday.'

Their trial had barely caused a ripple in the life of the judiciary but, even if their appeal for mercy succeeded, George knew that their own lives were about to be torn asunder. He did not underestimate the suffering that lay ahead, expecting that some of his men would wish for death long before payment of their debt to society had been exacted in full.

Jem

As they were led back to their cells, Wilson stumbled in the yard. Jem was at his side in a flash. They were forbidden to speak and had only minutes before being locked up again. Thrilled to be reunited in the disorganised squalor of Newgate, they were parted all too soon when Jem was sent on to Maidstone. When he arrived at the imposing new gaol, his friends occupied two clean but Spartan cells, each built to hold six men. That seemed to suggest that the Governor preferred not to let lesser offenders mingle with the notorious smugglers sent down from London. Along with Pierce and Higgins, Jem found himself shoved in with Dennard, Gilham and the Baileys. When Wilson eventually turned up with Quested, they were thrown in with Ransley, Giles, Hogben, Wheeler and the Wyors. Eight in each cell was tight enough, without them being the robust outdoorsmen that they were. It seemed as if they might have been sorted by size, with each group containing three of the largest and one of the smallest men in the Blues.

Jem had debated trying to force a change in their accommodation, perhaps by starting a fight with his cell-mates, but had two reasons for not doing so. Firstly, he might be thrown into solitary confinement and never see Wilson again. Secondly, at least Wilson was with Quested, the best man to care for him. All in all, stirring things up might only make matters worse.

Wilson gave him a sidelong smile.

'You all right?' Jem murmured, keeping his face turned away from the guards.

'Aye, better than I've been in an age. Thou hast been given a second chance.' His eyes shone with happiness. 'Promise me thou wilt make the best of it? Thy word?'

The surge of resentment Jem felt for this man who kept demanding promises that he might not be able to keep was instantly washed away by the knowledge that he'd want the same in Wilson's place. He nodded. 'And I'll think of you every day that I'm granted. Now let's get along. God's making life hard enough on you without giving these bastards an excuse to help him out.'

He helped Wilson to his feet and half-carried him inside. Wilson might have managed without his support but Jem knew that there would be few more moments of closeness before their final parting. After their capture, Wilson was at the point of death for weeks. Jem had been sure that their journey to trial would kill him but, against the odds, he not only held on but rallied in Maidstone gaol. Conditions were good. Relatives brought in food and other comforts, with Wilson's family as attentive as any, and their loving care helped to counter the effects of weeks on the run, although it could do nothing to stem the tide of Wilson's tuberculosis.

Jem spent every hour of every day in silent misery at being separated in his lover's dying days. He had accepted during the last night of their flight that Wilson's death was inevitable and now awaited it with mixed emotions, alternately hoping for a merciful release and then desperately wishing for more time. With contact limited to fleeting glimpses when they were moved around the gaol for one reason or another, his spirits initially rose each time Wilson seemed better and then plummeted each time he seemed worse. But, as time passed, those simple responses became confused and he wondered how many more false hopes and bitter disappointments he could take. When he found himself resenting Wilson for surviving another downturn, his heart grew heavy with guilt. Through it all, he shut himself off from his friends, no longer caring what they knew or what they thought.

George

George followed a guard through seemingly interminable corridors until they reached an interview room at the front of Maidstone prison. After the conviction, he and his men were returned there to await the outcome of their appeal. He assumed their captors deemed the risk of the journey back to London to be greater than the risk of a gaolbreak being organised by their supporters in the vicinity. If so, they were right: with all their best men incarcerated, there was no one to set them free. Their only hope might have been Rob Bailey but he had been under constant surveillance since his release. He still visited faithfully and brought provisions for his kin but his assistance could go no further. Along with most of his men, George had kin on the outside but, while they had strong backs good for carrying a pair of tubs of a night, they were not men to mastermind escapes from heavily guarded prisons. Only his son, young Georgie, plotted complicated schemes for their liberation but George had strictly forbidden him to take any action. Even if his discipline failed, Eliza would watch the boy like a hawk. One thing on which George's mind was set — if Georgie was ever to embark for the colonies, it would be as a free man.

While Newgate was a survivor of the last century, woefully inadequate for the burgeoning London underworld of the King's regency and reign, Maidstone was the newest prison in the country. Solidly built from Kentish ragstone quarried on the site itself, the buildings were not only impressive but more comfortable than some of his men's homes. On arrival, they had been ordered to scrub themselves from head to toe. There was no need for the order to be enforced. Only too keen to be rid of the fleas and lice crawling over his body, they rubbed until the scabs and encrusted sores came away and the blood flowed freely. Once George was dressed in the fresh clothes that Eliza had dropped off, he began to feel something of his old self.

Now, the first phase of the plan had been achieved and he awaited news of the second, all the while knowing that a long and uncertain road lay ahead even if they succeeded. He had the wit and vision to see beyond their present plight to a brighter future but knew that the chances of any, much less all, of them reaching that singular outcome were slim indeed.

Now he walked with the same quiet self-respect he'd always projected, resisting the temptation to scratch at the raw flesh left by the first of what he expected to be many ordeals. When he entered the room and sat opposite his visitor, he followed the man's eyes as they evaluated him and then raised an eyebrow enquiringly.

'You look better every time I call,' Platt said, his tone sincere.

'Smell better too, I'll wager.'

Platt gave a wry shrug. Far too much the gentleman to have commented on George's decline after the committal, he now made no attempt to deny the depths from which his client had risen.

George had spent much of the past week considering the day of the trial, from the length of the charges to the numbers of witnesses arrayed against them. Many times, his thoughts drifted back to what Platt had said about the meagre information that Horne and Bushell had so reluctantly furnished to the authorities. Any anger that he might have felt towards Horne had long since faded, remembering the man's admission that he was afraid after Giles's brush with death and finding it difficult to blame a man for fearing the same fate. With Platt's assurance that Horne's evidence post-dated the first set of arrests, he became more interested in how they came to be apprehended in the first place. Finding it played more on his mind as time went by, he began to wonder what Platt knew of the matter and decided to find out.

'Do you know who turned us in?'

Platt studied him for a few seconds. 'Retribution?'

George pursed his lips and then slowly shook his head. 'No sense in bolting the stable door after the horse has bolted.' Whether their fate was the hangmen or the colonies, there was no longer any point in sending warnings to the local people.

'Officially, no, I don't know. The prosecution guaranteed anonymity. That's why they had to subpoena half the county, ready to back up their information a piece at a time. Unofficially, I hear that there were two approvers.' He paused, presumably to build the mystery, before giving up what he did know. 'One is said to hail from Deal and I have heard the name William Marsh. Local opinion has the other as James Spratford.'

George frowned, considering what might link the former leader of the Burmarsh traders, now turned respectable butcher, and Bill Marsh, a recent newcomer to the Blues. Only moments passed before he saw the common denominator: Hogben. He had served under Spratford and he had recruited Marsh. George did not suspect him of betrayal for two reasons: firstly, he had always been loyal to the men he served, sometimes to a fault, and secondly because he would not be with them now if the plan was his. No, he might be the link but he was not the cause.

Spratford's reasons were transparent enough. In recent years, he'd been trying to better himself by taking on minor civic duties and George guessed that his motives for informing on them had more to do with gaining political advantage than any direct financial inducements. He might have miscalculated there because, no matter how disillusioned the locals might have become in recent years, he doubted that they'd carry on buying their meat from a butcher turned approver. Perhaps revenge on the man who had triumphed over the Blockade for so much longer than himself would be reward enough.

'The local women seem particularly resentful about Mr Spratford,' Platt commented with a wink, 'But no doubt you'll hear more about that from your nearest and dearest in due course. His establishment has suffered several indignities and I expect things to get worse before they get better.'

George smiled at the understatement. Spratford might have taken on more than he bargained for in the wives, sweethearts, mothers and sisters he crossed by turning on the trade — those of the Blues, to be sure, but probably a good many others who knew it could just as easily be their men rotting in gaol. Marsh's strategy was probably wiser: take the Blockade's reward and use it to start a new life far from Aldington.

Coming to the reason for his visit, Platt said, 'Good news.'

'Our appeal?'

The barrister nodded. 'Twiss was as good as his word and, luckily for us, it counts for something. Your execution has been respited until further signification of His Majesty's pleasure. Off the record, I'd say you won't be feeling the rope, whatever else.'

'All of us?'

'All of you. The governor of the gaol received a letter from the Secretary of State this morning. With the Solicitor-General's recommendation for clemency behind your appeal, no one is likely to oppose it.'

George felt winded, as if a physical blow had landed on his pigeon chest. He hadn't expected relief to pack such a punch. His troubled sleep ever since the trial had testified to his doubts about their strategy. None of them stood much chance of acquittal but pleading guilty even to limited charges had been a gamble. While he and

Dickon Wyor, perhaps Sam Bailey and Jem Smeed too, might have been convicted of murder, there had been a possibility that some of the others might have persuaded a jury of their innocence as Dick Wraight had done before them. As it was, they had traded the hanging of some for the transportation of all. Now a brighter future, while still over a distant horizon, seemed to beckon more strongly.

'What will that mean for us?' He had a good idea of the answer to his question but wanted to hear Platt's latest thinking, in the light of recent developments.

Platt sat back in his chair and took out a tobacco pouch. He passed George a cheap clay pipe and then took his time over filling the deep bowl of his own brier. George accepted the offer and matched his solicitor's movements.

'I'll not lie to you, George.'

In all the years they'd known one another, Platt always retained the same formal courtesy, addressing his client as 'Mr Ransley' or 'Sir' as if he were a gentleman. George knew that his given name was used now in comfort and not disrespect.

'It means your sentence is commuted to transportation for life to Van Diemen's Land. You can never return to England. To do so would be to risk hanging, or permanent imprisonment in a place you would be wise to avoid. Before transportation will be temporary imprisonment on a hulk anchored at Portsmouth. Temporary might mean months. However, it might just as easily mean years.'

He studied the pipe in his hand for some time before he continued. 'The hulks are an abomination, an affront to a civilised nation. They are nothing like Maidstone prison. Beside them, even Newgate gaol might be an 'otel.'

George felt his brief flame of optimism gutter. What lay ahead might be beyond their endurance. Even if their bodies held up, their minds might not. Before it died completely, the flicker of hope ignited coals of anger in the pit of his stomach. Yes, he chose to steal — and later to order men to kill to protect their hauls — but he had not chosen to be born poor in a society where poverty meant grinding hardship and early death. He refused to accept that institutionalised brutality was a fair response to a man's desperate attempts to eke out some kind of living from his lowly station.

The two men smoked in silence, barrister giving convict time to absorb his situation. Finally, George spoke.

'If we live long enough to make the voyage, and if we survive it, what awaits us at our journey's end?'

Platt inhaled deeply, clearly considering the question.

'That is, perhaps, in the hands of you and your men. In Van Diemen's Land, you will find penal colonies that men dread even more profoundly than they dread the hulks. You will also find a fertile country where labour is short. I advise you to use every means at your disposal to make your men understand that there is a chance, a slim chance but a chance nonetheless, of a good life for them there. Their future depends as much on their conduct as on the vagaries of fate. I am told they have comported themselves commendably in gaol. You would do well to persuade them to maintain that record through the tribulations to come.'

George considered the picture that Platt painted. Months or years rotting aboard a foetid hulk, then months more at sea, only to be ejected in a foreign land with nothing but a criminal record to recommend them. He knew that some of his men would prefer to hang and be done with it. Only one thing might make it bearable.

'I heard talk in gaol of men's families joining them in the colonies.'

Platt nodded. 'That is true in some, possibly many, cases. That too is partially in your hands. When you reach the colony, provided that the ship's register remembers you favourably, you are likely to be assigned as a worker to a prospering settler. If you satisfy your employer, and if your application is approved by the appropriate offices, your family may be permitted to join you.'

Despite the numerous caveats, George felt hope stir once more. Nothing, not one thing in the entire world, was more important to him than to be reunited with Eliza and the children. 'How would a convict pay for their passage?'

'That, at least, is not an obstacle. His Majesty's Government permits such families to travel on convict ships, with their expenses paid by the parish. Their journey would be as arduous as yours but it would not cost you a farthing.'

George gave a slow, deliberate nod of his head. 'That gives a man a reason to go on living. I'll put your points to the others in the strongest terms.' He allowed himself a grim smile. The strongest terms indeed. He would not allow the likes of Hogben to endanger his chance of seeing his family again. He knew he would have solid backup from the likes of Pierce, Quested and Giles to protect their shared goal.

'Meanwhile, there's little enough I can do,' Platt continued. 'But I hear you and your men are to be held on the *York* and *Leviathan*. I know the master of the *Leviathan* from his days at Dover and he's a man of business, no more and no less. I'll make arrangements for you to be in the *Leviathan* party and receive the best possible treatment. I'll do what I can for the other party but I can give no assurances there. What I hear of the master of the *York* is not encouraging.'

George nodded his appreciation. Even after so much had gone awry, his contacts and the generosity with which he'd recompensed those who helped the Blues still paid dividends from time to time but he was left with one sadness.

'Is there nothing to be done for Wilson?'

Platt's regret was clear. 'The only mercy for him would have been in a hemp cravat but, if he'd taken that route, you'd all have followed in his footsteps. I'll press for you to be kept as you have been. That way he'll go aboard the *Leviathan* with you.'

Sickened, George nodded grimly. The gentle waggoner's mate deserved better than a lingering death in filth and ignominy. He wondered whether to ask for the groups to be changed but doubted that Platt wielded such influence. As defence counsel, his motives in suggesting any alteration might be questioned. And, while he could defend a request to keep a sick man with his leader, it would be harder to explain why another man, not even of his kin, should be moved to keep him company. George would not relish trying to explain that himself.

He said only, 'It won't be long now.'

It was a surprise to all that Wilson was still with them.

Hog

The closed cart jolted to a halt and would have pitched its occupants forward had they not been packed in almost too tight to breathe. Like his companions, Hog wore irons on wrists and ankles, chains between the chafing bands weighing him down and punctuating his every move with the clank of link on link. Any faint hope of escape he might have harboured soon faded with the realisation that he would remain manacled, unable to swim to freedom and unlikely to find help in the Warren, a maze of naval workshops that depended on cheap convict labour to fill their orders.

The rear doors swung open to reveal two pistol-bearing guards. One was a head taller than the other but otherwise they were alike: two fat, dirty peas in a pod. Hog glared belligerently into the barrel pointed directly at his face. Every guard he encountered quickly realised that he was a truly dangerous man, not sufficiently concerned about his own or anyone else's skin to be easily coerced. Now, though, he was more interested in finding out where he was to spend the months awaiting a ship to Van Diemen's Land than in causing trouble for hapless guards. He climbed meekly out of the cart and studied the quayside, seeing for the first time the hulks of which they'd heard so much in gaol.

Hog had seen plenty of ships of the line during the years after his impressment, many of them third-raters like the two now before his eyes. Any resemblance ended with their type. The *York* and *Leviathan* made a sorry sight, causing Hog to glance involuntarily at another in their number who was well-acquainted with the former glories of such vessels. As usual, Smeed gave little outward sign of emotion but his sad scrutiny did not escape Hog, who returned to his own inspection.

Unsurprisingly, the ships were not rigged but, more than that, they had been brutally de-masted to leave only jagged remnants of the main and fore masts. If that was not indignity enough, a line of washing hung between the sorry stumps on the nearest vessel. The soiled rags that passed for clean laundry did not bode well for the state of dirty clothes. Hog squinted at the stern of a boat alongside the hulk and identified the vessel as the *York*. He let his eyes wander over the hull, past empty gun-ports secured with iron grilles and up to the ramshackle huts clustered on the decks.

What a fate for warships that had defended Britain's shores from Napoleon — to lie at anchor in Portsmouth until they were too rotten even to serve as receptacles for the lowest levels of human society.

Hog had no such fine thoughts on the subject. Uppermost in his mind was the throbbing pain in his thigh. He had managed to procure enough spirits and opiates during his weeks in gaol to dull its edge but, unable to bring any on the journey, he was now rediscovering the worst extremes of his condition. On the hulks, he expected there to be few visitors and probably therefore few opportunities to bring in supplies from outside. No doubt it would be possible to obtain the substances he needed ashore but how would he pay with no money or rob with no weapons? He knew that he might be embarking on one of the worst periods in a life replete with bad times and that knowledge only fuelled his depression.

A second pair of guards came past the *York* and joined their fellows. Alone they would have seemed rough and filthy but, beside their colleagues, they looked almost respectable. Perhaps the *Leviathan* was not quite such a hell-hole as its sister ship. Hog stared down into the stinking water around the *York*. Effluent floated on its surface, drifting lazily on the current towards the *Leviathan*. He hoped the ships did not draw water for their inmates from the estuary.

The elder of the second pair of guards read names from a roster.

'Ransley, George. Wilson, James.'

One by one, the Blues stepped forward for the *Leviathan*.

'Giles, Charles. Wyor, Richard.'

It became clear that they were to remain in the same groups to which they'd been assigned in gaol.

'Hogben, James.'

Hog joined the others.

'Quested, James. Wyor, William.'

One of the first pair of guards spoke up in an unfamiliar accent that Hog was not to know marked him as coming from Birmingham. 'The rest with us.'

Hog had no interest in how they were split but knew even before he looked that Pierce would not welcome continued separation from Quested and Giles. A quick study of both groups revealed that the Baileys and Wyors were content to stay with their kin, while Smeed resented having to abandon his sickly workmate.

There had been a time when Hog valued friendship as much as the next man but that time was long past. He was infinitely more troubled by being separated from his chemical comforters than from any human company. If pressed for an opinion, he would have declared himself equally satisfied with either group.

Not that his opinion mattered. They had no say in how they were divided and had soon learned that things went easier for them if they did as they were told. Ransley took the lead in their walk from the drop-off point to the *Leviathan*. Behind him, Quested and Giles flanked Wilson, who looked as if a puff of wind might blow him over at any moment. The Wyors followed, the younger trailing behind the elder.

When they were free, Hog had liked the Wyors as much as he liked any man but, during their time in prison, he had tired of what he saw as their weakness. Billy seemed more afraid than a man of their ilk had a right to be, subservient with the guards and sly with their fellow convicts. Dickon was belligerent enough for them both when it came to others but his loyalty to his brother irritated Hog, who had never had anyone offer him such unswerving devotion.

The more he thought about that devotion, the more infuriated he became with men like Giles and Quested, who showed such friendship to others in the group. He stared angrily at Wilson's back and thought how much he'd like to vent his irritation on that pathetic excuse for a man. It would have been easy to do so were it not that Wilson was never alone, tended dutifully day after day, as if such care would make any difference to the outcome. The man would die, soon, and Hog was at a loss to understand why his companions wasted their energy in fighting his fate.

When they drew closer to the *Leviathan*, Hog saw that it was in marginally better order than the *York*. For one thing, it was cleaner. For another, the huts on deck were strongly built and properly roofed. Unknown to Hog, the *Leviathan* was the older vessel by nearly two decades and had served as a prison since its return from war in eighteen-sixteen, three years longer than the *York*. Rather than any natural advantage, its condition was due to its captain's belief that running a ship well — even one that would never sail again — was easier than running it badly. Oblivious to the reason for his good fortune, Hog was torn between relief that he might not have drawn the short straw for once and suspicion that it would be harder than ever to acquire alcohol or opium aboard a competently administered hulk.

His companions eyed their new accommodation with the same wordless curiosity as himself, following the guards' instructions without question, making their way on board and then forward to where ladders led below decks. As they passed a line full of the *Leviathan's* washing, Hog saw that the clothes were somewhat cleaner than the rags fluttering above the *York*. Looking closer, he noted grimly that they were speckled as if with pepper — he shuddered when a long-forgotten memory surfaced in his mind. Wherever bodies were packed closely together, vermin surely followed. Men fought a running battle with the bloodthirsty parasites in the Navy and Hog gagged when he recalled how he and a friend had tried to rid themselves of the incessant irritation. Convinced that a hot flat-iron would put an end to their misery, they were appalled to find that the crackling explosions of the swollen bodies simply soaked the shirts with blood. With barely enough soap to freshen the washing as it was, there was no hope of removing the rusty stains and their endeavours were ultimately proved futile when reinforcements infested them as soon as they cleared a space.

The new arrivals descended only one ladder before moving into a corridor that ran the full length of the upper deck; it was narrow enough that even a small man might rest a hand on either wall without stretching. Heavy iron grilles divided off the wards on either side. The guard stopped by a grille on the right, opened a door set into it and then turned to face them.

'You'll spend your nights locked in the ward and your days working ashore. The irons stay on. Do as you're told and we'll rub along fine.'

For once, Hog followed his friends' example and kept his head down. There'd be time enough later to test the limits.

It was Quested who spoke up. 'This man's sick. Is there a doctor on board?'

The guard's gaze settled on Wilson briefly and then returned to a fixed point in space, refusing to acknowledge them as human beings worthy of eye contact. He gave a cold laugh and said, 'Aye, a doctor comes aboard now 'n' then, but I wouldn't wager on him getting to your friend any time soon.'

The set of Quested's shoulders declared his anger but he too seemed to decide that their first day was not the time to make trouble. They trooped dejectedly into the ward and stood in silence while the heavy iron locks slid into place and the guards' footsteps receded along the corridor. Presumably work would start tomorrow but it seemed as if they would be left in peace for the time being.

Hog watched Ransley take in their surroundings without comment, then made his own evaluation. The ward was some fifteen by eighteen feet, not generous but bearable. Then he saw the limp hammocks hanging from hooks along the hull and, counting twelve, his spirits sank. What might be tolerable for seven friends would be torture when their group was made up to a dozen by strangers. He was thankful not to be on the *York* with Higgins. The gamekeeper had reacted badly to their confinement, something that seemed as much as a shock to him as to his cell-mates. Countrymen all, many of them had never lived at such close quarters before so perhaps it was a mercy that only one was thus afflicted. Longing for the open air himself, Hog understood how Higgins felt but, wracked by withdrawal symptoms and freshly rediscovered pain, he had no tolerance for the man's nocturnal whimpering and whining. He lacked the discernment to know it but he was showing the same conditioned response to brutality that perpetuated the life they led: if he could endure the wretched conditions of a man-of-war after being impressed, Higgins could endure the same misery aboard a hulk and should be grateful that he wasn't likely to be cut down by a cannonball any time soon.

Tales of the hulks were not exaggerated. If anything, they failed to convey how rank and putrid the wards were in the absence of adequate sanitation and ventilation. The dimly lit, foul-smelling space was choking. Even the air coming through the barred gun-ports was poisoned by stale sewage. Had Hog hailed from the East End, he would have been all too familiar with the onslaught on his senses. As it was, he had never smelled its like, even in his Navy days. The cramped gun-decks on a ship-of-the-line reeked of unwashed bodies and, in rough seas, a good measure of vomit but not the rotting waste that assailed him now. Such products were jettisoned neatly overboard, while the ship ploughed onwards into the endless ocean. Only at anchor did things get a little ripe but nothing to compare with the hulk moorings. Hog longed for the fierce winds that bathed the marshes in bracing salt air fresh from the Channel. Thinking of them brought a rush of homesickness, memories of how their character changed — from the hail-heavy gales of winter to hot puffs of breath on a summer's day. He gave a bitter laugh, then shrugged as he found his companions' eyes on him. He could think of only one good thing to say about their predicament.

'Thank Christ it's winter.'

It was a feeble attempt at humour but Wilson responded with a faint smile. With most to fear from the cold, perhaps even he would not trade it for the insects and infestations that spring would surely bring. Tracing a line in the greasy residue that coated the deck with the tip of his boot, Hog wondered idly whether a man became used to such filth and hoped that time would make him oblivious to the stench.

Buckets stood in two corners of the ward, the floor around them stained and rotting from constant spills. Quested inspected them disdainfully, his expression revealing that the first contained soil. He lifted a ladle from the second.

'I wouldn't be in a hurry to drink that,' he said sourly.

Hog was silent but knew that they might have little choice. Barely a day passed when one or another of them was not suffering from sickness or diarrhoea. That was unlikely to improve under the conditions in which they now found themselves.

Wilson leaned against the iron bars over the gun-port, breath rasping as he tried to fill the bloody remnants of his lungs with icy air from outside. Hog grimaced when the man began to cough, the first shallow barks quickly escalating into hawking retches that brought the bile into his own throat. He glanced around his companions, wondering not for the first time whether he was the only one repulsed by witnessing death play with its victim. In Ransley, he saw uncharacteristic pity; Hog had never understood Wilson's popularity but he could not deny it. Seeing no reaction in the elder Wyor, only in the younger brother did he find a faint reflection of his own discomfort with the closing act now being played out in front of them.

Giles moved to Wilson's side, showing no reaction when the ailing man spat a bloody wad of phlegm through the grille, giving silent comfort through his presence. Quested looped the free end of the hammock furthest from the gun-port over its hook, instinctively allocating the warmest spot to Wilson. Hog couldn't be bothered to protest and didn't much care anyway. He'd spent too many nights passed out under the stars to worry about the cold now. He watched as Quested helped his patient into the high, flimsy bed. At least, on the plus side, Wilson was a dignified invalid who, as yet, had never missed the bucket with the waste products of his puny body. Hog hoped that held up but bagged the hammock at the far side of the ward as a precaution anyway.

Soon they were all stretched out in the grubby canvas slings.

Everything aboard was well worn and stained with an array of human by-products but the residues on the hammocks were old and odourless, at least in comparison with the ambient stench. Hog stared at the ceiling and began to catalogue his agonies. It was a technique he'd developed in the aftermath of his gunshot wound, before he learned that bathing pain in a drug-induced haze was easier than disciplining his mind to ignore it.

As always, the dog-leg thigh bone was at the centre of his suffering. It resonated with each beat of his slowing pulse, sending pains rippling towards knee and hip. Perhaps the bone might have healed properly if he had not run all those years before, eager to escape from the surgeon into whose care he had been discharged by a magistrate who'd been convinced that he would not recover enough to resume his nefarious ways. Ignorant of medicine, it never occurred to him that a broken bone could cause such unending agony. He thought he'd be left with a limp and that was that. Stone cold sober for the first time in years, he grudgingly admitted that he'd made the wrong decision. It had ruined his life.

That was a dangerous line of thought for Hog, taking him to places he did not want to visit. With more regrets than he could count, he was most troubled by the old woman's death six months earlier. He still found it hard to believe that he would kill an eighty-year-old woman but, as he had no memory of so much of his life since his injury, he could not be sure of his innocence. No one had publicly accused him of the murder but he knew that most of the Blues believed he was the guilty party. Some were disgusted by it, while others couldn't see why the demise of someone already so close to death provoked such outrage. It was the fact that he shared the feeling of outrage that made him so doubtful that, even in a drunken rampage, he could possibly have committed such a crime but also made it equally impossible for him to envisage that one of his fellow Blues could have done it.

Blocking the doubts from his mind, Hog drifted on to a happier memory — his wife's last visit to Maidstone. It was years since they had looked at each other closely and he'd been surprised to find that he still liked what he saw. Ann was tired, burdened by her fears for the future and how she was to manage his seven children, but she remained strong and handsome in her way. He wished he had not let her down, repeatedly and in more ways than he wanted to count, and that he'd been as prudent with his money as some of his friends. It went without saying that Eliza Ransley was well provided for, their leader's shrewd mind arranging his personal affairs with the same efficiency as it organised his business but Hog knew that several of the others had done almost as well for their families, who would continue to live comfortably while his kin would depend on the parish for their daily bread.

Only one thing cheered him now. He had not expected Ann to follow him to Van Diemen's Land, even if she were given leave to do so, but he saw a spark of fondness for him flicker into life during her regular visits to the prison. Knowing that he had given her every reason to hate him, he felt undeserving of her readiness to forgive and, slowly, a resolve to do better grew inside him. He doubted that his two eldest children, separated from the others by the war years and ready to strike out alone, would embark for a strange land to join a convict father who had done little but knock them about since his return from his enforced naval service. Perhaps, though, Ann would join him with the younger ones and he could make a fresh start.

Gallows humour fought to the surface again as he contemplated the notion of a fresh start as a convict. Only a reprobate as dissolute as he was could see being a felon in that light. Still, the fact remained that in the new land he would be indistinguishable from a man like Giles, a respectable tradesman who would no doubt soon live down his single conviction for a crime that was, after all, better than theft.

The brief amusement faded when Hog looked down at his hands, clasped on his chest in a vain attempt to stop them shaking. During his first month in Maidstone gaol, he imbibed a steady if unobtrusive stream of alcohol and laudanum brought in by Rob Bailey. Thinking of the fresh start and wanting Ann to have something better than an opium-eater awaiting her, he abruptly stopped taking the laudanum. Unfortunately, the only way he could withstand his craving for it was to increase his alcohol consumption. That didn't trouble him too much at the time, given that in his mind it was only drink, but, now robbed of anaesthetic, he would gladly have swallowed any drug to return to the oblivion that had so long protected him.

With a self-discipline he had not known he possessed, he forced the self-pity and regret from his mind. He must be prepared for it to take time to obtain any remedy for his ills and, meanwhile, he would have to live with them. Had he but known it, his mindset was not so far from that of his sick cell-mate: what could not be cured must be endured.

To distract himself, Hog began to listen to the jumbled sounds of the ship. He realised that it was as quiet then, in the middle of the afternoon, as it was ever likely to be. Beginning with those closest to him, he isolated the sounds and gauged their significance. Hours of unsprung travel on the rutted roads between London and Portsmouth were hard on even the fittest of men and three of his friends were soon snoring, Ransley deep and pig-like, the Wyors low and rhythmic. Wilson's breathing was still fitful but he sounded as close to sleep as he seemed able to get. In the hammock next to his patient, Quested might have been asleep but Hog suspected he was only resting. Giles was humming melodiously, something Hog would ordinarily have sworn at him for but now found strangely soothing.

He shifted his attention beyond the ward. When they were brought in, he had thought the deck empty but now he realised that there were sounds of breathing and snoring outside their accommodation. Given that no one seemed to have noticed or commented on their arrival, Hog assumed that the men still on board were too sick to work. Thinking on that, he supposed there were probably some who did not work for other reasons. In Maidstone, they'd encountered the insane and imbecilic, as well as the criminal. Judging by what they'd heard about the hulks, here there would also be those so incorrigible that they were never released from their wards. One thing that all those categories had in common was noise: they liked to shout, be it about weird fantasies, understandable fears or coarse abuse of their fellows. The quiet on the upper deck seemed to support his original thought of sickness.

Resolutely repressing the natural fear of infection, he listened again. Now he picked out the rumble of voices below. Too indistinct for him to understand the words, still he knew from the tone that he'd located the type of men he'd been thinking about. He was untroubled by the senseless howling, which was already familiar from Maidstone. Some men seemed to get comfort from wailing and others lost their minds to such an extent they probably didn't even know that they were wailing.

He was beginning to block out the sound when it was punctuated by a scream. In the scream, he heard the squeal of a stuck pig and the shriek of a trapped fox. It resonated with fear and horror, as well as pain. Perhaps the man was being beaten, for fun or as a lesson, or perhaps he was being robbed, though of what Hog could not imagine. More likely he was experiencing a fate of which they'd heard talk. Thankfully, seven of them, or six without the sickly Wilson, arrayed against their five cell-mates meant that unnatural crimes were unlikely to be committed in their ward.

Clearly the most troublesome convicts were relegated to the bowels of the vessel. It was a blessing that the Blues were considered useful enough for the upper deck. Everything would be better there: more space, more light and more air. As poor as their circumstances were, they could be worse and that lifted Hog's spirits almost as much as the longed-for bottle of brandy would have done.

In a final mental sweep of the vicinity, Hog found only the routine sounds of ship and port. They were as familiar to him as the instruments of an orchestra to a conductor: wood creaking, waves lapping, seagulls screeching and workers calling to each other. The more disturbing noises close to him receded and he began to drift amidst memories of trips to Folkestone from his childhood home in nearby Acrise.

Unaware that he fallen asleep, Hog had been dozing for hours when he woke to the sounds of men shuffling across the deck above, chains clanking around them. He roused himself groggily and looked around to see his companions waiting in tense anticipation. He traced the workers' progress, coming aboard midships, following a line along the centre of the ship towards the bow and then descending the ladder that he and his friends had used earlier.

When the corridor outside their ward filled with tramping boots, Giles and the younger Wyor dropped lightly down from their hammocks, reaching the grille just as men began to pass. There was a uniformity to the figures, heads bowed and feet dragging. Hog studied them closely, gauging their mood. Some were cowed by their imprisonment, probably as slumped at the day's start as at its end, but most were simply dog-tired. A few returned his gaze, with curiosity, hostility or both. None spoke.

He waited, expecting their door to be unlocked for their cell-mates at any moment, an expectation that he knew his friends shared. Grilles creaked open and clanged closed. Men jostled and

447

hammocks rustled. Streams of piss hit bucket-bottoms. It was only when he noted the new bodily noises and smells that Hog realised he was already becoming used to the background racket and stink. Before long, he would think it normal to go weeks without changing, his clothes as filthy as after his worst binge.

Still no one came. When the deck became quieter, Hog looked at Ransley, only to realise that his companions had also turned instinctively to their leader for an opinion. There was a pause while Ransley considered their situation.

'Looks like we've got a private room, lads.'

There was no surprise in his voice. Only then did Hog suspect that Ransley had been calling in favours. Perhaps it was not luck that found them on the upper deck, midships where the wards were largest, five down on the number sometimes crammed into the space although, unbeknown to them, only one less than intended when the plans for converting warships into prisons were drawn.

Paul

Paul was about to go below when he heard voices behind him. Without discussion, the Blues had fallen into defensive patterns on board the hulks, making sure they were usually with at least one of their fellows and keeping as low a profile as they could. Those on the *York* fared even worse than those on the *Leviathan*. The ship ran with filth and its occupants were regularly terrorised by gangs under no more than token control. Now he knew the men on the hulks, Paul wasn't sure whether the thought that the Blues had been portrayed as desperadoes was comic or tragic. Some convicts were on a third or fourth incarceration, often awaiting a second or third transportation. In the company of habitual killers and rapists, even Hogben began to seem more like a mischievous schoolboy than a dangerous criminal. In fact, while his enforced sobriety was a misery to himself, it had revealed him to his companions as a better man than most had realised.

Unusually, Paul was alone. He'd dropped behind on their return from work, seeking a moment's privacy to empty bowels swollen with a particularly foul bout of diarrhoea. Even the least delicate of men tired of having every aspect of his bodily functions on view twenty-

448

four hours a day. Seeing some buckets stacked in a corner of the deck, he'd grabbed the chance to use one. That tiny luxury was about to cost him dear.

Eager to catch up with his companions before they were locked in and his absence noticed, he was poised to mount the ladder leading down to the upper deck when two men appeared in the gloom below. Paul couldn't recognise them with certainty but guessed they were from the lower decks. They were simply two massive outlines, one with legs so bowed that his knees were half a yard apart and one with shoulders so vast that he seemed to have no neck. They had no reason to be on the upper deck and could only be looking for trouble.

Paul watched them ascend the ladder and then glanced over his shoulder at the deck behind him, just in time to see two more men come into view. For a fleeting instant, he hoped they might help but that hope was soon dashed when he saw the short length of chain that swung menacingly from one man's grip.

'Taking a turn around the deck, are we sir?,' the other jeered. He walked with a limp, not from an injury but from a club-foot, and his voice identified him as one of the many Londoners on board. 'Getting brave, are we sir? Leaving our friends at 'ome?'

Paul looked from one to another. All had half-a-foot and several stones on him. He could have taken any of them, alone or perhaps even as a pair, but four-to-one were poor odds. His only defence was a three-inch folding blade, hardly enough to prick them unless he managed a very precise cut. He didn't expect to have an opportunity to do that and anticipated retaliation with more formidable weapons.

Sandwiched between the deck-rooms and a makeshift tool-shed, there would be no witnesses to the assault. He could try shouting for help but doubted that his friends would hear from their ward below. In any case, the ship rang with the cries of the sick and dying, not to mention the insane and despairing, and who would notice one more voice amongst so many? Even if someone responded, there was no guarantee that they would come in on his side.

No-neck grinned at Club-foot. 'He's an ugly one, mind. I 'ad my eye on that young'un with the smile.'

Paul's stomach churned at the significance of the gibe. He hadn't known whether they intended to rob him of his meagre possessions or give him a beating for fun. Only then did he realise what he was in for. It came as no surprise — even if he hadn't seen it in the Army, there'd been plenty of evidence of it since coming aboard — but knowing proved inadequate preparation for facing the threat. The idea of the filthy specimens breaching his defences at such a personal level appalled him and the knowledge that his humiliation might spare Dennard brought scant comfort.

Like the other younger men in their number, Dennard had lived a relatively happy and secure life on the marshes. The people of Kent were luckier than many of their countrymen. With little industrialisation in the area, there was still demand for farm-workers and mariners, even if the wages were an insult. Added to that, the hop farms offered out-of-season work to see people through the mild southern winters. Their diet might lack variety but they had roofs over their heads and clean water to drink. They did not live in their own filth, victims of poverty and crime, as Paul knew many city-dwellers did. The gaols and hulks were the first time that the likes of Dennard had seen the rank underbelly of humanity and Paul had no wish for them to become more intimately acquainted.

He steeled himself for the confrontation, telling himself that a man of his age and experience could endure it without permanent harm. Firming his stance, he tensed and relaxed muscles all over his body, limbering up as best he could, intending to inflict as much damage as possible before submitting to his fate. His eyes darted from one assailant to the next, gauging their positions, waiting for a move.

When the move came, it was from two of the men in precise synchronisation. No-neck and Club-foot swept in as one, threatening a pair of punches to gut and kidneys from which Paul knew he would be lucky to get up. If he'd had any doubts about his chances, they cleared at that moment. His attackers did not expect him to survive the beating and were unlikely to care whether he was alive or dead when they relieved their frustrations on his battered body. Perhaps being dead wouldn't be so bad at that.

But Paul was not the kind of man who gave up any undertaking, however hopeless. Leaving his response as late as he dared, he sidestepped the brunt of the assault, catching a glancing blow to his side instead of his kidneys, while blocking the frontal punch with his scarred left forearm. He sent his right fist thundering into the underside of Club-foot's jaw. The pain flowering from his knuckles confirmed how well the blow had connected. Paul wasn't sure if he imagined the crunch of bone into soft tissue but the strong start swelled his confidence. Even while retracting his fist, he accelerated the elbow backwards and upwards, burying it painfully into No-neck's sternum. The wheeze that followed was unsatisfying but the man's bulk collapsing against the oak bulkhead was more rewarding.

Paul smiled grimly at the pain he'd inflicted but had no illusions: both men were still conscious and the quartet would soon be inflicting something closer to agony on him. Still, he wasted no time before building on his initial success.

The next wave of attack was badly timed, enabling its victim to land two solid punches. He flowed forward to meet Bow-legs, sweeping away a fist with his forearm and then planting a swift left jab in the gut. As his adversary doubled forward, Paul drew back and around in one fluid move, reaching out with his right hand, grabbing the swinging chain and pulling the fourth man into a fierce head-butt.

Stunned by the impact as he was, Paul knew his resistance was all but exhausted. Ringed closely by four men, now as angry as they were mean, he'd be lucky to land another blow. There was a sickness in the pit of his stomach at what that meant for him but he was still glad to have given them some tokens to remember him by. As the blows began to rain down on him, he could do little more than block the most obvious and inept. The first few sent sharp stabs of pain through his body but it was only seconds before his brain reached overload and gave up trying to process the signals flooding in from nerves all over his body.

Slowly Paul became aware that the blows had stopped. The pain was still there but no new explosions were added. He wondered if his attackers had been interrupted — a guard perhaps? — but felt only detached curiosity rather than any real optimism. Perhaps that was as well, since hope would only have brought disappointment when rough hands dragged him towards the hatch to the lower deck. Just before those hands sent him tumbling past the ladder, he managed to roll a small piece of wood almost silently towards the deck-rooms.

He fell awkwardly, sending spasms of agony through his right shoulder and forcing the breath from his lungs. Lying winded, his cheek rested on grimy worm-riddled oak lit faintly by a small circle of dim light coming from above. Without moving his head, he peered into the murky depths of the hulk. He knew from what other convicts said that the Blues were lucky to be housed on the upper deck. None of them had felt inclined to investigate what they had been spared, when their quarters were grim enough. Even now, he could see little but his nose told him all he needed to know.

Unsurprisingly, the stale air carried an even heavier load of sweat, urine, faeces and vomit than the deck above but those odours seemed almost comfortingly familiar alongside a new stench: the reek of decay drifting up from the orlop deck below.

A younger or less experienced man might have struggled to place the smell but Paul's war years meant that he recognised it immediately. A vague voice far inside his head seemed almost casually to draw his attention to the fact that there were two distinct threads to the stink of rotten flesh. Some of the flesh was alive, most likely from injuries putrid with gangrene, but some was dead. The guards ventured down into the bowels of the hulk only for as long as it took to lock the worst elements into their wards, which wasn't long given that most were never brought out anyway. It was the work of minutes to provide the fresh buckets and stale rations to see the occupants through another day in hell. Paul doubted that they hung around long enough to find out whether any of the lowest of the low were in need of a doctor, or a coffin.

Immobilised by the force of his fall and the fear of his fate, Paul lay sprawled on the deck while his assailants noisily descended the ladder. He was encircled by them before he gathered his thoughts enough to consider taking any action. He tried vainly to swat at the hands that ripped his trousers open and then yanked them savagely over his hips. Ordinarily, the coarse cloth pulling at his genitals would have provoked a yell of pain but Paul could not even feel that twinge amidst his other agonies. The hands shoved him onto all fours and then thrust down on his shoulders until his face hit the deck again. He could do nothing but squint along it and wait.

Watching Chain-wielder drop his trousers, Paul did not feel the horror he expected. The lack of a reaction puzzled and troubled him, but he knew too little about shock to understand why he had become so detached from the events going on around him. When he saw the ulcerated penis about to enter his body, the voice inside his head murmured something about the pox but the meaning eluded him.

A distant memory played in his mind as he watched the man align himself. The scene echoed the night when he watched Higgins with the fruit-picker. There was brief guilt as Paul remembered his own role in that play, seeing his present subjugation in the girl's and the vice-like paws pinning him down in Smeed's hand on her shoulder, but then his mind cleared. She had been smiling when she welcomed his touch and he had been tender in taking her ripe little body. Smeed's hand rested there only for an instant, just to tell her that her services were still in demand, and later acted just as effectively as a cushion when it shot out to protect her. They were rough men but they were not animals.

Without moving a muscle, Paul evaluated the holds his captors had on him. No-neck and Bow-legs were so heavy on his shoulders that it was hard to breathe, let alone move, but there was only Club-foot on his legs and it would be difficult for him to pin both legs securely while his mate knelt between them. He had already made a mistake by concentrating on the left-leg of a right-handed man. Paul waited, poised for that momentary relaxation, anticipating it as Club-foot began to shift his weight. An ache tightened his chest, somehow distinct from the stew of sensations around it, and Paul recognised it as his body's response to the stress of timing that final attempt at escape. His mind accepted that there was no chance of success and yet his heart twisted in knots at the thought that he might squander his only opportunity.

In the end, the decision was taken for him. When he felt a hand on his buttock, reason failed and instinct took over. Perhaps Club-foot had thought him more badly injured than he was, or perhaps despair gave birth to unexpected strength, but his right foot broke easily free of the hand around its calf and landed heavily on Chain-wielder. Paul couldn't see but guessed from the feel that the contact point was the thigh. He'd have preferred the groin but the thick layer of muscle in a man's thigh could generate impressive amounts of pain. However, despite the accuracy of his attack, Paul did not expect it to be as successful as it was. His assailant seemed to fly through the air, before crashing heavily into the bulkhead.

It was only when Club-foot followed his friend that Paul realised something was amiss. He had not so much as touched the man, meaning that he could not possibly have dispatched him. Still, as confused as he was, he knew he had to build on whatever had gone awry with his foes' plans. With a supreme effort, he forced his chest off the deck, using every muscle in those distinctive forearms to fight against the huge men weighing him down. He was still struggling when his left shoulder was freed, making it lift suddenly into the air. The momentum twisted his torso, sending his right shoulder crashing towards the deck with No-neck after it. He instantly rolled on top of the man and began to throttle him with the chain of his manacles. The chain was still buried between hunched shoulders and bluntly conical head when the body fell limp. Feeling the seconds drag by as his senses cleared, he cautiously released his grip and rolled slowly onto knees ringed by crumpled trousers. For the first time, he surveyed the corridor.

Chain-wielder looked as if he was crouching by the bulkhead but closer study showed he was simply propped where he had fallen. The emptiness of his open eyes confirmed that he too was dead, something that was in little doubt given the state of his shirt-front. A neat incision ran around the front of his neck, with the grimy skin above looking almost white in contrast to the crimson below. Despite prohibition on weapons, few convicts went unarmed after their first few days. Searches were sporadic and opportunities to acquire knives and tools from the workshops plentiful.

Club-foot was sprawled across the floor, his hair looking oddly matted, and only a small pool of thick blood around his head indicated how he had met his end.

Between Paul and Club-foot was Bow-legs, a knife still protruding from his chest, its owner sitting alongside and panting heavily.

Smeed!

Confusion rushed back into Paul's mind. Five minutes earlier, he'd have been in no doubt that he wanted one of his friends to chance by. Now, trousers down and on the brink of being violated, he wasn't so sure. He knew only that he would have given anything for the Good Samaritan to have been his lifelong friend Quested, a man from whom he had no secrets and in whose solid presence he would have found most comfort. Instead, Quested was on the *Leviathan*, most likely tending to the man whose impending death placed such a burden on Smeed's broad shoulders. Quite possibly, it was the sorrow that Paul had to thank for his rescue. From time to time, when the chance arose, Smeed faded away from the group for a while and later reappeared looking tired and occasionally red around the eyes.

Smeed got up and shook his head as if to clear it. Paul watched him retrieve his knife and then weave over uncertainly, putting one hand on the bulkhead and offering the other. Paul looked at the hand but made no move to take it, cringing from the touch of another man so soon after the threat of a far more intimate contact. He looked down when Smeed met his eye, not ready to face even a friend.

It was only when Smeed turned away sharply, making for the ladder, that Paul realised how he read the situation. He thought his aid unwelcome because he was a molly, more enemy than friend, not seeing that Paul's shame stemmed from having a man he admired see him compromised. Even as beaten and dazed as he was, Paul could not let that stand. Out of respect for the man's privacy, he never offered any comfort to Smeed in his torments but he could not add to them.

'Jem,' he called hoarsely. His throat was sore from a blow to his larynx but his lack of voice had as much to do with dented self-confidence as it did with bruised flesh.

Smeed stopped, still facing away, and waited.

'Jem,' he repeated.

Smeed turned slowly, came a few paces nearer and stared at the deck between them.

'Give us a hand.' Paul reached out for the help offered seconds earlier.

There was a long and awkward pause but Paul kept his hand where it was. Eventually Smeed closed the distance between them and took it. Paul gingerly hauled himself to his feet, then leaned on Smeed's arm as he pulled his trousers up.

'Don't,' he began. 'Don't tell.'

'Tell the others? What do you take me for?' As soon as he'd uttered the question, he added, 'No, don't answer that.'

Paul grabbed his arm and spoke earnestly. 'It's got nothing to do with that. I've got no problem with it — honest, I haven't. I, it, it's not my first choice but, well, a man gets lonely when he's far from hearth and home.'

Smeed's stare said plainly that Paul had his attention.

'But this. I don't want the others to know how close I came to, being *taken*.'

455

Smeed's arm relaxed as he absorbed the words, becoming firm rather than rigid, and he shifted to provide a better support. Paul found himself looking right into the sad depths of Smeed's eyes when his friend offered the one reassurance that could help.

'I'll not be saying aught. Take my word on it, I know how you feel.'

Seeing into his friend's soul for an instant, Paul had no doubt that was the truth.

'And Paul,' Smeed added, 'You were nowhere close to being taken. You were watching them as cool and calm as we've watched over a run together a score of times. I couldn't have stepped in alone but that you gave me the opening.'

Paul saw the reassurance for what it was. He hadn't been cool and calm — he'd been scared and desperate — and yet, even so, he had created the opportunity that Smeed had exploited so effectively. He had played his own part in averting the humiliation. He gripped his friend's arm tighter still and spoke in something nearer to his normal voice.

'I owe you.'

Smeed raised one eyebrow. 'Not worried what I might ask in payment?'

Paul managed a bit of a grin in response to the taunt, knowing it was only that. He knew how far Smeed's loyalty to his ailing lover went and didn't doubt that he'd get plenty of offers elsewhere if he sought them anyway.

Smeed reached inside his jacket and then held out his fist. Paul put his palm under it, keen to retrieve the token that had probably saved his life. A few months earlier, it would have been meaningless, recognised by no one except perhaps Quested, but Paul had gambled that his companions' keen eyes would have noticed the small piece of wood he had so often clasped through their long days and nights in prison.

It felt good to have the keepsake back in his grip. After years in a leather pouch at Sarah's neck, it was smoother even than the day he'd carved it. During her last visit, hours before he left Maidstone for Portsmouth, she had tearfully passed him the pouch, not as a rejection of the love he had symbolised in the cherry-wood heart but as a reminder of her enduring loyalty through whatever lay ahead. He put it carefully back into the pouch hidden inside his shirt.

'Let's get out of this…' Smeed's voice trailed off, as he failed to find a word in his vocabulary adequate to describe their surroundings. Paul nodded.

Making their way back to the ladder, they leaned on each other and somehow managed to stay on their feet. There would be no hiding the fact that they'd hit trouble but then few men managed to avoid that aboard the hulks. Having already delivered retribution, the matter was closed. There would be no interest from the guards in tracking down the killers of men who were nothing but trouble to them.

Smeed studied him in the light from above, then gave a sad smile.

'Christ, Paul, you weren't much to look at to start with. A man your age needs to take care of himself.'

Paul landed a feeble punch in Smeed's gut, trying to take the joke in good part but remembering the sorrow on Sarah's face when she saw the marks of his last beating on her first gaol visit. As it happened, it was his body not his face that had taken the brunt of this one. Of course, even if he'd been beaten beyond recognition, few would notice in a place where half the men were disfigured by injury or disease, old and new.

Bish

On board the *Leviathan*, in the corner of a cluttered storeroom, Bish lay propped on his side. Bloody spittle dribbled slowly from the corner of his mouth, only to hang in viscous globules before falling onto the rag tucked under his cheek. He winced, as another cough rattled through his body, then spewed out a foul-tasting piece of lung. He'd been right about the cost to him of another marsh winter; probably too weak to see the season through in Marseilles, he'd stood no chance in the unending cycle of torrential rain and solid ice that formed the backdrop to their wretched months of flight and imprisonment.

Looking up, he saw Quested on his left, kindly face filled with frustration while gentle hands wiped away the drool. As he had withered aboard the hulks, despite Quested's diligent nursing, Bish saw the pain of a healer failing to heal fuelled by that failure being with a friend.

On his right sat Giles, dark eyes filled with sorrow.

Not so long before, his death would have been a mere foretaste of what awaited them all but now they were embarking on a new adventure and only he would stay behind in England. He had never yearned for travel before but now his heart ached at being left behind. His twin comforts were his faith in the better place to which he hoped he was headed and the promise he'd extracted from Smeed to make the best of the unexpected second chance. At least his death would free Smeed from an earlier promise.

'Trouble thee not. I shall lie with my kin, as I wanted.'

Quested nodded. 'Remember how we brings Cephas home?'

Those days of youth and comparative fitness were long past but every detail was vivid in Bish's memory. He nodded.

'And how we thinks Wraight is for the scaffold?' Quested went on thoughtfully. 'Perhaps we has more luck than we knew, all in.'

Giles snorted. 'Stopping six slugs doesn't sound so lucky to me.'

'Ah, but none of them finishes off you, does they? Thirteen of us left. That's a Devil's Dozen. Perhaps he looks after his own.'

Bish would have argued if he'd had the strength — it was God he thanked for his friends' salvation. Instead, he squinted as the lamplight dimmed, puzzled that his friends did not trim or fill it. As the gloom deepened, he realised that the darkness was only for him. Death approached and he wondered idly if it was carrying a nice big scythe. The thought brought Smeed's image into his mind as sharp as on that day when, still no more than friends, they talked of death while they fished. He saw the smoky grey eyes, first filled with sadness at what life held for him and then crinkled in wry amusement at what their owner expected it to hold for himself. The comfort that Bish found in his memories was tinged with anxiety. Had he left things right between them? Their final moments together were a blur of hiding places, courtrooms and prisons. He thought he must have said how he felt but, now that there was so little time, he couldn't be sure.

'Quacks,' he rasped.

'I'm here.'

'Tell Jem...'

Tell Jem what?

He could not risk making trouble now, after they'd evaded it for so long. A new life awaited Smeed in Van Diemen's Land and he must do nothing to threaten it. A strong hand rested on his shoulder and it was Giles who spoke.

'I'll tell him, Bish, but he already knows.'

He nodded weakly, reassured, and then the darkness was complete.

Jem

Jem waited on the aft deck of the *Leviathan*, Phillippe's words echoing in his head as they had all morning, ever since the news came: *l'amor che muove il sole e l'autre stelle.* Now it was as if the sun, and every last star in the sky, had been snuffed out. He felt as useless as the decrepit hulk on which he stood, unable even to be by Wilson's side at the end. He'd paid for a final farewell with the only thing he had left to trade. The bloody rag lining his trousers testified to how high the price had been but he cared nothing for that, worried only that the guard would not keep his side of the bargain. Whether through integrity or fear of a gang that still had friends in high places in spite of its present straits, the man delivered and now stood nearby.

In a boat bobbing alongside the decommissioned vessel waited Wilson's brothers. Jem had met them often enough but, playing his role of workmate, he never hung around during their visits. He'd never deliberately revealed his personal life to anyone and such a staunchly Christian family would hardly be a likely starting point. When they looked up, the sorrow in their eyes matched his own. They would lay Wilson to rest with his kin in the churchyard at Aldington, fulfilling at least one of his promises.

Finally the trap door in the main deck opened and he saw signs of activity below. Quested's head appeared first, as he climbed up the ladder and knelt beside the hatch. When the ends of a stretcher poked up, he caught hold of them and took its weight. As it rose through the opening, Jem saw the outline of a body, covered in a blanket and tied to the stretcher with ropes. He swallowed, throat dry, eyes pricking with tears. Another half-minute or so passed before the full length emerged, with Giles struggling up the ladder behind it.

As they manipulated their load, the stretcher bearers glanced sorrowfully in his direction. They carried the stretcher over to where

459

a ladder hung down to the waiting boat. Quested went first, ready to take the lion's share of the weight on his strong shoulders. As they manoeuvred the stretcher up to the railings, they paused with it slanted towards him. Giles slipped the top of the blanket from under the ropes and folded it back to reveal Wilson's face, gaunt but peaceful, looking just as it had so many times when Jem had watched him sleep. Around his neck was the scarf, neatly tied with the ends crossed over his chest just as he'd so often worn it. Jem studied the face carefully, committing every detail to memory, replacing the pain he'd seen in their recent meetings with the serenity he saw now. After taking as long as he dared, he raised his eyes to Giles's and gave a slight nod, offering both thanks for the stolen moment and permission to proceed.

It took a minute or two for the men on the ladder to pass the stretcher down to the men below. They climbed back on board and watched the boat until it disappeared into the forest of masts in the harbour. From the corner of his eye, Jem saw them turn sadly away but he continued to stare into the distance long after they'd gone. He pictured Wilson as he had so often during the past year, the ravages of his illness stripped away, standing on the beach at New Romney in the dawn of that far-off day. Recalling the smiling face and wind-whipped hair, he wondered how he would carry on living without his first and only love. When comfort came, it was from an unexpected source.

Wilson's faith in his God had never wavered, his hope of salvation undimmed by what the Bible had to say about men like them or by the crimes they committed as Blues. Not a man in the Blues believed that defrauding the Revenue was a sin but, puzzled by Wilson's ease with God over the sins they committed together, Jem had once asked him why he didn't fear judgement. Wilson looked surprised by the question, as if the answer should be obvious to him of all people.

'Hast thou a choice in what thou feelest?'

He'd frowned, unsure of the point of the question.

'Couldst thou lie with a woman as easily as thou liest with me?'

He'd been honest, as he always was with Wilson, conceding that he'd be of little use to the woman if he did.

'Dost thou believe that the Lord would make thee so and then deny thee happiness?'

He'd shrugged, saying that he supposed he could go without.

'It's my belief that there will be no judgement for love at the gates of heaven.'

The memory triggered another, of a day when he found Wilson in the church, staring at a plaque and lost in thought. Without trying, Jem had remembered the words and now he hoped their optimism was justified: *Beloved, when we meet again, sunlight will flood the hills of paradise.*

A tiny flicker of hope ignited deep inside him. Perhaps it wasn't too late. He couldn't change what they were but Wilson had never shot anyone, whatever a court might say, and he still had time to make amends for his own actions. If Wilson was waiting for him in paradise, he planned to be there.

'I'll come, Jamie. Thou hast my oath.'

With those whispered words, he allowed the guard to return him to his earthly purgatory.

George

It was still dark when George opened his eyes, a strange tightness in the pit of his stomach. It was a moment or two before he placed the sensation — anticipation. Years had passed since he felt it so strongly: the day of his takeover bid for the Blues perhaps; the night before his wedding probably; feast days as a child definitely.

He'd tracked every day of his two months aboard the *Leviathan* and so he knew it to be the first day of spring, 21 March, but there was something far more significant than that. It was the day that they were to leave the stinking hulks. At anchor in the main harbour, the *Governor Ready* awaited them. George's enquiries had brought forth encouraging news. A 500-ton transport ship built only two years earlier on Prince Edward Island, the vessel was swift and seaworthy. Her master, Captain John Young, was efficient and her surgeon-superintendent, Dr Thomas Wilson, was conscientious in his duty to ensure the welfare and discipline of his human cargo.

George tried to keep his optimism in check, hoping that the transfer might mark the start of the better future at which Platt had hinted but knowing those hopes could be dashed at any moment. He swung easily down from his hammock, practice perfecting the manoeuvre in spite of the rheumatism brought on by their dank captivity. Quested dropped down beside him. As they looked at each other in the first pale light of dawn, George felt an idiotic grin spread over his face, a pair to the one lifting his friend's flat features. Their excitement was as foolish as their grins, when there was every chance that their new accommodation would be no better than their present squalor, but they could not suppress it.

The morning routine dragged — never had breakfast seemed so tiresome, swabbing decks so futile or stowing hammocks so pointless. Certainly seven o'clock had never been so slow in coming as it was that day. Only when they finally mustered on deck did the end start to seem real. Instead of separating for their work details, they stayed together and joined another dozen or so men who were headed out with them. Once their irons had been checked, they went ashore — as usual and yet quite different. Gazing along the waterfront, George saw a similar party disembarking from the *York*. Screwing up his eyes, he was sure he could see Dennard's slim silhouette and Pierce's compact bulk in a knot of men to one side. To his relief and delight, it looked as if they were to be reunited for their journey to the other side of the world.

Minutes later, the *Leviathan* men fell in behind the *York* contingent and they were bound for the harbour. It was a walk of a mile or so, barely a stroll for the men they had been but now a slog for the half-starved, iron-chafed weaklings they'd become. George knew they were lucky that only Wilson, a man who flirted with death long before they were captured, had lost his life on the hulks. During their short stay, they'd seen several convicts who were well when they arrived succumb to disease and injury. For all but one of their number to embark on the voyage in fair health was a better result than he'd dared hoped for. Half of them suffered with the same aching joints as he did — and the rest had troubles of their own with festering sores and violent gastric disorders — but they had survived and that was all that mattered.

Feeling a coldness on his left ankle, George looked down to see a trickle of blood wending its way over the dirt-blackened skin. The proverbial March wind quickly chilled the damp spot. As he watched, a matching dribble ran down from his right leg-iron. Glancing around, he saw that most men were in the same state. Raising his eyes to their faces, he saw too that most did not care. For men who had passed time on a prison hulk, it was impossible to conceive that a change in circumstance could be anything but for the better — they all looked forward to the transport ship with renewed vigour.

Half an hour later, George knew those hopes were not misplaced. The *Governor Ready* was indeed a sound vessel and its crew was hard at work on the countless tasks that needed to be completed before they set sail. Gone was the stagnant water and sewer-stench of the hulk moorings. In its place, a bracing sea breeze snatched away the reek of their unwashed bodies before it reached his nostrils. They huddled at the stern, awaiting instructions. The middle-aged warrant officer who appeared ran his eyes over them appraisingly, in a manner that marked him out as a medical man. When he spoke, it was with brisk civility.

'I am Dr Wilson, surgeon in the service of the Royal Navy, and it is my job to deliver you to the colony in good working order. Play fair with me and I'll play fair with you. Make trouble and you'll spend the next four months below decks in irons.' He paused for emphasis. 'Now strip.' He nodded curtly at a large basket by the bulkhead.

George would once have resented an order to strip in front of his fellows. Such reservations had long since been eroded by their enforced intimacy and now he could not wait to be rid of his lice-infested rags. When they were gone, he felt as if the fierce wind was scouring the filth from his exposed flesh. Looking down, he saw his misshapen sternum more prominent than ever and the flesh stretched over it blackened by countless knocks and falls. The paunch past which he had not been able to see for years was long gone, folds of wrinkled skin its only legacy, and now he saw his bony toes beyond. He felt a stab of humiliation when he realised that his private parts had retreated inside his body in search of warmth. Glancing around, embarrassment faded when he saw that most men were in the same boat.

Lifting his eyes modestly to their chests, he studied his friends. They all bore the same traces from their ordeal: ribs clearly visible, skin coated in grime, joints swollen and scabbed. When buckets of water and dishes of soap appeared, there was no need for an order to wash, as each of them began rubbing eagerly to rid himself of the unwelcome passengers he'd been carrying for months. There came a point at which the roughest character longed for a wash and a clean set of clothes. Not even the blood coursing from their scabs and sores could dampen their enthusiasm.

When they were done, which was sooner than it might have been on a warmer day, they stood shivering. George hoped they were not expected to put back on the filthy rags, now torn to shreds after being ripped from limbs still encircled by irons. The doctor had been watching them while they washed and now spoke again.

'Line up over here.'

George noted how quickly and automatically they obeyed. Although there was no reason not to do so, given that the order was fair and they wanted no trouble, he was conscious that most of them would have rebelled even at such a simple instruction in their past lives. Imprisonment, first in gaol and then on the hulks, had taken its toll. They had learned, from their own experience and from watching others, that resistance almost invariably brought even greater misery. Most of them were too smart to make their time harder than it needed to be. Those who weren't had been brought into line before they could earn black marks for the group.

Now he stood patiently in line, stepping forward when his turn came and allowing the doctor to examine him. The man was thorough, not flinching from the unenviable task of probing their wasted bodies. He ran through a series of questions for each convict, starting with his general health, lingering on his bowel movements and culminating in questions about his private parts, accompanied by a firm examination of the said parts. George was surprised to feel faint amusement at the ridiculous sight he must make, standing naked while a stranger grasped his scrotum. He answered the questions brusquely but honestly, his problems mundane and common to every farm worker of his vintage. He would have given the same answers anyway, whatever the truth, in his determination to leave the hulks behind him. Every man amongst them did the same, standing tall and making no mention of the dysentery and gaol fever rife in those hell-holes.

George's examination was completed just as a dozen men trooped aboard, staggering under enormous bundles of clothing. Working with military precision, it took them only a few minutes to organise themselves into a distribution line and start handing out the clean garments. The convicts quickly formed another queue of their own accord and George soon reached the head of it. The standard issue he received seemed like Sunday best after what he had been wearing: shirt, waistcoat and jacket on top, with trousers and stockings below. The finishing touch was a snug woollen cap that he pulled as far over his ears as it would reach. Chilled to the bone, it would be a while before his body heat warmed the new outfit but he began to feel better as soon as he buttoned the jacket.

Striking the irons from an arm and leg on each man to allow him to dress was time-consuming but inside an hour they were all dressed and headed down to their new quarters. As they descended to the lower decks, conditions inevitably became darker and more cramped but they saw nothing like the squalor they'd left behind. Every inch of the *Governor Ready* was scrubbed in readiness for its long voyage and packed with provisions to ensure its safe arrival. Like many of his men, George had never made more than short voyages before but no one who'd crossed the Channel in a winter gale could doubt how hard the journey ahead might become when they hit foul weather. Still, he was reassured by the evident experience and professionalism of the crew. If anyone was to deliver the convict labour so desperately needed by the colony in sound working order, the *Governor Ready* seemed to be the vessel to do it.

Two weeks later, George stood by the tiny ventilation grille in their berth. Their departure delayed by a storm, they'd had plenty of time to adjust to the new routine. Conditions were far better than on the hulks but the days were longer without work ashore to pass the time. Now confident that the voyage would *be* tolerable, he knew it would *seem* interminable, with little for two hundred passengers to do despite Dr Wilson's best efforts to devise ways to keep them out of mischief. Publicly, gambling was the main entertainment. Privately, other vices had already begun in dark corners and would no doubt become more common and more visible with each passing week. With no interest in where other men found their pleasure, George felt secure in the company and protection of his friends. They remained in the same groups as before but now lodged in adjacent berths.

He and his five companions had taken turns to peer through the grille, able to make out a small crowd at the quayside but too distant to see if their families were amongst them, but now the others sat in the gloom with their thoughts.

He heard a sniff — that'd be the younger Wyor. Back home, he'd

465

never been able to fathom the boy, suspecting him no better than his brother but finding his expectations confounded when Billy showed no interest in bearing firearms. On the hulks, he was first shocked to see how Billy fawned to the worst scum aboard and then disgusted to see how the boy exploited his new-found friends for whatever he could get.

Gradually, he realised that he'd misjudged the Wyor brothers. He'd seen them as younger versions of the Baileys, hard to control but useful in their way. Only too late, after the fateful night in Dover, did he see that Dickon was an utter liability — a braggart incapable of judging the consequences of his actions and too brash even to keep quiet about a capital crime. Now, after months of imprisonment, he'd glimpsed inside Billy's soul and was chilled by what he saw. There seemed no trace of dignity or conscience — qualities plentiful in the Blues whatever the judiciary might think — only calculated self-interest. He now had no doubt that the boy would do anything to improve his position and took care not to let any opportunities arise that might damage the prospects of himself or his friends. Dickon still bore the scars from the Baileys' warning to keep quiet. If they were not to hand, George had no doubt that Hogben could do a fair job.

Nonetheless, Billy's tears might well be genuine, especially as such a show seemed unlikely to reap any rewards in the present company. For all their faults, the Wyors were loyal sons leaving a much-loved mother to fend for herself. But how much worse for the others? Giles and Quested might have been carved from marble, rigid in joint refusal to give in to their grief but devastated at being parted from their wives and children, three for Giles and five for Quested. No one had spoken of it in George's hearing but he had no doubt that the question of whether their families would be given permission to join them occupied the other fathers' minds as much as it did his own. Transportation seemed so much harder on them than on their single friends who, for all he knew, might build a better life in the colony than they'd had in England.

He thought of the men in the next berth. Not long married, Higgins and Gilham both left new babes fatherless as well as older children or stepchildren; while Gilham showed his customary strength, so unexpected in such a reticent man, Higgins was foundering without Rhoda's calming influence to keep him steady.

Faced with the prospect of living without his three youngsters, Sam descended into melancholy and even John, usually so brash, seemed dazed by the parting from his family. Pierce was scarcely better, wretched at leaving his wife to cope with their seven and denied even the chance to share his incarceration with his friends, Quested and Giles.

As in his own berth, only two of the men beyond the bulkhead were unmarried but there any similarity between them and the Wyors ended. Both Dennard and Smeed were resourceful men of integrity, with skills that should serve them well in their new home if given a chance, and he hoped they would make the most of any such chance. He had confidence in Dennard's ability to rise above anything life threw at him, with the same irrepressible optimism tempered by common sense that he'd shown through every twist and turn of the Blues' fates. He was equally sure that Smeed could make a go of it, if he chose to, but wondered whether that decision had yet been made — as self-possessed as ever, Smeed's state of mind was never easy to judge. In George's opinion, what the man needed was hard work not the endless days of a long voyage to dwell on his loss.

Finally, George's reflections turned to himself. He had always provided well for his wife and their ten children, and his eldest boy knew the business inside out. Still, it would be hard for Eliza to manage alone with three babes under the age of five, and another on the way. They'd been partners in marriage for eighteen years, living comfortably almost from the outset and doing better still later on, but now she was the wife of a convicted felon and his children were as fatherless as if he had been dead. Craning to see beyond the stern, to the horizon over which Portsmouth had long since disappeared, he wondered if he would have lived the same life if he'd known how it would end.

Quested rose to his feet, knees creaking, and joined him.

'You wishes you does it different, Bats?'

George smiled at the total absence of recrimination in the man's voice. They'd made their own choices and now they'd been called to account for them. They would bear the voyage as they had borne the weeks on the hulks awaiting it.

'No. I was born in the trade and I thought to die in it too.'

He was sorry they'd been caught but not for how they'd lived, and yet... He recalled with a shudder their discovery that boy convicts, some as young as seven, were held on their own, equally squalid, hulk at Woolwich. He had not fully appreciated until that moment just how lucky his son had been to escape charges. True, he was only two years younger than Billy Wyor but that mattered at their age. At fifteen, Georgie was still a boy while, at seventeen, Billy was a man. The gulf between them had been widened by Billy's years following Dickon around without a father's discipline, while Georgie minded his parents and watched over his flock of younger siblings.

'But I have no wish for my boys to know the troubles we've seen. I'm glad young Georgie's out of it. Let him take care of his mother and find himself a safer living.'

George felt Quested's large hand rest heavy on his shoulder in an unexpected gesture of friendship that emphasised how the differences between them had been levelled by incarceration.

'P'r'aps the new country in't so bad. The old one hasn't been so good for us, when all's said and done.'

'England? Perhaps,' George admitted. 'But the marshes? Shall we ever find their like?'

He considered his own question, using an arm to brace himself against the motion of the ship as they moved clear of the land and onto the high seas. He twisted to see the horizon beyond the bow, feeling for the first time a trace of anticipation at the thought of their destination, the distant shore at the end of their journey.

'Who knows?' he admitted.

Dick

Dick Higgins lay shaking in the darkness, oblivious to the physical discomfort of trying to sleep in a narrow hammock in a space between two other men that was barely wider than his shoulders. His mind was fixed on one fact, and one fact only: above him, below him and on all four sides were oak planks several inches thick. There was no window to open and the door was locked and barred. The ceiling was too low to stand without stooping, especially for a man of his height. He told himself not to think of the cell, to think of anything but the cell, but his mind was locked in the same circles that it travelled every night. During the hours of daylight, gloomy as it was in their berth, he fought to keep his fear under control but, when darkness came, he lost the battle and gave in to the terror.

Gaol had been bad enough but the cells were twice the size of the berth on the *Governor Ready*. At the time, Dick had believed that nothing could be worse. Of course, that was before he spent two months aboard a hulk but at least there they were led ashore each day to work in the Warren. He would never have thought he could look forward to an honest day's work as much as he found himself anticipating that comparative liberty. He was glad to be assigned work outside, even if it was shovelling mud in a futile effort to dig a drainage ditch in mid-winter. He should have hated it, under-dressed and ill-fed as he was for such labour, but it seemed like paradise in comparison with the oppressive nights.

Through it all, he'd retained some semblance of dignity and self-control and only his friends knew of the terrors that plagued him after nightfall. It was the *Governor Ready* that brought him to his present sorry pass although, ironically, it was not a bad ship. Dr Wilson ordered the irons struck from all but the worst offenders on the second day out of Portsmouth. Supervision from Lieutenant Butler's detachment of the 39th Regiment was thorough, and could be brutal when warranted, but convicts who obeyed the rules and kept their heads down were fed, watered and treated with terse civility. With the sea for unlimited washing water and the wind for drying, no longer did they live in a cloud of filth like that around the hulks at Portsmouth.

There was a strict rotation of exercise periods, which were as generous as space and security allowed, and good conduct could win small privileges, from extra rations to longer exercise periods. Most of the convicts were city thieves with little to offer so the Blues, with their skills and trades, did better than many. Quested was assistant to Dr Wilson, Smeed slipped straight back into the role of mariner and Gilham switched between seaman and carpenter as required. All three were busy for most of the daylight hours and, while he envied their freedoms, Dick appreciated how their absence improved conditions for him.

Best of all from his perspective was the luxury of using the seats-of-ease in the bow during exercise periods. Unscreened though they were, they afforded more privacy than squatting in the corner of a cell full of men — something they still had to do when nature called during the long hours they spent locked down — but it was neither privacy nor cleanliness that gave Dick such delight. No, his pleasure came from sitting there with nothing, not a single soul, between himself and the distant horizon. Perched on his throne with the wind in his hair, he found brief respite from the horrors that lurked below. There were two piss-dales on deck, at which crewmen and convicts alike stood in full view to send cascades plunging into the waves below, but he took any and every opportunity to linger in the bows over his eliminations. One or two of his friends quietly warned him that he'd get a name for himself, hanging around up there, but even that did not deter him. Nothing, not even the harshest beating, could be worse than the private hell that he already occupied.

Such interludes notwithstanding, the hours on deck were not enough to counter his fears. When the weather permitted, they spent most of their days above decks and the nights were almost bearable. Then, just as he began to think he might survive the voyage, along came a storm and they were locked down for a whole day, and sometimes the next or even the one after. Interminable days and nights in a berth six feet square with his fellows quickly took him to the edge of his sanity. He dreaded any sign of rebellion; an uprising would see them all locked down indefinitely, a prospect he dare not contemplate. His berth was the worst aboard, with seven men in place of the regulation six. The reason was sound enough: they saw right away how carefully Dr Wilson segregated his cargo, following the new ideas in convict management by keeping first-time offenders away from hardened criminals and letting those he expected to make no trouble look out for themselves. Dick was glad to remain with his friends but would have given anything to be in the other berth, where Wilson's death meant precious extra space for the survivors.

In his more lucid moments, he knew his friends had done all they could to help him. Their hammocks were slung in two rows, giving the four men above some eighteen inches of space apiece while the three below had more like two feet. His was on the lower row, putting him further from the oppressive planks above, and hung between the door and the ventilation grille. When the wind came from the right direction, a refreshing breeze cooled his sweaty brow. As he lay on his back, staring into the darkness, the grille was only inches behind him.

Above him was Gilham and, beyond him next to the bulkhead, Smeed. Well used to the sea, Smeed showed no reaction to any of their privations, from mouldy biscuit to cramped quarters, and, although his experience was shorter and closer to land, Gilham adapted just as well. Packed in head-to-toe to make the most of the space, they looked as if they'd been born to the life. Seemingly oblivious to even the most severe physical hardships, they had slept as peacefully under a thin blanket in the north Atlantic of early April as they did now, a month later, lying nearly naked in the sweltering heat of equatorial waters.

On Gilham's other side was John Bailey, with Sam beyond. With his massive height and bulk, John suffered the restrictions of each confinement worse than any of them. Permanently stooped when standing and unable to stretch out in a hammock designed for someone a head shorter than he was, he was often to be seen rubbing at stiff muscles in his neck and shoulders, back and legs.

In contrast to John's complaints, Sam said little. At first, Dick wondered if that was a reaction to their circumstances, an indication that even the man who had fearlessly led them through scores of affrays was crushed by the misery of imprisonment. Soon he realised that Sam was the same as he'd always been. Never one to speak if silence would serve as well, he simply found the monotonous regime presented few situations in which anything needed to be said. Through glances and nods, he communicated his needs or thanks without words. Occasionally, he rested an appreciative or reassuring hand on one of his friends' shoulders but that was the extent of his interaction. Dick had felt that touch once and was surprised by the comfort that the solid contact brought him.

On Dick's left was Pierce, as steady and reliable as always despite his deep sorrow at being parted from his family. On his right, last but by no means least, was Dennard. Dick had come to depend on Dennard in a way he would never have chosen to depend on anyone. He hoped the extent of his dependence was not fully known even to the men locked in with them. It was too dark for them to see that Dennard held his hand through many of his sleepless nights but he could not conceal the panic attacks that assailed him nor the comfort Dennard gave him then.

It was an hour or so since they had turned in, the worst time of each day for him. Every night, he lay awake in the darkness, listening as his friends dropped one by one into sleep. He knew their routines by heart. First would come Smeed's even breathing, reflecting his ease with a sailor's lot and his fatigue from a hard day's work, then Gilham's faint snoring soon after. Neither man relieved his frustration at night but sometimes Dick heard faint rustles in the minutes before dawn.

Against the far bulkhead, Sam rarely made a sound. Dick suspected that he slept badly but the only evidence was that, perhaps once a week, he would wake suddenly, often with a gasp and occasionally a shout. He never offered any explanation for his restlessness and no one ever asked him for one.

John usually lulled himself to sleep with an undercurrent of curses about the design of hammocks, certain that men would be born with curved spines if God intended them to sleep in such contraptions. He thrashed about throughout the night, although his turmoil seemed purely physical.

Pierce generally dozed off soon after Smeed and Gilham. A casual observer would have thought he was coping with his incarceration well but Dick's insomnia meant that he heard the subdued weeping that sometimes came from one of the strongest of their number as each week took him further from his loved ones. There had been a time when Dick would have mocked that as weakness but now he despised himself more than he could ever despise even the most emotional response to separation.

Dennard was the revelation, not because he coped with imprisonment better than the rest but because Dick expected him to take it hardest. His merry sense of humour survived, battered but intact, and he treated his enforced celibacy as a joke. Sometimes he would regale them with fantasies of memorable past encounters while he played himself off. Although Dick wasn't really one for bawdy reminiscences, he knew that Dennard — always the most discreet of lovers in the past — sought only to lift their mood. Sometimes he threw in memories of his own or played himself off alongside his friend. Occasionally, for a few precious seconds, he even forgot that the walls were closing in on him for another night.

Whatever the pattern of a particular evening, Dick's true torment began when the last of his companions found peace in sleep. Then, feeding on his solitude, the anxieties multiplied. He had given little thought to the effects of close confinement before he was arrested

472

but he had since discovered just how afraid a man could be: not just too afraid to sleep but too afraid to move, too afraid even to breathe. During the darkest nights, when there was not so much as a faint glow of moonlight from the ventilation grille, he lay rigid in his hammock and prayed for the dawn.

Through it all, his companions said nothing. He saw their shock at the state of him, a man who'd never backed down from anyone or anything in his life, and their relief that they did not share his torments. Not even John Bailey scorned him as, frustrated by their inability to help, they gave him whatever space or distraction was in their power.

As fearful of his dreams as he was of reality, he clawed at the path from wakefulness into slumber until eventually, inevitably, his exhaustion overcame his fear and he slipped uneasily into fitful sleep. His drained body lay inert through its first hours of rest but, as soon as his system began to recover, his mind resumed its troubled meanderings. Rather than a single recurring dream, he was plagued by an impressive array of morbid fantasies. That night brought one of the more regular visitations. He lay on a floor of bare earth, all his limbs amputated, a helpless torso abandoned to its fate. A vast boulder rested on his chest, so heavy that he could barely draw breath. He felt his ribs straighten from their natural curvature and begin to bend inwards, pushing the air from his lungs. He heard his bones creaking and, desperate to find help before they cracked, began to scream but the only sound from his open mouth was the rush of his final exhalation before death.

He jerked awake to find arms around him and a murmur in his ear.

'Steady now. Calm down and take a breath.'

Dick gasped at the stifling air, only just beginning to cool after another tropical day. His body streamed with sweat. Dennard's embrace brought him back to reality, to the wretched cell that seemed small improvement on his tortured dreams.

'Christ,' he panted. 'I can't live like this. Put an end to it for me.'

The plea was nothing new. He found himself in a place few men would envy, too afraid to live and too afraid to die. His crowning fear was facing the Day of Judgement after taking his own life. Never having known real fear before, now he staggered under the crippling burden he carried.

'Hush. You'll feel better come the morning.'

Dennard shifted to get more comfortable, standing close beside the hammock to encompass him, as if the physical barrier of his arms could shield a man from his own mind. Morning was hours away, far too distant to be a comfort.

'Oh, God.' He was disgusted by the whimper he heard in his voice but couldn't stop himself. 'What if it's like this in the new country? What if they send me to, you know, Norfolk Island?'

Few men spoke the name of the grim penal colony that represented a fate worse than death. Tales of its horrors were sometimes spun by those who knew men who'd gone there, but none had returned to tell the truth behind the myths. In only two years of existence, its reputation had plumbed new depths in a penal system that was already justly notorious for its failings.

Dick's voice climbed in pitch and volume. 'I can't go there.' Grabbing Dennard fiercely, he shouted, 'I can't go there, Tommy!'

A fist thundered on the bulkhead beyond Smeed's hammock. Hogben's roar rose over it. 'For God's sake, shut him up! Some of us are trying to sleep, as if this buggering heat in't bad enough.'

Dick knew that Hogben, having learned to live with his own demons, was the last man to feel pity for a fellow — living in constant pain only made his temper worse than ever. He was glad of the stout oak between them, ensuring that he would feel no more than the lash of Hogben's tongue.

'Shit in your teeth, Hog.'

Smeed's matter-of-fact reply was devoid of any emotion, although his voice was raised to penetrate the bulkhead.

Dick never heard a murmur of complaint about his nightly outbursts from Smeed, despite the man's own unwavering self-control. Dick had watched the scene that played out on the deck of the *Leviathan* after Wilson's death. On ditch-digging duty ashore, he leaned on his shovel in puzzlement as Smeed waited on deck and Giles turned back the blanket from Wilson's face. It struck him as odd, even though the two men were friends from the same farm. Back home on the estate, he would certainly have gone to a friend's funeral and would probably have paid his respects at the open coffin. On the hulks, however, such courtesies would cost dear. Smeed was held on the *York* and Dick wondered how he could have paid for the privilege of standing on the *Leviathan*. They had little money left —

his own three shillings wouldn't go far — and Smeed had no family to bring him more.

Those thoughts coalesced into an idea that had never occurred to him before. The two men had been more than friends and Smeed's payment had been of a kind he'd die rather than submit to. Dick had no idea what to do with the knowledge, although hitting Smeed would have figured in it if he'd been within reach. As it was, by the time an opportunity arose, he'd worked out that some of his companions must have been in on the secret for quite a while. It cast a different light on their reactions at the meeting where he'd accused Smeed of bedding Rhoda. At least half a dozen of the men present had known Smeed had no interest in her, and why. It seemed they hadn't thought it their business and, over the weeks since Wilson's death, Dick had reconciled himself to the idea that it might not be any concern of his either. In truth, he had no heart for starting trouble with Smeed, let alone with the men who might side with him.

In the darkness to his left, Pierce tried to reassure him.

'Norfolk Island's for worse than the likes of us.'

'You don't know that. None of us knows what'll happen when we get there. What if they throw us in a dungeon? A hole in the ground–'

Pierce maintained his soothing tone. 'Think on all the men we've met who've taken this journey before and still not been sent there. It'll not happen to us. Norfolk Island's for killers.'

Dennard adopted the same timbre when he picked up the thread. 'When did you ever kill any more than a brace of bunnies?'

Dick relaxed a fraction, feeling some small comfort at their words but then an aching nostalgia for the nights Dennard's words evoked. Whether poaching or game-keeping, they were spent roaming free through open countryside. He began to sob. The arms around him drew tighter and he buried his face against his friend's chest.

'Christ, I'm going off the hook.'

'Aye, but then you was always halfway off it anyhow.'

There would be more dreams before dawn, and still more through each night yet to come, but he slowly drew enough strength from his friends to face another hour. Not until he was calm did Dennard swing back into his hammock and then clasp his hand in the darkness. They settled to await sleep once more.

475

Sam

Days aboard the *Governor Ready* were almost as predictable as they'd been on the hulks. The weather, and the captain's responses to it, brought some variation but there were few surprises. The highlights were exercise periods and mealtimes. On fine days, Sam Bailey liked nothing more than to lean on the railings and gaze at the horizon. The disconcerting detachment that had made him such a formidable presence in the Blues guaranteed him the place of his choice, however crowded the deck might be. On wet days, mealtimes became his focal point. It was on one such day, when a steady rain kept them below but without drenching the lower decks as heavier downpours were apt to do, that he lingered over a bowl of Dennard's stew.

Placed next to a meal prepared by any of their wives, the stew would have seemed inedible but, after eight months of prison food, it looked and smelled pretty decent. Their modest daily ration of salt meat was better preserved than the ship's biscuit and they had soup on some days and gruel on others. Dennard had surprised them all, both with his willingness to take on the role of mess cook and with his culinary skills, presumably honed during his years of bachelor living. Only Gilham's efforts came close — and he already worked a harder day than most — so the arrangement suited them all. Each man compensated Dennard in some way for his trouble, sometimes by helping with tasks he was assigned by the crew but more often by sprinkling some of their sugar ration in his over-sweetened tea.

They all took different approaches to the fare which, while more than enough to keep them alive and healthy, was far from satisfying. Some shovelled it down so fast that it barely touched the sides. Others stared sadly at it, no doubt thinking of their families eating meals without them thousands of miles away. Sam liked to savour his, letting the aroma hone his appetite and then holding each spoonful of gravy in his mouth until the flavour had fully marinated his tongue.

He was engrossed in the familiar ritual when his pleasure was interrupted by an itch on his left cheek. He swiped at the spot, then reached again for his spoon. Glancing down, he saw a broad smear of blood across the back of his hand.

'It's about time you learned to shave, Sam.' John spoke through a mouthful. 'Seems like you've cut yourself every day for a week.'

One of the luxuries of life aboard was a daily shave. Throughout their landward incarceration, it had been once a week at best, on the eve of the Sabbath, but now they had a bowl of seawater and a shared blade every morning. It helped to pass the time and certainly improved the appearance of the human cargo.

'It's the same buggering cut,' Sam muttered as he rubbed at the side of his face with his sleeve. The rubbing made the itching worse and that only made him rub harder. The blood flowed freely, soaking the cuff that he pressed to the wound.

Pierce looked at him for a second, then leaned over to push his hand aside. He studied the spot closely. 'You feel all right, Sam?'

'Aye,' Sam replied without thinking but then added, 'Well, a touch hot but then when in't it damned well hot out here?'

All of his cell-mates were looking at his cheek now. Dennard frowned. 'It's not hot today. That westerly's got quite a nip.'

Only then did Sam notice that they were all clad in waistcoats and jackets, while he wore just a shirt. A bead of sweat rolled down the other side of his face and dropped onto the grubby linen. He shivered. His face was burning but his body was feeling the chill in the air.

'Let Quacks take a look at that.'

Pierce's voice was as soft as always but his words were more instruction than suggestion. They'd declined to elect a mess captain alongside their cook but it was Pierce who usually spoke for them. The main reason was that he argued their corner well but he was also a man they could all accept without complaint.

'I'm not sick,' Sam protested, as if saying so would make it true.

'Can't hurt to check.'

Sam pushed his bowl away, resentful that his precious meal had been ruined but lacking the appetite to finish it. Any of the hundreds of men he'd led would have sworn that he feared nothing but, in truth, there was one thing that sent horror through him as surely as their confinement did through Higgins: sickness.

As a matter of fact, it didn't even have to be real sickness. Any bodily incapacity had the same effect, from injury to pregnancy. Even the sight of his wife feeding a baby made his stomach churn, too vivid a reminder of the vomit, blood and discharges that preceded each new arrival. From the day their first daughter distended Sarah's belly, he no longer saw her as a woman and, once he had a son, he'd given up trying.

'It's just a bloody cut.'

Smeed looked up. 'Seems like that's the point. It *is* bloody, after a week or more. And there's no sign of it closing.'

'All right,' Sam snapped. 'I'll show him tomorrow. Good enough?'

As aloof as he could often be, Sam was a surprisingly even-tempered man most of the time. He could be savage when facing a preventive man, brutal when drunk and unpredictable when his memories left him sleepless for too long. For the rest of the time, he acknowledged useful remarks with a curt nod and disregarded everything else. In the curious looks that his friends now turned on him, he saw first their surprise and then their suspicion that illness was making him irritable. Christ, they'd have him nailed inside his coffin in no time. He rose abruptly to his feet and stalked to the far side of the berth, frustrated as always by the close quarters that denied them solitude.

By morning, irritation had faded in the face of anxiety. Sam had spent the first half of the night telling himself that the prickling in his cheek and the heat in his forehead were imagined, put into his mind by what the others had said. By the time he heard the watch change at eight bells, he could no longer deny the combination of fever and chills that shook his body. He spent the remaining hours of darkness, alone after even Higgins had found his usual troubled sleep, speculating on the nature of his disease. Surrounded by sickness at Newgate and on the hulks, he had plenty of ideas to fuel his fears now. His first thought was gaol fever: convicts fell victim to it in their hundreds and the early stages were much like his own symptoms. Forcing himself to remain calm, he dismissed the possibility firmly. They'd been weeks at sea in their closed world without a case of gaol fever. If it were amongst them, he thought they'd have known before now.

He rubbed his cheek with the heel of his hand and then examined it gingerly in the early light leaking through the grille behind Higgins' head. Dark blood was mixed with lighter pus. Wiping it on his trousers, he tried not to think about the festering wounds he'd seen during the war years. Plenty of men had limbs sawn off to halt the progress of the black rot that spread from their injuries, although a sizeable proportion of them died anyway. He shuddered at the realisation that a cheek could hardly be amputated: if he had the black rot there, he would surely die.

He'd been reflecting on the possibility of his imminent demise for a while when the other men began to stir around him, their hammocks creaking with every shift in weight. Beside him, John grumbled at his sore muscles and stiff limbs. Below, Higgins came to with a gasp. The usual morning chorus of yawns and scratches, belches and farts seemed different that day, each movement and emission a sign of the life in his friends' bodies just as the life in his own threatened to ebb away. While he was no coward, he was a morose and pessimistic man for whom death had never seemed that distant and now seemed all too close. He lay motionless, listening to the others as they swung down from their hammocks, pissed into the bucket, swiped dampened rags across their faces and swilled tepid water around their mouths. Countrymen to the core, they beat the call to breakfast every morning, poised for a day of hard work that never came for most of them.

'Sam?' Pierce gave his canvas cocoon a shove. 'You getting up?'

A few seconds passed as Sam considered whether to answer the question or ignore it. Eventually he did neither, instead swinging his legs around to drop down to the deck. Having spent as long at sea as Smeed and Gilham, moving around on board was second nature to him. It was completely unexpected when his knees buckled and he fell against John. Even half asleep, his huge relative caught him without complaint and lowered him to sit against the bulkhead.

Finding it hard to focus, Sam blinked up at the six figures gathered around him. Some stood and some squatted but all stared in the dim light. He wanted to ask what was wrong but his mouth didn't seem to be working. The inside of his cheek was so swollen and sore that it was difficult to move his jaw.

'Christ,' Dennard said. 'No question now but you'd best see Quacks, or the doctor even.'

A shiver ran down Sam's spine. None of them had called on the doctor for whom Quested now worked each day, their belief in their friend far surpassing their faith in any paper qualifications the stranger might possess, but clearly Dennard thought whatever it was he saw might be beyond Quested's skill to heal. Sam raised a hot hand to his still hotter face and tried to explore the offending cheek, but a lifetime in the fields had left his fingertips thick with ancient calluses in which there was little sensitivity. His face seemed lumpy, with a strange step in the skin of his cheek, but he couldn't discern the details. He squinted at his fingers and found them wet with a thin, colourless discharge. His head spun unnervingly, though whether that was from the sickness or from his fear of the sickness he couldn't tell. He tried to draw up one leg, in preparation to stand, but barely managed to drag the heel six inches towards himself before the effort sent a convulsion through his whole body. He regretted trying to move when the spasm loosened muscles over which he normally exerted no conscious control. Warmth spread across his chilled right thigh.

'Blast.' His lips moved to shape the word but no sound came.

Smeed dropped to a squat beside him and rested a hand on his shoulder.

Pierce thumped the side of his fist on the bulkhead. 'Hey! Quacks!'

'Bugger off,' came Hogben's muffled retort.

'Wasn't talking to you,' Pierce shouted back, an edge in his usually mild voice.

Most of the men in the next berth were late risers by choice and, after a while, Giles and Quested had fallen into the same routine. When Quested's voice came back, it was thick with sleep.

'Paul?' He sounded befuddled for a moment, then repeated, 'Paul? Aught wrong?'

'Aye,' Pierce called back. 'Sam's not so good.' He hesitated and glanced at Sam. 'Looks right queer, truth be told.'

There was a loud thud from beyond the bulkhead, the sound of a large man gracelessly exiting a hammock, and then a quieter one as he settled himself against the bulkhead.

'Sam!' Quested called. 'What's the trouble?'

Sam gasped soundlessly, then licked his lips and tried again. Whether it was the fog in his mind or the wadding in his mouth, he found himself unable to reply. As if things weren't bad enough, his head began to throb in time with his racing pulse.

'Quacks, can you hear me?' Pierce had to raise his voice to penetrate the bulkhead but he kept it low. The last thing they needed was to set off a panic about an outbreak of fever on board.

'Aye,' Quested matched his tone. 'What goes on through there?'

'Looks like a fever. He seems confused, like he can't think what he's trying to say.'

'Just fever, or fever and chills?'

Sam lay limply as Pierce knelt in front of him and felt his forehead, neck, chest and limbs. He shivered as the movement of his damp clothes send draughts over his skin.

'Chills too, by the look of it,' Pierce called back, while Dennard draped the blanket from Sam's hammock around his shoulders. 'That's not all though.'

Sam felt all his friends staring at his face again. Even alongside his dread of what they were looking at, he felt a strange sense of relief that it couldn't be gaol fever. He'd never seen anything noteworthy about the faces of its victims, although he'd sometimes seen red spots on their arms and chests.

Pierce returned to the bulkhead. 'Sam cut himself shaving a week or so back. We were looking at it yesterday, saying how it wasn't healing and he should see what you thought, but it's come up something wicked now.'

'Black?' There was apprehension in the question.

'No, it's not the black rot. Not yet, at least. His cheek's gone red, all hard and shiny.' Groping for an adequate description, Pierce suddenly hit on an inspiration in the barrels of fruit stowed away as protection against scurvy. 'It's like the skin of a lime.'

'Thought you says it was red.'

'Aye,' Pierce cut him off impatiently, 'But puffy and pitted like lime skin.'

Silence.

'Quacks?' Pierce prompted.

'I never sees anything like that. Best we gets him to the doctor.'

There was a pause and then a thin metallic sound came from the next berth. After another few seconds of silence, a louder clang rang out. Quested was banging on the barred opening in the door with something. Pierce cast around the berth until he saw a large serving spoon and then joined his friend in making as much noise as possible. The racket drew curses from the berths around them immediately but they had to wait longer for it to bring any help. The two guards who eventually appeared wore surly expressions and vented their irritation in a stream of abuse as they clumped along the corridor. When they reached the source of the noise, the swearing stopped and a surprised shout came through the bars.

'All right, all right. You've made your point, boys. What the hell's up that you want to get yourselves locked down for a week?'

There was no real malice in the words. Weeks of good behaviour, and hard work when given the opportunity, had won the Blues friends on board. A four-month voyage at such close quarters meant that maintaining captor-captive relationships was more effort than it was worth for most of the crew. They preferred a friendlier arrangement if their charges had the sense to go along with it. Pierce had played many a hand of cards with the man now at the door. He put his face to the opening.

'Sorry, Joe. Sam's come over bad and Quacks wants to take him up to the doctor.'

Sam peered up at the guards who were now looking past Pierce to examine him. He wondered if they would suspect a trap of some kind but he needn't have worried. Both men hastily stepped back from the door, then Joe muttered his reply.

'Reckon it's best the doctor comes down here.'

Sam's heart sank. He could tell from the man's reaction what his friends' restraint had concealed. Whatever he had was bad enough to make men fear for their own safety. Perhaps they might feel better if he was tossed overboard. That thought did not distress him as much as he might have expected, not nearly as badly as the one that followed. He hoped his friends wouldn't be right behind him, whether infected by him or innocent victims of an irrational fear that they might have been.

The doctor was with them in minutes. Although he'd proved both conscientious and professional during the voyage, Sam knew the man's prompt appearance was down to Quested's diligence and dedication. Dr Wilson surely knew that his assistant would not raise an alarm without reason and might also be repaying the concern Quested showed for every patient with special treatment for one of his friends. The guard to whom Pierce had spoken unbarred the door and loitered uneasily in the corridor while the doctor swept over to the patient's side.

Sam waited while firm fingers explored his temperature and pulse, then pressed gently at the raised skin on his cheek.

'Does that hurt?' the doctor asked.

Sam swallowed and channelled all his failing concentration into his whispered reply. 'Bit. Not bad.'

The doctor tutted, no doubt making his own assessment as to how much pain it would take to make one of this party admit to something hurting. He glanced up at Pierce, who seemed to have taken charge of the situation. 'So he cut himself recently, the wound hasn't healed and then a fever started yesterday?'

Pierce nodded, his surprise evident at the ease with which the doctor divined the onset of the illness.

'Did he complain of a headache?'

Seeing Pierce start to shake his head, Sam nodded weakly. The throbbing had become steadily worse, until it felt as if his head was too full of blood and might explode at any moment.

'How is he, sir?' Quested's voice drifted in from the next berth, filled with anxiety for a friend and frustration at his inability to see the man's condition for himself.

The doctor looked through the door, at the guard leaning against the far wall of the corridor. 'Let Quested out, Cooper. Just him, mind.'

The guard nodded but did not move, clearly wanting no contact with anyone who might have the mysterious illness.

'Move, man!' the doctor snapped. 'And there's no need for you lot to start gossiping like old fishwives. You won't catch anything off this poor fellow.'

His words were the best thing Sam could have heard. Even if the mystery disease killed him, he wouldn't be taking his friends with him. A moment later, Quested knelt on the opposite side of him from the doctor.

'What is it, sir?'

Convicts were expected to address their betters, which was basically everyone, as 'sir' but Quested's tone held genuine respect rather than enforced servitude. Sam had heard him tell Pierce one evening that he'd never seen a doctor who knew as much as Dr Wilson, adding in awe that the man wrote his journal in Latin. That seemed a dubious achievement, if it meant that few people could read it, but Quested's respect was not easily won and it comforted Sam to know he was in such good hands.

'It's called erysipelas. You can't mistake it — the shiny red inflammation, with such clearly defined edges, is unique to this condition. We see it most often in babies but it can take hold whenever skin is broken. The mothers know it as the eel thing.'

Sam was amazed to hear an educated man like the doctor share his knowledge with one of their number. The doctor leaned closer before continuing his lecture, using the fourth finger of his fisted right hand to indicate each point as he made it.

'The cut hasn't healed because of its position over the cheek muscles, where the movement of the jaw disrupts scabbing, not to mention the repeated application of a razor. Meanwhile, the open wound has let the erysipelas reach the subcutaneous layers below.'

Sam's line of sight was filled with Quested's large head twisting and turning to examine the evidence supporting the doctor's explanation.

'Will he recover?'

There was a detachment in Quested's voice, as he asked after a patient's prognosis rather than a friend's future. The doctor's reply was equally clinical.

'There is no guarantee with a condition of this type. It can lead to fevers of many kinds… brain, lung and scarlet to mention but a few. There is also the potential for mortification, which would almost certainly be inoperable in such a sensitive location, and, of course, there is always a risk that fever and vomiting will induce terminal decline in any patient.'

Even Sam's stoic temperament faltered as he heard his prospects discussed do dispassionately. He was relieved when the doctor's words, if not his tone, became slightly more reassuring.

'However, this man is as strong as an ox so I think we should be optimistic for the present. We'll have him moved up to the surgery and design a regime to control both the fever and the dermal inflammation. I'll need you to get as much fluid into him as you can and apply warm compresses to the affected area. With luck, we'll see some improvement soon but it may be a considerable time before he regains full strength.'

Sam saw Quested nod his understanding and then wave for John to take his other arm. Between them, they hauled him to his feet. He was ashamed of his uselessness and vulnerability, not to mention the damp patch covering most of his right thigh, but had no strength for any protest or resistance.

Their progress to the surgery astern was painful and laborious.

His heart beat faster with each step, intensifying the throbbing in his head, and his stomach turned at every movement. Too late, he tried to call for a rest stop. Even as he opened his mouth to speak, his throat contracted and the bitter remnants of the previous night's stew filled his mouth. It spilled over his lower lip and dribbled onto his chest.

'Sorry, Sam,' Quested forestalled the apology that Sam couldn't utter. 'I has you cleaned up in no time once we gets there.'

Quested was as good as his word. Sam lay on a piece of sail canvas while his friend stripped and washed him, before bundling him onto a freshly made cot. He let the man work his limbs into clean underclothes and slip a generous pad of wadding around his crotch, before pulling a wind-crispened sheet and two blankets snugly over him.

'Now don't you be worrying over things that can't be helped,' Quested said euphemistically. Placing a wide-necked bottle beside the cot, he added, 'You uses this if you can and asks me if you can't. If all else fails, the wadding takes care of it. All right?'

Sam managed a weak nod. He hadn't felt so vulnerable since his belly halted the swing of a French blade more than a decade before. Two weeks in a stinking cabin packed with battle casualties had left him with his horror of sickness. Now he was the sole patient in an immaculate surgery, far better in every way but one: there was nothing to distract him from his body's failings. Surrounded by wounded men covered in blood, urine and faeces, he'd barely registered his own but now he was painfully aware of his friend washing and changing him like a baby. He was almost glad when Quested's attention returned to his face.

'Yell if I hurts you,' Quested murmured as he explored the raised flesh.

His ear was only inches from Sam's mouth. The prone man swallowed and then licked his lips apprehensively. With a supreme effort, he managed to shape them into words.

'Show me.'

Quested looked doubtful for a moment but then picked up a tray from a table at the side of the cabin. He sat on the edge of the cot and held it up.

Sam hesitated, wondering what he would see, but then examined himself. The polished metal made a poor mirror but it was enough to make out the familiar waves of near-black hair, now streaked with grey, and equally dark eyes, now darting anxiously over the reflection. The right side of his face was unchanged but he gasped at the left. His whole cheek was deep red, with an even deeper discolouration defining the edges of a plate of swollen skin that extended from his eye to his jawbone and from his nose to his ear. At the centre, a raw gash still oozed pus. He stared in horror, appalled by his disfigurement and surprised that his friends had shown so little reaction to its extent.

Quested set the tray to one side and gently but firmly forced him back onto the pillow. When he spoke, eager medical student had been replaced by dutiful nurse.

'You hears what the doctor says. We takes good care of you and this clears up in no time.' He filled a cup with water and held it to Sam's lips. 'All the while, you has the best food and bunk aboard. Not even the captain has it so good.' He chuckled. 'But I has to warn you, the doctor believes in the power of a bath. Sure as eggs is eggs, I washes you down twice daily and you lets me do it.'

Sam let out an unsteady sigh. Appreciating Quested's concern and respecting his experience, he would cooperate in whatever regime the doctor prescribed — however undignified it might be.

Tommy

Tommy Dennard stood at the ventilation grille, peering into the distance. A week had passed since the latest rumour that they were nearing the end of their voyage. When they began, every murmur had him watching and waiting. Soon he saw it was just talk; most men had no idea where they were or how much longer they must endure their miserable quarters, soaked in the foul waste of soil buckets and bilge water every time they hit rough seas however hard the tightly packed occupants tried to avoid it.

This time, he had a reason to take more notice: he'd seen a change in their two mariners. Although Smeed and Gilham had passed no comment in his hearing, they listened to the murmurs for the first time. Watching carefully, he saw what seemed like anticipation in the reserved pair. Ever since, he'd studied the horizon intently every time he got a turn around the deck and, back in the berth, spent long hours gazing through the grille.

Noting how the July days had grown shorter and colder as their south-easterly course took them into the southern winter, Tommy smiled to himself. He'd only discovered that south could be as cold as north when they were headed for the Cape of Good Hope. With yet another stifling day giving way to yet another suffocating night, he was ladling seawater over his burning skin at dusk when Gilham joined him for a share in the shower. Tommy obligingly drenched his back.

'Damnation take it, Datchy, but I'll be as barmy as Dick by the time we reach the new country. We've not been going a month and I'm sweating a gallon a day. How bad will it be another couple of months south?'

Gilham twisted around in surprise, then grinned when he saw that his friend was serious. The grin quickly blossomed into a laugh, not a common sound on the ship.

Knowing he was the butt of the joke, but not why, Tommy took it in good part and grinned back. 'What?'

'It don't w-work that w-way.'

'What don't?'

Tommy was confused. He hadn't travelled himself it was true, but he knew from other men that, to the south of England, Spain was hot and, to the north, Scotland was cold.

'The sun. We'll soon be across the Equator.'

Tommy frowned. He'd heard of the Equator, to be sure, but had no idea what it was.

Gilham smiled and picked up an apple that Tommy was saving for later — an occasional treat on top of their ration of lime juice from a captain who knew the dangers of long sea voyages and who intended to deliver his cargo of potential labourers to the colony in working order. He pulled out a knife that he was not supposed to carry and carved two small craters into the fruit, directly opposite each other and near the ends of the core. Gripping the fruit between his thumb and forefinger, he held it up and indicated the craters in turn.

'England. Van Diemen's Land.'

He held the apple in the dying rays of the sun, casting one side in gold while the other fell into deep shadow, and then rotated it slowly.

'That's how the sun lights the earth. Day and night.'

Tommy looked at the model thoughtfully. He wasn't a complete Philistine; he knew the earth was round and that days and nights came from the movement of the sun, although he hadn't appreciated that the earth spun in the sun's light. The thought made him feel faintly giddy. He did not doubt Gilham's word though, knowing the man to be too kind and too honest to make a fool of him.

'When it's day in England, it's night in Van Diemen's Land.'

Gilham then held up a finger and moved the apple around it. He waggled the finger.

'Say this is the sun now. At the same time as it turns, the earth moves slowly round the sun, once a year.'

He struggled to maintain both rotation and orbit but conveyed the general idea.

'The way the earth faces the sun brings the seasons.' He tilted the apple on its core. 'When we lean towards it, the days are longer and hotter. When we lean away, they're shorter and colder. Summer and winter.'

Tommy gaped. He'd no idea Gilham possessed such knowledge.

'W-when England leans towards the sun, Van Diemen's Land leans away. The Equator's hot all the time.' He held the apple still again and traced a path between the two craters. 'So we left England in early spring. When we get to the new country, it'll be just past mid-summer at home but just past mid-winter there. Up to now, we've been sailing towards the Equator, getting hotter, but soon we'll be sailing away from it. The days'll get shorter and colder.'

When Gilham looked up to check his understanding, Tommy nodded slowly. It was a big idea to grasp but he could see that it worked with the apple.

'W-won't be a steady thing mind. We've to go as much east as south, our course changes with the winds and currents, and the weather depends on how close we are to land and such like. But, take my word for it, you won't be hot when we get there.' He grinned at his own ironic reassurance, then added, 'From what I hear, it's not so different from home — they're nearly as far south as we are north.'

Tommy smiled at the memory of Gilham's impromptu lesson. Engrossed in his explanation, his friend almost lost his stammer.

Tommy was impressed by the lucid explanation, which conveyed the incredible concept with such conviction that it was accepted without a murmur. As time passed, he'd seen with his own eyes the evidence of its veracity. Now, wearing every stitch of clothing he possessed for his late exercise and wrapped in a blanket, he still shivered. Remembering Gilham's speculation that the new country would not be so different from the old, he felt sure the rumours were right this time — they were nearing the end of their journey. Despite the July date, it felt like mid-winter.

The final confirmation had come from Smeed a few days before. His watch finished, the mariner was leaning on the rail and gazing towards the north-western horizon, where the sun hung low in a sky that would delight any shepherd. Tommy joined him, taking position a little to the left, offering companionship without intrusion. He'd been relieved to see Smeed's misery slowly lift into a deep but healthy sadness, returning him almost to the man he had been before.

'All right?'

Smeed nodded. There was a long pause before he glanced across and added. 'You?'

Tommy shrugged and gave a wry grin. All things were relative; life on board was hard but he was alive and keeping well. Luckier than some, he'd had nothing worse than a bout of sea sickness during the voyage. Most could say the same. There'd been just one death and that was a man who was already weak when they left England. Of their number, only Sam Bailey had required the doctor's care for his skin complaint and that, while dramatic and unpleasant, had never posed a threat to his life. Three weeks of Quested's diligent nursing returned him to their berth and now he had only faint scarring to show for his experience. Perhaps thanks to fatigue brought on by restricted rations, Tommy hadn't even felt the lack of female company as much as he'd thought he might. Men confined as tightly as they had few secrets but he spent no more time relieving his frustration than anyone else.

They stared into the distance in silence.

'But I miss Bish.'

Smeed sighed. 'Aye.' He looked down at his hands. 'I never met Jamie's like before. I'm not expecting to meet it again.'

Seeing Smeed in a reflective frame of mind, Tommy probed.

'Neither of you cared what any of us thought anyway, did you?'

Smeed shifted so that his right elbow was on the rail and he half-faced Tommy. 'We weren't so keen to feel the edge of a blade in our sleep, if that's what you mean.'

'Who would be? I meant you'd have left sooner than give him up, wouldn't you?'

'I'd have died sooner than give him up.'

The conviction in Smeed's voice took even Tommy by surprise. He said only, 'I hope I find that one day.'

Smeed's eyes crinkled warmly. 'And I hope you have longer than we did when you do.'

Tommy nodded, heart bursting with compassion for the loneliness that engulfed even a man as slow to self-pity as Smeed. He kept silent for a while, giving the undemanding company that he knew his friend preferred. When he eventually spoke, he shifted to something less personal but no less important.

'You've heard what men are saying? That we're nearly there?'

Smeed nodded.

'Well?'

'Well what?'

'For God's sake! *Are* we nearly there?'

A broad smile crept over Smeed's face. 'Aye, days at most, I'd say.' The smile faded. 'Nigh on a year to the day since the night that cost us so dear, and none too soon for Dick at that.'

The answer was not unexpected but the emotions that choked Tommy were. Swamped by a potent blend of anticipation and apprehension, he leant on the rail for a while. Eventually, he patted Smeed's arm and turned away, unable to discuss it further but sharing the relief that they would reach the end of their voyage before their friend had quite reached the end of his tether.

Now, back beside the grille, he pressed against the hull, twisting to see ahead. His fingers played casually over indentations in the bulkhead. Each night, when they turned in, Higgins celebrated his triumph over another day's captivity with a savage gouge in the timber. Tommy knew that he was not alone in watching the marks accumulate into first weeks and then months. Smeed had struck up something of a friendship with one of the ordinary seamen, who told him that eighteen-twenty-seven was bringing some of the best sailing weather for years and that several ships had reached the southern continent in less than six-score days. Both crew and convicts had been laying bets on the *Governor Ready* joining their ranks. Tommy counted the marks under his fingertips. Just as he passed one hundred and fifteen, his eyes widened as he saw the horizon ahead thicken. A faint smudge split the sky from the sea, bringing to a sudden end the emptiness that had changed in nothing but colour for most of their sixteen long weeks at sea.

Even as he grasped what he was looking at, a faint call came from far above.

'Land ho!'

His knees wobbled, making him raise a hand to the rough oak. The other men gathered around him but let him keep his prime spot at the grille. It would be hours before they reached shore and yet still they stood, the time remaining but an instant compared with the time past. As the distant smudge slowly revealed itself to be a harbour, the other men came and went, sitting for a while or using the bucket in the corner, but Tommy was transfixed.

He was a different man from the merry rascal known to every woman on the marshes. Always slender, now he was gaunt. Always sensitive, now he was vulnerable. Yet still he had found it in him to support Higgins, standing beside his friend through each night's horrors, never losing patience with the terror that their confinement inspired in him. Now, for the first time since the heavy door slammed behind him on the *York*, he felt hope. They had little idea what to expect in the new country but some things seemed sure. There would be ground under his feet and sky over his head. He would be able to breathe fresh air without the stench of overcrowded men and slop buckets. He might even find work with the horses he'd missed far more than he'd expected to.

As they sailed into a bay, the others pressed tighter around him. Now they did not need to squint forwards: the coast was all around. They saw no tangled jungles bristling with wild beasts. Instead, ships sat at anchor, while boats too many to count were moored along the shore. The docks buzzed with activity, milling with people going about their business in what appeared to be a thriving community. Everything they'd left behind was present: fishermen and fish-markets, hangs and guts. The land was different, sweeping up towards distant mountains instead of stretching flat for mile after mile, but the slopes were tilled just the same. Where there were fish and farms, mariners and labourers must surely be needed.

Beside him, Higgins was trembling in his relief at leaving the wretched berth forever. The Baileys stood impassive, only their darting eyes revealing their interest. Pierce and Gilham wore the same open-mouthed wonder as he felt in himself, while Smeed stared enigmatically into the distance.

Through the heavy bulkhead came Quested's bellow, gruffer than ever as he raised his voice to penetrate the oak.

'You sees that, boys? Paul? Tommy? You sees it?'

Tommy looked at Pierce, who closed his mouth and swallowed. They all stared at each other for a moment or two, then Pierce cleared his throat and shouted back.

'We see it. By Christ, Quacks, we all see it.'

Author's Notes

This book, while a work of fiction, is true to the records describing the people and events in its pages. Inevitably, characters and scenes have been added to tell the story. There are inconsistencies in the records, some men used aliases and, in the tight-knit community, different men could have identical names. Consequently, some minor characters have been merged to simplify the story. The characterisations were developed in the light of the reminiscences of contemporaries so, while they are fictional, many facets have some basis in local rumour.

The demise of the Aldington Blues marked the end of large-scale smuggling in Kent and Sussex. The loss of this source of income may have contributed to the riots of 1830, in which agricultural workers from Kent to Devon rebelled against low pay and mechanisation. Job done and cost unjustifiable, the Coast Blockade was replaced by the Coastguard in 1831. Various changes followed over the years until, in 1971, the Customs and Excise was organised into its modern form.

All of the convicted Blues received good conduct reports from their captors in gaol and on the hulks. Although they evaded the hangman, they may have found the sentence of transportation as daunting: it is said that some men feared the prison hulks more than the noose. However, if they managed to find any hope in those dark days, it appears to have been justified. They were fortunate to sail on the *Governor Ready*, a two-year-old vessel with a competent master (John Young) and a progressive surgeon (Thomas B Wilson) in charge of convict welfare, and in a year when the prevailing weather conditions were excellent. The ship was lost off Australia only a few years later, in a sequence of events that saw a group shipwrecked no less than five times before reaching safety. Most of the Blues had long lives in Van Diemen's Land, now Tasmania, although many had brushes with the law. Their footprints linger in the official records and newspapers of their new home.

John Bailey was joined by his family in 1829, travelling aboard the *Harmony*. He was twice charged with offences, for 'damage done by Mr Gunns cattle in his charge on the wheat of Jas. Tasker' and 'by Mrs Campbell with having abused and insulted her'; he was fined seven shillings for the cattle (which had been a night's work for a tubman), while the other case was dismissed with costs. He received a conditional pardon on 24 May 1838 and a free pardon on 5 January 1843. His youngest son, William, married Maria Gilham (daughter of Thomas and Frances) in 1874. John died in New Norfolk on 8 February 1866, aged about 74.

Samuel Bailey applied in October 1828 for his wife and family to join him; the application was unsuccessful, reason unknown. The *Governor Ready*'s medical journal shows his bout of erysipelas as the sole illness amongst the Blues during the voyage. Sam was charged with two offences in Tasmania on the same day, 'on suspicion of stealing a quantity of wheat the property of Mr James Mitchell' and 'on suspicion of stealing certain wheat the property of Mr David Lord'; he was discharged of the first and pardoned of the second. He received a conditional pardon on 30 November 1839 and died in Oatlands, Tasmania, on 27 January 1866, aged about 82.

Thomas Dennard was assigned to a prominent settler Joseph Archer at Lake River in 1827. He married Ellen McCabe, a free settler, on 9 June 1838. He received a conditional pardon on 22 June 1838 (later extended, on 18 November 1845). He was declared insolvent in 1842, still owing £124 2s 8½d at the end of the year (a substantial amount then). The 1843 census shows him living at Oatlands with his wife, three young daughters and a male ex-convict. Oatlands Superior Court found him not guilty of receiving a stolen harness in 1845. The family later moved to Victoria, where six children were baptised in 1846: Bridget, Ellen, Jane, Lucy, Mary Ann and Thomas. Mary Ann died in 1847, aged 7, and 14-day-old Henry Dennard in 1850. A last child, Sarah, was born in 1852. Thomas died in Ballarat in 1880, aged 76.

Note: The Dennard name is also spelled Denard.

Charles Giles was joined by his family in 1829, travelling aboard the *Harmony*. At that time, he was working for James Grant. His sister later wrote, 'He did very well out there. He took up with his shoemaking and settled down at Hobart Town.' Said to be 'a bit more civilised than the rest', he received a conditional pardon on

22 April 1837 and a free pardon on 15 September 1842. He died in Hobart in 1874, aged about 76.

Thomas Gilham was assigned, along with Dennard, to Joseph Archer in 1827. He was transferred to Lieutenant William Thomas Lyttleton, another prominent settler, who applied in April 1828 for Thomas's wife and children to be brought to Tasmania. He described Thomas as 'an industrious and well conducted man' and indicated that, should the Lt Governor grant the request, he was prepared to 'enter into a bond for any amount required for their maintenance and support on arrival'. He was advised to resubmit his application 'when the man has been twelve months in the Colony, at which time it will be complied with'. This was done and, in October, Lt Governor Arthur transmitted Thomas's details to the Colonial Office. When Frances arrived on the *Harmony* in 1829, she brought her illegitimate children, the couple's children and an infant girl whose father is unknown. They had seven more children. Thomas was assigned to his wife (a practice that was later stopped) and they lived at Norfolk Plains (now Longford, Tasmania), where he became a farmer. Although he was admonished for missing church muster and fined once for drunkenness, he did well, owning several small properties that he rented out and taking over the Prince of Wales inn in Carrick, Tasmania. He received a conditional pardon on 28 January 1839 (later extended, on 10 February 1846). Two of the children married the children of other Blues: Frances married James Hogben (son of James and Ann) and Maria married William Bailey (son of John and Katherine) in 1874. Thomas died of 'natural decay' on 15 May 1865, aged about 62. Note: The Gilham name later changed to Gillam.

Richard Higgins was assigned to Samuel Hill in 1827. He was joined by his family in 1829, travelling aboard the *Harmony*. Rhoda brought their two daughters and the couple had five more children. On 9 October 1837, Richard was suspected of sheep stealing but pardoned and sent to reside in the Morvern district. On 2 May 1839, he was fined five shillings for being drunk. He received a conditional pardon on 15 May 1839. He died on 17 August 1841, aged only about 46, after being run over by a cart in Hobart.

James Hogben was joined by his family in 1830, travelling aboard the *Mellish*. At the time, Ann and her seven children were being supported by the Parish. Hogben was first assigned as a servant to H Simpson of Launceston but then transferred to his wife on 4 December 1830. Between 1828 and 1841, Hogben notched up more offences than all the other Blues put together. He was reported drunk seven times, stealing apples once, being in a public house after hours twice (once when drunk), using insulting or obscene language twice (once when drunk) and disorderly conduct — a total of 11 offences for which he was variously fined twenty shillings, put in a cell for four days on bread and water and deprived of his ticket of leave. He received a conditional pardon on 11 October 1843, some five years after the other Blues' received theirs. His son, James, married Frances Gilham (daughter of Thomas and Frances). James died in Launceston on 22 May 1858, aged about 73.

Paul Pierce was said to be 'good' on the voyage. He was assigned to the Colonial Secretary, John Burnett Esquire, where he was reprimanded on 5 February 1828 for 'indecent and immoral conduct with Elizabeth Frankland in the service of his master'. He was joined by his wife and five of his seven children in 1829 (two died after he left England), travelling aboard the *Harmony*. The couple had two more children, Alfred and Henry. He received a conditional pardon on 20 December 1838 and died on 18 October 1864, aged 80.

James Quested assisted the *Governor Ready's* surgeon superintendent, Dr Thomas Braidwood Wilson, and was assigned on arrival to Dr Francis Desailly at Jericho. He was joined by his wife and five children in 1830, travelling aboard the *Mellish*. He received a conditional pardon on 9 March 1839 and was granted 200 acres at Pembroke, Tasmania. In 1853, he was appointed Messenger to the Government Printing Office. One of his sons became a schoolmaster and another a schooner captain. James died on 29 October 1877, aged about 86.

George Ransley was joined by his family in 1829, travelling aboard the *Harmony*. All bar one of his eleven children made the journey but the youngest, Elizabeth, died during the voyage. George prospered, farming 500 acres at River Plenty, Hobart. He was charged with only one offence in Tasmania, disorderly conduct on 30 January 1833, and received a conditional pardon on 22 June 1838. He died on 25 October 1856 from yellow jaundice, aged about 74, when he was said to be 'respected and loved by all who knew him'. Some said that he returned to Aldington and died there but there is no evidence to support this romantic claim.

James Smeed became a constable. In July 1830, he was fined twenty shillings (which had been a night's work for a man in the armed parties) from his salary for drunkenness. In July 1831, he was 'recommended to be dismissed from the office of constable and to be suspended until the pleasure of his Excellency the Lieut Gover be signified'; his offence was 'gross disobedience of orders in conveying Geo Woodward charged with forgery from Launceston to Hobart Town by way of the Clyde and N Norfolk instead of the direct road.' However, he went on to receive a free pardon on 19 February 1835, only eight years after his conviction and several years before most of the other Blues received conditional pardons. He earned this by aiding in the capture of the bushrangers Jeffkins and Brown, for which he received £63 6s 8d (£33 6s 8d as his share of the posted reward and £30 as a bonus). It is thought that he accompanied the pioneering Henty family to Victoria; the Hentys emigrated to Tasmania from Sussex and left a series of journals about the years they spent whaling and farming in Portland Bay. Several references to a James Smeed appear in newspaper reports, where he is described as a stockman and bullock driver, and reports relating to the Hentys have him as Stephen Henty's usual companion, 'a trusted fellow … who looked after his master well'. He was said to have been the first white man to reach Mount Gambier, South Australia; he reported having seen its dim bluish outline through the trees to his employer, who sent him to investigate, and his 'pithy verdict' was reported as, 'Good land, well worth occupying.'

Note: There is no evidence to support the relationship between Smeed and Wilson described in this book but they were single and said to have been found on the run together. Smeed would surely have stood a better chance alone than with Wilson, who is said to have been in poor health at the time of their arrest and died aboard the *Leviathan* on 15 February 1827 aged 29.

Richard Wyor was single when transported and no record of a later marriage has been found. In December 1835, he was reported as 'being drunk in the presence of a magistrate'; it was recommended that his ticket of leave be suspended for 14 days. He was later fined five shillings for being drunk in March 1836. He received a conditional pardon on 15 May 1839 and died on 4 December 1889 of 'poplexy', aged about 81.

William Wyor was single when transported and no record of a later marriage has been found. Like his brother, he received a conditional pardon on 15 May 1839. He died of erysipelas, the same condition as Sam Bailey suffered, in Launceston county on 30 December 1845, aged about 34. His death was registered by his brother. According to a conversation reported between Robert Bailey and Thomas Wheeler, William 'used to go along with them, but he never carried arms: he was only about eighteen years of age; and a small chap too — not a big man like his brother'. Prison records show the two men as similar in height.

Note: The Wyor name is also spelled Wyer and Wire. A contemporary said it was just as well the Wyor brothers were transported 'for they never did no good after the old man was killed: that was their father, who was struck by lightning harvest time, when he had a fork in his hand'.

About Bretwalda Books

Bretwalda Books is an exciting new publishing company devoted to exploring the lesser known areas of British and European history. We aim to produce books targetted at the general market embracing popular writing styles and attractive design formats while upholding the highest standards of accuracy and reliability. Our books will deal with unusual topics in an open and engaging manner.

Why Bretwalda?

The term "Bretwalda" is one of the more mysterious titles in Dark Age British History. It has been translated in various ways and although entire nations were plunged into war and thousands of men were killed fighting for the right to use the title, nobody is entirely certain what it meant. We thought it summed up our mission to uncover the little known nooks and crannies of history. In fact, that gives us an idea for a book ...

Finding Bretwalda

Bretwalda has a constantly growing range of innovative books.

We have a website on
www.BretwaldaBooks.com

We have a blog on
http://bretwaldabooks.blogspot.com/

We have a Facebook Page as
Bretwalda Books

We have a Twitter account as
@Bretwaldabooks

You can email us on
info@bretwaldabooks.com

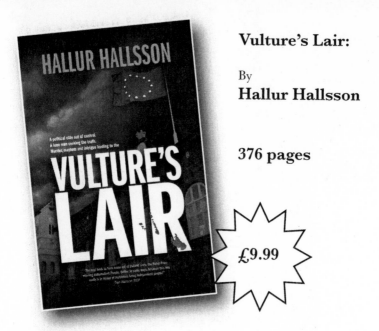

Vulture's Lair:

By
Hallur Hallsson

376 pages

£9.99

The first great eurosceptic novel that the world has been waiting for.

BRUSSELS. Krummi the fisherman leads a protest against corrupt EU regulations and uncovers a desperate secret.

BERLIN. A sinister figure in a black suit deep inside the hierarchy plots a coup with politics, big business and the Mafia to plunge Europe into dictatorship.

Can Krummi stay alive long to find out what is really happening? Can he stop the Vulture? And will he ever discover where to find the Vulture's Lair?

About the Author
HALLUR HALLSSON is a leading journalist and TV-personality in Iceland. Hallsson was one of the founders of the daily Dagbladid in 1975 which became the second biggest newspaper in Iceland. He was a leading journalist at the influential Morgunbladid and a journalist and anchor at Channel 2 and State Television.

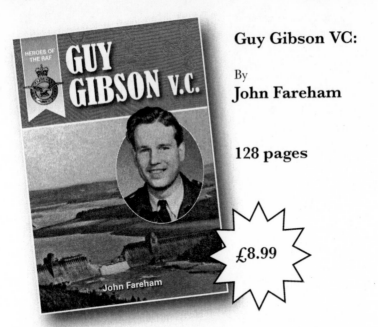

Guy Gibson VC:

By
John Fareham

128 pages

£8.99

Thrilling biography of the man who led the Dambusters Raid.
Having joined the RAF in 1936, Gibson was a bomber pilot when
war broke out. He won a DFC in July 1940 then volunteered for
Fighter Command and flew nightfighters on 99 sorites before
returning to Bomber Command to fly 46 more missions before the
Dambusters Raid. This book looks at the life and career of the man
who led the most famous bombing raid of World War II. It is a
gripping account of his life and exploits, revealing new and little
known facts about Guy Gibson for the first time.

About the Author
JOHN FAREHAM is the son of an RAF veteran who grew up on
RAF bases around the world. He now lives only a short drive from
RAF Scampton from which Gibson flew his famous Dambuster
Raid.

Bretwalda Books Ltd

Bretwalda Books Ltd